The Editor

ROBERT W. HILL JR. is Henry Norman Hudson Professor of English at Middlebury College. He received his Ph.D. from Harvard and was a recipient of the John Harvard honorary scholarship. He previously taught at Amherst and Harvard.

A NORTON CRITICAL EDITION

TENNYSON'S POETRY

AUTHORITATIVE TEXTS

CONTEXTS

CRITICISM

Second Edition

Selected and Edited by

ROBERT W. HILL JR.

MIDDLEBURY COLLEGE

W • W • NORTON & COMPANY • *New York* • *London*

W. W. Norton & Company has been independent since its founding in 1923, when William Warder Norton and Mary D. Herter Norton first published lectures delivered at the People's Institute, the adult education division of New York City's Cooper Union. The Nortons soon expanded their program beyond the Institute, publishing books by celebrated academics from America and abroad. By mid-century, the two major pillars of Norton's publishing program — trade books and college texts — were firmly established. In the 1950s, the Norton family transferred control of the company to its employees, and today — with a staff of four hundred and a comparable number of trade, college, and professional titles published each year — W. W. Norton & Company stands as the largest and oldest publishing house owned wholly by its employees.

The text of this book is composed in Electra with the display set in Bernhard Modern.
Composition by Publishing Synthesis Ltd., New York.
Manufacturing by the Courier Companies — Westford division.
Book design by Antonina Krass.
Cover illustration: Alred Tennyson, 1st Baron Tennyson, by Samuel Laurence. Reproduced by permission of the National Portrait Gallery, London.

Production Manager: Diane O'Connor.

Library of Congress Cataloging-in-Publication Data

Tennyson, Alfred Tennyson, Baron, 1809–1892.
    [Poems. Selections]
    Tennyson's poetry : authoritative texts, contexts, criticism /
  selected and edited by Robert W. Hill, Jr. — 2nd ed.
        p.   cm. — (A Norton critical edition)
    Includes bibliographical references.

    ISBN 0-393-97279-8 (pbk.)

    1. Tennyson, Alfred Tennyson, Baron, 1809–1892 — Criticism and
  interpretation.   I. Hill, Robert W.
PS3553.H5   1998
821'.8 — dc21   98-21561
                                                              CIP

W. W. Norton & Company, Inc., 500 Fifth Avenue, New York, N.Y. 10110
www.wwnorton.com

W. W. Norton & Company Ltd., Castle House, 75/76 Wells Street, London W1T 3QT

1 2 3 4 5 6 7 8 9 0

Contents

Contexts   579

Criticism   611

Preface

All but by definition, all selections of a poet's works, sooner than later, became dated. Any edition containing criticism is palpably ephemeral. Perhaps only two popular exceptions exist in the English language: *England's Helicon* (1600) and Palgrave's *Golden Treasury of Songs and Lyrics* (1861). Bartlett's *Familiar Quotations* (1855) has at last count gone through sixteen editions, new ones appearing as others drop into literary history's fathomless maw. Behind the first Tennyson Norton Critical Edition was a conscious effort to represent lesser poems, even indisputably "bad" ones. Not counting those (they have been removed), while girding myself for the humbling task that lay ahead, a truth became clear. For perhaps fifty, maybe even seventy-five years, any work of this scope would most likely contain fully 90 percent of the same Tennyson poetry; yet, as is demonstrably (one hopes) apparent here, over the past quarter century a wealth of new information about the poems has been accumulating. Although the old order in regard to the poems themselves may have changed only somewhat, preliminary study revealed a countertruth, even if partly anticipated — the breadth and depth of resurgent interest in *The Princess*. Of the poetry, its inclusion is by far what distinguishes this book from its predecessor. Here I have been most strongly influenced by a remark Sir Charles Tennyson made to me long ago in a letter of April 28, 1972: "The recovery of Tennyson's fame in recent years is very marked — & I believe the upward movement is not yet finished — particularly in regard to *The Princess* and the late poems." How extraordinarily prescient his comment on *The Princess* has been amply proved to be. I have also, therefore, taken heart from his guidance and retain a dozen of the late poems, which do not, for example, appear in Christopher Ricks's single-volume selection.

The poetry is arranged as far as possible in the order of composition. The date after each selection is that of first publication. For poems not published fairly soon after they were written, conjectural or known dates of composition precede dates of publication. Dates in parentheses indicate substantial changes in subsequent publication. I have deliberately not modernized Tennyson's spelling (e.g., "tho'," and "thro'," remain for "though" and "through," etc.), believing there is value retained in seeing the poems on the page as Tennyson and his readers read them.

References to *In Memoriam* (*IM*) are usually made by section number, followed, where appropriate, by stanza numbers. Elsewhere the practice is to refer to poem and line numbers, whether to Tennyson or in allusion to other poems. Page references are always given to the *Memoir* (the two-volume edition of 1897) partly because its index is not dependable. Notes by Tennyson himself or by his son Hallam either are identified by source or, where no explanation is given, are found in the nine-volume *Eversley* edition of the poet's complete works, on which this text is based. *Alfred Tennyson* refers to the biography by the poet's grandson, whereas other biographical references will be identified by author.

If choice from the poetry of the major British Victorian poet is subject to some change through various shifting tastes and predilections over the decades, most literary criticism has a relative shelf life measured in nanoseconds. Hallam's, Wilson's, Croker's, Mill's, Sterling's, Spedding's, and Knowles's retained articles on Tennyson have currency today, exclusively because of our historical interest in the poet. T. S. Eliot's piece on *In Memoriam* stands apart and is, in the sense above, unique. The

job of supplanting all the old "modern criticism" with the new has not been an easy
one. Turn where so e'er one may, the quest for current representative voices was apt
to stall with a persistent refrain: "O, that way madness lies." One is not unaware of
Isobel Armstrong's injunction: "The most arresting discussions of Victorian poetry
recently have come from Marxists, feminists and deconstruction. A critical history
cannot be written from outside these debates with a false neutrality, for these are the
contexts in which readers will read new discussions and the poets themselves" (*Victorian Poetry: Poetry, Poetics and Politics*, 1993, p. 9). Nonetheless, two principles,
shaky though they be, have guided the critical selections: (1) choose what may stand
the best chance to have continuing relevance for perhaps the next twenty-five years;
and (2) focus on the major poems and let the articles retain their integrity, i.e., be
represented in most instances in full, eschewing the temptation to promote more
choices and points of view in chopped excerpts. If I have unwittingly succumbed to
"a false neutrality," so be it, for I am far more nervous with the responsibility of
choosing the poetry. Consequently, given here are Eve Sedgwick on *The Princess*,
Isobel Armstrong on *In Memoriam*, Herbert F. Tucker on *Maud*, and Christopher
Ricks on *Idylls of the King*. Gertrude Himmelfarb's and my own effort, with focus
on the last poems, are tentative attempts to approach Tennyson today in the largest
contexts and at great risk, daring to guess where future interest in his work may lie.

In re-assembling this edition, composing the notes and prefaces, my debts are
extensive and indeed numerous. Rather than try to list them all in this space, I leave
the textual notations simply to speak for themselves and have tried hard to give due
credits. For an example, my reliance on Shatto and Shaw, superseding as they have
Eleanor Mattes's efforts (1951), should be nearly everywhere in evidence with my
updating of the notes to *In Memoriam*. And I must here dutifully own obeisance to
Ricks's three-volume, definitive edition of the poems. As I. A. Richards said of Coleridge, "He illustrates that daunting imitation-Greek epigram: 'where ever I go in
my mind, I meet Plato on his way back.' Where ever I have gone in mine, I have
met Christopher Ricks on his way back. To a friend and scholar: "*il miglior fabbro*."
Similarly, with several biographies, notes indicate sources; and again exceptionally,
there would be beggary in any attempt to reckon my admiration of Sir Charles Tennyson's enduringly splendid biography of his grandfather. Here, too, I must reaffirm
the incalculable value of my relations with two Tennysonians, Jerome H. Buckley
and the late Douglas Bush. For current help, I wish to acknowledge Lynette Felber,
Linda Hughes, Thomas Jeffers, Jack Kolb, Linda Peterson, and Paul Schlicke. Donald Lawler may need to take the remainder of his life to discover his singular contribution. The following list of names can discover for themselves what they may of
what their friendship, varied and vast knowledge of literature, and they themselves
have meant to me for many years: John Barlow; John Bertolini; William Catton; the
late "Doc" Cook; Emory Fanning; Robert Ferm; Edmund Harvey; Robert Hill III;
Travis Jacobs; John McCardell; Howard, Marion, Martha (née), and David Mun-
ford; Elizabeth Napier; Robert Pack; Jay Parini; Richard Poirier; David Price; Henry
Prickitt; Marguerite Tassi; Susan Ward; John Wilders; and Larry Yarbrough. On the
public front, as before, I thank Houghton Library and its staff for easy access to the
packets and notebooks in the Harvard collection. More recently, I extend formal acknowledgment to the Master and Fellows of Trinity College, Cambridge, and their
permission to quote from the Trinity manuscripts, granted by David McKitterick, Li-
brarian of Trinity College Library. When Sub-Librarian Mrs. Alison Sproston implied she would pave my way to the Trinity Collection, she gave understatement a
new dimension. To my student Pauls H. Toutonghi for some superefficient biblio-
graphic research; and to those scores of Middlebury students who, over many years
in classes and honors theses, have challenged me to keep learning. For copy editing,
corrections, contributions, and support, Candace Levy's "silent" presence is nearly
everywhere. To snitch and alter a couple of lines from Frost's "A Tuft of Flowers":

"we worked together, I tell you from my heart, whether we worked together or apart." To my editor, Carol Bemis, for tolerance, patience, and lots of helpful suggestions along the way—well, the book wouldn't be here but for her. Finally, to Helen Reiff, for proofreading the manuscript, words fail. To Middlebury College, for travel funds, several grants, and a leave of absence I record my appreciation. Special, and certainly close to home, for putting up with me during the last couple of years, thank-yous are insufficient: to my daughters Lisa and Catie.

Dedicated to Ruth Speakman

(Both of them, mother and daughter, who
out of the deep passed in the night.)

The Texts of the
POEMS

Earliest Poems (ca. 1823ff.): From *Unpublished Early Poems* (1931) and *The Devil and the Lady* (1930)

Translation from Claudian's "Proserpine"[1]

The gloomy chariot of the God of night,
And the wan stars that sicken'd at the sight,
And the dark nuptials of th' infernal King,[2]
With senses rapt in holy thought, I sing.
Away! away! profane ones! ye whose days   5
Are spent in endless sin and error's maze,
Seraphic transports through my bosom roll,
All Phoebus[3] fills my heart and fires my soul.
Lo! the shrines tremble and a heavenly light
Streams from their vaulted roofs serenely bright,   10
The God! the God, appears! the yawning ground
Moans at the view, the temples quake around,
And high in air the Eleusinians[4] raise
The sacred torch with undulating blaze;
Hiss the green snakes to sacred rapture giv'n   15
And meekly lift their scaly necks to heav'n,
With easy lapse they win their gentle way
And rear their rosy crests and listen to my lay.
See! see! where triform Hecate[5] dimly stands,
And mild Iacchus[6] leads the tuneful bands!   20
Immortal glories round his temples shine,
And flow'ring ivy wreaths his brows entwine;
From Parthia's[7] land he clasps beneath his chin
The speckled honours of the tiger's skin;
A vine-clad thyrsus with celestial grace   25

1. Tennyson's earliest extant poem, perhaps written when he was eleven. Although a translation of the first 93 lines of Claudian's "De Raptu Proserpinae," it contains a number of original lines and phrases. Of his debt to Pope, Tennyson later said, at "about ten or eleven Pope's *Homer's Iliad* became a favourite of mine and I wrote hundreds and hundreds of lines in the regular Popeian metre" (*Memoir* I, 11).
2. Pluto, who carried Proserpine off to the underworld while she was gathering flowers in Sicily.
3. Apollo, the sun god, also god of music and poets; invoked to illuminate the speaker's vision of the underworld.
4. Those practicing the Eleusinian mysteries; in ancient Greece the secret rites celebrated every spring at Eleusis in honor of Demeter and Persephone.
5. Patroness of witches and magicians.
6. Dionysus, god of fertility and wine.
7. An ancient kingdom southeast of the Caspian Sea.

Sustains his reeling feet and props his falling pace.
Ye mighty demons, whose tremendous sway
The shadowy tribes of airy ghosts obey,
To whose insatiate portion ever fall
All things that perish on this earthly ball,   30
Whom livid Styx with lurid torrent bounds
And fiery Phlegethon for aye surrounds,
Dark, deep and whirling round his flaming caves
The braying vortex of his breathless waves,
Eternal spirits! to your bard explain   35
The dread Arcana[8] of the Stygian reign,
How that stern Deity, Infernal Jove,
First felt the power, and own'd the force of love;
How Hell's fair Empress first was snatch'd away
From Earth's bright regions, and the face of day;   40
How anxious Ceres[9] wander'd far and near
Now torn by grief and tortur'd now by fear,
Whence laws to man are giv'n, and acorns yield
To the rich produce of the golden field.
Hell's haughty Lord in times of old began   45
To rouse 'gainst Heav'n the terrors of his clan;
Stern fury shook his soul—that he alone
Of every God upon his glitt'ring throne,
Should lead a dull and melancholy life,
Without the fond endearments of a wife—   50
Wretch that he was, who knew not how to claim
A consort's or a father's dearer name!
Now Hell's misshapen monsters rush to arms
And fill the wide abyss with loud alarms;
The haggard train of midnight Furies meet   55
To shake the Thunderer from his starry seat,
And pale Tisiphone,[1] with baleful breath
Calls the thin Ghosts within the Camp of Death;
High in her hand amid the shades of night
The gleaming pine shoots forth a dismal light,   60
Around her head the snaky volumes rise
And dart their tongues of flame and roll their gory eyes,
Now had all nature gone to wrack again
And Earth's fell offspring burst their brazen chain,
And from the deep recesses where they lay   65
Uprisen in wrath to view the beam of day,
Now had the fierce Aegaeon[2] thrown aside
The adamantine limits of his pride,
Uprear'd his hundred-handed form on high
And dar'd the forkéd terrors of the sky;   70
But the dire Parcae[3] with a piercing yell

8. Secrets or mysteries beyond the perception of ordinary people.
9. Mother of Proserpine and Roman goddess of agriculture equivalent to Greek Demeter (see n. 4, p. 3). In search of her lost daughter, Ceres vainly roamed the earth, at last appealing to Zeus, who decreed that Proserpine should be queen of Hades for three months of the year and live the other nine months on earth.
1. One of the three Furies.
2. A giant son of Uranus by Gaea.
3. Latin name for the three Fates.

Before the throne of gloomy Pluto fell,
Around his knees their suppliant hands were thrown,
Those awful hands which make the world their own,
Whose dreadful power the shades of Hades fear   75
And men on earth, and Gods in Heav'n revere,
Which mark the lot of fate's unerring page
And ply their iron tasks through every age.
First Lachesis[4] began (while all around
Hell's hollow caverns shudder'd at the sound),   80
"Dark Power of night and God of Hell, for whom
We draw the fated threads of human doom,
Thou end and origin of all on earth,
Redeeming death below by human birth!
Thou Lord of life and dissolution! King   85
Of all that live! (for first from thee they spring
And to thee they return, and in thy reign
Take other shapes and seek the world again)
Break not, ah! break not with unholy deed
That peace our laws have fix'd, our threats decreed.   90
Oh, wake not thou the trumpet's impious swell
Nor raise thy standard in the gulph of Hell
Nor rouse the Titans[5] from their dread abode,
The hideous Titans, foes to man and God.
Jove, — Jove himself shall grant thine ardent wish   95
And some fond wife shall crown thy nuptial bliss."
She spake — the God was struck with sudden shame
And his wild fury lost its former flame.
So when with whirlwinds in his icy train
Stern Boreas[6] sweeps along the sounding plain,   100
Bright o'er his wings the glittering frost is spread
And deathless winters crown his hoary head,
Then bow the groves, the woods his breath obey,
The heaving Ocean tosses either way.
But lo! if chance on far Aeolia's shores   105
The God of winds[7] should close his brazen doors,
With sudden pause the jarring tumults cease,
And Earth, Air, Ocean, find one common peace.
Then Maia's[8] son he calls, in haste to bear
His fix'd commands through all the deep of air;   110
Prompt at the word Cyllenius is at hand
Adorn'd with pinion'd brow and magic wand.
Himself the God of terrors, rear'd on high,
Sits thron'd in shades of midnight majesty,
Dim wreaths of mist his mighty sceptre shroud,   115
He veils his horrors in a viewless cloud.
Then thus in haughty tone the God began
(Through Hell's wide halls the echoing accents ran,

4. The Fate who measured the length of the thread of life. Atropos cut the thread, Clotho spun it.
5. The giant gods who warred against Zeus and were thrown into Hades.
6. God of the north wind.
7. Aeolus, who confined the winds in a cave in the Aeolian Islands.
8. Mother of Hermes, Cyllenius of line 111, the messenger of the gods.

The bellowing beast[9] that guards the gates of Hell
Repress'd the thunder of his triple yell,   120
And sad Cocytus at the sudden cry
Recall'd his wailing stream of misery.
From Acheron's banks no sullen murmurs spread,
His hoarse waves slumbered on his noiseless bed,
'Gan Phlegethon in surly haste retire   125
And still his whirling waves and check his flood of fire),
"Grandson of Atlas, thou whose footsteps stray
Through Hell's deep shadows, and the realms of day,
To whom alone of all the Gods 'tis giv'n
To tread the shores of Styx[1] and halls of Heav'n,   130
Chain of each world and link of either sphere,
Whom Tegea's[2] sons in silent awe revere,
Go, cleave the winds and bear my will to Jove,
That haughty God who sways the realms above. . . .

1820–23; 1931

From The Devil and the Lady[1]

From Act 1, Scene 4

AMORET   Go thy ways![2]
      Thou yellowest leaf on Autumn's wither'd tree!
      Thou sickliest ear of all the sheaf! thou clod!
      Thou fireless mixture of Earth's coldest clay!
      Thou crazy dotard, crusted o'er with age[3]   5
      As thick as ice upon a standing pool!
      Thou shrunken, sapless, wizen Grasshopper,[4]
      Consuming the green promise of my youth!
      Go, get thee gone, and evil winds attend thee,
      Thou antidote to love! thou bane of Hope,   10
      Which like the float o' th' fisher's rod buoys up
      The sinking line and by its fluctuations
      Shows when the pang of Disappointment gnaws
      Beneath it! But to me are both unknown:
      I never more can hope and therefore never   15

---

9. Cerberus, the three-headed dog guarding the entrance to the underworld.
1. Cocytus, Acheron, Phlegethon, and Styx are rivers of Hades.
2. A city of Arcadia founded by Tegeus and noted for the exceptional bravery of its inhabitants.
1. This curious "Elizabethan" comedy in blank verse, strongly influenced by extensive reading in Shakespeare, Beaumont and Fletcher, and perhaps Ben Jonson, is the longest and most carefully written work of the juvenilia. An incredible achievement for a boy fourteen years old, the unfinished play is about an aged necromancer called Magus who leaves his young and wanton bride, Amoret, in the care of the Devil, conjured from the underworld. The Devil summarily sends Amoret off to bed and, disguised in her clothes, meets the inevitable troop of suitors who appear during the husband's absence. The play ends abruptly in the third scene of Act 3, when Magus returns; and one can only guess how the poet intended to finish it.
2. The magician has departed on some mysterious journey; and in this soliloquy Amoret reveals her true feelings, the nature but hardly the intensity of which Magus had suspected.
3. Magus is in his eighties and Amoret is just twenty, one of several interesting parallels to Merlin and Vivien in Idylls of the King.
4. Tithonus, to whom Jupiter granted immortality but not eternal youth, withered away and was turned into a cicada. See Tennyson's "Tithonus."

Can suffer Disappointment.
He bears a charmed life and will outlast me
In mustiness of dry longevity,
Like some tough mummy wither'd, not decay'd—
His years are countless as the dusty race   20
That people an old Cheese and flourish only
In the unsoundest parts on't.
The big waves shatter thy frail skiff! the winds
Sing anything but lullabies unto thee!
The dark-hair'd Midnight grant no ray to thee,   25
But that of lightning, or the dreadful splendour
Of the conflicting wave! the red bolt scathe thee!
Why was I link'd with such a frowzy mate,
With such a fusty partner of my days?

From *Act 2, Scene 1*[5]

[MAGUS's *cottage with the wood and lake in the distance.*
Enter DEVIL *and takes his station before the cottage door attired in a cap and gown.*]

DEVIL   The starry fires of yon Chrystalline vault
Are waning,[6] and the airy-footed Night
Will soon withdraw the dismal solitude
Of her capacious pall, wherewith she clouds
Yon mighty and illimitable sky,   5
Placing a death-like colour in all things,
Monopolizing all the varied Earth
With her dim mantle—
                                    [A *pause*
              Oh! ye eyes of Heaven,
Ye glorious inextinguishable lights,
High blazing mid the lone solemnity   10
Of night and silence, shall the poor worm, Man,
The creature of this solitary earth,
Presume to think his destiny enroll'd
In your almighty everlasting fires?
Shall this poor thing of melancholy clay,   15
This lone ephemeris of one small hour,
Proudly suppose his little fate inscribed
In the magnificent stars? What have the worlds
Of yon o'er arching Heavn'n—the ample spheres
Of never-ending space, to do with Man?[7]   20
And some romantick visionaries have deem'd
This petty clod the centre of all worlds.
Nay—even the Sun himself, the gorgeous Sun,
Pays homage to it. Ha! Ha! Ha! Poor Man,

5. Here, as elsewhere in the play, the Devil becomes the young Tennyson's mouthpiece as he speculates on the nature of human existence and the illusory qualities of the visible universe. The passage is espe-cially important because many of the questions foreshadow the concerns of the late poetry.
6. The time, as established at the end of Act 1, is "half after midnight" and not, as one might suspect, be-fore dawn.
7. A question at the center of several sections of *IM* and of such late pieces as "Despair" and "Vastness."

Thou summer midge![8]—Oh, ye shine bravely now   25
Through the deep purple of the summer sky,
I know that ye are Earths as fair and fairer
And mightier than this I tread upon—
For I have scaled your mountains, to whose cones
Of most insuperable altitude   30
This Earth's most glorious Eminences and heights
All pil'd and heap'd upon each other's brows,
And massed and kneaded to one common substance,
Were but a molehill.
And I have swum your boundless seas, whose waves   35
Were each an ocean of this little orb,
Yet know I not your natures, or if that
Which we call palpable and visible
Is condensation of firm particles.
O suns and spheres and stars and belts and systems,[9]   40
Are ye or are ye not?
Are ye realities or semblances
Of that which men call real?
Are ye true substance? are ye anthing
Except delusive shows and physical points   45
Endow'd with some repulsive potency?
Could the Omnipotent fill all space, if ye
Or the least atom in ye or the least
Division of that atom (if least can dwell
In infinite divisibility) should be impenetrable?   50
I have some doubt if ye exist when none
Are by to view ye; if your Being alone
Be in the mind and the intelligence
Of the created? should some great decree
Annihilate the sentient principle   55
Would ye or would ye not be non-existent?
'Tis a shrewd doubt—

From *Act 3, Scene 2*[1]

MAGUS   Half the powers o' th' other world
Were leagued against my journeying: but had not
The irresistible and lawless might
Of brazen-handed fix'd Fatality[2]

8. Two manuscript versions of the play exist. The earlier version contained in notebook number 1 in the Harvard collection ends with "midge," and what follows, perhaps added one or two years later, is from the Trinity manuscript, from which Sir Charles Tennyson had the play printed.
9. Lines 40–57 anticipate some of Tennyson's later metaphysical speculations. "There are moments when the flesh is nothing to me," he said in 1869, "when I feel and know the flesh to be the vision, God and the Spiritual the only real and true. Depend upon it, the Spiritual *is* the real" (*Memoir* II, 90). Frederick Locker-Lampson reported that in the same year Tennyson told him in a discussion about the Material-ists, "I think it [matter] is merely the shadow of something greater than itself, and which we poor short-sighted creatures cannot see" (*Memoir* II, 69). For similar views expressed in poetry see, for example, King Arthur's speech in "The Holy Grail," lines 906–15.
1. Magus is back home outside his cottage, now filled with the suitors. He is explaining to the Devil the reasons for his untimely return. "The powers o' th' other world" are apparently from Heaven, though the spirits Magus describes as having thwarted his passage seem hardly to have come from there.
2. Like Milton's Satan after his defeat in Heaven, Magus ascribes the cause of his failure to Fate, not God—a comparison Tennyson may have had in mind. The influence of *Paradise Lost* is clearly evident through-out this passage, which draws on Milton's description of Satan's journey through Chaos to Eden.

Oppos'd me, I had done it. The black storm,   5
From out whose mass of volum'd vapour sprang
The lively curling thunderbolt had ceas'd
Long ere from out the dewy depth of Pines
Emerging on the hollow'd banks, that bound
The leapings of the saucy tide, I stood—   10
The mighty waste of moaning waters lay
So goldenly in moonlight, whose clear lamp
With its long line of vibratory lustre
Trembled on the dun surface, that my Spirit
Was buoyant with rejoicings. Each hoar wave   15
With crisped undulation arching rose,
Thence falling in white ridge with sinuous slope
Dash'd headlong to the shore and spread along
The sands its tender fringe of creamy spray.[3]
Thereat my shallop lightly I unbound,   20
Spread my white sail and rode exulting on
The placid murmurings of each feathery wave
That hurried into sparkles round the cleaving
Of my dark Prow; but scarcely had I past
The third white line of breakers when a squall,   25
Fell on me from the North, an inky Congress
O' the Republican clouds unto the zenith
Rush'd from th' horizon upwards with the speed
Of their own thunder-bolts.
The seas divided and dim Phantasies   30
Came thronging thickly round me, with hot eyes
Unutterable things came flitting by me;
Semblance of palpability was in them,
Albeit the wavering lightnings glitter'd thro'
Their shadow'd immaterialities.   35
Black shapes clung to my boat; a sullen owl[4]
Perch'd on the Prow, and overhead the hum
As of infernal Spirits in mid Heaven
Holding aerial council caught mine ear.
Then came a band of melancholy sprites,   40
White as their shrouds and motionlessly pale
Like some young Ashwood when the argent[5] Moon
Looks in upon its many silver stems,
And thrice my name was syllabled i' th' air
And thrice upon the wave, like that loud voice   45
Which thro' the deep dark night i' th' olden time
Came sounding o'er the lone Ionian.
Thereat I girded round my loins the scarf
Thy Mother Hecate gave me and withstood
The violent tempest: the insulting surge   50
Rode over me in glassy arch but dar'd not
Sprinkle one drop of its nefarious spray

3. Tennyson, one of the great landscape painters in verse, shows in these five lines the precise visual detail and careful choice of adjectives that will characterize his mature art.
4. Here a bird of ill omen.
5. Silver.

Upon my charmèd person: the red heralds
O' th' heavy footed thunder glanc'd beside me,
Kiss'd my bar'd front and curl'd around my brow   55
In lambent wreaths of circling fire, but could not
Singe one loose lock of vagrant grey, that floated
To the wind's dalliance. But nor magic spells
Vigour of heart or vigilance of hand,
Could back the Ocean's spumy menacings,   60
Which drove my leaky skiff upon the sands.
Soon as I touch'd firm Earth, each mounting billow
Fell laxly back into its windless bed,
And all the moon-lit Ocean slumber'd still.
Thrice with bold prow I breasted the rough spume   65
But thrice a vitreous wall of waves up sprung
Ridging the level sea—so far'd it with me
Foil'd of my purpose. Some unwholesome star,
Some spells of darker Gramarie[6] than mine,
Rul'd the dim night and would not grant me passage.   70

*   *   *

MAGUS[7]   "Tis even thus—
And they would pluck from th' casket the sole gem[8]
Of mine affections, taint its innocent lustre,
And give it back dishonour'd, they would canker
My brightest flower, would muddy the clear source   5
Whence flows my only stream of earthly bliss;
Would let the foul consuming worm into
The garner of my love. O Earthliness!
Man clambers over the high battlements
That part the principalities of good   10
And ill—perchance a few hot tears, and then
The sear'd heart yields to 't and Crime's signet stamps
Her burning image there. The summer fly
That skims the surface of the deep black pool
Knows not the gulf beneath its slippery path.   15
Man sees,[9] but plunges madly into it.
We follow thro' a night of crime and care
The voice of soft Temptation, still it calls,
And still we follow onwards, till we find
She is a Phantom and—we follow still.   20
When couched in Boyhood's passionless tranquility,
The natural mind of man is warm and yielding,
Fit to receive the best impressions,
But raise it to the atmosphere of manhood
And the rude breath of dissipation   25
Will harden it to stone. 'Tis like the seaplant

---

6. Magic.
7. The Devil has told Magus about the situation at the cottage, and the magician is left alone to speculate on sex and morality. These lines also appear only in the Trinity Manuscript; were therefore probably written when Tennyson was fifteen or sixteen; and chiefly reflect the poet's views, not the character's.
8. Amoret. "They": the suitors.
9. Because, for Tennyson, unlike animals, humans have moral sense and can perceive evil.

Which in its parent and unshaken depths
Is mouldable as clay, but when rude hands
Have pluck'd it from its billowless Abyss
Unto the breathings of Heaven's airs, each gust   30
Which blows upon 't will fix it into hardness.
I'll to the Northern casement which looks over
The shrubby banks o' th' mountain Lake, for thence
The slightest whisper from within may reach me.

                                      1823–24; 1930

Armageddon[1]

Spirit of Prophecy whose mighty grasp
Enfoldeth all things, whose capacious soul
Can people the illimitable abyss
Of vast and fathomless futurity
With all the Giant Figures that shall pace   5
The dimness of its stage,—whose subtle ken
Can throng the doubly-darkened firmament
Of Time to come with all its burning stars
At awful intervals. I thank thy power,
Whose wondrous emanation hath poured   10
Bright light on what was darkest, and removed
The cloud that from my mortal faculties
Barred out the knowledge of the Latter Times.

    I stood upon the mountain which o'erlooks
The valley of destruction and I saw   15
Things strange, surpassing wonder; but to give
Utterance to things unutterable, to paint
In dignity of language suitable
The majesty of what I then beheld,
Were past the power of man. No fabled Muse   20
Could breathe into my soul such influence
Of her seraphic nature, as to express
Deeds inexpressible by loftiest rhyme.[2]

    I stood upon the mountain which o'erlooks
The valley of Megiddo.—Broad before me   25
Lay a huge plain whereon the wandering eye,
Weary with gazing, found no resting-place,
Unbroken by the ridge of mound or hill

---

1. The plain of Megiddo, where, according to the Bible (Revelation 16:16), the final decisive battle between
   the forces of good and evil will be fought before the Day of Judgment. This very early fragmentary dream-
   vision in Miltonic blank verse later became the basis for Tennyson's Prize Poem "Timbuctoo," for which
   he won the Chancellor's Medal at Cambridge in 1829. The traditional verse form for all applicants had
   been the heroic couplet, so Tennyson's achievement has an added dimension. Dwight Culler's chapter
   "The Poetry of Apocalypse" in *The Poetry of Tennyson* (1977) renders a fascinating account for that impulse in a number of these earliest poems.
2. See *Paradise Lost* VIII, line 113: "Distance inexpressible," and "Lycidas" line 11: "lofty rhyme"
   [Ricks].

Or far-off cone of some aerial mount
Varying the horizon's sameness.

                       Eve came down.   30
Upon the valleys and the sun was setting;
Never set sun with such portentous glare
Since he arose on that gay morn, when Earth
First drunk the light of his prolific ray.
Strange figures thickly thronged his burning orb,   35
Spirits of discord seem'd to weave across
His fiery disk a web of bloody haze,
Thro' whose reticulations struggled forth
His ineffectual, intercepted beams,
Curtaining in one dark terrific pall   40
Of dun-red light heaven's azure and earth's green.

The beasts fled to their dens; the little birds
All wing'd their way home shrieking: fitful gusts
Of violent tempest shook the scanty palm
That cloth'd the mountain ridge whereon I stood: 45
And in the red and murky Even light,
Black, formless, unclean things came flitting by;
Some seemed of bestial similitude
And some half human, yet so horrible,
So shadowy, indistinct and undefin'd,   50
It were a mockery to call them ought
Save unrealities, which took the form
And fashioning of such ill-omened things
That it were sin almost to look on them.[3]

    There was a mingling too of such strange sounds   55
(Which came at times upon my startled hearing)
Half wailing and half laughter; such a dissonance
Of jarring confus'd voices, part of which
Seem'd hellish and part heavenly, whisperings,
Low chauntings, strangled screams, and other notes   60
Which I may liken unto nothing which
I ever heard on Earth, but seem'd most like
A mixture of the voice of man and beast;
And then again throughout the lurid waste
Of air, a breathless stillness reigned, so deep,   65
So deathlike, so appalling, that I shrunk
Into myself again, and almost wish'd
For the recurrence of those deadly sounds,
Which fix'd my senses into stone, and drove
The buoyant life-drops back into my heart.   70

    Nor did the glittering of white wings escape
My notice far within the East, which caught
Ruddy reflection from the ensanguin'd West;

---

3. Tennyson was most probably already familiar with Dante, and the above verse-paragraph may have been influenced by the Francesca episode, *Inferno* V, lines 121ff.

Nor, ever and anon, the shrill clear sound
Of some aerial trumpet, solemnly   75
Pealing throughout the Empyrean void.

    Thus to some wakeful hind who on the heights
Outwatches the wan planet, comes the sound
Of some far horn along the distant hills
Echoing, in some beleaguer'd country, where   80
The pitiless Enemy by night hath made
Sudden incursion and unsafe inroad.

    The streams, whose imperceptible advance
Lingering in slow meanders, once was wont
To fertilize the plain beneath—whose course   85
Was barely mark'd save by the lazy straws
That wandered down them—now, as instinct with life,
Ran like the lightning's wing, and dash'd upon
The curvature of their green banks a wreath
Of lengthen'd foam; and yet, although they rush'd   90
Incalculably swift and fring'd with spray
The pointed crags, whose wave-worn slippery height
Parted their glassy channels, there awoke
No murmurs round them—but their sapphire depths
Of light were changed to crimson, as the sky   95
Glow'd like a fiery furnace.
                    In the East
Broad rose the moon, first like a beacon flame
Seen on the far horizon's utmost verge,
Of red eruption from the fissur'd cone
Of Cotopaxi's[4] cloud-cap't altitude;   100
Then with dilated orb and mark'd with lines
Of mazy red athwart her shadowy face,
Sickly, as though her secret eyes beheld
Witchcrafts, abominations, and the spells
Of sorcerers, what time they summon up   105
From out the stilly chambers of the earth
Obscene, inutterable phantasies.

    The sun went down; the hot and feverish night
Succeeded; but the parch'd, unwholesome air
Was unrecruited by the tears of heaven.   110
There was a windless calm, a dismal pause,
A dreary interval, wherein I held
My breath and heard the beatings of my heart.
The moon show'd clearer yet, with deadlier gleam,
Her ridgéd and uneven surface stain'd   115
With crosses, fiery streaks, and wandering lines—
Bloody impressions! and a star or two
Peer'd through the thick and smoky atmosphere.

4. An active volcano in the Andes, probably the world's highest (19,347 feet) live volcano.

Strange was that lunar light: the rock which stood
Fronting her sanguine ray, seem'd chang'd unto   120
A pillar of crimson, while the other half
Averted, and whatever else around
Stood not in opposition to her beams,
Was shrouded in the densest pall of night
And darkness almost palpable.
                              Deep fear   125
And trembling came upon me, when I saw
In the remotest chambers of the East
Ranges of silver tents beside the moon,
Clear, but at distance so ineffable,
That save when keenly view'd, they else might seem   130
But little shining points or galaxies,
The blending of the beams of many stars.

Full opposite within the lurid West,
In clear relief against the long rich vein
Of melancholy red that fring'd the sky,   135
A suite of dark pavilions met mine eyes,
That covered half the western tide of Heaven,
Far stretching, in the midst of which tower'd one
Pre-eminent, which bore aloft in air
A standard, round whose staff a mighty snake   140
Twin'd his black folds, the while his ardent crest
And glossy neck were swaying to and fro.

2⁵

The rustling of white wings! The bright descent
Of a young seraph! and he stood beside me
In the wide foldings of his argent robes   145
There on the ridge, and look'd into my face
With his unutterable shining eyes,
So that with hasty motion I did veil
My vision with both hands, and saw before me
Such coloured spots as dance before the eyes   150
Of those that gaze from the noonday sun.

"O Son of Man, why stand you here alone
Upon the mountain, knowing not the things
Which will be, and the gathering of the nations
Unto the mighty battle of the Lord?   155
Thy sense is clogg'd with dull Mortality,[6]
Thy spirit fetter'd with the bond of clay—
Open thine eyes and see!"
                         I look'd, but not
Upon his face, for it was wonderful

---

5. Tennyson drew most heavily on sections 2 and 3 when reworking this poem in "Timbuctoo."
6. A phrase probably from Beaumont and Fletcher's *The Faithful Shepherdess* I, ii, lines 104–05: "so to make
   thee free / From dying flesh and dull mortality." Also compare this passage and the following to Tennyson's "The Ancient Sage" lines 229–32. And compare Keats's "On Seeing the Elgin Marbles": "mortality / Weighs heavily on me."

With its exceeding brightness, and the light   160
Of the great Angel Mind that look'd from out
The starry glowing of his restless eyes.
I felt my soul grow godlike, and my spirit[7]
With supernatural excitation bound
Within me, and my mental eye grew large   165
With such a vast circumference of thought,
That, in my vanity, I seem'd to stand
Upon the outward verge and bound alone
Of God's omniscience. Each failing sense,
As with a momentary flash of light,   170
Grew thrillingly distinct and keen:[8] I saw
The smallest grain that dappled the dark Earth,
The indistinctest atom in deep air,
The Moon's white cities, and the opal width
Of her small, glowing lakes, her silver heights   175
Unvisited with dew of vagrant cloud,
And the unsounded, undescended depth
Of her black hollows. Nay—the hum of men
Or other things talking in unknown tongues,
And notes of busy Life in distant worlds,   180
Beat, like a far wave, on my anxious ear.

  I wondered with deep wonder at myself:
My mind seem'd wing'd with knowledge and the strength
Of holy musings and immense Ideas,
Even to Infinitude.[9] All sense of Time   185
And Being and Place was swallowed up and lost
Within a victory of boundless thought.
I was a part of the Unchangeable,
A scintillation of Eternal Mind,
Remix'd and burning with its parent fire.   190
Yea! in that hour I could have fallen down
Before my own strong soul and worshipp'd it.

  Highly and holily the Angel look'd.
Immeasurable Solicitude and Awe,
And solemn Adoration and high Faith,   195
Were trac'd on his imperishable front—
Then with a mournful and ineffable smile,
Which but to look on for a moment fill'd
My eyes with irresistible sweet tears,
In accents of majestic melody,   200
Like a swollen river's gushings in still night
Mingled with floating music, thus he spoke.

7. Lines 163ff. record a mystical experience that in some respects resembles Wordsworth's in "Ode: Intimations of Immortality," especially "Those obstinate questionings / Of sense and outward things, / Falling
   from us, vanishings" (lines 141–43).
8. In "The Coming of Arthur" Tennyson speaks of the king's enlightenment in similar terms: "The world /
   Was all so clear about him that he saw / The smallest rock far on the faintest hill" (lines 96–98).
9. An expression recalling the young Keats's remark in his early poem "Sleep and Poetry": "There ever rolls
   a vast idea before me / And I glean therefrom my liberty" (lines 290–92). Although a number of passages
   in "Armageddon" and others in the very early poetry beg comparison with Keats, Tennyson may not have
   read either Keats or Wordsworth until after he entered Cambridge in November 1827.

3

"O Everlasting God, and thou not less
The Everlasting Man (since that great spirit
Which permeates and informs thine inward sense,   205
Though limited in action, capable
Of the extreme of knowledge—whether join'd
Unto thee in conception or confin'd
From former wanderings in other shapes
I know not—deathless as its God's own life,   210
Burns on with inextinguishable strength),
O Lords of Earth and Tyrannies of Hell,
And thrones of Heaven, whose triple pride shall clash
In the annihilating anarchy
Of unimaginable war, a day   215
Of darkness riseth on ye, a thick day,
Pall'd with dun wreaths of dusky fight, a day
Of many thunders and confuséd noise,
Of bloody grapplings in the interval
Of the opposéd Battle, a great day   220
Of wonderful revealings and vast sights
And inconceivable visions, such as yet
have never shone into the heart of Man—
THE DAY of the Lord God!"
                     His voice grew deep
With volumes of strong sound, which made the rock   225
To throb beneath me, and his parted locks
Of spiral light fell raylike, as he mov'd,
On each white shoulder: his ambrosial lip
Was beautifully curv'd, as in the pride
And power of his mid Prophecy: his nostril   230
Dilated with Expression; half upturn'd
The broad beneficence of his clear brow
Into the smoky sky; his sunlike eyes
With tenfold glory lit; his mighty arm
Outstretch'd described half-circles; small thin flashes   235
Of intense lustre followed it.

4

I look'd,
And lo! the vision of the night was chang'd.
The sooty mantle of infernal smoke
Whose blank, obliterating, dewless cloud
Had made the plain like some vast crater, rose   240
Distinct from Earth and gather'd to itself
In one dense, dry, interminable mass
Sailing far Northward, as it were the shadow
Of this round Planet cast upon the face
Of the bleak air. But this was wonderful,   245
To see how full it was of living things,
Strange shapings, and anomalies of Hell,
And dusky faces, and protruded arms
Of hairy strength, and white and garish eyes,

And silent intertwisted thunderbolts,   250
Wreathing and sparkling restlessly like snakes
Within their grassy depths. I watch'd it till
Its latest margin sank beneath the sweep
Of the horizon.
                    All the crimson streaks
And bloody dapplings faded from the disk.   255
Of the immaculate morn.
                    An icy veil
Of pale, weak, lifeless, thin, unnatural blue
Wrapt up the rich varieties of things
In grim and ghastly sameness.
                    The clear stars
Shone out with keen but fix'd intensity,   260
All-silence, looking steadfast consciousness
Upon the dark and windy waste of Earth.
There was a beating in the atmosphere,
An indefinable pulsation
Inaudible to outward sense, but felt   265
Thro' the deep heart of every living thing,
As if the great soul of the Universe
Heav'd with tumultuous throbbings on the vast
Suspense of some grand issue.[1] . . .

                                        1824?; 1931

1. Compare Wordsworth, who celebrates his awakening power during his seventeenth year to see relationships among objects "By observation of affinities / In objects where no brotherhood exists / To passive minds" (*Prelude* II, lines 382–402).

From *Poems by Two Brothers* (1827)[1]

Memory[2]

The memory is perpetually looking back when we have nothing present
to entertain us: it is like those repositories in animals that are filled with
stores of food, on which they may ruminate when their present pasture
fails.

—ADDISON

Memory! dear enchanter!
   Why bring back to view
Dreams of youth, which banter
   All that e'er was true?

Why present before me   5
   Thoughts of years gone by,
Which, like shadows o'er me,
   Dim in distance fly?

Days of youth, now shaded
   By twilight of long years,[3]   10
Flowers of youth, now faded,
   Though bathed in sorrow's tears:

Thoughts of youth, which waken
   Mournful feelings now
Fruits which time hath shaken   15
   From off their parent bough:

1. Since the dates of publication, 1826 and 1827, have been used indiscriminately, confusion exists over the actual date the volume appeared. As Tennyson himself tells us, "The book was issued late in 1826, but *ante*-dated (as is the fashion of publishers) as coming out in 1827. . . . When the poems were published Charles was eighteen, I was seventeen." See the 1898 edition of the *Memoir* I, 22–23. For dates of composition, which cannot be precisely known, the advertisement explains: "The following Poems were written from the ages of fifteen to eighteen." And in the preface to his facsimile edition of 1893, Hallam Tennyson notes: "My father writes, 'The Preface states "written from 15 to 18." I was between 15 and 17, Charles between 15 and 18.'" When originally published the volume contained no references anywhere to the authors' names. In the 1893 edition Hallam, working with the publishers' manuscript and the help of Frederick Tennyson, Alfred's other older brother, then in his late eighties, assigned initials to the poems. Alfred had contributed over half the volume, and Frederick, it turned out, had written three or four of the poems. The authorship of several pieces, however, remains in doubt.
2. Although Hallam Tennyson tentatively assigned authorship of the poem to Charles, later editors have tended to ascribe it to Alfred. The poem's relationship to "Ode to Memory," as well as its length and content, strongly links it to Alfred.
3. Often in *Poems by Two Brothers* Tennyson adopts the mask of an older man, as in the opening lines of the following poem, "Remorse."

Memory! why, oh why,
  This fond heart consuming,
Shew me years gone by,
  When those hopes were blooming.   20

Hopes which now are parted,
  Hopes which then I priz'd,
Which this world, cold-hearted,
  Ne'er has realiz'd?

I knew not then its strife,   25
  I knew not then its rancour;
In every rose of life,
  Alas! there lurks a canker.

Round every palm-tree, springing
  With bright fruit in the waste,   30
A mournful asp⁴ is clinging,
  Which sours it to our taste.

O'er every fountain, pouring
  Its waters thro' the wild,
Which man imbibes, adoring,   35
  And deems it undefil'd,

The poison-shrubs are dropping
  Their dark dews day by day;
And Care is hourly lopping
  Our greenest boughs away!   40

Ah! these are thoughts that grieve me
  Then, when others rest.
Memory! why deceive me
  By thy visions blest?

Why lift the veil, dividing   45
  The brilliant courts of spring—
Where gilded shapes are gliding
  In fairy colouring—

From age's frosty mansion,
  So cheerless and so chill?   50
Why bid the bleak expansion
  Of past life meet us still?

Where's now that peace of mind
  O'er youth's pure bosom stealing

---

4. The word *mournful* qualifies the conventional association of serpents with evil. Tennyson had read Shakespeare's *Antony and Cleopatra* and perhaps was thinking of that asp too. For an interesting discussion of the imagery in the early work, W. D. Paden's psychologically inclined *Tennyson in Egypt* is well worth consulting.

So sweet and so refin'd,   55
    So exquisite a feeling?

Where's now the heart exulting
    In pleasure's bouyant sense,
And gaiety, resulting
    From conscious innocence?   60

All, all have past and fled,
    And left me lorn and lonely;
All those dear hopes are dead,
    Remembrance wakes them only!

I stand like some lone tower   65
    Of former days remaining,
Within whose place of power
    The midnight owl is plaining;—

Like oak-tree old and grey,
    Whose trunk with age is failing,   70
Thro' whose dark boughs for aye
    The winter winds are wailing.

Thus, Memory, thus thy light
    O'er this worn soul is gleaming,
Like some far fire at night   75
    Along the dun deep streaming.

1827

Remorse

—sudant tacita præcordia culpa[1]
                                                    —JUVENAL

Oh! 't is a fearful thing to glance
    Back on the gloom of mis-spent years:[2]
What shadowy forms of guilt advance,
    And fill me with a thousand fears!
The vices of my life arise,   5
    Pourtray'd in shapes, alas! too true;
    And not one beam of hope breaks through,
To cheer my old and aching eyes,
T' illume my night of wretchedness,
My age of anguish and distress.   10
If I am damn'd, why find I not
Some comfort in this earthly spot?

1. The hearts sweat in unspeaking guilt.
2. Compare the last stanza from the Prologue to *IM*: "Forgive these wild and wandering cries, / Confusions of a wasted youth."

But no! this world and that to come
Are both to me one scene of gloom!
Lest ought of solace I should see,   15
　Or lose the thoughts of what I do,
Remorse, with soul-felt agony,
　Holds up the mirror to my view.
And I was cursed from my birth,
A reptile made to creep on earth,   20
An hopeless outcast, born to die
A living death eternally!³
With too much conscience to have rest,
Too little to be ever blest,
To you vast world of endless woe,   25
　Unlighted by the cheerful day,
　My soul shall wing her weary way;
　　To those dread depths where aye the same,
Throughout the waste of darkness, glow
　　The glimmerings of the boundless flame.   30
And yet I cannot here below
Take my full cup of guilt, as some,
And laugh away my doom to come.
I would I'd been all-heartless! then
I might have sinn'd like other men;   35
But all this side the grave is fear,
A wilderness so dank and drear,
That never wholesome plant would spring;
　And all behind—I dare not think!
I would not risk th' imagining—   40
　From the full view my spirits shrink;
And starting backwards, yet I cling
To life, whose every hour to me
Hath been increase of misery.
But yet I cling to it, for well   45
　I know the pangs that rack me now
Are trifles, to the endless hell
　That waits me, when my burning brow
And my wrung eyes shall hope in vain
For one small drop to cool the pain,   50
The fury of that madd'ning flame
That then shall scorch my writhing frame!
Fiends! who have goaded me to ill!
Distracting fiends, who goad me still!
If e'er I work'd a sinful deed,   55
　Ye know how bitter was the draught;
Ye know my inmost soul would bleed,
　And ye have look'd at me and laugh'd,
Triumphing that I could not free

---

3. One suspects the influence of Tennyson's aunt Mary Bourne in such passages. A rigid Calvinist of the
hellfire and damnation school, she would weep for hours over God's infinite goodness. "'Has He not
damned,' she cried, 'most of my friends? But *me, me* He has picked out for eternal salvation, *me* who am
no better than my neighbors.' One day she said to her nephew, 'Alfred, Alfred, when I look at you, I think
of the words of Holy Scripture— "Depart from me, ye cursed, into everlasting fire"'" (*Memoir* I, 15).
Whatever Aunt Mary's effect on Tennyson may have been, he probably took his Byron more seriously.

My spirit from your slavery!   60
Yet is there that in me which says,
     Should these old feet their course retread
From out the portal of my days,
     That I should lead the life I've led:
My agony, my torturing shame,   65
My guilt, my errors all the same![4]
Oh, God! that thou wouldst grant that ne'er
     My soul its clay-cold bed forsake,
     That I might sleep, and never wake
Unto the thrill of conscious fear;[5]   70
     For when the trumphet's piercing cry[6]
Shall burst upon my slumb'ring ear,
     And countless seraphs throng the sky,
How shall I cast my shroud away,
And come into the blaze of day?   75
How shall I brook to hear each crime,
Here veil'd by secrecy and time,
Read out from thine eternal book?
     How shall I stand before thy throne,
         While earth shall like a furnace burn?   80
How shall I bear the with'ring look
     Of men and angels, who will turn
Their dreadful gaze on me alone?

                                           1827

"I Wander in Darkness and Sorrow"

I wander in darkness and sorrow,
     Unfriended, and cold, and alone,
As dismally gurgles beside me
     The bleak river's desolate moan.
The rise of the volleying thunder   5
     The mountain's lone echoes repeat:
The roar of the wind is around me,
     The leaves of the year at my feet.

I wander in darkness and sorrow,
     Uncheer'd by the moon's placid ray;   10

4. Not reproduced here are several pieces from *Poems by Two Brothers* composed in obvious immitation of Byron, who, more powerfully than any other poet Tennyson was currently reading, directly addressed the subject of sexual impulses. For one of numberless examples, see *IM* 51 and notes: "Is there no baseness we would hide? / No inner vileness that we dread?" Tennyson was keenly sensitive to the sexual dilemmas of adolescence, and, as he said, "Byron expressed what I felt" (*Memoir* I, 16). On the day he learned of Byron's death, Tennyson, then fourteen, went out and carved on a rock, "Byron is dead"; he later recalled that it was "a day when the whole world seemed to be darkened for me" (*Memoir* I, 4).
5. An inchoate expression of the tension between desiring the escape offered by unconsciousness and accepting the burdens of consciousness, a tension at the center of Tennyson's thought in his mature poetry. "Supposed Confessions" will be his first concerted effort to work out the dilemma that also becomes the subject of "The Lotos-Eaters" and numerous other poems.
6. On the Day of Judgment.

Not a friend that I lov'd but is dead,
   Not a hope but has faded away!
Oh! when shall I rest in the tomb,
   Wrapt about with the chill winding sheet?
For the roar of the wind is around me,   15
   The leaves of the year at my feet.

I heed not the blasts that sweep o'er me,
   I blame not the tempests of night;
They are not the foes who have banish'd
   The visions of youthful delight: 20
I hail the wild sound of their raving,
   Their merciless presence I greet;
Though the roar of the wind be around me,
   The leaves of the year at my feet.

In this waste of existence, for solace,   25
   On whom shall my lone spiril call?
Shall I fly to the friends of my bosom?
   My God! I have buried them all![1]
They are dead, they are gone, they are cold,
   My embraces no longer they meet;   30
Let the roar of the wind be around me,
   The leaves of the year at my feet!

Those eyes that glanc'd love unto mine,
   With motionless slumbers are prest;
Those hearts which once throbb'd but for me,   35
   Are chill as the earth where they rest.
Then around on my wan wither'd form
   Let the pitiless hurricanes beat;
Let the roar of the wind be around me,
   The leaves of the year at my feet!   40

Like the voice of the owl in the hall,
   Where the song and the banquet have ceas'd,
Where the green weeds have mantled the hearth,
   Whence arose the proud flame of the feast;
So I cry to the storm, whose dark wing   45
   Scatters on me the wild-driving sleet—
'Let the roar of the wind be around me,
   The fall of the leaves at my feet!'

1827

---

1. The degree to which Tennyson was aware of the incongruities in the pose of a boy of seventeen speaking out on a wasted youth filled with vice and mortal sin is open to speculation.

From *Poems, Chiefly Lyrical* (1830)

Ode to Memory[1]

ADDRESSED TO————.

1

Thou who stealest fire,
From the fountains of the past,
To glorify the present, O, haste,
    Visit my low desire!
Strengthen me, enlighten me!   5
I faint in this obscurity,
Thou dewy dawn of memory.

2

Come not as thou camest of late,
    Flinging the gloom of yesternight
On the white day, but robed in soften'd light   10
    Of orient state.
Whilome thou camest with the morning mist,
    Even as a maid, whose stately brow
The dew-impearled winds of dawn have kiss'd,
    When she, as thou,   15
Stays on her floating locks the lovely freight
Of overflowing blooms, and earliest shoots
Of orient green, giving safe pledge of fruits,
Which in wintertide shall star
The black earth with brilliance rare.   20

3

Whilome thou camest with the morning mist,
    And with the evening cloud,
Showering thy gleaned wealth into my open breast;
Those peerless flowers which in the rudest wind
    Never grow sere,[2]   25
When rooted in the garden of the mind,

---

1. First published in the 1830 volume with the subtitle "Written very Early in Life," which subsequently became "Addressed to————" with Arthur Hallam in mind. The verse form, five-stress and three-stress iambics, was perhaps suggested by "Lycidas" [Ricks].
2. Compare "Lycidas" line 2: "with Ivy never seer."

Because they are the earliest of the year.
    Nor was the night thy shroud.
In sweet dreams softer than unbroken rest
Thou leddest by the hand thine infant Hope.   30
The eddying of her garments caught from thee
The light of thy great presence; and the cope[3]
    Of the half-attain'd futurity,
    Tho' deep not fathomless,
Was cloven with the million stars which tremble   35
O'er the deep mind of dauntless infancy.
Small thought was there of life's distress;
For sure she deem'd no mist of earth could dull
Those spirit-thrilling eyes so keen and beautiful;
Sure she was nigher to heaven's spheres,   40
Listening the lordly music flowing from
    The illimitable years.
    O, strengthen me, enlighten me!
    I faint in this obscurity,
    Thou dewy dawn of memory.   45

4

Come forth, I charge thee, arise,
Thou of the many tongues, the myriad eyes!
Thou comest not with shows of flaunting vines
    Unto mine inner eye,
    Divinest Memory!   50
    Thou wert not nursed by the waterfall
Which ever sounds and shines
    A pillar of white light upon the wall
Of purple cliffs, aloof descried:
Come from the woods that belt the gray hillside,[4]   55
The seven elms, the poplars four
That stand beside my father's door,
And chiefly from the brook that loves
To purl o'er matted cress and ribbed sand,
Or dimple in the dark of rushy coves,   60
Drawing into his narrow earthen urn,
    In every elbow and turn,
The filter'd tribute of the rough woodland;
    O, hither lead thy feet!
Pour round mine ears the livelong bleat   65
Of the thick-fleeced sheep from wattled folds,
    Upon the ridged wolds,
When the first matin-song hath waken'd loud
Over the dark dewy earth forlorn,

---

3. Cloak.
4. The following lines describe in some detail the landscape about the Somersby rectory, the family home until 1837. Tennyson would draw throughout his life on his memories of the Lincolnshire countryside as a source for natural imagery, and Arthur Hallam's romanticized notion of Somersby is essentially accurate in stressing its centrality in the molding of the young poet's mind. "Many years perhaps, or shall I say many ages, after we all have been laid in dust," Hallam wrote to Alfred's sister Emily in 1831, "young lovers of the beautiful and the true may seek in faithful pilgrimage the spot where Alfred's mind was moulded in silent sympathy with the everlasting forms of nature" (*Memoir* I, 74).

What time the amber morn   70
Forth gushes from beneath a low-hung cloud.

5

Large dowries doth the raptured eye
    To the young spirit present
        When first she is wed,
            And like a bride of old   75
        In triumph led,
            With music and sweet showers
            Of festal flowers,
    Unto the dwelling she must sway.
Well hast thou done, great artist Memory   80
    In setting round thy first experiment
        With royal framework of wrought gold;
Needs must thou dearly love thy first essay,
And foremost in thy various gallery
    Place it, where sweetest sunlight falls   85
        Upon the storied walls;
            For the discovery
And newness of thine art so pleased thee
That all which thou hast drawn of fairest
Or boldest since but lightly weighs   90
With thee unto the love thou bearest
The first-born of thy genius. Artist-like,
Ever retiring thou dost gaze
On the prime labor of thine early days,
No matter what the sketch might be: 95
Whether the high field on the bushless pike,[5]
Or even a sand-built ridge[6]
Of heaped hills that mound the sea,
Overblown with murmurs harsh,
Or even a lowly cottage whence we see   100
Stretch'd wide and wild the waste enormous marsh,
Where from the frequent bridge,
Like emblems of infinity,
The trenched waters run from sky to sky;
Or a garden bower'd close   105
With plaited alleys of the trailing rose,
Long alleys falling down to twilight grots,
Or opening upon level plots

---

5. A Cumberland word for "peak."
6. Here follows a description of the seaside on the North Sea at Mablethorpe where the family regularly went
during the summer. "I used to stand on this sand-built ridge and think that it was the spine-bone of the world"
(*Memoir* I, 20). A fragment of a poem about Mablethorpe composed in 1837 provides an interesting gloss.
    Here often when a child I lay reclined:
        I took delight in this fair strand and free;
    Here stood the infant Ilion of the mind,
        And here the Grecian ships all seem'd to be.
    And here again I come, and only find
        The drain-cut level of the marshy lea,
    Gray sand-banks, and pale sunsets, dreary wind,
        Dim shores, dense rains, and heavy-clouded sea.
(*Memoir* I, 161)

Of crowned lilies, standing near
Purple-spiked lavender: 110
Whither in after life retired
From brawling storms,
From weary wind,
With youthful fancy re-inspired,
We may hold converse with all forms   115
Of the many-sided mind,
And those whom passion hath not blinded,
Subtle-thoughted, myriad-minded.

My friend, with you to live alone[7]
Were how much better than to own   120
A crown, a sceptre, and a throne!
O, strengthen me, enlighten me!
I faint in this obscurity,
Thou dewy dawn of memory.

                                                      1826?; 1830

Song[1]

1

A spirit haunts the year's last hours
Dwelling amid these yelowing bowers.
        To himself he talks;
For at eventide, listening earnestly,
At his work you may hear him sob and sigh   5
        In the walks;
    Earthward he boweth the heavy stalks
Of the mouldering flowers.
        Heavily hangs the broad sunflower
            Over its grave i' the earth so chilly;   10
        Heavily hangs the hollyhock,
            Heavily hangs the tiger-lily.

2

The air is damp, and hush'd and close,
As a sick man's room when he taketh repose
        An hour before death;   15
My very heart faints and my whole soul grieves
At the moist rich smell of the rotting leaves,
        And the breath
    Of the fading edges of box beneath,
And the year's last rose.   20
        Heavily hangs the broad sunflower.
            Over its grave i' the earth so chilly;

---

7. These lines to Arthur Hallam were probably added just before the poem was published.
1. Written on the lawn outside the rectory at Somersby, this poem, like "Ode to Memory," shows clearly
   that Tennyson's most accomplished early work derived from firsthand experiences.

Heavily hangs the hollyhock,
Heavily hangs the tiger-lily.

1828; 1830

The Dying Swan

1

The plain was grassy, wild and bare,
Wide, wild, and open to the air
Which had built up everywhere
    An under-roof of doleful gray.
With an inner voice the river ran,   5
Adown it floated a dying swan,
        And loudly did lament.
    It was the middle of the day.
Ever the weary wind went on,
        And took the reed-tops as it went.   10

2

Some blue peaks in the distance rose,
And white against the cold-white sky
Shone out their crowning snows.
    One willow over the river wept,
And shook the wave as the wind did sigh;   15
Above in the wind was the swallow,
        Chasing itself at its own wild will,[1]
    And far thro' the marish green and still
    The tangled water-courses slept,
Shot over with purple, and green, and yellow.   20

3

The wild swan's death-hymn took the soul
Of that waste place with joy
Hidden in sorrow. At first to the ear
The warble was low, and full and clear;
And floating about the under-sky,   25
Prevailing in weakness, the coronach[2] stole
Sometimes afar, and sometimes anear;
But anon her awful jubilant voice,
With a music strange and manifold,
Flow'd forth on a carol free and bold;   30
As when a mighty people rejoice
With shawms,[3] and with cymbals, and harps of gold,
And the tumult of their acclaim is roll'd
Thro' the open gates of the city afar,
To the shepherd who watcheth the evening star.   35

---

1. Compare Wordsworth's line "The river glideth at his own sweet will," from "Composed upon Westminster Bridge."
2. A dirge.
3. Kinds of oboes.

And the creeping mosses and clambering weeds,
And the willow-branches hoar and dank,
And the wavy swell of the soughing[4] reeds,
And the wave-worn horns of the echoing bank,
And the silvery marish-flowers that throng   40
The desolate creeks and pools among,
Were flooded over with eddying song.[5]

                                    1830

The Sleeping Beauty[1]

                1

Year after year unto her feet,
    She lying on her couch alone,
Across the purple coverlet
    The maiden's jet-black hair has grown,
On either side her tranced form   5
    Forth streaming from a braid of pearl;
The slumbrous light is rich and warm,
    And moves not on the rounded curl.

                2

The silk star-broider'd coverlid
    Unto her limbs itself doth mould   10
Languidly ever; and, amid
    Her full black ringlets downward roll'd,
Glows forth each softly-shadow'd arm
    With bracelets of the diamond bright.
Her constant beauty doth inform   15
    Stillness with love, and day with light.

                3

She sleeps; her breathings are not heard
    In palace chambers far apart.
The fragrant tresses are not stirr'd
    That lie upon her charmed heart.   20
She sleeps; on either hand upswells
    The gold-fringed pillow lightly prest;
She sleeps, nor dreams, but ever dwells
    A perfect form in perfect rest.

                                    1830

4. Murmuring, sighing.
5. As in "The Ode to Memory" and "A Spirit Haunts the Year's Last Hours," the imagery of section 3 particularly seems to be drawn from the rectory garden at Somersby.
1. Altered slightly from the 1830 version, the piece reappears in 1842 as the third section of the much longer and elaborately wrought poem "The Day-Dream."

A Character[1]

With a half-glance upon the sky
At night he said, "The wanderings
Of this most intricate Universe
Teach me the nothingness of things;"
Yet could not all creation pierce　　　　　　　　　　5
Beyond the bottom of his eye.

He spake of beauty: that the dull
Saw no divinity in grass,
Life in dead stones, or spirit in air;
Then looking as 't were in a glass,　　　　　　　　10
He smooth'd his chin and sleek'd his hair,
And said the earth was beautiful.

He spake of virtue: not the gods
More purely when they wish to charm
Pallas and Juno sitting by;　　　　　　　　　　　　15
And with a sweeping of the arm,
And a lack-lustre dead-blue eye,
Devolved his rounded periods.[2]

Most delicately hour by hour
He canvass'd human mysteries,　　　　　　　　　　20
And trod on silk, as if the winds
Blew his own praises in his eyes,
And stood aloof from other minds
In impotence of fancied power.

With lips depress'd as he were meek,　　　　　　　25
Himself unto himself he sold:
Upon himself himself did feed;
Quiet, dispassionate, and cold,
And other than his form of creed,
With chisell'd features clear and sleek.　　　　　30

1830

---

1. Sunderland, the most able and most brilliant speaker in the Cambridge Union Debating Society, has been identified as the character in the poem, one of Tennyson's few attempts at satire. When showed the lines and told Tennyson was the author, Sunderland reportedly asked, "Which Tennyson? The slovenly one?" Edward FitzGerald called Sunderland "a very plausible, parliament-like, self-satisfied speaker" (*Memoir* I, 37).
2. Sunderland apparently spoke in a cold drawl, which Tennyson found particularly obnoxious.

Supposed Confessions[1]

Of a Second-Rate Sensitive Mind

O God! my God! have mercy now.
I faint, I fall.[2] Men say that Thou
Didst die for me, for such as *me*,
Patient of ill, and death, and scorn,
And that my sin was as a thorn   5
Among the thorns that girt Thy brow,
Wounding Thy soul.—That even now,
In this extremest misery
Of ignorance, I should require
A sign! and if a bolt of fire[3]   10
Would rive the slumbrous summer noon
While I do pray to Thee alone,
Think my belief would stronger grow!
Is not my human pride brought low?
The boastings of my spirit still?   15
The joy I had in my free-will
All cold, and dead, and corpse-like grown?
And what is left to me but Thou,
And faith in Thee? Men pass me by;
Christians with happy countenances—   20
And children all seem full of Thee!
And women smile with saint-like glances
Like Thine own mother's when she bow'd
Above Thee, on that happy morn
When angels spake to men aloud,   25
And Thou and peace to earth were born.
Good-will to me as well as all—
I one of them; my brothers they;
Brothers in Christ—a world of peace
And confidence, day after day;   30
And trust and hope till things should cease,
And then one Heaven receive us all.

How sweet to have a common faith!
To hold a common scorn of death!
And at a burial to hear   35
The creaking cords[4] which wound and eat
Into my human heart, whene'er
Earth goes to earth, with grief, not fear,
With hopeful grief, were passing sweet!

1. Reprinted in 1884 with the omission of seventeen lines and a few minor changes, the poem was originally titled "Supposed Confessions of a Second-rate Sensitive Mind not in Unity with Itself." Authur Hallam praised the poem in his review of 1831 (excerpts of which are included in this volume; see p. 581)
for being "full of deep insight into human nature." He thought the title, however, "ill chosen" and "in-
correct," for the mood portrayed to him "rather the clouded reason of a strong mind than the habitual
condition of one feeble and second-rate."
2. Compare Shelley's line "I fall upon the thorns of life! I bleed!" in "Ode to the West Wind."
3. Perhaps a reference to Luther's experience with the bolt of lightning. See 1 Corinthians 1:22: "For the
Jews require a sign."
4. The straps that lower the casket into the grave.

Thrice happy state[5] again to be   40
The trustful infant on the knee,
Who lets his rosy fingers play
About his mother's neck, and knows
Nothing beyond his mother's eyes!
They comfort him by night and day;   45
They light his little life alway;
He hath no thought of coming woes;
He hath no care of life or death;
Scarce outward signs of joy arise,
Because the Spirit of happiness   50
And perfect rest so inward is;
And loveth so his innocent heart,
Her temple and her place of birth,
Where she would ever wish to dwell,
Life of the fountain there, beneath   55
Its salient springs, and far apart,
Hating to wander out on earth,
Or breathe into the hollow air,
Whose chillness would make visible
Her subtil, warm, and golden breath,   60
Which mixing with the infant's blood,
Fulfils him with beatitude.
O, sure it is a special care
Of God, to fortify from doubt,
To arm in proof, and guard about   65
With triple-mailed trust, and clear
Delight, the infant's dawning year.

Would that my gloomed fancy were
As thine, my mother, when with brows
Propt on thy knees, my hands upheld   70
In thine, I listen'd to thy vows,
For me outpour'd in holiest prayer—
For me unworthy!—and beheld
Thy mild deep eyes upraised, that knew
The beauty and repose of faith,   75
And the clear spirit shining thro'.
O, wherefore do we grow awry
From roots which strike so deep?[6] why dare
Paths in the desert? Could not I
Bow myself down, where thou has knelt,   80
To the earth—until the ice would melt
Here, and I feel as thou hast felt?
What devil had the heart to scathe
Flowers thou hadst rear'd—to brush the dew
From thine own lily, when thy grave   85
Was deep, my mother, in the clay?
Myself? Is it thus? Myself? Had I

5. Lines 40–67 seem clearly indebted to Wordsworth's "Ode: Intimations of Immortality."
6. Compare "Intimations Ode" lines 67–69: "Heaven lies about us in our infancy; / Shades of the prison-house begin to close / Upon the growing Boy."

So little love for thee? But why
Prevail'd not thy pure prayers? Why pray
To one who heeds not, who can save   90
But will not? Great in faith, and strong
Against the grief of circumstance
Wert thou, and yet unheard. What if
Thou pleadest still, and seest me drive
Thro' utter dark a full-sale'd skiff,   95
Unpiloted i' the echoing dance
Of reboant whirlwinds,[7] stooping low

Unto the death, not sunk! I know
At matins and at evensong,
That thou, if thou wert yet alive,   100
In deep and daily prayers wouldst strive
To reconcile me with thy God.
Albeit, my hope is gray, and cold
At heart, thou wouldest murmur still—
"Bring this lamb back into Thy fold,   105
My Lord, if so it be Thy will."
Wouldst tell me I must brook the rod
And chastisement of human pride;
That pride, the sin of devils, stood
Betwixt me and the light of God;   110
That hitherto I had defied
And had rejected God—that grace
Would drop from His o'er-brimming love,
As manna on my wilderness,
If I would pray—that God would move   115
And strike the hard, hard rock, and thence,
Sweet in their utmost bitterness,
Would issue tears of penitence
Which would keep green hope's life. Alas!
I think that pride hath now no place   120
Nor sojourn in me. I am void,
Dark, formless, utterly destroyed.

Why not believe then? Why not yet
Anchor thy frailty there, where man
Hath moor'd and rested? Ask the sea   125
At midnight, when the crisp slope waves
After a tempest rib and fret
The broad-imbased beach, why he
Slumbers not like a mountain tarn?
Wherefore his ridges are not curls   130
And ripples of an inland mere?[8]

7. For this image, Tennyson was probably thinking of Milton's *Samson Agonistes* lines 197–200:
How could I once look up, or have the head,
Who like a foolish Pilot have shipwrack't
My vessel trusted to me from above,
Gloriously rigg'd; . . .
Compare *IM* 4, 1.
8. A small lake or pool, as distinguished from a "tarn" or mountain lake.

Wherefore he moaneth thus, nor can
Draw down into his vexed pools
All that blue heaven which hues and paves
The other? I am too forlorn,   135
Too shaken: my own weakness fools
My judgment, and my spirit whirls,
Moved from beneath with doubt and fear.
"Yet," said I, in my morn of youth,
The unsunn'd freshness of my strength,   140
When I went forth in quest of truth,
"It is man's privilege to doubt,[9]
If so be that from doubt at length
Truth may stand forth unmoved of change,
An image with profulgent[1] brows   145
And perfect limbs, as from the storm
Of running fires and fluid range
Of lawless airs, at last stood out
This excellence and solid form
Of constant beauty. For the ox[2]   150
Feeds in the herb, and sleeps, or fills
The horned valleys all about,
And hollows of the fringed hills
In summer heats, with placid lows
Unfearing, till his own blood flows   155
About his hoof. And in the flocks
The lamb rejoiceth in the year,
And raceth freely with his fere,
And answers to his mother's calls
From the flower'd furrow. In a time   160
Of which he wots not, run short pains
Thro' his warm heart; and then, from whence
He knows not, on his light there falls
A shadow; and his native slope,
Where he was wont to leap and climb,   165
Floats from his sick and filmed eyes,
And something in the darkness draws
His forehead earthward, and he dies.
Shall man live thus, in joy and hope
As a young lamb, who cannot dream,   170
Living, but that he shall live on?
Shall we not look into the laws
Of life and death, and things that seem,
And things that be, and analyze
Our double nature, and compare   175
All creeds till we have found the one,
If one there be? Ay me! I fear

9. See *IM* 96, 3.
1. Radiant.
2. This passage on the ox and lamb is indebted to Pope's *Essay on Man* I, lines 81–84:
      The lamb thy riot dooms to bleed today,
      Had he thy Reason, would skip and play?
      Pleased to the last, he crops the flowery food,
      And licks the hand just raised to shed his blood.

All my not doubt, but everywhere
Some must clasp idols. Yet, my God,
Whom call I idol? let Thy dove   180
Shadow me over, and my sins
Be unremember'd, and Thy love
Enlighten me. O, teach me yet
Somewhat before the heavy clod
Weighs on me, and the busy fret   185
Of that sharp-headed worm begins
In the gross blackness underneath.

O weary life! O weary death!
O spirit and heart made desolate!
O damned vacillating state!³   190

1830

The Kraken¹

Below the thunders of the upper deep,
Far, far beneath in the abysmal sea,
His ancient, dreamless, uninvaded sleep
The Kraken sleepeth: faintest sunlights flee
About his shadowy sides; above him swell   5
Huge sponges of millennial growth and height;
And far away into the sickly light,
From many a wondrous grot and secret cell
Unnumber'd and enormous polypi²
Winnow with giant arms the slumbering green.   10
There hath he lain for ages, and will lie
Battening upon huge sea-worms in his sleep.³
Until the latter fire⁴ shall heat the deep;
Then once by man and angels to be seen,
In roaring he shall rise and on the surface die.⁵   15

1830

3. Compare *Hamlet* I, ii, lines 133–34: "How weary, stale, flat and unprofitable, / Seem to me all the uses
of this world!"
1. A mythical Norwegian sea beast from Scandinavian folklore; here identified with the beast of the Apocalypse. See Revelation 13:1: "And I stood upon the sand of the sea, and saw a beast rise up out of the sea."
2. Sea animals such as the hydra or octopus.
3. See Shelley's line "the dull weed some sea-worm battens on," in *Prometheus Unbound* IV, i, line 542.
4. Fire that will consume the world at its end. See Revelation 16:8–9.
5. Revelation 8:8–9: "And the second angel sounded, and as it were a great mountain burning with fire was
cast into the sea: and the third part of the sea became blood; And the third part of the creatures which
were in the sea, and had life, died."

Mariana[1]

Mariana in the moated grange.
—MEASURE FOR MEASURE

With blackest moss the flower-plots
　　Were thickly crusted, one and all;
The rusted nails fell from the knots
　　That held the pear to the gable-wall.
The broken sheds look'd sad and strange:　　　　5
　　Unlifted was the clinking latch;
　　Weeded and worn the ancient thatch
Upon the lonely moated grange.
　　　　She only said, "My life is dreary,
　　　　　　He cometh not," she said;　　　　10
　　　　She said, "I am aweary, aweary,
　　　　　　I would that I were dead![2]

Her tears fell with the dews at even;
　　Her tears fell ere the dews were dried;
She could not look on the sweet heaven,　　　　15
　　Either at morn or eventide.
After the flitting of the bats,
　　When thickest dark did trance[3] the sky,
　　She drew her casement-curtain by,
And glanced athwart the glooming flats.　　　　20
　　　　She only said, "The night is dreary,
　　　　　　He cometh not," she said;
　　　　She said, "I am aweary, aweary,
　　　　　　I would that I were dead!"

Upon the middle of the night,　　　　25
　　Waking she heard the night-fowl crow;
The cock sung out an hour ere light;
　　From the dark fen the oxen's low
Came to her; without hope of change,
　　In sleep she seem'd to walk forlorn,　　　　30
　　Till cold winds woke the gray-eyed morn[4]
About the lonely moated grange.
　　　　She only said, "The day is dreary,
　　　　　　He cometh not," she said;
　　　　She said, "I am aweary, aweary,　　　　35
　　　　　　I would that I were dead!"

About a stone-cast from the wall
　　A sluice with blacken'd waters slept,

1. In Shakespeare's play (III, i, line 277) "there, at the moated grange, resides this dejected Mariana," who waits for Angelo who has deserted her. The notion of desertion is the only parallel to the play; the theme of isolation is thoroughly Tennysonian. ("The Moated Grange," Tennyson said, "is an imaginary house in the fen"; *Memoir* I, 4–5.) In mood and atmosphere the poem is often cited as anticipating the Pre-Raphaelites and the Symbolist movement fifty years later.
2. Compare the last lines of "Supposed Confessions."
3. Entrance, line cited in O.E.D.
4. *Romeo and Juliet* II, iii, line 1: "The grey-eyed morn smiles on the frowning night."

And o'er it many, round and small,
    The cluster'd marish-mosses[5] crept.   40
Hard by a poplar shook alway,
    All silver-green with gnarled bark:
For leagues no other tree did mark
The level waste, the rounding gray.
        She only said, "My life is dreary,   45
        He cometh not," she said;
        She said, "I am aweary, aweary,
        I would that I were dead!"

And ever when the moon was low,
    And the shrill winds were up and away,   50
In the white curtain, to and fro,
    She saw the gusty shadow sway.
But when the moon was very low,
    And wild winds bound within their cell,
The shadow of the poplar fell   55
Upon her bed, across her brow.
        She only said, "The night is dreary,
        He cometh not," she said;
        She said, "I am aweary, aweary,
        I would that I were dead!"   60

All day within the dreamy house,
    The doors upon their hinges creak'd;
The blue fly sung in the pane; the mouse
    Behind the mouldering wainscot shriek'd,
Or from the crevice peer'd about.   65
    Old faces glimmer'd thro' the doors,
    Old footsteps trod the upper floors,
Old voices called her from without.
        She only said, "My life is dreary,
        He cometh not," she said;   70
        She said, "I am aweary, aweary,
        I would that I were dead!"

The sparrow's chirrup on the roof,
    The slow clock ticking, and the sound
Which to the wooing wind aloof   75
    The poplar made, did all confound
Her sense; but most she loathed the hour
    When the thick-moted sunbeam lay
    Athwart the chambers, and the day
Was sloping toward his western bower.   80
        Then said she, "I am very dreary,
        He will not come," she said;
        She wept, "I am aweary, aweary,
        O God, that I were dead!"

          1830

---

5. Lumps of moss floating on water.

Sir Launcelot and Queen Guinevere[1]

A Fragment

Like souls that balance joy and pain,
With tears and smiles from heaven again
The maiden Spring upon the plain
Came in a sunlit fall of rain.
    In crystal vapor everywhere   5
Blue isles of heaven laugh'd between,
And far, in forest-deeps unseen,
The topmost elm-tree gather'd green
    From draughts of balmy air.

Sometimes the linnet piped his song;   10
Sometimes the throstle whistled strong;
Sometimes the sparhawk,[2] wheel'd along.
Hush'd all the groves from fear of wrong;
    By grassy capes with fuller sound
In curves the yellowing river ran,   15
And drooping chestnut-buds began
To spread into the perfect fan,
    Above the teeming ground.

Then, in the boyhood of the year,
Sir Launcelot and Queen Guinevere   20
Rode thro' the coverts of the deer,
With blissful treble ringing clear.
    She seem'd a part of joyous Spring;
A gown of grass-green silk she wore,
Buckled with golden clasps before;   25
A light-green tuft of plumes she bore
    Closed in a golden ring.

Now on some twisted ivy-net,
Now by some tinkling rivulet,
In mosses mixt with violet   30
Her cream-white mule his pastern[3] set;
    And fleeter now she skimm'd the plains
Than she whose elfin prancer springs
By night to eery warblings,
When all the glimmering moorland rings   35
    With jingling bridle-reins.

As she fled fast thro' sun and shade,
The happy winds upon her play'd,

---

1. According to Hallam Tennyson, the fragment was "partly if not wholly written in 1830" (*Memoir* II, 122). FitzGerald recalled that some verses of it were handed about at Cambridge, and a fragment from FitzGerald's collection appears in the *Memoir* I, 59. This poem marks the beginning of Tennyson's life-long interest in the Arthurian legends for poetic purposes and anticipates in verse-form "The Lady of Shalott."
2. Sparrow hawk.
3. Hoofprint.

Blowing the ringlet from the braid.
She look'd so lovely, as she sway'd   40
   The rein with dainty finger-tips,
A man had given all other bliss,
And all his worldly worth for this,
To waste his whole heart in one kiss
   Upon her perfect lips.   45

1830; 1842

From *Poems* (1832, dated 1833)

"My Life Is Full of Weary Days"[1]

My life is full of weary days,
    But good things have not kept aloof,
Nor wander'd into other ways;
    I have not lack'd thy mild reproof,
Nor golden largess of thy praise   5

And now shake hands across the brink
    Of that deep grave to which I go,
Shake hands once more; I cannot sink
    So far—far down, but I shall know
Thy voice, and answer from below.   10

When in the darkness over me
    The four-handed mole shall scrape,
Plant thou no dusky cypress-tree,
    Nor wreathe thy cap with doleful crape,
But pledge me in the flowing grape.   15

And when the sappy field and wood
    Grow green beneath the showery gray,
And rugged barks begin to bud,
    And thro' damp holts new-flush'd with may,
Ring sudden scritches of the jay,   20

Then let wise Nature work her will,
    And on my clay her darnel grow;
Come only, when the days are still,
    And at my headstone whisper low,
And tell me if the woodbines blow.   25

1832 (1865, 1872)

---

1. In the 1832 volume printed with the heading "To————." ("All good things have not kept aloof.") In the *Quarterly* for April 1833 Croker savagely derided this piece for its indulgence in the pathetic fallacy. Among numerous revisions, Tennyson changed "sudden laughters of the jay" to "sudden scritches of the jay." Spedding wrote on April 1, 1832, that the lines were addressed "to the lordly-browed and gracious Hallam . . . worthy subject of worthy poet" [Ricks].

The Lady of Shalott[1]

Part I

On either side the river lie
Long fields of barley and of rye,
That clothe the wold and meet the sky;
And thro' the field the road runs by
    To many-tower'd Camelot;[2]   5
And up and down the people go,
Gazing where the lilies blow[3]
Round an island there below,
    The island of Shalott.

Willows whiten,[4] aspens quiver,   10
Little breezes dusk and shiver
Thro' the wave that runs for ever
By the island in the river
    Flowing down to Camelot.
Four gray walls, and four gray towers,   15
Overlook a space of flowers,
And the silent isle imbowers
    The Lady of Shalott.

By the margin, willow-veil'd,
Slide the heavy barges trail'd   20
By slow horses; and unhail'd
The shallop[5] flitteth silken-sail'd
    Skimming down to Camelot:
But who hath seen her wave her hand?
Or at the casement seen her stand?   25
Or is she known in all the land,
    The Lady of Shalott?

Only reapers, reaping early
In among the bearded barley,
Hear a song that echoes cheerly   30
From the river winding clearly,
    Down to tower'd Camelot;
And by the moon the reaper weary,
Piling sheaves in uplands airy,
Listening, whispers "'T'is the fairy   35
    Lady of Shalott."

1. The 1842 version as printed here is significantly altered from the original, and comparison with the 1832 text reveals much about the poet's methods of revision. For the poem's source, Palgrave in his notes says it was suggested by "an Italian romance upon the Donna di Scalotta," confirming, as Tennyson said to his son, that he had not drawn on Malory's *Morte d'Arthur*: "I do not think that I had ever heard of the latter [Malory's Elaine] when I wrote the former." *Shallot* from the Italian *Scalotta* is the same as *Astolat*: the lady later becomes Elaine, "the lily maid of Astolat," in "Lancelot and Elaine" (1859).
2. The legendary city and site of Arthur's palace, variously located in Winchester, Somersetshire, and elsewhere. Unlike the kingdom of Celtic mythology, Camelot is placed by the sea in the Italian story.
3. Bloom.
4. The white underside of the leaves show in the wind.
5. A light, open boat.

Part II

There she weaves by night and day
A magic web with colors gay.
She has heard a whisper say,
A curse is on her if she stay   40
    To look down to Camelot.
She knows not what the curse may be,
And so she weaveth steadily,
And little other care hath she,
    The Lady of Shalott.   45

And moving thro a mirror[6] clear
That hangs before her all the year,
Shadows of the world appear.
There she sees the highway near
    Winding down to Camelot;   50
There the river eddy whirls,
And there the surly village-churls,
And the red cloaks of market girls,
    Pass onward from Shalott.

Sometimes a troop of damsels glad,   55
An abbot on an ambling pad.[7]
Sometimes a curly shepherd-lad,
Or long hair'd page in crimson clad,
    Goes by to tower'd Camelot;
And sometimes thro' the mirror blue   60
The knights come riding two and two:
She hath no loyal knight and true,
    The Lady of Shalott.

But in her web she still delights
To weave the mirror's magic sights,   65
For often thro' the silent nights
A funeral, with plumes and lights
    And music, went to Camelot;
Or when the moon was overhead,
Came two young lovers lately wed: 70
"I am half sick of shadows,"[8] said
    The Lady of Shalott.

Part III

A bow-shot from her bower-eaves,
He rode between the barley-sheaves.
The sun came dazzling thro' the leaves,   75
And flamed upon the brazen greaves[9]

6. Ricks cites the influence of Spenser's *Faerie Queen* III, ii, on Britomart and Artegall: "The wondrous myrrhour, by which she in love with him did fall."
7. An easy-paced horse.
8. Tennyson commented: "The newborn love for something, for some one in the wide world from which she has been so long secluded, takes her out of the region of shadows into that of realities" (*Memoir* I, 117).
9. Shin-guard armor.

Of bold Sir Lancelot.
A red-cross[1] knight for ever kneel'd
To a lady in his shield,
That sparkled on the yellow field,   80
    Beside remote Shalott.

The gemmy bridle glitter'd free,
Like to some branch of stars we see
Hung in the golden Galaxy.
The bridle bells rang merrily.   85
    As he rode down to Camelot;

And from his blazon'd baldric[2] slung
A mighty silver bugle hung,
And as he rode his armor rung,
    Beside remote Shalott.   90

All in the blue unclouded weather
Thick-jewell'd shone the saddle-leather,
The helmet and the helmet-feather
Burn'd like one burning flame together,
    As he rode down to Camelot;   95

As often thro' the purple night,
Below the starry clusters bright,
Some bearded meteor, trailing light,
    Moves over still Shalott.

His broad clear brow in sunlight glow'd;   100
On burnish'd hooves his war-horse trode;
From underneath his helmet flow'd
His coal-black curls as on he rode,
    As he rode down to Camelot.
From the bank and from the river   105
He flash'd into the crystal mirror,
"Tirra lirra,"[3] by the river
    Sang Sir Lancelot.

She left the web, she left the loom,
She made three paces thro' the room,   110
She saw the water-lily bloom,
She saw the helmet and the plume,
    She look'd down to Camelot.
Out flew the web and floated wide;
The mirror crack'd from side to side;   115
"The curse is come upon me," cried
    The Lady of Shalott.

---

1. Not one of Lancelot's usual emblems, though Malory once gives him such a shield. Perhaps Tennyson
   was thinking of Spenser's Red-Crosse Knight in Book I of the *Faerie Queene*.
2. A richly ornamented shoulder belt.
3. *Winter's Tale* IV, iii, line 9: "The lark, that tirra-lyra chants."

Part IV

In the stormy east-wind straining,
The pale yellow woods were waning,
The broad stream in his banks complaining,   120
Heavily the low sky raining
          Over tower'd Camelot;
Down she came and found a boat
Beneath a willow left afloat,
And round about the prow she wrote   125
          The Lady of Shalott.

And down the river's dim expanse
Like some bold seër in a trance,
Seeing all his own mischance—
With a glassy countenance   130
          Did she look to Camelot.
And at the closing of the day
She loosed the chain, and down she lay;
The broad stream bore her far away,
          The Lady of Shalott.   135

Lying, robed in snowy white
That loosely flew to left and right—
The leaves upon her falling light—
Thro' the noises of the night
          She floated down to Camelot;   140
And as the boat-head wound along
The willowy hills and fields among,
They heard her singing her last song,
          The Lady of Shalott.

Heard a carol, mournful, holy,   145
Chanted loudly, chanted lowly,
Till her blood was frozen slowly,
And her eyes were darken'd wholly,
          Turn'd to tower'd Camelot.
For ere she reach'd upon the tide   150
The first house by the water-side,
Singing in her song she died,
          The Lady of Shalott.

Under tower and balcony,
By garden-wall and gallery,
A gleaming shape she floated by,   155
Dead-pale between the houses high,
          Silent into Camelot.
Out upon the wharfs they came,
Knight and burgher, lord and dame   160
And round the prow[4] they read her name,
          The Lady of Shalott.[5]

4. The 1832 version read, "Below the stern." In *Tennyson and the Reviewers*, Edgar F. Shannon observes that
    J. W. Croker "had noted with derision that the name, *The Lady of Shallot*, was 'below the stern' of the boat."
5. Compare the stanza to "Lancelot and Elaine," lines 1236–74.

Who is this? and what is here?
And in the lighted palace near
Died the sound of royal cheer;   165
And they cross'd themselves for fear,
　　All the knights at Camelot:
But Lancelot mused a little space;
He said, "She has a lovely face;
God in his mercy lend her grace,   170
　　The Lady of Shalott."[6]

1832 (1842)

Mariana in the South[1]

With one black shadow at its feet,
　　The house thro' all the level shines,
Close-latticed to the brooding heat,
　　And silent in its dusty vines;
A faint-blue ridge upon the right,   5
　　An empty river-bed before,
　　And shallows on a distant shore,
In glaring sand and inlets bright.
　　　But "Ave Mary," made she moan,
　　　And "Ave Mary," night and morn,   10
　　And "Ah," she sang, "to be all alone,
　　To live forgotten, and love forlorn."

She, as her carol sadder grew,
　　From brow and bosom slowly down
Thro' rosy taper fingers drew   15
　　Her streaming curls of deepest brown
To left and right, and made appear
　　Still-lighted in a secret shrine
　　Her melancholy eyes divine,
The home of woe without a tear.   20
　　　And "Ave Mary," was her moan,
　　　"Madonna, sad is night and morn,"

6. The 1832 text ended with the following stanza, which undercuts the sympathetic outside world by making it a bunch of Philistines:
　　They crossed themselves, their stars they blest,
　　Knight, minstrel, abbot, squire and guest.
　　There lay a parchment on her breast,
　　That puzzled more than all the rest,
　　　　The wellfed wits at Camelot;
　　"The web was woven curiously
　　The charm is broken utterly,
　　Draw near and fear not—this is I,
　　　　The Lady of Shalott."
1. Much revised and improved from the 1832 text, this poem, as Arthur Hallam explains in a letter to W. B. Donne (1831), was obviously intended "as a kind of pendant to his former poem of 'Mariana,' the idea of both being the expression of desolate loneliness" (*Memoir* I, 500). Conceived when "travelling between Narbonne and Perpignan" (*Memoir* I, 117), the second "Mariana" draws heavily on the scenery of southern France (see notes to "Œnone," p. 48) just as the earlier "Mariana" reflected the Lincolnshire countryside.

And "Ah," she sang, "to be all alone,
        To live forgotten, and love forlorn."

Till all the crimson changed, and past   25
        Into deep orange o'er the sea,
Low on her knees herself she cast,
        Before Our Lady murmur'd she;
Complaining, "Mother, give me grace
        To help me of my weary load."   30
And on the liquid mirror glow'd
The clear perfection of her face.
        "Is this the form," she made her moan,
            "That won his praises night and morn?"
        And "Ah," she said, "but I wake alone,   35
            I sleep forgotten, I wake forlorn."

Nor bird would sing, nor lamb would bleat,
        Nor any cloud would cross the vault,
But day increased from heat to heat,
        On stony drought and steaming salt;   40
Till now at noon she slept again,
        And seem'd knee-deep in mountain grass,
        And heard her native breezes pass,
And runlets babbling down the glen.[2]
        She breathed in sleep a lower moan,   45
            And murmuring, as at night and morn,
        She thought, "My spirit is here alone,
            Walks forgotten, and is forlorn."

Dreaming, she knew it was a dream;
        She felt he was and was not there.   50
She woke; the babble of the stream
        Fell, and, without, the steady glare
Shrank one sick willow sere and small.
        The river-bed was dusty-white;
        And all the furnace of the light   55
Struck up against the blinding wall.
        She whisper'd, with a stifled moan
            More inward than at night or morn,
        "Sweet Mother, let me not here alone
            Live forgotten and die forlorn."   60

And, rising, from her bosom drew
        Old letters, breathing of her worth,

2. A comparison with the original eight lines of this stanza readily indicates the quality of the poet's revisions:
        At noon she slumbered. All along
            The silvery field, the large leaves talked
        With one another, as among
            The spiked maize in dreams she walked.
        The lizard leapt: the sunlight played:
            She heard the callow nestling lisp,
        And brimful meadow-runnels crisp,
            In the full-leavèd platan-shade.

For "Love," they said, "must needs be true
  To what is loveliest upon earth."
An image seem'd to pass the door,   65
  To look at her with slight, and say
  "But now thy beauty flows away,
So be alone for evermore."
      "O cruel heart," she changed her tone,
        "And cruel love, whose end is scorn,   70
      Is this the end, to be left alone,
        To live forgotten, and die forlorn?"

But sometimes in the falling day
  An image seem'd to pass the door,
To look into her eyes and say,   75
  "But thou shalt be alone no more."
And flaming downward over all
  From heat to heat the day decreased,
  And slowly rounded to the east
The one black shadow from the wall.   80
      "The day to night," she made her moan,
        "The day to night, the night to morn,
      And day and night I am left alone
        To live forgotten, and love forlorn."

At eve a dry cicala[3] sung,   85
  There came a sound as of the sea;
Backward the lattice-blind she flung,
  And lean'd upon the balcony.
There all in spaces rosy-bright
  Large Hesper glitter'd on her tears.   90
  And deepening thro' the silent spheres
Heaven over heaven rose the night.
      And weeping then she made her moan,
        "The night comes on that knows not morn,
      When I shall cease to be all alone,   95
        To live forgotten, and love forlorn."

1832 (1842)

---

3. A cicada or locust.

Œnone[1]

There lies a vale in Ida, lovelier
Than all the valleys of Ionian[2] hills.
The swimming vapor slopes athwart the glen,
Puts forth an arm, and creeps from pine to pine,
And loiters, slowly drawn. On either hand   5
The lawns and meadow-ledges midway down
Hang rich in flowers, and far below them roars
The long brook falling thro' the cloven ravine
In cataract after cataract to the sea.
Behind the valley topmost Gargarus[3]   10
Stands up and takes the morning; but in front
The gorges, opening wide apart, reveal
Troas and Ilion's column'd citadel,
The crown of Troas.[4]
                    Hither came at noon
Mournful Œnone, wandering forlorn   15
Of Paris, once her playmate on the hills.
Her cheek had lost the rose, and round her neck
Floated her hair or seem'd to float in rest.
She, leaning on a fragment twined with vine,
Sang to the stillness, till the mountain shade   20
Sloped downward to her seat from the upper cliff.

"O mother Ida, many-fountain'd Ida,
Dear mother Ida, harken ere I die.
For now the noonday quiet holds the hill;
The grasshopper is silent in the grass;   25
The lizard, with his shadow on the stone,
Rests like a shadow, and the winds are dead.
The purple flower droops, the golden bee
Is lily-cradled; I alone awake.
My eyes are full of tears, my heart of love,   30
My heart is breaking, and my eyes are dim,
And I am all aweary of my life.

---

1. Much altered from the 1832 version, "Œnone" is the first of the great classical idyls or little pictures
in verse more or less indebted to Theocritus. Tennyson's primary sources for the story were probably
Ovid's *Heroides* and James Beattie's *The Judgment of Paris*. Œnone, a nymph of Troas and the daughter of Mount Ida, was deserted by her husband, Paris, for Helen of Troy. Helen's abduction precipitated the Trojan War and the dire consequences darkly prophesied by the wild Cassandra at the end of
the poem.
    During the summer of 1830, from early July to the end of September, Tennyson and Arthur Hallam
journeyed to the Pyrenees to aid a small band of insurgents led by Torrijos, a daring revolutionary whose
abortive attempt to overthrow the Spanish government ended with his surrender and execution. On this
dangerous and romantic excursion the two youths carried secret coded documents from an unknown
source, perhaps from sympathizers within the British government, but the precise nature of their mission remains mysterious (see *Memoir* I, 51–55).
    Tennyson started work on "Œnone" in the valley of Cauteretz, which provides the landscape infus-
ing the poem. The scenery of the Pyrenees became a lasting source of natural imagery, but it took Tennyson thirty-one years to face up to a return trip to commemorate that first daring journey with Hallam
(see "In the Valley of Cauteretz," 1864).
2. The west coast of Asia Minor on the Aegean Sea.
3. The highest peak in the Ida Mountains.
4. The district of Troy. "Ilion": the city itself.

"O mother Ida, many-fountain'd Ida,
Dear mother Ida, harken ere I die.
Hear me, O earth, hear me, O hills, O caves   35
That house the cold crown'd snake! O mountain brooks,
I am the daughter of a River-God,[5]
Hear me, for I will speak, and build up all
My sorrow with my song, as yonder walls
Rose slowly to a music[6] slowly breathed,   40
A cloud that gather'd shape; for it may be
That, while I speak of it, a little while
My heart may wander from its deeper woe.

"O mother Ida, many-fountain'd Ida,
Dear mother Ida, harken ere I die.   45
I waited underneath the dawning hills;
Aloft the mountain lawn was dewy-dark,
And dewy dark aloft the mountain pine.
Beautiful Paris, evil-hearted Paris,
Leading a jet-black hoat white-horn'd white-hooved,   50
Came up from reedy Simois all alone.

"O mother Ida, harken ere I die.
Far-off the torrent call'd me from the cleft;
Far up the solitary morning smote
The streaks of virgin snow. With downdropt eyes   55
I sat alone; white-breasted like a star
Fronting the dawn he moved; a leopard skin
Droop'd from his shoulder, but his sunny hair
Cluster'd about his temples like a God's;
And his cheeks brighten'd as the froam-bow brightens   60
When the wind blows the foam, and all my heart
Went forth to embrace him coming ere he came.

"Dear mother Ida, harken ere I die.
He smiled, and opening out his milk-white palm
Disclosed a fruit of pure Hesperian gold,[7]   65
That smelt ambrosially, and while I look'd
And listen'd, the full-flowing river of speech
Came down upon my heart:
                    "My own Œnone,
Beautiful-brow'd Œnone, my own soul,
Behold this fruit, whose gleaming rind ingraven   70
"For the most fair," would seem to award it thine,
As lovelier than whatever Oread[8] haunt
The knolls of Ida, loveliest in all grace
Of movement, and the charm of married brows.[9]

5. Simois, one of the two rivers on the plain of Troy.
6. Compare "Tiresias," line 96.
7. The golden apples of the Hesperides. See notes to Tennyson's poem "The Hesperides" (p. 63) for part of the mythology.
8. A nymph.
9. In the classical age, eyebrows that met were considered a mark of beauty. Chaucer, in his description of Criseyde, wasn't so sure: "And save hire browes joyneden yfere, / Ther was no lakke, in aught I kan espien."

"Dear mother Ida, harken ere I die.   75
He prest the blossom of his lips to mine,
And added, 'This was cast upon the board,
When all the full-faced presence of the Gods,
Ranged in the halls of Peleus;[1] whereupon
Rose feud, with question unto whom't were due;   80
But light-foot Iris brought it yester-eve,
Delivering, that to me, by common voice
Elected umpire, Herè comes to-day,
Pallas and Aphrodite, claiming each
This meed of fairest. Thou, within the cave   85
Behind yon whispering tuft of oldest pine,
Mayst well behold them unbeheld, unheard
Hear all, and see thy Paris judge of Gods.'

"Dear mother Ida, harken ere I die.
It was the deep midnoon; one silvery cloud   90
Had lost his way between the piny sides
Of this long glen. Then to the bower they came,
Naked they came to that smooth-swarded bower,
And at their feet the crocus brake like fire,
Violet, amaracus, and asphodel,   95
Lotos and lilies; and a wind arose,
And overhead the wandering ivy and vine,
This way and that, in many a wild festoon
Ran riot, garlanding the gnarled boughs
With bunch and berry and flower thro' and thro'.   100

"O mother Ida, harken ere I die.
On the tree-tops a crested peacock lit,
And o'er him flow'd a golden cloud, and lean'd
Upon him, slowly dropping fragrant dew.
Then first I heard the voice of her to whom   105
Coming thro' heaven, like a light that grows
Larger and clearer, with one mind the Gods
Rise up for reverence. She to Paris made
Proffer of royal power, ample rule
Unquestion'd, overflowing revenue   110
Wherewith to embellish state, 'from many a vale
And river-sunder'd champaign clothed with corn,
Or labor'd mine undrainable of ore.
Honor,' she said, 'and homage, tax and toll,
From many an inland town and haven large,   115
Mast-throng'd beneath her shadowing citadel
In glassy bays among her tallest towers.'

"O mother Ida, harken ere I die.
Still she spake on and still she spake of power,
'Which in all action is the end of all;   120

---

1. The king of Thessaly who married Thetis; parents of Achilles. At their marriage Eris, the goddess of discord ("the abominable" of line 220), brought the golden apple marked "for the fairest." Hera (identified
as Juno by the Romans), Athene, and Aphrodite all claimed it.

Power fitted to the season; wisdom-bred
And throned of wisdom — from all neighbor crowns
Alliance and allegiance, till thy hand
Fail from the sceptre-staff. Such boon from me,
From me, heaven's queen, Paris,[2] to thee king-born,   125
A shepherd all thy life, but yet king-born.
Should come most welcome, seeing men, in power
Only, are likest Gods, who have attain'd
Rest in happy place and quiet seats
Above the thunder, with undying bliss   130
In knowledge of their own supremacy.'

   "Dear mother Ida, harken ere I die.
She ceased, and Paris held the costly fruit
Out at arm's-length, so much the thought of power
Flatter'd his spirit; but Pallas where she stood   135
Somewhat apart, her clear and bared limbs
O'erthwarted with the brazen-headed spear
Upon her pearly shoulder leaning cold,
The while, above, her full and earnest eye
Over her snow-cold breast and angry cheek   140
Kept watch, waiting decision, made reply:

   "Self-reverence, self-knowledge, self-control,
These three alone lead life to sovereign power.
Yet not for power (power of herself
Would come uncall'd for) but to live by law,   145
Acting the law we live by without fear;
And, because right is right, to follow right
Were wisdom in the scorn of consequence.'

   "Dear mother Ida, harken ere I die.
Again she said: 'I woo thee not with gifts.   150
Sequel of guerdon could not alter me
To fairer. Judge thou me by what I am,
So shalt thou find me fairest.
                              Yet, indeed,
If gazing on divinity disrobed
Thy mortal eyes are frail to judge of fair,   155
Unbias'd by self-profit, O, rest thee sure
That I shall love thee well and cleave to thee,
So that my vigor, wedded to thy blood,
Shall strike within thy pulses, like a God's,
To push thee forward thro' a life of shocks,   160
Dangers, and deeds, until endurance grow
Sinew'd with action, and the full-grown will,
Circled thro' all experiences, pure law,
Commeasure perfect freedom.'
                              "Here she ceas'd,

---

2. One of Priam's fifty sons. Paris as a child was left to die on Mount Ida because of a prophecy that he
would bring destruction on Troy; he was saved and brought up by shepherds.

And Paris ponder'd, and I cried, 'O Paris,   165
Give it to Pallas!' but he heard me not,
Or hearing would not hear me, woe is me!

"O mother Ida, many-fountain'd Ida,
Dear mother Ida, harken ere I die.
Idalian Aphrodite beautiful,   170
Fresh as the foam, new-bathed in Paphian³ wells,
With rosy slender fingers backward drew
From her warm brows and bosom her deep hair
Ambrosial, golden round her lucid throat
And shoulder; from the violets her light foot   175
Shone rosy-white, and o'er her rounded form
Between the shadows of the vine-bunches
Floated the glowing sunlights, as she moved.

"Dear mother Ida, harken ere I die.
She with a subtle smile in her mild eyes,   180
The herald of her triumph, drawing nigh
Half-whisper'd in his ear, 'I promise thee
The fairest and most loving wife in Greece.'
She spoke and laugh'd; I shut my sight for fear;
But when I look'd, Paris had raised his arm,   185
And I beheld great Herè's angry eyes,
As she withdrew into the golden cloud,
And I was left alone within the bower;
And from that time to this I am alone,
And I shall be alone until I die.   190

"Yet, mother Ida, harken ere I die.
Fairest—why fairest wife? am I not fair?
My love hath told me so a thousand times.
Methinks I must be fair, for yesterday,
When I past by, a wild and wanton pard,   195
Eyed like the evening star, with playful tail
Crouch'd fawning in the weed. Most loving is she?
Ah me, my mountain shepherd, that my arms
Were wound about thee, and my hot lips prest
Close, close to thine in that quick-falling dew   200
Of fruitful kisses, thick as autumn rains
Flash in the pools of whirling Simois!

"O mother, hear me yet before I die.
They came, they cut away my tallest pines,
My tall dark pines, that plumed the craggy ledge   205
High over the blue gorge, and all between
The snowy peak and snow-white cataract
Foster'd the callow eaglet—from beneath
Whose thick mysterious boughs in the dark morn
The panther's roar came muffled, while I sat   210

---

3. Paphos, like Idalium, was a city in Cyprus sacred to Aphrodite.

Low in the valley. Never, never more
Shall lone Œnone see the morning mist
Sweep thro' them; never see them overlaid
With narrow moonlit slips of silver cloud,
Between the loud stream and the trembling stars.   215

        "O mother, hear me yet before I die.
I wish that somewhere in the ruin'd folds,
Among the fragments tumbled from the glens,
Or the dry thickets, I could meet with her
The Abominable, that uninvited came   220
Into the fair Peleïan banquet-hall,
And cast the golden fruit upon the board,
And bred this change; that I might speak my mind,
And tell her to her face how much I hate
Her presence, hated both of Gods and men.   225

        "O mother, hear me yet before I die.
Hath he not sworn his love a thousand times,
In this green valley, under this green hill,
Even on this hand, and sitting on this stone?
Seal'd it with kisses? water'd it with tears?   230
O happy tears, and how unlike to these!
O happy heaven, how canst thou see my face?
O happy earth, how canst thou bear my weight?
O death, death, death, thou ever-floating cloud,
There are enough unhappy on this earth,   235
Pass by the happy souls, that love to live;
I pray thee, pass before my light of life,
And shadow all my soul, that I may die.
Thou weighest heavy on the heart within,
Weigh heavy on my eyelids; let me die.   240

        "O mother, hear me yet before I die.
I will not die alone[4] for fiery thoughts
Do shape themselves within me, more and more,
Whereof I catch the issue, as I hear
Dead sounds at night come from the inmost hills,   245
Like footsteps upon wool. I dimly see
My far-off doubtful purpose, as a mother
Conjectures of the features of her child
Ere it is born. Her child!—a shudder comes
Across me: never child be born of me,   250
Unblest, to vex me with his father's eyes!

        "O mother, hear me yet before I die.
Hear me, O earth. I will not die alone,
Lest their shrill happy laughter come to me
Walking the cold and starless road of death   255
Uncomforted, leaving my ancient love

---

4. Fatally wounded by Philoctetes' poisoned arrow, Paris finally sought help from Œnone, who alone had
the gift to heal him.

With the Greek woman. I will rise and go
Down into Troy, and ere the stars come forth
Talk with the wild Cassandra,[5] for she says
A fire dances before her, and a sound   260
Rings ever in her ears of armed men.
What this may be I know not, but I know
That, wheresoe'er I am by night and day,
All earth and air seem only burning fire."

                                                    1832 (1842)

To ———

With the Following Poem[1]

I send you here a sort of allegory—
For you will understand it—of a soul,
A sinful soul possess'd of many gifts,
A spacious garden full of flowering weeds,
A glorious devil, large in heart and brain,   5
That did love beauty only—beauty seen
In all varieties of mould and mind—
And knowledge for its beauty; or if good,
Good only for its beauty, seeing not
That Beauty, Good, and Knowledge are three sisters   10
That doat upon each other, friends to man,
Living together under the same roof,
And never can be sunder'd without tears.
And he that shuts Love out, in turn shall be

Shut out from Love, and on her threshold lie   15
Howling in outer darkness.[2] Not for this
Was common clay ta'en from the common earth
Moulded by God, and temper'd with the tears
Of angels to the perfect shape of man.

                                                        1832

5. One of Priam's daughters. She denied Apollo her love; he then rendered valueless his earlier gift of prophecy by causing her prophecies never to be believed. Turner clarifies the similarities between Dido (see her dream, *Aeneid* IV, lines 465–68) and Œnone: both were deserted by Trojan lovers and both committed suicide on funeral pyres. Cassandra knew specifically that Paris's rape of Helen would initiate the Trojan War; Tennyson's Œnone's vision is less precise.

1. Dedicated to Richard Trench, a member of the Cambridge Apostles. Trench, Tennyson noted late in his life, "said to me, when we were at Trinity together, 'Tennyson, we cannot live in art'" (*Memoir* I, 118). See IM 87, 6.
   The so-called art for art's sake movement came from the French phrase *l'art pour l'art*, which originally derived from Edgar Allan Poe in The *Poetic Principle* (1850): "There neither exists nor can exist any work more thoroughly dignified . . . than the poem which is a poem and nothing more—the poem written solely for the poem's sake." The theory, which evolved with the early Romantics, especially Coleridge, would flourish a half century later among the French Symbolist poets and in England especially with Walter Pater's *Marius the Epicurean* (1885).

2. Compare IM 54, 5: "an infant crying in the night . . . with no language but a cry," and IM 124, 5–6. In 1890 Tennyson wrote: "'The Palace of Art' is the embodiment of my own belief that the Godlike life is with man and for man" (*Memoir* I, 118–19).

The Palace of Art[1]

I built my soul a lordly pleasure-house,[2]
    Wherein at ease for aye to dwell.
I said, "O Soul, make merry and carouse,
    Dear soul, for all is well."

A huge crag-platform, smooth as burnish'd brass,   5
    I chose. The ranged ramparts bright
From level meadow-bases of deep grass
    Suddenly scaled the light.

Thereon I built it firm. Of ledge or shelf
    The rock rose clear, or winding stair.   10
My soul would live alone unto herself
    In her high palace there.

And "while the world runs round and round," I said,
    "Reign thou apart, a quiet king,
Still as, while Saturn whirls, his steadfast shade   15
    Sleeps on his luminous ring."[3]

To which my soul made answer readily:
    "Trust me, in bliss I shall abide
In this great mansion, that is built for me,
    So royal-rich and wide."   20
   . . . .
Four courts I made, East, West and South and North,
    In each a squared lawn, wherefrom
The golden gorge of dragons spouted forth
    A flood of fountain-foam.

And round the cool green courts there ran a row   25
    Of cloisters, branch'd like mighty woods,
Echoing all night to that sonorous flow
    Of spouted fountain-floods;

And round the roofs a gilded gallery
    That lent broad verge to distant lands,   30

1. Circulating in manuscript by May 1832, the poem was extensively revised between 1832 and 1853. A number of stanzas were transposed, many were dropped, and several new ones were added. A couple of significant deletions are given in the notes; but a full comparison of the 1832 and 1842 texts is needed to reveal the extent of Tennyson's artistic development during the so-called ten years' silence.
    In a note to the 1832 version the poet acknowledged, "It is the most difficult of all things to *devise* a statue in verse." "When I first conceived the plan of the poem, I intended to have introduced both sculptures and paintings into it" (*Memoir* I, 119). Many of the changes record the poet's often successful attempts at painting pictures in verse.
2. Compare the opening lines of Coleridge's "Kubla Khan": "In Xanadu did Kubla Khan / A stately pleasure-dome decree."
3. Saturn revolves every ten and a half hours, but the planet's shadow cast on its rings appears stationary. Tennyson often, especially in *In Memoriam*, alludes to astronomical phenomena, a tendency that, for Yeats, contributed to what he called "that brooding over scientific opinion that so often extinguished the central flame in Tennyson."

Far as the wild swan wings, to where the sky
    Dipt down to sea and sands.

From those four jets four currents in one swell
    Across the mountain stream'd below
In misty folds, that floating as they fell   35
    Lit up a torrent-bow.

And high on every peak a statue seem'd
    To hang on tiptoe, tossing up
A cloud of incense of all odor steam'd
    From out a golden cup.   40

So that she thought, "And who shall gaze upon
    My palace with unblinded eyes,
While this great bow will waver in the sun,
    And that sweet incense rise?"

For that sweet incense rose and never fail'd,   45
    And, while day sank or mounted higher,
The light aerial galley, golden-rail'd,
    Burnt like a fringe of fire.

Likewise the deep-set windows, stain'd and traced,
    Would seem slow-flaming crimson fires   50
From shadow'd grots of arches interlaced,
    And tipt with frost-like spires.
            . . . .
Full of long-sounding corridors it was,
    That over-vaulted grateful gloom,
Thro' which the livelong day my soul did pass,   55
    Well-pleased, from room to room.

Full of great rooms and small the palace stood,
    All various, each a perfect whole
From living Nature, fit for every mood
    And change of my still soul.   60

For some were hung with arras green and blue,
    Showing a gaudy summer-morn,
Where with puff'd cheek the belted hunter blew
    His wreathed bugle-horn.

One seem'd all dark and red—a tract of sand,   65
    And some one pacing there alone,
Who paced for ever in a glimmering land,
    Lit with a low large moon.

One show'd an iron coast and angry waves,
    You seem'd to hear them climb and fall   70
And roar rock-thwarted under bellowing caves,
    Beneath the windy wall.

And one, a full-fed river winding slow
   By herds upon an endless plain,
The ragged rims of thunder brooding low,   75
   With shadow-streaks of rain.

And one, the reapers at their sultry toil.
   In front they bound the sheaves. Behind
Were realms of upland, prodigal in oil,
   And hoary to the wind.[4]   80

And one a foreground black with stones and slags;
   Beyond, a line of heights; and higher
All barr'd with long white cloud the scornful crags;
   And highest, snow and fire.

And one, an English home—gray twilight pour'd   85
   On dewy pastures, dewy trees,
Softer than sleep—all things in order stored,
   A haunt of ancient Peace.

Nor these alone, but every landscape fair,
   As fit for every mood of mind,   90
Or gay, or grave, or sweet, or stern, was there,
   Not less than truth design'd.
   . . . .
Or the maid-mother by a crucifix,
   In tracts of pasture sunny-warm,
Beneath branch-work of costly sardonyx[5]   95
   Sat smiling, babe in arm.

Or in a clear-wall'd city on the sea,
   Near gilded organ-pipes, her hair
Wound with white rose, slept Saint Cecily;[6]
   An angel look'd at her.   100

Or thronging all one porch of Paradise
   A group of Houris[7] bow'd to see
The dying Islamite, with hands and eyes
   That said, We wait for thee.

Or mythic Uther's deeply-wounded son[8]   105
   In some fair space of sloping greens
Lay, dozing in the vale of Avalon,
   And watch'd by weeping queens.

Or hollowing one hand against his ear,
   To list foot-fall, ere he saw   110

4. Probably an Italian landscape; the olive trees show their white undersides in the wind.
5. A kind of stone with orange-red layers.
6. St. Cecilia, the patron saint of music.
7. Nymphs of the Muslim paradise who welcome the faithful.
8. King Arthur. For Tennyson's rendering of this part of the myth, see "The Passing of Arthur," especially lines 361 to the end.

The wood-nymph, stay'd the Ausonian king[9] to hear
    Of wisdom and of law.

Or over hills with peaky tops and engrail'd,
    And many a tract of palm and rice,
The throne of Indian Cama[1] slowly sail'd   115
    A summer fann'd with spice.

Or sweet Europa's mantle blew unclasp'd,
    From off her shoulder backward borne;
From one hand droop'd a crocus; one hand grasp'd
    The mild bull's golden horn.[2]   120

Or else flush'd Ganymede,[3] his rosy thigh
    Half-buried in the eagle's down,
Sole as a flying star shot thro' the sky
    Above the pillar'd town.

Nor these alone; but every legend fair   125
    Which the supreme Caucasian mind
Carved out of Nature for itself was there,
    Not less than life design'd.
        .   .   .   .
Then in the towers I placed great bells that swung,
    Moved of themselves, with silver sound;   130
And with choice paintings of wise men I hung
    The royal dais round.

For there was Milton like a seraph strong,
    Beside him Shakespeare bland and mild;
And there the world-worn Dante grasp'd his song,   135
    And somewhat grimly smiled.

And there the Ionian father[4] of the rest;
    A million wrinkles carved his skin;
A hundred winters snow'd upon his breast,
    From cheek and throat and chin.   140

Above, the fair hall-ceiling stately-set
    Many an arch high up did lift,
And angels rising and descending met
    With interchange of gift.

Below was all mosaic choicely plann'd   145
    With cycles of the human tale
Of this wide world, the times of every land
    So wrought they will not fail.

9. Numa Pompilius, the second king of Rome.
1. Indian god of love.
2. Zeus loved Europa, the daughter of the king of Tyre; in the form of a white bull he carried her off to Crete.
3. A mortal who, because of his extraordinary beauty, was carried off by Zeus in the guise of an eagle and
    made cupbearer to the gods.
4. Homer.

The people here, a beast of burden slow,
    Toil'd onward, prick'd with goads and stings;   150
Here play'd, a tiger, rolling to and fro
    The heads and crowns of kings;[5]

Here rose, an athlete, strong to break or bind
    All force in bonds that might endure,
And here once more like some sick man declined,   155
    And trusted any cure.

But over these she trod; and those great bells
    Began to chime. She took her throne;
She sat betwixt the shining oriels,
    To sing her songs alone.   160

And thro' the topmost oriels' colored flame
    Two godlike faces gazed below;
Plato the wise, and large-brow'd Verulam,[6]
    The first of those who know.

And all those names that in their motion were   165
    Full-welling fountain-heads of change,
Betwixt the slender shafts were blazon'd fair
    In diverse raiment strange;

Thro' which the lights, rose, amber, emerald, blue,
    Flush'd in her temples and her eyes,   170
And from her lips, as morn from Memnon,[7] drew
    Rivers of melodies.

No nightingale delighteth to prolong
    Her low preamble all alone,
More than my soul to hear her echo'd song   175
    Throb thro' the ribbed stone;

Singing and murmuring in her feastful mirth,
    Joying to feel herself alive,
Lord over Nature, lord of the visible earth,
    Lord of the senses five;   180

Communing with herself: "All these are mine,
    And let the world have peace or wars,
'T is one to me." She—when young night divine
    Crown'd dying day with stars,

5. Perhaps a reference to the French Revolution of 1789, in which case the athlete and sick man in the following stanza may be democracy and anarchy, respectively.
6. Francis Bacon, suggested by his bust just outside the Trinity College library. Tennyson may also have
   been recalling his science tutor during his first year at Cambridge, William Whewell, whose bust is just
   outside the interior entrance to the Trinity Library.
7. King of the Ethiopians and immortalized by Zeus. His statue supposedly gave forth a musical sound
   when struck by the first rays of the morning sun (see *The Princess* III, line 100).

Making sweet close of his delicious toils—   185
    Lit light in wreaths and anadems,[8]
And pure quintessences of precious oils
    In hollow'd moons of gems,

To mimic heaven; and clapt her hands and cried,
    "I marvel if my still delight   190
In this great house so royal-rich and wide
    Be flatter'd to the height.

"O all things fair to sate my various eyes!
    O shapes and hues that please me well!
O silent faces of the Great and Wise,   195
    My Gods, with whom I dwell![9]

"O Godlike isolation which art mine,
    I can but count thee perfect gain,
What time I watch the darkening droves of swine
    That range on yonder plain.   200

"In filthy sloughs they roll a prurient skin,
    They gaze and wallow, breed and sleep;
And oft some brainless devil enters in
    And drives them to the deep."[1]

Then of the moral instinct would she prate   205
    And of the rising from the dead,
As hers by right of full-accomplish'd Fate;
    And at the last she said:

"I take possession of man's mind and deed.
    I care not what the sects may bawl.   210
I sit as God holding no form of creed,
    But contemplating all."
        . . . .
Full oft the riddle of the painful earth
    Flash'd thro' her as she sat alone,

---

8. Crowns.
9. After this stanza the following two verses appeared in the 1842 text:
    "From shape to shape at first within the womb
        The brain is moulded," she began,
    "And thro' all phases of all thought
        I come
    Unto the perfect man.

    All nature widens upward. Evermore
        The simpler essence lower lies,
    More complex is more perfect, owning more
        Discourse, more widely wise."
    Ricks, citing Killham, notes: "'The discovery of the four-fold resemblance of the foetal human brain to the
    brains of other vertebrates was made by Friedrich Tiedemann.' Tennyson 'sought to exorcise those [doubts]
    raised by Tiedemann's theory by making the erring Soul foolishly base its own hubristic confidence upon
    it.'" The matter may be debatable; Tennyson was not apt to dismiss any scientific idea lightly.
        In the 1832 version the first of these stanzas began: "From change to change four times within the womb."
1. From two possessed men Christ cast out the Devils who went into a herd of swine, "and behold, the
    whole herd of swine ran violently down a steep place into the sea, and perished in the waters" (Matthew
    8:28–34).

Yet not the less held she her solemn mirth,   215
     And intellectual throne.

And so she throve and prosper'd; so three years
     She prosper'd; on the fourth she fell,
Like Herod,[2] when the shout was in his ears,
     Struck thro' with pangs of hell.   220

Lest she should fail and perish utterly,
     God, before whom ever lie bare
The abysmal deeps of personality,
     Plagued her with sore despair.

When she would think, where'er she turn'd her sight   225
     The airy hand confusion wrought,
Wrote, "Mene, mene,"[3] and divided quite
     The kingdom of her thought.

Deep dread and loathing of her solitude
     Fell on her, from which mood was born   230
Scorn of herself; again, from out that mood
     Laughter at her self-scorn.

"What! is not this my place of strength," she said,
     "My spacious mansion built for me,
Whereof the strong foundation-stones were laid   235
     Since my first memory?"

But in dark corners of her palace stood
     Uncertain shapes; and unawares
On white-eyed phantasms weeping tears of blood,
     And horrible nightmares,   240

And hollow shades enclosing hearts of flame,
     And, with dim fretted foreheads all,
On corpses three-months-old at noon she came,
     That stood against the wall.

A spot of dull stagnation, without light   245
     Or power of movement, seem'd my soul,
Mid onward-sloping motions infinite
     Making for one sure goal;

A still salt pool, lock'd in with bars of sand,
     Left on the shore, that hears all night   250
The plunging seas draw backward from the land
     Their moon-led waters white;

2. Known as "The Great" (73?–4 B.C.); king of Judea (40–4), who, in the New Testament, attempts to kill the infant Jesus by commanding all children under two years old in Bethlehem be put to death. The people claimed Herod's voice was God's: "Immediately the angel of the Lord smote him, because he gave not God the glory: and he was eaten of worms, and gave up the ghost" (Acts 12:18–23).
3. "This is the interpretation of the thing: mene; God hath numbered thy kingdom, and finished it" (Daniel 5:26).

A star that with the choral starry dance
  Join'd not, but stood, and standing saw
The hollow orb of moving Circumstance   255
  Roll'd round by one fix'd law.

Back on herself her serpent pride had curl'd.
  "No voice," she shriek'd in that lone hall,
"No voice breaks thro' the stillness of this world;
  One deep, deep silence all!"   260

She, mouldering with the dull earth's mouldering sod,
  Inwrapt tenfold in slothful shame,
Lay there exiled from eternal God,
  Lost to her place and name;

And death and life she hated equally,   265
  And nothing saw, for her despair,
But dreadful time, dreadful eternity,
  No comfort anywhere;

Remaining utterly confused with fears,
  And ever worse with growing time,   270
And ever unrelieved by dismal tears,
  And all alone in crime.

Shut up as in a crumbling tomb, girt round
  With blackness as a solid wall,
Far off she seem'd to hear the dully sound   275
  Of human footsteps fall:

As in strange lands a traveller walking slow,
  In doubt and great perplexity,
A little before moonrise hears the low
  Moan of an unknown sea;   280

And knows not if it be thunder, or a sound
  Of rocks thrown down, or one deep cry
Of great wild beasts; then thinketh, "I have found
  A new land, but I die."

She howl'd aloud, "I am on fire within.   285
  There comes no murmur of reply.
What is it that will take away my sin,
  And save me lest I die?"

So when four years were wholly finished,
  She threw her royal robes away.   290
"Make me a cottage in the vale," she said,
  "Where I may mourn and pray.

"Yet pull not down my palace towers, that are
  So lightly, beautifully built;

Perchance I may return with others[4] there   295
  When I have purged my guilt."

                                                    1832 (1842, 1853)

The Hesperides[1]

> Hesperus and his daughters three,
> That sing about the golden tree.
>   —COMUS [MILTON]

The North-wind fall'n, in the new-starréd night
Zidonian Hanno,[2] voyaging beyond
The hoary promontory of Soloë
Past Thymiaterion,[3] in calméd bays,
Between the southern and the western Horn,   5
Heard neither warbling of the nightingale,
Nor melody of the Libyan lotus flute
Blown seaward from the shore; but from a slope
That ran bloom-bright into the Atlantic blue,
Beneath a highland leaning down a weight   10
Of cliffs, and zoned below with cedar shade,
Came voices, like the voices in a dream,
Continuous, till he reached the outer sea.

Song

1
The golden apple, the golden apple, the hallowed fruit,
Guard it well, guard it warily,   15
Singing airily,
Standing about the charméd root.
Round about all is mute,
As the snow-field on the mountain-peaks,
As the sand-field at the mountain-foot.   20
Crocodiles in briny creeks
Sleep and stir not: all is mute.
If ye sing not, if ye make false measure,

---

4. See *IM* 108: "I will not shut me from my kind." Also compare Wordsworth's "Elegiac Stanzas": "Farewell, farewell the heart that lives alone, / Housed in a dream, at distance from the Kind [i.e., humankind]."
1. The poem was never republished during the poet's lifetime. Tennyson expressed regret that he had done away with it from among his juvenilia (see *Memoir* I, 61). As a celebration of pure art, "The Hesperides" should be contrasted with "A Palace of Art."
    In Greek mythology the Hesperides were the four daughters of the evening star Hesperus, and they lived near the Atlas Mountains on the northwest coast of Africa. With the dragon Ladon, they guarded the tree of the golden apples given by the Titan goddess of the earth Gaea to Hera when she married Zeus. The eleventh labor of Heracles was to get the golden apples, which he did—according to one version—by slaying Ladon. In another version he induced Atlas to fetch the apples while assuming the latter's burden of holding up the world. The apples supposedly had the power of healing and were symbolic of happiness, love, and wisdom. Tennyson's primary source was probably in Hesiod's rendering of the myth.
2. A Carthaginian commander who, around 500 B.C., navigated the west coast of Africa and recorded his experiences in the *Periplus*.
3. Like Soloë, a point on the African coast Hanno passed as he penetrated beyond the colony of Senegal on "the western Horn."

We shall lose eternal pleasure,
Worth eternal want of rest.   25
Laugh not loudly: watch the treasure
Of the wisdom of the West.[4]
In a corner wisdom whispers. Five[5] and three
(Let it not be preached abroad) make an awful mystery.
For the blossom unto threefold music bloweth;   30
Evermore it is born anew;
And the sap to threefold music floweth,
From the root
Drawn in the dark,
Up to the fruit,   35
Creeping under the fragrant bark,
Liquid gold, honeysweet, thro' and thro'.
Keen-eyed Sisters, singing airily,
Looking warily
Every way,   40
Guard the apple night and day,
Lest one from the East[6] come and take it away.

                                    2
Father Hesper, Father Hesper, watch, watch, ever and aye,
Looking under silver hair with a silver eye.
Father, twinkle not thy steadfast sight;   45
Kingdoms lapse, and climates change, and races die;
Honor comes with mystery;
Hoarded wisdom brings delight.
Number, tell them over and number
How many the mystic fruit-tree holds   50
Lest the red-combed dragon slumber
Rolled together in purple folds.
Look to him, father, lest he wink, and the golden apple be stol'n away,
For his ancient heart is drunk with overwatchings night and day,
Round about the hallowed fruit-tree curled—   55
Sing away, sing loud evermore in the wind, without stop,
Lest his scaléd eyelid drop,
For he is older than the world.
If he waken, we waken,
Rapidly levelling eager eyes.   60
If he sleep, we sleep,
Dropping the eyelid over the eyes.
If the golden apple be taken,
The world will be overwise.
Five links a golden chain, are we,   65
Hesper, the dragon, and sisters three,
Bound about the golden tree.

---

4. In the symbolic geography here and in other early poems, the west stands for stability, twilight, rest, and
   civilization; whereas Tennyson connects the east with images of dawn, strength, vigor, and strife.
5. The number five traditionally has mystic significance as the first number that contains the two primary
   odd and even numbers and is thus the original unification of opposites. The poet may also be thinking
   of the five senses.
6. Alludes to Heracles, who came from Greece.

3
Father Hesper, Father Hesper, watch, watch, night and day,
Lest the old wound[7] of the world be healéd,
The glory unsealéd,   70
The golden apple stolén away,
And the ancient secret revealéd.
Look from west to east along:
Father, old Himala weakens, Caucasus[8] is bold and strong.
Wandering waters unto wandering waters call;   75
Let them clash together, foam and fall.
Out of watchings, out of wiles,
Comes the bliss of secret smiles.
All things are not told to all.
Half-round the mantling night is drawn,   80
Purple fringéd with even and dawn.
Hesper hateth Phosphor,[9] evening hateth morn.

4
Every flower and every fruit the redolent breath
Of this warm sea-wind ripeneth,
Arching the billow in his sleep;   85
But the land-wind wandereth,
Broken by the highland-steep,
Two streams upon the violet deep;
For the western sun and the western star,
And the low west-wind, breathing afar,   90
The end of day and beginning of night
Make the apple holy and bright;
Holy and bright, round and full, bright and blest,
Mellowed in a land of rest; ·
Watch it warily day and night;   95
All good things are in the west.
Till mid noon the cool east light
Is shut out by the round of the tall hillbrow.
But when the full-faced sunset yellowly
Stays on the flowering arch of the bough,   100
The lucious fruitage clustereth mellowly,
Golden-kernelled, golden-cored,
Sunset-ripened above on the tree.
The world is wasted with fire and sword,
But the apple of gold hangs over the sea   105
Five links, a golden chain are we,

---

7. A hint, as in line 27, where "wisdom of the West" suggests knowledge of good and evil, of the Fall from Eden. This line defies precise explication but is in keeping with the idea that mysteriousness somehow preserves vitality in art.
8. From the Himalayas to the Caucasus Mountains. Perhaps an allusion to the popular nineteenth-century notion that civilization was also moving northward. In many of the pieces in *Poems by Two Brothers* Tennyson conceives of the north and east as regions from which the barbarian hordes come to threaten the Western civilizations. *Idylls of the King* esssentially preserves this notion; see the end of the "Epilogue" for one of numerous allusions.
9. The morning star, specifically Venus. Classical astrologers believed the morning and evening star were two different stars.

Hesper, the dragon, and sisters three,
Daughters three,
Bound about
All round about   110
The gnarléd bole of the charméd tree.
The golden apple, the golden apple, the hallowed fruit,
Guard it well, guard it warily,
Watch it warily,
Singing airily,   115
Standing about the charméd root.

1832

A Dream of Fair Women[1]

I read, before my eyelids dropt heir shade,[2]
"*The Legend of Good Women*," long ago
Sung by the morning star of song, who made
    His music heard below.;

Dan[3] Chaucer, the first warbler, whose sweet breath   5
    Preluded those melodious bursts that fill
The spacious times to great Elizabeth
    With sounds that echo still.

And, for a while, the knowledge of his art
    Held me above the subject, as strong gales   10
Hold swollen clouds from raining, tho' my heart,
    Brimful of those wild tales,

Charged both mine eyes with tears. In every land
    I saw, wherever light illumineth,
Beauty and anguish walking hand in hand   15
    The downward slope to death.

Those far-renowned brides of ancient song
    Peopled the hollow dark, like burning stars,
And I heard sounds of insult, shame, and wrong,
    And trumpets blown for wars;   20

1. A dream-vision in the medieval tradition. The poem was suggested by Chaucer's "Legend of Good Women"; though Chaucer praises women faithful in love, and from his list only Cleopatra appears. Croker bludgeoned Tennyson's poem (see excerpt from *Quarterly Review* of 1833, in the "Contexts" section of this book), and it underwent considerable revision for republication in 1842. Retouched in 1845, 1853, and 1884, these sketches of uneven quality never materialized into an organic whole.
2. The pose, reading leading to dream-visions, strongly resembles Keats's in such poems as "Sleep and Poetry." In line 18, for example, "the hollow dark" appears in Keats's *The Fall of Hyperion* I, line 455: "Thea arose, / And stretch'd her white arm through the hollow dark." In so noting, and as Ricks observes, *The Fall* was not published until 1856; the language and imagery, however, "suggests the status of romantic poetic diction" in Tennyson here, as well as throughout many poems from this period.
3. From *dominus*, "master." Spenser first used the appellation: "Dan Chaucer, well of English undefiled" (*The Faerie Queen* IV, ii, xxxii).

And clattering flints batter'd with clanging hoofs;
    And I saw crowds in column'd sanctuaries,
And forms that pass'd at windows and on roofs
    Of marble palaces;

Corpses across the threshold, heroes tall   25
    Dislodging pinnacle and parapet
Upon the tortoise[4] creeping to the wall,
    Lances in ambush set;

And high shrine-doors burst thro' with heated blasts
    That run before the fluttering tongues of fire;   30
White surf wind-scatter'd over sails and masts,
    And ever climbing higher;

Squadrons and squares of men in brazen plates,
    Scaffolds, still sheets of water, divers woes,
Ranges of glimmering vaults with iron grates,   35
    And hush'd seraglios.[5]

So shape chased shape as swift as, when to land
    Bluster the winds and tides the selfsame way,
Crisp foam-flakes scud along the level sand,
    Torn from the fringe of spray.   40

I started once, or seem'd to start in pain,
    Resolved on noble things, and strove to speak,
As when a great thought strikes along the brain
    And flushes all the cheek.

And once my arm was lifted to hew down   45
    A cavalier from off his saddle-bow,
That bore a lady from a leaguer'd town;
    And then, I know not how,

All those sharp fancies, by down-lapsing thought
    Stream'd onward, lost their edges, and did creep   50
Roll'd on each other, rounded, smooth'd, and brought
    Into the gulfs of sleep.

At last methought that I had wander'd far
    In an old wood;[6] fresh-wash'd in coolest dew
The maiden splendors of the morning star   55
    Shook in the steadfast blue.

Enormous elm-tree boles did stoop and lean
    Upon the dusky brushwood underneath
Their broad curved branches, fledged with clearest green,
    New from its silken sheath.   60

4. The "testudo," a close troop formation made by soldiers overlapping their shields above their heads.
5. Harems.
6. I.e., into the past.

The dim red Morn had died, her journey done,
    And with dead lips smiled at the twilight plain,
Half-fallen across the threshold of the sun,
    Never to rise again.

There was no motion in the dumb dead air,   65
    Not any song of bird or sound of rill;
Gross darkness of the inner sepulchre
    Is not so deadly still

As that wide forest. Growths of jasmine turn'd
    Their humid arms festooning tree to tree,   70
And at the root thro' lush green grasses burn'd
    The red anemone.

I knew the flowers, I knew the leaves, I knew
    The tearful glimmer of the languid dawn
On those long, rank, dark wood-walks drench'd in dew,   75
    Leading from lawn to lawn.

The smell of violets, hidden in the green,
    Pour'd back into my empty soul and frame
The times when I remember to have been
    Joyful and free from blame.   80

And from within me a clear undertone
    Thrill'd thro' mine ears in that unblissful clime,
"Pass freely thro'; the wood is all thine own
    Until the end of time."

At length I saw a lady[7] within call,   85
    Stiller than chisell'd marble, standing there;
A daughter of the gods, divinely tall,
    And most divinely fair.

Her loveliness with shame and with surprise
    Froze my swift speech; she turning on my face   90
The star-like sorrows of immortal eyes,
    Spoke slowly in her place:

"I had great beauty; ask thou not my name:
    No one can be more wise than destiny.
Many drew swords and died. Where'er I came   95
    I brought calamity."

"No marvel, sovereign lady: in fair field
    Myself for such a face had boldly died,"
I answer'd free; and turning I appeal'd
    To one[8] that stood beside.   100

---

7. Helen of Troy.
8. Iphigenia, Agamemnon's daughter, sacrificed to Artemis by her father so that the Greek fleet might have favorable winds in setting sail for Troy.

But she, with sick and scornful looks averse,
    To her full height her stately stature draws;
"My youth," she said, "was blasted with a curse:
        This woman was the cause.

"I was cut off from hope in that sad place   105
    Which men call'd Aulis in those iron years:
My father held his hand upon his face;
        I, blinded with my tears,

"Still strove to speak: my voice was thick with sighs
    As in a dream. Dimly I could descry   110
The stern black-bearded kings with wolfish eyes,
        Waiting to see me die.

"The high masts flicker'd as they lay afloat;
    The crowds, the temples, waver'd, and the shore;
The bright death quiver'd at the victim's throat—   115
        Touch'd—and I knew no more."

Whereto the other with a downward brow:
    "I would the white cold heavy-plunging foam,
Whirl'd by the wind, had roll'd me deep below,
        Then when I left my home."   120

Her slow full words sank thro' the silence drear,
    As thunder-drops fall on a sleeping sea:
Sudden I heard a voice that cried, "Come here,
        That I may look on thee."

I turning saw, throned on a flowery rise,   125
    One[9] sitting on a crimson scarf unroll'd;
A queen, with swarthy cheeks and bold black eyes,
        Brow-bound with burning gold.

She, flashing forth a haughty smile, began:
    "I govern'd men by change, and so I sway'd   130
All moods. 'T is long since I have seen a man.
        Once, like the moon, I made

"The ever-shifting currents of the blood
    According to my humor ebb and flow.
I have no men to govern in this wood: 135
        That makes my only woe.

"Nay—yet it chafes me that I could not bend
    One will; nor tame and tutor with mine eye

---

9. Cleopatra. Tennyson acknowledged he was thinking of Shakespeare's lines, "Think on me / That am
with Phoebus' amorous pinches black" (*Antony and Cleopatra* I, v, lines 27–28).

That dull cold-blooded Cæsar.[1] Prythee, friend,
    Where is Mark Antony?   140

"The man, my lover, with whom I rode sublime
    On fortune's neck; we sat as God by God:
The Nilus would have risen before his time
    And flooded at our nod.

"We drank the Libyan Sun to sleep, and lit   145
    Lamps which out-burn'd Canopus.[2] O, my life
In Egypt! O, the dalliance and the wit,
    The flattery and the strife,

"And the wild kiss, when fresh from war's alarms,
    My Hercules, my Roman Antony,   150
My mailed Bacchus leapt into my arms,
    Contended there to die!

"And there he died: and when I heard my name
    Sigh'd forth with life I would not brook my fear
Of the other; with a worm I balk'd his fame.   155
    What else was left? look here!" —

With that she tore her robe apart, and half
    The polish'd argent of her breast to sight
Laid bare. Thereto she pointed with a laugh,
    Showing the aspick's bite. —   160

"I died a Queen. The Roman soldier found
    Me lying dead, my crown about my brows,
A name for ever! — lying robed and crown'd,
    Worthy a Roman spouse."

Her warbling voice, a lyre of widest range   165
    Struck by all passion, did fall down and glance
From tone to tone, and glided thro' all change
    Of liveliest utterance.

When she made pause I knew not for delight;
    Because with sudden motion from the ground   170
She raised her piercing orbs, and fill'd with light
    The interval of sound.

Still with their fires Love tipt his keenest darts;
    As once they drew into two burning rings
All beams of love, melting the mighty hearts   175
    Of captains and of kings.

1. Not Julius, whom she had loved, but Octavius, "the other" of line 155, whom Cleopatra failed to seduce.
  Consequently she took her own life rather than be led captive through the streets of Rome.
2. A first-magnitude star visible in the Southern Hemisphere.

Slowly my sense undazzled. Then I heard
　　A noise of some one[3] coming thro' the lawn,
And singing clearer than the crested bird
　　That claps his wings at dawn: 180

"The torrent brooks of hallow'd Israel
　　From craggy hollows pouring, late and soon,
Sound all night long, in falling thro' the dell,
　　Far-heard beneath the moon.

"The balmy moon of blessed Israel   185
　　Floods all the deep-blue gloom with beams divine;
All night the splinter'd crags that will the dell
　　With spires of silver shine."

As one that museth where broad sunshine laves
　　The lawn by some cathedral, thro' the door   190
Hearing the holy organ rolling waves
　　Of sound on roof and floor

Within, and anthem sung, is charm'd and tied
　　To where he stands, — so stood I, when that flow
Of music left the lips of her that died   195
　　To save her father's vow;

The daughter of the warrior Gileadite,
　　A maiden pure; as when she went along
From Mizpeh's[4] tower'd gate with welcome light,
　　With timbrel and with song.   200

My words leapt forth: "Heaven heads the count of crimes
　　With that wild oath." She render'd answer high:
"Not so, nor once alone; a thousand times
　　I would be born and die.

"Single I grew, like some green plant, whose root   205
　　Creeps to the garden water-pipes beneath,
Feeding the flower; but ere my flower to fruit
　　Changed, I was ripe for death.

"My God, my land, my father — these did move
　　Me from my bliss of life that Nature gave,   210
Lower'd softly with a threefold cord of love
　　Down to a silent grave.

"And I went mourning, 'No fair Hebrew boy
　　Shall smile away my mainden blame among

---

3. Jephthah's daughter (Judges 11:30–40). Jephthah, "the warrior Gileadite," vowed he would sacrifice the first person to greet him on his return home were he victorious in the war against the children of Ammon. Subsequently, he fulfilled his vow, sacrificing his only child, a daughter.
4. A town in Gilead where Jephthah's house was.

The Hebrew mothers'—emptied of all joy,   215
    Leaving the dance and song,

"Leaving the olive-gardens far below,
    Leaving the promise of my bridal bower,
The valleys of grape-loaded vines that glow
    Beneath the battled tower.   220

"The light white cloud swam over us. Anon
    We heard the lion roaring from his den;
We saw the large white stars rise one by one,
    Or, from the darken'd glen,

"Saw God divide the night with flying flame,   225
    And thunder on the everlasting hills.
I heard Him, for He spake, and grief became
    A solemn scorn of ills.

"When the next moon was roll'd into the sky,
    Strength came to me that equall'd my desire.   230
How beautiful a thing it was to die
    For God and for my sire!

"It comforts me in this one thought to dwell,
    That I subdued me to my father's will;
Because the kiss he gave me, ere I fell,   235
    Sweetens the spirit still.

"Moreover it is written that my race
    Hew'd Ammon, hip and thigh, from Aroer
On Arnon unto Minneth." Here her face
    Glow'd, as I look'd at her.   240

She lock'd her lips; she left me where I stood:
    "Glory to God," she sang, and past afar,
Thridding[5] the sombre boskage of the wood,
    Toward the morning-star.

Losing her carol I stood pensively,   245
    As one that from a casement leans his head,
When midnight bells cease ringing suddenly,
    And the old year is dead.

"Alas! alas!" a low voice, full of care,
    Murmur'd beside me: "Turn and look on me;   250
I am that Rosamond[6] whom men call fair,
    If what I was I be.

"Would I had been some maiden coarse and poor!
    O me, that I should ever see the light!

5. Threading or making her way through the dark thicket.
6. Mistress of Henry II who was allegedly poisoned by his queen, Eleanor of Aquitaine.

Those dragon eyes of anger'd Eleanor   255
  Do hunt me, day and night."

She ceased in tears, fallen from hope and trust;
  To whom the Egyptian:[7] "O, you tamely died!
You should have clung to Fulvia's waist, and thrust
  The dagger thro' her side."   260

With that sharp sound the white dawn's creeping beams,
  Stolen to my brain, dissolved the mystery
Of folded sleep. The captain[8] of my dreams
  Ruled in the eastern sky.

Morn broaden'd on the borders of the dark   265
  Ere I saw her[9] who clasp'd in her last trance
Her murder'd father's head, or Joan of Arc,
  A light of ancient France;

Or her[1] who knew that Love can vanquish Death,
  Who kneeling, with one arm about her king,   270
Drew forth the poison with her balmy breath,
  Sweet as new buds in spring.

No memory labors longer from the deep
  Gold-mines of thought to lift the hidden ore
That glimpses, moving up, that I from sleep   275
  To gather and tell o'er

Each little sound and sight. With what dull pain
  Compass'd, how eagerly I sought to strike
Into that wondrous track of dreams again!
  But no two dreams are like.   280

As when a soul laments, which hath been blest,
  Desiring what is mingled with past years,
In yearnings that can never be exprest
  By signs or groans or tears;

Because all words, tho' cull'd with choicest art,   285
  Failing to give the bitter of the sweet,
Wither beneath the palate, and the heart
  Faints, faded by its heat.

1832 (1842)

---

7. Cleopatra. She substitutes Fulvia, Antony's wife, for Eleanor.
8. "Venus, the star of the morning" (Tennyson).
9. Margaret Roper, Sir Thomas More's daughter. She claimed her father's head, which, after his execution
  (1535), had been shown on London Bridge for two weeks. Allegedly, when her vault was opened in 1715,
  she was found clasping a leaden box containing the head.
1. Eleanor of Castile, wife of Edward I. When Edward was stabbed with a poisoned dagger, she sucked the
  poison from his wound.

To ———[1]

As when with downcast eyes we muse and brood,
And ebb into a former life, or seem
To lapse far back in some confusèd dream
To states of mystical similitude,
If one but speaks or hems or stirs his chair,   5
Ever the wonder waxeth more and more,
So that we say, "All this hath been before,
All this hath been, I know not when or where;"
So, friend, when first I look'd upon your face,
Our thought gave answer each to each, so true —   10
Opposed mirrors each reflecting each —
That, tho' I knew not in what time or place,
Methought that I had often met with you,
And either lived in either's heart and speech.

                                                    1832

To J. S.[1]

The wind that beats the mountain blows
    More softly round the open wold,
And gently comes the world to those
    That are cast in gentle mould.

And me this knowledge bolder made,   5
    Or else I had not dared to flow
In these words toward you, and invade
    Even with a verse your holy woe.

'T is strange that those we lean on most,
    Those in whose laps our limbs are nursed,   10
Fall into shadow, soonest lost;
    Those we love first are taken first.

God gives us love. Something to love
    He lends us; but, when love is grown
To ripeness, that on which it throve   15
    Falls off, and love is left alone.

This is the curse of time. Alas!
    In grief I am not all unlearn'd;
Once thro' mine own doors Death did pass;
    One[2] went who never hath return'd.   20

---

1. The poem is probably addressed to Arthur Hallam.
1. James Spedding, a Cambridge Apostle and later famous as the biographer of Bacon. He was a close friend
   of Tennyson's from undergraduate days to Spedding's death in 1881. Selections from his favorable review
   of the 1842 volumes appear in the "Contexts" section of this book. This elegy is on the death of Spedding's younger brother, Edward.
2. Tennyson's father, who had died on March 16, 1831. As the poet's grandson observed, these lines show
   "how deep and sincere the son's feelings had been, in spite of all the father's weaknesses and the suffering which he had brought upon his family" (*Alfred Tennyson*, p. 134).

He will not smile—not speak to me
    Once more. Two years his chair is seen
Empty before us. That was he
    Without whose life I had not been.

Your loss is rarer; for this star   25
    Rose with you thro' a little arc
Of heaven, nor having wander'd far
    Shot on the sudden into dark.

I knew your brother; his mute dust
    I honor and his living worth;   30
A man more pure and bold and just
    Was never born into the earth.

I have not look'd upon you nigh
    Since that dear soul hath fallen asleep.
Great Nature is more wise than I;   35
    I will not tell you not to weep.

And tho' mine own eyes fill with dew,
    Drawn from the spirit thro' the brain,
I will not even preach to you,
    "Weep, weeping dulls the inward pain."   40

Let Grief be her own mistress still.
    She loveth her own anguish deep
More than much pleasure. Let her will
    Be done—to weep or not to weep.

I will not say, "God's ordinance   45
    Of death is blown in every wind;"
For that is not a common chance
    That takes away a noble mind.

His memory long will live alone
    In all our hearts, as mournful light   50
That broods above the fallen sun,
    And dwells in heaven half the night.

Vain solace! Memory standing near
    Cast down her eyes, and in her throat
Her voice seem'd distant, and a tear   55
    Dropt on the letters as I wrote.

I wrote I know not what. In truth,
    How *should* I soothe you any way,
Who miss the brother of your youth?
    Yet something I did wish to say;   60

For he too was a friend to me.
    Both are my friends, and my true breast

Bleedeth for both; yet it may be
    That only silence suiteth best.

Words weaker than your grief would make   65
    Grief more. 'T were better I should cease
Although my self could almost take
    The place of him that sleeps in peace.

Sleep sweetly, tender heart, in peace;
    Sleep, holy spirit, blessed soul,   70
While the stars burn, the moons increase,
    And the great ages onward roll.[3]

Sleep till the end, true soul and sweet.
    Nothing comes to thee new or strange.
Sleep full of rest from head to feet;   75
    Lie still, dry dust, secure of change.

                                              1832

The Lotos-Eaters[1]

"Courage!" he[2] said, and pointed toward the land,
"This mounting wave will roll us shoreward soon."
In the afternoon they came into a land
In which it seemed always afternoon.
All round the coast the languid air did swoon,   5
Breathing like one that hath a weary dream.
Full-faced above the valley stood the moon;
And, like a downward smoke, the slender stream
Along the cliff to fall and pause and fall did seem.[3]

A land of streams! some, like a downward smoke,   10
Slow-dropping veils of thinnest lawn,[4] did go;
And some thro' wavering lights and shadows broke,
Rolling a slumbrous sheet of foam below.
They saw the gleaming river seaward flow

---

3. Compare the end of the "Epilogue" of *IM*.
1. Although the subject is based on the episode in the *Odyssey* (IX, 82ff.) where Odysseus describes his
    weary mariners' brief stay with the Lotos-Eaters, only the opening stanzas and the sixth stanza of the
    choric song contain Homeric elements. The five introductory Spenserian stanzas were begun during the
    1830 journey with Hallam though the Pyrenees (see notes to "Œnone") and reflect that scenery and draw
    on Spenser's descriptions in *The Faerie Queene* II, vi. Tennyson undoubtedly was also influenced by
    Thomson's *Castle of Indolence*. Of numerous revisions for republication in 1842, the additions of the
    sixth and eighth stanzas of the choric song were the most important.
2. Of Odysseus's words, Turner observes that "the note of heroism sounds in the first word," reflecting the
    fact that the mariners had been suffering through a storm for nine days.
3. As Tennyson noted, the image was "taken from the waterfall at Gavarnie, in the Pyrenees."
4. "When I printed this, a critic informed me that 'lawn' was the material used in theatres to imitate a wa-
    terfall, and graciously added, 'Mr. T. should not go to the boards of a theatre but to nature herself for his
    suggestions.'" Tennyson, who seldom erred in his natural descriptions, could honesty say, as he did, "And
    I *had* gone to Nature herself"—to the Pyrenees in the Cirque de Gavarnie where "lying among these
    mountains before a waterfall that comes down one thousand or twelve hundred feet I sketched it . . .
    in these words" (*Memoir* I, 259).

From the inner land; for off, three mountain-tops,   15
Three silent pinnacles of aged snow,
Stood sunset-flush'd; and, dew'd with showery drops,
Up-clomb the shadowy pine above the woven copse.

The charmed sunset linger'd low adown
In the red West; thro' mountain clefts the dale   20
Was seen far inland, and the yellow down
Border'd with palm, and many a winding vale
And meadow, set with slender galingale;⁵
A land where all things always seem'd the same!
And round about the keel with faces pale,   25
Dark faces pale against that rosy flame,
The mild-eyed melancholy Lotos-eaters came.

Branches they bore of that enchanted stem,
Laden with flower and fruit, whereof they gave
To each, but whoso did receive of them   30
And taste, to him the gushing of the wave
Far far away did seem to mourn and rave
On alien shores; and if his fellow spake,
His voice ws thin, as voices from the grave;
And deep-asleep he seem'd, yet all awake,   35
And music in his ears his beating heart did make.

They sat them down upon the yellow sand,
Between the sun and moon upon the shore;
And sweet it was to dream of Fatherland,
Of child, and wife, and slave; but evermore   40
Most weary seem'd the sea, weary the oar,
Weary the wandering fields of barren foam.
Then some one said, "We will return no more;"
And all at once they sang, "Our island home⁶
Is far beyond the wave; we will no longer roam."   45

Choric Song⁷

1

There is sweet music here that softer falls
Than petals from blown roses on the grass,
Or night-dews on still waters between walls
Of shadowy granite, in a gleaming pass;
Music that gentlier on the spirit lies,   50
Than tired eyelids upon tired eyes;
Music that brings sweet sleep down from the blissful skies.
Here are cool mosses deep,
And thro' the moss the ivies creep,

---

5. An aromatic herb.
6. Ithaca. "But those who ate this honeyed plant, the Lotos, never cared to report, nor to return; they longed
   to stay forever, browsing on that native bloom, forgetful of their homeland" (*Odyssey* IX, lines 97–100).
7. Sung by the mariners.

And in the stream the long-leaved flowers weep,   55
And from the craggy ledge the poppy hangs in sleep.

                                        2

Why are we weigh'd upon with heaviness,
And utterly consumed with sharp distress,
While all things else have rest from weariness?
All things have rest: why should we toil alone,   60
We only toil, who are the first of things,
And make perpetual moan,
Still from one sorrow to another thrown;
Nor ever fold our wings,
And cease from wanderings,   65
Nor steep our brows in slumber's holy balm;
Nor harken what the inner spirit sings,
"There is no joy but calm!" —
Why should we only toil, the roof and crown of things?

                                        3

Lo! in the middle of the wood,   70
The folded leaf is woo'd from out the bud
With winds upon the branch, and there
Grows green and broad, and takes no care,
Sun-steep'd at noon, and in the moon
Nightly dew-fed; and turning yellow   75
Falls, and floats adown the air.
Lo! sweeten'd with the summer light,
The full-juiced apple, waxing over-mellow,
Drops in a silent autumn night.
All its allotted length of days   80
The flower ripens in its place
Ripens and fades, and falls, and hath no toil,
Fast-rooted in the fruited soil.

                                        4

Hateful is the dark-blue sky,
Vaulted o'er the dark-blue sea.   85
Death is the end of life; ah, why
Should life all labor be?
Let us alone. Time driveth onward fast,
And in a little while our lips are dumb.
Let us alone. What is it that will last?   90
All things are taken from us, and become
Portions and parcels of the dreadful past.
Let us alone. What pleasure can we have
To war with evil? Is there any peace
In ever climbing up the climbing wave?[8]   95
All things have rest, and ripen toward the grave

---

8. Compare "The Two Voices," lines 184–86.

In silence—ripen, fall, and cease:
Give us long rest or death, dark death, or dreamful ease.

5

How sweet it were, hearing the downward stream,
With half-shut eyes ever to seem   100
Falling asleep in a half-dream!
To dream and dream, like yonder amber light,
Which will not leave the myrrh-bush on the height;
To hear each other's whisper'd speech;
Eating the Lotos day by day,   105
To watch the crisping ripples on the beach,
And tender curving lines of creamy spray;
To lend our hearts and spirits wholly
To the influence of mild-minded melancholy;
To muse and brood and live again in memory,   110
With those old faces of our infancy
Heap'd over with a mound of grass,
Two handfuls of white dust, shut in an urn of brass!

6

Dear is the memory of our wedded lives,
And dear the last embraces of our wives   115
And their warm tears; but all hath suffer'd change;
For surely now our household hearths are cold,
Our sons inherit us, our looks are strange,
And we should come like ghosts to trouble joy.
Or else the island princes⁹ over-bold   120
Have eat our substance, and the minstrel sings
Before them of the ten years' war in Troy,
And our great deeds, as half-forgotten things.
Is there confusion in the little isle?
Let what is broken so remain.   125
The Gods are hard to reconcile;
'T is hard to settle order once again.
There *is* confusion worse than death,
Trouble on trouble, pain on pain,
Long labor unto aged breath,   130
Sore task to hearts worn out by many wars
And eyes grown dim with gazing on the pilot-stars.

7

But, propt on beds of amaranth and moly,¹
How sweet—while warn airs lull us, blowing lowly—
With half-dropt eyelid still,   135
Beneath a heaven dark and holy,
To watch the long bright river drawing slowly
His waters from the purple hill—

9. Princes from the islands neighboring Ithaca. The mariners cannot know, of course, that they accurately
   describe the activities of Penelope's suitors.
1. A magical herb mentioned in the *Odyssey* (X), given by Hermes to Odysseus to protect him from Circe.
   "Amaranth": the legendary flower that never faded.

To hear the dewy echoes calling
From cave to cave thro' the thick-twined vine—   140
To watch the emerald-color'd water falling
Thro' many a women acanthus-wreath[2] divine!
Only to hear and see the far-off sparkling brine,
Only to hear were sweet, stretch'd out beneath the pine.

                                    8
The Lotos blooms below the barren peak,   145
The Lotos blows by every winding creek;
All day the wind breathes low with mellower tone;
Thro' every hollow cave and alley lone
Round and round the spicy downs the yellow Lotos-dust is blown.
We have had enough of action, and of motion we,   150
Roll'd to starboard, roll'd to larboard, when the surge was seething free,
Where the wallowing monster spouted his foam-fountains in the sea.
Let us swear an oath, and keep it with an equal mind,
In the hollow Lotos-land to live and lie reclined
On the hills like Gods[3] together, careless of mankind.   155
For they lie beside their nectar, and the bolts[4] are hurl'd
Far below them in the valleys, and the clouds are lightly curl'd
Round their golden houses, girdled with the gleaming world;
Where they smile in secret, looking over wasted lands,
Blight and famine, plague and earthquake, roaring deeps and fiery sands,   160
Clanging fights, and flaming towns, and sinking ships, and praying hands.
But they smile, they find a music centred in a doleful song
Steaming up, a lamentation and an ancient tale of wrong,
Like a tale of little meaning tho' the words are strong;
Chanted from an ill-used race of men that cleave the soil,   165
Sow the seed, and reap the harvest with enduring toil,
Storing yearly little dues of wheat, and wine and oil;
Till they perish and they suffer—some, 't is whisper'd—down in hell
Suffer endless anguish, others in Elysian valleys dwell,
Resting weary limbs at last on beds of asphodel.[5]   170
Surely, surely, slumber is more sweet than toil, the shore
Than labor in the deep mid-ocean, wind and wave and oar;
O, rest ye, brother mariners, we will not wander more.

                                                    1832 (1842)

---

2. A prickly herbaceous plant the likeness of which often ornaments Corinthian columns.
3. This description of the indifferent gods derives from Lucretius's *De Rerum Natura*.
4. Thunderbolts.
5. The yellow lilylike flower covering the Elysian Fields; the English daffodil or the narcissus is approxi-
mate.

The Eagle[1]

Fragment

He clasps the crag with crooked hands;
Close to the sun in lonely lands,
Ring'd with the azure world, he stands.

The wrinkled sea beneath him crawls;
He watches from his mountain walls,   5
And like a thunderbolt he falls.

1833–42?; 1846 (and 1851)

---

1. The composition dates are conjectural; as Ricks observes, its triplets being those of "The Two Voices" could place it in the early 1830s. Purely for the sake of contrast, see Keats's "On Seeing the Elgin Marbles": "And each imagin'd pinnacle and steep / Of godlike hardship, tells me I must die / Like a sick Eagle looking at the sky," a poem Tennyson surely would have known.

From *Poems* (1842), Including Several Other Pieces Written between 1833 and 1846

Ulysses[1]

It little profits that an idle king,
By this still hearth, among these barren crags,
Match'd with an aged wife, I mete and dole
Unequal[2] laws unto a savage race,
That hoard, and sleep, and feed, and know not me.[3]   5
I cannot rest from travel; I will drink
Life to the lees. All times I have enjoy'd
Greatly, have suffer'd greatly, both with those
That loved me, and alone; on shore, and when
Thro' scudding drifts the rainy Hyades[4]   10
Vext the dim sea. I am become a name;
For always roaming with a hungry heart
Much have I seen and known, — cities of men
And manners, climates, councils, governments,
Myself not least, but honor'd of them all, —   15
And drunk delight of battle with my peers,

---

1. "Ulysses," Tennyson said, "was written soon after Arthur Hallam's death, and gave my feeling about the need of going forward, and braving the struggle of life perhaps more simply than anything in *In Memoriam*" (*Memoir*, I, 196). Tennyson learned of Hallam's death (September 15, 1833) on October 6, and an early draft in Harvard Notebook 16 suggests it was begun a few days later. A substantially complete copy of the poem appears, however, in Trinity manuscript T 22, dated in Tennyson's hand beneath inkblots (but clearly legible), "Anno domini 1833–June 25th." In his *Catalogue of Tennyson Manuscripts at Trinity College*, John Yearwood accurately describes this manuscript: "a small octavo brown-sheep notebook of the type used by Tennyson from 1823–1833. It is probable that all of the drafts contained here were in place by the end of June, 1833" (p. 171). Ricks does not confront the chronological problem, perhaps assuming Yearwood is wrong.
   Speaking of *IM*, Tennyson told James Knowles, "There is more about myself in 'Ulysses', which was written under the sense of loss and that all had gone by, but that still life must be fought out to the end" (from "A Personal Reminiscence," much of which is reprinted in the "Contexts" section of this book).
   Tennyson's source is first the *Odyssey* XI, lines 100–37, where Ulysses learns from Tiresias's ghost that, after killing the suitors, he must undertake a final sea voyage. In Canto 26 of the *Inferno*, Dante has Ulysses give an account of that mysterious journey, and that episode forms the basis of Tennyson's poem.
2. I.e., fitting different nations. Ulysses' description of Ithaca bears little resemblance to Homer's nor is Penelope depicted as aged when Ulysses returns. Perhaps Tennyson has Ulysses living in Ithaca for a long time before he departs, but there is no basis for that in the *Odyssey*.
3. Compare *Hamlet* IV, iv, lines 33ff.: "What is a man, / If his chief good and market of his time / Be but to sleep and feed? A beast, no more."
4. A V-shaped cluster of stars that, when they rose with the sun, were supposed to indicate the coming of the rainy season.

Far on the ringing plains of windy Troy.
I am a part of all that I have met;
Yet all experience is an arch wherethro'
Gleams that untravell'd world whose margin fades   20
For ever and for ever when I move.
How dull it is to pause, to make an end,
To rust unburnish'd, not to shine in use.[5]
As tho' to breathe were life! Life piled on life
Were all too little, and of one to me   25
Little remains; but every hour is saved
From that eternal silence, something more,
A bringer of new things; and vile it were
For some three suns to store and hoard myself,
And this gray spirit yearning in desire   30
To follow knowledge like a sinking star,
Beyond the utmost bound of human thought.
    This is my son, mine own Telemachus,
To whom I leave the sceptre and the isle,—
Well-loved of me, discerning to fulfil   35
This labor, by slow prudence to make mild
A rugged people, and thro' soft degrees
Subdue them to the useful and the good.
Most blameless is he, centred in the sphere
Of common duties, decent not to fail   40
In offices of tenderness, and pay
Meet adoration to my household gods,
When I am gone. He works his work, I mine[6]
    There lies the port; the vessel puffs her sail;
There gloom the dark, broad seas. My mariners,   45
Souls that have toil'd, and wrought, and thought with me,—
That ever with a frolic welcome took
The thunder and the sunshine, and opposed
Free hearts, free foreheads,—you and I are old;
Old age hath yet his honor and his toil.   50
Death closes all; but something ere the end,
Some work of noble note, may yet be done,
Not unbecoming men that strove with Gods[7]
The lights begin to twinkle from the rocks;
The long day wanes; the slow moon climbs; the deep   55
Moans round with many voices. Come, my friends.
'T is not too late to seek a newer world.
Push off, and sitting well in order smite
The sounding furrows; for my purpose holds
To sail beyond the sunset, and the baths   60
Of all the western stars,[8] until I die.

5. Compare Shakespeare's *Troilus and Cressida*, III, iii, lines 151ff., where Ulysses speaks to Achilles: "To
have done is to hang / Quite out of fashion, like a rusty mail / In monumental mock'ry."
6. The above passage about Telemachus has led a few critics to charge Ulysses with being irresponsible, the
poem being, in the words of one commentator, "a dramatic portrayal of a type of human being who held
a set of ideas which Tennyson regarded as destructive of the whole fabric of his society."
7. Compare Ulysses' words to his mariners in the *Inferno* XXVI, lines 119–21: "Consider your lineage; you
were not made to live as brutes, but to follow virtue and knowledge."
8. The Homeric view of the ocean as a great river around the flat earth. In Dante, Ulysses sailed to these
outer limits, glimpsed the Mount of Purgatory, and drowned in the "gulfs" for his presumption.

It may be that the gulfs will wash us down;
It may be we shall touch the Happy Isles,
And see the great Achilles, whom we knew[9]
Tho' much is taken, much abides; and tho'   65
We are not now that strength which in old days
Moved earth and heaven, that which we are, we are,—
One equal temper of heroic hearts,
Made weak by time and fate, but strong in will
To strive, to seek, to find, and not to yield.   70

                                        1833; 1842

The Two Voices[1]

A still small voice spake unto me,
"Thou art so full of misery,
Were it not better not to be?"

Then to the still small voice I said:
"Let me not cast in endless shade   5
What is so wonderfully made."

To which the voice did urge reply:
"To-day I saw the dragon-fly
Come from the wells where he did lie.

"An inner impulse rent the veil   10
Of his old husk; from head to tail
Came out clear plates of sapphire mail.

"He dried his wings; like gauze they grew;
Thro' crofts and pastures wet with dew
A living flash of light he flew."[2]   15

---

9. Carlyle said, "These lines do not make me weep, but there is in me what would fill whole Lachrymatories as I read" (*Memoir* I, 214). The "Happy Isles," or Elysium, were supposed to be in the far west, the abode for the great heroes like Achilles whom Paris had slain in the Trojan War.
1. Begun in 1833, before June 22, the poem in manuscript was called "Thoughts of a Suicide" and was written, as Hallam Tennyson says, "under the cloud of this overwhelming sorrow, which, as my father told me, for a while blotted out all joy from his life, and made him long for death" (*Memoir* I, 109). In Tennyson's words, "When I wrote 'The Two Voices' I was so utterly miserable, a burden to myself and to my family, that I said, 'Is life worth anything?'" (*Memoir* I, 193).
   Disproving Hallam Tennyson's long accepted dating, Ricks refers to a letter from Kemble to Donne postmarked June 22, 1833, in which the poem is cited: "Clearly a version of 'The Two Voices' was already in existence." With that information, pondering over the Trinity manuscripts leads one to question further the accepted dates for the writing of "Ulysses."
   Many of the issues raised by the poem were anticipated in "Supposed Confessions" and would shortly be articulated more fully and thoughtfully as work on *IM* progressed. The struggle within the individual between faith and skepticism reminded Carlyle "of passages in *Job*" (*Memoir* I, 213). And Tennyson clearly has *Hamlet* in mind as he speculates on the nature of human existence and the attractiveness of suicide, which, in this poem at least, the reader is convinced was real enough. See Spedding's commentary in the "Contexts" section of this book.
2. The implication is that the dragonfly is as wonderfully made as the human, the beginning of the negative voice's long argument to reduce humankind to the level of beasts.

I said: "When first the world began,
Young Nature thro' five cycles[3] ran,
And in the sixth she moulded man.

"She gave him mind, the lordliest
Proportion, and, above the rest,   20
Dominion in the head and breast."

Thereto the silent voice replied:
"Self-blinded are you by your pride;
Look up thro' night; the world is wide.

"This truth within thy mind rehearse,   25
That in a boundless universe
Is boundless better, boundless worse.

"Think you this mould of hopes and fears
Could find no statelier than his peers
In yonder hundred million spheres?"[4]   30

It spake, moreover, in my mind:
"Tho' thou wert scatter'd to the wind,
Yet is there plenty of the kind."

Then did my response clearer fall:
"No compound of this earthly ball   35
Is like another, all in all."

To which he answer'd scoffingly:
"Good soul! suppose I grant it thee,
Who'll weep for thy deficiency?

"Or will one beam be less intense,   40
When thy peculiar difference
Is cancell'd in the world of sense?"

I would have said, "Thou canst not know,"
But my full heart, that work'd below,
Rain'd thro' my sight its overflow.   45

Again the voice spake unto me:
"Thou art so steep'd in misery,
Surely 't were better not to be.

"Thine anguish will not let thee sleep,
Nor any train of reason keep;   50
Thou canst not think, but thou wilt weep."

3. The Creation as described in Genesis.
4. Of numerous parallels in *IM*, see sections 3 and 61. Among the late poems, the opening stanzas of "Vastness" (1885) show the poet's lasting concern with our significance in a universe the proportions of which the "new" science made increasingly incomprehensible.

I said: "The years with change advance;
If I make dark my countenance,
I shut my life from happier chance.

"Some turn this sickness yet might take,   55
Even yet." But he: "What drug can make
A wither'd palsy cease to shake?"

I wept: "Tho' I should die, I know
That all about the thorn will blow
In tufts of rosy-tinted snow;   60

"And men, thro' novel spheres of thought
Still moving after truth long sought,
Will learn new things when I am not."

"Yet," said the secret voice, "some time,
Sooner or later, will gray prime   65
Make thy grass hoar with early rime.

"Not less swift souls that yearn for light,
Rapt after heaven's starry flight,
Would sweep the tracts of day and night.

"Not less the bee would range her cells,   70
The furzy prickle fire the dells,
The foxglove cluster dappled bells."

I said that "all the years invent;
Each month is various to present
The world with some development.   75

"Were this not well, to bide mine hour,
Tho' watching from a ruin'd tower
How grows the day of human power?"

"The highest-mounted mind," he said,
"Still sees the sacred morning spread   80
The silent summit overhead.

"Will thirty seasons render plain
Those lonely lights that still remain,
Just breaking over land and main?[5]

"Or make that morn, from his cold crown   85
And crystal silence creeping down,
Flood with full daylight glebe and town?

---

5. The Trinity manuscript contains three additional stanzas, among them the lines: "Six thousand suns have failed to pour / Clear lustre on the boundless shore." The reference was to Archbishop Ussher's calculation that the world was created at 8 P.M. on Saturday, October 22, 4004 B.C.

"Forerun thy peers, thy time, and let
Thy feet, millenniums hence, be set
In midst of knowledge, dream'd not yet.   90

"Thou hast not gain'd a real height,
Nor art thou nearer to the light,
Because the scale is infinite.

"'T were better not to breathe or speak,
Than cry for strength, remaining weak,   95
And seem to find, but still to seek.[6]

"Moreover, but to seem to find
Asks what thou lackest, thought resign'd,
A healthy frame, a quiet mind."

I said: "When I am gone away,   100
'He dared not tarry,' men will say,
Doing dishonor to my clay."

"This is more vile," he made reply,
"To breathe and loathe, to live and sigh,
Than once from dread of pain to die.   105

"Sick art thou—a divided will
Still heaping on the fear of ill
The fear of men, a coward still.

"Do men love thee? Art thou so bound
To men that how thy name may sound   110
Will vex thee lying underground?

"The memory of the wither'd leaf
In endless time is scarce more brief
Than of the garner'd autumn-sheaf.

"Go, vexed spirit, sleep in trust;   115
The right ear that is fill'd with dust
Hears little of the false or just."

"Hard task, to pluck resolve," I cried,
"From emptiness and the waste wide
Of that abyss, or scornful pride!   120

"Nay—rather yet that I could raise
One hope that warm'd me in the days
While still I yearn'd for human praise.

6. Contrast the conclusion of "Ulysses."

"When, wide in soul and bold of tongue,
Among the tents I paused and sung,   125
The distant battle flash'd and rung.

"I sung the joyful Pæan clear,
And, sitting, burnish'd without fear
The brand, the buckler, and the spear—

"Waiting to strive a happy strife,   130
To war with falsehood to the knife,
And not to lose the good of life—

"Some hidden principle to move,
To put together, part and prove,
And mete the bounds of hate and love—   135

"As far as might be, to carve out
Free space for every human doubt,
That the whole mind might orb about—

"To search thro' all I felt or saw,
The springs of life, the depths of awe,   140
And reach the law within the law;[7]

"At least, not rotting like a weed,
But, having sown some generous seed,
Fruitful of further thought and deed,

"To pass, when Life her light withdraws,   145
Not void of righteous self-applause,
Nor in a merely selfish cause—

"In some good cause, not in mine own,
To perish, wept for, honor'd, known,
And like a warrior overthrown;   150

"Whose eyes are dim with glorious tears,
When, soil'd with noble dust, he hears
His country's war-song thrill his ears:

"Then dying of a mortal stroke,
What time the foeman's line is broke,   155
And all the war is roll'd in smoke."

"Yea!" said the voice, "thy dream was good,
While thou abodest in the bud.
It was the stirring of the blood.

---

7. See "Supposed Confessions," lines 172ff.

"If Nature put not forth her power   160
About the opening of the flower,
Who is it that could live an hour?

"Then comes the check, the change, the fall,
Pain rises up, old pleasures pall.
There is one remedy for all.   165

"Yet hadst thou, thro' enduring pain,
Link'd month to month with such a chain
Of knitted purport, all were vain.

"Thou hadst not between death and birth
Dissolved the riddle of the earth.[8]   170
So were thy labor little worth.

"That men with knowledge merely play'd,
I told thee—hardly nigher made,
Tho' scaling slow from grade to grade;

"Much less this dreamer, deaf and blind,   175
Named man, may hope some truth to find,
That bears relation to the mind.

"For every worm beneath the moon
Draws different threads, and late and soon
Spins, toiling out his own cocoon.   180

"Cry, faint not: either Truth is born
Beyond the polar gleam forlorn,
Or in the gateways of the morn.

"Cry, faint not, climb: the summits slope
Beyond the furthest flights of hope,[9]   185
Wrapt in dense cloud from base to cope:[1]

"Sometimes a little corner shines,
As over rainy mist inclines
A gleaming crag with belts of pines.

"I will go forward, sayest thou,   190
I shall not fail to find her now.
Look up, the fold is on her brow.

8. Compare "The Palace of Art," line 213, and Pallas's words in "Œnone," lines 142ff.
9. Compare John Donne's *Satire III, Religion*, lines 79–81: "On a huge hill, / Cragged and steep, Truth stands, and he that will / Reach her, about must, and about must go." See "The Lotos-Eaters," line 95.
1. Crown or top; ironically presented here by the negative voice is the argument to which the Lotos-Eaters succumbed (see particularly stanza 4).

"If straight thy track, or if oblique,
Thou know'st not. Shadows thou dost strike,
Embracing cloud, Ixion-like;[2]   195

"And owning but a little more
Than beasts,[3] abidest lame and poor,
Calling thyself a little lower

"Than angels. Cease to wail and brawl!
Why inch by inch to darkness crawl?   200
There is one remedy for all."

"O dull, one-sided voice," said I,
"Wilt thou make everything a lie,
To flatter me that I may die?

"I know that age to age succeeds,   205
Blowing a noise of tongues and deeds,
A dust of systems and of creeds.

"I cannot hide that some have striven,
Achieving calm, to whom was given
The joy that mixes man with Heaven;   210

"Who, rowing hard against the stream,
Saw distant gates of Eden gleam,
And did not dream it was a dream;

"But heard, by secret transport led,
Even in the charnels of the dead,   215
The murmur of the fountain-head—

"Which did accomplish their desire,
Bore and forebore, and did not tire,
Like Stephen,[4] an unquenched fire.

"He needed not reviling tones,   220
Nor sold his heart to idle moans,
Tho' cursed and scorn'd, and bruised with stones;

"But looking upward, full of grace,
He pray'd, and from a happy place
God's glory smote him on the face."   225

The sullen answer slid betwixt:
"Not that the grounds of hope were fix'd,
The elements were kindlier mix'd."

---

2. When Ixion attempted to seduce Hera, Zeus formed of the clouds a phantom resembling her, and by it
   Ixion became the father of the Centaurs.
3. See *IM* 27, 2, and 34, 4.
4. See Acts 7:55–60.

I said: "I toil beneath the curse,
But, knowing not the universe,   230
I fear to slide from bad to worse;

"And that, in seeking to undo
One riddle, and to find the true,
I knit a hundred others new;

"Or that this anguish fleeting hence,   235
Unmanacled from bonds of sense,
Be fix'd and frozen to permanence:

"For I go, weak from suffering here;
Naked I go, and void of cheer:
What is it that I may not fear?   240

"Consider well," the voice replied,
"His face, that two hours since hath died;
Wilt thou find passion, pain or pride?

"Will he obey when one commands?
Or answer should one press his hands?   245
He answers not, nor understands.

"His palms are folded on his breast;
There is no other thing express'd
But long disquiet merged in rest.

"His lips are very mild and meek;   250
Tho' one should smite him on the cheek,
And on the mouth, he will not speak.

"His little daughter, whose sweet face
He kiss'd, taking his last embrace,
Becomes dishonor to her race—   255

"His sons grow up that bear his name,
Some grow to honor, some to shame,—
But he is chill to praise or blame.

"He will not hear the north-wind rave,
Nor, moaning, household shelter crave   260
From winter rains that beat his grave.

"High up the vapors fold and swim;
About him broods the twilight dim;
The place he knew forgetteth him."

"If all be dark, vague voice," I said,   265
"These things are wrapt in doubt and dread,
Nor canst thou show the dead are dead.

"The sap dries up: the plant declines.
A deeper tale my heart divines.
Know I not death? the outward signs?   270

"I found him[5] when my years were few;
A shadow on the graves I knew,
And darkness in the village yew.

"From grave to grave the shadow crept;
In her still place the morning wept;   275
Touch'd by his feet the daisy slept.

"The simple senses crown'd his head:
'Omega! thou art Lord,' they said,
'We find no motion in the dead!'

"Why, if man rot in dreamless ease,   280
Should that plain fact, as taught by these,
Not make him sure that he shall cease?

"Who forged that other influence,
That heat of inward evidence,
By which he doubts against the sense?   285

"He owns the fatal gift of eyes,
That read his spirit blindly wise,
Not simple as a thing that dies.

"Here sits he shaping wings to fly;
His heart forebodes a mystery;   290
He names the name Eternity.

"That type of Perfect in his mind
In Nature can he nowhere find.[6]
He sows himself on every wind.

"He seems to hear a Heavenly Friend,   295
And thro' thick veils to apprehend
A labor working to an end.

"The end and the beginning vex
His reason: many things perplex,
With motions, checks, and counterchecks.   300

"He knows a baseness in his blood[7]
At such strange war with something good,
He may not do the thing he would.

---

5. Death; possibly an allusion to his father's death in March 1831.
6. See *IM* 124, 2.
7. See *IM* 51, 1.

"Heaven opens inward, chasms yawn,
Vast images in glimmering dawn,   305
Half shown, are broken and withdrawn.

"Ah! sure within him and without,
Could his dark wisdom find it out,
There must be answer to his doubt,[8]

"But thou canst answer not again.   310
With thine own weapon art thou slain,
Or thou wilt answer but in vain.

"The doubt would rest, I dare not solve.
In the same circle we revolve.
Assurance only breeds resolve."   315

As when a billow, blown against,
Falls back, the voice with which I fenced
A little ceased, but recommended:

"Where wert thou when thy father play'd
In his free field, and pastime made,   320
A merry boy in sun and shade?

"A merry boy they call'd him then,
He sat upon the knees of men
In days that never come again;

"Before the little ducts began   325
To feed thy bones with lime, and ran
Their course, till thou wert also man:

"Who took a wife, who rear'd his race,
Whose wrinkles gather'd on his face,
Whose troubles number with his days;   330

"A life of nothings, nothing worth,
From that first nothing ere his birth
To that last nothing under earth!⁹

"These words," I said, "are like the rest;
No certain clearness, but at best   335
A vague suspicion of the breast:

---

8. An early manuscript in Harvard Papers 254 ends here as the poet struggled to bring the poem to some
   satisfactory conclusion. Trinity manuscript 22 ends here as well.
9. A somewhat later manuscript in Harvard Notebook 21 ends here with the stanza,
   From when his baby pulses beat
   To when his hands in their last heat
   Pick at the death-mote on the sheet,
   suppressed as being perhaps too gruesome in its accurate depiction of old age facing death (*Memoir* I,
   109). Conceivably Tennyson was still working on a conclusion as late as 1837.

"But if I grant, thou mightst defend
The thesis which thy words intend—
That to begin implies to end:

"Yet how should I for certain hold,   340
Because my memory is so cold,
That I first was in human mould?

"I cannot make this matter plain,
But I would shoot, howe'er in vain,
A random arrow from the brain.   345

"It may be that no life is found,
Which only to one engine bound
Falls off, but cycles always round.

"As old mythologies relate,
Some draught of Lethe might await   350
The slipping thro' from state to state;

"As here we find in trances, men
Forget the dream that happens then,
Until they fall in trance again;

"So might we, if our state were such   355
As one before, remember much,
For those two likes might meet and touch.

"But, If I lapsed from nobler place,
Some legend of a fallen race
Alone might hint of my disgrace;   360

"Some vague emotion of delight
In gazing up an Alpine height,
Some yearning toward the lamps of night;

"Or if thro' lower lives I came—
Tho' all experience past became   365
Consolidate in mind and frame—

"I might forget my weaker lot;
For is not our first year forgot?
The haunts of memory echo not.

"And men, whose reason long was blind,   370
From cells of madness unconfined,
Oft lose whole years of darker mind.

"Much more, if first I floated free,
As naked essence, must I be
Incompetent of memory;   375

"For memory dealing but with time,
And he with matter, could she climb
Beyond her own material prime?

"Moreover, something is or seems,
That touches me with mystic gleams,   380
Like glimpses of forgotten dreams—

"Of something felt, like something here;
Of something done, I know not where;
Such as no language may declare."

The still voice laugh'd. "I talk," said he,   385
"Not with thy dreams. Suffice it thee
Thy pain is a reality."

"But thou," said I, "hast missed thy mark,
Who sought'st to wreck my mortal ark,
By making all the horizon dark.   390

"Why not set forth, if I should do
This rashness, that which might ensue
With this old soul in organs new?

"Whatever crazy sorrow saith,
No life that breathes with human breath   395
Has ever truly long'd for death.

"'T is life, whereof our nerves are scant,
O, life, not death, for which we pant;
More life, and fuller, that I want."

I ceased, and sat as one forlorn.   400
Then said the voice, in quiet scorn,
"Behold, it is the Sabbath morn."

And I arose, and I released
The casement, and the light increased
With freshness in the dawning east.   405

Like soften'd airs that blowing steal,
When meres begin to uncongeal,
The sweet church bells began to peal.

On to God's house the people prest;
Passing the place where each must rest,   410
Each enter'd like a welcome guest.

One walk'd between his wife and child,
With measured footfall firm and mild,
And now and then he gravely smiled.

The prudent partner of his blood   415
Lean'd on him, faithful, gentle, good,
Wearing the rose of womanhood.

And in their double love secure,
The little maiden walk'd demure,
Pacing with downward eyelids pure.   420

These three made unity so sweet,
My frozen heart began to beat,
Remembering its ancient heat.

I blest them, and they wander'd on;
I spoke, but answer came there none;   425
The dull and bitter voice was gone.

A second voice was at mine ear,
A little whisper silver-clear,
A murmur, "Be of better cheer."

As from some blissful neighborhood,   430
A notice faintly understood,
"I see the end, and know the good."

A little hint to solace woe,
A hint, a whisper breathing low,
"I may not speak of what I know".   435

Like an æolian harp that wakes
No certain air, but overtakes
Far thought with music that it makes;

Such seem'd the whisper at my side:
"What is it thou knowest, sweet voice?" I cried.   440
"A hidden hope," the voice replied;

So heavenly-toned, that in that hour
From out my sullen heart a power
Broke, like the rainbow from the shower,

To feel, altho' no tongue can prove,   445
That every cloud that spreads above
And veileth love, itself is love.

And forth into the fields I went,
And Nature's living motion lent
The pulse of hope to discontent.   450

I wonder'd at the bounteous hours,
The slow result of winter showers;
You scarce could see the grass for flowers.

I wonder'd, while I paced along;
The woods were fill'd so full with song,   455
There seem'd no room for sense of wrong;

And all so variously wrought,
I marvell'd how the mind was brought
To anchor by one gloomy thought;

And wherefore rather I made choice   460
To commune with that barren voice,
Than him that said, "Rejoice! Rejoice!"

                                                    1833–34; 1842

Saint Simeon Stylites[1]

Altho' I be the basest of mankind,
From scalp to sole one slough and crust of sin,
Unfit for earth, unfit for heaven, scarce meet
For troops of devils, mad with blasphemy,
I will not cease to grasp the hope I hold   5
Of saintdom, and to clamor, mourn, and sob,
Battering the gates of heaven with storms of prayer,
Have mercy, Lord, and take away my sin!
   Let this avail, just, dreadful, mighty God,
This not be all in vain, that thrice ten years,   10
Thrice multiplied by superhuman pangs,
In hungers and in thirsts, fevers and cold,
In coughs, aches, stitches, ulcerous throes and cramps,[2]
A sign betwixt the meadow and the cloud
Patient on this tall pillar I have borne   15
Rain, wind, frost, heat, hail, damp, and sleet, and snow;
And I had hoped that ere this period closed
Thou wouldst have caught me up into thy rest,
Denying not these weather-beaten limbs
The meed of saints, the white robe and the palm.   20
   O, take the meaning, Lord! I do not breathe,
Not whisper, any murmur of complaint.
Pain heap'd ten-hundred-fold to this, were still
Less burthen, by ten-hundred-fold, to bear,
Than were those lead-like tons of sin that crush'd   25

---

1. Circulating by November 1833 among several of Tennyson's Cambridge friends, who called St. Simeon not "the watcher on the pillar to the end," but "to the *n*th" (*Memoir* I, 130), the poem expresses satirically the poet's distrust of asceticism, with possibly a gibe at his Aunt Mary Bourne's brand of Calvinism (see n. 3, p. 21).
   Simeon Stylites of Syria (c. 390–459) outdid all his contemporaries in the extremes to which he aspired to mortify the flesh. Tennyson's source was probably Edward Gibbon's derisive account in *The Decline and Fall of the Roman Empire:* "This voluntary martyrdom must have gradually destroyed the sensibility both of mind and body; nor can it be presumed that the fanatics, who torment themselves, are susceptible of any lively affection from the rest of mankind." Predictably, Robert Browning, the acknowledged master of the grotesque in his dramatic monologues, was fond of this poem.
2. "This is one of the poems A. T. would read with grotesque grimness, especially such passages as 'coughs, aches, stitches,' etc., laughing aloud at times" (FitzGerald's note, *Memoir* I, 193).

My spirit flat before thee.
                  O Lord, Lord,
Thou knowest I bore this better at the first,
For I was strong and hale of body then;
And tho' my teeth, which now are dropt away,
Would chatter with the cold, and all my beard   30
Was tagg'd with icy fringes in the moon,
I drown'd the whoopings of the owl with sound
Of pious hymns and psalms, and sometimes saw
An angel stand and watch me, as I sang.
Now am I feeble grown; my end draws nigh.   35
I hope my end draws nigh; half deaf I am,
So that I scarce can hear the people hum
About the column's base, and almost blind,
And scarce can recognize the fields I know;
And both my thighs are rotted with the dew;   40
Yet cease I not to clamor and to cry,
While my stiff spine can hold my weary head,
Till all my limbs drop piecemeal from the stone,
Have mercy, mercy! take away my sin!
    O Jesus, if thou wilt not save my soul,   45
Who may be saved? who is it may be saved?
Who may be made a saint if I fail here?
Show me the man hath suffer'd more than I.
For did not all thy martyrs die one death?
For either they were stoned, or crucified,   50
Or burn'd in fire, or boil'd in oil, or sawn
In twain beneath the ribs; but I die here
To-day, and whole years long, a life of death.
Bear witness, if I could have found a way—
And heedfully I sifted all my thought—   55
More slowly-painful to subdue this home
Of sin, my flesh, which I despise and hate,
I had not stinted practice, O my God!
    For not alone this pillar-punishment,
Not this alone I bore; but while I lived   60
In the white convent down the valley there,
For many weeks about my loins I wore
The rope that haled the buckets from the well,
Twisted as tight as I could knot the noose,
And spake not of it to a single soul,   65
Until the ulcer, eating thro' my skin,
Betray'd my secret penance, so that all
My brethren marvell'd greatly. More than this
I bore, whereof, O God, thou knowest all.
    Three winters, that my soul might grow to thee,   70
I lived up there on yonder mountain-side.
My right leg chain'd into the crag, I lay
Pent in a roofless close of ragged stones;
Inswathed sometimes in wandering mist, and twice
Black'd with thy branding thunder, and sometimes   75
Sucking the damps for drink, and eating not,

Except the spare chance-gift of those that came
To touch my body and be heal'd, and live.
And they say then that I work'd miracles,
Whereof my fame is loud amongst mankind,   80
Cured lameness, palsies, cancers. Thou, O God,
Knowest alone whether this was or no.
Have mercy, mercy! cover all my sin!
    Then, that I might be more alone with thee,
Three years I lived upon a pillar, high   85
Six cubits, and three years on one of twelve;
And twice three years I crouch'd on one that rose
Twenty by measure; last of all, I grew
Twice ten long weary, weary years to this,
That numbers forty cubits³ from the soil.   90
    I think that I have borne as much as this—
Or else I dream—and for so long a time,
If I may measure time by yon slow light,
And this high dial,⁴ which my sorrow crowns—
So much—even so.
                         And yet I know not well,   95
For that the evil ones come here, and say,
'Fall down, O Simeon; thou hast suffer'd long
For ages and for ages!' then they prate
Of penances I cannot have gone thro',
Perplexing me with lies; and oft I fall,   100
Maybe for months, in such blind lethargies
That Heaven, and Earth, and Time are choked.
                                        But yet
Bethink thee, Lord, while thou and all the saints
Enjoy themselves in heaven, and men on earth
House in the shade of comfortable roofs,   105
Sit with their wives by fires, eat wholesome food,
And wear warm clothes, and even beasts have stalls,
I, 'tween the spring and downfall of the light,
Bow down one thousand and two hundred times,
To Christ, the Virgin Mother, and the saints;   110
Or in the night, after a little sleep,
I wake; the chill stars sparkle; I am wet
With drenching dews, or stiff with crackling frost.
I wear an undress'd goatskin on my back;
A grazing iron collar grinds my neck;   115
And in my weak, lean arms I lift the cross,
And strive and wrestle with thee till I die.
O, mercy, mercy! wash away my sin!
    O Lord, thou knowest what a man I am;
A sinful man, conceived and born in sin.   120
'T is their own doing; this is none of mine;

---

3. One cubit is approximately eighteen inches, so the pillar is now about sixty feet high. Kemble, one of
the Cambridge friends mentioned above, wrote: "Could you only have made the height of the pillar a
geometrical progression" (*Memoir* I, 130). There is clearly no basis for the assumption, which a few critics have held, that Tennyson's portrait is in any sense sympathetic.
4. I.e., a sundial.

Lay it not to me. Am I to blame for this,
That here come those that worship me? Ha! ha!
They think that I am somewhat. What am I?
The silly people take me for a saint,   125
And bring me offerings of fruit and flowers;
And I, in truth—thou wilt bear witness here—
Have all in all endured as much, and more
Than many just and holy men, whose names
Are register'd and calendar'd for saints.   130
    Good people, you do ill to kneel to me.
What is it I can have done to merit this?
I am a sinner viler than you all.
It may be I have wrought some miracles,
And cured some halt and maim'd; but what of that?   135
It may be no one, even among the saints,
May match his pains with mine; but what of that?
Yet do not rise; for you may look on me,
And in your looking you may kneel to God.
Speak! is there any of you halt or maim'd?   140
I think you know I have some power with Heaven
From my long penance; let him speak his wish.
    Yes, I can heal him. Power goes forth from me.
They say that they are heal'd. Ah, hark! they shout
'Saint Simeon Stylites.' Why, if so,   145
God reaps a harvest in me. O my soul,
God reaps a harvest in thee! If this be,
Can I work miracles and not be saved?
This is not told of any. They were saints.
It cannot be but that I shall be saved,   150
Yea, crown'd a saint. They shout, 'Behold a saint!'
And lower voices saint me from above.
Courage, Saint Simeon! This dull chrysalis[5]
Cracks into shining wings, and hope ere death
Spreads more and more and more, that God hath now   155
Sponged and made blank of crimeful record all
My mortal archives.
                O my sons, my sons,
I, Simeon of the pillar, by surname
Stylites, among men; I, Simeon,
The watcher on the column till the end;   160
I, Simeon, whose brain the sunshine bakes;
I, whose bald brows in silent hours become
Unnaturally hoar with rime, do now
From my high nest of penance here proclaim
That Pontius and Iscariot by my side   165
Show'd like fair seraphs.[6] On the coals I lay,
A vessel full of sin; all hell beneath
Made me boil over. Devils pluck'd my sleeve,

---

5. A cocoon. Ironically the metaphor reduces him to an insect in the midst of his maniacal effort to purge himself of the bestiality within.
6. Pontius Pilate and Judas Iscariot—respectively, Christ's judge and betrayer—are angels compared to him.

Abaddon and Asmodeus[7] caught at me.
I smote them with the cross; they swarm'd again.   170
In bed like monstrous apes they crush'd my chest;[8]
They flapp'd my light out as I read; I saw
Their faces grow between me and my book;
With coltlike whinny and with hoggish whine
They burst my prayer. Yet this way was left,   175
And by this way I 'scaped them. Mortify
Your flesh, like me, with scourges and with thorns;
Smite, shrink not, spare not. If it may be, fast
Whole Lents, and pray. I hardly, with slow steps,
With slow, faint steps, and much exceeding pain,   180
Have scrambled past those pits of fire, that still
Sing in mine ears. But yield not me the praise;
God only thro' his bounty hath thought fit,
Among the powers and princes of this world,
To make me an example to mankind,   185
Which few can reach to. Yet I do not say
But that a time may come—yea, even now,
Now, now, his footsteps smite the threshold stairs
Of life—I say, that time is at the doors
When you may worship me without reproach;   190
For I will leave my relics in your land,
And you may carve a shrine about my dust,
And burn a fragrant lamp before my bones,
When I am gather'd to the glorious saints.
    While I spake then, a sting of shrewdest pain   195
Ran shrivelling thro' me, and a cloudlike change,
In passing, with a grosser film made thick
These heavy, horny eyes. The end! the end!
Surely the end! What's here? a shape, a shade,
A flash of light. Is that the angel there   200
That holds a crown? Come, blessed brother, come!
I know thy glittering face. I waited long;
My brows are ready. What! deny it now?
Nay, draw, draw, draw nigh. So I clutch it. Christ!
'T is gone; 't is here again; the crown! the crown!   205
So now 't is fitted on and grows to me,
And from it melt the dews of Paradise,
Sweet! sweet! spikenard, and balm, and frankincense.
Ah! let me not be fool'd, sweet saints; I trust
That I am whole, and clean, and meet for Heaven.   210
    Speak, if there be a priest, a man of God,
Among you there, and let him presently
Approach, and lean a ladder on the shaft,
And climbing up into my airy home,
Deliver me the blessed sacrament;   215

---

7. In Jewish demonology, an evil spirit, demon of anger and lust. He appears in the apocryphal Book of
Tobit and stands opposed to Raphael in *Paradise Lost* (VI, 365) during the battle in heaven, which Tennyson may have had in mind here. See also *Paradise Lost* IV, 153–71. "Abaddon": a fallen angel in the
abyss of hell; the name means "destruction" (see Revelation 9:11).
8. Ironic in that St. Simeon hallucinates fiends far more provocative than anything external.

For by the warning of the Holy Ghost,
I prophesy that I shall die to-night,

A quarter before twelve.
           But thou, O Lord,
Aid all this foolish people;[9] let them take
Example, pattern; lead them to thy light.   220

                     1833; 1842

Tithonus[1]

The woods decay, the woods decay and fall,
The vapors weep their burthen to the ground,
Man comes and tills the field and lies beneath,
And after many a summer dies the swan.[2]
Me only cruel immortality   5
Consumes; I wither slowly in thine arms,
Here at the quiet limit of the world,
A white-hair'd shadow roaming like a dream
The ever-silent spaces of the East,
Far-folded mists, and gleaming halls of morn.   10
   Alas! for this gray shadow, once a man—
So glorious in his beauty and thy choice,
Who madest him thy chosen, that he seem'd
To his great heart none other than a God!
I ask'd thee, "Give me immortality."   15
Then didst thou grant mine asking with a smile,
Like wealthy men who care not how they give.
But thy strong Hours indignant work'd their wills,
And beat me down and marr'd and wasted me,
And tho' they could not end me, left me maim'd   20
To dwell in presence of immortal youth,
Immortal age beside immortal youth,
And all I was in ashes. Can thy love,
Thy beauty, make amends, tho' even now,
Close over us, the silver star,[3] thy guide,   25

9. Psalm 74:18: "O Lord, and that the foolish people have blasphemed thy name."
1. Started shortly after Hallam's death, "Tithonus" was, as Tennyson explained, "originally a pendent to the 'Ulysses' in my former volumes" and reflected his own desire to be released from the burdens of life. In 1860 he wrote that Thackeray had urged him to send a poem for publication in *Cornhill Magazine*, and he "found this 'Tithonus,' written upwards of a quarter of a century ago" (*Memoir* I, 459; II, 9).
    Eos or Aurora, the daughter of Hyperion and goddess of the dawn, begged Zeus to grant Tithonus eternal life but forgot to ask for eternal youth. In pity for his plight, the gods turned him into a grasshopper.
2. Douglas Bush, my teacher of long ago, once observed in a lecture addressing this poem: "Try to imagine, if you will, what would become of this line had Tennyson written: 'After many a summer dies the duck.'" The context involved Thomas Gray's "Elegy Written in a Country Churchyard," the first stanza:
    The curfew tolls the knell of parting day,
      The lowing herd wind slowly o'er the lea,
    The plowman homeward plods his weary way,
      And leaves the world to darkness and to me.
Praising Gray and Tennyson, Bush made this point to emphasize the risks any poet takes, whether of "the sentimental school of poetry" or where ever. His "throwaway" annotations have always been to me educational.
3. Venus, the morning star.

Shines in those tremulous eyes that fill with tears
To hear me? Let me go; take back thy gift.
Why should a man desire in any way
To vary from the kindly race of men,
Or pass beyond the goal of ordinance[4]   30
Where all should pause, as is most meet for all?
    A soft air fans the cloud apart; there comes
A glimpse of that dark world where I was born.
Once more the old mysterious glimmer steals
From thy pure brows, and from thy shoulders pure,   35
And bosom beating with a heart renew'd.
Thy cheek begins to redden thro' the gloom,
Thy sweet eyes brighten slowly close to mine.
Ere yet they blind the stars, and the wild team[5]
Which love thee, yearning for thy yoke, arise,   40
And shake the darkness from their loosen'd manes,
And beat the twilight into flakes of fire.
    Lo! ever thus thou growest beautiful
In silence, then before thine answer given
Departest, and thy tears are on my cheek.   45
    Why wilt thou ever scare me with thy tears,
And make me tremble lest a saying learnt,
In days far-off, on that dark earth, be true?
"The Gods themselves cannot recall their gifts."
    Ay me! ay me! with what another heart   50
In days far-off, and with what other eyes
I used to watch—if I be he that watch'd—
The lucid outline forming round thee; saw
The dim curls kindle into sunny rings;
Changed with thy mystic change, and felt my blood   55
Glow with the glow that slowly crimson'd all
Thy presence and thy portals, while I lay,
Mouth, forehead, eyelids, growing dewy-warm
With kisses balmier than half-operating buds
Of April, and could hear the lips that kiss'd   60
Whispering I knew not what of wild and sweet,
Like that strange song I heard Apollo sing,
While Ilion like a mist rose into towers.[6]
    Yet hold me not for ever in thine East;
How can my nature longer mix with thine?   65
Coldly thy rosy shadows bathe me, cold
Are all thy lights, and cold my wrinkled feet
Upon thy glimmering thresholds, when the steam
Floats up from those fields about the homes
Of happy men that have the power to die,   70
And grassy barrows[7] of the happier dead.
Release me, and restore me to the ground.
Thou seest all things, thou wilt see my grave;

4. The appointed span of life.
5. Eos and her team of horses announce the sunrise.
6. Troy was built to the music of Apollo's lyre. Compare "Œnone," lines 39–41, and "Tiresias," lines 95ff.
7. Burial mounds.

Thou wilt renew thy beauty morn by morn,
I earth in earth forget these empty courts,   75
And thee returning on thy silver wheels.

1833ff.; 1860

Tithon[1]

Ay me! ay me! the woods decay and fall,
The vapours weep their substance to the ground,
Man comes and tills the earth and lies beneath,
And after many summers dies the rose.
Me only fatal immortality   5
Consumes: I wither slowly in thine arms,
Here at the quiet limit of the world,
A white-haired shadow roaming like a dream
The ever-silent spaces of the East,
Far-folded mists, and gleaming halls of morn.   10

Ay me! ay me! what everlasting pain,
Being immortal with a mortal heart,
To live confronted with eternal youth:
To look on what is beautiful nor know
Enjoyment save through memory. Can thy love,   15
Thy beauty, make amends, though even now,
Close over us, the silver star, thy guide,
Shines in those tremulous eyes that fill with tears?
Release me: let me go: take back thy gift:
Why should a man desire in any shape   20
To vary from his kind, or beat the roads
Of life, beyond the goal of ordinance
Where all should pause, as is most meet for all?
Or let me call thy ministers, the hours,
To take me up, to wind me in their arms,   25
To shoot the sunny interval of day,
And lap me deep within the lonely west.

A soft air fans the cloud apart; there comes
A glimpse of that dark world where I was born.
Once more the old mysterious glimmer steals   30
From thy pure brows, and from thy shoulders pure,
And bosom throbbing with a fresher heart.
Thy cheek begins to bloom a fuller red,
Thy sweet eyes brighten slowly close to mine,
Ere yet they blind the stars, and thy wild team,   35
Spreading a rapid glow with loosened manes,
Fly, trampling twilight into flakes of fire.

1. Written in 1833 and first printed from the Heath manuscript by M. J. Donahue, *PMLA* 64 (1949), the poem more properly belongs to this period than does the expanded version.

'Tis ever thus: thou growest more beautiful,
Thou partest: when a little warmth returns
Thou partest, and thy tears are on my cheek.   40

Ay me! ay me! with what another heart,
By thy divine embraces circumfused,
Thy black curls burning into sunny rings,
With thy change changed, I felt this wondrous glow
That, gradually blooming, flushes all   45
Thy pale fair limbs: what time my mortal frame
Molten in thine immortal, I lay wooed,
Lips, forehead, eyelids, growing dewy-warm
With kisses balmier than opening buds;
Anon the lips that dealt them moved themselves   50
In wild and airy whisperings more sweet
Than that strange song I heard Apollo sing,
While Ilion like a mist rose into towers.

Ah! keep me not for ever in the East:
How can my nature longer mix with thine?   55
Coldly thy rosy shadows bathe me, cold
Are all thy lights, and cold my wrinkled feet
Upon these glimmering thresholds, when the steam
Floats up from those still fields that dream below.
Relase me! so restore me to the ground;   60
Thou seest all things, thou wilt see my grave:
Thou wilt renew thy beauty with the morn;
I earth in earth forget these empty courts,
And thee returning on thy silver wheels.

                                                               1833

Tiresias[1]

To E. FitzGerald

Old Fitz, who from your suburb grange,
    Where once I tarried for a while,
Glance at the wheeling orb of change,
    And greet it with a kindly smile;
Whom yet I see as there you sit   5
    Beneath your sheltering garden-tree,
And watch your doves about you flit,
    And plant on shoulder, hand, and knee,
Or on your head their rosy feet,
    As if they knew your diet spares   10

---

1. "The Prologue," Tennyson noted, "describes Edward FitzGerald, as we had seen him at Woodbridge in 1876" (*Memoir* II, 316), and was composed shortly before FitzGerald's death on June 14, 1883. Much of the narrative poem, "dating many a year ago," was written at the time of "Ulysses"; the Epilogue was added for publication in 1885.

Whatever moved in that full sheet
   Let down to Peter at his prayers;[2]
Who live on milk and meal and grass;
   And once for ten long weeks I tried
Your table of Pythagoras,[3]   15
   And seem'd at first "a thing enskied,"[4]
As Shakespeare has it, airy-light
   To float above the ways of men,
Then fell from that half-spiritual height
   Chill'd, till I tasted flesh again   20
One night when earth was winter-black,
   And all the heavens flash'd in frost;
And on me, half-asleep, came back
   That wholesome heat the blood had lost,
And set me climbing icy capes   25
   And glaciers, over which there roll'd
To meet me long-arm'd vines with grapes
   Of Eshcol hugeness;[5] for the cold
Without, and warmth within me, wrought
   To mould the dream; but none can say   30
That Lenten fare makes Lenten thought
   Who reads your golden Eastern lay,[6]
Than which I know no version done
   In English more divinely well;
A planet equal to the sun   35
   Which cast it, that large infidel
Your Omar; and your Omar drew
   Full-handed plaudits from our best
In modern letters, and from two,
   Old friends outvaluing all the rest,   40
Two voices[7] heard on earth no more;
   But we old friends are still alive,
And I am nearing seventy-four,
   While you have touch'd at seventy-five,
And so I send a birthday line   45
   Of greeting; and my son, who dipt
In some forgotten book of mine
   With sallow scraps of manuscript,
And dating many a year ago,
   Has hit on this, which you will take,   50
My Fitz, and welcome, as I know,
   Less for its own than for the sake
Of one recalling gracious times,

---

2. A reference to meat, fish, and fowl (see Acts 10:11–12). FitzGerald was a vegetarian.
3. Sixth-century B.C. Greek philosopher and vegetarian.
4. See *Measure for Measure* I, iv, line 34.
5. Of his vegetarian dream Tennyson said: "I had gone without meat for six weeks, living only on vegetables; and at the end of the time, when I came to eat a mutton-chop, I shall never forget the sensation. I never felt such joy in my blood. When I went to sleep, I dreamt that I saw the vines of the South, with huge Eshcol branches, trailing over the glaciers of the North" (*Memoir* II, 317). For Eshcol, a fruitful valley, see Numbers 13:23.
6. FitzGerald's translation of the *Rubaiyat of Omar Khayyam*, published in 1859.
7. In the 1880s, many of the closest of the old friends were dying. Here Tennyson is probably thinking of Thomas Carlyle and James Spedding, both of whom had died in 1881. See *Memoir* II, 262–63.

When, in our younger London days,
You found some merit in my rhymes,   55
And I more pleasure in your praise.[8]

Tiresias[9]

I wish I were as in the years of old,
While yet the blessed daylight made itself
Ruddy thro' both the roofs of sight, and woke
These eyes, now dull, but then so keen to seek
The meanings ambush'd under all they saw,   5
The flight of birds, the flame of sacrifice,
What omens may foreshadow fate to man
And woman, and the secret of the Gods.
　　My son,[1] the Gods, despite of human prayer,
Are slower to forgive than human kings.   10
The great God Arês burns in anger still
Against the guiltless heirs of him from Tyre,
Our Cadmus, out of whom thou art, who found
Beside the springs of Dircê, smote, and still'd
Thro' all its folds the multitudinous beast,   15
The dragon, which our trembling fathers call'd
The God's own son.
　　　　　　　A tale, that told to me,
When but thine age, by age as winter-white
As mine is now, amazed, but made me yearn
For larger glimpses of that more than man   20
Which rolls the heavens, and lifts and lays the deep,
Yet loves and hates with mortal hates and loves,
And moves unseen among the ways of men.
　　Then, in my wanderings all the lands that lie
Subjected to the Heliconian[2] ridge   25
Have heard this footstep fall, altho' my wont
Was more to scale the highest of the heights
With some strange hope to see the nearer God.
　　One naked peak—the sister of the Sun
Would climb from out the dark, and linger there   30
To silver all the valleys with her shafts—
There once, but long ago, five-fold thy term[3]
Of years, I lay; the winds were dead for heat;
The noonday crag made the hand burn; and sick
For shadow—not one bush was near—I rose,   35
Following a torrent till its myriad falls

8. FitzGerald had been an admirer of Tennyson's earlier poetry (through the 1842 volumes); but, as he said, "I am considered a great heretic, because like Carlyle, I gave up all hopes of him after 'The Princess'" (1847), for none of the songs had "the old champagne flavour" (*Memoir* I, 253).
9. Tiresias, blinded by Athena when he surprised her while she was bathing, was granted the gift of prophecy but, like Cassandra, could not compel belief. In the poem he tries to persuade Menoeceus to sacrifice himself to save Thebes in its War of the Seven. Among many possible sources, Tennyson drew from the *Odyssey* XI, lines 90–151.
1. Menoeceus, familiarly addressed. He was the son of Creon and descended from Cadmus, against whose offspring Ares (Mars) held his grudge.
2. I.e., the lands that lie below the Helicon mountain range, regarded as sacred to the Muses.
3. In some legends, Tiresias was in his seventieth year.

Found silence in the hollows underneath.
   There in a secret olive-glade I saw
Pallas Athene climbing from the bath
In anger; yet one glittering foot disturb'd   40
The lucid well; one snowy knee was prest
Against the margin flowers; a dreadful light
Came from her golden hair, her golden helm
And all her golden armor on the grass,
And from her virgin breast, and virgin eyes   45
Remaining fixt on mine, till mine grew dark
For ever, and I heard a voice that said,
"Henceforth be blind, for thou hast seen too much,
And speak the truth that no man may believe."
   Son, in the hidden world of sight that lives   50
Behind this darkness, I behold her still,
Beyond all work of those who carve the stone,
Beyond all dreams of Godlike womanhood,
Ineffable beauty, out of whom, at a glance,
And as it were, perforce, upon me flash'd   55
The power of prophesying—but to me
No power—so chain'd and coupled with the curse
Of blindness and their unbelief who heard
And heard not, when I spake of famine, plague,
Shrine-shattering earthquake, fire, flood, thunderbolt,   60
And angers of the Gods for evil done
And expiation lack'd—no power on Fate
Theirs, or mine own! for when the crowd would roar
For blood, for war, whose issue was their doom,
To cast wise words among the multitude   65
Was flinging fruit to lions; nor, in hours
Of civil outbreak, when I knew the twain
Would each waste each, and bring on both the yoke
Of stronger states, was mine the voice to curb
The madness of our cities and their kings.[4]   70
   Who ever turn'd upon his heel to hear
My warning that the tyranny of one
Was prelude to the tyranny of all?
My counsel that the tyranny of all
Led backward to the tyranny of one?   75
   This power hath work'd no good to aught that lives
And these blind hands were useless in their wars.
O, therefore, that the unfulfill'd desire,
The grief for ever born from griefs to be,
The boundless yearning of the prophet's heart—   80
Could *that* stand forth, and like a statute, rear'd
To some great citizen, win all praise from all
Who past it, saying, "That was he!"

---

4. Passages like the above suggest the late Tennyson of "Locksley Hall Sixty Years After" and were perhaps altered from or added to the original. Here he identifies himself with the blind seer, feeling, like Tiresias, that his own prophecies and warnings fell on the deaf ears of his contemporaries. Since the Cambridge days, Tennyson had had a sometimes exaggerated notion that he was going blind, a fear that was particularly acute in the 1880s (see *Memoir* II, 311).

In vain!
Virtue must shape itself in deed, and those
Whom weakness or necessity have cramp'd   85
Within themselves, immerging, each, his urn
In his own well, draws solace as he may.
    Menœceus, thou hast eyes, and I can hear
Too plainly what full tides of onset sap
Our seven high gates, and what a weight of war   90
Rides on those ringing axles! jingle of bits,
Shouts, arrows, tramp of the horn-footed horse
That grind the glebe to powder! Stony showers
Of that ear-stunning hail of Arês crash
Along the sounding walls. Above, below,   95
Shock after shock, the song-built towers⁵ and gates
Reel, bruished and butted with the shuddering
War-thunder of iron rams; and from within
The city comes a murmur void of joy,
Lest she be taken captive—maidens, wives,   100
And mothers with their babblers of the dawn,
And oldest age in shadow from the night,
Falling about their shrines before their Gods,
And wailing, "Save us."
                            And they wail to thee!
These eyeless eyes, that cannot see thine own,   105
See this, that only in thy virtue lies
The saving of our Thebes; for, yesternight,
To me, the great God Arês, whose one bliss
Is war and sacrifice—himself
Blood-red from battle, spear and helmet tipt   110
With stormy light as on a mast at sea,
Stood out before a darkness, crying, "Thebes,
Thy Thebes shall fall and perish, for I loathe
The seed of Cadmus—yet if one of these
By his own hand—if one of these—"
                            My son,   115
No sound is breathed so potent to coerce,
And to conciliate, as their names who dare
For that sweet mother land which gave them birth
Nobly to do, nobly to die. Their names,
Graven on memorial columns, are a song   120
Heard in the future; few, but more than wall
And rampart, their examples reach a hand
Far thro' all years, and everywhere they meet
And kindle generous purpose, and the strength
To mould it into action pure as theirs.   125
    Fairer thy fate than mine, if life's best end
Be to end well! and thou refusing this,
Unvenerable will thy memory be
While men shall move the lips; but if thou dare—
Thou, one of these, the race of Cadmus—then   130

---

5. In legend, the walls of Thebes were built to the music of Amphion's harp (see n. 6, p. 103).

No stone is fitted in yon marble girth
Whose echo shall not tongue thy glorious doom,
Nor in this pavement but shall ring thy name
To every hoof that clangs it, and the springs
Of Dircê laving yonder battle-plain,   135
Heard from the roofs by night, will murmur thee
To thine own Thebes, while Thebes thro' thee shall stand
Firm-based with all her Gods.
                              The Dragon's cave
Half hid, they tell me, now in flowing vines—
Where once he dwelt and whence he roll'd himself   140
At dead of night—thou knowest, and that smooth rock
Before it, altar-fashion'd, where of late
The woman-breasted Sphinx, with wings drawn back,
Folded her lion paws, and look'd to Thebes.
There blanch the bones of whom she slew, and these   145
Mixt with her own, because the fierce beast found
A wiser[6] than herself, and dash'd herself
Dead in her rage; but thou art wise enough,
Tho' young, to love thy wiser, blunt the curse
Of Pallas, bear, and tho' I speak the truth   150
Believe I speak it, let thine own hand strike
Thy youthful pulses into rest and quench
The red God's anger, fearing not to plunge
Thy torch of life in darkness, rather—thou
Rejoicing that the sun, the moon, the stars   155
Send no such light upon the ways of men
As one great deed.
                   Thither, my son, and there
Thou, that hast never known the embrace of love,
Offer thy maiden life.
                       This useless hand!
I felt one warm tear fall upon it. Gone!   160
He will achieve his greatness.
                               But for me,
I would that I were gather'd to my rest,
And mingled with the famous kings of old,
On whom about their ocean-islets flash
The faces of the Gods—the wise man's word,   165
Here trampled by the populace underfoot,
There crown'd with worship—and these eyes will find
The men I knew, and watch the chariot whirl
About the goal again, and hunters race
The shadowy lion, and the warrior-kings,   170
In height and prowess more than human, strive
Again for glory, while the golden lyre
Is ever sounding in heroic ears
    Heroic hymns, and every way the vales
Wind, clouded with the grateful incense-fume   175
Of those who mix all odor to the Gods

---

6. Oedipus and his solving of the riddle of the Sphinx.

On one far height in one far-shining fire.[7]

_____

"One height and one far-shining fire!"
    And while I fancied that my friend
For this brief idyll would require   180
    A less diffuse and opulent end,
And would defend his judgment well,
    If I should deem it over nice —
The tolling of his funeral bell
    Broke on my Pagan Paradise,   185
And mixt the dream of classic times,
    And all the phantoms of the dream,
With present grief, and made the rhymes,
    That miss'd his living welcome, seem
Like would-be guests an hour too late,   190
    Who down the highway moving on
With easy laughter find the gate
    Is bolted, and the master gone.
Gone into darkness, that full light
    Of friendship! past, in sleep, away   195
By night, into the deeper night![8]
    The deeper night? A clearer day
Than our poor twilight dawn on earth —
    If night, what barren toil to be!
What life, so maim'd by night, were worth   200
    Our living out? Not mine to me
Remembering all the golden hours
    Now silent, and so many dead,
And him the last; and laying flowers,
    This wreath, above his honor'd head,   205
And praying that, when I from hence
    Shall fade with him into the unknown,
My close of earth's experience
    May prove as peaceful as his own.

                                              1833ff.; 1885

Break, Break, Break[1]

Break, break, break,
    On thy cold gray stones, O Sea!
And I would that my tongue could utter
    The thoughts that arise in me.

O, well for the fisherman's boy,   5
    That he shouts with his sister at play!

_____

7. Tennyson liked to quote the above seventeen lines "as a sample of his blank verse" (*Memoir* II, 318).
8. In a letter to Fanny Kemble fondly describing Tennyson's short visit in 1876, FitzGerald concluded, "I suppose I may never see him again" (*Memoir* II, 317).
1. Although the lyric is a seascape, Tennyson said it was "made in a Lincolnshire lane at 5 o'clock in the morning between blossoming hedges" (*Memoir* I, 190).

O, well for the sailor lad,
   That he sings in his boat on the bay!

And the stately ships go on
   To their haven under the hill;   10
But O for the touch of a vanish'd hand,
   And the sound of a voice[2] that is still!

Break, break, break,
   At the foot of thy crags, O Sea!
But the tender grace of a day that is dead   15
   Will never come back to me.

                       1834?; 1842

The Epic[1]

At Francis Allen's on the Christmas-eve, —
The game of forfeits done—the girls all kiss'd
Beneath the sacred bush[2] and past away—
The parson Holmes, the poet Everard Hall,[3]
The host, and I sat round the wassail-bowl,   5
Then half-way ebb'd; and there we held a talk,
How all the old honor had from Christmas gone,
Or gone or dwindled down to some odd games
In some odd nooks like this; till I tired out
With cutting eights that day upon the pond,   10
Where, three times slipping from the outer edge,
I bump'd the ice into three several stars,
Fell in a doze; and half-awake I heard
The parson taking wide and wider sweeps,
Now harping on the church-commissioners,[4]   15
Now hawking at geology[5] and schism;
Until I woke, and found him settled down
Upon the general decay of faith
Right thro' the world: "at home was little left,
And none abroad; there was no anchor, none,   20
To hold by." Francis, laughing, clapt his hand
On Everard's shoulder, with "I hold by him."
"And I," quoth Everard, "by the wassail-bowl."
"Why yes," I said, "we knew your gift that way

---

2. Arthur Hallam's. See *IM* 130; line 1: "Thy voice is on the rolling air."
1. FitzGerald has said that when the "Morte d'Arthur" was read to him in 1835 from manuscript, it had no introduction or epilogue; "The Epic" was added later "to give a reason for telling an old-world tale" (*Memoir* I, 194). Tennyson's early interest in the Arthurian legends as material for a grand epic had been abandoned or postponed by 1838, as the casual, almost flippant, tone of "The Epic" suggests. See *Alfred Tennyson*, p. 193.
2. Mistletoe.
3. May represent Tennyson himself with his friends at Cambridge.
4. Refers to the Ecclesiastical Commission, established in 1835 to administer the revenues of the Anglican Church.
5. Tennyson had been reading Lyell's *The Principles of Geology* (1830–33), one of the major contributions to the "new" science that challenged the biblical interpretation of creation. Here and below, compare *IM* 55 and 56.

At college; but another which you had—   25
I mean of verse (for so we held it then),
What came of that?" "You know," said Frank, "he burnt
His epic, his King Arthur, some twelve books"—
And then to me demanding why: "O, sir,
He thought that nothing new was said, or else   30
Something so said 't was nothing—that a truth
Looks freshest in the fashion of the day;
God knows; he has a mint of reasons; ask.
It pleased *me* well enough." "Nay, nay," said Hall,
"Why take the style of those heroic times?   35
For nature brings not back the mastodon,
Nor we those times; and why should any man
Remodel models? these twelve books of mine
Were faint Homeric echoes, nothing-worth,
Mere chaff and draff, much better burnt." "But I,"   40
Said Francis, "pick'd the eleventh[6] from this hearth,
And have it; keep a thing, its use will come.
I hoard it as a sugar-plum for Holmes."
He laugh'd, and I, tho' sleepy, like a horse
That hears the corn-bin open, prick'd my ears;   45
For I remember'd Everard's college fame
When we were Freshmen. Then at my request
He brought it; and the poet, little urged,
But with some prelude of disparagement,
Read, mouthing out his hollow oes and as,   50
Deep-chested music, and to this result.[7]

[Here follows "Morte d'Arthur," lines 170–440 of "The Passing of Arthur," below.
Then "The Epic" continues.]

Here ended Hall, and our last light, that long
Had wink'd and threaten'd darkness, flared and fell;
At which the parson, sent to sleep with sound,
And waked with silence, grunted "Good!" but we   55
Sat rapt: it was the tone with which he read—
Perhaps some modern touches here and there
Redeem'd it from the charge of nothingness—
Or else we loved the man, and prized his work;
I know not; but we sitting, as I said,   60
The cock crew loud, as all that time of year
The lusty bird takes every hour for dawn.
Then Francis, muttering, like a man ill-used,
"There now—that's nothing!" drew a little back,
And drove his heel into the smoulder'd log,   65
That sent a blast of sparkles up the flue.
And so to bed, where yet in sleep I seem'd
To sail with Arthur under looming shores,

6. The "Morte d'Arthur," which in 1869 was incoporated into the *Idylls* but did not actually become the twelfth book until 1888.
7. "His voice, very deep and deep-chested, but rather murmuring than mouthing" was FitzGerald's comment on the poet's reading (*Memoir* I, 194).

Point after point; till on to dawn, when dreams
Begin to feel the truth and stir of day,   70
To me, methought, who waited with the crowd,
There came a bark that, blowing forward, bore
King Arthur, like a modern gentleman[8]
Of stateliest port; and all the people cried,
"Arthur is come again: he cannot die."   75
Then those that stood upon the hills behind
Repeated—"Come again, and thrice as fair;"
And, further inland, voices echoed—"Come

With all good things, and war shall be no more."
At this a hundred bells began to peal,   80
That with the sound I woke, and heard indeed
The clear church-bells ring in the Christmas morn.

                                              1835–38; 1842

"Move Eastward, Happy Earth"[1]

Move eastward, happy earth, and leave
    Yon orange sunset waning slow;
From fringes of the faded eve,
    O happy planet, eastward go,
Till over thy dark shoulder glow   5
    Thy silver sister-world,[2] and rise
    To glass herself in dewy eyes
That watch me from the glen below.

Ah, bear me with thee, smoothly borne,
    Dip forward under starry light,   10
And move me to my marriage-morn,
    And round again to happy night.

                                              1836; 1842

A Farewell[1]

Flow down, cold rivulet, to the sea,
    Thy tribute wave deliver;
No more by thee my steps shall be,
    For ever and for ever.

---

8. A phrase that in some ways anticipates the dedication of the *Idylls* in 1862 to Prince Albert.
1. Chiefly of biographical interest, the poem suggests Tennyson's engagement to Emily Sellwood, whom he did not marry, however, until 1850. The poem was probably occasioned by the marriage in May 1836 of his brother Charles to Emily's sister Louisa.
2. The moon, or possibly Venus, as reflected in Emily's eyes. As Sir Charles confirms: "Alfred's engagement to Emily Sellwood was recognized by the Sellwoods early in 1838" (see *Alfred Tennyson*, p. 177).
1. The Tennyson family moved out of the rectory at Somersby during the spring of 1837. See *IM* 103 for the dream the poet had the night before they left. The brook is also described in "Ode to Memory."

Flow, softly flow, by lawn and lea,   5
   A rivulet, then a river;
Nowhere by thee my steps shall be,
   For ever and for ever.

But here will sigh thine alder-tree,
   And here thine aspen shiver;   10
And here by thee will hum the bee,
   For ever and for ever.

A thousand suns will stream on thee,
   A thousand moons will quiver;
But not by thee my steps shall be,   15
   For ever and for ever.

                                        1837; 1842

Locksley Hall[1]

Comrades, leave me here a little, while as yet 't is early morn;
Leave me here, and when you want me, sound upon the bugle-horn.

'T is the place, and all around it, as of old, the curlews call,
Dreary gleams[2] about the moorland flying over Locksley Hall;

Locksley Hall, that in the distance overlooks the sandy tracts,   5
And the hollow ocean-ridges roaring into cataracts.

Many a night from yonder ivied casement, ere I went to rest,
Did I look on great Orion sloping slowly to the west.

Many a night I saw the Pleiads,[3] rising thro' the mellow shade,
Glitter like a swarm of fireflies tangled in a silver braid.   10

Here about the beach I wander'd, nourishing a youth sublime
With the fairy tales of science, and the long result of time;

When the centuries behind me like a fruitful land reposed;
When I clung to all the present for the promise that it closed;

When I dipt into the future far as human eye could see,   15
Saw the vision of the world and all the wonder that would be. —

1. The poem is a dramatic monologue that represents, according to Tennyson, "young life, its good side, its deficiencies, and its yearnings" (*Memoir* I, 195). Speaker, place, and incidents are fictional. As the poet noted, "'Locksley Hall' is an imaginary place (tho' the coast is Lincolnshire) and the hero is imaginary" (*Memoir* I, 195). Having been jilted by Amy, the speaker does, however, bear some resemblance to Tennyson's older brother Frederick, whose impetuous infatuation for his cousin Julia was thwarted by her parents. Similarly, Tennyson's more genuine relationship with Rosa Barring, to whom he had written several love poems between 1834 and 1836, was squelched by her parents. See *Alfred Tennyson*, pp. 162–63.
2. Tennyson said that the "gleams" do not refer to the curlews, as some commentators insist; he meant the line to read: "while dreary gleams of light are flying across a dreary moorland."
3. I.e., the Pleiades, a constellation that, like Orion, is especially brilliant in winter and early spring.

In the spring a fuller crimson comes upon the robin's breast;
In the spring the wanton lapwing gets himself another crest;

In the spring a livelier iris changes on the burnish'd dove;
In the spring a young man's fancy lightly turns to thoughts of love.   20

Then her cheek was pale and thinner than should be for one so young,
And her eyes on all my motions with a mute observance hung.

And I said, "My cousin Amy, speak, and speak the truth to me,
Trust me, cousin, all the current of my being sets to thee."

On her pallid cheek and forehead came a color and a light,   25
As I have seen the rosy red flushing in the northern night.

And she turn'd—her bosom shaken with a sudden storm of sighs—
All the spirit deeply dawning in the dark of hazel eyes—

Saying, "I have hid my feelings, fearing they should do me wrong,"
Saying, "Dost thou love me, cousin?" weeping, "I have loved thee long."   30

Love took up the glass of Time, and turn'd it in his glowing hands;
Every moment, lightly shaken, ran itself in golden sands.

Love took up the harp of Life, and smote on all the chords with might;
Smote the chord of Self, that, trembling, past in music out of sight.

Many a morning on the moorland did we hear the copses ring,   35
And her whisper throng'd my pulses with the fulness of the spring.

Many an evening by the waters did we watch the stately ships,
And our spirits rush'd together at the touching of the lips.

O my cousin, shallow-hearted! O my Amy, mine no more!
O the dreary, dreary moorland! O the barren, barren shore!   40

Falser than all fancy fathoms,[4] falser than all songs have sung,
Puppet to a father's threat, and servile to a shrewish tongue!

Is it well to wish thee happy?—having known me—to decline
On a range of lower feelings and a narrower heart than mine!

Yet it shall be; thou shalt lower to his level day by day,   45
What is fine within thee growing coarse to sympathize with clay.

As the husband is, the wife is; thou art mated with a clown,
And the grossness of his nature will have weight to drag thee down.

He will hold thee, when his passion shall have spent its novel force,
Something better than his dog, a little dearer than his horse.   50

---

4. A verb, not a noun.

What is this? his eyes are heavy; think not they are glazed with wine.
Go to him, it is thy duly; kiss him, take his hand in thine.

It may be my lord is weary, that his brain is overwrought;
Soothe him with thy finer fancies, touch him with thy lighter thought.

He will answer to the purpose, easy things to understand—   55
Better thou wert dead before me, tho' I slew thee with my hand!

Better thou and I were lying, hidden from the heart's disgrace,
Roll'd in one another's arms, and silent in a last embrace.

Cursed be the social wants that sin against the strength of youth!
Cursed be the social lies that warp us from the living truth!   60

Cursed be the sickly forms that err from honest Nature's rule!
Cursed be the gold that gilds the straiten'd⁵ forehead of the fool!

Well—'t is well that I should bluster!—Hadst thou less unworthy proved—
Would to God—for I had loved thee more than ever wife was loved.

Am I mad, that I should cherish that which bears but bitter fruit?   65
I will pluck it from my bosom, tho' my heart be at the root.

Never, tho' my mortal summers to such length of years should come
As the many-winter'd crow⁶ that leads the clanging rookery home.

Where is comfort? in division of the records of the mind?
Can I part her from herself, and love her, as I knew her, kind?   70

I remember one that perish'd; sweetly did she speak and move;
Such a one do I remember, whom to look at was to love.

Can I think of her as dead, and love her for the love she bore?
No—she never loved me truly; love is love for evermore.

Comfort? comfort scorn'd of devils! this is truth the poet⁷ sings,   75
That a sorrow's crown of sorrow is remembering happier things.

Drug thy memories, lest thou learn it, lest thy heart be put to proof,
In the dead unhappy night, and when the rain is on the roof.

Like a dog, he hunts in dreams, and thou art staring at the wall,
Where the dying night-lamp flickers, and the shadows rise and fall.   80

Then a hand shall pass before thee, pointing to his drunken sleep,
To thy widow'd⁸ marriage-pillows, to the tears that thou wilt weep.

5. Narrowed, i.e., a "lowbrow."
6. The long-lived English rook.
7. Dante in the *Inferno* V, lines 121–23.
8. His lack of attention has figuratively widowed her. For a nocturnal visit of the rejected lover, compare John Donne's poem "The Apparition."

Thou shalt hear, the "Never, never," whisper'd by the phantom years,
And a song from out the distance in the ringing of thine ears;

And an eye shall vex thee, looking ancient kindness on thy pain.   85
Turn thee, turn thee on thy pillow; get thee to thy rest again.

Nay, but Nature brings thee solace; for a tender voice will cry.
'T is a purer life than thine, a lip to drain thy trouble dry.

Baby lips will laugh me down; my latest rival brings thee rest.
Baby fingers, waxen touches, press me from the mother's breast.   90

O, the child too clothes the father with a dearness not his due.
Half is thine and half is his; it will be worthy of the two.

O, I see thee old and formal, fitted to thy petty part,
With a little hoard of maxims preaching down a daughter's heart.

"They were dangerous guides the feelings—she herself was not exempt—   95
Truly, she herself had suffer'd"—Perish in thy self-contempt!

Overlive it—lower yet—be happy! wherefore should I care?
I myself must mix with action, lest I wither by despair.

What is that which I should turn to, lighting upon days like these?
Every door is barr'd with gold, and opens but to golden keys.   100

Every gate is throng'd with suitors, all the markets overflow.
I have but an angry fancy; what is that which I should do?

I had been content to perish, falling on the foeman's ground,
When the ranks are roll'd in vapor, and the winds are laid with sound.[9]

But the jingling of the guinea helps the hurt that Honor feels,   105
And the nations do but murmur, snarling at each other's heels.

Can I but relive in sadness? I will turn that earlier page.
Hide me from my deep emotion, O thou wondrous Mother-Age!

Make me feel the wild pulsation that I felt before the strife,
When I heard my days before me, and the tumult of my life;   110

Yearning for the large excitement that the coming years would yield,
Eager-hearted as a boy when first he leaves his father's field,

And at night along the dusky highway near the nearer drawn,
Sees in heaven the light of London flaring like a dreary dawn;[1]

---

9. Cannon firing supposedly stilled the winds.
1. This couplet describes a night journey from High Beech, where the Tennysons moved after leaving Somersby, to London. The simile, Tennyson noted, was "from old times and the top of the mail-coach."

And his spirit leaps within him to be gone before him then,   115
Underneath the light he looks at, in among the throngs of men;

Men, my brothers, men the workers, ever reaping something new;
That which they have done but earnest[2] of the things that they shall do.

For I dipt into the future, far as human eye could see,
Saw the Vision of the world, and all the wonder that would be;   120

Saw the heavens fill with commerce, argosies of magic sails,[3]
Pilots of the purple twilight, dropping down with costly bales;

Heard the heavens fill with shouting, and there rain'd a ghastly dew
From the nations' airy navies grappling in the central blue;

Far along the world-wide whisper of the south-wind rushing warm,   125
With the standards of the peoples plunging thro' the thunder-storm;

Till the war-drum throbb'd no longer, and the battle-flags were furl'd
In the Parliament of man, the Federation of the world.

There the common sense of most shall hold a fretful realm in awe,
And the kindly earth shall slumber, lapt in universal law.   130

So I triumph'd ere my passion sweeping thro' me left me dry,
Left me with the palsied heart, and left me with the jaundiced eye;

Eye, to which all order festers, all things here are out of joint.[4]
Science moves, but slowly, slowly, creeping on from point to point;

Slowly comes a hungry people, as a lion, creeping nigher,   135
Glares at one that nods and winks behind a slowly-dying fire.[5]

Yet I doubt not thro' the ages one increasing purpose runs,
And the thoughts of men are widen'd with the process of the suns.[6]
What is that to him that reaps not harvest of his youthful joys,
Tho' the deep heart of existence beat for ever like a boy's?   140

They that go by train seldom see this." In *Modern Painters*, John Ruskin would soon deplore the same sort of loss by those who traveled by train, for example: "All travelling becomes dull in exact proportion to its rapidity. Going by railroad I do not consider as travelling at all; it is merely 'being sent' to a place, and very little different from becoming a parcel."
2. A pledge, i.e., assurance of future achievements.
3. Much has been claimed for this line as making Tennyson a prophet of modern aviation. Manned balloon flights were a novelty in the England of the 1830s, and he was probably thinking only of lighter-than-air craft.
4. Compare *Hamlet* I, v, lines 189–90: "The time is out of joint: O cursed spite / That ever I was born to set it right."
5. Suggests the gradual encroachment of democracy on the dying aristocratic establishment. Contrast "Locksley Hall Sixty Years After," lines 247ff., for a similarly expressed but completely unsympathetic point of view.
6. Compare Tennyson's dream on the night before leaving Somersby as recorded in *IM* 103. Both the vision and the dream are involved with journeys, are conceivably variations of the single experience, and suggest that this part of "Locksley Hall" may have been composed concurrently with section 103 sometime in 1837.

Knowledge comes, but wisdom lingers, and I linger on the shore,
And the individual withers, and the world is more and more.[7]
Knowledge comes, but wisdom lingers, and he bears a laden breast,
Full of sad experience, moving toward the stillness of his rest.

Hark, my merry comrades call me, sounding on the bugle-horn,   145
They to whom my foolish passion were a target for their scorn.

Shall it not be scorn to me to harp on such a moulder'd string?
I am shamed thro' all my nature to have loved so slight a thing.

Weakness to be wroth with weakness! woman's pleasure, woman's pain—
Nature made them blinder motions bounded in a shallower brain.[8]   150

Woman is the lesser man, and all thy passions, match'd with mine,
Are as moonlight unto sunlight, and as water unto wine—

Here at least, where nature sickens, nothing. Ah, for some retreat
Deep in yonder shining Orient, where my life began to beat,

Where in wild Mahratta-battle[9] fell my father evil-starr'd;—   155
I was left a trampled orphan, and a selfish uncle's ward.

Or to burst all links of habit—there to wander far away,
On from island unto island at the gateways of the day.

Larger constellations burning, mellow moons and happy skies,
Breadths of tropic shade and palms in cluster, knots of Paradise.   160

Never comes the trader, never floats an European flag,
Slides the bird o'er lustrous woodland, swings the trailer[1] from the crag;

Droops the heavy-blossom'd bower, hangs the heavy-fruited tree—
Summer isles of Eden lying in dark-purple spheres of sea.

There methinks would be enjoyment more than in this march of mind,   165
In the steamship, in the railway, in the thoughts that shake mankind.

There the passions cramp'd no longer shall have scope and breathing space;
I will take some savage woman, she shall rear my dusky race.

7. A belief shared by a number of Tennyson's contemporaries, notably by John Stuart Mill in his "Essay on
   Civilization" (1836). See Matthew Arnold, "To Marguerite—Continued" (c. 1849):
       Yes! in the sea of life enisled,
       With echoing straits between us thrown,
       Dotting the shoreless watery wild,
       We mortal millions live *alone.*
8. It was commonly held throughout the nineteenth century (Darwin included) that cranial capacity,
   specifically brain mass, bore a direct relation to intelligence. Generally, women (and some "savages")
   have brains of less weight than European men have. It was not until early in the twentieth century that
   anthropologists, namely Franz Boas (the founder of nonracist, relativistic general anthropology), discovered that brain mass had a direct relationship to body mass, i.e., women and men were equally intelligent (see line 177).
9. Alludes to wars in India violently fought in 1803 and 1817 by a Hindu tribe against the British.
1. A vine.

Iron-jointed, supple-sinew'd, they shall dive, and they shall run,
Catch the wild goat by the hair, and hurl their lances in the sun;   170
Whistle back the parrot's call and leap the rainbows of the brooks,
Not with blinded eyesight poring over miserable books—

Fool, again the dream, the fancy! but I *know* my words are wild,
But I count the gray barbarian lower than the Christian child.

I, to herd with narrow foreheads, vacant of our glorious gains,   175
Like a beast with lower pleasures, like a beast with lower pains![2]

Mated with a squalid savage—what to me were sun or clime?
I the heir of all the ages, in the foremost files of time—

I that rather held it better men should perish one by one,
Than that earth should stand at gaze like Joshua's moon in Ajalon![3]   180

Not in vain the distance beacons. Forward, forward let us range,
Let the great world spin for ever down the ringing grooves[4] of change.

Thro' the shadow of the globe we sweep into the younger day;
Better fifty years of Europe than a cycle of Cathay.[5]

Mother-Age,—for mine I knew not,—help me as when life begun;   185
Rift the hills, and roll the waters, flash the lightnings, weigh the sun.

O, I see the crescent promise of my spirit hath not set.
Ancient founts of inspiration well thro' all my fancy yet.

Howsoever these things be, a long farewell to Locksley Hall!
Now for me the woods may wither, now for me the roof-tree fall.   190

Comes a vapor from the margin, blackening over heath and holt,
Cramming all the blast before it, in its breast a thunderbolt.

Let it fall on Locksley Hall, with rain or hail, or fire or snow;
For the mighty wind arises, roaring seaward, and I go.

1835ff.; 1842

2. Compare the opening of "Ulysses."
3. Joshua commanded that the sun and moon stand still while the Israelites continued the slaughter of their
   enemies in the valley of Ajalon (see Joshua 10:12–13).
4. "When I went by the first train from Liverpool to Manchester (1830), I thought that the wheels ran in a
   groove" (*Memoir* I, 195).
5. Ancient name for China; to the progressive minds of the nineteenth century a remote, static civilization.

The Vision of Sin[1]

1

I had a vision when the night was late;
A youth came riding toward a palace-gate.

He rode a horse[2] with wings, that would have flown,
But that his heavy rider kept him down.
And from the palace came a child of sin,   5
And took him by the curls, and led him in,
Where sat a company with heated eyes,
Expecting when a fountain[3] should arise.
A sleepy light upon their brows and lips—
As when the sun, a crescent of eclipse,   10
Dreams over lake and lawn, and isles and capes—
Suffused them, sitting, lying, languid shapes,
By heaps of gourds, and skins of wine, and piles of grapes.

2

Then methought I heard a mellow sound,
Gathering up from all the lower ground;   15
Narrowing in to where they sat assembled,
Low voluptuous music winding trembled,
Woven in circles. They that heard it sigh'd,
Panted hand-in-hand with faces pale,
Swung themselves, and in low tones replied;   20
Till the fountain spouted, showering wide
Sleet of diamond-drift and pearly hail.
Then the music touch'd the gates and died,
Rose again from where it seem'd to fail,
Storm'd in orbs of song, a growing gale;   25
Till thronging in and in, to where they waited,
As 't were a hundred-throated nightingale,
The strong tempestuous treble throbb'd and palpitated;
Ran into its giddiest whirl of sound,
Caught the sparkles, and in circles,   30
Purple gauzes, golden hazes, liquid mazes,
Flung the torrent rainbow round.
Then they started from their places,
Moved with violence, changed in hue,
Caught each other with wild grimaces,   35
Half-invisible to the view,
Wheeling with precipitate paces

---

1. This dream-allegory may be read as a companion poem to "The Palace of Art," and much of it may have been written in the 1830s. The young aesthete can be the artist whose sin is the denial of the creative principle —the failure of the ideal poet to realize the true purposes of art. "This describes the soul of a youth," Tennyson noted, "who has given himself up to pleasure and Epicureanism. He at length is worn out and wrapt in the mists of satiety. Afterwards he grows into a cynical old man afflicted with the 'curse of nature,' and joining in the Feast of Death. Then we see the landscape which symbolizes God, Law and the future life."
2. Pegasus, the horse associated with the Muses, would have carried the poet aloft toward the realization of his poetic aspirations.
3. Here, as in stanza 2, descriptions of the fountain and palace suggest possible debts to Coleridge's "Kubla Khan" and Keats's "Lamia."

To the melody, till they flew,
Hair and eyes and limbs and faces,
Twisted hard in fierce embraces,   40
Like to Furies, like to Graces,[4]
Dash'd together in blinding dew;
Till, kill'd with some luxurious agony,
The nerve-dissolving melody
Flutter'd headlong from the sky.   45

3

And then I look'd up toward a mountain-tract,
That girt the region with high cliff and lawn.
I saw that every morning, far withdrawn
Beyond the darkness and the cataract,
God made Himself an awful rose of dawn,   50
Unheeded; and detaching, fold by fold,
From those still heights, and, slowly drawing near,
A vapor heavy, hueless, formless, cold,
Came floating on for many a month and year,
Unheeded; and I thought I would have spoken,   55
And warn'd that madman ere it grew too late,
But, as in dreams, I could not. Mine was broken,
When that cold vapor touch'd the palace-gate,
And link'd again. I saw within my head
A gray and gap-tooth'd man as lean as death,   60
Who slowly rode across a wither'd heath,
And lighted at a ruin'd inn, and said:

4

"Wrinkled ostler, grim and thin!
    Here is custom come your way;
Take my brute, and lead him in,   65
    Stuff his ribs with mouldy hay.

"Bitter barmaid, waning fast!
    See that sheets are on my bed.
What! the flower of life is past;
    It is long before you wed.   70

"Slip-shod waiter, lank and sour,
    At the Dragon[5] on the heath!
Let us have a quiet hour,
    Let us hob-and-nob with Death.

"I am old, but let me drink;   75
    Bring me spices, bring me wine;
I remember, when I think,
    That my youth was half divine.

4. Three goddesses who personified loveliness. "Furies": three winged women, often represented with snakes about them, who were the avengers of crime.
5. Name of the inn.

"Wine is good for shrivell'd lips.
  When a blanket wraps the day,   80
When the rotten woodland drips,
  And the leaf is stamp'd in clay.

"Sit thee down, and have no shame,
  Cheek by jowl, and knee by knee;
What care I for any name?   85
  What for order or degree?

"Let me screw thee up a peg;
  Let me loose thy tongue with wine;
Callest thou that thing a leg?
  Which is thinnest? thine or mine?   90

"Thou shalt not be saved by works,
  Thou hast been a sinner too;
Ruin'd trunks on wither'd forks,
  Empty scarecrows, I and you!

"Fill the cup and fill the can,   95
  Have a rouse before the morn;
Every moment dies a man,
  Every moment[6] one is born.

"We are men of ruin'd blood;
  Therefore comes it we are wise.   100
Fish are we that love the mud,
  Rising to no fancy-flies.

"Name and fame! to fly sublime
  Thro' the courts, the camps, the schools,
Is to be the ball of Time,   105
  Bandied by the hands of fools.

"Friendship! — to be two in one —
  Let the canting liar pack!
Well I know, when I am gone,
  How she mouths behind my back.   110

"Virtue! — to be good and just —
  Every heart, when sifted well,
Is a clot of warmer dust,
  Mix'd with cunning sparks of hell.

"O, we two as well can look   115
  Whited thought and cleanly life

---

6. The mathematician Charles Babbage objected to the original word, *minute:* "I would therefore take the liberty of suggesting in the next edition of your excellent poem the erroneous caculation to which I refer should be corrected as follows: 'Every minute dies a man / and one and a sixteenth is born'" (Martin's *Tennyson,* p. 462). Even Tennyson couldn't construct meter for *that* line, as both knew, but the poet did change *minute* to *moment* (Reiff).

As the priest, above his book
   Leering at his neighbor's wife.

"Fill the cup and fill the can,
   Have a rouse before the morn: 120
Every moment dies a man,
   Every moment one is born.

"Drink, and let the parties rave;
   They are fill'd with idle spleen,
Rising, falling, like a wave,   125
   For they know not what they mean.

"He that roars for liberty
   Faster binds a tyrant's power,
And the tyrant's cruel glee
   Forces on the freer hour.   130

"Fill the can and fill the cup;
   All the windy ways of men
Are but dust that rises up,
   And is lightly laid again.

"Greet her with applausive breath,   135
   Freedom, gaily doth she tread;
In her right a civic wreath,
   In her left a human head.[7]

"No, I love not what is new;
   She is of an ancient house,   140
And I think we know the hue
   Of that cap upon her brows.

"Let her go! her thirst she slakes
   Where the bloody conduit runs,
Then her sweetest meal she makes   145
   On the first-born of her sons.

"Drink to lofty hopes that cool,—
   Visions of a perfect State;
Drink we, last, the public fool,
   Frantic love and frantic hate.   150

"Chant me now some wicked stave,
   Till thy drooping courage rise,
And the glow-worm of the grave
   Glimmer in thy rheumy[8] eyes.

7. Probably an allusion to the French Revolution. Compare "The Palace of Art," lines 151–52. Until the Reign of Terror, several of the first generation of Romantic poets, notably Coleridge and Wordsworth, had high hopes for the Revolution, the "lofty hopes" of line 147.
8. Diseased and watery.

"Fear not thou to loose thy tongue,   155
    Set thy hoary fancies free;
What is loathsome to the young
    Savors well to thee and me.

"Change, reverting to the years,
    When thy nerves could understand   160
What there is in loving tears,
    And the warmth of hand in hand.

"Tell me tales of thy first love—
    April hopes, the fools of chance—
Till the graves begin to move,   165
    And the dead begin to dance.

"Fill the can and fill the cup;
    All the windy ways of men
Are but dust that rises up,
    And is lightly laid again.   170

"Trooping from their mouldy dens
    The chap-fallen circle spreads—
Welcome, fellow-citizens,
    Hollow hearts and empty heads!

"You are bones, and what of that?   175
    Every face, however full,
Padded round with flesh and fat,
    Is but modell'd on a skull.

"Death is king, and Vivat Rex!
    Tread a measure on the stones,   180
Madam—if I know your sex
    From the fashion of your bones.

"No, I cannot praise the fire
    In your eye—nor yet your lip;
All the more do I admire   185
    Joints of cunning workmanship.

"Lo! God's likeness—the ground-plan—
    Neither modell'd, glazed, nor framed;
Buss⁹ me, thou rough sketch of man,
    Far too naked to be shamed!   190

"Drink to Fortune, drink to Chance,
    While we keep a little breath!
Drink to heavy Ignorance!
    Hob-and-nob with brother Death!

9. Kiss.

"Thou art mazed, the night is long,   195
  And the longer night is near—
What! I am not all as wrong
  As a bitter jest is dear.

"Youthful hopes, by scores, to all,
  When the locks are crisp and curl'd;   200
Unto me my maudlin gall
  And my mockeries of the world.

"Fill the cup and fill the can;
  Mingle madness, mingle scorn!
Dregs of life, and lees of man;   205
  Yet we will not die forlorn."

                       5
The voice grew faint; there came a further change;
Once more uprose the mystic mountain-range.
Below were men and horses pierced with worms,
And slowly quickening into lower forms: 210
By shards and scurf[1] of salt, and scum of dross,
Old plash of rains, and refuse patch'd with moss.
Then some one spake: "Behold! it was a crime
Of sense avenged by sense that wore with time."
Another said: "The crime of sense became   215
The crime of malice, and is equal blame."
And one: "He had not wholly quench'd his power;

A little grain of conscience made him sour."
At last I heard a voice upon the slope
Cry to the summit, "Is there any hope?"[2]   220
To which an answer peal'd from that high land,
But in a tongue no man could understand;
And on the glimmering limit far withdrawn
God made Himself an awful rose of dawn.[3]

                                            1842

1. Flakes. "Shards": scales. A devolution of life into the primeval state.
2. Compare *IM* 55, 5: "And faintly trust the larger hope." Also "The Two Voices," line 185: "Beyond the
   furthest flights of hope."
3. When John Tyndall asked Tennyson to explain the line, he answered evasively: "the power of explaining such concentrated expressions of the imagination was very different from that of writing them" (*Memoir* II, 475). More revealing is a passage from a letter to Emily Sellwood in 1839: "To me often the far-off
   world seems nearer than the present, for in the present is always something unreal and indistinct, but the
   other seems a good solid planet, rolling round its green hills and paradises to the harmony of more steadfast laws. There steam up from about me mists of weakness, or sin, or despondency, and roll between me
   and the far planet, but it is there still" (*Memoir* I, 171–72).

To ———[1]

After Reading a Life and Letters

Cursed be he that moves my bones.
—Shakespeare's Epitaph

You might have won the Poet's name,
    If such be worth the winning now,
    And gain'd a laurel for your brow
Of sounder leaf than I can claim;

But you have made the wiser choice,   5
    A life that moves to gracious ends
    Thro' troops of unrecording friends,
A deedful life, a silent voice.

And you have miss'd the irreverent doom
    Of those that wear the Poet's crown;   10
    Hereaftter, neither knave nor clown
Shall hold their orgies at your tomb.

For now the Poet cannot die,
    Nor leave his music as of old,
    But round him ere he scarce be cold   15
Begins the scandal and the cry:

"Proclaim the faults he would not show;
    Break lock and seal, betray the trust;
    Keep nothing scared, 't is but just
The many-headed beast should know."   20

Ah, shameless! for he did but sing
    A song that pleased us from its worth;
    No public life was his on earth,
No blazon'd statesman he, nor king.

He gave the people of his best;   25
    His worst he kept, his best he gave.
    My Shakespeare's curse on clown and knave
Who will not let his ashes rest!

Who make it seem more sweet to be
    The little life of bank and brier,   30
    The bird that pipes his lone desire
And dies unheard within his tree,

1. Probably addressed to the poet's brother Charles, who had exchanged the life of a poet for that of a country clergyman. The "Life and Letters" may be Richard Monckton Milnes's *Life, Letters and Literary Remains of John Keats* (1848). Tennyson "was indignant that Keats's wild love-letters should have been published," but he disclaimed any particular reference. He often expressed his own dread of trial by biographers, wanting his work to stand for his life. Compare "The Dead Prophet" (1885).

Than he that warbles long and loud
And drops at Glory's temple-gates,

For whom the carrion vulture waits   35
To tear his heart before the crowd!

1849

THE PRINCESS

Hallam Tennyson says his father believed the subject of *The Princess* was "original" and "it may have suggested itself when the project of a Women's College was in the air." In a note: "He talked over the plan of the poem with my mother in 1839" (*Memoir* I, 247–48). "I believe the *Vindication of the Rights of Woman*, by Mary Wollstonecraft (1792) first turned the attention of the people of England to the 'wrongs of women'" [Tennyson headnote]. But Hallam also remarked: "It may have arisen in its mock-heroic form from a Cambridge joke." If, indeed, the poem had been first conceived of as a nonserious treatment of a serious issue, it clearly evolved into something more than that.

Just how far any Victorian male, given the temper of the times, could be capable of any disinterested, objective discourse addressing the rights of women remains, of course, a heatedly debated point. John Stuart Mill's essay *The Subjection of Women*, conceived of and written all but contemporaneously with Tennyson's poem, may indeed be the *sine qua non*, in the Latin, root sense of the phrase. Yet, among writers with a large public audience, Daniel Defoe had been perhaps the first Englishman to publish genuine concern for the absence of educational opportunities for women. In *An Essay on Projects* (1697) arguing for "an academy for Women," Defoe wrote:

> I have often thought of it as one of the most barbarous customs in the world, considering us as a civilized and Christian country, that we deny the advantages of education to women. . . . The academy I propose should differ little from public schools [Eton and Harrow], wherein such ladies as were willing to study should have all the advantages of learning suitable to their genius.

Although the idea of constructing a poem on the subject may have been "original"—the subject itself was certainly not.

After publication in 1847, the "medley" was much altered through numerous editions, making it the most worked over of the longer poems. (See Ricks's *Tennyson* for an exhaustive account.) The constant tinkering does show the poet's continuing dissatisfaction with the work. Frederick Locker-Lampson records that in 1869, "He talked of *The Princess* with something of regret, of its fine blank verse, and the many good things in it: 'but,' said he, 'though truly original, it is, after all, only a medley' (*Memoir* II, 70–71). Although highly regarded throughout the three decades following its printing, the poem declined in popularity thereafter and was marked by Gilbert and Sullivan's successful parody in the operetta *Princess Ida* (1884). Perhaps the multitude of points of view, possibly the result of a half-serious, half-mocking tone, *The Princess* continues to puzzle. FitzGerald reportedly said that "he gave up all hope of Tennyson after *The Princess*" (*Memoir* I, 253). "My book is out and I hate it, and so no doubt will you," Tennyson wrote FitzGerald (*Memoir* I, 260). The poet's long, sustained though fractious friendship with the

author of the *Rubaiyat of Omar Khayyam* (1859) shows Tennyson knew his
friend— and certainly the other way around. "Old Fitz" was faithful to the last (see
"Tiresias" and notes).

No other single poem of Tennyson's has received greater critical attention over
the last quarter century than has *The Princess.* Justifiably, scholars have "rediscovered" the poem, finding its concerns over women's rights of signal importance. (See
Eve Sedgwick in the "Criticism" section of this book.) It would not be an exaggeration to say that the poem currently enjoys its pre-1884 popularity, a rare event for
any poem from the Victorian period. The "Selected Bibliography" of this book attempts, at the very least, to indicate the wide-ranging critical interest in it. The over-
all quality of *The Princess* as a poem in its own right evidently remains, as at the
outset, an open issue for debate—with a vengeance.

The Princess

A Medley

PROLOGUE[1]

Sir Walter Vivian all a summer's day
Gave his broad lawns until the set of sun
Up to the people; thither flock'd at noon
His tenants, wife and child, and thither half

The neighboring borough with their Institute,   5
Of which he was the patron. I was there
From college, visiting the son,—the son
A Walter too,—with others of our set,
Five others; we were seven at Vivian-place.
    And me that morning Walter show'd the house,   10
Greek, set with busts. From vases in the hall
Flowers of all heavens, and lovelier than their names,
Grew side by side; and on the pavement lay
Carved stones of the Abbey-ruin in the park,
Huge Ammonites[2] and the first bones of Time;   15
And on the tables every clime and age
Jumbled together; celts and calumets,[3]
Claymore and snow-shoe, toys in lava, fans
Of sandal, amber, ancient rosaries,
Laborious orient ivory sphere in sphere,   20
The cursed Malayan crease[4] and battle-clubs
From the isles of palm; and higher on the walls,
Betwixt the monstrous horns of elk and deer,
His own forefathers' arms and armor hung.

1. "The Prologue was written about a feast of the Mechanic's Institute held in the Lushingtons' grounds at
   Park House, near Maidstone, 6th July 1842" (Tennyson).
2. The coiled, flat, chambered fossil shells of an extinct mollusk from the Cretaceous Period.
3. Tennyson said, "Longfellow sent me one of these pipes of peace, which belonged to a Red Indian Chief."
   "Celts": prehistoric or metal tools shaped like a chisel or ax head.
4. I.e., kris, a Malayan dagger with a wavy double-edged blade.

And 'this,' he said, 'was Hugh's at Agin-court;   25
And that was old Sir Ralph's at Ascalon.[5]
A good knight he! we keep a chronicle
With all about him,'—which he brought, and I
Dived in a hoard of tales that dealt with knights
Half-legend, half-historic, counts and kings   30
Who laid about them at their wills and died;
And mixt with these a lady, one that arm'd
Her own fair head, and sallying thro' the gate,
Had beat her foes with slaughter from her walls.

        'O miracle of women,' said the book,   35
'O noble heart who, being strait-besieged
By this wild king to force her to his wish,
Nor bent, nor broke, nor shunn'd a soldier's death,
But now when all was lost or seem'd as loss—
Her stature more than mortal in the burst   40
Of sunrise, her arm lifted, eyes on fire—
Brake with a blast of trumpets from the gate,
And, falling on them like a thunderbolt,
She trampled some beneath her horses' heels.
And some were whelm'd with missiles of the wall,   45
And some were push'd with lances from the rock,
And part were drown'd within the whirling brook;
O miracle of noble womanhood!'

        So sang the gallant glorious chronicle;
And, I all rapt in this, 'Come out,' he said   50
'To the Abbey; there is Aunt Elizabeth
And sister Lilia with the rest.' We went—
I kept the book and had my finger in it—
Down thro' the park. Strange was the sight to me;
For all the sloping pasture murmur'd, sown   55
With happy faces and with holiday.
There moved the multitude, a thousand heads;
The patient leaders of their Institute
Taught them with facts. One rear'd a font of stone
And drew, from butts of water on the slope,   60
The fountain of the moment, playing, now
A twisted snake, and now a rain of pearls,
Or steep-up spout whereon the gilded ball
Danced like a wisp; and somewhat lower down
A man with knobs and wires and vials fire   65
A cannon; Echo answer'd in her sleep
From hollow fields; and here were telescopes
For azure views; and there a group of girls
In circle waited, whom the electric shock
Dislink'd with shrieks and laughter; round to lake   70
A little clock-work steamer paddling plied
And shook the lilies; perch'd about the knolls

5. An ancient city of southwest Palestine on the Mediterranean and seat of worship for the goddess Astarte. Here perhaps referring to Richard I's victory over the Saracens in 1192 (Ricks).

A dozen angry models jetted steam;
A petty railway ran; a fire-balloon[6]
Rose gem-like up before the dusky groves   75
And dropt a fairy parachute and past;
And there thro' twenty posts of telegraph
They flash'd a saucy message to and fro
Between the mimic stations; so that sport
Went hand in hand with science; other-where   80
Pure sport; a herd of boys with clamor bowl'd
And stump'd the wicket; babies roll'd about
Like tumbled fruit in grass; and men and maids
Arranged a country dance, and flew thro' light
And shadow, while the twangling violin   85
Struck up with Soldier-laddie, and overhead
The broad ambrosial aisles of lofty lime
Made noise with bees and breeze from end to end.

    Strange was the sight and smacking of the time;
And long we gazed, but satiated at length   90
Came to the ruins. High-arch'd and ivy-claspt,
Of finest Gothic lighter than a fire,
Thro' one wide chasm of time and frost they gave
The park, the crowd, the house; but all within
The sward was trim as any garden lawn.   95
And here we lit on Aunt Elizabeth,
And Lilia with the rest, and lady friends
From neighbor seats; and there was Ralph himself,
A broken statue propt against the wall,
As gay as any. Lilia, wild with sport,   100
Half child, half woman as she was, had wound
A scarf of orange round the stony helm,
And robed the shoulders in a rosy silk,
That made the old warrior from his ivied nook
Glow like a sunbeam. Near his tomb a feast   105
Shone, silver-set; about it lay the guests,
And there we join'd them; then the maiden aunt
Took this fair day for text, and from it preach'd
An universal culture for the crowd,
And all things great. But we, unworthier, told   110
Of college: he had climb'd across the spikes,
And he had squeezed himself betwixt the bars,
And he had breathed[7] the Proctor's dogs; and one
Discuss'd his tutor, rough to common men,
But honeying at the whisper of a lord;   115
And one the Master, as rogue in grain
Veneer'd with sanctimonious theory.

    But while they talk'd, above their heads I saw
The feudal warrior lady - clad; which brought
My book to mind, and opening this I read   120

6. A balloon that rises by heated air and not lighter-than-air gas.
7. "Made the proctor's attendants out of breath" (Tennyson).

Of old Sir Ralph a page or two that rang
With tilt and tourney; then the tale of her
That drove her foes with slaughter from her walls,
And much I praised her nobleness, and 'Where,'
Ask'd Walter, patting Lilia's head—she lay   125
Beside him—'lives there such a woman now?'

    Quick answer'd Lilia: 'There are thousands now
Such women, but convention beats them down;
It is but bringing up; no more than that.
You men have done it—how I hate you all!   130
Ah, were I something great! I wish I were
Some mighty poetess, I would shame you then,
That love to keep us children! O, I wish
That I were some great princess, I would build
Far off from men a college like a man's,   135
And I would teach them all that men are taught;
We are twice as quick!' And here she shook aside
The hand that play'd the patron with her curls.

    And one said smiling: 'Pretty were the sight
If our old halls could change their sex, and flaunt   140
With prudes for proctors, dowagers for deans,
And sweet girl-graduates in their golden hair.[8]
I think they should not wear our rusty gowns,
But move as rich as Emperor-moths, or Ralph
Who shines so in the corner; yet I fear,   145
If there were many Lilias in the brood,
However deep you might embower the nest,
Some boy would spy it.'
                    At this upon the sward
She tapt her tiny silken-sandall'd foot:
'That's your light way; but I would make it death   150
For any male thing but to peep at us.'

    Petulant she spoke, and at herself she laugh'd;
A rosebud set with little wilful thorns,
And sweet as English air could make her, she!
But Walter hail'd a score of names upon her,   155
And 'petty Ogress,' and 'ungrateful Puss,'
And swore he long'd at college, only long'd,
And else was well, for she-society.
They boated and they cricketed; they talk'd
At wine, in clubs, of art, of politics;   160
They lost their weeks; they vext the souls of deans;
They rode; they betted; made a hundred friends,
And caught the blossom of the flying terms,
But miss'd the mignonette of Vivian-place,
The little hearth-flower Lilia. Thus he spoke,   165

---

8. Compare Keats's *Lamia* I, lines 197–98: "as though in Cupid's college she had spent / Sweet days a lovely
graduate" (as noted by Ricks).

Part banter, part affection.
                    "'True,' she said,
'We doubt not that. O, yes, you miss'd us much!
I'll stake my ruby ring upon it you did.'

        She held it out; and as a parrot turns
Up thro' gilt wires a crafty loving   170
And takes a lady's finger with all care,
And bites it for true heart and not for harm,
So he with Lilia's. Daintily she shriek'd
And wrung it. 'Doubt my word again!' he said.
'Come, listen! here is proof that you were miss'd: 175
We seven stay'd at Christmas up to read;
And there we took one tutor as to read.
The hard-grain'd Muses of the cube and square
Were out of season; never man, I think,
So moulder'd in a sinecure as he;   180
For while our cloisters echo'd frosty feet,
And our long walks were stript as bare as brooms,
We did but talk you over, pledge you all
In wassail; often, like as many girls—
Sick for the hollies and the yews of home—   185
As many little trifling Lilias—play'd
Charades and riddles as at Christmas here,
And *what's my thought* and *when and where and how*,
And often told a tale[9] from mouth to mouth
As here at Christmas.
                    She remember'd that;   190
A pleasant game, she thought. She liked it more
Than magic music, forfeits, all the rest.
But these—what kind of tales did men tell men,
She wonder'd, by themselves?
                    A half-disdain
Perch'd on the pouted blossom of her lips;   195
And Walter nodded at me: '*He* began,
The rest would follow, each in turn; and so
We forged a sevenfold story. Kind? what kind?
Chimeras, crotchets, Christmas solecisms;
Seven-headed monsters only made to kill   200
Time by the fire in winter.'
                    'Kill him now,
The tyrant! kill him in the summer too,'
Said Lilia; 'Why not now?' the maiden aunt.
'Why not a summer's as a winter's tale?[1]
A tale for summer as befits the time,   205
And something it should be to suit the place,
Heroic, for a hero lies beneath,
Grave, solemn!'
                    Walter warp'd his mouth at this

9. "A game which I have more than once played when I was at Trinity College, Cambridge, with my
   brother-under-graduates" (Tennyson).
1. *Winter's Tale* II, i, lines 25–26: "A sad tale's best for winter: I have one / Of sprites and goblins."

To something so mock-solemn, that I laugh'd,
And Lilia woke with sudden-shrilling mirth   210
An echo like a ghostly woodpecker
Hid in the ruins; till the maiden aunt—
A little sense of wrong had touch'd her face
With color—turn'd to me with 'As you will;
Heroic if you will, or what you will,   215
Or be yourself your hero if you will.'

    'Take Lilia, then, for heroine,' clamor'd he,
'And make her some great princess, six feet high,
Grand, epic, homicidal; and be you
The prince to win her!'
                    'Then follow me, the prince,   220
I answer'd, 'each be hero in his turn!
Seven and yet one, like shadows in a dream.—
Heroic seems our princess as required—
But something made to suit with time and place,
A Gothic ruin and a Grecian house,   225
A talk of college and of ladies' rights,
A feudal knight in silken masquerade,
And, yonder, shrieks and strange experiments
For which the good Sir Ralph had burnt them all—
This *were* a medley! we should have him back   230
Who told the "Winter's Tale" to do it for us.
No matter; we will say whatever comes.
And let the ladies sing us, if they will,
From time to time, some ballad or a song
To give us breathing-space.'
                    So I began,   235
And the rest follow'd; and the women sang
Between the rougher voices of the men,
Like linnets in the pauses of the wind:
And here I give the story and the songs.

                    I

A Prince I was, blue-eyed, and fair in face,
Of temper amorous as the first of May,
With lengths of yellow ringlet, like a girl,
For on my cradle shone the Northern star.

    There lived an ancient legend in our house.   5
Some sorcerer, whom a far-off grandsire burnt
Because he cast no shadow, had foretold,
Dying, that none of all our blood should know
The shadow from the substance, and that one
Should come to fight with shadows and to fall;   10
For so, my mother said, the story ran.
And, truly, waking dreams were, more or less,
An old and strange affection of the house.
Myself too had weird seizures, Heaven knows what!

On a sudden in the midst of men and day,   15
And while I walk'd and talk'd as heretofore,
I seem'd to move among a world of ghosts,
And feel myself the shadow of a dream.
Our great court-Galen[2] poised his gilt-head cane,
And paw'd his bear, and mutter'd 'catalepsy.'   20
My mother pitying made a thousand prayers.
My mother was as mild as any saint,
Half-canonized by all that look'd on her,
So gracious was her tact and tenderness;
But my good father thought a king a king.   25
He cared not for the affection of the house;
He held his sceptre like a pedant's wand
To lash offence, and with long arms and hands
Reach'd out and pick'd offenders from the mass
For judgment.
                Now it chanced that I had been,   30
While life was yet in bud and blade, betroth'd
To one, a neighboring Princess. She to me
Was proxy-wedded[3] with a bootless calf
At eight years old; and still from time to time
Came murmurs of her beauty from the South,   35
And of her brethren, youths of puissance;
And still I wore her picture by my heart,
And one dark tress; and all around them both
Sweet thoughts would swarm as bees about their queen.

But when the days drew nigh that I should wed,   40
My father sent ambassadors with furs
And jewels, gifts, to fetch her. These brought back
A present, a great labor of the loom;
And therewithal an answer vague as wind.
Besides, they saw the king; he took the gifts;   45
He said there was a compact; that was true;
But then she had a will; was he to blame?
And maiden fancies; loved to live alone
Among her women; certain, would not wed.

That morning in the presence room I stood   50
With Cyril and with Florian, my two friends:
The first, a gentleman of broken means—
His father's fault—but given to starts and bursts
Of revel; and the last, my other heart,
And almost my half-self, for still we moved   55
Together, twinn'd as horse's ear and eye.

2. "The great doctor of Pergamus, 131 to 200 A.D." (Tennyson).
3. "The proxy of the king used to place his bare leg under the coverlet of the king's betrothed" (Tennyson).
"Bacon in his *Henry VII* writes of the proxy marriage of Maximilian the king of the Romans, with Anne
of Brittany, 1489: 'For she was not only publicly contracted, but stated as a bride, and solemnly bedded;
and after she was laid, there came in Maximilian's ambassador, with letters of procuration, and in the
presence of sundry noble personages, men and women, put his leg, stript naked to the knee, between the
espousal sheets; to the end that the ceremony might be thought to amount to a consummation and actual knowledge'" (Hallam Tennyson).

  Now, while they spake, I saw my father's face
Growing long and troubled like a rising room,
Inflamed with wrath. He started on his feet,
Tore the king's letter, snow'd it down, and rent   60
The wonder of the loom thro' warp and woof
From skirt to skirt; and at the last he sware
That he would send a hundred thousand men,
And bring her in a whirlwind; then he chew'd
The thrice-turn'd cud of wrath, and cook'd his spleen,   65
Communing with his captains of the war.

  At last I spoke: 'My father, let me go.
It cannot be but some gross error lies
In this report, this answer of a king
Whom all men rate as kind and hospitable;   70
Or, maybe, I myself, my bride once seen,
Whate'er my grief to find her less than fame,
May rue the bargain made.' And Florian said:
'I have a sister at the foreign court,
Who moves about the Princess; she, you know,   75
Who wedded with a nobleman from thence.
He, dying lately, left her, as I hear,
The lady of three castles in that land;
Thro' her this matter might be sifted clean.'
And Cyril whisper'd: 'Take me with you too.'   80
Then laughing, 'What if these weird seizures come
Upon you in those lands, and no one near
To point you out the shadow from the truth!
Take me; I'll serve you better in a strait;
I grate on rusty hinges here.' But 'No!   85
Roar'd the rough king, 'you shall not; we ourself
Will crush her pretty maiden fancies dead
In iron gauntlets; break the council up.'

  But when the council broke, I rose and past
Thro' the wild woods that hung about the town;   90
Found a still place, and pluck'd her likeness out;
Laid it on flowers, and watch'd it lying bathed
In the green gleam of dewy-tassell'd trees.
What were those fancies? wherefore break her troth?
Proud look'd the lips; but while I meditated   95
A wind arose and rush'd upon the South,
And shook the songs, the whispers, and the shrieks
Of the wild woods together, and a Voice
Went with it, 'Follow, follow, thou shalt win.'

  Then, ere the silver sickle of that month   100
Became her golden shield, I stole from court
With Cyril and with Florian, unperceived,
Cat-footed thro' the town and half in dread
To hear my father's clamor at our backs
With 'Ho!' from some bay-window shake the night;   105

But all was quiet. From the bastion'd walls
Like threaded spiders, one by one, we dropt,
And flying reach'd the frontier; then we crost
To a livelier land; and so by tilth and grange,
And vines, and blowing bosks[4] of wilderness,   110
We gain'd the mother-city thick with towers,
And in the imperial palace found the king.

    His name was Gama; crack'd and small his voice,
But bland the smile that like a wrinkling wind
On glassy water drove his cheek in lines;   115
A little dry old man, without a star,
Not like a king. Three days he feasted us,
And on the fourth I spake of why we came,
And my betroth'd. 'You do us, Prince,' he said,
Airing a snowy hand and signet gem,   120
'All honor. We remember love ourself
In our sweet youth. There did a compact pass
Long summers back, a kind of ceremony—
I think the year in which our olives fail'd.
I would you had her, Prince, with all my heart,   125
With my full heart; but there were widows here,
Two widows, Lady Psyche, Lady Blanche;
They fed her theories, in and out of place
Maintaining that with equal husbandry
The woman were an equal to the man.   130
They harp'd on this; with this our banquets rang;
Our dances broke and buzz'd in knots of talk;
Nothing but this; my very ears were hot
To hear them. Knowledge, so my daughter held,
Was all in all; they had but been, she thought,   135
As children; they must lose the child, assume
The woman. Then, sir, awful odes she wrote,
Too awful, sure, for what they treated of,
But all she is and does is awful; odes
About this losing of the child; and rhymes   140
And dismal lyrics, prophesying change
Beyond all reason. These the women sang;
And they that know such things—I sought but peace;
No critic I—would call them masterpieces.
They master'd *me*. At last she begg'd a boon,   145
A certain summer-palace which I have
Hard by your father's frontier. I said no,
Yet being an easy man, gave it; and there,
All wild to found an University
For maidens, on the spur she fled; and more   150
We know not,—only this: they see no men,
Not even her brother Arac, nor the twins
Her brethren, tho' they love her, look upon her
As on a kind of paragon; and I—

4. "Blossoming thickets" (Tennyson).

Pardon me saying it—were much loth to breed   155
Dispute betwixt myself and mine; but since—
And I confess with right—you think me bound
In some sort, I can give you letters to her;
And yet, to speak the truth, I rate your chance
Almost at naked nothing.'
                                Thus the king;   160
And I, tho' nettled that he seem'd to slur
With garrulous ease and oily courtesies
Our formal compact, yet, not less—all frets
But chafing me on fire to find my bride—
Went forth again with both my friends.
                                    We rode   165
Many a long league back to the North.
                                    At last
From hills that look'd across a land of hope
We dropt with evening on a rustic town
Set in a gleaming river's crescent-curve,
Close at the boundary of the liberties;[5]   170
There, enter'd an old hostel, call'd mine host
To council, plied him with his richest wines,
And show'd the late-writ letters of the king.

He with a long low sibilation, stared
As blank as death in marble; then exclaim'd,   175
Averring it was clear against all rules
For any man to go; but as his brain
Began to mellow, 'If the king,' he said,
'Had given us letters, was he bound to speak?
The king would bear him out;' and at the last—   180
The summer of the vine in all his veins—
'No doubt that we might make it worth his while.
She once had past that way; he heard her speak;
She scared him; life! he never saw the like;
She look'd as grand as doomsday and as grave!   185
And he, he reverenced his liege-lady there;
He always made a point to post with mares;
His daughter and his housemaid were the boys;[6]
The land, he understood, for miles about
Was till'd by women; all the swine were sows,   190
And all the dogs'—
                            But while he jested thus,
A thought flash'd thro' me which I clothed in act,
Remembering how we three presented Maid,
Or Nymph, or Goddess, at high tide of feast,
In masque or pageant at my father's court.   195
We sent mine host to purchase female gear;
He brought it, and himself, a sight to shake

5. "Blackstone in his *Commentaries*, ii 37, defines a 'liberty' as a 'Royal privilege or branch of the King's prerogative, subsisting in the hands of a subject.' The term 'liberties' is here applied to the estate over which the privilege can be exercised" (Hallam Tennyson).
6. To guide the horses drawing a coach, the boy rides the near horse of the leaders; a postilion.

The midriff of despair with laughter, holp
To lace us up, till each in maiden plumes
We rustled; him we gave a costly bribe[7]   200
To guerdon silence, mounted our good steeds,
And boldly ventured on the liberties.

We follow'd up the river as we rode,
And rode till midnight, when the college lights
Began to glitter firefly-like in copse   205
And linden alley; then we past an arch,
Whereon a woman-statue rose with wings
From four wing'd horses dark against the stars,
And some inscription ran along the front,
But deep in shadow. Further on we gain'd   210
A little street half garden and half house,
But scarce could hear each other speak for noise
Of clocks and chimes, like silver hammers falling
On silver anvils, and the splash and stir
Of fountains spouted up and showering down   215
In meshes of the jasmine and the rose;
And all about us peal'd the nightingale,
Rapt in her song and careless of the snare.

There stood a bust of Pallas for a sign,
By two sphere lamps blazon'd like Heaven and Earth   220
With constellation and with continent,
Above an entry. Riding in, we call'd;
A plump-arm'd ostleress and a stable wench
Came running at the call, and help'd us down.
Then stept a buxom hostess forth, and sail'd,   225
Full-blown, before us into rooms which gave
Upon a pillar'd porch, the bases lost
In laurel. Her we ask'd of that and this,
And who were tutors. 'Lady Blanche' she said,
'And Lady Psyche.' 'Which was prettiest,   230
Best natured?' 'Lady Psyche.' 'Hers are we,'
One voice, we cried; and I sat down and wrote
In such a hand as when a field of corn
Bows all its ears before the roaring East:

'Three ladies of the Northern empire pray   235
Your Highness would enroll them with your own,
As Lady Psyche's pupils.'
                            This I seal'd;
The seal was Cupid bent above a scroll,

---

7. Lines 197–200 originally read: "we tweezered out / What slender blossom lived on lip or cheek / Of manhood, gave mine host a costly bribe." The *Quarterly Review*, Shannon observes (pp. 118–19), was probably responsible for the omission of these lines as ridiculed by the reviewer: "A hero 'blue-eyed and fair
   of face, with lengths of yellow ringlet like a girl,' who when he has '*tweezered* out the slender blossom of
   manhood that lives on his lip or cheek,' passes well for a tall young lady, can hardly grow in the course
   of a few months into a fitting mate for a magnificent princess." Shannon concludes that the poet thereby
   "was able to diminish the impression of the Prince's lack of manliness."

And o'er his head Uranian⁸ Venus hung,
And raised the blinding bandage from his eyes. 240
I gave the letter to be sent with dawn;
And then to bed, where half in doze I seem'd
To float about a glimmering night, and watch
A full sea glazed with muffled moonlight swell
On some dark shore just seen that it was rich. 245

    As thro' the land at eve we went,
      And pluck'd the ripen'd ears,
    We fell out, my wife and I,
      O, we fell out, I know not why,
    And kiss'd again with tears. 250
      And blessings on the falling out
    That all the more endears,
      When we fall out with those we love
    And kiss again with tears!
      For when we came where lies the child 255
    We lost in other years,
      There above the little grave,
    O, there above the little grave,
      We kiss'd again with tears.

II

At break of day the College Portress came;
She brought us academic silks, in hue
The lilac, with a silken hood to each,
And zoned with gold; and now when these were on,
And we as rich as moths from dusk cocoons, 5
She, curtseying her obeisance, let us know
The Princess Ida waited. Out we paced,
I first, and following thro' the porch that sang
All round with laurel, issued in a court
Compact of lucid marbles, boss'd with lengths 10
Of classic frieze, with ample awnings gay
Betwixt the pillars, and with great urns of flowers.
The Muses and the Graces, group'd in threes,
Enring'd a billowing fountain in the midst,
And here and there on lattice edges lay 15
Or book or lute; but hastily we past,
And up a flight of stairs into the hall.

    There at a board by tome and paper sat,
With two tame leopards couch'd beside her throne,
All beauty compass'd in a female form, 20
The Princess; liker to the inhabitant
Of some clear planet close upon the sun,
Than our man's earth; such eyes were in her head,
And so much grace and power, breathing down
From over her arch'd brows, with every turn 25

8. Urania was the heavenly love of Plato's *Symposium*.

Lived thro' her to the tips of her long hands,
And to her feet. She rose her height, and said:

We give you welcome; not without redound
Of use and glory to yourselves ye come,
The first-fruits of the stranger; aftertime,   30
And that full voice which circles round the grave,
Will rank you nobly, mingled up with me.
What! are the ladies of your land so tall?'
'We of the court,' said Cyril. 'From the court,'
She answer'd, 'then ye know the Prince?' and he: 35
'The climax of his age! as tho' there were
One rose in all the world, your Highness that,
He worships your ideal.' She replied:
'We scarcely thought in our own hall to hear
This barren verbiage, current among men,   40
Light coin, the tinsel clink of compliment.
Your flight from out your bookless wilds would seem
As arguing love of knowledge and of power;
Your language proves you still the child. Indeed,
We dream not of him; when we set our hand   45
To this great work, we purposed with ourself
Never to wed. You likewise will do well,
Ladies, in entering here, to cast and fling
The tricks which make us toys of men, that so
Some future time, if so indeed you will,   50
You may with those self-styled our lords ally
Your fortunes, justlier balanced, scale with scale.'

At those high words, we, conscious of ourselves,
Perused the matting; then an officer
Rose up, and read the statutes, such as these: 55
Not for three years to correspond with home;
Not for three years to cross the liberties;
Not for three years to speak with any men;
And many more, which hastily subscribed,
We enter'd on the boards.[9] And 'Now,' she cried,   60
'Ye are green wood, see ye warp not.
                                        Look, our hall!
Our statues! — not of those that men desire,
Sleek Odalisques,[1] or oracles of mode,
Nor stunted squaws of West or East; but she[2]
That taught the Sabine how to rule, and she   65
The foundress of the Babylonian wall,
The Carian Artemisia[3] strong in war,
The Rhodope[4] that built the pyramid,

---

9. "The college register" (Ricks).
1. "Female slaves of the harem" (Tennyson).
2. "The wood-nymph Egeria, who was said to have given the laws to Numa Pompilius" (Tennyson).
3. "She who fought so bravely for Xerxes at Salamis that he said that his women had become men and his men women" (Tennyson). "Foundress": "Semiramis" (Tennyson).
4. "A celebrated Greek courtesan of Thracian origin, who was said to have built a pyramid near Memphis"

Clelia, Cornelia, with the Palmyrene[5]
That fought Aurelian, and the Roman brows   70
Of Agrippina.[6] Dwell with these, and lose
Convention, since to look on noble forms
Makes noble thro' the sensuous organism
That which is higher. O, lift your natures up;
Embrace our aims; work out your freedom. Girls,   75
Knowledge is now no more a fountain seal'd!
Drink deep, until the habits of the slave,
The sins of emptiness, gossip and spite
And slander, die. Better not be at all
Than not be noble. Leave us; you may go.   80
To-day the Lady Psyche will harangue
The fresh arrivals of the week before;
For they press in from all the provinces,
And fill the hive.'
             She spoke, and bowing waved
Dismissal; back again we crost the court   85
To Lady Psyche's. As we enter'd in,
There sat along the forms, like morning doves
That sun their milky bosoms on the thatch,
A patient range of pupils; she herself
Erect behind a desk of satin-wood,   90
A quick brunette, well-moulded, falcon-eyed,
And on the hither side, or so she look'd,
Of twenty summers. At her left, a child,
In shining draperies, headed like a star,[7]
Her maiden babe, a double April old,   95
Aglaïa[8] slept. We sat; the lady glanced;
Then Florian, but no livelier than the dame
That whisper'd 'Asses' ears'[9] among the sedge,
'My sister.' 'Comely, too, by all that's fair,'
Said Cyril. 'O, hush, hush!' and she began.   100

'This world was once a fluid haze of light,[1]
Till toward the centre set the starry tides,
And eddied into suns, that wheeling cast
The planets; then the monster, then the man;
Tattoo'd or woaded, winter-clad in skins,   105
Raw from the prime, and crushing down his mate,
As yet we find in barbarous isles, and here
Among the lowest.'
            Thereupon she took
A bird's-eye view of all the ungracious past;

(Tennyson). Tennyson quotes from 1 Henry VI I, vi, lines 21–22: "A statlier pyramis to her I'll rear / Than Rhodope's of Memphis ever was."
5. "Zenobia, Queen of Palmyra" (Tennyson). "Clelia": She "who swam the Tiber [on horseback] in escaping from Porsenna's camp (Livy, ii, 13)" (Tennyson). "Cornelia": "mother of the Graacchi" (Tennyson).
6. "Grand-daughter of Augustus, married to Germanicus" (Tennyson).
7. "With bright golden hair" (Tennyson).
8. Brightness, one of the Three Graces.
9. "Midas in The Wyf of Bathe's Tale confides the secret of his asses' ears only to his wife" (Tennyson).
1. "The nebular theory as formulated by Laplace" (Tennyson). Compare IM 118, 9–12 and 89, 45–48 (and notes).

Glanced at the legendary Amazon[2]   110
As emblematic of a nobler age;
Appraised the Lycian custom,[3] spoke of those
That lay at wine with Lar and Lucumo;[4]
Ran down the Persian, Grecian, Roman lines
Of empire, and the woman's state in each,   115
How far from just, till warming with her theme
She fulmined out her scorn of laws Salique[5]
And little-footed[6] China, touch'd on Mahomet
With much contempt,[7] and came to chivalry,
When some respect, however slight, was paid   120
To woman, superstition all awry.
However, then commenced the dawn; a beam
Had slanted forward, falling in a land
Of promise;[8] fruit would follow. Deep, indeed,
Their debt of thanks to her who first had dared   125
To leap the rotten pales of prejudice,
Disyoke their necks from custom, and assert
None lordlier than themselves but that which made
Woman and man. She had founded; they must build.
Here might they learn whatever men were taught.   130
Let them not fear, some said their heads were less;
Some men's were small, not they the least of men;
For often fineness compensated size.
Besides the brain was like the hand, and grew
With using; thence the man's, if more was more.[9]   135
He took advantage of his strength to be
First in the field; some ages had been lost;
But woman ripen'd earlier, and her life
Was longer; and albeit their glorious names
Were fewer, scatter'd stars, yet since in truth   140
The highest is the measure of the man,
And not the Kaffir, Hottentot, Malay,
Nor those horn-handed breakers of the glebe,
But Homer, Plato, Verulam, even so
With woman; and in arts of government   145
Elizabeth and others, arts of war
The peasant Joan and others, arts of grace
Sappho and others vied with any man;
And, last not least, she who had left her place,
And bow'd her state to them, that they might grow   150
To use and power on this oasis, lapt
In the arms of leisure, sacred from the blight

2. "On feminism, 19th and 20th century, and the Amazons, see M. R. Lefkowitz, *TLS*, 27 Nov. 1981" (Ricks).
3. "Herodotus (i 173) says that the Lycians took their names from their mothers instead of their fathers"
   (Tennyson).
4. "An Etruscan prince or priest" (Tennyson). "Lar": "signifies Noble" (Hallam Tennyson).
5. "The laws of the Salian Franks forbad inheritance by women" (Tennyson).
6. Reference to the Chinese practice of binding the feet of very young girls; as they grow the bones may
   break, forming the desired malformation.
7. "Had she heard that, according to the Mohammedan doctrine, hell was chiefly occupied by women?"
   (Tennyson). "True? So Byron wished" (Wilders).
8. Hebrews 11:9.
9. "Greater in size meant greater in power" (Tennyson).

Of ancient influence and scorn.
                                   At last
She rose upon a wind of prophecy
Dilating on the future: 'everywhere   155
Two heads in council, two beside the hearth,
Two in the tangled business of the world,
Two in the liberal offices of life,
Two plummets dropt for one to sound the abyss
Of science and the secrets of the mind;   160
Musician, painter, sculptor, critic, more;
And everywhere the broad and bounteous Earth
Should bear a double growth of those rare souls,
Poets, whose thoughts enrich the blood of the world.'

    She ended here, and beckon'd us; the rest   165
Parted; and, glowing full-faced welcome, she
Began to address us, and was moving on
In gratulation, till as when a boat
Tacks and the slacken'd sail flaps, all her voice
Faltering and fluttering in her throat, she cried,   170
'My brother!' 'Well, my sister,' 'O,' she said,
'What do you here? and in this dress? and these?
Why, who are these? a wolf within the fold!
A pack of wolves! the Lord be gracious to me!
A plot, a plot, a plot, to ruin all!'   175
'No plot, no plot,' he answer'd. 'Wretched boy,
How saw you not the inscription on the gate,
LET NO MAN ENTER IN ON PAIN OF DEATH?'
'And if I had,' he answer'd, 'who could think
The softer Adams of your Academe,   180
O sister, Sirens tho' they be, were such
As chanted on the blanching bones of men?'
'But you will find it otherwise,' she said.
'You jest; ill jesting with edge-tools! my vow
Binds me to speak, and O that iron will,   185
That axelike edge unturnable, our Head,
The Princess!' 'Well then, Psyche, take my life,
And nail me like a weasel on a grange
For warning; bury me beside the gate,
And cut this epitaph above my bones: 190
Here lies a brother by a sister slain,
All for the common good of womankind.'
'Let me die too,' said Cyril, 'having seen
And heard the Lady Psyche.'
                               I struck in:
'Albeit so mask'd, madam, I love the truth;   195
Receive it, and in me behold the Prince
Your countryman, affianced years ago
To the Lady Ida. Here, for here she was,
And thus—what other way was left?—I came.'
'O sir, O Prince, I have no country, none;   200
If any, this; but none, Whate'er I was

Disrooted, what I am is grafted here.
Affianced, sir? love-whispers may not breathe
Within this vestal limit, and how should I,
Who am not mine, say, live? The thunderbolt   205
Hangs silent; but prepare. I speak, it falls.'
'Yet pause,' I said: 'for that inscription there,
I think no more of deadly lurks therein,
Than in a clapper clapping in a garth,
To scare the fowl from fruit; if more there be,   210
If more and acted on, what follows? war;
Your own work marr'd; for this your Academe,
Whichever side be victor, in the halloo
Will topple to the trumpet down, and pass
With all fair theories only made to gild   215
A stormless summer.' 'Let the Princess judge
Of that,' she said: 'farewell, sir—and to you.
I shudder at the sequel, but I go.'

    'Are you that Lady Psyche,' I rejoin'd,
'The fifth in line from that old Florian,   220
Yet hangs his portrait in my father's hall—
The gaunt old baron with his beetle brow
Sun-shaded in the heat of dusty fights—
As he bestrode[1] my grandsire, when he fell,
And all else fled? we point to it, and we say,   225
The loyal warmth of Florian is not cold,
But branches current yet in kindred veins.
'Are you that Psyche,' Florian added; 'she
With whom I sang about the morning hills,
Flung ball, flew kite, and raced the purple fly,   230
And snared the squirrel of the glen? are you
That Psyche, wont to bind my throbbing brow,
To smooth my pillow, mix the foaming draught
Of fever, tell me pleasant tales, and read
My sickness down to happy dreams? are you   235
That brother-sister Psyche, both in one?
You were that Psyche, but what are you now?'
'You are that Psyche,' Cyril said, 'for whom
I would be that forever which I seem,
Woman, if I might sit beside your feet,   240
And glean your scatter'd sapience.'
                              Then once more,
'Are you that Lady Psyche,' I began,
'That on her bridal morn before she past
From all her old companions, when the king
Kiss'd her pale cheek, declared that ancient ties   245
Would still be dear beyond the southern hills;
That were there any of our people there
In want or peril, there was one to hear
And help them? look! for such are these and I.'

---

1. "In defence" (Tennyson). "Cf. Shakespeare, *I Henry IV*, V, i, 122, and *Comedy of Errors*, V, i, 192: 'when I bestrid thee in the wars'" (Hallam Tennyson).

'Are you that Psyche,' Florian ask'd, 'to whom,   250
In gentler days, your arrow-wounded fawn
Came flying while you sat beside the well?
The creature laid his muzzle on your lap
And sobb'd, and you sobb'd with it, and the blood
Was sprinkled on your kirtle, and you wept.   255
That was fawn's blood, not brother's, yet you wept.
O, by the bright head of my little niece,
You were that Psyche, and what are you now?'
'You are that Psyche,' Cyril said again,
'The mother of the sweetest little maid   260
That ever crow'd for kisses.'
                         'Out upon it!'
She answer'd, 'peace! and why should I not play
The Spartan Mother with emotion, be
The Lucius Junius Brutus[2] of my kind?
Him you call great; he for the common weal,   265
The fading politics of mortal Rome,
As I might slay this child, if good need were,
Slew both his sons; and I, shall I, on whom
The secular[3] emancipation turns
Of half this world, be swerved from right to save   270
A prince, a brother? a little will I yield.
Best so, perchance, for us, and well for you.
O, hard when love and duty clash! I fear
My conscience will not count me fleckless; yet—
Hear my conditions: promise—otherwise   275
You perish—as you came, to slip away
To-day, to-morrow, soon. It shall be said,
These women were too barbarous, would not learn;
They fled, who might have shamed us. Promise, all.'

    What could we else, we promised each; and she,   280
Like some wild creature newly-caged, commenced
A to-and-fro, so pacing till she paused
By Florian; holding out her lily arms
Took both his hands, and smiling faintly said:
'I knew you at the first; tho' you have grown   285
You scarce have alter'd. I am sad and glad
To see you, Florian. I give thee to death,
My brother! it was duty spoke, not I.
My needful seeming harshness, pardon it.
Our mother, is she well?'
                         With that she kiss'd   290
His forehead, then, a moment after, clung
About him, and betwixt them blossom'd up
From out a common vein of memory
Sweet household talk, and phrases of the hearth,
And far allusion, till the gracious dews   295
Began to glisten and to fall; and while

2. "Who condemned his sons to death for conspiracy against the city (Livy, ii, 5)" (Tennyson).
3. The infrequent dictionary definition: from century to century. "Lasting through ages" (Ricks).

They stood, so rapt, we gazing, came a voice,
'I brought a message here from Lady Blanche.'
Back started she, and turning round we saw
The Lady Blanche's daughter where she stood,   300
Melissa, with her hand upon the lock,
A rosy blonde, and in a college gown,
That clad her like an April daffodilly[4]—
Her mother's color—with her lips apart,
And all her thoughts as fair within her eyes,   305
As bottom agates seen to wave and float
In crystal currents of clear morning seas.[5]

   So stood that same fair creature at the door.
Then Lady Psyche, 'Ah—Melissa—you!
You heard us?' and Melissa, 'O, pardon me!   310
I heard, I could not help it, did not wish;
But, dearest lady, pray you fear me not,
Nor think I bear that heart within my breast,
To give three gallant gentlemen to death.'
'I trust you,' said the other, 'for we two   315
Were always friends, none closer, elm and vine;
But yet your mother's jealous temperament—
Let not your prudence, dearest, drowse, or prove
The Danaïd[6] of a leaky vase, for fear
This whole foundation ruin, and I lose   320
My honor, these their lives,' 'Ah, fear me not,'
Replied Melissa; 'no—I would not tell,
No, not for all Aspasia's[7] cleverness,
No, not to answer, madam, all those hard things
That Sheba[8] came to ask of Solomon.'   325
'Be it so,' the other, 'that we still may lead
The new light up, and culminate in peace,
For Solomon may come to Sheba yet.'
Said Cyril, 'Madam, he the wisest man
Feasted the woman wisest then, in halls   330
Of Lebanonian cedar; nor should you—
Tho', madam *you* should answer, *we* would ask—
Less welcome find among us, if you came
Among us, debtors for our lives to you,
Myself for something more." He said not what,   335
But 'Thanks,' she answer'd, 'go; we have been too long

---

4. Responding to the *Quarterly Review* objection to "April daffodilly," Tennyson noted that "in the North of England [they] belong as much to April as to March." Shannon records that for the third edition, of thirty-five passages "singled out by the reviewers for stricture . . . eight, or slightly less than a fourth, were altered" (p. 118). To challenge Tennyson's accuracy about flowers, despite his extreme nearsightedness, was as risky as questioning Wordsworth's with birds.
5. "It has been said that I took this simile partly from Beaumont and Fletcher, partly from Shakespeare, whereas I made it while I was bathing in Wales" (Tennyson).
6. As Hallam Tennyson notes, the allusion is "to the myth of the daughters of Danaus, condemned eternally [for murdering their husbands] to the hopeless task of filling a leaky vessel with water."
7. "Hostess to the finest literary and philosophical minds in Athens, and (as Turner notes) a hetaera and the mistress of Pericles" (Ricks).
8. "And when the queen of Sheba heard of the fame of Solomon concerning the name of the Lord, she came to prove him with hard questions. . . . And Solomon told her all the questions: there was not any thing hid from the king, which he told her not" (1 Kings 10:1, 3).

Together; keep your hoods about the face;
They do so that affect abstraction here.
Speak little; mix not with the rest; and hold
Your promise. All, I trust, may yet be well.'   340

    We turn'd to go, but Cyril took the child,
And held her round the knees against his waist,
And blew the swollen cheek of a trumpeter,
While Psyche watch'd them, smiling, and the child
Push'd her flat hand against his face and laugh'd;   345
And thus our conference closed.
                         And then we strolled
For half the day thro' stately theatres
Bench'd crescent-wise. In each we sat, we heard
The grave professor. On the lecture slate
The circle rounded under female hands   350
With flawless demonstration; follow'd then
A classic lecture, rich in sentiment,
With scraps of thunderous epic lilted out
By violet-hooded Doctors, elegies
And quoted odes, and jewels five-words-long   355
That on the stretch'd forefinger of all Time
Sparkle forever. Then we dipt in all
That treats of whatsoever is, the state,
The total chronicles of man, the mind,
The morals, something of the frame, the rock,   360
The star, the bird, the fish, the shell, the flower,
Electric, chemic laws, and all the rest,
And whatsoever can be taught and known;
Till like three horses that have broken fence,
And glutted all night long breast-deep in corn,   365
We issued gorged with knowledge, and I spoke:
'Why sirs, they do all this as well as we.'
'They hunt old trails,' said Cyril, 'very well;
But when did woman ever yet invent?'
'Ungracious!' answer'd Florian; 'have you learnt   370
No more from Psyche's lecture, you that talk'd
The trash that made me sick, and almost sad?'
'O, trash,' he said, 'but with a kernel in it!
Should I not call her wise who made me wise?
And learnt? I learnt more from her in a flash   375
Than if my brainpan were an empty hull,
And every Muse tumbled a science in.
A thousand hearts lie fallow in these halls,
And round these halls a thousand baby loves
Fly twanging headless arrows at the hearts,   380
Whence follows many a vacant pang; but O,
With me, sir enter'd in the bigger boy,
The head of all the golden-shafted firm,
The long-limb'd lad that had a Psyche[9] too;

9. For the legend of Cupid and Psyche, compare Keats's "Ode to Psyche," ll, lines 21–23: "the wingéd boy

He cleft me thro' the stomacher. And now   385
What think you of it, Florian? do I chase
The substance or the shadow? will it hold?
I have no sorcerer's malison on me,
No ghostly hauntings like his Highness. I
Flatter myself that always everywhere   390
I know the substance when I see it. Well,
Are castles shadows? Three of them? Is she
The sweet proprietress a shadow? If not,
Shall those three castles patch my tatter'd coat?
For dear are those three castles to my wants,   395
And dear is sister Psyche to my heart,
And two dear things are one of double worth;
And much I might have said, but that my zone[1]
Unmann'd me. Then the Doctors! O, to hear
The Doctors! O, to watch the thirsty plants   400
Imbibing! once or twice I thought to roar,
To break my chain, to shake my mane; but thou,
Modulate me, soul of mincing mimicry!
Make liquid treble of that bassoon, my throat;
Abase those eyes that ever loved to meet   405
Star-sisters answering under crescent brows;
Abate the stride which speaks of man, and loose
A flying charm of blushes o'er this cheek,
Where they like swallows coming out of time
Will wonder why they came. But hark the bell   410
For dinner, let us go!'
      And in we stream'd
Among the columns, pacing staid and still
By twos and threes, till all from end to end
With beauties every shade of brown and fair
In colors gayer than the morning mist,   415
The long hall glitter'd like a bed of flowers.[2]
How might a man not wander from his wits
Pierced thro' with eyes, but that I kept mine own
Intent on her, who rapt in glorious dreams,
The second-sight of some Astræan[3] age,   420
Sat compass'd with professors; they, the while,
Discuss'd a doubt and tost it to and fro.
A clamor thicken'd, mixt with inmost terms
Of art and science; Lady Blanche alone
Of faded form and haughtiest lineaments,   425
With all her autumn tresses falsely brown,
Shot sidelong daggers at us, a tiger-cat
In act to spring.
     At last a solemn grace

I knew; / But who wast thou, O happy, happy dove? / His Psyche true!" Given Tennyson's oft-noted echoes
of Keats, that line may have resonated in his ears.
1. A belt or girdle (archaic).
2. "Lady Psyche's 'side' (pupils) wore lilac robes, and Lady Blanche's robes of daffodil colour" (Tennyson).
3. "Astraea, daughter of Zeus and Themis, is to come back first of the celestials on the return of the Golden
Age [even as she was the last to leave earth in the Age of Iron]" (Tennyson; brackets enclose Hallam Tennyson's addition).

Concluded, and we sought the gardens. There
One walk'd reciting by herself, and one   430
In this hand held a volume as to read,
And smoothed a petted peacock down with that.
Some to a low song oar'd a shallop by,
Or under arches of the marble bridge
Hung, shadow'd from the heat; some hid and sought   435
In the orange thickets; others tost a ball
Above the fountain-jets, and back again
With laughter; others lay about the lawns,
Of the older sort, and murmur'd that their May
Was passing—what was learning unto them?   440
They wish'd to marry; they could rule a house;
Men hated learned women. But we three
Sat muffled like the Fates; and often came
Melissa hitting all we saw with shafts
Of gentle satire, kin to charity,   445
That harm'd not. They day droopt; the chapel bells
Call'd us; we left the walks; we mixt with those
Six hundred maidens clad in purest white,
Before two streams of light from wall to wall,
While the great organ almost burst his pipes   450
Groaning for power, and rolling thro' the court
A long melodious thunder to the sound
Of solemn psalms and silver litanies,
The work of Ida, to call down from heaven
A blessing on her labors for the world.   455

    Sweet and low, sweet and low,[4]
      Wind of the western sea,
   Low, low, breathe and blow,
      Wind of the western sea!

    Over the rolling waters go,   460
    Come from the dying moon, and blow,
      Blow him again to me;
   While my little one, while my pretty one sleeps.

    Sleep and rest, sleep and rest,
      Father will come to thee soon;   465
   Rest, rest, on mother's breast,
   Father will come to thee soon;
      Father will come to his babe in the nest,
   Silver sails all out of the west
      Under the silver moon;   470
   Sleep, my little one, sleep, my pretty one, sleep.

III

Morn in the white wake of the morning star
Came furrowing all the orient into gold.

---

4. This piece was written in 1849 and added in 1850. "Compare *Hero to Leander*, 33: 'Thy voice is sweet and
low' (contrasted with the sea). Also *The Lover's Tale*, i, 552: 'her voice was very sweet and low'" (Ricks).

We rose, and each by other drest with care
Descended to the court that lay three parts
In shadow, but the Muses' heads were touch'd   5
Above the darkness from their native East.

There while we stood beside the fount, and watch'd
Or seem'd to watch the dancing bubble, approach'd
Melissa, tinged with wan from lack of sleep,
Or grief, and glowing round her dewy eyes   10
The circled Iris⁵ of a night of tears;
And 'Fly,' she cried, 'O fly, while yet you may!
My mother knows.' And when I ask'd her 'how,'
'My fault,' she wept, 'my fault! and yet not mine;
Yet mine in part. O, hear me, pardon me!   15
My mother, 't is her wont from night to night
To rail at Lady Psyche and her side.
She says the Princess should have been the Head,
Herself and Lady Psyche the two arms;
And so it was agreed when first they came;   20
But Lady Psyche was the right hand now,
And she the left, or not or seldom used;
Hers more than half the students, all the love.
And so last night she fell to canvass you,
Her countrywomen! she did not envy her.   25
"Who ever saw such wild barbarians?
Girls?—more like men!" and at these words the snake,
My secret, seem'd to stir within my breast;
And O, sirs, could I help it, but my cheek
Began to burn and burn, and her lynx eye   30
To fix and make me hotter, till she laugh'd:
"O marvellously modest maiden, you!
Men! girls, like men! why, if they had been men
You need not set your thoughts in rubric⁶ thus
For wholesale comment." Pardon, I am shamed   35
That I must needs repeat for my excuse
What looks so little graceful: "men"—for still
My mother went revolving on the world—
"And so they are,—very like men indeed—
And with that woman closeted for hours!"   40
Then came these dreadful words out one by one,
"Why—these—*are*—men;" I shudder'd, "and you know it."
"O, ask me nothing," I said. "And she knows too,
And she conceals it." So my mother clutch'd
The truth at once, but with no word from me;   45
And now thus early risen she goes to inform
The Princess. Lady Psyche will be crush'd;
But you may yet be saved, and therefore fly;
But heal me with your pardon ere you go.'

5. Rainbow. "Compare *All's Well*, I, iii, 147–50: 'What's the matter, / That this distempered messenger of wet, / The many-coloured Iris, rounds thine eye? / Why? that you are my daughter?'" (Ricks).
6. In red, as in the rubrics in a prayer book.

'What pardon, sweet Melissa, for a blush?'   50
Said Cyril: 'Pale one, blush again; than wear
Those lilies, better blush our lives away.
Yet let us breathe for one hour more in heaven,'
He added, 'lest some classic angel speak
In scorn of us, "They mounted, Ganymedes,   55
To tumble, Vulcans,[7] on the second morn."
But I will melt this marble into wax
To yield us farther furlough;'[8] and he went.

Melissa shook her doubtful curls, and thought
He scarce would prosper. 'Tell us,' Florian ask'd,   60
'How grew this feud betwixt the right and left.'
'O, long ago,' she said, 'betwixt these two
Division smoulders hidden; 't is my mother,
Too jealous, often fretful as the wind
Pent in a crevice: much I bear with her.   65
I never knew my father, but she says—
God help her!—she was wedded to a fool;
And still she rail'd against the state of things.
She had the care of Lady Ida's youth,
And from the Queen's decease she brought her up.   70
But when your sister came she won the heart
Of Ida; they were still together, grew—
For so they said themselves—inosculated;[9]
Consonant chords that shiver to one note;[1]
One mind in all things. Yet my mother still   75
Affirms your Psyche thieved her theories,
And angled with them for her pupil's love;
She calls her plagiarist, I know not what.
But I must go; I dare not tarry,' and light,
As flies the shadow of a bird, she fled.   80

Then murmur'd Florian, gazing after her:
'An open-hearted maiden, true and pure.
If I could love, why this were she. How pretty
Her blushing was, and how she blush'd again,
As if to close with Cyril's random wish!   85
Not like your Princess cramm'd with erring pride,
Nor like poor Psyche whom she drags in tow.'

'The crane,' I said, 'may chatter of the crane,
The dove may murmur of the dove, but I
An eagle clang an eagle to the sphere.   90
My princess, O my princess! true she errs,
But in her own grand way; being herself

7. Ganymede was the beautiful Trojan boy whom Zeus took from earth to be cupbearer to the gods. Vulcan, in contrast, was hurled from heaven.
8. "Leave of absence, here permission in general" (Ricks).
9. Blended together, as in kissing.
1. "If two stringed instruments are together, and a note is struck on one, the other will vibrate with the same harmony" (Tennyson).

Three times more noble than three score of men,
She sees herself in every woman else,
And so she wears her error like a crown   95
To blind the truth and me. For her, and her,
Hebes[2] are they to hand ambrosia, mix
The nectar; but—ah, she—whene'er she moves
The Samian Herè[3] rises, and she speaks
A Memmon[4] smitten with the morning sun.   100

      So saying from the court we paced, and gain'd
The terrace ranged along the northern front,
And leaning there on those balusters, high
Above the empurpled champaign, drank the gale
That blown about the foliage underneath,   105
And sated with the innumerable rose,
Beat balm upon our eyelids. Hither came
Cyril, and yawning, 'O hard task,' he cried:
'No fighting shadows here. I forced a way
Thro' solid opposition crabb'd and gnarl'd.   110
Better to clear prime forests, heave and thump
A league of street in summer solstice down,
Than hammer at this reverend gentlewoman.
I knock'd and, bidden, enter'd; found her there
At point to move, and settled in her eyes   115
The green malignant light of coming storm.
Sir, I was courteous, every phrase well-oil'd,
As man's could be; yet maiden-meek I pray'd
Concealment. She demanded who we were,
And why we came? I fabled nothing fair,   120
But your example pilot, told her all.
Up went the hush'd amaze of hand and eye.
But when I dwelt upon your old affiance,
She answer'd sharply that I talk'd astray.
I urged the fierce inscription on the gate,   125
And our three lives. True—we had limed ourselves
With open eyes, and we must take the chance.
But such extremes, I told her, well might harm
The woman's cause. "Not more than now," she said,
"So puddled as it is with favoritism."   130
I tried the mother's heart. Shame might befall
Melissa, knowing, saying not she knew;
Her answer was, "Leave me to deal with that."
I spoke of war to come and many deaths,
And she replied, her duty was to speak,   135
And duty duty, clear of consequences.
I grew discouraged, sir; but since I knew
No rock so hard but that a little wave
May beat admission in a thousand years,

2. In Greek mythology, the goddess of spring and youth; also cupbearer to the Olympian gods.
3. "The Greek Herè, whose favourite abode was Samos" (Tennyson).
4. An Ethiopian king slain by Achilles and immortalized by Zeus. "The statue in Egypt which gave forth a
   musical note when 'smitten with the morning sun'" (Tennyson). See "The Palace of Art," line 171.

I recommended: "Decide not ere you pause.   140
I find you here but in the second place,
Some say the third—the authentic foundress you.
I offer boldly; we will seat you highest.
Wink at our advent; help my prince to gain
His rightful bride, and here I promise you   145
Some palace in our land, where you shall reign
The head and heart of all our fair sheworld,
And your great name flow on with broadening time
For ever." Well, she balanced this a little,
And told me she would answer us to-day,   150
Meantime be mute; thus much, nor more I gain'd.'

　　He ceasing, came a message from the Head.
'That afternoon the Princess rode to take
The dip of certain strata to the north.
Would we go with her? we should find the land   155
Worth seeing, and the river made a fall
Out yonder;' then she pointed on to where
A double hill ran up his furrowy forks
Beyond the thick-leaved platans of the vale.

　　Agreed to, this, the day fled on thro' all   160
Its range of duties to the appointed hour.
Then summon'd to the porch we went. She stood
Among her maidens, higher by the head,
Her back agains a pillar, her foot on one
Of those tame leopards. Kitten-like he roll'd   165
And paw'd about her sandal. I drew near;
I gazed. On a sudden my strange seizure came
Upon me, the weird vision of our house.
The Princess Ida seem'd a hollow show,
Her gay-furr'd cats a painted fantasy,   170
Her college and her maidens empty masks,
And I myself the shadow of a dream,
For all things were and were not. Yet I felt
My heart beat thick with passion and with awe;
Then from my breast the involuntary sigh   175
Brake, as she smote me with the light of eyes
That lent my knee desire to kneel, and shook
My pulses, till to horse we got, and so
Went forth in long retinue following up
The river as it narrow'd to the bills.   180

　　I rode beside her and to me she said:
'O friend, we trust that you esteem'd us not
Too harsh to your companion yestermorn;
Unwillingly we spake.' 'No—not to her,'
I answer'd, 'but to one of whom we spake   185
Your Highness might have seem'd the thing you say.'
'Again?' she cried, 'are you ambassadresses
From him to me? we give you, being strange,

A license; speak, and let the topic die.'
    I stammer'd that I knew him—could have wish'd—   190
'Our king expects—was there no precontract?
There is no truer-hearted—ah, you seem
All he prefigured, and he could not see
The bird of passage flying south but long'd
To follow. Surely, if your Highness keep   195
Your purport, you will shock him even to death,
Or baser courses, children of despair.'

    'Poor boy,' she said, 'can he not read—no books?
Quoit, tennis,[5] ball—no games? nor deals in that
Which men delight in, martial exercise?   200
To nurse a blind ideal like a girl,
Methinks he seems no better than a girl;
As girls were once, as we ourself have been.
We had our dreams; perhaps he mixt with them.
We touch on our dead self, nor shun to do it   205
Being other—since we learnt our meaning here,
To lift the woman's fallen divinity
Upon an even pedestal with man.'

    She paused, and added with a haughtier smile,
'And as to precontracts, we move, my friend,   210
At no man's beck, but know ourself and thee,
O Vashti, noble Vashti! Summon'd out
She kept her state, and left the drunken king
To brawl at Shushan underneath the palms.'

    'Alas, your Highness breathes full East,'[6] I said,   215
'On that which leans to you! I know the Prince,
I prize his truth. And then how vast a work
To assail this gray preëminence of man!
You grant me license; might I use it? think;
Ere half be done perchance your life may fail;   220
Then comes the feebler heiress of your plan,
And takes and ruins all; and thus your pains
May only make that footprint upon sand
Which old-recurring waves of prejudice
Resmooth to nothing. Might I dread that you,   225
With only Fame for spouse and your great deeds
For issue, yet may live in vain, and miss
Meanwhile what every woman counts her due,
Love, children, happiness?'
                  And she exclaim'd,
'Peace, you young savage of the Northern wild!   230
What! tho' your Prince's love were like a god's,
Have we not made ourself the sacrifice?
You are bold indeed; we are not talk'd to thus.

5. "The earlier game, played in a walled court" (Ricks).
6. "A playful reference to the cold manner of an Eastern queen and the east wind" (Tennyson).

Yet will we say for children, would they grew
Like field - flowers everywhere! we like them well: 235
But children die; and let me tell you, girl,
Howe'er you babble, great deeds cannot die;
They with the sun and moon renew their light
For ever, blessing those that look on them.
Children—that men may pluck them from our hearts,   240
Kill us with pity, break us with ourselves—
O—children—there is nothing upon earth
More miserable than she that has a son
And sees him err.[7] Nor would we work for fame;
Tho' she perhaps might reap the applause of Great,   245
Who learns the one POU STO[8] whence afterhands
May move the world, tho' she herself effect
But little; wherefore up and act, nor shrink
For fear our solid aim be dissipated
By frail successors. Would, indeed, we had been,   250
In lieu of many mortal flies, a race
Of giants living each a thousand years,
That we might see our own work out, and watch
The sandy footprint harden into stone.'
    I answer'd nothing, doubtful in myself   255
If that strange poet-princess with her grand
Imaginations might at all be won.
And she broke out interpreting my thoughts:

    'No doubt we seem a kind of monster to you;
We are used to that; for women, up till this   260
Cramp'd under worse than South-sea-isle taboo,
Dwarfs of the gynæceum,[9] fail so far
In high desire, they know not, cannot guess
How much their welfare is a passion to us.
If we could give them surer, quicker proof—   265
O, if our end were less achievable
By slow approaches than by single act
Of immolation, any phase of death,
We were as prompt to spring against the pikes,
Or down the fiery gulf as talk of it.[1]   270
To compass our dear sisters' liberties.

    She bow'd as if to veil a noble tear;
And up we came to where the river sloped
To plunge in cataract, shattering on black blocks
A breadth of thunder. O'er it shook the woods,   275
And danced the color, and, below, stuck out
The bones of some vast bulk that lived and roar'd
Before man was. She gazed awhile and said,
'As these rude bones to us, are we to her

---

7. Proverbs 10:1: "A wise son maketh a glad father: but a foolish son is the heaviness of his mother."
8. "('Give me where I may stand and I will move the world'), an often-quoted saying of Archimedes" (Tennyson).
9. "Women's quarters in a Greek house" (Tennysyon).
1. "The acts of self-sacrifice by Publius Decius Mus and by Mareus Curtius" (Ricks).

That will be.' 'Dare we dream of that,' I ask'd,   280
'Which wrought us, as the workman and his work,
That practice betters?' 'How,' she cried, 'you love
The metaphysics! read and earn our prize,
A golden brooch. Beneath an emerald plane
Sits Diotima,[2] teaching him that died   285
Of hemlock—our device, wrought to the life—
She rapt upon her subject, he on her;
For there are schools for all.' 'And yet,' I said,
'Methinks I have not found among them all
One anatomic.' 'Nay, we thought of that,'   290
She answer'd, 'but it pleased us not; in truth
We shudder but to dream our maids should ape
Those monstrous males that carve the living hound,
And cram him with the fragments of the grave,[3]
Or in the dark dissolving human heart,   295
And holy secrets of this microcosm,
Dabbling a shameless hand with shameful jest,
Encarnalize their spirits. Yet we know
Knowledge is knowledge, and this matter hangs.
Howbeit ourself, foreseeing casualty,   300
Nor willing men should come among us, learnt,
For many weary moons before we came,
This craft of healing. Were you sick, ourself
Would tend upon you. To your question now,
Which touches on the workman and his work.   305
Let there be light and there was light; 't is so,
For was, and is, and will be, are but is,
And all creation is one act at once,
The birth of light; but we that are not all,
As parts, can see but parts, now this, now that,   310
And live, perforce, from thought to thought, and make
One act a phantom of succession. Thus
Our weakness somehow shapes the shadow, Time;
But in the shadow will we work, and mould
The woman to the fuller day.'
                                        She spake   315
With kindled eyes: we rode a league beyond,
And, o'er a bridge of pinewood crossing, came
On flowery levels underneath the crag,
Full of all beauty. 'O, how sweet,' I said,—
For I was half-oblivious of my mask,—   320

---

2. "Said to have been an instructress of Socrates. She was a priestess of Mantinea. (Cf. Plato's *Symposium*)"
   (Tennyson).
3. "See Hogarth's picture in the 'Stages of Cruelty.' It was asserted that they used to give dogs the remnants
   of the dissecting-room" (Tennyson). All his life Tennyson was opposed to vivisection; his fondness for
   dogs is legendary. In 1877 "A beautiful setter was given him. It suddenly struck him at midnight that the
   new dog might feel hungry and lonely, so he went downstairs and stole a chicken for the dog" (*Memoir*
   II, 219).
   And from Darwin's *The Descent of Man* (ed. Philip Appleman, NCE, p. 246): "In the agony of death
   a dog has been known to caress his master, and every one has heard of the dog suffering under vivisection, who licked the hand of the operator; this man, unless the operation was fully justified by an increase of our knowledge, or unless he had a heart of stone, must have felt remorse to the last hour of his
   life."

'To linger here with one that loved us!' 'Yea,'
She answer'd, 'or with fair philosophies
That lift the fancy; for indeed these fields
Are lovely, lovelier not the Elysian lawns,
Where paced the demigods of old, and saw   325
The soft white vapor streak the crowned towers
Built to the Sun.' Then, turning to her maids,
'Pitch our pavilion here upon the sward;
Lay out the viands.' At the word, they raised
A tent of satin, elaborately wrought   330
With fair Corinna's[4] triumph; here she stood,
Engirt with many a florid maiden-cheek,
The woman-conqueror; woman-conquer'd there
The bearded Victor of ten-thousand hymns,
And all the men mourn'd at his side. But we   335
Set forth to climb; then, climbing, Cyril kept
With Psyche, with Melissa Florian, I
With mine affianced. Many a little hand
Glanced like a touch of sunshine on the rocks,
Many a light foot shone like a jewel set   340
In the dark crag. And then we turn'd, we wound
About the cliffs, the copses, out and in,
Hammering and clinking, chattering stony names
Of shale and hornblende, rag and trap and tuff,
Amygdaloid and trachyte, till the sun   345
Grew broader toward his death and fell, and all
The rosy heights came out above the lawns.

      The splendor falls on castle walls[5]
        And snowy summits old in story;
      The long light shakes across the lakes,   350
        And the wild cataract leaps in glory.
    Blow, bugle, blow, set the wild echoes flying,
    Blow, bugle; answer, echoes, dying, dying, dying.

      O, hark, O hear! how thin and clear,
        And thinner, clearer, farther going!   355
      O, sweet and far from cliff and scar
        The horns of Elfland faintly blowing!
    Blow, let us hear the purple glens replying,
    Blow, bugle; answer, echoes, dying, dying, dying.

      O love, they die in yon rich sky,   360
        They faint on hill or field or river;
      Our echoes roll from soul to soul,

---

4. "She is the Boeotian poetess who is said to have triumphed over Pindar in poetical composition (Pausanias, ix, 22). The Princess probably exaggerates" (Tennyson).
5. Inspired by the echoes of the boatman's bugle over the lakes at Killarney, Ireland, which Tennyson visited in 1848. See Memoir I, 291–92. "When I was there, I heard a bugle blown beneath the 'Eagle's Nest,' and eight distinct echoes" (Tennyson). "So you're the gentleman that brought the money to the place," a boatman told Tennyson on his last visit there—a measure of the lyric's popularity in terms of the tourist trade. Known as "The Bugle Song," it was the one song FitzGerald praised; none of the others, he felt, had "the old champagne flavour" (Memoir I, 253).

And grow for ever and for ever.
Blow, bugle, blow, set the wild echoes flying,
And answer, echoes, answer, dying, dying, dying.   365

1850

IV

'There sinks the nebulous star we call the sun,[6]
If that hypothesis of theirs be sound,'
Said Ida; 'let us down and rest;' and we
Down from the lean and wrinkled precipices,
By every coppice-feather'd chasm and cleft,   5
Dropt thro' the ambrosial gloom to where below
No bigger than a glowworm shone the tent
Lamp-lit from the inner. Once she lean'd on me,
Descending; once or twice she lent her hand,
And blissful palpitations in the blood   10
Stirring a sudden transport rose and fell.

But when we planted level feet, and dipt
Beneath the satin dome and enter'd in,
There leaning deep in broider'd down we sank
Our elbows; on a tripod in the midst   15
A fragrant flame rose, and before us glow'd
Fruit, blossom, viand, amber wine, and gold.

Then she, 'Let some one sing to us; lightlier move
The minutes fledged with music;' and a maid,
Of those beside her, smote her harp and sang.   20

'Tears, idle tears, I know not what they mean,[7]
Tears from the depth of some divine despair
Rise in the heart, and gather to the eyes,
In looking on the happy autumn-fields,
And thinking of the days that are no more.   25

'Fresh as the first beam glittering on a sail,
That brings our friends up from the underworld,
Sad as the last which reddens over one
That sinks with all we love below the verge;
So sad, so fresh, the days that are no more.   30

6. "Norman Locker says that this is a true description of the sun" (Tennyson).
7. One of the most Virgilian of Tennyson's poems (I'm indebted to Douglas Bush for pointing that out in a lecture), it was written at Tintern Abbey, "full for me of its bygone memories" (Tennyson). Wordsworth's "Tintern Abbey" had to have been in the poet's thoughts when he said what his poem was about: "The passion
of the past, the abiding in the transient" (Memoir I, 253). For but one of Wordsworth's passages: "That time
is past, / And all its aching joys are now no more, / And all its dizzy raptures" ("Tintern Abby," lines 83–85).
Also compare, from Wordsworth's "Immortality Ode," line 205: "Thoughts that do often lie too deep for
tears."
    Frederick Locker-Lampson recorded: "He told me that he was moved to write 'Tears, idle Tears' at Tin-
tern Abbey; and that it was not real woe, as some people might suppose; it 'was rather the yearning that
young people occasionally experience for that which seems to have passed away from them for ever.' That
in him it was strongest when he was quite a youth" (Memoir II, 73). Nevertheless, as Bush suggests, the
"bygone memories" might well include those of Hallam, who is buried near there. See IM 19, and notes;
and Bush, Major British Writers.

'Ah, sad and strange as in dark summer dawns
The earliest pipe of half-awaken'd birds[8]
The dying ears, when unto dying eyes
The casement slowly grows a glimmering square;
So sad, so strange, the days that are no more.   35

'Dear as remember'd kisses after death,
And sweet as those by hopeless fancy feign'd
On lips that are for others; deep as love,
Deep as first love, and wild with all regret;
O Death in Life, the days that are no more!'   40

She ended with such passion that the tear
She sang of shook and fell, an erring pearl
Lost in her bosom; but with some disdain
Answer'd the Princess: 'If indeed there haunt
About the moulder'd lodges of the past   45
So sweet a voice and vague, fatal to men,
Well needs it we should cram our ears with wool[9]
And so pace by. But thine are fancies hatch'd
In silken-folded idleness; nor is it
Wiser to weep a true occasion lost,   50
But trim our sails, and let old bygones be,
While down the streams that float us each and all
To the issue, goes, like glittering bergs of ice,
Throne after throne, and molten on the waste
Becomes a cloud; for all things serve their time   55
Toward that great year of equal mights and rights.
Nor would I fight with iron laws, in the end
Found golden. Let the past be past, let be
Their cancell'd Babels; tho' the rough kex[1] break
The starr'd mosaic, and the beard-blown goat   60
Hang on the shaft,[2] and the wild fig-tree split
Their monstrous idols, care not while we hear
A trumpet in the distance pealing news
Of better, and Hope, a poising eagle, burns
Above the unrisen morrow.' Then to me,   65
'Know you no song of your own land,' she said,
'Not such as moans about the retrospect,
But deals with the other distance and the hues
Of promise; not a death's-head at the wine?'
Then I remember'd one myself had made,   70
What time I watch'd the swallow winging south
From mine own land, part made long since, and part

8. During September 1883, while on a cruise up the coast of Scotland and Norway, "One morning after breakfast Harcourt met Tennyson on deck having a smoke and asked, 'The earliest pipe of half-awakened bards?' Tennyson was not amused and for some years insisted that 'Harcourt has spoilt a beautiful line by making a burlesque of it'" (Martin's *Tennyson* 540). The laureate's sense of humor was notoriously unpredictable.
9. Lashed to the mast, Odysseus stopped the ears of his crew with wax, ordering them to disobey any commands he might give, so that he alone could hear the Sirens' song.
1. "Hemlock" (Tennyson).
2. "The wind blew his beard on the height of the ruined pillar" (Tennyson).

Now while I sang, and maiden-like as far
As I could ape their treble did I sing.

'O Swallow, Swallow, flying, flying south,[3]   75
Fly to her, and fall upon her gilded eaves,
And tell her, tell her, what I tell to thee.

'O, tell her, Swallow, thou that knowest each,
That bright and fierce and fickle is the South,
And dark and true and tender is the North.   80

'O Swallow, Swallow, if I could follow, and light
Upon her lattice, I would pipe and trill,
And cheep and twitter twenty million loves.

'O were I thou that she might take me in,
And lay me on her bosom, and her heart   85
Would rock the snowy cradle till I died!

'Why lingereth she to clothe her heart with love,
Delaying as the tender ash delays
To clothe herself, when all the woods are green?

'O, tell her, Swallow, that thy brood is flown;   90
Say to her, I do but wanton in the South,
But in the North long since my nest is made.

'O tell her, brief is life but love is long,
And brief the sun of summer in the North,
And brief the moon of beauty in the South.   95

'O Swallow, flying from the golden woods,
Fly to her, and pipe and woo her, and make her mine,
And tell her, tell her, that I follow thee.'

I ceased, and all the ladies, each at each,
Like the Ithacensian suitors in old time,   100
Stared with great eyes, and laugh'd with alien lips,[4]
And knew not what they meant; for still my voice
Rang false. But smiling, 'Not for thee,' she said,
'O Bulbul, any rose of Gulistan[5]
Shall burst her veil; marsh-divers, rather, maid,   105
Shall croak thee sister, or the meadow-crake[6]
Grate her harsh kindred in the grass—and this
A mere love-poem! O, for such, my friend,
We hold them slight; they mind us of the time
When we made bricks in Egypt. Knaves are men,   110

3. Tennyson said the song was "first composed in rhyme" (*Memoir* II, 74). As with "Tears, idle Tears," that
   both poems are in blank verse can easily be overlooked.
4. Alludes to the *Odyssey* XX, line 347: "And now they laughed with alien lips" (Hallam Tennyson).
5. As Ricks notes, "Bulbul" and "Gulistan" are Persian for nightingale and rose garden, respectively.
6. "Corn-crake or landrail" (Tennyson).

That lute and flute fantastic tenderness,
And dress the victim to the offering up,
And paint the gates of Hell with Paradise,
And play the slave to gain the tyranny.
Poor soul! I had a maid of honor once;   115
She wept her true eyes blind for such a one,
A rogue of canzonets and serenades.
I loved her. Peace be with her. She is dead.
So they blaspheme the muse! But great is song
Used to great ends; ourself have often tried   120
Valkyrian hymns,[7] or into rhythm have dash'd
The passion of the prophetess; for song
Is duer unto freedom, force and growth
Of spirit, than to junketing and love.
Love is it? Would this same mock-love, and this   125
Mock-Hymen were laid up like winter bats,
Till all men grew to rate us at our worth,
Not vassals to be beat, nor pretty babes
To be dandled, no, but living wills, and sphered
Whole in ourselves and owed to none. Enough!   130
But now to leaven play with profit, you,
Know you no song, the true growth of your soil,
That gives the manners of your countrywomen?'

      She spoke and turn'd her sumptuous head with eyes
Of shining expectation fixt on mine.   135
Then while I dragg'd my brains for such a song,
Cyril, with whom the bell-mouth'd glass had wrought,
Or master'd by the sense of sport, began
To troll a careless, careless tavern-catch
Of Moll and Meg, and strange experiences   140
Unmeet for ladies. Florian nodded at him,
I frowning; Psyche flush'd and wann'd and shook;
The lilylike Melissa droop'd her brows.
'Forbear,' the Princess cried; 'Forbear, sir,' I;
And heated thro' and thro' with wrath and love,   145
I smote him on the breast. He started up;
There rose a shriek as of a city sack'd;
Melissa clamor'd, 'Flee the death;' 'To horse!'
Said Ida, 'home! to horse!' and fled, as flies   150
A troop of snowy doves athwart the dusk
When some one batters at the dovecote doors,
Disorderly the women. Alone I stood
With Florian, cursing Cyril, vext at heart
In the pavilion. There like parting hopes
I heard them passing from me; hoof by hoof,   155
And every hoof a knell to my desires,
Clang'd on the bridge; and then another shriek,
'The Head, the Head, the Princess, O the Head!'

---

7. "Like those sung by the Valkyrian maidens, 'the choosers of the slain,' in the Northern Mythology" (Hallam Tennyson).

For blind with rage she miss'd the plank, and roll'd
In the river.[8] Out I sprang from glow to gloom;   160
There whirl'd her white robe like a blossom'd branch
Rapt to the horrible fall. A glance I gave,
No more, but woman-vested as I was
Plunged, and the flood drew; yet I caught her; then
Oaring one arm, and bearing in my left   165
The weight of all the hopes of half the world,
Strove to buffet to land in vain. A tree
Was half-disrooted from his place and stoop'd
To drench his dark locks in the gurgling wave
Mid-channel. Right on this we drove and caught,   170
And grasping down the boughs I gain'd the shore.

There stood her maidens glimmeringly group'd
In the hollow bank. One reaching forward drew
My burthen from mine arms; they cried, 'She lives.'
They bore her back into the tent: but I,   175
So much a kind of shame withim me wrought,
Not yet endured to meet her opening eyes,
Nor found my friends; but push'd alone on foot—
For since her horse was lost I left her mine—
Across the woods, and less from Indian craft   180
Than beelike instinct hiveward, found at length
The garden portals. Two great statues, Art
And Science, Caryatids,[9] lifted up.
A weight of emblem, and betwixt were valves[1]
Of open-work in which the hunter[2] rued   185
His rash intrusion, manlike, but his brows
Had sprouted, and the branches thereupon
Spread out at top, and grimly spiked the gates.

A little space was left between the horns,
Thro' which I clamber'd o'er at top with pain,   190
Dropt on the sward, and up the linden walks,
And, tost on thoughts that changed from hue to hue,
Now poring on the glowworm, now the star,
I paced the terrace, till the Bear had wheel'd
Thro' a great arc his seven slow suns.
                        A step   195
Of lightest echo, then a loftier form
Than female, moving thro' the uncertain gloom,
Disturb'd me with the doubt 'if this were she,'
But it was Florian. 'Hist, O, hist!' he said,
'They seek us; out so late is out of rules.   200
Moreover, "Seize the strangers" is the cry.

---

8. Arguing against the assertion that the poem is "entirely without humor," Turner (pp. 112–13) singles out this passage as an example of the poet's intentional humor: "One of the best comic scenes is where Ida, 'blind with rage,' misses a plank and falls into the river."
9. "Female figures used as bearing shafts (Vitruvius, i), e.g. the maidens supporting the light entablature of the portico of the Erechteum at Athens" (Tennyson).
1. "Gates" (Ricks).
2. "Actaeon turned into a stag for looking at Diana bathing" (Tennyson).

How came you here?' I told him. 'I,' said he,
'Last of the train, a moral leper, I,
To whom none spake, half-sick at heart, return'd.
Arriving all confused among the rest   205
With hooded brows I crept into the hall,
And, couch'd behind a Judith, underneath
The head of Holofernes peep'd and saw.
Girl after girl was call'd to trial; each
Disclaim'd all knowledge of us; last of all,   210
Melissa; trust me, sir I pitied her.
She question'd if she knew us men, at first
Was silent; closer prest, denied it not,
And then, demanded if her mother knew,
Or Psyche, she affirm'd not, or denied;   215
From whence the Royal mind, familiar with her,
Easily gather'd either guilt. She sent
For Psyche, but she was not there; she call'd
For Psyche's child to cast it from the doors;
She sent for Blanche to accuse her face to face;   220
And I slipt out. But whither will you now?
And where are Psyche, Cyril? both are fled;
What, if together? that were not so well.
Would rather we had never come! I dread
His wildness, and the chances of the dark.'   225

        'And yet,' I said, 'you wrong him more than I
That struck him; this is proper to the clown,
Tho' smock'd, or furr'd and purpled, still the clown,
To harm the thing that trusts him, and to shame
That which he says he loves. For Cyril, howe'er   230
He deal in frolic, as to-night—the song
Might have been worse and sinn'd in grosser lips
Beyond all pardon—as it is, I hold
These flashes on the surface are not he.
He has a solid base of temperament;   235
But as the water-lily³ starts and slides
Upon the level in little puffs of wind,
Tho' anchor'd to the bottom, such is he.'

        Scarce bad I ceased when from a tamarisk near
Two Proctors leapt upon us, crying, 'Names!'   240
He, standing still, was clutch'd; but I began
To thrid the musky-circled mazes, wind
And double in and out the boles, and race
By all the fountains. Fleet I was of foot;
Before me shower'd the rose in flakes; behind   245
I heard the puff'd pursuer: at mine ear
Bubbled the nightingale⁴ and heeded not,

3. "Waterlilies in my own pond, and seen by me on a gusty day. They started and slid in the sudden puffs of wind till caught and stayed by the tether of their own stalks" (Tennyson). The note was provoked by a claim that he had taken the image from Wordsworth's *Excursion*
4. "When I was in a friend's garden in Yorkshire, I heard a nightingale singing with such a frenzy of passion

And secret laughter tickled all my soul.
At last I hook'd my ankle in a vine
That claspt the feet of a Mnemosyne,[5]   250
And falling on my face was caught and known.

They haled us to the Princess where she sat
High in the hall; above her droop'd a lamp,
And made the single jewel on her brow
Burn like the mystic fire[6] on a mast-head,   255
Prophet of storm; a handmaid on each side
Bow'd toward her, combing out her long black hair
Damp from the river; and close behind her stood
Eight daughters of the plough, stronger than men,
Huge women blowzed[7] with health, and wind, and rain,   260
And labor. Each was like a Druid rock;
Or like a spire of land that stands apart
Cleft from the main, and wail'd about with mews.

Then, as we came, the crowd dividing clove
An advent to the throne; and therebeside,   265
Half-naked as if caught at once from bed
And tumbled on the purple footcloth, lay
The lily-shining child; and on the left,
Bow'd on her palms and folded up from wrong,
Her round white shoulder shaken with her sobs,   270
Melissa knelt; but Lady Blanche erect
Stood up and spake, an affluent orator:

'It was not thus, O Princess, in old days;
You prized my counsel, lived upon my lips.
I led you then to all the Castalies;[8]   275
I fed you with the milk of every Muse;
I loved you like this kneeler, and you me
Your second mother, those were gracious times.
Then came your new friend; you began to change—
I saw it and grieved—to slacken and to cool;   280
Till taken with her seeming openness
You turn'd your warmer currents all to her,
To me you froze; this was my meed for all.
Yet I bore up in part from ancient love,
And partly that I hoped to win you back,   285
And partly conscious of my own deserts,
And partly that you were my civil head,
And chiefly you were born for something great,
In which I might your fellow-worker be,
When time should serve; and thus a noble scheme   290

---

that it was unconscious of everything else, and not frightened though I came and stood quite close beside it. I saw its eye flashing and felt the air bubble in my ear through the vibration" (Tennyson).
5. "Goddess of memory, mother of the Muses" (Tennyson).
6. "St. Elmo's fire" (Tennyson). "St. Elmo's phosphorescent light flickers on the tops of masts when a storm
   is brewing. Cf. *Tempest*, I, ii, 197" (Hallam Tennyson).
7. "Brown-red" (Tennyson).
8. In Greek mythology, a nymph who, pursued by Apollo, threw herself into a spring on Mt. Parnasus. Subsequently, the spring was held sacred to Apollo and the Muses.

Grew up from seed we two long since had sown;
In us true growth, in her a Jonah's gourd,
Up in one night and due to sudden sun.
We took this palace; but evem from the first
You stood in your own light and darken'd mine.   295
What student came but that you planed her path
To Lady Psyche, younger, not so wise,
A foreigner, and I your countrywoman,
I your old friend and tried, she new in all?
But still her lists were swell'd and mine were lean;   300
Yet I bore up in hope she would be known.
Then came these wolves; *they* knew her; *they* endured,
Long-closeted with her the yestermorn,
To tell her what they were, and she to hear.
And me none told. Not less to an eye like mine,   305
A lidless⁹ watcher of the public weal,
Last night, their mask was patent, and my foot
Was to you. But I thought again; I fear'd
To meet a cold "We thank you, we shall hear of it
From Lady Psyche;" you had gone to her,   310
She told, perforce, and winning easy grace,
No doubt, for slight delay, remain'd among us
In our young nursery still unknown, the stem
Less grain than touchwood, while my honest heat
Were all miscounted as malignant haste   315
To push my rival out of place and power.
But public use required she should be known;
And since my oath was ta'en for public use,
I broke the letter¹ of it to keep the sense.
I spoke not then at first, but watch'd them well,   320
Saw that they kept apart, no mischief done;
And yet this day—tho' you should hate me for it—
I came to tell you; found that you had gone,
Ridden to the hills, she likewise. Now, I thought,
That surely she will speak; if not, then I.   325
Did she? These monsters blazon'd what they were,
According to the coarseness of their kind,
For thus I hear; and known at last—my work—
And full of cowardice and guilty shame—
I grant in her some sense of shame—she flies;   330
And I remain on whom to wreak your rage,
I, that have lent my life to build up yours,
I, that have wasted here health, wealth, and time,
And talent, I—you know it—I will not boast;
Dismiss me, and I prophesy your plan,   335
Divorced from my experience, will be chaff
For every gust of chance, and men will say
We did not know the real light, but chased
The wisp that flickers where no foot can tread.'

---

9. "Wakeful, wide-eyed" (Tennyson). Ricks observes that in this sense the OED quotes only Coleridge and
   Shelley before Tennyson.
1. See 2 Corinthians 3:6: "Not of the letter, but of the spirit: for the letter killeth, but the spirit giveth life."

　　She ceased; the Princess answer'd coldly, 'Good;   340
Your oath is broken; we dismiss you, go.
For this lost lamb'—she pointed to the child—
'Our mind is changed; we take it to ourself.'
　　Thereat the lady stretch'd a vulture throat,
And shot from crooked lips a haggard smile.   345
'The plan was mine. I built the nest,' she said,
'To hatch the cuckoo. Rise! and stoop'd to updrag
Melissa. She, half on her mother propt,
Half-drooping from her, turn'd her face, and cast
A liquid look on Ida, full of prayer,   350
Which melted Florian's fancy as she hung,
A Niobeän² daughter, one arm out,
Appealing to the bolts of heaven; and while
We gazed upon her came a little stir
About the doors, and on a sudden rush'd   355
Among us, out of breath, as one pursued,
A woman-post in flying raiment. Fear
Stared in her eyes, and chalk'd her face, and wing'd
Her transit to the throne, whereby she fell
Delivering seal'd dispatches which the Head   360
Took half-amazed, and in her lion's mood
Tore open, silent we with blind surmise
Regarding, while she read, till over brow
And cheek and bosom brake the wrathful bloom
As of some fire against a stormy cloud,   365
When the wild peasant rights himself, the rick³
Flames, and his anger reddens in the heavens;
For anger most it seem'd, while now her breast,
Beaten with some great passion at her heart,
Palpitated, her hand shook, and we heard   370
In the dead hush the papers that she held
Rustle. At once the lost lamb at her feet
Sent out a bitter bleating for its dam.
The plaintive cry jarr'd on her ire; she crush'd
The scrolls together, made a sudden turn   375
As if to speak, but, utterance failing her,
She whirl'd them on to me, as who should say
'Read,' and I read—two letters—one her sire's:

　　'Fair daughter, when we sent the Prince your way
We knew not your ungracious laws, which learnt,   380
We, conscious of what temper you are built,
Came all in haste to hinder wrong, but fell
Into his father's hand, who has this night,
You lying close upon his territory,
Slipt round and in the dark invested you,   385
And here he keeps me hostage for his son.'

2. "Niobe was proud of her twelve children, and in consequence boasted herself as superior to Leto, mother
of Apollo and Artemis, who in revenge shot them all dead" (Tennyson).
3. 'I remember seeing thirty ricks burning near Cambridge, and I helped to pass the bucket from the well
to help to quench the fire" (Tennyson).

The second was my father's running thus:
'You have our son; touch not a hair of his head;
Render him up unscathed; give him your hand;
Cleave to your contract—tho' indeed we hear   390
You hold the woman is the better man;
A rampant heresy, such as if it spread
Would make all women kick against their lords
Thro' all the world, and which might well deserve
That we this night should pluck your palace down; 395
And we will do it, unless you send us back
Our son, on the instant, whole.'
       So far I read;
And then stood up and spoke impetuously:

'O, not to pry and peer on your reserve,
But led by golden wishes, and a hope   400
The child of regal compact, did I break
Your precinct; not a scorner of your sex
But venerator, zealous it should be
All that it might be. Hear me, for I bear,
Tho' man, yet human, whatsoe'er your wrongs, 405
From the flaxen curl to the gray lock a life
Less mine than yours. My nurse would tell me of you;
I babbled for you, as babies for the moon,
Vague brightness; when a boy, you stoop'd to me
From all high places, lived in all fair lights, 410
Came in long breezes rapt from inmost south
And blown to inmost north; at eve and dawn
With Ida, Ida, Ida, rang the woods;
The leader wild-swan in among the stars
Would clang it, and lapt in wreaths of glowworm light 415
The mellow breaker murmur'd Ida. Now,
Because I would have reach'd you, had you been
Sphered up with Cassiopeia,[4] or the enthroned
Persephone in Hades, now at length,
Those winters of abeyance all worn out,   420
A man I came to see you; but, indeed,
Not in this frequence can I lend full tongue,
O noble Ida, to those thoughts that wait
On you, their centre. Let me say but this,
That many a famous man and woman, town 425
And landskip, have I heard of, after seen
The dwarfs of presage;[5] tho' when known, there grew
Another kind of beauty in detail
Made them worth knowing; but in you I found
My boyish dream involved and dazzled down 430
And master'd while that after-beauty makes
Such head from act to act, from hour to hour,
Within me, that except you slay me here,

4. "A mythical Queen of Ethiopia, subsequently a constellation" (Ricks).
5. "Afterwards seen to be far short of expectation" (Hallam Tennyson).

According to your bitter statute-book,
I cannot cease to follow you, as they say   435
The seal does music; who desire you more
Than growing boys their manhood; dying lips,
With many thousand matters left to do,
The breath of life; O, more than poor men wealth,
Than sick men health—yours, yours, not mine—but half   440
Without you; with you, whole; and of those halves
You worthiest; and howe'er you block and bar
Your heart with system out from mine, I hold
That it becomes no man to nurse despair,
But in the teeth of clench'd antagonisms   445
To follow up the worthiest till he die.
Yet that I came not all unauthorized
Behold your father's letter.'
                                        On one knee
Kneeling, I gave it, which she caught, and dash'd
Unopen'd at her feet. A tide of fierce   450
Invective seem'd to wait behind her lips,
As waits a river level with the dam
Ready to burst and flood the world with foam;
And so she would have spoken, but there rose
A hubbub in the court of half the maids   455
Gather'd together; from the illumined hall
Long lanes of splendor slanted o'er a press
Of snowy shoulders, thick as herded ewes,
And rainbow robes, and gems and gemlike eyes,
And gold and golden heads. They to and fro   460
Fluctuated, as flowers in storm, some red, some pale,
All open-mouth'd, all gazing to the light,
Some crying there was an army in the land,
And some that men were in the very walls,
And some they cared not; till a clamor grew   465
As of a new-world Babel, woman-built,
And worse-confounded. High above them stood
The placid marble Muses, looking peace.

      Not peace she look'd, the Head; but rising up
Robed in the long night of her deep hair, so   470
To the open window moved, remaining there
Fixt like a beacon-tower above the waves
Of tempest, when the crimson-rolling eye
Glares ruin, and the wild birds on the light
Dash themselves dead. She stretch'd her arms and call'd   475
Across the tumult, and the tumult fell.

      'What fear ye, brawlers? am not I your Head?
On me, me, me, the storm first breaks; I dare
All these male thunderbolts; what is it ye fear?
Peace! there are those to avenge us and they come;   480
If not,—myself were like enough, O girls,
To unfurl the maiden banner of our rights,

And clad in iron burst the ranks of war,
Or, falling, protomartyr of our cause,
Die; yet I blame you not so much for fear;   485
Six thousand years[6] of fear have made you that
From which I would redeem you. But for those
That stir this hubbub—you and you—I know
Your faces there in the crowd—to-morrow morn
We hold a great convention; then shall they   490
That love their voices more than duty, learn
With whom they deal, dismiss'd in shame to live
No wiser than their mothers, household stuff,
Live chattels, mincers of each other's fame,
Full of weak poison, turnspits for the clown,   495
The drunkard's football, laughing-stocks of Time,
Whose brains are in their hands and in their heels,
But fit to flaunt, to dress, to dance, to thrum,
To tramp, to scream, to burnish, and to scour,
For ever slaves at home and fools abroad.'   500

      She, ending, waved her hands; thereat the crowd
Muttering, dissolved; then with a smile, that look'd
A stroke of cruel sunshine on the cliff,
When all the glens are drown'd in azure gloom
Of thunder-shower, she floated to us and said: 505

      'You have done well and like a gentleman,
And like a prince; you have our thanks for all.
And you look well too in your woman's dress.
Well have you done and like a gentleman.
You saved our life; we owe you bitter thanks.   510
Better have died and spilt our bones in the flood—
Then men had said—but now—what hinders me
To take such bloody vengeance on you both?—
Yet since our father—wasps in our good hive,
You would-be quenchers of the light to be,   515
Barbarians, grosser than your native bears—
O, would I had his sceptre for one hour!
You that have dared to break our bound, and gull'd
Our servants, wrong'd and lied and thwarted us—
I wed with thee! I bound by precontract   520
Your bride, your bondslave! not tho' all the gold
That veins the world were pack'd to make your crown,
And every spoken tongue should lord you. Sir,
Your falsehood and yourself are hateful to us;
I trample on your offers and on you.   525
Begone; we will not look upon you more.
Here, push them out at gates.'
                              In wrath she spake.
Then those eight mighty daughters of the plough

6. Alludes to Archbishop Ussher's caculation of the time since the creation (see n. 5, p. 86). In *Darwin among the Poets*, Lionel Stevenson observes that here "Ida's grasp of evolution is not consistently maintained" (p. 73).

Bent their broad faces toward us and address'd
Their motion. Twice I sought to plead my cause,   530
But on my shoulder hung their heavy hands,
The weight of destiny; so from her face
They push'd us, down the steps, and thro' the court,
And with grim laughter thrust us out at gates.

        We cross'd the street and gain'd a petty mound   535
Beyond it, whence we saw the lights and heard
The voices murmuring. While I listen'd, came
On a sudden the weird seizure and the doubt.
I seem'd to move among a world of ghosts;
The Princess with her monstrous woman-guard,   540
The jest and earnest working side by side,
The cataract and the tumult and the kings
Were shadows; and the long fantastic night
With all its doings had and had not been,
And all things were and were not.
                                    This went by   545
As strangely as it came, and on my spirits
Settled a gentle cloud of melancholy—
Not long; I shook it off; for spite of doubts
And sudden ghostly shadowings I was one
To whom the touch of all mischance but came   550
As night to him that sitting on a hill
Sees the midsummer, midnight, Norway sun
Set into sunrise; then we moved away.

INTERLUDE

    Thy voice is heard thro' rolling drums[7]
        That beat to battle where he stands;
    Thy face across his fancy comes,
        And gives the battle to his hands.
    A moment, while the trumpets blow,   5
        He sees his brood about thy knee;
    The next, like fire he meets the foe,
        And strikes him dead for thine and thee.

So Lilia sang. We thought her half-possess'd,
She struck such warbling fury thro' the words;   10
And, after, feigning pique at what she call'd
The raillery, or grotesque, or false sublime—
Like one that wishes at a dance to change
The music—clapt her hands and cried for war,
Or some grand fight to kill and make an end.   15
And he that next inherited the tale,
Half turning to the broken statue, said,
'Sir Ralph has got your colors; if I prove

---

7. For various versions of the song ("My first version of this song was published in *Selections*, 1865"), see
   Ricks's edition.

Your knight, and fight your battle, what for me?'
It chanced, her empty glove upon the tomb   20
Lay by her like a model of her hand.
She took it and she flung it. 'Fight,' she said,
'And make us all we would be, great and good.'
He knightlike in his cap instead of casque,
A cap of Tyrol borrow'd from the hall,   25
Arranged the favor, and assumed the Prince.

V

Now, scarce three paces measured from the mound,
We stumbled on a stationary[8] voice,
And 'Stand, who goes?' 'Two from the palace,' I.
'The second two; they wait,' he said, 'pass on;
His Highness wakes;' and one, that clash'd in arms,   5
By glimmering lanes[9] and walls of canvas led
Threading the soldier-city, till we heard
The drowsy folds of our great ensign shake
From blazon'd lions o'er the imperial tent
Whispers of war.
                    Entering, the sudden light   10
Dazed me half-blind. I stood and seem'd to hear,
As in a poplar grove when a light wind wakes
A lisping of the innumerous leaf and dies,
Each hissing in his neighbor's ear; and then
A strangled titter, out of which there brake   15
On all sides, clamoring etiquette to death,
Unmeasured mirth; while now the two old kings
Began to wag their baldness up and down,
The fresh young captains flash'd their glittering teeth,
The huge bush-bearded barons heaved and blew,   20
And slain with laughter roll'd the gilded squire.

    At length my sire, his rough cheek wet with tears,
Panted from weary sides, 'King, you are free!
We did but keep you surety for our son,
If this be he,—or a draggled mawkin,[1] thou,   25
That tends her bristled grunters in the sludge;'
For I was drench'd with ooze, and torn with briers,
More crumpled than a poppy from the sheath,
And all one rag, disprinced from head to heel.
Then some one sent beneath his vaulted palm   30
A whisper'd jest to some one near him, 'Look,
He has been among his shadows.' 'Satan take
The old women and their shadows!'—thus the king
Roar'd—'make yourself a man to fight with men.
Go; Cyril told us all.'
                    As boys that slink   35

8. "Pertaining to a military post (*OED*, 4b)" (Ricks).
9. "The lines of tents just visible in the darkness" (Tennyson).
1. "Kitchen-wench" (Hallam Tennyson).

From ferule and the trespass-chiding eye,
Away we stole, and transient[2] in a trice
From what was left to faded woman-slough
To sheathing splendors and the golden scale
Of harness, issued in the sun, that now   40
Leapt from the dewy shoulders of the earth,
And hit the Northern hills. Here Cyril met us,
A little shy at first, but by and by
We twain, with mutual pardon ask'd and given
For stroke and song, resolder'd peace, whereon   45
Follow'd his tale. Amazed he fled away
Thro' the dark land, and later in the night
Had come on Psyche weeping: 'then we fell
Into your father's hand, and there she lies,
But will not speak nor stir.'
                              He show'd a tent   50
A stone-shot off; we enter'd in, and there
Among piled arms and rough accoutrements,
Pitiful sight, wrapp'd in a soldier's cloak,
Like some sweet sculpture draped from head to foot,
And push'd by rude hands from its pedestal,   55
All her fair length upon the ground she lay;
And at her head a follower of the camp,
A charr'd and wrinkled piece of woman-hood,
Sat watching like a watcher by the dead.

Then Florian knelt, and 'Come,' he whisper'd to her,   60
'Lift up your head, sweet sister; lie not thus.
What have you done but right? you could not slay
Me, nor your prince; look up, he comforted.
Sweet is it to have done the thing one ought,
When fallen in darker ways.' And likewise I: 65
'Be comforted; have I not lost her too,
In whose least act abides the nameless charm
That none has else for me?' She heard, she moved,
She moan'd, a folded voice; and up she sat,
And raised the cloak from brows as pale and smooth   70
As those that mourn half-shrouded over death
In deathless marble. 'Her,' she said, 'my friend—
Parted from her—betray'd her cause and mine—
Where shall I breathe? why kept ye not your faith?
O base and bad! what comfort? none for me!'   75
To whom remorseful Cyril, 'Yet I pray
Take comfort; live, dear lady, for your child!'
At which she lifted up her voice and cried:

'Ah me, my babe, my blossom, ah, my child,
My one sweet child, whom I shall see no more!   80
For now will cruel Ida keep her back;
And either she will die from want of care,

2. "Passing from one thing or person to another. Now rare (*OED*, 3)" (Ricks).

Or sicken with ill-usage, when they say
The child is hers—for every little fault,
The child is hers; and they will beat my girl   85
Remembering her mother—O my flower!
Or they will take her, they will make her hard,
And she will pass me by in after-life
With some cold reverence worse than were she dead.
Ill mother that I was to leave her there,   90
To lag behind, scared by the cry they made,
The horror of the shame among them all.
But I will go and sit beside the doors,
And make a wild petition night and day,
Until they hate to hear me like a wind   95
Wailing for ever, till they open to me,
And lay my little blossom at my feet,
My babe, my sweet Aglaïa, my one child;
And I will take her up and go my way,
And satisfy my soul with kissing her.   100
Ah! what might that man not deserve of me
Who gave me back my child?' 'Be comforted,'
Said Cyril, 'you shall have it;' but again
She veil'd her brows, and prone she sank, and so,
Like tender things that being caught feign death,   105
Spoke not, nor stirr'd.
                       By this a murmur ran
Thro' all the camp, and inward raced the scouts
With rumor of Prince Arac hard at hand.
We left her by the woman, and without
Found the gray kings at parle; and 'Look you,' cried   110
My father, 'that our compact be fulfill'd.
You have spoilt this child; she laughs at you and man;
She wrongs herself, her sex, and me, and him.
But red-faced war has rods of steel and fire;
She yields, of war.'
                     Then Gama turn'd to me: 115
'We fear, indeed, you spent a stormy time
With our strange girl; and yet they say that still
You love her. Give us, then, your mind at large:
How say you, war or not?'
                          'Not war, if possible,
O king,' I said, 'lest from the abuse of war,   120
The desecrated shrine, the trampled year,
The smouldering homestead, and the household flower
Torn from the lintel—all the common wrong—
A smoke go up thro' which I loom to her
Three times a monster. Now she lightens scorn   125
At him that mars her plan, but then would hate—
And every voice she talk'd with ratify it,
And every face she look'd on justify it—
The general foe. More soluble is this knot
By gentleness than war. I want her love.   130
What were I nigher this altho' we dash'd

Your cities into shards with catapults? —
She would not love — or brought her chain'd, a slave,
The lifting of whose eyelash is my lord?
Not ever would she love, but brooding turn   135
The book of scorn, till all my flitting chance
Were caught within the record of her wrongs
And crush'd to death; and rather, Sire, than this
I would the old god of war himself were dead,
Forgotten, rusting on his iron hills,[3]   140
Rotting on some wild shore with ribs of wreck,
Or like an old-world mammoth bulk'd in ice,[4]
Not to be molten out.'
                            And roughly spake
My father: 'Tut, you know them not, the girls.
Boy, when I hear you prate I almost think   145
That idiot legend credible. Look you, sir!
Man is the hunter; woman is his game.
The sleek and shining creatures of the chase,
We hunt them for the beauty of their skins;
They love us for it, and we ride them down.   150
Wheedling and siding with them! Out! for shame!
Boy, there's no rose that's half so dear to them
As he that does the thing they dare not do,
Breathing and sounding beauteous battle, comes
With the air of the trumpet round him, and leaps in   155
Among the women, snares them by the score
Flatter'd and fluster'd, wins, tho' dash'd with death
He reddens what he kisses. Thus I won
Your mother, a good mother, a good wife,
Worth winning; but this firebrand — gentleness   160
To such as her! if Cyril spake her true,
To catch a dragon in a cherry net,
To trip a tigress with a gossamer,
Were wisdom to it.'
                        'Yea, but, Sire,' I cried,
'Wild natures need wise curbs. The soldier? No!   165
What dares not Ida do that she should prize
The soldier? I beheld her, when she rose
The yesternight, and storming in extremes
Stood for her cause, and flung defiance down
Gagelike to man, and had not shunn'd the death,   170
No, not the soldier's; yet I hold her, king,
True woman; but you clash them all in one,
That have as many differences as we.
The violet varies from the lily as far
As oak from elm. One loves the soldier, one   175
The silken priest of peace, one this, one that,
And some unworthily; their sinless faith,

3. Compare *IM* 56, 5: "Or seal'd within the iron hills?"
4. "Bulky mammoth buried in ice" (Tennyson). Ricks notes: "Lyell's *Principles of Geology* (4th edn, 1835),
    i, 147, mentions that 'the entire carcass of a mammoth was obtained in 1803. It fell from a mass of ice,
    in which it had been encased, on the banks of the Lena.'" See also the notes to *IM* 56.

A maiden moon that sparkles on a sty,
Glorifying clown and satyr; whence they need
More breadth of culture. Is not Ida right?   180
They worth it? truer to the law within?
Severer in the logic of a life?
Twice as magnetic to sweet influences
Of earth and heaven? and she of whom you speak,
My mother, looks as whole as some serene   185
Creation minted in the golden moods
Of sovereign artists; not a thought, a touch,
But pure as lines of green that streak the white
Of the first snowdrop's inner leaves; I say,
Not like the piebald miscellany, man,   190
Bursts of great heart and slips in sensual mire,
But whole and one; and take them all-in-all,
Were we ourselves but half as good, as kind,
As truthful, much that Ida claims as right
Had ne'er been mooted, but as frankly theirs   195
As dues of Nature. To our point; not war,
Lest I lose all.'
                    'Nay, nay, you spake but sense,'
Said Gama. 'We remember love ourself
In our sweet youth; we did not rate him then
This red-hot iron to be shaped with blows.   200
You talk almost like Ida; *she* can talk;
And there is something in it as you say:
But you talk kindlier; we esteem you for it.—
He seems a gracious and a gallant Prince,
I would he had our daughter. For the rest,   205
Our own detention, why, the causes weigh'd,
Fatherly fears—you used us courteously—
We would do much to gratify your Prince—
We pardon it; and for your ingress here
Upon the skirt and fringe of our fair land,   210
You did but come as goblins in the night,
Nor in the furrow broke the ploughman's head,
Nor burnt the grange, nor buss'd the milking-maid,
Nor robb'd the farmer of his bowl of cream.
But let your Prince—our royal word upon it,   215
He comes back safe—ride with us to our lines,
And speak with Arac. Arac's word is thrice
As ours with Ida; something may be done—
I know not what—and ours shall see us friends.
You, likewise, our late guests, if so you will,   220
Follow us. Who knows? we four may build some plan
Four square to opposition.'
                        Here he reach'd
White hands of farewell to my sire, who growl'd
An answer which, half-muffled in his beard,
Let so much out as gave us leave to go.   225
   Then rode we with the old king across the lawns
Beneath huge trees, a thousand rings of Spring

In every bole, a song on every spray
Of birds that piped their Valentines, and woke
Desire in me to infuse my tale of love   230
In the old king's ears, who promised help, and oozed
All o'er with honey'd answer as we rode;
And blossom-fragrant slipt the heavy dews
Gather'd by night and peace, with each light air
On our mail'd heads. But other thoughts than peace   235
Burnt in us, when we saw the embattled squares
And squadrons of the Prince, trampling the flowers
With clamor; for among them rose a cry
As if to greet the king; they made a halt;
The horses yell'd; they clash'd their arms; the drum   240
Beat; merrily-blowing shrill'd the martial fife;
And in the blast and bray of the long horn
And serpent-throated bugle, undulated
The banner. Anon to meet us lightly pranced
Three captains out; nor ever had I seen   245
Such thews of men. The midmost and the highest
Was Arac; all about his motion clung
The shadow of his sister, as the beam
Of the East, that play'd upon them, made them glance
Like those three stars of the airy Giant's[5] zone,   250
That glitter burnish'd by the frosty dark;
And as the fiery Sirius alters hue,
And bickers into red and emerald, shone
Their morions,[6] wash'd with morning, as they came.

And I that prated peace, when first I heard   255
War-music, felt the blind wild-beast of force,
Whose home is in the sinews of a man,
Stir in me as to strike. Then took the king
His three broad sons; with now a wandering hand
And now a pointed finger, told them all.   260
A common light of smiles at our disguise
Broke from their lips, and, ere the windy jest
Had labor'd down within his ample lungs,
The genial giant, Arac, roll'd himself
Thrice in the saddle, then burst out in words: 265

'Our land invaded, 'sdeath! and he himself
Your captive, yet my father wills not war!
And, 'sdeath! myself, what care I, war or no?
But then this question of your troth remains;
And there's a downright honest meaning in her.   270
She flies too high, she flies too high! and yet
She ask'd but space and fair-play for her scheme;
She prest and prest it on me—I myself,
What know I of these things? but, life and soul!
I thought her half-right talking of her wrongs;   275

5. "The stars in the belt of Orion" (Tennyson).
6. "Steel helmets" (Hallam Tennyson).

I say she flies too high, 'sdeath! what of that?
I take her for the flower of womankind,
And so I often told her, right or wrong;
And, Prince, she can be sweet to those she loves,
And, right or wrong, I care not; this is all,   280
I stand upon her side; she made me swear it—
'Sdeath!—and with solemn rites by candle-light—
Swear by Saint something—I forget her name—
Her that talk'd down the fifty wisest men;
She[7] was a princess too; and so I swore.   285
Come, this is all; she will not; waive your claim.
If not, the foughten field, what else, at once
Decides it, 'sdeath! against my father's will.'

   I lagg'd answer, loth to render up
My precontract, and loth by brainless war   290
To cleave the rift of difference deeper yet;
Till one of those two brothers, half aside
And fingering at the hair about his lip,
To prick us on the combat, 'Like to like!
The woman's garment hid the woman's heart.'   295
A taunt that clench'd his purpose like a blow!
For fiery-short was Cyril's counter-scoff,
And sharp I answer'd, touch'd upon the point
Where idle boys are cowards to their shame,
'Decide it here; why not? we are three to three.'   300

   Then spake the third: 'But three to three? no more?
No more, and in our noble sister's cause?
More, more, for honor! every captain waits
Hungry for honor, angry for his king.
More, more, some fifty on a side, that each   305
May breathe himself, and quick! by overthrow
Of these or those, the question settled die.'

   'Yea,' answer'd I, 'for this wild wreath of air,
This flake of rainbow flying on the highest
Foam of men's deeds—this honor, if ye will.   310
It needs must be for honor if at all;
Since, what decision? if we fail we fail,[8]
And if we win we fail; she would not keep
Her compact.' "Sdeath! but we will send to her,'
Said Arac, 'worthy reasons why she should   315
Bide by this issue; let our missive thro'
And you shall have her answer by the word.'
   'Boys!' shriek'd the old king, but vainlier than a hen
To her false daughters in the pool; for none
Regarded; neither seem'd there more to say.   320

7. "St. Catherine of Alexandria, niece of Constantine the Great" (Tennyson). "The Emperor Maxentius
   during his persecution is related to have sent fifty of his wisest men to convert her from Christianity, but
   she combated and confuted them all" (Hallam Tennyson).
8. See Shakespeare's *Macbeth*: "If we should fail?" and Lady Macbeth's, "We fail!" (I, vii, line 59).

Back rode we to my father's camp, and found
He thrice had sent a herald to the gates,
To learn if Ida yet would cede our claim,
Or by denial flush her babbling wells
With her own people's life; three times he went.   325
The first, he blew and blew, but none appear'd;
He batter'd at the doors, none came; the next
An awful voice within had warn'd him thence;
The third, and those eight daughters of the plough
Came sallying thro' the gates, and caught his hair,   330
And so belabor'd him on rib and cheek
They made him wild. No less one glance he caught
Thro' open doors of Ida station'd there
Unshaken, clinging to her purpose, firm
Tho' compass'd by two armies and the noise   335
Of arms; and standing like a stately pine
Set in a cataract on an island-crag,[9]
When storm is on the heights, and right and left
Suck'd from the dark heart of the long hills roll
The torrents, dash'd to the vale; and yet her will   340
Bred will in me to overcome it or fall.

But when I told the king that I was pledged
To fight in tourney for my bride, he clash'd
His iron palms together with a cry;
Himself would tilt it out among the lads;   345
But overborne by all his bearded lords
With reasons drawn from age and state, perforce
He yielded, wroth and red, with fierce demur;
And many a bold knight started up in heat,
And sware to combat for my claim till death.   350

All on this side the palace ran the field
Flat to the garden-wall; and likewise here,
Above the garden's glowing blossom-belts,
A column'd entry shone and marble stairs,
And great bronze valves, emboss'd with Tomyris[1]   355
And what she did to Cyrus after fight,
But now fast barr'd. So here upon the flat
All that long morn the lists were hammer'd up,
And all that morn the heralds to and fro,
With message and defiance, went and came;   360
Last, Ida's answer, in a royal hand,
But shaken here and there, and rolling words
Oration-like. I kiss'd it and I read:

9. "Taken from a torrent above Cauteretz" (Tennyson). "Cf. *Remains of Arthur Hugh Clough*, Sept. 7, 1861,
   p. 269: 'CAUTERETS, *September* 7.—I have been out for a walk with A. T. to a sort of island between
   two waterfalls, with pines on it, of which he retained a recollection from his visit thirty-one years ago,
   and which, moreover, furnished a simile to *The Princess*. He is very fond of the place evidently, as it is
   more in the mountains than any other, and so far superior.' In 1875 he took me to this same island and
   talked of Arthur Hallam and Clough" (Hallam Tennyson).
1. "Queen of the Massagetae, who cut off the head of Cyrus the Great after defeating him, and dipped it
   in a skin which she had filled with blood and bade him, as he was insatiate of blood, to drink his fill,
   gorge himself with blood" (Tennyson).

'O brother, you have known the pangs we felt,
What heats of indignation when we heard   365
Of those that iron-cramp'd their women's feet;
Of lands in which at the altar the poor bride
Gives her harsh groom for bridal-gift a scourge;[2]
Of living hearts[3] that crack within the fire
Where smoulder their dead despots; and of those,—   370
Mothers,—that, all prophetic pity, fling
Their pretty maids in the running flood,[4] and swoops
The vulture, beak and talon, at the heart
Made for all noble motion. And I saw
That equal baseness lived in sleeker times   375
With smoother men; the old leaven leaven'd all;[5]
Millions of throats would bawl for civil rights,
No woman named; therefore I set my face
Against all men, and lived but for mine own.
Far off from men I built a fold for them;   380
I stored it full of rich memorial;
I fenced it round with gallant institutes,[6]
And biting laws to scare the beasts of prey,
And prosper'd, till a rout of saucy boys
Brake on us at our books, and marr'd our peace,   385
Mask'd like our maids, blustering I know not what
Of insolence and love, some pretext held
Of baby troth, invalid, since my will
Seal'd not the bond—the striplings!—for their sport!—
I tamed my leopards; shall I not tame these?   390
Or you? or I? for since you think me touch'd
In honor—what! I would not aught of false—
Is not our cause pure? and whereas I know
Your prowess, Arac, and what mother's blood
You draw from, fight! You failing, I abide   395
What end soever; fail you will not. Still,
Take not his life, he risk'd it for my own;
His mother lives. Yet whatsoe'er you do,
Fight and fight well; strike and strike home. O dear
Brothers, the woman's angel guards you, you   400
The sole men to be mingled with our cause,
The sole men we shall prize in the aftertime,
Your very armor hallow'd, and your statues
Rear'd, sung to, when, this gadfly brush'd aside,
We plant a solid foot into the Time,   405
And mould a generation strong to move
With claim on claim from right to right, till she
Whose name is yoked with children's know herself;
And Knowledge in our own land make her free,
And, ever following those two crowned twins,   410

2. "An old Russian custom" (Tennyson).
3. "Suttee in India" (Tennyson).
4. "Ganges" (Tennyson).
5. 1 Corinthians 5:6–7: "Know ye not that a little leaven leaveneth the whole lump? Purge out therefore
the old leaven."
6. Laws, as in the *Institutes of Justinian*.

Commerce and Conquest, shower the fiery grain
Of freedom broadcast over all that orbs
Between the Northern and the Southern morn.'

Then came a postcript dash'd across the rest:
'See that there be no traitors in your camp.   415
We seem a nest of traitors—none to trust
Since our arms fail'd—this Egypt-plague of men!
Almost our maids were better at their homes,
Than thus man-girdled here. Indeed I think
Our chiefest comfort is the little child   420
Of one unworthy mother, which she left.
She shall not have it back; the child shall grow
To prize the authentic mother of her mind.
I took it for an hour in mine own bed
This morning; there the tender orphan hands   425
Felt my heart, and seem'd to charm from thence
The wrath I nursed against the world. Farewell.'

I ceased; he said, 'Stubborn, but she may sit
Upon a king's right hand in thunderstorms,
And breed up warriors! See now, tho' yourself   430
Be dazzled by the wildfire Love to sloughs
That swallow common sense, the spindling king,
This Gama swamp'd in lazy tolerance.
When the man wants weight, the woman takes it up,
And topples down the scales; but this is fixt   435
As are the roots of earth and base of all,—
Man for the field and woman for the hearth;
Man for the sword, and for the needle she;
Man with the head, and woman with the heart;
Man to command, and woman to obey;   440
All else confusion. Look you! the gray mare[7]
Is ill to live with, when her whinny shrills
From tile to scullery, and her small goodman
Shrinks in his arm-chair while the fires of hell
Mix with his hearth. But you—she's yet a colt—   445
Take, break her; strongly groom'd and straitly curb'd
She might not rank with those detestable
That let the bantling scald at home, and brawl
Their rights or wrongs like potherbs in the street.
They say she's comely; there's the fairer chance.   450
I Like her none the less for rating at her!
Besides, the woman wed is not as we,
But suffers change of frame. A lusty brace
Of twins may weed her of her folly. Boy,
The bearing and the training of a child   455
Is woman's wisdom.'
                        Thus the hard old king.
I took my leave, for it was nearly noon;

---

7. "The proverb, 'the grey mare is the better horse,' said of the domineering wife" (Ricks).

I pored upon her letter which I held,
And on the little clause, 'take not his life;'
I mused on that wild morning in the woods,   460
And on the 'Follow, follow, thou shalt win;'
I thought on all the wrathful king had said,
And how the strange betrothment was to end.
Then I remember'd that burnt sorcerer's curse
That one should fight with shadows and should fall;   465
And like a flash the weird affection came.
King, camp, and college turn'd to hollow shows;
I seem'd to move in old memorial tilts,
And doing battle with forgotten ghosts,
To dream myself the shadow of a dream;   470
And ere I woke it was the point of noon,
The lists[8] were ready. Empanoplied and plumed
We enter'd in, and waited, fifty there
Opposed to fifty, till the trumpet blared
At the barrier like a wild horn in a land   475
Of echoes, and a moment, and once more
The trumpet, and again; at which the storm
Of galloping hoofs bare on the ridge of spears
And riders front to front, until they closed
In conflict with the crash of shivering points,   480
And thunder. Yet it seem'd a dream, I dream'd
Of fighting. On his haunches rose the steed,
And into fiery splinters leapt the lance,
And out of stricken helmets sprang the fire.
Part sat like rocks; part reel'd but kept their seats;   485
Part roll'd on the earth and rose again and drew;
Part stumbled mixt with floundering horses. Down
From those two bulks at Arac's side, and down
From Arac's arm, as from a giant's flail,
The large blows rain'd, as here and everywhere   490
He rode the mellay, lord of the ringing lists,
And all the plain—brand, mace, and shaft, and shield—
Shock'd, like an iron-clanging anvil bang'd
With hammers; till I thought, can this be he
From Gama's dwarfish loins? if this be so,   495
The mother makes us most—and in my dream
I glanced aside, and saw the palace-front
Alive with fluttering scarfs and ladies' eyes,
And highest, among the statues, statue-like,
Between a cymbal'd Miriam and a Jael,   500
With Psyche's babe, was Ida watching us,
A single band of gold about her hair,
Like a saint's glory up in heaven, but she,
No saint—inexorable—no tenderness—
Too hard, too cruel. Yet she sees me fight   505
Yea, let her see me fall. With that I drave

8. Derived from the Eglinton tournament in September 1839, an event sponsored to recapture medieval jousts with knights in full armor: "that pathetically funny attempt to breathe new life into chivalry and jousting" (Martin's *Tennyson*, p. 211). See also Peter Levi's *Tennyson* for an account of the event.

Among the thickest and bore down a prince,
And Cyril one. Yea, let me make my dream
All that I would. But that large-moulded man,
His visage all agrin as at a wake,   510
Made at me thro' the press, and, staggering back
With stroke on stroke the horse and horseman, came
As comes a pillar of electric cloud,
Flaying the roofs and sucking up the drains,
And shadowing down the champaign till it strikes   515
On a wood, and takes, and breaks, and cracks, and splits,
And twists the grain with such a roar that Earth
Reels, and the herdsmen cry; for everything
Gave way before him. Only Florian, he
That loved me closer than his own right eye,   520
Thrust in between; but Arac rode him down.
And Cyril seeing it, push'd against the Prince,
With Psyche's color round his helmet, tough,
Strong, supple, sinew-corded, apt at arms;
But tougher, heavier, stronger, he that smote   525
And threw him. Last I spurr'd; I felt my veins
Stretch with fierce heat; a moment hand to hand,
And sword to sword, and horse to horse we hung,
Till I struck out and shouted; the blade glanced,
I did but shear a feather, and dream and truth   530
Flow'd from me; darkness closed me, and I fell.

     Home they brought her warrior dead;[9]
       She nor swoon'd nor utter'd cry.
     All her maidens, watching, said,
       'She must weep or she will die.'   535

     Then they praised him, soft and low,
       Call'd him worthy to be loved,
     Truest friend and noblest foe;
       Yet she neither spoke nor moved.

     Stole a maiden from her place,   540
     Lightly to the warrior stept,
     Took the face-cloth from the face;
       Yet she neither moved nor wept.

     Rose a nurse of ninety years,
     Set his child upon her knee—   545
     Like summer tempest came her tears—
       'Sweet my child, I live for thee.'

VI

My dream had never died or lived again;
As in some mystic middle state I lay.
Seeing I saw not, hearing not I heard;

9. Ricks notes the resemblances to Sir Walter Scott's *Lay of the Last Minstrel*.

Tho', if I saw not, yet they told me all
So often that I speak as having seen.   5

For so it seem'd, or so they said to me,
That all things grew more tragic and more strange;
That when our side was vanquish'd and my cause
For ever lost, there went up a great cry,
'The Prince is slain!' My father heard and ran   10
In on the lists, and there unlaced my casque
And grovell'd on my body, and after him
Came Psyche, sorrowing for Aglaïa.[1]
    But high upon the palace Ida stood
With Psyche's babe in arm; there on the roofs   15
Like that great dame of Lapidoth[2] she sang.

'Our enemies have fallen, have fallen: the seed,
The little seed they laugh'd at in the dark,
Has risen and cleft the soil, and grown a bulk
Of spanless girth, that lays on every side   20
A thousand arms and rushes to the sun.

'Our enemies[3] have fallen, have fallen: they came;
The leaves were wet with women's tears; they heard
A noise of songs they would not understand;
They mark'd it with the red cross to the fall,   25
And would have strown it, and are fallen themselves.

'Our enemies have fallen, have fallen: they came,
The woodmen with their axes: lo the tree!
But we will make it faggots for the hearth,
And shape it plank and beam for roof and floor,   30
And boats and bridges for the use of men.

'Our enemies have fallen, have fallen; they struck;
With their own blows they hurt themselves, nor knew
There dwelt an iron nature in the grain;
The glittering axe was broken in their arms,   35
Their arms were shatter'd to the shoulder blade.

'Our enemies have fallen, but this shall grow
A night of Summer from the heat, a breadth
Of Autumn, dropping fruits of power; and roll'd
With music in the growing breeze of Time,   40
The tops shall strike from star to star, the fangs
Shall move the stony bases of the world.

'And now, O maids, behold our sanctuary
Is violate, our laws broken; fear we not

---

1. See n. 8, p. 143.
2. Tennyson noted Judges 4:4 "And Deborah, a prophetess, the wife of Lapidoth, she judged Israel at that time."
3. Tennyson noted Judges 5:31: "So let all thine enemies perish, O Lord"; and Isaiah 21:9: "Babylon is fallen, is fallen."

To break them more in their behoof, whose arms   45
Champion'd our cause and won it with a day
Blanch'd[4] in our annals, and perpetual feast,
When dames and heroines of the golden year
Shall strip a hundred hollows bare of Spring,
To rain an April of ovation round   50
Their statues, borne aloft, the three; but come,
We will be liberal, since our rights are won.
Let them not lie in the tents with coarse mankind,
Ill nurses; but descend, and proffer these
The brethren of our blood and cause, that there   55
Lie bruised and maim'd, the tender ministries
Of female hands and hospitality.'

   She spoke, and with the babe yet in her arms,
Descending, burst the great bronze valves,[5] and led
A hundred maids in train across the park.   60
Some cowl'd, and some bare-headed, on they came,
Their feet in flowers, her loveliest. By them went
The enamor'd air[6] sighing, and on their curls
From the high tree the blossom wavering fell,
And over them the tremulous isles of light[7]   65
Slided, they moving under shade; but Blanche
At distance follow'd. So they came: anon
Thro' open field into the lists they wound
Timorously; and as the leader of the herd
That holds a stately fretwork to the sun,   70
And follow'd up by a hundred airy does,
Steps with a tender foot, light as on air,
The lovely, lordly creature floated on
To where her wounded brethren lay; there stay'd,
Knelt on one knee,—the child on one,—and prest   75
Their hands, and call'd them dear deliverers,
And happy warriors,[8] and immortal names,
And said, 'You shall not lie in the tents, but here,
And nursed by those for whom you fought, and served
With female hands and hospitality.'   80

   Then, whether moved by this, or was it chance,
She past my way. Up started from my side
The old lion, glaring with his whelpless eye,
Silent; but when she saw me lying stark,
Dishelm'd and mute, and motionlessly pale,   85
Cold even to her, she sigh'd; and when she saw
The haggard father's face and reverend beard
Of grisly twine, all dabbled with the blood

---

4. "Marked in white chalk as propitious days" (Ricks).
5. "Leaves of a door" (Ricks). See also n. 1, p. 164.
6. Compare *Antony and Cleopatra* II, ii, lines 199 and 202: "The winds were love-sick"; the water "As amorous of their strokes."
7. "Spots of sunshine coming through the leaves, and seeming to slide from one to the other, as the procession of girls 'moves under shade'" (Tennyson).
8. "Compare Wordsworth's 'Who is the happy Warrior?'" (Ricks)

Of his own son, shudder'd, a twitch of pain
Tortured her mouth, and o'er her forehead past   90
A shadow, and her hue changed, and she said:
'He saved my life; my brother slew him for it.'
No more; at which the king in bitter scorn
Drew from my neck the painting and the tress,
And held them up. She saw them, and a day   95
Rose from the distance on her memory,
When the good queen, her mother, shore the tress
With kisses, ere the days of Lady Blanche.
And then once more she look'd at my pale face;
Till understanding all the foolish work   100
Of Fancy, and the bitter close of all,
Her iron will was broken in her mind;
Her noble heart was molten in her breast;
She bow'd, she set the child on the earth; she laid
A feeling finger on my brows, and presently   105
'O Sire,' she said, 'he lives; he is not dead!
O, let me have him with my brethren here
In our own palace; we will tend on him
Like one of these; if so, by any means,
To lighten this great clog of thanks, that make   110
Our progress falter to the woman's goal.'

   She said; but at the happy word 'he lives!
My father stoop'd, re-father'd o'er my wounds.
So those two foes above my fallen life
With brow to brow like night and evening mixt   115
Their dark and gray, while Psyche ever stole
A little nearer, till the babe that by us,
Half-lapt in glowing gauze and golden brede[9]
Lay like a new-fallen meteor on the grass,
Uncared for, spied its mother and began   120
A blind and babbling laughter, and to dance
Its body, and reach its fatling innocent arms
And lazy lingering fingers. She the appeal
Brook'd not, but clamoring out 'Mine—mine—not yours!
It is not yours, but mine; give me the child!'   125
Ceased all on tremble; piteous was the cry.
So stood the unhappy mother open-mouth'd,
And turn'd each face her way. Wan was her cheek
With hollow watch; her blooming mantle torn,
Red grief and mother's hunger in her eye,   130
And down dead-heavy sank her curls, and half
The sacred mother's bosom, panting, burst
The laces toward her babe; but she nor cared
Nor knew it, clamoring on, till Ida heard,
Look'd up, and rising slowly from me, stood   135
Erect and silent, striking with her glance
The mother, me, the child. But he that lay

9. "Embroidery" (Tennyson).

Beside us, Cyril, batter'd as he was,
Trail'd himself up on one knee; then he drew
Her robe to meet his lips, and down she look'd   140
At the arm'd man sideways, pitying as it seem'd,
Or self-involved; but when she learnt his face,
Remembering his ill-omen'd song, arose
Once more thro' all her height, and o'er him grew
Tall as a figure lengthen'd on the sand   145
When the tide ebbs in sunshine, and he said:

   'O fair and strong and terrible! Lioness
That with your long locks play the lion's mane!
But Love and Nature, these are two more terrible
And stronger. See, your foot is on our necks,   150
We vanquish'd, you the victor of your will.
What would you more? give her the child! remain
Orb'd in your isolation; he is dead,
Or all as dead: henceforth we let you be.
Win you the hearts of women; and beware   155
Lest, where you seek the common love of these,
The common hate with the revolving wheel
Should drag you down, and some great Nemesis
Break from a darken'd future, crown'd with fire,
And tread you out for ever. But howsoe'er   160
Fixt in yourself, never in your own arms
To hold your own, deny not hers to her,
Give her the child! O, if, I say, you keep
One pulse that beats true woman, if you loved
The breast that fed or arm that dandled you,   165
Or own one port[1] of sense not flint to prayer,
Give her the child! or if you scorn to lay it,
Yourself, in hands so lately claspt with yours,
Or speak to her, your dearest, her one fault
The tenderness, not yours, that could not kill,   170
Give *me* it, *I* will give it her.'
                              He said.
At first her eye with slow dilation roll'd
Dry flame, she listening' after sank and sank
And, into mournful twilight mellowing, dwelt
Full on the child. She took it: 'Pretty bud!   175
Lily of the vale! half-opcn'd bell of the woods!
Sole comfort of my dark hour, when a world
Of traitorous friend and broken system made
No purple in the distance, mystery,
Pledge of a love not to be mine, farewell!   180
These men are hard upon us as of old,
We two must part; and yet how fain was I
To dream thy cause embraced in mine, to think
I might be something to thee, when I felt
Thy helpless warmth about my barren breast   185

---

1. "Port for haven. Misprinted 'part' in earlier editions" (Tennyson).

In the dead prime; but may thy mother prove
As true to thee as false, false, false to me!
And, if thou needs must bear the yoke, I with it
Gentle as freedom'—here she kiss'd it; then—
'All good go with thee! take it, sir,' and so   190
Laid the soft babe in his hard - mailed hands,
Who turn'd half-round to Psyche as she sprang
To meet it, with an eye that swum in thanks;
Then felt it sound and whole from head to foot,
And hugg'd and never hugg'd it close enough,   195
And in her hunger mouth'd and mumbled it,
And hid her bosom with it; after that
Put on more calm and added suppliantly:

   'We two were friends: I go to mine own land
For ever. Find some other; as for me   200
I scarce am fit for your great plans: yet speak to me,
Say one soft word and let me part forgiven.'

   But Ida spoke not, rapt upon the child.
Then Arac: 'Ida—'sdeath! you blame the man;
You wrong yourselves—the woman is so hard   205
Upon the woman. Come, a grace to me!
I am your warrior; I and mine have fought
Your battle. Kiss her; take her hand, she weeps.
'Sdeath! I would sooner fight thrice o'er than see it.'

   But Ida spoke not, gazing on the ground;   210
And reddening in the furrows of his chin,
And moved beyond his custom, Gama said:

   'I've heard that there is iron in the blood,
And I believe it. Not one word? not one?
Whence drew you this steel temper? not from me,   215
Not from your mother, now a saint with saints.
She said you had a heart—I heard her say it—
"Our Ida has a heart"—just ere she died—
"But see that some one with authority
Be near her still" and I—I sought for one—   220
All people said she had authority—
The Lady Blanche—much profit! Not one word;
No! tho' your father sues. See how you stand
Stiff as Lot's wife, and all the good knights maim'd,
I trust that there is no one hurt to death,   225
For your wild whim. And was it then for this,
Was it for this we gave our palace up,
Where we withdrew from summer heats and state,
And had our wine and chess beneath the planes,
And many a pleasant hour with her that's gone,   230
Ere you were born to vex us? Is it kind?
Speak to her, I say; is this not she of whom,
When first she came, all flush'd you said to me,

Now had you got a friend of your own age,
Now could you share your thought, now should men see   235
Two women faster welded in one love
Than pairs of wedlock? she you walk'd with, she
You talk'd with, whole nights long, up with the tower
Of sine and arc, spheroid and azimuth,[2]
And right ascension, heaven knows what; and now   240
A word, but one, one little kindly word,
Not one to spare her! Out upon you, flint!
You love nor her, nor me, nor any; nay,
You shame your mother's judgment too. Not one?
You will not? well—no heart have you, or such   245
As fancies like the vermin in a nut[3]
Have fretted all to dust and bitterness.'
So said the small king moved beyond his wont.

   But Ida stood nor spoke, drain'd of her force
By many a varying influence and so long.   250
Down thro' her limbs a drooping langour wept;
Her head a little bent; and on her mouth
A doubtful smile dwelt like a clouded moon
In a still water. Then brake out my sire,
Lifting his grim head from my wounds: 'O you,   255
Woman, whom we thought woman even now,
And were half fool'd to let you tend our son,
Because he might have wish'd it—but we see
The accomplice of your madness unforgiven,
And think that you might mix his draught with death,   260
When your skies change again; the rougher hand
Is safer. On to the tents; take up the Prince.'

   He rose, and while each ear was prick'd to attend
A tempest, thro' the cloud that dimm'd her broke
A genial warmth and light once more, and shone   265
Thro' glittering drops on her sad friend.
                              'Come hither,
O Psyche,' she cried out, 'embrace me, come,
Quick while I melt; make reconcilement sure
With one that cannot keep her mind an hour;
Come to the hollow heart they slander so!   270
Kiss and be friends, like children being chid!
I seem no more, I want forgiveness too;
I should have had to do with none but maids,
That have no links with men. Ah false but dear,
Dear traitor, too much loved, why?—why?—yet see   275
Before these kings we embrace you yet once more
With all forgiveness, all oblivion,
And trust, not love, you less.

---

2. "The azimuth of any point on a horizontal plane is the angle between a line drawn to that point, and a
   fixed line in the horizontal plane, usually chosen to be a line drawn due North" (Hallam Tennyson). Evidently the discussion must have involved, at least in part, celestial navigation.
3. "The worm eats a nut and leaves behind but dry and bitter dust" (Tennyson).

And now, O Sire,
Grant me your son, to nurse, to wait upon him,
Like mine own brother. For my debt to him,   280
This nightmare weight of gratitude, I know it.
Taunt me no more; yourself and yours shall have
Free adit;[4] we will scatter all our maids
Till happier times each to her proper hearth.
What use to keep them here—now? grant my prayer.   285
Help, father, brother, help; speak to the king;
Thaw this male nature to some touch of that
Which kills me with myself, and drags me down
From my fixt height to mob me up with all
The soft and milky rabble of womankind,   290
Poor weakling even as they are.'
                    Passionate tears
Follow'd; the king replied not; Cyril said:
'Your brother, lady,—Florian,—ask for him
Of your great Head—for he is wounded too—
That you may tend upon him with the Prince.'   295
'Ay, so,' said Ida with a bitter smile,
'Our laws are broken; let him enter too.'
Then Violet, she that sang the mournful song,
And had a cousin tumbled on the plain,
Petition'd too for him. 'Ay, so,' she said,   300
'I stagger in the stream; I cannot keep
My heart an eddy from the brawling hour.
We break our laws with ease, but let it be.'
'Ay, so?' said Blanche: 'Amazed am I to hear
Your Highness; but your Highness breaks with ease   305
The law your Highness did not make; 't was I.
I had been wedded wife, I knew mankind,
And block'd them out; but these men came to woo
Your Highness,—verily I think to win.'

   So she, and turn'd askance a wintry eye;   310
But Ida, with a voice that, like a bell
Toll'd by an earthquake in a trembling tower,
Rang ruin, answer'd full of grief and scorn:

   'Fling our doors wide! all, all, not one, but all,
Not only he, but by my mother's soul,   315
Whatever man lies wounded, friend or foe,
Shall enter, if he will! Let our girls flit,
Till the storm die! but had you stood by us,
The roar that breaks the Pharos from his base
Had left us rock. She fain would sting us too,   320
But shall not. Pass, and mingle with your likes.
We brook no further insult, but are gone.'
   She turn'd; the very nape of her white neck
Was rosed with indignation; but the Prince

4. Access. In precisely this sense of the word, Tennyson's is the earliest example in the OED (Ricks).

Her brother came; the king her father charm'd   325
Her wounded soul with words; nor did mine own
Refuse her proffer, lastly gave his hand.

   Then us they lifted up, dead weights, and bare
Straight to the doors; to them the doors gave way
Groaning, and in the vestal entry shriek'd   330
The virgin marble under iron heels.
And on they moved and gain'd the hall, and there
Rested; but great the crush was, and each base,
To left and right, of those tall columns drown'd
In silken fluctuation and the swarm   335
Of female whisperers. At the further end
Was Ida by the throne, the two great cats
Close by her, like supporters on a shield,
Bow-back'd with fear; but in the centre stood
The common men with rolling eyes; amazed   340
They glared upon the women, and aghast
The women stared at these, all silent, save
When armor clash'd or jingled, while the day,
Descending, struck athwart the hall, and shot
A flying splendor out of brass and steel,   345
That o'er the statues leapt from head to head,
Now fired an angry Pallas on the helm,
Now set a wrathful Dian's moon on flame;
And now and then an echo started up,
And shuddering fled from room to room, and died   350
Of fright in far apartments.
                    Then the voice
Of Ida sounded, issuing ordinance;
And me they bore up the broad stairs, and thro'
The long-laid galleries past a hundred doors
To one deep chamber shut from sound, and due   355
To languid limbs and sickness, left me in it;
And others otherwhere they laid; and all
That afternoon a sound arose of hoof
And chariot, many a maiden passing home
Till happier times; but some were left of those   360
Held sagest, and the great lords out and in,
From those two hosts that lay beside the wall,
Walk'd at their will, and everything was changed.

    Ask me no more: the moon may draw the sea;[5]
       The cloud may stoop from heaven and take the shape,   365
       With fold to fold, of mountain or of cape;
    But O too fond, when have I answered thee?
                            Ask me no more.

    Ask me no more: what answer should I give?
       I love not hollow cheek or faded eye:

5. "Compare Carew's Song, of which each stanza begins, 'Aske me no more'" (Ricks).

Yet, O my friend, I will not have thee die!   370
Ask me no more, lest I should bid thee live;
                                         Ask me no more.

Ask me no more: thy fate and mine are seal'd;
    I strove against the stream and all in vain;
    Let the great river take me to the main.
No more, dear love, for at a touch I yield;
                                         Ask me no more.   375

                            VII

So was their sanctuary violated,
So their fair college turn'd to hospital,
At first with all confusion; by and by
Sweet order lived again with other laws,
A kindlier influence reign'd, and everywhere   5
Low voices with the ministering hand
Hung round the sick. The maidens came, they talk'd,
They sang, they read; till she not fair began
To gather light, and she that was became
Her former beauty treble; and to and fro   10
With books, with flowers, with angel offices,
Like creatures native unto gracious act,
And in their own clear element, they moved.

    But sadness on the soul of Ida fell,
And hatred of her weakness, blent with shame.   15
Old studies fail'd; seldom she spoke; but oft
Clomb to the roofs, and gazed alone for hours
On that disastrous leaguer, swarms of men
Darkening her female field. Void was her use,[6]
And she as one that climbs a peak to gaze   20
O'er land and main, and sees a great black cloud[7]
Drag inward from the deeps, a wall of night,
Blot out the slope of sea from verge to shore,
And suck the blinding splendor from the sand,
And quenching lake by lake and tarn by tarn   25
Expunge the world; so fared she gazing there,
So blacken'd all her world in secret, blank
And waste it seem'd and vain; till down she came,
And found fair peace once more among the sick.

    And twilight dawn'd; and morn by morn the lark   30
Shot up and shrill'd in flickering gyres, but I
Lay silent in the muffled cage of life.
And twilight gloom'd, and broader-grown the bowers
Drew the great night into themselves, and heaven,
Star after star, arose and fell; but I,   35
Deeper than those weird doubts could reach me, lay

6. "Her usual occupations neglected" (Ricks)
7. "An approaching storm seen from the summit of Snowden" (Tennyson).

Quite sunder'd from the moving Universe,
Nor knew what eye was on me, nor the hand
That nursed me, more than infants in their sleep.

But Psyche tended Florian; with her oft   40
Melissa came, for Blanche had gone, but left
Her child among us, willing she should keep
Court-favor. Here and there the small bright head,
A light of healing, glanced about the couch,
Or thro' the parted silks the tender face   45
Peep'd, shining in upon the wounded man
With blush and smile, a medicine in themselves
To wile the length from languorous hours, and draw
The sting from pain; nor seem'd it strange that soon
He rose up whole, and those fair charities   50
Join'd at her side; nor stranger seem'd that hearts
So gentle, so employ'd, should close in love,
Than when two dewdrops on the petal shake
To the same sweet air, and tremble deeper down,
And slip at once all-fragrant into one.   55

Less prosperously the second suit obtain'd[8]
At first with Psyche. Not tho' Blanche had sworn
That after that dark night among the fields
She needs must wed him for her own good name;
Not tho' he built upon the babe restored;   60
Not tho' she liked him, yielded she, but fear'd
To incense the Head once more; till on a day
When Cyril pleaded, Ida came behind
Seen but of Psyche; on her foot she hung
A moment, and she heard, at which her face   65
A little flush'd, and she past on; but each
Assumed from thence a half-consent involved
In stillness, plighted troth, and were at peace.

Nor only these; Love in the sacred halls
Held carnival at will, and flying struck   70
With showers of random sweet on maid and man.
Nor did her father cease to press my claim,
Nor did mine own now reconciled; nor yet
Did those twin brothers, risen again and whole;
Nor Arac, satiate with his victory.   75

But I lay still, and with me oft she sat.
Then came a change; for sometimes I would catch
Her hand in wild delirium, gripe it hard,
And fling it like a viper off, and shriek,
'You are not Ida;' clasp it once again,   80
And call her Ida, tho' I knew her not,
And call her sweet, as if in irony,

8. "Prevailed" (Tennyson).

And call her hard and cold, which seem'd a truth;
And still she fear'd that I should lose my mind,
And often she believed that I should die;   85
Till out of long frustration of her care,
And pensive tendance in the all-weary noons,
And watches in the dead, the dark, when clocks
Throbb'd thunder thro' the palace floors, or call'd
On flying Time from all their silver tongues—   90
And out of memories of her kindlier days,
And sidelong glances at my father's grief,
And at the happy lovers heart in heart—
And out of hauntings of my spoken love,
And lonely listenings to my mutter'd dream,   95
And often feeling of the helpless hands,
And wordless broodings on the wasted check—
From all a closer interest flourish'd up,
Tenderness touch by touch, and last, to these,
Love, like an Alpine harebell hung with tears   100
By some cold morning glacier; frail at first
And feeble, all unconscious of itself,
But such as gather'd color day by day.

     Last I woke sane, but well-nigh close to death
For weakness. It was evening; silent light   105
Slept on the painted walls, wherein were wrought
Two grand designs; for on one side arose
The women up in wild revolt, and storm'd
At the Oppian[9] law. Titanic shapes, they cramm'd
The forum, and half-crush'd among the rest   110
A drawf-like Cato cower'd. On the other side
Hortensia[1] spoke against the tax; behind,
A train of dames. By axe and eagle sat,
With all their foreheads drawn in Roman scowls,
And half the wolf's-milk curdled in their veins,   115
The fierce triumvirs; and before them paused
Hortensia, pleading; angry was her face.

     I saw the forms; I knew not where I was.
They did but look like hollow shows; nor more
Sweet Ida. Palm to palm she sat; the dew   120
Dwelt in her eyes, and softer all her shape
And rounder seem'd. I moved, I sigh'd; a touch
Came round my wrist, and tears upon my hand.
Then all for languor and self-pity ran
Mine down my face, and with what life I had,   125
And like a flower that cannot all unfold,

9. "When Hannibal was nearing Rome a law was carried by C. Oppius, Trib. Pleb., B.C. 215, forbidding
    women to wear more than half an ounce of gold, or brilliant dresses, and no woman was to come within
    a mile of Rome or of any town save on account of public sacrifices in a conveyance drawn by horses"
    (Tennyson). "In B.C. 195 the Oppian Law was, in spite of Cato's protests, repealed. Livy, xxxiv, 8" (Hal-
    lam Tennyson).
1. "She pleaded against the proposed tax on Roman matrons after the assassination of Julius Caesar which
    was to be raised in order to pay for the expenses of the war against Brutus and Cassius" (Hallam Tennyson).

So drench'd it is with tempest, to the sun,
Yet, as it may, turns toward him, I on her
Fixt my faint eyes, and utter'd whisperingly:

'If you be what I think you, some sweet dream,   130
I would but ask you to fulfill yourself;
But if you be that Ida whom I knew,
I ask you nothing; only, if a dream,
Sweet dream, be perfect. I shall die tonight.
Stoop down and seem to kiss me ere I die.'   135

I could no more, but lay like one in trance,
That hears his burial talk'd of by his friends,
And cannot speak, nor move, nor make one sign,
But lies and dreads his doom. She turn'd, she paused,
She stoop'd; and out of languor leapt a cry,   140
Leapt fiery Passion from the brinks of death,
And I believed that in the living world
My spirit closed with Ida's at the lips;
Till back I fell, and from mine arms she rose
Glowing all over noble shame; and all   145
Her falser self split from her like a robe,
And left her woman, lovelier in her mood
Than in her mould that other,[2] when she came
From barren deeps to conquer all with love,
And down the streaming crystal dropt; and she   150
Far-fleeted by the purple island-sides,
Naked, a double light in air and wave,
To meet her Graces, where they deck'd her out
For worship without end—nor end of mine,
Stateliest, for thee! but mute she glided forth,   155
Nor glanced behind her, and I sank and slept,
Fill'd thro' and thro' with love, a happy sleep.

Deep in the night I woke: she, near me, held
A volume of the poets of her land.
There to herself, all in low tones, she read: 160

'Now sleeps the crimson petal, now the white;[3]
Nor waves the cypress in the palace walk;
Nor winks the gold fin in the porphyry font.
The fire-fly wakens; waken thou with me.

'Now droops the milk-white peacock like a ghost,   165
And like a ghost she glimmers on to me.

2. "Aphrodite passed before his brain, drowsy with weakness" (Tennyson). The following lines picture her
rising from the ocean.
3. "This song draws on eastern sources; the best summary is by Killham (pp. 219–20). The form is that of
a ghazal—'the requisite number of couplets, the repetitions of a single final word at short intervals to produce what is tantamount to rhyme, and the standard images and ornaments of the Persian love poem:
roses, lilies, peacocks, the stars, the cypress'" (Ricks).

'Now lies the Earth all Danaë[4] to the stars,
And all thy heart lies open unto me.

'Now slides the silent meteor on, and leaves
A shining furrow, as thy thoughts in me.   170

'Now folds the lily all her sweetness up,
And slips into the bosom of the lake.
So fold thyself, my dearest, thou, and slip
Into my bosom and be lost in me.'

I heard her turn the page; she found a small   175
Sweet idyl, and once more, as low, she read:

'Come down, O maid, from yonder mountain height.[5]
What pleasure lives in height (the shepherd sang),
In height and cold, the splendor of the hills?
But cease to move so near the heavens, and cease   180
To glide a sunbeam by the blasted pine,
To sit a star upon the sparkling spire;
And come, for Love is of the valley, come,
For Love is of the valley, come thou down
And find him; by the happy threshold, he,   185
Or hand in hand with Plenty in the maize,
Or red with spirted purple of the vats,
Or foxlike in the vine, nor cares to walk[6]
With Death and Morning on the silver Horns,[7]
Nor wilt thou snare him in the white ravine,   190
Nor find him dropt upon the firths of ice,
That huddling slant in furrow-cloven falls
To roll the torrent out of dusky doors.[8]
But follow; let the torrent dance thee down
To find him in the valley; let the wild   195
Lean-headed eagles yelp alone, and leave
The monstrous ledges there to slope, and spill
Their thousand wreaths of dangling water-smoke.
That like a broken purpose waste in air.
So waste not thou, but come; for all the vales   200
Await thee; azure pillars of the hearth
Arise to thee; the children call, and I
Thy shepherd pipe, and sweet is every sound,
Sweeter thy voice, but every sound is sweet;
Myriads of rivulets hurrying thro' the lawn,   205

4. "Zeus came down to Danaë when shut up in a tower in a shower of golden stars" (Tennyson). Warned by an oracle that his daughter's male offspring would kill him, Acrisius locked her up in a brass tower; Danaë's son by Zeus, Perseus, accidently killed his grandfather with a discus while taking part in some games.
5. "Come down, O maid is said to be taken from Theocritus, but there is no real likeness except perhaps in the Greek Idyllic feeling" (Tennyson). Nevertheless, see Theocritus' Idyll XI. The song was "written in Switzerland (chiefly at Lauterbrunnen and Grindewald) and descriptive of the waste Alpine heights and gorges" (Memoir I, 252). Tennyson considered the poem to be among his "most successful work."
6. Hallam Tennyson noted Hamlet I, i, line 167; "But look, the morn in russet mantle clad / Walks o'er the dew of yon high eastward hill." "Vine": Song of Solomon 2:15: "Take us the foxes, the little foxes, that spoil the vines: for our vines have tender grapes."
7. The snowy mountain peaks. "'Silver,' by the bye, ought not to be spelt as it is with capital letters" (Tennyson). "Death": "Death is the lifelessness on the high snow peaks" (Tennyson). Also see Letters II, 49.
8. Passageways cut by melting ice through the mud and rocks at the foot of a glacier. "The opening of the gorge is called dusky as a contrast with the snows all about" (Tennyson).

The moan of doves[9] in immemorial elms,
And murmuring of innumerable bees.'

So she low-toned, while with shut eyes I lay
Listening, then look'd. Pale was the perfect face;
The bosom with long sighs labor'd; and meek   210
Seem'd the full lips, and mild the luminous eyes,
And the voice trembled and the hand. She said
Brokenly, that she knew it, she had fail'd
In sweet humility, had fail'd in all;
That all her labor was but as a block   215
Left in the quarry; but she still were loth,
She still were loth to yield herself to one
That wholly scorn'd to help their equal rights
Against the sons of men and barbarous laws.
She pray'd me not to judge their cause from her   220
That wrong'd it, sought far less for truth than power
In knowledge. Something wild within her breast,
A greater than all knowledge, beat her down.
And she had nursed me there from week to week;
Much had she learnt in little time. In part   225
It was ill counsel had misled the girl
To vex true hearts; yet was she but a girl—
'Ah fool, and made myself a queen of farce!
When comes another such? never, I think,
Till the sun drop, dead, from the signs.'
                              Her voice   230
Choked, and her forehead sank upon her hands,
And her great heart thro' all the faultful past
Went sorrowing in a pause I dared not break;
Till notice of a change in the dark world
Was lispt about the acacias, and a bird,   235
That early woke to feed her little ones,
Sent from a dewy breast a cry for light.
She moved, and at her feet the volume fell.

'Blame not thyself too much,' I said, 'nor blame
Too much the sons of men and barbarous laws;   240
These were the rough ways of the world till now.
Henceforth thou hast a helper, me, that know
The woman's cause is man's; they rise or sink
Together, dwarf'd or godlike, bond or free[1]
For she that out of Lethe scales with man   245
The shining steps of Nature, shares with man
His nights, his days, moves with him to one goal,
Stays all the fair young planet in her hands[2]—
If she be small, slight-natured, miserable,

---

9. "'Nec gemere aëria cessabit turtur ab ulmo.' Virgil, *Eclogue*, I, 59" (Tennyson). "While still the cooing wood-pigeons, your pets, and the turtle-dove shall cease not their moaning from the skyey elm" (*Loeb Classical Library*, 57–58).
1. 1 Corinthians 12:13: "Whether we be Jews or Gentiles, whether we be bond or free."
2. "Cf. Ross Wallace's lines: 'The hand that rocks the cradle / Is the hand that rules the world.'" (Hallam Tennyson).

How shall men grow?[3] but work no more alone!   250
Our place is much; as far as in us lies
We two will serve them both in aiding her—
Will clear away the parasitic forms
That seem to keep her up but drag her down—
Will leave her space to burgeon out of all   255
Within her—let her make herself her own
To give or keep, to live and learn and be
All that not harms distinctive womanhood.
For woman is not undevelopt man,
But diverse. Could we make her as the man,   260
Sweet Love were slain; his dearest bond is this,
Not like to like, but like in difference.
Yet in the long years liker must they grow;
The man be more of woman, she of man;
He gain in sweetness and in moral height,   265
Nor lose the wrestling thews that throw the world;
She mental breadth, nor fail in childward care,
Nor lose the childlike in the larger mind;
Till at the last she set herself to man,
Like perfect music unto noble words;   270
And so these twain, upon the skirts of Time,
Sit side by side, full-summ'd in all their powers,
Dispensing harvest, sowing the to-be,
Self-reverent each and reverencing each,
Distinct in individualities,   275
But like each other even as those who love.
Then comes the statelier Eden back to men;
Then reign the world's great bridals, chaste and calm;
Then springs the crowning race of humankind.
May these things be!'
                        Sighing she spoke: 'I fear   280
They will not.'
                'Dear, but let us type them now
In our own lives, and this proud watchword rest
Of equal; seeing either sex alone
Is half itself, and in true marriage lies
Nor equal, nor unequal. Each fulfills   285
Defect in each, and always thought in thought,
Purpose in purpose, will in will, they grow,
The single pure and perfect animal,
The two-cell'd heart beating, with one full stroke,
Life.'   290
    And again sighing she spoke: 'A dream
That once was mine! what woman taught you this?'

---

3. The prevailing science of the day held that acquired characteristics could be transmitted to offspring, promoted by Darwin as "pangenesis." Tennyson could have picked up this information from a number of sources, probably from Robert Chambers's *Vestiges of Creation* (1844), which he was reading just after its publication. See *Alfred Tennyson*, p. 250. Mendel (1822–1884) and his science of genetics (based on work with peas) was not discovered until around 1902, although his work was accomplished by 1865.

'Alone,' I said, 'from earlier than I know,
Immersed in rich foreshadowings of the world,
I loved the woman. He, that doth not, lives   295
A drowning life, besotted in sweet self,
Or pines in sad experience worse than death,
Or keeps his wing'd affections clipt with crime.
Yet was there one thro' whom I loved her, one
Not learned, save in gracious household ways,   300
Not perfect, nay, but full of tender wants,
No angel, but a dearer being, all dipt
In angel instincts, breathing Paradise,
Interpreter between the gods and men,
Who look'd all native to her place, and yet   305
On tiptoe seem'd to touch upon a sphere
Too gross to tread, and all male minds perforce
Sway'd to her from their orbits as they moved,
And girdled her with music. Happy he
With such a mother! faith in womankind   310
Beats with his blood, and trust in all things high
Comes easy to him, and tho' he trip and fall
He shall not blind his soul with clay.'
                                        'But I,'
Said Ida, tremulously, 'so all unlike—
It seems you love to cheat yourself with words;   315
This mother is your model. I have heard
Of your strange doubts; they well might be; I seem
A mockery to my own self. Never, Prince!
You cannot love me.'
                        'Nay, but thee,' I said,
'From yearlong poring on thy pictured eyes,   320
Ere seen I loved, and loved thee seen, and saw
Thee woman thro' the crust of iron moods
That mask'd thee from men's reverence up, and forced
Sweet love on pranks of saucy boyhood; now,
Given back to life, to life indeed, thro' thee,   325
Indeed I love. The new day comes, the light
Dearer for night, as dearer thou for faults
Lived over. Lift thine eyes; my doubts are dead,
My haunting sense of hollow shows; the change,[4]
This truthful change in thee has kill'd it. Dear,   330
Look up, and let thy nature strike on mine,
Like yonder morning on the blind half-world.
Approach and fear not; breathe upon my brows;
In that fine air I tremble, all the past
Melts mist-like into this bright hour, and this   335
Is morn to more, and all the rich to-come
Reels, as the golden Autumn woodland reels
Athwart the smoke of burning weeds. Forgive me,

---

4. "You have become a real woman to me" (Tennyson). "The realization of her womanhood was the magic
touch which gave her reality and dispelled his haunting sense of the unreality of things" (Hallam Tennyson). Just as the prince's "masculinity" has been the subject of continued debate, so with Princess Ida
as an "ersatz male."

I waste my heart in signs; let be. My bride,
My wife, my life! O, we will walk this world,   340
Yoked in all exercise of noble end,
And so thro' those dark gates across the wild
That no man knows. Indeed I love thee; come,
Yield thyself up; my hopes and thine are one.
Accomplish thou my manhood and thyself;   345
Lay thy sweet hands in mine and trust to me.'

CONCLUSION

So closed our tale, of which I give you all
The random scheme as wildly as it rose.
The words are mostly mine; for when we ceased
There came a minute's pause, and Walter said,
'I wish she had not yielded!' then to me,   5
'What if you drest it up poetically!'
So pray'd the men, the women; I gave assent.
Yet how to bind the scatter'd scheme of seven
Together in one sheaf? What style could suit?
The men required that I should give throughout   10
The sort of mock-heroic gigantesque,
With which we banter'd little Lilia first;
The women—and perhaps they felt their power,
For something in the ballads which they sang,
Or in their silent influence as they sat,   15
Had ever seem'd to wrestle with burlesque,
And drove us, last, to quite a solemn close—
They hated banter, wish'd for something real,
A gallant fight, a noble princess—why
Not make her true-heroic—true-sublime?   20
Or all, they said, as earnest as the close?
Which yet with such a framework scarce could be.
Then rose a little feud betwixt the two,
Betwixt the mockers and the realists;
And I, betwixt them both, to please them both,   25
And yet to give the story as it rose,
I moved as in a strange diagonal,
And maybe neither pleased myself nor them.

But Lilia pleased me, for she took no part
In our dispute; the sequel of the tale   30
Had touch'd her, and she sat, she pluck'd the grass,
She flung it from her, thinking; last, she fixt
A showery glance upon her aunt, and said,
'You—tell us what we are'—who might have told.[5]
For she was cramm'd with theories out of books,   35
But that there rose a shout. The gates were closed
At sunset, and the crowd were swarming now,

5. In a change from the earlier version, "the forty-six lines, 'who might have told' to 'garden rails,' were inserted, written just after the disturbances in France, February 1848, when Louis Philippe was compelled to abdicate" (Tennyson).

To take their leave, about the garden rails.
So I and some went out to these; we climb'd
The slope to Vivian-place, and turning saw   40
The happy valleys, half in light and half
Far-shadowing from the west, a land of peace;
Gray halls alone among their massive groves;
Trim hamlets, here and there a rustie tower
Half-lost in belts of hop and breadths of wheat;   45
The shimmering glimpses of a stream; the seas;
A red sail, or a white; and far beyond,
Imagined more than seen, the skirts of France.

'Look there, a garden!' said my college friend,
The Tory member's elder son, 'and there!   50
God bless the narrow sea which keeps her off,
And keeps our Britain, whole within herself,
A nation yet, the rulers and the ruled—
Some sense of duty, something of a faith,
Some reverence for the laws ourselves have made,   55
Some patient force to change them when we will,
Some civic manhood firm against the crowd—
But yonder, whiff! there comes a sudden heat,
The gravest citizen seems to lose his head,
The king is scared, the soldier will not fight,   60
The little boys begin to shoot and stab,
A kingdom topples over with a shriek
Like an old woman, and down rolls the world
In mock heroics stranger than our own;
Revolts, republics, revolutions, most   65
No graver than a schoolboys' barring out;
Too comic for the solemn things they are,
Too solemn for the comic touches in them,
Like our wild Princess with as wise a dream
As some of theirs—God bless the narrow seas!   70
I wish they were a whole Atlantic broad.'

'Have patience,' I replied, 'ourselves are full
Of social wrong; and maybe wildest dreams
Are but the needful preludes of the truth.
For me, the genial day, the happy crowd,   75
The sport half-science, fill me with a faith,
This fine old world of ours is but a child
Yet in the go-cart. Patience! Give it time
To learn its limbs; there is a hand that guides.'

In such discourse we gain'd the garden rails,   80
And there we saw Sir Walter where he stood,
Before a tower of crimson holly-oaks,
Among six boys, head under head, and look'd
No little lily-handed baronet he,[6]

6. "An imaginary character" (Tennyson).

A great broad-shoulder'd genial Englishman,   85
A lord of fat prize-oxen and of sheep,
A raiser of huge melons and of pine,[7]
A patron of some thirty charities,
A pamphleteer on guano and on grain,
A quarter-sessions chairman, abler none;   90
Fair-hair'd and redder than a windy morn;
Now shaking hands with him, now him, of those
That stood the nearest—now address'd to speech—
Who spoke few words and pithy, such as closed
Welcome, farewell, and welcome for the year   95
To follow. A shout rose again, and made
The long line of the approaching rookery swerve
From the elms, and shook the branches of the deer
From slope to slope thro' distant ferns, and rang
Beyond the bourn of sunset—O, a shout   100
More joyful than the city-roar that hails
Premier or king! Why should not these great sirs
Give up their parks some dozen times a year
To let the people breathe? So thrice they cried,
I likewise, and in groups they stream'd away.   105

But we went back to the Abbey, and sat on,
So much the gathering darkness charm'd; we sat
But spoke not, rapt in nameless reverie,
Perchance upon the future man. The walls
Blacken'd about us, bats wheel'd, and owls whoop'd,   110
And gradually the powers of the night,
That range above the region of the wind,
Deepening the courts of twilight broke them up
Thro' all the silent spaces of the worlds,
Beyond all thought into the heaven of heavens.   115

Last little Lilia, rising quietly,
Disrobed the glimmering statue of Sir Ralph
From those rich silks, and home well-pleased we went.
1847; 1849–51

1847

In Memoriam A. H. H.

Arthur Henry Hallam died suddenly and unexpectedly from a cerebral hemorrhage on September 15, 1833, while on a visit to Vienna with his father. Some five years earlier, shortly after his arrival at Trinity College in October, 1828, Hallam had befriended Tennyson. "Alfred was already a prominent figure in the College by that time and Hallam's passion for poetry must almost certainly have brought the two together before long" (*Alfred Tennyson*, p. 66). Thereafter, the two remained insep-

---

7. "Pine-apple" (Tennyson).

arable. During the last couple of decades, an extraordinary amount of attention has been devoted to speculations about a homosexual dimension to their friendship. It should always be recalled that, throughout the nineteenth century, friendships between young men would be viewed by twentieth-century standards as exceptionally close. A rigorously imposed etiquette, particularly in regard to prolonged separation of the sexes, was the most important cause. High points in their relationship included the trip to the Pyrenees in 1830 (see n. 1, p. 48) and a tour of the Rhineland in 1832.

At Cambridge, Hallam was considered by all who knew him to be the most promising figure of his generation, a statement substantiated by numerous reminiscences. As titular leader of the Apostles, the Cambridge undergraduate literary group, he introduced Tennyson to that society and its stimulating atmosphere. Hallam's influence was profound. It was Hallam who helped Tennyson through the difficult period following publication of *Poems, Chiefly Lyrical* in 1830 and who worked over the new volume for 1832. Hostile reviewers—the two most vicious were Wilson and Croker (who had earlier savaged Keats)—stung hard and stung deep. (See excerpts from both in the "Contexts" section of this book.) Hallam's role in meliorating their otherwise negative effects simply cannot be overrated, both at the time and for the future's sake. He was friend, critic, and philosopher to a sometimes confused and lonely poet who desperately needed the guidance, warmth, and compassion that Hallam freely offered. (See also Hallam's essay on p. 581.) Hallam's engagement to Tennyson's sister Emily had been "recognized" in 1833. As he was shortly to become a member of the family, his loss was shattering.

The Hallam family learned of his death on September 28; Hallam's uncle posted Tennyson the news on October 1, although Tennyson probably did not receive it until several days later. The composition of elegy 9, on October 6, remains the best guess at the inception of *In Memoriam*, the lyrics that would eventually be assembled into his greatest work (see *Memoir* I, 107). As he said much later, "The sections were written at many different places, and as the phases of our intercourse came to my memory and suggested them. I did not write them with any view of weaving them into a whole or for publication, until I found I had written so many" (*Memoir* I, 304).

Through internal evidence, the composition of several sections can be dated rather precisely; others by the poet's specific remarks. The majority of the elegies were written before 1842. And by 1849, with the composition of "The Prologue," the lyrics had been arranged for publication. One should not, therefore, expect a tightly knit structure. Rather, the poem is loosely organized around the three Christmas sections: 28, 78, and 104. What other unity is present largely results from recurrent themes, symbols, images, and atmosphere. For "the way of the soul," as the poet first subtitled his work, properly—humanly—moves from doubt to tentative assertions of faith in an irregular fashion. Unlike Wordsworth in his *Prelude*, Tennyson had not set out to program the growth of a poet's mind, building from "least suggestions" to some monumental moments of profound insight. This is a point that should—must—be taken into account by those who would fault the work for its lack of structure. The movement among the elegies is, frequently and figuratively, two steps forward to three steps backward. "It is not religious because of the quality of its faith," to quote Eliot's memorable sentence, "but because of the quality of its doubt." On the subject of our individual immortality, it has been said that no other single poem has opened—and closed—so many doors. Although disputed by his son, Tennyson reportedly told Knowles: "'It's too hopeful, this poem, more than I am myself.'" For a poet who met the Furies on their own dark grounds, Tennyson could be all but paralyzingly tentative (see section 95) in dread of uttering unqualified dogma or even validating his own mystical experience.

In Memoriam is best read as a whole, preferably at one sitting. Perhaps only then does the modern reader have a chance of grasping— possibly even feeling— the magnitude of the issue. In 1850 the "night of fear" had descended. Theories of evolution were very much in the air. Sir Charles Lyell's famous *Principles of Geology* (1830–33) had made it extremely difficult for any self-respecting intelligence to take the biblical version of the Creation literally. At issue was the immortality of the soul, given special and immediate poignancy by Hallam's death. If that issue no longer moves us as deeply as it did Tennyson and his contemporaries, we nonetheless owe this great poem a willing suspension of our disbelief. As in our reading of Dante's *Divine Comedy*, we believe in a belief— or here, perhaps more accurately, in the expression of doubt.

In Memoriam A. H. H.

Obiit MDCCCXXXIII

Strong Son of God, immortal Love,[1]
Whom we, that have not seen thy face,
By faith, and faith alone, embrace,
Believing where we cannot prove;[2]

Thine are these orbs[3] of light and shade;   5
Thou madest Life in man and brute;
Thou madest Death; and lo, thy foot[4]
Is on the skull which thou hast made.

Thou wilt not leave us in the dust:[5]
Thou madest man, he knows not why,   10
He thinks he was not made to die;
And thou hast made him: thou art just.

Thou seemest human and divine,
The highest, holiest manhood, thou.
Our wills are ours, we know not how;   15
Our wills are ours, to make them thine.

Our little systems[6] have their day;
They have their day and cease to be;

1. Probably influenced by George Herbert's poem "Love," which begins:
   Immortal Love, Author of this great frame,
     Sprung from that beauty which can never fade,
     How hath Man parcell'd out Thy glorious name,
   And thrown it on the dust which Thou hast made . . .
   "This might be taken in a St. John sense" (Tennyson). Hallam Tennyson alludes to 1 John 4–5. On the meter of the *IM* stanza, Tennyson commented: "I believed myself the originator of the metre, until after 'In Memoriam' came out, when some one told me that Ben Jonson and Sir Philip Sidney had used it" (*Memoir* I, 306).
2. See John 20:29, where Jesus speaks of His resurrection to the doubting Thomas: "Because thou hast seen me, thou hast believed: blessed are they that have not seen, and yet have believed." Of Christ, see also 1 Peter 1:8: "Whom having not seen, ye love; in whom, though now ye see him not, yet believing."
3. "The sun and moon" (Tennyson).
4. Possibly suggested by Revelation 10:2, a chapter Tennyson particularly admired and often quoted. An angel appeared "and he set his right foot upon the sea, and his left foot on the earth."
5. Psalm 16:10: "Thou wilt not leave my soul in hell."
6. Of philosophy and theology.

They are but broken lights of thee,
And thou, O Lord, art more than they.   20

We have but faith: we cannot know,
   For knowledge is of things we see;
   And yet we trust it comes from thee,
A beam in darkness: let it grow.

   Let knowledge grow from more to more,   25
   But more of reverence in us dwell;
   That mind and soul, according well,
May make one music as before,[7]

But vaster. We are fools and slight;
   We mock thee when we do not fear: 30
   But help thy foolish ones to bear;
Help thy vain worlds[8] to bear thy light.

Forgive what seem'd my sin in me,
   What seem'd my worth since I began;
   For merit lives from man to man,   35
And not from man, O Lord, to thee.

Forgive my grief for one removed,
   Thy creature, whom I found so fair.
   I trust he lives in thee, and there
I find him worthier to be loved.   40

Forgive these wild and wandering cries,
   Confusions of a wasted[9] youth;
   Forgive them where they fail in truth,
And in thy wisdom make me wise.

                                          1849

1

I held it truth, with him[1] who sings
   To one clear harp in divers tones,[2]
   That men may rise on stepping-stones
Of their dead selves to higher things.

   But who shall so forecast the years   5
   And find in loss a gain to match?
   Or reach a hand thro' time to catch
The far-off interest[3] of tears?

7. "As in the ages of faith" (Tennyson). Before the split between faith and knowledge that the "new science" was rapidly widening. Compare Matthew Arnold's "Dover Beach" for a similar expression in a different metaphor: "The Sea of Faith / Was once, too, at the full."
8. Tennyson often implied that he believed in a number of inhabited planets.
9. Desolated. Bradley remarks, "surely, not 'squandered,'" but see line 2 in "Remorse."
1. Goethe, according to Tennyson (see *Memoir* II, 391), but the reference never has been located.
2. "Goethe is consummate in so many different styles" (Tennyson).
3. "The good that grows for us out of grief" (Tennyson). The use of economic terms in religious context also suggests the influence of George Herbert. Of Ricks's three possible reminiscences of Shakespeare,

Let Love clasp Grief lest both be drown'd,[4]
  Let darkness keep her raven gloss.   10
  Ah, sweeter to be drunk with loss,
To dance with Death, to beat the ground,

Than that the victor Hours should scorn
  The long result of love, and boast,
  "Behold the man that loved and lost,   15
But all he was is overworn."

2

Old yew,[5] which graspest at the stones
  That name the underlying dead,
  Thy fibres net the dreamless head,[6]
Thy roots are wrapt about the bones.

The seasons bring the flower again,   5
  And bring the firstling to the flock;
  And in the dusk of thee the clock[7]
Beats out the little lives of men.

O, not for thee the glow, the bloom,
  Who changest not in any gale,   10
  Nor branding summer suns avail
To touch thy thousand years of gloom;[8]

And gazing on thee, sullen tree,
  Sick for[9] thy stubborn hardihood,
  I seem to fail from out my blood   15
And grow incorporate into thee.

3

O Sorrow, cruel fellowship,
  O Priestess in the vaults of Death,
  O sweet and bitter in a breath,
What whispers from thy lying lip?

"The stars," she whispers, "blindly run;   5
  A web is woven across the sky;
  From out waste places comes a cry,
And murmurs from the dying sun;[1]

---

see *Sonnet* 31, lines 5–7: "How many a holy and obsequious tear / Hath dear religious love stol'n from mine eye, / As interest of the dead."
4. "Yet it is better to bear the wild misery of extreme grief than that Time should obliterate the sense of loss and deaden the power of love" (Hallam Tennyson).
5. Hallam was buried January 3, 1834, at Clevedon Church, Somersetshire, overlooking the Bristol Channel. The scene of this section is, however, probably a composite picture in part suggested by the graveyard at Somersby where Tennyson's father was buried. See "The Two Voices," lines 271ff, "darkness in the village yew." "I myself did not see Clevedon till years after the burial" (*Memoir* I, 305).
6. Tennyson compares the *Odyssey* X line 521: "The powerless heads of the dead."
7. In the church tower behind the yew.
8. "No autumn tints ever change the green gloom of the yew" (Hallam Tennyson).
9. In envy of.
1. An allusion to the nebular hypothesis.

"And all the phantom, Nature, stands —
  With all the music in her tone,   10
  A hollow echo of my own, —
A hollow form with empty hands."[2]

And shall I take a thing so blind,
  Embrace her[3] as my natural good;
  Or crush her, like a vice of blood,[4]   15
Upon the threshold of the mind?

4

To Sleep I give my powers away;
  My will is bondsman to the dark;
  I sit within a helmless bark,
And with my heart I muse and say:

O heart, how fares it with thee now,   5
  That thou shouldst fail[5] from thy desire,
  Who scarcely darest to inquire,
"What is it makes me beat so low?"

Something it is which thou hast lost,
  Some pleasure from thine early years.   10
  Break thou deep vase of chilling tears,
That grief hath shaken into frost![6]

Such clouds of nameless trouble cross
  All night below the darken'd eyes;
  With morning wakes the will, and cries,   15
"Thou shalt not be the fool of loss."

5

I sometimes hold it half a sin
  To put in words the grief I feel:
  For words, like Nature, half reveal
And half conceal the Soul within.

But, for the unquiet heart and brain,   5
  A use in measured language lies;
  The sad mechanic exercise,
Like dull narcotics, numbing pain.[7]

2. Sorrow's words reflect Tennyson's growing concern with the mechanistic theory of the universe, which held that all life works out its predestined course according to natural laws over which neither God nor man has any control.
3. Sorrow.
4. "Compare *Othello*, I, iii, 123: 'I do confess the vices of my blood'" (Ricks).
5. Lose the capacity for desiring.
6. "Water can be brought below freezing-point and not turn into ice — if it be kept still; but if it be moved suddenly it turns into ice and may break the vase" (Tennyson).
7. "Compare Keats's 'Ode to a Nightingale,' lines 1–3: 'a drowsy numbness pains / My sense, as though of hemlock I had drunk, / Or emptied some dull opiate to the drains'" (Shatto and Shaw).

In words, like weeds,[8] I'll wrap me o'er,
   Like coarsest clothes against the cold;   10
   But the large grief which these enfold
Is given in outline and no more.

6

One writes, that "other friends remain,"
   That "loss is common to the race"[9]—
   And common is the commonplace,
And vacant chaff well meant for grain.

That loss is common would not make   5
   My own less bitter, rather more.
   Too common! Never morning wore
To evening, but some heart did break.[1]

O father, wheresoe'er thou be,
   Who pledgest now thy gallant son,   10
   A shot, ere half thy draught be done,
Hath still'd the life that beat from thee.

O mother, praying God will save
   Thy sailor,—while thy head is bow'd,
   His heavy-shotted hammock-shroud   15
Drops in his vast and wandering grave.

Ye know no more than I who wrought
   At that last hour[2] to please him well;
   Who mused on all I had to tell,
And something written, something thought;   20

Expecting still his advent home;
   And ever met him on his way
   With wishes, thinking, "here to-day,"
Or "here to-morrow will he come."

O, somewhere, meek, unconscious dove,   25
   That sittest ranging[3] golden hair;
   And glad to find thyself so fair,
Poor child, that waitest for thy love!

For now her father's chimney glows
   In expectation of a guest;   30

8. Garments, strongly implying "widow's weeds" in mourning (OED, 5, 2). Contrast section 38. From his initial feeling that writing is merely an antidote for despair, the poet later moves toward a more positive conception of his art.
9. "See Numbers, 16:29 'If these men die the common death of all men'" (Shatto and Shaw).
1. "Of these two stanzas, Tennyson compares Lucretius, II, 578–80. 'No night ever followed day, or dawn followed night, but has heard mingled with their sickly wailings the lamentations that attend upon death and the black funeral.' Also compare Hamlet, I, ii, 72: 'Thou know'st 'tis common, all that lives must die'" (Ricks).
2. "My father was writing to Arthur Hallam in the hour that he died" (Hallam Tennyson).
3. Arranging. This section was probably written sometime between summer 1840 and Christmas 1841. See Memoir I, 201–02.

And thinking "this will please him best,"
She takes a riband or a rose,[4]

For he will see them on to-night;
    And with the thought her color burns;
    And, having left the glass, she turns   35
Once more to set a ringlet right;

And, even when she turn'd, the curse
    Had fallen, and her future lord
    Was drown'd in passing thro' the ford,
Or kill'd in falling from his horse.   40

O, what to her shall be the end?
    And what to me remains of good?
    To her perpetual maidenhood,
And unto me no second friend.

7

Dark house,[5] by which once more I stand
    Here in the long unlovely street,
    Doors, where my heart was used to beat
So quickly, waiting for a hand,

A hand that can be clasp'd no more —   5
    Behold me, for I cannot sleep,
    And like a guilty thing[6] I creep
At earliest morning to the door.

He is not here; but far away
    The noise of life begins again,   10
    And ghastly thro' the drizzling rain
On the bald street breaks the blank day.

8

A happy lover who has come
    To look on her that loves him well,
    Who 'lights and rings the gateway bell,
And learns her gone and far from home;

He saddens, all the magic light   5
    Dies off at once from bower and hall,

---

4. "'We were waiting for her,' writes one of her [Emily Tennyson's] friends, 'in the drawing room the first day since her loss that she had been able to meet anyone, and she came at last, dressed in deep mourning, a shadow of her former self, but with one white rose in her black hair as her Arthur loved to see her'" (*Memoir* I, 108–09).
5. Hallam's home at 67 Wimpole Street, London. See section 119.
6. Tennyson was thinking of Horatio's description of Hamlet's father's ghost in *Hamlet* I, i, line 148: "And then it started like a guilty thing." Ricks cites Wordsworth's *Immortality Ode* lines 148–51: "Blank misgivings of a Creature / Moving about in worlds not realised, / High instincts before which our mortal Nature / Did tremble like a guilty thing surprised."

And all the place is dark, and all
The chambers emptied of delight:[7]

So find I every pleasant spot
    In which we two were wont to meet,   10
    The field, the chamber, and the street,
For all is dark where thou art not.

Yet as that other, wandering there
    In those deserted walks, may find
    A flower beat with rain and wind,   15
Which once she foster'd up with care;

So seems it in my deep regret,
    O my forsaken heart, with thee
    And this poor flower of poesy
Which, little cared for, fades not yet.   20

But since it pleased a vanish'd eye,
    I go to plant it on his tomb,
    That if it can it there may bloom,
Or, dying, there at least may die.

9

Fair ship,[8] that from the Italian shore
    Sailest the placid ocean-plains
    With my lost Arthur's[9] loved remains,
Spread thy full wings, and waft him o'er.

So draw him home to those that mourn   5
    In vain; a favorable speed
    Ruffle thy mirror'd mast, and lead
Thro' prosperous floods his holy urn.

All night no ruder air perplex
    Thy sliding keel, till Phosphor,[1] bright   10
    As our pure love, thro' early light
Shall glimmer on the dewy decks.

Sphere all your lights around, above;
    Sleep, gentle heavens, before the prow;
    Sleep, gentle winds, as he sleeps now,   15
My friend, the brother of my love;

7. "Compare Keats's *Lamia*, II, 307: 'and Lycius' arms were empty of delight'" (Bradley).
8. Sections 9–17 form a group all concerned with the return of Hallam's body. They are probably among
   the first written of the elegies, mostly composed, one assumes, before the end of the year. Tennyson told
   Knowles that elegy 9 was "the first written" (see also the headnote). On December 31, 1833, Tennyson
   received a letter from Hallam's father saying his son's body had arrived.
9. "The first mention of the deceased by name. It appears twice in this section and twice more in the poem:
   80. [line] 2; 89. [line] 6" (Shatto and Shaw).
1. The morning star, Venus.

My Arthur, whom I shall not see
    Till all my widow'd[2] race be run;
    Dear as the mother to the son,
More than my brothers are to me.   20

10

I hear the noise about thy keel;
    I hear the bell struck in the night;
    I see the cabin-window bright;
I see the sailor at the wheel.

Thou bring'st the sailor to his wife,   5
    And travell'd men from foreign lands;
    And letters unto trembling hands;
And, thy dark freight, a vanish'd life.

So bring him; we have idle dreams;
    This look of quiet flatters thus   10
    Our home-bred fancies. O, to us,
The fools of habit, sweeter seems

To rest beneath the clover sod,
    That takes the sunshine and the rains,
    Or where the kneeling hamlet drains   15
The chalice of the grapes of God;[3]

Than if with thee the roaring wells
    Should gulf him fathom-deep in brine,
    And hands so often clasp'd in mine,
Should toss with tangle[4] and with shells.   20

11

Calm is the morn without a sound,
    Calm as to suit a calmer grief,
    And only thro' the faded leaf
The chestnut pattering to the ground;

Calm and deep peace on this high wold,[5]   5
    And on these dews that drench the furze,
    And all the silvery gossamers
That twinkle into green and gold;

2. The speaker alternately thinks of himself as a widow or widower (see opening of section 13), and a care-less reviewer of the first edition referred to the poem: "These touching lines evidently come from the full heart of the widow of a military man" (*Memoir* I, 298).
3. The speaker imagines the possibility of burial inside the church where the villagers kneel to receive the sacrament.
4. Seaweed. Citing Tillotson, Ricks quotes: Tennyson "cannot bear the thought that the seaweed might clasp with its fingers the hands so often clasped in his." Here, as in other contexts, Tennyson's imagined burial at sea recalls *Lycidas* and Milton's untimely loss of his Cambridge friend Edward King drowned at sea: "Sunk though he be beneath the watery floor" (line 167). Hallam would, in fact, be buried in the Elton family vault in the south transept of Clevedon Parish Church.
5. The scene reflects the landscape near Somersby. In Tennyson's words: "A Lincolnshire wold or upland from which the whole range of marsh to the sea is visible." The ship returning Hallam's body actually departed later in the year, and not in autumn, as the poet imagines.

Calm and still light on yon great plain
    That sweeps with all its autumn bowers,   10
    And crowded farms and lessening[6] towers,
To mingle with the bounding main;

Calm and deep peace in this wide air,
    These leaves that redden to the fall,
    And in my heart, if calm at all,   15
If any calm, a calm despair;

Calm on the seas, and silver sleep,
    And waves that sway themselves in rest,
    And dead calm in that noble breast
Which heaves but with the heaving deep.   20

12

Lo, as a dove[7] when up she springs
    To bear thro' heaven a tale of woe,
    Some dolorous message knit below
The wild pulsation of her wings;

Like her I go, I cannot stay;   5
    I leave this mortal ark behind,[8]
    A weight of nerves without a mind,
And leave the cliffs, and haste away

O'er ocean-mirrors rounded large,
    And reach the glow of southern skies,   10
    And see the sails at distance rise,
And linger weeping on the marge,

And saying, "Comes he thus, my friend?
    Is this the end of all my care?"
    And circle moaning in the air,   15
"Is this the end? Is this the end?"

And forward dart again, and play
    About the prow, and back return
    To where the body sits, and learn
That I have been an hour away.   20

13

Tears of the widower, when he sees
    A late-lost form that sleep reveals,
    And moves his doubtful arms, and feels
Her place is empty, fall like these;

---

6. As his vision reaches toward the sea in the distance, the church towers in the foreground appear to grow smaller.
7. See Genesis 8:8–9: "Also he sent forth a dove from him, to see if the waters were abated from off the face of the ground; but the dove found no rest for the sole of her foot, and she returned unto him into the ark, for the waters were on the face of the whole earth."
8. "My spirit flies from out my material self" (Tennyson).

Which weep a loss for ever new,   5
   A void where heart on heart reposed;
   And, where warm hands have prest and closed,
Silence, till I be silent too;

Which weep the comrade of my choice,
   An awful thought, a life removed,   10
   The human-hearted man I loved,
A Spirit, not a breathing voice.[9]

Come, Time, and teach me, many years,[1]
   I do not suffer in a dream;
   For now so strange do these things seem,   15
Mine eyes have leisure for their tears,

My fancies time[2] to rise on wing,
   And glance about the approaching sails,
   As tho' they brought but merchants' bales,
And not the burthen that they bring.   20

14

If one should bring me this report,
   That thou[3] hadst touch'd the land to-day,
   And I went down the quay,
And found thee lying in the port;

And standing, muffled round with woe,   5
   Should see thy passengers in rank
   Come stepping lightly down the plank
And beckoning unto those they know;

And if along with these should come
   The man I held as half-divine,[4]   10
   Should strike a sudden hand in mine,
And ask a thousand things of home;

And I should tell him all my pain,
   And how my life had droop'd of late,
   And he should sorrow o'er my state   15
And marvel what possess'd my brain;

And I perceived no touch of change,
   No hint of death in all his frame,
   But found him all in all the same,
I should not feel it to be strange.   20

9. For this and the following stanza, compare Milton's *Sonnet* 19: "Methought I saw my late espoused Saint
  . . . But O, as to embrace me she inclin'd, / I wak'd, she fled, and day brought back my night."
1. Through many years.
2. The sense is: Since the passage of years has not yet come to teach him to accept the full meaning of his
  loss, his fancy has the time or leisure to imagine the ship brings only merchants' wares.
3. The ship.
4. "My father said, 'He was as near perfection as mortal man could be'" (Hallam Tennyson).

15

To-night the winds begin to rise
    And roar from yonder dropping day;
    The last red leaf[5] is whirl'd away,
The rooks are blown about the skies;

The forest crack'd, the waters curl'd,   5
    The cattle huddled on the lea;[6]
    And wildly dash'd on tower and tree
The sunbeam strikes along the world:

And but for fancies, which aver
    That all thy[7] motions gently   10
    Athwart a plane[8] of molten glass,
I scarce could brook the strain and stir

That makes the barren branches loud;
    And but for fear it is not so,[9]
    The wild unrest that lives in woe   15
Would dote and pore on yonder cloud[1]

That rises upward always higher,
    And onward drags a laboring breast,
    And topples round the dreary west,
A looming bastion fringed with fire.   20

16

What words are these have fallen from me?
    Can calm despair and wild unrest[2]
    Be tenants of a single breast,
Or Sorrow such a changeling be?

Or doth she only seem to take   5
    The touch of change in calm or storm,
    But knows no more of transient form
In her deep self, than some dead lake

That holds the shadow of a lark
    Hung in the shadow of a heaven?   10

---

5. Tennyson may have been indebted to Coleridge's "Christabel" for this image, "The one red leaf, the last of its clan, / That dances as often as dance it can" (lines 49–50).
6. Compare Gray's "Elegy Written in a Country Churchyard," line 2: "The lowing herd wind slowly o'er the lea."
7. The ship's.
8. "A calm sea" (Tennyson).
9. "Tennyson glossed this, 'all is not peace with thee' (University of London Library, Works, 1884)" (Ricks).
1. "The stormy night, except it were for my fear for the 'sacred bark' would be in sympathy with me" (Hallam Tennyson). Also compare Coleridge's "Dejection: An Ode," lines 15–20:
    And oh! that even now the gust were swelling,
        And the slant night shower driving loud and fast!
    Those sounds which oft have raised me, whilst they awed,
        And sent my soul abroad,
    Might now perhaps their wonted impulse give,
    Might startle this dull pain, and make it move and live!
2. The moods of sections 11 and 15.

Or has the shock, so harshly given,
Confused me like the unhappy bark[3]

That strikes by night a craggy shelf,
    And staggers blindly ere she sink?
    And stunn'd me from my power to think   15
And all my knowledge of myself;

And made me that delirious man
    Whose fancy fuses old and new,
    And flashes into false and true,
And mingles all without a plan?   20

17

Thou comest, much wept for; such a breeze
    Compell'd thy canvas, and my prayer
    Was as the whisper of an air
To breathe thee over lonely seas.

For I in spirit saw thee move   5
    Thro' circles of the bounding sky,
    Week after week; the days go by;
Come quick, thou bringest all I love.

Henceforth, wherever thou mayst roam,
    My blessing, like a line of light,   10
    Is on the waters day and night,
And like a beacon guards thee home.

So may whatever tempest mars
    Mid-ocean spare thee, sacred bark,
    And balmy drops in summer dark   15
Slide from the bosom[4] of the stars;

So kind an office hath been done,
    Such precious relics brought by thee,
    The dust of him I shall not see
Till all my widow'd race be run.   20

18

'T is well; 't is something; we may stand
    Where he in English earth is laid,[5]
    And from his ashes may be made
The violet[6] of his native land.

3. Compare "Lycidas," line 100: "that fated and perfidious bark."
4. "The image alludes to the legendary origin of the Milky Way as being formed from the milk expressed from the breasts of Juno" (Shatto and Shaw).
5. Hallam was buried inside the church. Tennyson was not present at Hallam's interment, on January 3, 1834. His first visit to Clevedon seems to have been on June 14, 1850, the day after his marriage to Emily Sellwood. At her wish, together "they saw Arthur Hallam's resting-place." "'It seemed a kind of consecration to go there'" (Memoir I, 332).
6. "'Lay her in the earth, / And from her fair and unpolluted flesh / May violets spring,' Hamlet, V, i, 261–63" (Tennyson).

'T is little; but it looks in truth   5
    As if the quiet bones were blest
    Among familiar names to rest
And in the places of his youth.

Come then, pure hands, and bear the head
    That sleeps or wears the mask of sleep,   10
    And come, whatever loves to weep,
And hear the ritual of the dead.

Ah yet, even yet, if this might be,
    I, falling on his faithful heart,
    Would breathing thro' his lips impart   15
The life that almost dies in me;

That dies not, but endures with pain,
    And slowly forms the firmer mind,
    Treasuring the look it cannot find,
The words that are not heard again.   20

19

The Danube to the Severn[7] gave
    The darken'd heart that beat no more;
    They laid him by the pleasant shore,
And in the hearing of the wave.

There twice a day the Severn fills;   5
    The salt sea-water passes by,
    And hushes half the babbling Wye,
And makes a silence in the hills.[8]

The Wye is hush'd nor moved along,
    And, hush'd my deepest grief of all,   10
    When fill'd with tears that cannot fall,
I brim with sorrow drowning song.

The tide flows down, the wave again
    Is vocal in its wooded walls;
    My deeper anguish also falls,   15
And I can speak a little then.

20

The lesser griefs that may be said,
    That breathe a thousand tender vows.
    Are but as servants in a house
Where lies the master newly dead;

7. Vienna, where Hallam died, is on the Danube. The tides flow up the Bristol Channel, which, farther up, becomes the Severn, and eventually enter the Wye. Like "Tears, idle Tears," this section was written at Tintern Abbey, on the Wye River. "Taken from my own observation—the rapids of the Wye are stilled by the incoming sea" (Tennyson).
8. "Compare Wordsworth's description of the Wye in 'Tintern Abbey,' 3–4: 'These waters, rolling from their mountain-springs / With a soft inland murmur'" (Shatto and Shaw).

Who speak their feeling as it is,   5
    And weep the fulness from the mind.
    "It will be hard," they say, "to find
Another service such as this."

My lighter moods are like to these,
    That out of words a comfort win;   10
    But there are other griefs within,
And tears that at their fountain freeze;

For by the hearth the children sit
    Cold in that atmosphere of death,
    And scarce endure to draw the breath,   15
Or like to noiseless phantoms flit;

But open converse is there none,
    So much the vital spirits sink
    To see the vacant chair, and think,
"How good! how kind! and he is gone."   20

21

I sing to him that rests below,
    And, since the grasses round me wave,
    I take the grasses of the grave,[9]
And make them pipes whereon to blow.

The traveller hears me now and then,   5
    And sometimes harshly will he speak:
    "This fellow would make weakness weak,
And melt the waxen hearts of men."

Another answers: "Let him be,
    He loves to make parade of pain,   10
    That with his piping he may gain
The praise that comes to constancy."

A third is wroth: "Is this an hour
    For private sorrow's barren song,
    When more and more the people throng   15
The chairs and thrones of civil power?[1]

"A time to sicken and to swoon,
    When Science reaches forth her arms
    To feel from world to world, and charms
Her secret from the latest moon?"[2]   20

9. Sections 21–25 form an interlude. Working within the conventions of the classical pastoral elegy, the
   poet continues the theme begun in sections 5 and 8. His recourse to the pastoral convention allows him
   to think of his verses in terms of a larger, more durable context than that suggested by the previous comparison of his lines to a dying flower.
1. Possibly an allusion to the Chartist movement of 1838–39.
2. Apparently the section was written late, since the poet probably is referring to the discovery of Neptune
   in September 1846. Neptune's single moon was discovered a month later. Ricks challenges the allusion
   to Neptune; it "seems unfoundedly late for this section." By "moon" Tennyson may mean either planet

Behold, ye speak an idle thing;
    Ye never knew the sacred dust.
    I do but sing because I must,
And pipe but as the linnets sing;

And one is glad; her note is gay,   25
    For now her little ones have ranged;
    And one is sad; her note is changed,
Because her brood is stolen away.

22

The path by which we twain did go,
    Which led by tracts that pleased us well,
    Thro' four sweet years arose and fell,
From flower to flower, from snow to snow;

And we with singing cheer'd the way,   5
    And, crown'd with all the season lent,
    From April on to April went,
And glad at heart from May to May.

But where the path[3] we walk'd began
    To slant the fifth autumnal slope,[4]   10
    As we descended following Hope,
There sat the Shadow[5] fear'd of man;

Who broke our fair companionship,
    And spread his mantle dark and cold,
    And wrapt thee formless in the fold.   15
And dull'd the murmur on thy lip,

And bore thee where I could not see
    Nor follow, tho' I walk in haste,
    And think that somewhere in the waste
The Shadow sits and waits for me.   20

23

Now, sometimes in my sorrow shut,
    Or breaking into song by fits,
    Alone, alone, to where he sits,
The Shadow cloak'd from head to foot,

Who keeps the keys[6] of all the creeds,   5
    I wander, often falling lame,

---

or satellite. Late in life he reportedly said, "at least one of the planets belonging to each sun should be inhabited" (*Memoir* II, 336).
3. As in the opening of this section, "the path," very much including their Cambridge college days together, recalls Milton's similar memories of his days there with King: "And old Damoetas [possibly referring to a specific Cambridge tutor] loved to hear our song" (*Lycidas*, line 36).
4. Hallam died September 15, 1833, in the fifth year of the friendship.
5. Death, which at this stage the poet does not seem anxious to avoid.
6. "After death we shall learn the truth of all beliefs" (Tennyson).

And looking back to whence I came,
Or on to where the pathway leads;

And crying, How changed from where it ran
    Thro' lands where not a leaf was dumb,   10
    But all the lavish hills would hum
The murmur of a happy Pan;[7]

When each by turns was guide to each,
    And Fancy light from Fancy caught,
    And Thought leapt out to wed with Thought   15
Ere Thought could wed itself with Speech;

And all we met was fair and good,
    And all was good that Time could bring,
    And all the secret of the Spring[8]
Moved in the chambers of the blood;   20

And many an old philosophy
    On Argive[9] heights divinely sang,
    And round us all the thicket rang
To many a flute of Arcady.[1]

24

And was the day of my delight
    As pure and perfect as I say?
    The very source and fount of day
Is dash'd with wandering isles of night.[2]

If all was good and fair we met,   5
    This earth had been the Paradise
    It never look'd to human eyes
Since our first sun arose and set.

And is it that the haze of grief
    Makes former gladness loom so great?   10
    The lowness of the present state,
That sets the past in this relief?

Or that the past will always win
    A glory from its being far,
    And orb into the perfect star[3]   15
We saw not when we moved therein?

7. God of all nature.
8. "Re-awakening of life" (Tennyson).
9. Greek; specifically, of the city of Argos, known for its music.
1. Arcadia, the mountainous region in central Greece celebrated as the home of pastoral poetry.
2. "Sun-spots" (Tennyson).
3. From a distance the earth would appear a perfect disc, just as the rough edges of their past friendship appear to vanish with time.

25

I know that this was Life,[4]—the track
    Whereon with equal feet we fared;
    And then, as now, the day prepared
The daily burden for the back.

But this it was that made me move   5
    As light as carrier-birds in air;
    I loved the weight I had to bear,
Because it needed help of Love:

Nor could I weary, heart or limb,
    When mighty Love would cleave in twain   10
    The lading[5] of a single pain,
And part it, giving half to him.

26

Still onward winds the dreary way;
    I with it, for I long to prove
    No lapse of moons can canker Love,
Whatever fickle tongues may say.

And if that eye which watches guilt   5
    And goodness, and hath power to see
    Within the green the moulder'd tree,
And towers fallen as soon as built—

Oh, if indeed that eye foresee
    Or see—in Him is no before[6]—   10
    In more of life true life no more
And Love the indifference to be,[7]

Then might I find, ere yet the morn
    Breaks hither over Indian seas,
    That Shadow waiting with the keys,   15
To shroud me from my proper scorn.[8]

27

I envy not in any moods
    The captive void of noble rage,
    The linnet born within the cage,
That never knew the summer woods:

I envy not the beast that takes   5
    His license in the field of time,

---

4. "Chequered, but the burden was shared" (Tennyson).
5. The loading; burden.
6. "The Eternal Now. I AM" (Tennyson).
7. "And that the present Love will end in future indifference" (Hallam Tennyson).
8. "Scorn of myself" (Tennyson). This stanza poses one of the larger questions asked in the poem: Does love live outside of time?

Unfetter'd by the sense of crime,
To whom a conscience never wakes;

Nor, what may count itself as blest,
   The heart that never plighted troth   10
   But stagnates in the weeds of sloth:
Nor any want-begotten rest.[9]

I hold it true, whate'er befall;
   I feel it, when I sorrow most;
   'T is better to have loved and lost   15
Than never to have loved at all.[1]

28

The time draws near the birth of Christ.[2]
   The moon is hid, the night is still;
   The Christmas bells from hill to hill
Answer each other in the mist.

Four voices of four hamlets round,   5
   From far and near, on mead and moor,
   Swell out and fail, as if a door
Were shut between me and the sound;

Each voice four changes[3] on the wind,
   That now dilate, and now decrease,   10
   Peace and goodwill, goodwill and peace,
Peace and goodwill, to all mankind.

This year I slept and woke with pain,
   I almost wish'd no more to wake,
   And that my hold on life would break   15
Before I heard those bells again;

But they my troubled spirit rule,
   For they controll'd me when a boy;
   They bring me sorrow touch'd with joy,
The merry, merry bells of Yule.[4]   20

29

With such compelling cause to grieve
   As daily vexes household[5] peace,
   And chains regret to his decease,
How dare we keep our Christmas-eve,

9. Ill-deserved rest, resulting from "want" or deficiency.
1. "Many analogues have been found, among them Congreve: 'Tis better to be left, than never to have been lov'd,' *Way of the World*, II, i" (Ricks).
2. The second part of the poem begins here, and the predominant concern is for Hallam's immortality. The time is the first Christmas after his friend's death (1833); the scene is the Tennyson family home at Somersby.
3. In different sequence, four churches each with four bells ring the four syllables in each of the four phrases of lines 11 and 12.
4. "They always used to ring on Christmas eve" (Tennyson).
5. Our household, where thoughts of Hallam's death are daily present.

Which brings no more a welcome guest[6]   5
    To enrich the threshold of the night
    With shower'd largess of delight
In dance and song and game and jest?

Yet go, and while the holly boughs
    Entwine the cold baptismal font,   10
    Make one wreath more for Use and Wont,
That guard the portals of the house;

Old sisters[7] of a day gone by,
    Gray nurses, loving nothing new—
    Why should they miss their yearly due   15
Before their time? They too will die.

30

With trembling fingers did we weave
    The holly round the Christmas hearth;
    A rainy cloud possess'd the earth,
And sadly fell our Christmas-eve.

At our old pastimes in the hall[8]   5
    We gamboll'd, making vain pretence
    Of gladness, with an awful sense
Of one mute Shadow[9] watching all.

We paused: the winds were in the beech;
    We heard them sweep the winter land;   10
    And in a circle hand-in-hand
Sat silent, looking each at each.

The echo-like our voices rang;
    We sung, tho' every eye was dim,
    A merry song we sang with him   15
Last year; impetuously we sang.

We ceased; a gentler feeling crept
    Upon us: surely rest is meet.
    "They rest," we said, "their sleep is sweet,"
And silence follow'd, and we wept.   20

Our voices took a higher range;
    Once more we sang: "They do not die
    Nor lose their mortal sympathy,
Nor change to us, although they change;

6. Hallam had spent the previous Christmas Eve (1832) at Somersby.
7. I.e., Use and Wont.
8. "The dining-room at Somersby which my father built" (Tennyson).
9. Not Death but the spirit of Hallam. A draft of this section was probably made in 1833. See *Memoir* I, 109.

"Rapt from the fickle and the frail   25
    With gather'd power, yet the same,
    Pierces the keen seraphic flame
From orb to orb, from veil to veil."[1]

Rise, happy morn,[2] rise, holy morn,
    Draw forth the cheerful day from night: 30
    O Father, touch the east, and light
The light that shone when Hope was born.[3]

31

When Lazarus[4] left his charnel-cave,
    And home to Mary's house return'd,
    Was this demanded — if he yearn'd
To hear her weeping by his grave?

"Where wert thou, brother, those four days?"   5
    There lives no record of reply,
    Which telling what it is to die
Had surely added praise to praise.

From every house the neighbors met,
    The streets were fill'd with joyful sound,   10
    A solemn gladness even crown'd
The purple brows of Olivet.[5]

Behold a man raised up by Christ!
    The rest remaineth unreveal'd;
    He [6] told it not, or something seal'd   15
The lips of that Evangelist.[7]

32

Her[8] eyes are homes of silent prayer,
    Nor other thought, her mind admits
    But, he was dead, and there he sits,
And he that brought him back is there.

Then one deep love doth supersede   5
    All other, when her ardent gaze

1. The soul, freed from the instabilities and frailties of the flesh though unchanged in essence, is now empowered to assume different embodiments passing from world to world. "I can hardly understand how any great, imaginative man, who has deeply loved, suffered, thought and wrought, can doubt the Soul's continuous progress in the after-life" (*Memoir* I, 321). "Compare Shelley's elegy on Keats: 'Whilst burning through the inmost veil of Heaven, / The Soul of Adonais, like a star, / Beacons from the abode where the Eternal are,' 'Adonais,' 493–95" (Ricks).
2. Compare the first line of Milton's "On the Morning of Christ's Nativity": "This is the month, and this the happy morn."
3. "My father often said: 'the cardinal point of Christianity is the life after death'" (Hallam Tennyson).
4. Sections 31–36 are a group dealing directly with questions of love and individual immortality. For Christ's raising of Lazarus from the dead, see John 11.
5. The Mount of Olives, a hill near Jerusalem.
6. Lazarus.
7. St. John, who alone records the story.
8. Mary, Lazarus's sister.

Roves from the living brother's face,
And rests upon the Life[9] indeed.

All subtle thought, all curious fears,
  Borne down by gladness so complete,   10
  She bows, she bathes the Saviour's feet
With costly spikenard[1] and with tears.

Thrice blest whose lives are faithful prayers,
  Whose loves in higher love endure;
  What souls posses themselves so pure,   15
Or is there blessedness like theirs?

33

O thou[2] that after toil and storm
  Mayst seem to have reach'd a purer air,
  Whose faith has centre everywhere,
Nor cares to fix itself to form,

Leave thou thy sister when she prays   5
  Her early heaven, her happy views;
  Nor thou with shadow'd hint confuse
A life that leads melodious days.

Her faith thro' form is pure as thine,
  Her hands are quicker unto good.   10
  O, sacred be the flesh and blood
To which she links a truth divine!

See thou, that countest reason ripe
  In holding by the law within,[3]
  Thou fail not in a world of sin,   15
And even for want of such a type.

34

My own dim life should teach me this,
  That life shall live for evermore,[4]
  Else earth is darkness at the core,
And dust and ashes all that is;

This round of green, this orb of flame,[5]   5
  Fantastic beauty; such as lurks

9. John 11:25: "Jesus said unto her, I am the resurrection, and the life: he that believeth in me, though he were dead yet shall he live."
1. A fragrant ointment.
2. Addressed to no one in particular. Tennyson is supporting the less intellectualized faith of simple believers like the sister. "Arthur Hallam, writing to Emily Tennyson (22 January 1832), expressed the traditional notion that the innocence and ignorance of women in matters of religion should not be corrupted by philosophical inquiry or scepticism" (Shatto and Shaw). Lest that appear overly patronizing, Hallam also wrote in the same letter: "It is by the heart, not by the head, that we must all be convinced of the two great fundamental truths, the reality of Love, & the reality of Evil" (*Letters* 509).
3. "In holding an intellectual faith which does not care 'to fix itself to form'" (Hallam Tennyson).
4. "I have heard him say that he 'would rather know that he was to be lost eternally than not know that the whole human race was to live eternally'" (Hallam Tennyson).
5. The earth and the sun.

In some wild poet, when he works
Without a conscience or an aim.

What then were God to such as I?
   'T were hardlly worth my while to choose   10
   Of things all mortal, or to use
A little patience ere I die;

'T were best at once to sink to peace,
   Like birds the charming serpent[6] draws,
   To drop head-foremost in the jaws   15
Of vacant darkness and to cease.

35

Yet if some voice that man could trust
   Should murmur from the narrow house,
   "The cheeks drop in, the body bows;
Man dies, nor is there hope in dust;"

Might I not say? "Yet even here,   5
   But for one hour, O Love, I strive
   To keep so sweet a thing alive."
But I should turn mine ears and hear

The moanings of the homeless sea,
   The sound of streams that swift or slow   10
Draw down æonian[7] hills, and sow
   The dust of continents to be,

And Love would answer with a sigh,
   "The sound of that forgetful shore[8]
   Will change my sweetness more and more,   15
Half-dead to know that I shall die."

O me, what profits it to put
   An idle case? If Death were seen
   At first as Death,[9] Love had not been,
Or been in narrowest working shut,   20

Mere fellowship of sluggish moods,
   Or in his coarsest Satyr-shape
   Had bruised the herb and crush'd the grape,
And bask'd and batten'd[1] in the woods.

6. Some snakes, like the cobra, are supposed to be able to cast a spell over their prey.
7. Hills that have lasted for eons. This is one of several sections that seem clearly indebted to Tennyson's reading of Lyell's *Principles of Geology* (1830–33), in which, during some months of 1837, he was "deeply immersed" (*Memoir* I, 162). Lyell familiarized English readers with Lamarck's concept of "uniformitism" as opposed to "catastrophism," expounding the theory that the whole surface of the earth changed not by sudden catastrophe but gradually, in obedience to natural laws.
8. The shore of Lethe, the river of forgetfulness. "The land where all things are forgotten" (Tennyson). See *Paradise Lost* II, line 74: "that forgetful Lake."
9. I.e., only as extinction. The idea is: Love, to exist in more than a physical sense, must have perceived intimations of our immortality.
1. Fed on grossly. See "The Kraken."

36

Tho' truths in manhood darkly join,[2]
   Deep-seated in our mystic frame,
   We yield all blessing to the name
Of Him that made them current coin;

For Wisdom dealt with mortal powers,   5
   Where truth in closest words shall fail,
   Where truth embodied in a tale[3]
Shall enter in at lowly doors.[4]

And so the Word[5] had breath, and wrought
   With human hands the creed of creeds[6]   10
   In loveliness of perfect deeds,
More strong than all poetic thought;

Which he may read that binds the sheaf,
   Or builds the house, or digs the grave,
   And those wild eyes[7] that watch the wave   15
In roarings round the coral reef.

37

Urania[8] speaks with darken'd brow:
   "Thou pratest here where thou art least;
   This faith has many a purer priest,
And many an abler voice than thou.

"Go down beside thy native rill,   5
   On thy Parnassus[9] set thy feet,
   And hear thy laurel whisper sweet
About the ledges of the hill."

And my Melpomene[1] replies,
   A touch of shame upon her cheek: 10
   "I am not worthy even to speak
Of thy prevailing[2] mysteries;

2. Obscurely meet, hence dimly perceived. See "dim" in 34, line 1.
3. The Gospels, not just the Parables.
4. "For divine Wisdom had to deal with the limited powers of humanity, to which truth logically argued out
   would be ineffectual, whereas truth coming in the story of the Gospel can influence the poorest" (Tennyson).
5. Tennyson explained: "'The Word' as used by St. John, the Revelation of the Eternal Thought of the Universe" (*Memoir* I, 312).
6. Christ's life.
7. "By this is intended the Pacific Islanders, 'wild' having a sense of 'barbarian'" (Tennyson). The practice
   throughout this book has not been, as occasionally elsewhere, to expurgate or modify direct quotations
   that *The American Heritage Dictionary*, for example, designates "now considered offensive."
8. Originally, Muse of Astronomy. Tennyson is indebted to the invocation to Book VII of Milton's *Paradise
   Lost*, where she is made Muse of Heavenly Poetry. "The Heavenly muse bids the poet's muse sing on a
   less lofty theme" (Tennyson).
9. The mountain in Greece sacred to Apollo and the Muses. Laurel grows on its slopes, and poets are traditionally crowned with laurel wreaths.
1. Muse of Tragedy or, as here, of Elegy.
2. "Probably in the sense of the Latin *pravelens*, 'very strong,' since there is no reason why Urania should
   prevail over Melpomene" (Ricks). To the contrary, Tennyson may well be consciously qualifying his po-

"For I am but an earthly Muse,
    And owning but a little art
    To lull with song an aching heart,   15
And render human love his dues;

"But brooding on the dear one dead,
    And all he said of things divine, —
    And dear to me as sacred wine
To dying lips is all he said, —   20

"I murmur'd, as I came along,
    Of comfort clasp'd in truth reveal'd,
    And loiter'd in the master's field,
And darken'd sanctities with song."

38

With weary steps I loiter on,
    Tho' always under alter'd skies
    The purple from the distance dies,
My prospect and horizon gone.

No joy the blowing[3] season gives,   5
    The herald melodies of spring,
    But in the songs I love to sing
A doubtful gleam of solace[4] lives.

If any care for what is here
    Survive in spirits render'd free,   10
    Then are these songs I sing of thee
Not all ungrateful to thine ear.

39

Old warder[5] of these buried bones,
    And answering now my random stroke
    With fruitful cloud and living smoke,[6]
Dark yew, that graspest at the stones

And dippest toward the dreamless head,   5
    To thee too comes the golden hour
    When flower is feeling after flower;[7]
But Sorrow, — fixt upon the dead,

---

etic prowess in these elegies as measured against the power of Milton's epic. "Melpomene, the earthly muse of tragedy, answers the poet: 'I am compelled to speak—as I think of the dead and his words—of the comfort in the creed of creeds, although I feel myself unworthy to speak of such mysteries'" (Hallam Tennyson, saying the note is "by my mother").
3. "The blossoming season" (Tennyson).
4. Contrast sections 5 and 8.
5. The yew tree of section 2. Section 39 was written in 1868 and retained thereafter. See *Memoir* II, 53.
6. "The yew, when flowering, in a wind or if struck sends up its pollen like smoke" (Tennyson). Compare "The Holy Grail," line 15.
7. "The yew is dioecious" (Hallam Tennyson); i.e., male and female flowers sometimes grow on the same tree. In contrast to section 2, the poet sees a renewal of life taking place in the ancient yew.

And darkening the dark graves of men,—
    What whisper'd from her lying lips?   10
    Thy gloom is kindled at the tips,
And passes into gloom again.[8]

40[9]

Could we forget the widow'd hour
    And look on Spirits breathed away,
    As on a maiden in the day
When first she wears her orange-flower!

When crown'd with blessing she doth rise   5
    To take her latest leave of home,
    And hopes and light regrets that come
Make April of her tender eyes;

And doubtful joys the father move,
    And tears are on the mother's face,   10
    As parting with a long embrace
She enters other realms of love;

Her office there to rear, to teach,
    Becoming as is meet and fit
    A link among the days, to knit   15
The generations each with each;

And, doubtless, unto thee[1] is given
    A life that bears immortal fruit
    In those great offices that suit
The full-grown energies of heaven.   20

Ay me, the difference I discern!
    How often shall her old fireside
    Be cheer'd with tidings of the bride,
How often she herself return,

And tell them all they would have told,   25
    And bring her babe, and make her boast,
    Till even those that miss'd her most
Shall count new things as dear as old;

But thou and I have shaken hands,
    Till growing winters lay me low;   30
    My paths are in the fields I know,
And thine in undiscover'd lands.[2]

---

8. Sorrow's "lying lips" take us back to section 3. Sorrow lied before in suggesting the sun never touched the yew's "thousand years of gloom" (section 2). The speaker knows she also lies in lines 11 and 12 in disparaging the springtime phenomenon. In admitting her earlier distortion of nature, Sorrow confirms her untrustworthiness.
9. Sections 40–47 return to the theme of 31–36. The poet further speculates on some eventual reunion with Hallam's spirit.
1. Hallam.
2. "I have parted with thee until I die, and my paths are in the fields I know, whilst thine are in lands which

41

Thy spirit ere our fatal loss
   Did ever rise from high to higher,
   As mounts the heavenward altar-fire,
As flies the lighter thro' the gross.

But thou art turn'd to something strange,[3]   5
   And I have lost the links that bound
   Thy changes; here upon the ground,
No more partaker of thy change.

Deep folly![4] yet that this could be —
   That I could wing my will with might   10
   To leap the grades of life and light,
And flash[5] at once, my friend, to thee!

For tho' my nature rarely yields
   To that vague fear implied in death,
   Nor shudders at the gulfs beneath,   15
The howlings from forgotten fields;[6]

Yet oft when sundown skirts the moor
   An inner trouble I behold,
   A spectral doubt which makes me cold,
That I shall be thy mate no more,   20

Tho' following with an upward mind
   The wonders that have come to thee,
   Thro' all the secular to-be,[7]
But evermore a life behind.[8]

42

I vex my heart with fancies dim.
   He still outstript me in the race;
   It was but unity of place
That made me dream I rank'd with him.

I do not know" (Tennyson). See *Hamlet* III, i, lines 78–82:
   But that the dread of something after death —
   The undiscover'd country, from whose bourn
   No traveller returns — puzzles the will,
   And makes us rather bear those ills we have
   Than fly to others that we know not of?
3. Compare *The Tempest* I, ii, line 405: "something rich and strange."
4. Refers to the wish of lines 10–12.
5. See section 95, 9: "And all at once it seem'd at last / The living soul was flash'd on mine."
6. "The eternal miseries of the inferno" (Tennyson). Hallam Tennyson is sure the reminiscence is of
   Dante's *Inferno* III, lines 25–51, which describe "those wretched beings, who for ever shriek and wail
   and beat their breasts because they are despised and forgotten, and consigned to everlasting nothingness on account of their colourlessness and indifference during life."
7. "Aeons of the future" (Tennyson). "The secular abyss to come" (Hallam Tennyson).
8. The speaker has imagined Hallam in afterlife advancing through stages that he cannot follow or even
   comprehend while on earth himself (stanza 2). When he dies, even if he could follow in his friend's steps
   (which he doubts he would be able to), he would remain a step behind through all time.

And so may Place retain[9] us still,   5
  And he the much-beloved again,
  A lord of large experience, train
To riper growth the mind and will;

And what delights can equal those
  That stir the spirit's inner deeps,   10
  When one that loves, but knows not, reaps
A truth from one that loves and knows?

43

If Sleep and Death be truly one,
  And every spirit's folded bloom
  Thro' all its intervital[1] gloom
In some long trance should slumber on;

Unconscious of the sliding hour,   5
  Bare of the body, might it last,
  And silent traces of the past
Be all the color of the flower:

So then were nothing lost to man;
  So that still garden of the souls   10
  In many a figured leaf enrolls
The total world since life began;

And love will last as pure and whole
  As when he loved me here in Time,
  And at the spiritual prime[2]   15
Rewaken with the dawning soul.

44

How fares it with the happy dead?
  For here the man is more and more;
  But he forgets the days before
God shut the doorways of his head.[3]

The days have vanish'd, tone and tint,   5
  And yet perhaps the hoarding sense

9. Keep us together.
1. "In the passage between this life and the next" (Tennyson). "Tennyson apparently coined 'intervital'"
(Shatto and Shaw).
2. Dawn of the spiritual hereafter" (Tennyson).
3. Bradley offers several possible interpretations of this difficult section, the most plausible being: "The
man" of line 2 and "he" of line 3 refer to living man, who, as he grows up, forgets the first two years of
infancy before the closing of the sutures of the skull. Stanza 2 continues with the Wordsworthian notion
that we receive mystic impulses from those earliest years, but does not suggest flashings from a prenatal
existence. Stanza 3 then shifts to the dead, who have forgotten their earthly life ("taste Lethean springs")
but may have sudden glimpses of it parallel to our recollections from earliest childhood.
    Tennyson notes: "Closing of the skull after babyhood," and then continues in a long note, in part: "The
dead after this life may have no remembrance of life, like the living babe who forgets the time before the sutures of the skull are closed, yet the living babe grows in knowledge, and though the remembrance of his earliest days has vanished, yet with increasing knowledge there comes a dreamy vision of what has been . . ."
Compare Wordsworth's "Immortality Ode," especially line 58: "Our birth is but a sleep and a forgetting."

Gives out at times—he knows not whence—
A little flash, a mystic hint;

And in the long harmonious years—
   If Death so taste Lethean springs—   10
   May some dim touch of earthly things
Surprise thee ranging with thy peers.

If such a dreamy touch should fall,
   O, turn thee round, resolve the doubt;
   My guardian angel will speak out   15
In that high place, and tell thee all.

45

The baby new to earth and sky,
   What time his tender palm is prest
   Against the circle of the breast,
Has never thought that "this is I;"

But as he grows he gathers much,   5
   And learns the use of "I" and "me,"
   And finds "I am not what I see,
And other than the things I touch."

So rounds he to a separate mind
   From whence clear memory may begin,
   As thro' the frame that binds him in   10
His isolation[4] grows defined.

This use[5] may lie in blood and breath,
   Which else were fruitless of their due,
   Had man to learn himself anew   15
Beyond the second birth of death.[6]

46

We ranging down this lower track,
   The path we came by, thorn and flower,
   Is shadow'd by the growing hour,
Lest life should fail in looking back.[7]

So be it: there[8] no shade can last   5
   In that deep dawn behind the tomb,

4. Compare Wordsworth, "Ode: Intimations of Immortality" V, lines 67–68: "Shades of the prison-house begin to close / Upon the growing Boy."
5. "The purpose of the life here may be to realise personal consciousness" (Hallam Tennyson). Compare 34, line 8: "Without conscience or an aim" and 35, 6: "Mere fellowship of sluggish moods."
6. The speaker undercuts the proposition of section 44, arguing that if the dead did forget their earthly life, they would have to acquire an identity all over again.
7. Living man's concern with the present and future ("growing hour") makes memory imperfect. But neither can man live in the past.
8. In the spiritual world these imperfections do not exist.

But clear from marge to marge[9] shall bloom
The eternal landscape of the past;

A lifelong tract of time reveal'd,
    The fruitful hours of still increase;   10
Days order'd in a wealthy peace,
And those five years its richest field.

O love, thy province were not large,
    A bounded field, nor stretching far;
Look also, Love a brooding star,[1]   15
A rosy warmth from marge to marge.

47

That each, who seems a separate whole,
    Should move his rounds, and fusing all
    The skirts of self again, should fall
Remerging in the general Soul,[2]

Is faith as vague as all unsweet.   5
    Eternal form shall still divide
    The eternal soul from all beside;
And I shall know him when we meet;

And we shall sit at endless feast,
    Enjoying each the other's good.   10
    What vaster dream can hit the mood
Of Love on earth? He seeks at least

Upon the last and sharpest height,
    Before the spirits fade away,
    Some landing-place, to clasp and say,   15
"Farewell! We lose ourselves in light."

48

If these brief lays, of Sorrow born,
    Were taken to be such as closed,[3]
Grave doubts and answers here proposed,
Then these were such as men might scorn.

9. From birth to death. The word *shall* creates ambiguities. He cannot be thinking of his friend's present state but looks to the indefinite future. Then perhaps he, his friend, or both of them together will look back on the five-year friendship.
1. "As if Lord of the whole life" (Tennyson). "Not merely of these five years of friendship" (Hallam Tennyson). Venus, both morning and evening "star," which, appearing on both horizons, had been thought by classical poets to be two separate heavenly bodies.
2. A medieval theory known as Averroism denied individual immortality, claiming the spirit was merged back into the universal soul from whence it came. If this must be, and we cannot endlessly enjoy each other's company, let us at least share a moment of recognition before our souls are absorbed and "we lose ourselves in light." Apparently alluding to this section, Tennyson said: "If the absorption into the divine in the after-life be the creed of some, let them at all events allow us many existences of individuality before this absorption; since this short-lived individuality seems to be but too short a preparation for so mighty a union" (*Memoir* I, 319).
3. Concluded.

Her[4] care is not to part and prove;   5
   She takes, when harsher moods remit,
   What slender shade of doubt may flit,
And makes it vassal unto love;

And hence, indeed, she sports with words,
   But better serves a wholesome law,   10
   And holds it sin and shame to draw
The deepest measure[5] from the chords;

Nor dare she trust a larger lay,
   But rather loosens from the lip
   Short swallow-flights of song, that dip   15
Their wings in tears, and skim away.

49

From art, from nature, from the schools,[6]
   Let random influences glance,
   Like light in many a shiver'd lance
That breaks about the dappled pools.

The lightest wave of thought shall lisp,   5
   The fancy's tenderest eddy wreathe,
   The slightest air of song shall breathe
To make the sullen surface crisp.[7]

And look thy[8] look, and go thy way,
   But blame not thou the winds that make   10
   The seeming-wanton ripple break,
The tender-pencill'd shadow play.

Beneath all fancied hopes and fears
   Ay me, the sorrow deepens down,
   Whose muffled motions blindly drown   15
The bases of my life in tears.

50

Be near me when my light is low,
   When the blood creeps, and the nerves prick
   And tingle; and the heart is sick,
And all the wheels of being slow.

Be near me when the sensuous frame   5
   Is rack'd with pangs that conquer trust;
   And Time, a maniac scattering dust,
And Life, a Fury slinging flame.[9]

---

4. Sorrow's.
5. "For there are 'thoughts that do often lie too deep for' mere poetic words" (Hallam Tennyson, clearly alluding to Wordsworth's "Thoughts that do often lie too deep for tears" (*Intimations Ode*, last line).
6. Of theology and philosophy.
7. A verb; curl or ripple.
8. Any observer such as the traveler of section 21.
9. "The Furies carried torches" (Ricks).

Be near me when my faith is dry,
    And men the flies of latter spring,   10
    That lay their eggs, and sting and sing
And weave their petty cells and die.

Be near me when I fade away,
    To point the term[1] of human strife,
    And on the low dark verge of life   15
The twilight of eternal day.

51[2]

Do we indeed desire the dead
    Should still be near us at our side?
    Is there no baseness we would hide?
No inner vileness that we dread?[3]

Shall he for whose applause I strove,   5
    I had such reverence for his blame,
    See with clear eye some hidden shame
And I be lessen'd in his love?

I wrong the grave with fears untrue.
    Shall love be blamed for want of faith?   10
    There must be wisdom with great Death;
The dead shall look me thro' and thro'.

Be near us when we climb or fall;
    Ye watch, like God, the rolling hours
    With larger other eyes than ours,   15
To make allowance for us all.[4]

52

I cannot love thee as I ought,
    For love reflects the thing beloved;
    My words are only words, and moved
Upon the topmost froth of thought.

"Yet blame not thou thy plaintive song,"   5
    The Spirit of true love replied;

1. Reach the limit or end.
2. See n. 3, p. 209. Probably composed in December 1841. At Christmas time Tennyson showed it to Edmund Lushington, who wrote for the *Memoir* (I, 203) that Tennyson "liked it better than most he had done lately."
3. Compare "He knows a baseness in his blood," "The Two Voices," line 301. Ian Hamilton, reviewing Cecil Y. Lang's edition of *The Letters of Matthew Arnold* (TLS, July 1997), questions but cannot dismiss Lang's belief that a cross in a diary entry indicates masturbation. In Arthur Kenny's *Oxford Diaries of Arthur Hugh Clough*, there is no doubt that "with Clough, the asterisks indicate those days on which he fell victim to the 'wretched habit' of masturbation, 'the worst sin.'" Hallam Tennyson has so thoroughly 'cleansed' all of his father's private papers and correspondence that no such direct similar evidence for that "guilt" remains. But throughout the Victorian era, young men's obsession with this "sin," compounded by Lord Acton's dissertations on the subject, is difficult for today's reader to comprehend.
4. Of this stanza, Hallam Tennyson notes: "The Queen quoted this verse to my father about the Prince Consort, just after his death, and told him that it had brought her great comfort."

"Thou canst not move me from thy side,
Nor human frailty do me wrong.

"What keeps a spirit wholly true
    To that ideal which he bears?   10
    What record? not the sinless years[5]
That breathed beneath the Syrian blue;

"So fret not, like an idle girl,
    That life is dash'd with flecks of sin.
    Abide;[6] thy wealth is gather'd in,   15
When Time hath sunder'd shell from pearl."[7]

53[8]

How many a father have I seen,
    A sober man, among his boys,
    Whose youth was full of foolish noise,
Who wears his manhood hale and green;

And dare we to this fancy give,   5
    That had the wild oat not been sown,
    The soil, left barren, scarce had grown
The grain by which a man may live?

Or, if we held the doctrine sound
    For life outliving heats of youth,   10
    Yet who would preach it as a truth
To those that eddy round and round?

Hold thou the good, define it well;
    For fear divine Philosophy
    Should push beyond her mark, and be   15
Procuress to the Lords of Hell.

54

O, yet we trust that somehow good
    Will be the final goal[9] of ill,
    To pangs of nature, sins of will,
Defects of doubt, and taints of blood;

---

5. The record of Christ's sinless earthly life.
6. "Wait without wearying" (Tennyson).
7. Although the pearl is traditionally a symbol for the soul, Tennyson may also mean separating what is worthless from what is valuable in any human life.
8. Tennyson's comments on this section: "There is a passionate heart of nature in a rake sometimes. The nature that yields emotionally may turn out straighter than a prig's. Yet we must not be making excuses, but we must set before us a rule of good for young as for old."
9. A notion that makes little sense. How could evil ever have good as its goal—final or otherwise? Tennyson may have been thinking of Pope's conclusion to Part I of the *Essay on Man:*
    All Nature is but Art, unknown to thee;
    All Chance, Direction, which thou canst not see;
    All Discord, Harmony not understood;
    All partial Evil, universal Good.

That nothing walks with aimless feet;   5
   That not one life shall be destroy'd,
   Or cast as rubbish to the void,
When God hath made the pile complete;

That not a worm is cloven in vain;
   That not a moth with vain desire   10
   Is shrivell'd in a fruitless fire,
Or but subserves another's gain.

Behold, we know not anything;
   I can but trust that good shall fall
   At last—far off[1]—at last, to all,   15
And every winter change to spring.

So runs my dreams; but what am I?
   An infant crying in the night;
   An infant crying for the light,
And with no language but a cry.[2]   20

55

The wish, that of the living whole
   No life may fail beyond the grave,
   Derives it not from what we have
The likest God within the soul?[3]

Are God and Nature then at strife,   5
   That Nature lends such evil dreams?
   So careful of the type[4] she seems,
So careless of the single life,

That I, considering everywhere
   Her secret meaning in her deeds,   10
   And finding that of fifty[5] seeds
She often brings but one to bear,

I falter where I firmly trod,
   And falling with my weight of cares
   Upon the great world's altar-stairs   15
That slope thro' darkness up to God,

I stretch lame hands of faith, and grope,
   And gather dust and chaff, and call

1. See the poem's conclusion: "And one far-off divine event, To which the whole creation moves."
2. See 124, 5.
3. "The inner consciousness—the divine in man" (Tennyson).
4. Species. "The use of this term to mean a specific group or division of animals, plants, etc., having a common structure was introduced in the 1830's and is common in Lyell" (Shatto and Shaw). As in section 35, here and in section 56 Lyell's influence is apparent. "The lavish profusion too in the natural world appals me, from the growths of the tropical forest to the capacity of man to multiply, the torrent of babies. . . . If we look at Nature alone, full of perfection and imperfection, she tells us that God is disease, murder and rapine" (Tennyson in *Memoir* I, 314)
5. "'Fifty' should be 'myriad'" (Tennyson).

To what I feel is Lord of all,
And faintly trust the larger hope.[6]   20

56[7]

"So careful of the type?" but no.
From scarped[8] cliff and quarried stone
She[9] cries, "A thousand types are gone;
I care for nothing, all shall go.

"Thou makest thine appeal to me.   5
I bring to life, I bring to death;
The spirit does but mean the breath:
I know no more." And he, shall he,

Man, her last work, who seem'd so fair,
Such splendid purpose in his eyes,   10
Who roll'd the psalm to wintry skies,
Who built him fanes of fruitless prayer,

Who trusted God was love in indeed
And love Creation's final law—
Tho' Nature, red in tooth and claw   15
With ravine, shriek'd against his creed—

Who loved, who suffer'd countless ills,
Who battled for the True, the Just,
Be blown about the desert dust,
Or seal'd[1] within the iron hills?   20

No more? A monster then, a dream,
A discord. Dragons[2] of the prime,
That tare each other in their slime,
Were mellow music match'd with him.[3]

6 "He means," his son says, "that the whole human race would through, perhaps, ages of suffering, be at
  length purified and saved" (*Memoir* I, 321–22). The "hope" is larger than the wish in stanza 1 that no
  individual lose his immortality. See 34, 1 and n. 4, p. 225.
7. In 1844 Tennyson wrote his publisher to obtain a copy of Chambers's *Vestiges of Creation* (1844), a book
  that, Tennyson rightly noted from an advertisement, "seems to contain many speculations with which I
  have been familiar for years" (*Memoir* I, 222–23). Probably written before 1844, section 56 helps support
  the claim that Tennyson anticipated some implications of Darwinian theory and supports his assertion
  above.
8. Cut vertically, exposing the strata.
9. Nature. For the poet's response, see section 118. "The idea of the extinction of species originated with
  Georges Cuvier (1769–1832), who proved by the new methods of comparative anatomy that recently di-
  covered fossils derived from species distinct from any of those known now to be alive" (Shatto and Shaw).
1. As fossils.
2. "The geologic monsters of the early ages" (Tennyson). Reports of the discoveries of these huge fossils
  were circulating by the second decade of the century. Sir Richard Owen, though himself an early oppo-
  nent of Darwinism, coined the word *dinosaur* in 1841—from the Greek meaning "terrible lizard"—ob-
  serving that their structures bore remarkable similarities to those of crocodiles. See the "monstrous eft"
  in *Maud* 1, IV, line 6.
3. Man. The thought that man may perish as did the lost species makes the human condition monstrous
  and more terrifying to contemplate than the fate of prehistoric beasts, which at least worked out their des-
  tinies in harmony with natural law.

O life as futile, then, as frail!   25
    O for thy[4] voice to soothe and bless!
    What hope of answer, or redress?
Behind the veil, behind the veil.[5]

57[6]

Peace; come away: the song of woe
    Is after all earthly song.
    Peace;[7] come away: we do him wrong
To sing so wildly: let us go.

Come; let us go: your cheeks are pale;   5
    But half my life I leave behind.
    Methinks my friend is richly shrined;
But I shall pass, my work will fail.[8]

Yet in these ears, till hearing dies,
    One set slow bell will seem to toll   10
    The passing of the sweetest soul
That ever look'd with human eyes.

I hear it now, and o'er and o'er,
    Eternal greetings to the dead;
    And "Ave, Ave, Ave,"[9] said,   15
"Adieu, adieu," for evermore.

58[1]

In those sad words I took farewell.
    Like echoes in sepulchral halls,
    As drop by drop the water falls
In vaults and catacombs, they fell;

And, falling, idly broke the peace   5
    Of hearts that beat from day to day,
    Half-conscious of their dying clay,
And those cold crypts where they shall cease.

---

4. Hallam's.
5. "Here used as an image of successive stages of life after death: 'From orb to orb, from veil to veil'" (Shatto and Shaw).
6. This section comes at the end of the Trinity manuscript, and Tennyson seems once to have intended for it to conclude the whole poem. Knowles reports Tennyson saying: "I thought this was too sad for an ending." It is perhaps addressed to Tennyson's sister Emily, who had been Hallam's fiancée. See *Memoir* I, 306, for the unpublished section "The Grave," originally section 57.
7. In a letter to Tennyson (September 4, 1832), Hallam writes of Edward Spedding's death: "He looked to a future life, I should think, as calmly as to a future day. His epitaph is 'Peace'" (*Letters*, 638). See Tennyson's poem "To J. S."
8. "The poet speaks of these poems. Methinks I have built a rich shrine to my friend, but it will not last" (Tennyson).
9. Of Catullus's farewell to his brother Tennyson said that no "modern elegy, so long as men retain the least hope in the after-life of those whom they loved, [can] equal in pathos the desolation of that everlasting farewell, 'Atque in perpetuum frater ave atque vale'" (*Memoir* II, 239).
1. Of this section, Tennyson says: "*Ulysses* was written soon after Arthur Hallam's death, and gave my feelings about the need of going forward and braving the struggle of life perhaps more simply than anything in *In Memoriam*." See "Ulysses" and notes.

The high Muse[2] answer'd: "Wherefore grieve
    Thy brethren with a fruitless tear?   10
    Abide a little longer here,[3]
And thou shalt take a nobler leave."

59[4]

O Sorrow, wilt thou live with me
    No casual mistress, but a wife,
    My bosom-friend and half of life;
As I confess it needs must be?

O Sorrow, wilt thou rule my blood,   5
    Be sometimes lovely like a bride,
    And put thy harsher moods aside,
If thou wilt have me wise and good?

My centred passion cannot move,
    Nor will it lessen from to-day;   10
    But I'll leave at times to play
As with the creature of my love;

And set forth, for thou art mine,
    With so much hope for years to come,
    That, howsoe'er I know thee, some   15
Could hardly tell what name were thine.

60[5]

He past, a soul of nobler tone;
    My spirit loved and loves him yet,
    Like some poor girl whose heart is set
On one whose rank exceeds her own.

He mixing with his proper sphere,   5
    She finds the baseness of her lot,
    Half jealous of she knows not what,
And envying all that meet him there,

The little village looks forlorn;
    She sighs amid her narrow days,   10
    Moving about the household ways,
In that dark house where she was born.

The foolish neighbors come and go,
    And tease her till the day draws by;
    At night she weeps, "How vain am I!   15
How should he love a thing so low?"

2. Urania, as in the opening to section 37.
3. By the grave.
4. Contrast section 3. Section 59 was added in the fourth edition, 1851, "inserted as a pendant to Section III" (Hallam Tennyson).
5. Sections 60–65 form a group similar to group 40–47, but here the emphasis is on the speaker's desire that his friend think of him.

61

If, in thy second state sublime,
Thy ransom'd reason[6] change replies
With all the circle of the wise,[7]
The perfect flower of human time;

And if thou cast thine eyes below,   5
How dimly character'd and slight,
How dwarf'd a growth of cold and night,
How blanch'd with darkness must I grow!

Yet turn thee to the doubtful shore,[8]
Where thy first form was made a man;   10
I loved thee, Spirit, and love, nor can
The soul of Shakespeare love thee more.[9]

62

Tho' if an eye that's downward cast
Could make thee somewhat blench[1] or fail,
Then be my love an idle tale
And fading legend of the past;

And thou, as one that once declined,[2]   5
When he was little more than boy,
On some unworthy heart with joy,
But lives to wed an equal mind,

And breathes a novel world, the while
His other passion wholly dies,   10
Or in the light of deeper eyes
Is matter for a flying smile.

63

Yet pity for a horse o'er-driven,
And love in which my hound has part
Can hang no weight upon my heart
In its assumptions up to heaven;

And I am so much more than these,   5
As thou, perchance, art more than I,
And yet I spare them sympathy,
And I would set their pains at ease.

6. Compare "spirits render'd free" in 38, 3. "Change": exchange.
7. Tennyson probably had in mind Odysseus's, Aeneas's, and Dante's descents into the underworld and their conversing with the ghosts of great heroes and brave spirits from the past.
8. Earthly life, where man is in doubt and only dimly perceives.
9. "Tennyson's gloss to the entire section is particularly relevant here: 'In power of love not even the greatest dead can surpass the poet'" (Shatto and Shaw).
1. Flinch.
2. Stooped.

So mayst thou watch me where I weep,
 As unto vaster motions bound,[3]
 The circuits of thine orbit round
A higher height, a deeper deep.

64[4]

Dost thou look back on what hath been,
 As some divinely gifted man,
 Whose life in low estate began
And on a simple village green;

Who breaks his birth's individous bar,
 And grasps the skirts of happy chance,
 And breasts the blows of circumstance,
And grapples with his evil star;

Who makes by force his merit known
 And lives to clutch the golden keys,[5]
 To mould a mighty state's decrees,
And shape the whisper of the throne;

And moving up from high to higher,
 Becomes on Fortune's crowning slope
 The pillar of a people's hope,
The centre of a world's desire;

Yet feels, as in a pensive dream,
 When all his active powers are still,
 A distant dearness in the hill,
A secret sweetness in the stream,

The limit of his narrower fate,
 While yet beside its vocal springs
 He play's at counsellors and kings,
With one that was his earliest mate;

Who ploughs with pain his native lea
 And reaps the labor of his hands,
 Or in the furrow musing stands:
"Does my old friend remember me?"

65[6]

Sweet soul, do with me as thou wilt;
 I lull a fancy trouble-tost
 With "Love's too precious to be lost,
A little grain shall not be spilt."

3. Hallam's spirit may be re-embodied on a planet with an orbit larger than earth's.
4. "Composed by my father when he was walking up and down the Strand and Fleet Street" (Hallam Tennyson). "In Memoriam contains greater poems, but none perhaps more exquisitely imagined and written" (Bradley).
5. "Keys of office of state" (Hallam Tennyson).
6. "Perhaps the first section of In Memoriam that can described as cheerful or happy" (Bradley).

And in that solace can I sing,   5
   Till out of painful phases wrought
   There flutters up a happy thought,
Self-balanced on a lightsome wing;

Since we deserved the name of friends,
   And thine effect so lives in me,   10
   And part of mine may live in thee
And move thee on to noble ends.

66

You[7] thought my heart too far diseased;
   You wonder when my fancies play
   To find me gay among the gay,
Like one with any trifle pleased.

The shade by which my life was crost,   5
   Which makes a desert in the mind,
   Has made me kindly with my kind,
And like to him whose sight is lost;

Whose feet are guided thro' the land,
   Whose jest among his friends is free,   10
   Who takes the children on his knee,
And winds their curls about his hand.

He plays with threads, he beats his chair
   For pastime, dreaming of the sky;
   His inner day can never die,   15
His night of loss is always there.

67

When on my bed the moonlight falls,
   I know that in thy place of rest[8]
   By that broad water of the west[9]
There comes a glory on the walls:

Thy marble bright in dark appears,   5
   As slowly steals a silver flame
   Along the letters of thy name,
And o'er the number of thy years.

The mystic glory swims away,
   From off my bed the moonlight dies;   10
   And closing eaves of wearied eyes
I sleep till dusk is dipt in gray;

7. "You," Tennyson told Knowles, refers to "the auditor." Tennyson often voices concerns over how his elegies will be perceived or mis-perceived; e.g., see section 21, 3, as one who makes "parade of pain." The section marks a transition between groups. Sections 67–71 are loosely connected by references to night, sleep, and dreams.
8. At Clevedon, by the Severn River.
9. "The Severn" (Tennyson).

And then I know the mist is drawn
   A lucid veil from coast to coast,
   And in the dark church[1] like a ghost   15
Thy tablet[2] glimmers to the dawn.

68

When in the down I sink my head,
   Sleep, Death's twin-brother, times my breath;
   Sleep, Death's twin-brother, knows not Death,
Nor can I dream of thee as dead.

I walk as ere I walk'd forlorn,   5
   When all our path was fresh with dew,
   And all the bugle breezes blew
Reveillée to the breaking morn.

But what is this? I turn about,
   I find a trouble in thine eye,   10
   Which makes me sad I know not why,
Nor can my dream resolve the doubt;

But ere the lark hath left the lea
   I wake, and I discern the truth;
   It is the trouble of my youth   15
That foolish sleep transfers to thee.

69[3]

I dream'd there would be Spring no more,
   That nature's ancient power was lost;
   The streets were black with smoke and frost,
They chatter'd trifles at the door;

I wander'd from the noisy town,   5
   I found a wood with thorny boughs;
   I took the thorns to bind my brows,
I wore them like a civic crown;

I met with scoffs, I met with scorns
   From youth and babe and hoary hairs: 10
   They call'd me in the public squares
The fool that wears a crown of thorns.

They call'd me fool, they call'd me child:
   I found an angel[4] of the night;
   The voice was low, the look was bright;   15
He look'd upon my crown and smiled.

1. See notes to sections 2 and 18. "In later editions of 'In Memoriam' I altered the word 'chancel,' which was the word used by Mr. Hallam in his Memoir, to 'dark church'" (*Memoir* I, 305).
2. The tablet is "in the manor isle of the church." The epitaph, written by Hallam's father, is reproduced in the *Memoir* I, 296.
3. "To write poems abouth death and grief is 'to wear a crown of thorns,' which the people say ought to be laid aside" (Tennyson).
4. "But the Divine Thing in the gloom brought comfort" (Tennyson). The stanza recalls similar visions in Blake.

He reach'd the glory of a hand,
    That seem'd to touch it into leaf;
    The voice was not the voice of grief,
The words were hard to understand.   20

70

I cannot see the features right,
    When on the gloom I strive to paint
    The face I know; the hues are faint
And mix with hollow[5] masks of night;

Cloud-towers by ghostly masons wrought,   5
    A gulf that ever shuts and gapes,
    A hand that points, and palled[6] shapes
In shadowy thoroughfares of thought;

And crowds that stream from yawning doors,
    And shoals of pucker'd faces drive;   10
    Dark bulks that tumble half alive,
And lazy lengths on boundless shores;

Till all at once beyond the will
    I hear a wizard music roll,
    And thro' a lattice on the soul   15
Looks thy fair face and makes it still.

71

Sleep, kinsman thou to death and trance
    And madness, thou hast forged at last
    A night-long present of the past
In which we went thro' summer France.[7]

Hadst thou such credit with the soul?   5
    Then bring an opiate trebly strong,
    Drug down the blindfold sense of wrong,
That so my pleasure may be whole;

While now we talk as once we talk'd
    Of men and minds, the dust of change,   10
    The days that grow to something strange,
In walking as of old we walk'd

Beside the river's wooded reach,
    The fortress, and the mountain ridge,
    The cataract flashing from the bridge,   15
The breaker breaking on the beach.

5. Lacking substance.
6. Veiled, hence dimly seen.
7. In 1830, Tennyson and Hallam journeyed through the Pyrenees to see Torrijos, who was leading a revolt
against the Spanish king. See notes to "Œnone."

72

Risest thou thus, dim dawn,[8] again,
    And howlest, issuing out of night,
    With blasts that blow the poplar white,
And lash with storm the streaming pane?

Day, when my crown'd estate[9] begun   5
    To pine in that reverse of doom,
    Which sicken'd every living bloom,
And blurr'd the splendor of the sun;

Who usherest in the dolorous hour
    With thy quick tears that make the rose   10
    Pull sideways, and the daisy close
Her crimson fringes to the shower;

Who mightst have heaved a windless flame
    Up the deep East, or, whispering, play'd
    A chequer-work of beam and shade   15
Along the hills, yet look'd the same,

As wan, as chill, as wild as now;
    Day, mark'd as with some hideous crime,
    When the dark hand struck down thro' time,
And cancell'd nature's best: but thou,   20

Lift as thou mayst thy burthen'd brows
    Thro' clouds that drench the morning star,
    And whirl the ungarner'd sheaf afar,
And sow the sky with flying boughs,

And up thy vault with roaring sound   25
    Climb thy thick noon, disastrous day;
    Touch thy dull goal[1] of joyless gray,
And hide thy shame beneath the ground.

73

So many worlds, so much to do,
    So little done, such things to be,
    How know I what had need of thee,[2]
For thou wert strong as thou wert true?

The fame is quench'd that I foresaw,   5
    The head hath miss'd an earthly wreath:
    I curse not Nature, no, nor Death;
For nothing is that errs from law.[3]

8. September 15, 1834, the first anniversary of Hallam's death. See *Memoir* I, 305. Contrast section 99.
9. As a poet. "Crown'd" recalls those happy days recorded in section 22, 2.
1. The sun's zenith or noon; line 28 suggests the sunset, which Hallam Tennyson glossed "the dull sunset."
2. Hallam. Here and through section 77, Tennyson seems indebted to Milton's "Lycidas," particularly on the subject of fame.
3. "Cf. Zoroaster's saying, 'Nought errs from law'" (Tennyson).

We pass; the path that each man trod
    Is dim, or will be dim, with weeds.   10
    What fame is left for human deeds
In endless age? It rests with God.

O hollow wraith[4] of dying fame,
    Fade wholly, while the soul exults,
    And self-infolds the large results   15
Of force that would have forged a name.

74

As sometimes in a dead man's face,
    To those that watch it more and more,
    A likeness, hardly seen before,
Comes out—to some one of his race;

So, dearest,[5] now thy brows are cold,   5
    I see thee what thou art, and know
    Thy likeness to the wise below,[6]
Thy kindred with the great of old.

But there is more than I can see,
    And what I see I leave unsaid,   10
    Nor speak it, knowing Death has made
His darkness beautiful with thee.

75

I leave thy praises unexpress'd
    In verse that brings myself relief,[7]
    And by the measure of my grief
I leave thy greatness to be guess'd.

What practice howsoe'er expert   5
    In fitting aptest words to things,
    Or voice the richest-toned that sings,
Hath power to give thee as thou wert?

I care not in these fading days
    To raise a cry that lasts not long,   10
    And round thee with the breeze of song
To stir a little dust of praise.

4. Apparition. See 70, 1.
5. "If any body thinks I ever called him 'dearest' in his life they are much mistaken, for I never even called him 'dear'" (Tennyson to Knowles). Perhaps here is as good a place as any to note Hallam Tennyson's restrictions on the Trinity manuscripts, not lifted until 1969. They reveal his inordinate concerns over possible misconstruings of even the mildest of comments, for example James Spedding's notations and jokings on drafts of the elegies. Such characteristic protectiveness and sensitivity by nineteenth-century biographers, especially family, all too readily and erroneously suggest to modern perceptions that there must have been something to hide. Reading through the manuscript, one is utterly baffled. Besides, Hallam Tennyson had incorporated many of the significant marginal comments into the Memoir.
6. The famous dead; lines 7 and 8 are in apposition. See 61, 1.
7. Contrast the "sad mechanic exercise" of 5, 2.

Thy leaf has perish'd in the green,[8]
 And, while we breathe beneath the sun,
 The world which credits what is done   15
Is cold to all that might have been.

So here shall silence guard thy fame;
 But somewhere, out of human view,
 Whate'er thy hands are set to do
Is wrought with tumult of acclaim.   20

76

Take wings of fancy, and ascend,
 And in a moment set thy face
 Where all the starry heavens of space
Are sharpen'd to a needle's end;[9]

Take wings of foresight; lighten thro'   5
 The secular abyss to come,[1]
 And lo, thy deepest lays are dumb
Before the mouldering of a yew;

And if the matin songs,[2] that woke
 The darkness of our planet, last,   10
 Thine own shall wither in the vast,
Ere half the lifetime of an oak.

Ere these[3] have clothed their branchy bowers
 With fifty Mays, thy songs are vain;
 And what are they when these remain   15
The ruin'd shells of hollow towers?

77

What hope is here for modern rhyme
 To him who turns a musing eye
 On songs, and deeds, and lives, that lie
Foreshorten'd in the tract of time?[4]

These mortal lullabies of pain   5
 May bind a book, may line a box,
 May serve to curl a maiden's locks;
Or when a thousand moons shall wane

A man upon a stall may find,
 And, passing, turn the page that tells   10

---

8. "At twenty-three" (Tennyson)
9. "So distant in void space that all our firmanent would appear to be a needle-point thence" (Tennyson).
1. "The ages upon ages to be" (Tennyson).
2. "The great early poets" (Tennyson).
3. The long-lived yew and oak.
4. Tennyson would be the first of the major poets, well informed by Lyell's *Principles of Geology*, to be fully
   aware of geologic time as stretching back to unimaginable length. Contrast, for example, Shakespeare's
   Sonnet 55: "Not marble, nor the guilded monuments / Of princes, shall outlive this powerful rhyme."
   Such comparisons became relatively meaningless when thinking of a future in millions of years.

A grief, then changed to something else,[5]
Sung by a long-forgotten mind.

But what of that? My darken'd ways
   Shall ring with music all the same;
   To breathe my loss is more than fame,   15
To utter love more sweet than praise.

78

Again at Christmas[6] did we weave
   The holly round the Christmas hearth;
   The silent snow possess'd the earth,
And calmly fell our Christmas-eve.

The yule-clog[7] sparkled keen with frost,   5
   No wing of wind the region swept,
   But over all things brooding slept
The quiet sense of something lost.

As in the winters left behind,
   Again in our ancient games had place,   10
   The mimic picture's[8] breathing grace,
And dance and song and hoodman-blind.[9]

Who show'd a token of distress?
   No single tear, no mark of pain—
   O sorrow, then can sorrow wane?   15
O grief, can grief be changed to less?[1]

O last regret, regret can die!
   No—mixt with all this mystic frame,
   Her deep relations are the same,
But with long use her tears are dry.   20

79[2]

"More than my brothers are to me,"—
   Let this not vex thee, noble heart!

5. "The grief that is no longer a grief" (Hallam Tennyson).
6. The second Christmas (1834) after Hallam's death. The third part of the poem begins here. For Bradley, and others later, this section marks the "turning-point in the general feeling of In Memoriam. . . . It seems true that in spite of gradual change, the tone of the poem so far is, on the whole, melancholy, while after LXXVIII, the predominant tone can scarcely be called even sad." But see the notes to section 95.
7. Scottish dialect for yule-log.
8. "Tableaux vivants" (Tennyson). A game like charades in which the participants assume poses of well-known figures in paintings or statues while the rest of the group guesses their identity.
9. "Blind-man's buff" (Tennyson).
1. If only for the flavor and tone of Spedding's notations in the Trinity manuscript, he scribbled his objection to the original "the less": "'the less' I doubt whether this is good English. As far as I can remember 'the' is never prefixed except when a [deleted] "because of" or some equivalent expression follows,—exprest or understood—'Never the less' means I think 'not the less on that account.' When will you do it? on Monday. Will you not do it sooner? The sooner sweet for you! I hope you are better (not the better). How are you? Never the better for seeing you?"
2. "This section is addressed to my brother Charles (Tennyson Turner)" (Tennyson). Hallam Tennyson quotes his father: "He was the most lovable human being I have ever met." See the last line of section 9.

I know thee of what force thou art
To hold the costliest love in fee.[3]

But thou and I are one in kind,   5
    As moulded like in Nature's mint;
    And hill and wood and field did print
The same sweet forms in either mind.[4]

For us the same cold streamlet curl'd
    Thro' all his eddying coves, the same   10
    All winds that roam the twilight came
In whispers of the beauteous world.

At one dear knee we proffer'd vows,
    One lesson from one book we learn'd,
    Ere childhood's flaxen ringlet turn'd   15
To black and brown on kindred brows.

And so my wealth resembles thine,
    But he was rich where I was poor,
    And he supplied my want the more
As his unlikeness fitted mine.   20

80

If any vague desire should rise,
    That holy Death ere Arthur died
    Had moved me kindly from his side,
And dropt the dust on tearless eyes;

Then fancy shapes, as fancy can,   5
    The grief my loss in him had wrought,
    A grief as deep as life or thought,
But stay'd in peace with God and man.

I make a picture in the brain;
    I hear the sentence that he speaks;   10
    He bears the burthen of the weeks,
But turns his burthen into gain.

His credit[5] thus shall set me free;
    And, influence-rich to soothe and save,
    Unused example from the grave   15
Reach out dead hands to comfort me.

---

3. Full possession.
4. "Compare 'Lycidas,' 23–24: 'For were nurs'd upon the self-same hill, / fed the same flock by fountain, shade, and rill'" (Shatto and Shaw).
5. The capacity to turn burden into gain, which, in the poet's fancy, Hallam would have done had Tennyson died.

81

Could I have said[6] while he was here,
   "My love shall now no further range;
   There cannot come a mellower change,
For now is love mature in ear."[7]

Love, then,[8] had hope of richer store: 5
   What end is here to my complaint?
   This haunting whisper makes me faint,
"More years had made me love thee more."

But Death returns an answer sweet:
   "My sudden frost was sudden gain,   10
   And gave all ripeness to the grain[9]
It might have drawn from after-heat."

82

I wage not any feud with Death
   For changes wrought on form and face;
   No lower life that earth's embrace
May breed with him can fright my faith.

Eternal process moving on,   5
   From state to state the spirit walks;
   And these[1] are but the shatter'd stalks,
Or ruin'd chrysalis of one.

Nor blame I Death, because he bare
   The use of virtue out of earth: 10
   I know transplanted human worth
Will bloom to profit, otherwhere.

For this alone on Death I wreak
   The wrath that garners in my heart;
   He put our lives so far apart   15
We cannot hear each other speak.

83

Dip down upon the northern shore,
   O sweet new-year delaying long;
   Thou doest expectant nature wrong;
Delaying long, delay no more.

6. "Would that I could have said" (Tennyson).
7. Ear of grain.
8. At that time. The meaning of these complicated five lines seems to be: if, when Hallam was alive, I could have said our love was complete, I could have anticipated then a fuller store of love were he to die than I could have by assuming our relationship to be incomplete.
9. His love for Hallam was ripened through sudden death, as some fruit is ripened by a sudden frost.
1. "Changes" of line 2.

What stays thee from the clouded noons,[2]   5
    Thy sweetness from its proper place?
    Can trouble live with April days,
Or sadness in the summer moons?[3]

Bring orchis, bring the foxglove spire,
    The little speedwell's darling blue,   10
    Deep tulips dash'd with fiery dew,
Laburnums, dropping-wells of fire.

O thou, new-year, delaying long,
    Delayest the sorrow in my blood,
    That longs to burst a frozen bud   15
And flood a fresher throat with song.

84

When I contemplate all alone
    The life that had been thine below,
    And fix my thoughts on all the glow
To which thy crescent would have grown,

I see thee sitting crown'd with good,   5
    A central warmth diffusing bliss
    In glance and smile, and clasp and kiss,
On all the branches of thy blood;

Thy blood, my friend, and partly mine;
    For now the day was drawing on,   10
    When thou shouldst link thy life with one[4]
Of mine own house, and boys of thine

Had babbled "Uncle" on my knee;
    But that remorseless iron hour
    Made cypress of her orange flower,[5]   15
Despair of hope, and earth of thee.

I seem to meet their least desire,
    To clap their checks, to call them mine.
    I see their unborn faces shine
Beside the never-lighted fire.   20

I see myself an honor'd guest,
    Thy partner in the flowery walk
    Of letters, genial table-talk,
Or deep dispute, and graceful jest;

2. The "new year," or spring, has not caught up with these April days whose cloudiness suggests an earlier season.
3. Contrast section 38.
4. Emily Tennyson, to whom Hallam was engaged.
5. See 40, 1. The orange blossom is symbolic of weddings; the cypress, of death and mourning.

While now thy prosperous labor fills   25
   The lips of men with honest praise,
   And sun by sun the happy days
Descend below the golden hills

With promise of a morn as fair;
   And all the train of bounteous hours   30
   Conduct, by paths of growing powers,
To reverence and the silver hair;

Till slowly worn her earthly robe,
   Her lavish mission richly wrought,
   Leaving great legacies of thought,   35
Thy spirit should fail from off the globe;

What time mine own might also flee,
   As link'd with thine in love and fate,
   And, hovering o'er the dolorous strait
To the other shore, involved in thee,   40

Arrive at last the blessed goal,[6]
   And He that died in Holy Land
   Would reach us out the shinning hand,
And take us as a single soul.

What reed was that on which I leant?   45
   Ah, backward fancy, wherefore wake
   The old bitterness again, and break
The low beginnings of content?

85[7]

This truth came borne with bier and pall,
   I felt it, when I sorrow'd most,
   'T is better to have loved and lost,
Than never to have loved at all[8] —

O true in word, and tried in deed,   5
   Demanding, so to bring relief
   To this which is our common grief,
What kind of life is that I lead;

And whether trust in things above
   Be dimm'd of sorrow, or sustain'd;   10
   And whether love for him have drain'd
My capabilities of love;

Your words have virtue such as draws
   A faithful answer from the breast,

6. Tennyson compares *Paradise Lost* II, line 409: "ere he arrive / The happy isle."
7. Perhaps addressed to Edmund Lushington, who married Tennyson's sister Cecilia on October 10, 1842. See the "Epilogue." A draft of this section was made in 1833 but clearly was much altered later.
8. See 27, 4.

Thro' light reproaches, half exprest,   15
And loyal unto kindly laws.

My blood an even tenor kept,
    Till on mine ear this message falls,
    That in Vienna's fatal walls
God's finger[9] touch'd him, and he slept.   20

The great Intelligences[1] fair
    That range above our mortal state,
    In circle round the blessed gate,
Received and gave him welcome there;

And led him thro' the blissful climes,   25
    And show'd him in the fountain fresh
    All knowledge that the sons of flesh
Shall gather in the cycled times.[2]

But I remain'd, whose hopes were dim,
    Whose life, whose thoughts were little worth,   30
    To wander on a darken'd earth,
Where all things round me breathed of him.

O friendship, equal-poised control,
    O heart, with kindliest motion warm,
    O sacred essence, other form,   35
O solemn ghost, O crowned soul!

Yet none could better know than I,
    How much of act at human hands
    The sense of human will demands[3]
By which we dare to live or die.   40

Whatever way my days decline,
    I felt and feel, tho' left alone,
    His being working in mine own,
The footsteps of his life in mine;

A life that all the Muses deck'd   45
    With gifts of grace, that might express
    All-comprehensive tenderness,
All-subtilizing intellect:

And so my passion hath not swerved
    To works of weakness, but I find   50
    An image comforting the mind,
And in my grief a strength reserved.

9. "An image reversing Michelangelo's view of the creation" (Buckley's *Tennyson: The Growth of a Poet*, p. 114).
1. Tennyson compares "Lycidas," lines 178–81: "There entertain him all the Saints above / In solemn troops, and sweet societies, / That sing, and singing in their glory move, / And wipe the tears for ever from his eyes."
2. "Earthly periods" (Hallam Tennyson).
3. "Yet I know that the knowledge that we have free will demands from us action" (Tennyson).

Likewise the imaginative woe,
   That loved to handle spiritual strife,
   Diffused the shock thro' all my life,   55
But in the present broke the blow.

My pulses therefore beat again
   For other friends that once I met;
   Nor can it suit me to forget
The mighty hopes[4] that make us men.   60

I woo your love: I count it crime
   To mourn for any overmuch;
   I, the divided half of such
A friendship as had[5] master's Time;

Which masters Time indeed, and is   65
   Eternal, separate from fears.
   The all-assuming[6] months and years
Can take no part away from this;

But Summer on the steaming floods,
   And Spring that swells the narrow brooks,   70
   And Autumn, with a noise of rooks,
That gather in the waning woods,

And every pulse of wind and wave
   Recalls, in change of light or gloom,
   My old affection of the tomb,   75
And my prime passion in the grave.

My old affection of the tomb,
   A part of stillness, yearns to speak:
   "Arise, and get thee forth and seek
A friendship for the years to come.   80

"I watch thee from the quiet shore;
   Thy spirit up to mine can reach;
   But in dear words of human speech
We two communicate no more."

And I, "Can clouds of nature stain   85
   The starry clearness of the free?[7]
   How is it? Canst thou feel for me
Some painless sympathy with pain?"

And lightly does the whisper fall:
   "'T is hard for thee to fathom this;   90

---

4. Compare 55, 5, and see *Memoir* I, 321: "We cannot give up the mighty hopes that make us men."
5. Would have.
6. All-devouring.
7. From the body, as in 38, 3.

I triumph in conclusive bliss,
And that serene result of all."

So hold I commerce with the dead;
    Or so methinks the dead would say;
    Or so shall grief with symbols play   95
And pining life be fancy-fed.

Now looking to some settled end,
    That these things pass, and I shall prove
    A meeting somewhere, love with love,
I crave your pardon, O my friend;   100

If not so fresh, with love as true,
    I clasping brother-hands, aver
    I could not, if I would, transfer
The whole I felt for him to you.

For which be they that hold apart   105
    The promise of the golden hours?
    First love, first friendship, equal powers,
That marry with the virgin heart.

Still mine, that cannot but deplore,
    That beats within a lonely place,
    That yet remembers his embrace,   110
But at his footstep leaps no more,

My heart, tho' widow'd, may not rest
    Quite in the love of what is gone,
    But seeks to beat in time with one[8]   115
That warms another living breast.

Ah, take the imperfect gift I bring,
    Knowing the primrose yet is dear,
    The primrose of the later year,
As not unlike to that of Spring.   120

86[9]

Sweet after showers, ambrosial air,[1]
    That rollest from the gorgeous gloom
    Of evening over brake and bloom
And meadow, slowly breathing bare

---

8. Hallam Tennyson identified as his "bride to be" Emily Sellwood, whom his father would finally marry in June 1850. "This statement is refuted by Tennyson's marginal note in Gatty; moreover, the entire section is clearly addressed to another man . . . and the poet is making a plea for friendship, not conjugal love" (Shatto and Shaw). Similar doubts exist about Lushington being the addressee for the section (see also Ricks).
9. Answering section 83, this was written at Barmouth (see *Memoir* I, 313), which Tennyson first visited in 1839 and described as "a flat sand shore, a sea with breakers, looking Mablethorpe-like, and sand hills, and close behind them huge crags and a long estuary with cloud-capt hills" (*Memoir* I, 173–74).
1. "It was a west wind" (Tennyson).

The round of space, and rapt below 5
Thro' all the dewy tassell'd wood,
And shadowing down the horned[2] flood
In ripples, fan my brows and blow

The fever from my check, and sigh
The full new life that feeds thy breath 10
Throughout my frame, till Doubt and Death,
Ill brethren, let the fancy fly

From belt to belt of crimson seas
On leagues of odor streaming far,
To where in yonder orient star[3] 15
A hundred spirits whisper "Peace."

87

I past beside the reverend walls[4]
In which of old I wore the gown;
I roved at random thro' the town,
And saw the tumult of the halls;

And heard once more in college fanes 5
The storm their high-built organs make,
And thunder-music, rolling, shake
The prophet blazon'd on the panes;

And caught once more the distant shout,
The measured pulse of racing oars 10
Among the willows; paced the shores
And many a bridge, and all about

The same gray flats again, and felt
The same, but not the same; and last
Up that long walk of limes I past 15
To see the rooms[5] in which he dwelt.

Another name was on the door.
I linger'd; all within was noise
Of songs, and clapping hands, and boys
That crash'd the glass and beat the floor; 20

Where once we held debate, a band[6]
Of youthful friends, on mind and art,
And labor, and the changing mart,
And all the framework of the land;

2. "Between two promontories" (Tennyson).
3. "Any rising star is here intended" (Tennyson).
4. "Trinity College, Cambridge" (Tennyson). In November 1827 Tennyson enrolled at Trinity College and left in 1831 without graduating.
5. "Which were in New Court, Trinity" (Tennyson). Hallam entered into residence in October 1828, took his degree, and left Cambridge in January 1832.
6. "The 'Water Club,' because there was no wine. They used to make speeches there—I never did" (Tennyson to Knowles).

When one would aim an arrow fair,   25
  But send it slackly from the string;
And one would pierce on outer ring,
  And one an inner, here and there;

And last the master-bowman,[7] he,
  Would cleve the mark. A willing ear   30
We lent him. Who, but hung to hear
  The rapt oration flowing free

From point to point, with power and grace
  And music in the bounds of law,
To those conclusions when we saw   35
  The God within him light his face,

And seem to lift the form, and glow
  In azure orbits heavenly-wise;
And over those ethereal eyes
  The bar of Michael Angelo.[8]   40

88

Wild bird,[9] whose warble, liquid sweet,
  Rings Eden thro' the budded quicks,[1]
O tell me where the senses mix,
  O tell me where the passions meet,

Whence radiate: fierce extremes employ   5
  Thy spirits in the darkening leaf,
And in the midmost heart of grief
  Thy passion clasps a secret joy:

And I—my harp would prelude woe—
  I cannot all command the strings;   10
The glory of the sum of things
  Will flash along the chords and go.

89[2]

Witch-elms that counterchange[3] the floor
  Of this flat lawn with dusk and bright;
And thou, with all thy breath and height
  Of foliage, towering sycamore;[4]

---

7. The metaphor celebrates Hallam's prowess as a speaker and debater always hitting the mark.
8. "These lines I wrote from what Arthur Hallam said after reading of the prominent ridge of bone over the eyes of Michael Angelo: 'Alfred, look over my eyes; surely I have the bar of Michael Angelo'" (Memoir I, 38). "The broad bar of frontal bone over the eyes of Michael Angelo" (Tennyson's note); the single instance in the poem that directly addresses Hallam's physical appearance.
9. "To the Nightingale" (Tennyson).
1. Hedgerows.
2. "Somersby" (Tennyson). Probably written after the autumn of 1838.
3. Checker.
4. "The 'towering sycamore' is cut down, and the four poplars are gone, and the lawn is no longer flat" (Tennyson, in May 1883).

How often, hither wandering down, 5
    My Arthur found your shadows fair,[5]
    And shook to all the liberal air
The dust and din and steam of town!

He brought an eye for all he saw;
    He mixt in all our simple sports; 10
    They pleased him, fresh from brawling courts
And dusty purlieus of the law.[6]

O joy to him in this retreat,
    Immantled in ambrosial dark,
    To drink the cooler air, and mark 15
The landscape winking thro' the heat!

O sound to rout the brood of cares,
    The sweep of scythe in morning dew,
    The gust that round the garden flew,
And tumbled half the mellowing pears! 20

O bliss, when all in circle drawn
    About him, heart and ear were fed
    To hear him, as he lay and read
The Tuscan[7] poets on the lawn!

Or in the all-golden afternoon 25
    A guest, or happy sister, sung,
    Or here she brought the harp and flung
A ballad to the brightening moon.

Nor less it pleased in livelier moods,
    Beyond the bounding hill to stray, 30
    And break the livelong summer day
With banquet in the distant woods;

Whereat we glanced from theme to theme,
    Discuss'd the books to love or hate,
    Or touch'd the changes of the state, 35
Or threaded some Socratic dream;[8]

But if I praised the busy town,
    He loved to rail against it still,
    For "ground in yonder social mill
We rub each other's angles down, 40

5. "Hallam paid several visits to Somersby, primarily to see Emily Tennyson. His first meeting with her was probably on his first visit to Somersby in December 1829. . . . Hallam's last visit to Somersby was in July 1833, when Tennyson was not present" (Shatto and Shaw).
6. After leaving Cambridge, Hallam became a law student.
7. Dante and Petrarch.
8. "Arthur Hallam could take in the most abstruse ideas with the utmost rapidity and insight" (Tennyson in *Memoir* I, 45).

"And merge," he said, "in form and gloss
   The picturesque of man and man."
   We talk'd: the stream beneath us ran,
The wine-flask lying couch'd in moss,

Or cool'd within the glooming wave;   45
   And last, returning from afar,
   Before the crimson-circled star
Had fallen into her father's grave,[9]

And brushing ankle-deep in flowers,
   We heard behind the woodbine veil   50
   The milk that bubbled in the pail,
And buzzings of the honeyed hours.

90[1]

He tasted love with half his mind,
   Nor ever drank the inviolate spring
   Where nighest heaven, who first could fling
This bitter seed among mankind:

That could the dead, whose dying eyes   5
   Were closed with wail, resume their life,
   They would but find in child and wife
An iron welcome when they rise.[2]

'T was well, indeed, when warm with wine,
   To pledge them with a kindly tear,
   To talk them o'er, to wish them here,   10
To count their memories half divine;

But if they came who past away,
   Behold their brides in other hands;
   The hard heir strides about their lands,
And will not yield them for a day.   15

Yea, tho' their sons were none of these,
   Not less the yet-loved sire would make
   Confussion worse than death,[3] and shake
The pillars of domestic peace.   20

9. "Before Venus, the evening star, had dipt into the sunset. The planets, according to Laplace, were evolved from the sun" (Tennyson). The nebular hypothesis (see section 3, 2) held that the planets were born from the gaseous matter thrown from the sun. In *The Princess* (II, lines 101–04), Lady Psyche gives an account of the earth's beginnings:
   "This world was once a fluid haze of light,
   Til toward the centre set the starry tides,
   And eddied into suns, that wheeling cast
   The planets."
1. Sections 90–95 form a group concerned with communion between the living and the dead.
2. "He who first suggested that the dead would not be welcome if they came to life again knew not the highest love." Hallam Tennyson, who also compares "The Lotos-Eaters," lines 119–20: "our looks are strange, / And we should come like ghosts to trouble joy."
3. Compare "The Lotos-Eaters," line 128: "There *is* confusion worse than death."

Ah, dear, but come thou back to me!
    Whatever change the years have wrought,
    I find not yet one lonely thought
That cries agaist my wish for thee.

91

When rosy plumelets tuft the larch,
    And rarely[4] pipes the mounted thrush,
    Or underneath the barren bush
Flits by the sea-blue bird[5] of March;

Come, wear the form by which I know   5
    Thy spirit in time among thy peers;
    The hope of unaccomplish'd years
Be large and lucid round thy brow.

When summer's hourly-mellowing change
    May breathe, with many roses sweet,   10
    Upon the thousand waves of wheat
That ripple round the lowly grange,

Come; not in watches of the night,
    But where the sunbeam broodeth warm,
    Come, beauteous in thine after form,   15
And like a finer light in light.

92

If any vision should reveal
    Thy likeness, I might count in vain
    As but the canker of the brain;
Yea, tho' it spake and made appeal

To chances where our lots were cast   5
    Together in the days behind,
    I might but say, I hear a wind
Of memory murmuring the past.

Yea, tho' it spake and bared to view
    A fact within the coming year;   10
    And tho' the months, revolving near,
Should prove the phantom-warning true,

They might not seem thy prophecies,
    But spiritual presentiments,
    And such refraction [6] of events   15
As often rises ere they rise.

---

4. Exquisitely.
5. "Darts the sea-shining bird of March would best suit the Kingfisher" (Tennyson).
6. "The heavenly bodies are seen above the horizon, by refraction, before they actually arise" (Tennyson).

93

I shall not see thee. Dare I say
  No spirit ever brake the band
  That stays him from the native land
Where first he walk'd when claspt in clay?

No visual shade of some one lost,   5
  But he, Spirit himself, may come
  Where all the nerve of sense is numb,
Spirit to Spirit, Ghost to Ghost.

O, therefore from thy sightless range
  With gods in unconjectured bliss,   10
  O, from the distance of the abyss
Of tenfold-complicated change,

Descend, and touch, and enter; hear
  The wish too strong for words to name,
  That in this blindness of the frame   15
My Ghost may feel that thine is near.

94

How pure at heart and sound in head,
  With what divine affections bold
  Should be the man whose thought would hold
An hour's communion with the dead.

In vain shalt thou, or any, call   5
  The spirits from their golden day,
  Except, like them, thou too canst say,
My spirit is at peace with all.

They haunt the silence of the breast,[7]
  Imaginations calm and fair,   10
  The memory like a cloudless air,
The conscience as a sea at rest;

But when the heart is full of din,
  And doubt beside the portal waits,
  They can but listen at the gates,   15
And hear the household jar within.

95[8]

By night we linger'd on the lawn,[9]
  For underfoot the herb was dry;

---

7. "This was what I felt" (Tennyson).
8. Section 78 may mark the turning point in the poem, but its climax comes here. Tennyson says in the *Memoir* (I, 320) that he had from boyhood the capacity to put himself into "a kind of waking trance" in which "out of the intensity of the consciousness of individuality, the individuality itself seemed to dissolve and fade away into boundless being."
9. At Somersby, where a family gathering has taken place.

And genial warmth; and o'er the sky
The silvery haze of summer drawn;

And calm that let the tapers burn   5
Unwavering: not a cricket chirr'd;
The brook alone far-off was heard,[1]
And on the board the fluttering urn.[2]

And bats went round in fragrant skies,
And wheel'd or lit the filmy shapes[3]   10
That haunt the dusk, with ermine capes
And woolly breast and beaded eyes;

While now we sang old songs that peal'd
From knoll to knoll, where, couch'd at ease,
The white kine[4] glimmer'd and the trees   15
Laid their dark arms about the field.

But when those others, one by one,
Withdrew themeselves from me and night,[5]
And in the house light after light
Went out, and I was all alone,   20

A hunger seized my heart; I read
Of that glad year[6] which once had been,
In those fallen leaves which kept their green,
The noble letters of the dead.

And strangely on the silence broke   25
The silent-speaking words, and strange
Was love's dumb cry defying change
To test his worth; and strangely spoke

The faith, the vigor, bold to dwell
On doubts that drive the coward back,   30
And keen thro' wordy snares to track
Suggestion to her inmost cell.

So word by word, and line by line,
The dead man touch'd me from the past,
And all at once it seem'd at last   35
The living soul was flash'd on mine,

And mine in this[7]
About empyreal heights of thought,

1. "It was a marvellously still night, and I aked my brother Charles to listen to the brook, which we had never heard so far off before" (Tennyson).
2. A teapot that is boiling.
3. "Moths; perhaps the ermine or the puss-moth" (Tennyson).
4. Cattle.
5. Compare Gray's "Elegy Written in a Country Churchyard," line 4: "And leave the world to darkness and to me."
6. The five years of the friendship.
7. Originally "His living soul" and "mine in his." According to Bradley, Tennyson remarked to Knowles:

And came on that which is, and caught
   The deep pulsations of the world,   40

Æonian music[8] measuring out
   The steps of Time—the shocks of Chance—
   The blows of Death. At length my trance
Was cancell'd, stricken thro' with doubt.

Vague words! but ah, how hard to frame   45
   In matter-moulded forms of speech,
   Or even for intellect to reach
Thro' memory that which I became;

Till now the doubtful dusk reveal'd
   The knolls once more where, couch'd at ease,   50
   The white kine glimmer'd and the trees
Laid their dark arms about the field;

And suck'd from out the distant gloom
   A breeze began to tremble o'er
   The large leaves of the sycamore,   55
And fluctuate all the still perfume,

And gathering freshlier overhead,
   Rock'd the full-foliaged elms, and swung
   The heavy-folded rose, and flung
The lilies to and fro, and said,   60

"The dawn, the dawn," and died away;
   And East and West, without a breath,
   Mixt their dim lights, like life and death,
To broaden into boundless day.[9]

96

You[1] say, but with no touch of scorn,
   Sweet-hearted, you, whose light-blue eyes
   Are tender over drowning flies,
You tell me, doubt is Devil-born.

I know not: one[2] indeed I knew   5
   In many a subtle question versed,
   Who touch'd a jarring lyre at first,
But ever strove to make it true;

"perchance the Deity. . . . My conscience is troubled by 'his.'" Bradley suggests the poet's conscience was troubled by "a doubt whether the soul that seemed to be flashed on his, and seemed to be Hallam's, was Hallam's." "Of course the greater Soul may include the less. I have often had that feeling of being whirled up and wrapt into the Great Soul" (Tennyson). See also Shatto and Shaw.
8. The music of the spheres that has gone on for eons.
9. "The trance came to an end in a moment of critical doubt, but the doubt was dispelled by the glory of the dawn of the 'boundless day'" (Tennyson).
1. Perhaps some imaginary woman of simple beliefs (see 33). "In so far as a particular person is addressed, it is more likely to be Emily Sellwood (whose religious scruples about Tennyson had been one factor in delaying their marriage) and not Tennyson's mother" (Ricks).
2. Hallam, according to Tennyson.

Perplext in faith, but pure in deeds,
    At last he beat his music out.   10
    There lives more faith in honest doubt,
Believe me, than in half the creeds.

He fought his doubts and gather'd strength,
    He would not make his judgment blind,
    He faced the spectres of the mind   15
And laid them; thus he came at length

To find a stronger faith his own;
    And Power was with him in the night,
    Which makes the darkness and the light,
And dwells not in the light alone,   20

But in the darkness and the cloud,
    As over Sinai's peaks of old,
    While Israel made their gods of gold,
Altho' the trumpet blew so loud.[3]

97

My love[4] has talk'd with rocks and trees;
    He finds on misty mountain-ground
    His own vast shadow glory-crown'd[5]
He sees himself in all he sees.

Two partners of a married life—   5
    I look'd on these and thought of thee,[6]
    In vastness and in mystery,
And of my spirit as of a wife.

These two—they dwelt with eye on eye,
    Their hearts of old have beat in tune,   10
    Their meetings made December June,
Their every parting was to die.

Their love has never past away;
    The days she never can forget
    Are earnest that he loves her yet,   15
Whate'er the faithless people say.

Her life is lone, he sits apart;
    He loves her yet, she will not weep,

3. The stanza refers to Moses receiving the Commandments on Mount Sinai while the Israelites lawlessly idolized a golden calf. See Exodus 19:16–25 and 32:1–6.
4. A personification of love, not Hallam. Compare 60. "The relation of one on earth to one in the other higher world. Not my relation to him here. He looked up to me as I looked up to him" (Tennyson).
5. "Like the spectre of the Brocken" (Tennyson). Shatto and Shaw cite Coleridge's "Constancy to an Ideal Object," lines 29–30, where the woodman "Sees full before him, gliding without tread, / An image with a glory round its head." In an early poem, "On Sublimity," line 94: "The shadowy Colossus of the mountain" refers to the spectre of the Brocken.
6. Hallam.

Tho' rapt in matters dark and deep
He seems to slight her simple heat.   20

He thrids[7] the labyrinth of the mind,
   He reads the secret of the star,
   He seems so near and yet so far,
He looks so cold: she thinks him kind.

She keeps the gift of years before,   25
   A wither'd violet is her bliss;
   She knows not what his greatness is,
For that, for all, she loves him more.

For him she plays, to him she sings
   Of early faith and plighted vows;   30
   She knows but matters of the house,
And he, he knows a thousand things.

Her faith is fixt and cannot move.
   She darkly feels him great and wise,
   She dwells on him with faithful eyes,   35
"I cannot understand; I love."

98

You[8] leave us: you will see the Rhine,
   And those fair hills I sail'd below,
   When I was there with him; and go
By summer belts of wheat and vine

To where he breathed his latest breath,   5
   That city.[9] All her splendor seems
   No livelier than the wisp that gleams
On Lethe in the eyes of Death.

Let her great Danube rolling fair
   Enwind her isles, unmark'd of me;   10
   I have not seen, I will not see
Vienna; rather dream that there,

A treble darkness, Evil haunts
   The birth, the bridal; friend from friend
   Is oftener parted, fathers bend   15
Above more graves, a thousand wants

7. Threads.
8. Tennyson notes that the "'you' is imaginary," but elsewhere he indentifies his brother Charles, who was
married in 1836 and here is about to set off on his honeymoon for the Rhine valley (where Tennyson
travelled with Hallam in 1832) and Vienna (where Hallam died). See *Memoir* I, 148.
9. "To *that* city my father would never go, and he gave me a most emphatic 'no' when I once proposed a
tour there with him" (*Memoir* I, 149).

Gnarr[1] at the heels of men, and prey
  By each cold hearth, and sadness flings
  Her shadow on the blaze of kings.
And yet myself have heard him say,   20

That not in any mother town[2]
  With statelier progress to and fro
  The double tides of chariots flow
By park and suburb under brown

Of lustier leaves; nor more content,   25
  He told me, lives in any crowd,
  When all is with lamps, and loud
With sport and song, in booth and tent,

Imperial halls, or open plain;
  And wheels the circled dance, and breaks   30
  The rocket molten into flakes
Of crimson or in emerald rain.

99

Risest thou thus, dim dawn, again,[3]
  So loud with voices of the birds,
  So thick with lowings of the herds,
Day, when I lost the flower of men;

Who tremblest thro' thy darkling red   5
  On yon swollen brook that bubbles fast
  By meadows breathing of the past,
And woodlands holy to the dead;

Who murmurest in the foliage eaves
  A song that slights the coming care,[4]   10
  And Autumn laying here and there
A fiery finger on the leaves;

Who wakenest with thy balmy breath
  To myriads on the genial earth,
  Memories of bridal, or of birth,   15
And unto myriads more, of death.

O, wheresoever those may be,
  Betwixt the slumber[5] of the poles,
  To-day they count as kindred souls;
They know me not, but mourn with me.   20

---

1. "Snarl" (Tennyson).
2. "Metropolis" (Tennyson).
3. The second anniversary (September 15, 1835) of Hallam's death. See section 72.
4. "The hardship of winter" (Hallam Tennyson).
5. "The ends of the axis of the earth, which move so slowly that they seem not to move, but slumber" (Tennyson).

100[6]

I climb the hill: from end to end
    Of all the landscape underneath,
    I find no place that does not breathe
Some gracious memory of my friend;

No gray old grange[7] or lonely fold,   5
    Or low morass and whispering reed,
    Or simple stile from mead to mead,
Or sheepwalk up the windy wold;

Nor hoary[8] knoll of ash and haw
    That hears the latest linnet trill,   10
    Nor quarry trench'd along the hill
And haunted by the wrangling daw;

Nor runlet tinkling from the rock;[9]
    Nor pastoral rivulet that swerves
    To left and right thro' meadowy curves,   15
That feed the mothers of the flock;

But each has pleased a kindred eye,
    And each reflects a kindlier day;
    And, leaving these, to pass away,
I think once more he seems to die.   20

101

Unwatch'd the garden bough shall sway,
    The tender blossom flutter down,
    Unloved, that beech will gather brown,
This maple burn itself away;

Unloved, the sunflower, shining fair,   5
    Ray round with flames her disk of seed,
    And many a rose-carnation feed
With summer spice the humming air;

Unloved, by many a sandy bar,
    The brook[1] shall babble down the plain,   10
    At noon or when the Lesser Wain[2]
Is twisting round the polar star;

6. Sections 100–03 are concerned with the Tennyson family's move from Somersby to High Beech, north
of London. The group makes a transition to the last part of the poem. Compare "A Farewell."
7. "The house adjacent to Somersby Rectory known as 'Baumber's Farm,' a picturesque manor house"
(Shatto and Shaw).
8. An autumnal scene. The move from Somersby had been contemplated for many months. It actually
seems to have taken place in April 1837 (see *Alfred Tennyson*, 177).
9. "The rock is Holywell, which is a wooded ravine, commonly called there 'the Glen'" (Tennyson).
1. "The brook at Somersby, the charm and beauty of which was a joy to my father all his life" (Hallam Tennyson).
2. Ursa Minor, whose axis is the North Star. "My father often would spend his nights wandering about the
wolds, gazing at the stars. Edward FitzGerald writes: 'Like Wordsworth on the mountains, Alfred too,
when a lad abroad on the wold, sometimes of a night with the shepherd, watched not only the flock on
the greensward, but also "the fleecy star that bears / Andromeda far off Atlantic seas"'" (Hallam Tennyson).

Uncared for, gird the windy grove,
    And flood the haunts of hern and crake,[3]
    Or into silver arrows break   15
The sailing moon in creek and cove;

Till from the garden and the wild
    A fresh association blow,
    And year by year the landscape grow
Familiar to the stranger's child;   20

As year by year the laborer tills
    His wonted glebe, or lops the glades,
    And year by year our memory fades
From all the circle of the hills.

102

We leave the well-beloved place
    Where first we gazed upon the sky;
    The roofs that heard our earliest cry
Will shelter one of stranger race.

We go, but ere we go from home,   5
    As down the garden-walks I move,
    Two spirits[4] of a diverse love
Contend for loving masterdom.

One whispers, "Here thy boyhood sung
    Long since its matin song,[5] and heard   10
    The low love-language of the bird
In native hazels tassel-hung."

The other answers, "Yea, but here
    Thy feet have stray'd in after hours
    With thy lost friend among the bowers,   15
And this hath made them trebly dear.

These two have striven half the day,
    And each prefers his separate claim,
    Poor rivals in a losing game,
That will not yield each other way.   20

I turn to go; my feet are set
    To leave the pleasant fields and farms;
    They mix in one another's arms
To one pure image of regret.

3. The heron and corncrake, a kind of short-billed rail.
4. "Referring to the double loss of his father and of his friend" (*Memoir* I, 72). However, the poet glossed:
    "First, the love of the native place; second, this enhanced by the memory of A. H. H."
5. His earliest poetry.

103

On that last night[6] before we went
   From out the doors where I was bred,
   I dream'd a vision of the dead,
Which left my after-morn content.

Methought I dwelt within a hall,   5
   And maidens[7] with me; distant hills
   From hidden summits[8] fed with rills
A river sliding by the wall.

The hall with harp and carol rang.
   They sang of what is wise and good   10
   And graceful. In the centre stood
A statue[9] veil'd, to which they sang;

And which, tho' veil'd, was known to me,
   The shape of him I loved, and love
   For ever. Then flew in a dove   15
And brought a summons from the sea;

And when they learnt that I must go,
   They wept and wail'd, but led the way
   To where a little shallop lay
At anchor in the flood below[1]   20

And on by many a level mead,
   And shadowing bluff that made the banks,
   We glided winding under ranks
Of iris and the golden reed;

And still as vaster grew the shore   25
   And roll'd the floods in grander space,
   The maidens gather'd strength and grace
And presence, lordlier than before;

And I myself, who sat apart
   And watch'd them, wax'd in every limb;   30
   I felt the thews of Anakim,[2]
The pulses of a Titan's heart;

As one would sing the death of war,
   And one would chant the history

6. This section recalls a dream Tennyson actually had on the night before leaving Somersby for the last time.
7. Tennyson said: "They are the Muses, poetry, arts—all that make life beautiful here, which we hope will pass with us beyond the grave." According to Knowles, he explained them as, "all the human powers and talents that do not pass with life but go along with it." Clearly the dream concerns the poet's own life, his poetry, and especially these lyrics, which grow and depart with him.
8. "The high—the divine—the origin of Life"; the river is "Life"; the sea in line 16, "Eternity" (Tennyson to Knowles).
9. Of Hallam.
1. Compare the conclusion of "The Passing of Arthur."
2. Powerful giants, the sons of Anak. See Numbers 13:33.

Of that great race which is to be,[3]   35
And one the shaping of a star;

Until the forward-creeping tides
   Began to foam, and we to draw
   From deep to deep, to where we saw
A great ship lift her shining sides.   40

The man we loved was there on deck,
   But thrice as large as man he bent
   To greet us. Up the side I went,
And fell in silence on his neck;

Whereat those maiders with one mind   45
   Bewail'd their lot; I did them wrong:
   "We served thee here," they said, "so long,
And wilt thou leave us now behind?"[4]

So rapt I was, they could not win
   An answer from my lips, but he   50
   Replying, "Enter likewise ye
And go with us:" they enter'd in.

And while the wind began to sweep
   A music out of sheet and shroud,
   We steer'd her toward a crimson cloud   55
That landlike slept along the deep.

104[5]

The time draws near the birth of Christ;
   The moon is hid, the night is still;
   A single church[6] below the hill
Is pealing folded in the mist.

A single peal of bells below,   5
   That wakens at this hour of rest
   A single murmur in the breast,
That these are not the bells I know.

Like strangers' voices here they sound,
   In lands where not a memory strays,   10
   Nor landmark breathes of other days,
But all is new unhallow'd ground.[7]

---

3. Compare "Locksley Hall," lines 119–30, and the "Epilogue," lines 136ff.
4. "He was wrong to drop his earthly hopes and powers—they will be still of use to him" (Tennyson to Knowles).
5. The third Christmas (1835) after Hallam's death. The fourth part of the poem begins here. In the poem's chronology the time is 1835–36, in biographical time 1837–38, since the Tennyson family has moved to High Beech, the setting here.
6. "Waltham Abbey church" (Tennyson).
7. "High Beech, Epping Forest (where we were living)" (Tennyson).

105

To-night ungather'd let us leave
  This laurel, let this holly stand:
  We live within the stranger's land,
And strangely falls our Christmas-eve.

Our father's dust[8] is left alone   5
  And silent under other snows:
  There in due time the woodbine blows,
The violet comes, but we are gone.

No more shall wayward grief abuse
  The genial hour with mask and mime;   10
  For change of place, like growth of time,
Has broke the bond of dying use.

Let cares that petty shadows cast,
  By which our lives are chiefly proved,
  A little spare the night I loved,   15
And hold it solemn to the past.

But let no footstep beat the floor,
  Nor bowl of wassail mantle warm;
  For who would keep an ancient form
Thro' which the spirit breathes no more?   20

Be neither song, nor game, nor feast;
  Nor harp be touch'd, nor flute be blown;
  No dance, no motion, save alone
What lightens in the lucid East

Of rising worlds[9] by yonder wood.   25
  Long sleeps the summer in the seed;
  Run out your measured arcs, and lead
The closing cycle rich in good.[1]

106

Ring out, wild bells, to the wild sky,
  The flying cloud, the frosty light;
  The year is dying in the night;
Ring out, wild bells, and let him die.

Ring out the old, ring in the new,   5
  Ring, happy bells, across the snow:
  The year is going, let him go;
Ring out the false, ring in the true.

8. Tennyson's father died in March 1831 and was buried at Somersby.
9. "The scintillating motion of the stars that rise" (Tennyson).
1. Let the old cycle fulfill its appointed revolution and the new cycle, which closes the old, begin. See 106,
   7, and "Epilogue," lines 128ff.

Ring out the grief that saps the mind,
    For those that here we see no more;   10
Ring out the feud of rich and poor,
Ring in redress to all mankind.

Ring out a slowly dying cause,
    And ancient forms of party strife;
Ring in the nobler modes of life,   15
With sweeter manners, purer laws.

Ring out the want, the care, the sin,
    The faithless coldness of the times;
Ring out, ring out my mournful rhymes,
But ring the fuller minstrel in.   20

Ring out false pride in place and blood,
    The civic slander and the spite;
Ring in the love of truth and right,
Ring in the common love of good.

Ring out old shapes of foul disease;   25
    Ring out the narrowing lust of gold;
Ring out the thousand wars of old,
Ring in the thousand years[2] of peace.

Ring in the valiant man and free,
    The larger heart, the kindlier hand;   30
Ring out the darkness of the land,
Ring in the Christ that is to be.[3]

107

It is the day when he was born,[4]
    A bitter day that early sank
    Behind a purple-frosty bank
Of vapor, leaving night forlorn.

The time admits not flowers or leaves   5
    To deck the banquet. Fiercely flies
    The blast of North and East, and ice
Makes daggers at the sharpen'd eaves,

And bristles all the brakes[5] and thorns
    To yon hard crescent, as she hangs   10

2. See Revelation 20:3: "Till the thousand years should be fulfilled."
3. "The broader Christianity of the future" (Tennyson). "My father expressed his conviction . . . that the forms of Christian religion would alter; but that the spirit of Christ would still grow from more to more 'in the roll of the ages' . . . when Christianity without bigotry will triumph, when the controversies of creeds shall have vanished" (*Memoir* I, 325–26).
4. Hallam's birthday was February 1; he was born in 1811.
5. "Tennyson glossed this 'bushes' in his copy of Gatty" (Shatto and Shaw).

Above the wood which grides[6] and clangs
  Its leafless ribs and iron[7] horns

Together, in the drifts[8] that pass
  To darken on the rolling brine
  That breaks the coast. But fetch the wine,   15
Arrange the board and brim the glass;

Bring in great logs and let them lie,
  To make a solid core of heat;
  Be cheerful-minded, talk and treat
Off all things even as he were by;   20

We keep the day. With festal cheer,
  With books and music, surely we
  Will drink to him, whate're he be,
And sing the songs he loved to hear.

108

I will not shut me from my kind,[9]
  And, lest I stiffen into stone,
  I will not eat my heart alone,
Nor feed with sighs a passing wind:

What profit lies in barren faith,   5
  And vacant yearning, tho' with might
  To scale the heaven's highest height,
Or dive below the wells of death?

What find I in the highest place,
  But mine own phantom chanting hymns?   10
  And on the depths of death there swims
The reflex of a human face.

I'll rather take what fruit may be
  Of sorrow under human skies:
  'T is held that sorrow makes us wise,   15
Whatever wisdom sleep with thee.

109[1]

Heart-affluence in discursive talk
  From household fountains never dry;

6. "Grates" (Tennyson).
7. May describe either the frozen branches or the sound of their grinding together.
8. "Fine snow which passes in squalls to fall into the breaker, and darkens before melting in the sea" (Hallam Tennyson).
9. "Grief shall not make me a hermit, and I will not indulge in vacant yearnings and barren aspirations; it
   is useless trying to find him in the other worlds—I find nothing but the reflection of myself; I had better
   learn the lesson that sorrow teaches" (Tennyson). Compare Wordsworth's "Elegiac Stanzas," lines 53–54:
   "Farewell, farewell the heart that lives alone, / Housed in a dream, at distance from the Kind."
1. Sections 109–14 form a group in which the poet forthrightly attempts to describe his friend's character,
   a task that he shied away from as late as section 65.

The critic clearness of an eye
That saw thro' all the Muses' walk;

Seraphic intellect and force
   To seize and throw the doubts of man;
   Impassion'd logic, which outran
The hearer in its fiery course;

High nature amorous of the good,
   But touch'd with no ascetic gloom;
   And passion pure in snowy bloom
Thro' all the years of April blood;

A love of freedom rarely felt,
   Of freedom in her regal seat
   Of England; not the schoolboy heat,
The blind hysterics of the Celt;[2]

And manhood fused with female grace[3]
   In such a sort, the child would twine
   A trustful hand, unask'd, in thine,
And find his comfort in thy face;

All these have been, and thee mine eyes
   Have look'd on: if they look'd in vain,
   My shame is greater who remain,
Nor let thy wisdom make me wise.

110

Thy converse drew us with delight,
   The men of rathe[4] and riper years;
   The feeble soul, a haunt of fears,
Forgot his weakness in thy sight.

On thee the loyal-hearted hung,
   The proud was half disarm'd of pride,
   Nor cared the serpent at thy side
To flicker with his double tongue.

The stern were mild when thou wert by,
   The flippant put himself to school
   And heard thee, and the brazen fool
Was soften'd, and he knew not why;

While I, thy nearest, sat apart,
   And felt thy triumph was as mine;

2. Perhaps an allusion to the French Revolution of 1789; see 127, 2. Probably a more generalized prejudice; "that unstable Celtic blood"; "Kelts are all mad furious fools!" Cited by Shatto and Shaw. The poet's
francophobia is notorious; his dislike of Americans (in general) comes in a close second.
3. Tennyson speaks similarly of Christ: "What he called 'the man-woman' in Christ, the union of tenderness and strength" (*Memoir* I, 326).
4. Early.

And loved them more, that they were thine,   15
The graceful tact, the Christian art;

Nor mine the sweetness or the skill,
But mine the love that will not tire,
And, born of love, the vague desire
That spurs an imitative will.   20

111

The churl in spirit, up or down
Along the scale of ranks, thro' all,
To him who grasps a golden ball,[5]
By blood a king, at heart a clown,—

The churl in spirit, howe'er he veil   5
His want in forms for fashion's sake,
Will let his coltish nature break
At seasons thro' the gilded pale;

For who can always act? but he,
To whom a thousand memories call,   10
Not being less but more than all
The gentleness he seem'd to be,

Best seem'd the thing he was, and join'd
Each office of the social hour
To noble manners, as the flower   15
And native growth of noble mind;

Nor ever narrowness or spite,
Or villain[6] fancy fleeting by,
Drew in[7] the expression of an eye
Where God and Nature met in light;[8]   20

And thus he bore without abuse
The grand old name of gentleman,
Defamed by every charlatan,[9]
And soil'd with all ignoble use.

112

High wisdom[1] holds my wisdom less,
That I, who gaze with temperate eyes

---

5. The king's scepter, topped by a golden ball.
6. Ignoble; the antithesis of gentle, as in "gentleman."
7. "Contracted, narrowed" (Hallam Tennyson).
8. Compare 87, 9, and see 55, 2.
9. "A mountebank" (Tennyson).
1. "*High wisdom*, is ironical. 'High wisdom' has been twitting the poet that although he gazes with calm and indulgent eyes on unaccomplished greatness, yet he makes light of narrower natures more perfect in their own small way" (Hallam Tennyson).

On glorious insufficiencies,[2]
Set light by[3] narrower perfectness.

But thou, that fillest all the room   5
Of all my love, art reason why
I seem to cast a careless eye
On souls, the lesser lords of doom.

For what wert thou? some novel power
Sprang up for ever at a touch,   10
And hope could never hope too much.
In watching thee from hour to hour,

Large elements in order brought,
And tracts of calm from tempest made,
And world-wide fluctuation sway'd   15
In vassal tides that follow'd thought.

113

'T is held that sorrow makes us wise;[4]
Yet how much wisdom sleeps with thee
Which not alone had guided me,
But served the seasons thay may rise;

For can I doubt, who knew thee keen   5
In intellect, with force and skill
To strive, to fashion, to fulfill —
I doubt not what thou wouldst have been:

A life in civic action warm,
A soul on highest mission sent,   10
A potent voice of Parliament,
A pillar steadfast in the storm,

Should licensed boldness gather force,
Becoming, when the time has birth,
A lever to uplift the earth[5]   15
And roll it in another course,

With thousand shocks[6] that come and go,
With agonies, with energies,
With overthrowings, and with cries,
And undulations to and fro.   20

2. "Unaccomplished greatness such as Arthur Hallam's" (Tennyson).
3. "Make light of" (Tennyson). "In answer to 'high wisdom' the poet says: 'The power and grasp and origi-nality of A.H.H.'s intellect, and the greatness of his nature [which are not mere 'glorious insufficiencies'] make me seem careless about those that have a narrower perfectness" (Hallan Tennyson, noting "by my mother").
4. See 108, 4, "The idea is: 'I may grow wise as a result of my sorrow, but you had wisdom in such abun-dance that it would have benefitted not only myself, but also the entire nation in its coming troubles" (Shatto and Shaw).
5. The reference is to Archimedes' famous saying: "Give me where I may stand and I will move the worlds." See *The Princess* III, lines 245–47.
6. Compare *Hamlet* III, i, lines 62–63: "The thousand natural shocks / That flesh is heir to."

114

Who loves not Knowledge? Who shall rail
    Against her beauty? May she mix
    With men and prosper! Who shall fix
Her pillars?[7] Let her work prevail.

But on her forehead sits a fire;   5
    She sets her forward countenance
    And leaps into the future chance,
Submitting all things to desire.

Half-grown as yet, a child, and vain—
    She cannot fight the fear of death.   10
    What is she, cut from love and faith,
But some wild Pallas[8] from the brain

Of demons? fiery-hot to burst
    All barriers in her onward race
    For power. Let her know her place;   15
She is the second, not the first.

A higher hand[9] must make her mild,
    If all be not in vain, and guide
    Her footsteps, moving side by side
With Wisdom, like the younger child;   20

For she is earthly[1] of the mind,
    But Wisdom heavenly of the soul.
    O friend, who camest to thy goal
So early, leaving me behind,

I would the great would grew like thee,   25
    Who grewest not alone in power
    And knowledge, but by year and hour
In reverence and in charity.

115

Now fades the last long streak of snow,
    Now burgeons every maze of quick[2]
    About the flowering squares,[3] and thick
By ashen roots[4] the violets blow.

---

7. The Pillars of Hercules, which marked the known boundaries of the ancient world. "'Wisdom has
  builded her house, she hath hewn out her seven pillars' *Proverbs.* IX, 1" (Tennyson).
8. Athena, goddess of wisdom, who sprang fully armed from the brain of Zeus.
9. Wisdom's.
1. See "Prologue," 6–8, especially, "For knowledge is of things we see," and also "Locksley Hall," lines
  141–44.
2. Hedgerows sprouting and budding.
3. Fields.
4. Roots of the ash trees.

Now rings the woodland loud and long, 5
    The distance takes a lovelier hue,
    And drown'd in yonder living blue
The lark becomes a sightless song.[5]

Now dance the lights on lawn and lea,
    The flocks are whiter down the vale, 10
    And milkier every milky sail
On winding stream or distant sea;

Where now the seamew pipes, or dives
    In yonder greening gleam, and fly
    The happy birds, that change their sky 15
To build and brood, that live their lives

From land to land; and in my breast
    Spring wakens too, and my regret
    Becomes an April violet,
And buds and blossoms like the rest. 20

116

Is it, then, regret for buried time
    That keenlier in sweet April wakes,
    And meets the year[6] and gives and takes
The colors of the crescent prime?[7]

Not all: the songs, the stirring air, 5
    The life re-orient out of dust,
    Cry thro' the sense to hearten trust
In that which made the world so fair.

Not all regret: the face will shine
    Upon me, while I muse alone, 10
    And that dear voice, I once have known,
Still speak to me of me and mine.

Yet less of sorrow lives in me
    For days of happy commune dead,
    Less yearning for the friendship fled 15
Than some strong bond which is to be.

117

O days and hours, your work is this,
    To hold me from my proper place,
    A little while from his embrace,
For fuller gain of after bliss;

5. Compare Shelley's "To a Skylark," line 20: "Thou art unseen, but yet I hear thy shrill delight."
6. As in 83, 1, the year is thought of as beginning in spring.
7. "Growing spring" (Tennyson).

That out of distance might ensue   5
    Desire of nearness doubly sweet,
    And unto meeting, when we meet,
Delight a hundredfold accrue,

For every grain of sand that runs,
    And every span of shade that steals,   10
    And every kiss of toothed wheels,[8]
And all the courses of the suns.

118[9]

Contemplate all this work of Time,
    The giant laboring in his youth;
    Nor dream of human love and truth,
As dying Nature's earth and lime;

But trust that those we call the dead   5
    Are breathers of an ampler[1] day
    For ever nobler ends. They[2] say,
The solid earth whereon we tread

In tracts of fluent heat began,
    And grew to seeming[3] -random forms,
    The seeming prey of cyclic storms,   10
Till at the last arose the man;

Who throve and branch'd from clime to clime,
    The herald of a higher race,
    And of himself in higher place,   15
If so he type[4] this work of time

Within himself, from more to more;
    Or, crown'd with attributes of woe
    Like glories, move his course, and show
That life is not as idle ore,   20

But iron dug from central gloom,
    And heated hot with burning fears,
    And dipt in baths of hissing tears,
And batter'd with the shocks of doom

To shape and use. Arise and fly   25
    The reeling Faun, the sensual feast;
    Move upward, working out the beast,
And let the ape and tiger die.

8. Gears of a clock. The four lines of the stanza refer to different ways of measuring time: the hourglass; the sundial; the clock; and the movements of the stars, including our sun. Tennyson glosses "span of shade" with "The sun-dial" and "wheels" with "The Clock."
9. Compare sections 55, 56, and 123.
1. Virgil's "largior aether" (*Aeneid* VI, line 640).
2. Geologists and astronomers, particularly Lyell and Laplace in his nebular hypothesis.
3. That is, apparently without a plan or order.
4. Prefigure.

119

Doors,[5] where my heart was used to beat
So quickly, not as one that weeps
I come once more; the city sleeps;
I smell the meadow in the street;

I hear a chirp of birds; I see   5
Betwixt the black fronts long-withdrawn
A light-blue lane of early dawn,
And think of early days and thee,

And bless thee, for thy lips are bland,
And bright the friendship of thine eye;   10
And in my thoughts with scarce a sigh
I take the pressure of thine hand.

120

I trust I have not wasted breath:
I think we are not wholly brain,
Magnetic mockeries;[6] not in vain,
Like Paul with beasts, I fought with Death;[7]

Not only cunning casts in clay;   5
Let Science prove we are, and then
What matters Science unto men,
At least to me? I would not stay.

Let him, the wiser man[8] who springs
Hereafter, up from childhood shape   10
His action like the greater ape,
But I was *born*[9] to other things.

121

Sad Hesper[1] o'er the buried sun
And ready, thou, to die with him,

---

5. Hallam's house; see section 7.
6. Automatons; machines turned on by electrical impulse.
7. "Electricity and magnetism were closely associated phenomena in the 1830's and so were treated to-gether in popular manuals and by reputable authorities" (Shatto and Shaw). Tennyson paraphrases Paul in 1 Corinthians 15:32: "If after the manner of men I have fought with beasts at Ephesus, what advantageth it me, if the dead rise not? let us eat and drink; for to morrow we die."
8. According to Tennyson, "Spoken ironically against materialism, not against evolution."
9. Italicized sometime between 1875 and 1878. Tennyson had welcomed the publication of Darwin's *Origin of Species* (1859) but later grew increasingly hostile toward the theory as interpreted by those who sought to deny man's spiritual existence. To Tyndall he once said: "No evolutionist is able to explain the mind of Man or how any possible physiological change of tissue can produce conscious thought" (*Memoir* I, 323)—a sentiment in keeping with the stress on "*born*." See "By an Evolutionist." As here, and well before Darwin, to say or assume that one shaped one's "action like the greater ape" was a highly charged issue. For an illustrative anecdote, Alexander Dumas's (*pere*, 1802–1870) reputed response to a snide comment on his heritage is a rich repartee: "My father was a mulatto, my grand-mother was a Negress, and my great grandparents were monkeys. My pedigree begins where yours ends."
1. The evening star; see also Phosphor in line 9, the morning star. The ancients thought Venus to be two different stars.

Thou watchest all things ever dim
And dimmer, and a glory done.

The team is loosen'd from the wain,[2]   5
The boat is drawn upon the shore;
Thou listenest to the closing door,
And life is darken'd in the brain.

Bright Phosphor, fresher for the night,
By thee the world's great work is heard   10
Beginning, and the wakeful bird;[3]
Behind thee comes the greater light.

The market boat is on the stream,
And voices hail it from the brink;
Thou hear'st the village hammer clink,   15
And see'st the moving of the team.

Sweet Hesper-Phosphor, double name[4]
For what is one, the first, the last,
Thou, like my present and my past,
Thy place is changed; thou art the same.   20

122

O, wast thou with me, dearest,[5] then,
While I rose up against my doom,[6]
And yearn'd to burst the folded gloom,
To bare the eternal heavens again,[7]

To feel once more, in placid awe   5
The strong imagination roll
A sphere of stars about my soul,
In all her motion one with law?

If thou wert with me, and the grave
Divide us not, be with me now,   10
And enter in at breast and brow,
Till all my blood, a fuller wave,

Be quicken'd with a livelier breath,
And like an inconsiderate boy,

---

2. A farmer's wagon. "A classical commonplace for 'the end of day'" (Shatto and Shaw).
3. The nightingale. Compare *Paradise Lost* III, lines 38–39: "the wakeful bird / Sings darkling."
4. The evening star is also the morning star, death and sorrow brighten into death and hope" (Tennyson).
5. "If anybody thinks I even called him 'dearest' in his life they are much mistaken, for I never called him 'dear'"; see n. 5, p. 247.
6. His grief at Hallam's death.
7. "Again" and "once more" (line 5) probably refer to the time Hallam was alive. "Then" in line 1 strongly suggests the experience of section 95. Another possibility is that "again" presupposes an experience prior to "then" or that of section 95—perhaps that of section 86. In this case, although the first part of the present section alludes to 95 in either interpretation, the last nine lines may recall 86. See Shatto and Shaw for other interpretations.

As in the former flash of joy,   15
I slip[8] the thoughts of life and death;

And all the breeze of Fancy blows,
And every dewdrop paints a bow,[9]
The wizard lightnings[1] deeply glow,
And every thought breaks out a rose.   20

123[2]

There rolls the deep where grew the tree.
O earth, what changes hast thou seen!
There where the long street roars hath been
The stillness of the central sea.[3]

The hills are shadows, and they flow   5
From form to form, and nothing stands;
They melt like mist, the solid lands,
Like clouds they shape themselves and go.

But in my spirit will I dwell,
And dream my dream, and hold it true;   10
For tho' my lips may breathe adieu,
I cannot think the thing farewell.

124

That which we dare invoke to bless;
Our dearest faith; our ghastliest doubt;
He, They, One, All; within, without;
The Power in darkness whom we guess, —

I found Him not in world or sun,   5
Or eagle's wing, or insect's eye,
Nor thro' the questions men may try,
The petty cobwebs we have spun.[4]

If e'er when faith had fallen asleep,
I heard a voice, "believe no more,"[5]   10
And heard an ever-breaking shore
That tumbled in the Godless deep,

8. Escape from.
9. "Every dew-drop turns into a miniature rainbow" (Tennyson).
1. Probably not conventional lightning but the northern lights.
2. Another section in which the influence of Lyell's *Geology* appears obvious.
3. "Balloonists say that even in a storm the middle sea is noiseless" (Tennyson). Hallam Tennyson quotes
   George Darwin: "People always talk at sea of the howling of the wind and the lashing of the sea, but it is
   the ship that makes it all."
4. Here Tennyson is not saying that God is not present in nature but that he can find no proof of His existence using the old eighteenth-century argument from design. In March 1833, when he and Hallam
   were looking through microscopes at "moths' wings, gnats' heads, and at all the lions and tigers which
   lie perdus in a drop of spring water," Tennyson said: "Strange that these wonders should draw some men
   to God and repel others. No more reason in one than in other" (*Memoir* I, 102). As is well known, "Tennyson rejected Paley's arguments for the existence of God, based on design in the natural world" (Ricks).
5. Among numerous echoes from "The Two Voices," lines 292–93: "That type of Perfect in his mind / In
   Nature can he nowhere find."

A warmth within the breast would melt
   The freezing reason's colder part,[6]
   And like a man in wrath the heart   15
Stood up and answer'd, "I have felt."

No, like a child in doubt and fear:
   But that blind clamor made me wise;
   Then was I as a child that cries,
But, crying, knows his father near,[7]   20

And what I am beheld again
   What is, and no man understands;
   And out of darkness came the hands
That reach thro' nature, moulding men.

125

Whatever I have said or sung,
   Some bitter notes my harp would give,
   Yea, tho' there often seem'd to live
A contradiction on the tongue,

Yet Hope had never lost her youth,   5
   She did but look through dimmer eyes;
   Or Love but play'd with gracious lies,
Because he felt so fix'd in truth;

And if the song were full of care,
   He breathed the spirit of the song;   10
   And if the words were sweet and strong
He set his royal signet there;

Abiding with me till I sail
   To seek thee on the mystic deeps,
   And this electric force,[8] that keeps   15
A thousand pulses dancing, fail.

126

Love is and was my lord and king,
   And in his presence I attend
   To hear the tidings of my friend,
Which every hour his couriers bring.

Love is and was my king and lord,   5
   And will be, tho' as yet I keep
   Within the court on earth, and sleep
Encompass'd by his faithful guard,

---

6. Reason argues that the universe is in meaningless flux. Compare "The Two Voices," lines 422–23: "My frozen heart began to beat, / Remembering its ancient heat."
7. See section 54, 5.
8. "Alludes to the contemporary physiological theory that electricity is associated with the phenomena of life" (Shatto and Shaw).

And hear at times a sentinel
Who moves about from place to place,   10
And whispers to the worlds of space,
In the deep night, that all is well.

127

And all is well, tho' faith and form[9]
Be sunder'd in the night of fear;
Well roars the storm to those that hear
A deeper voice across the storm,

Proclaiming social truth shall spread,   5
And justice, ev'n tho' thrice[1] again
The red fool-fury of the Seine
Should pile her barricades with dead.[2]

But ill for him that wears a crown,[3]
And him, the lazar in his rags: 10
They tremble, the sustaining crags;
The spires of ice are toppled down,

And molten up, and roar in flood;
The fortress crashes from on high,
The brute earth lightens to the sky,   15
And the great Æon[4] sinks in blood,

And compass'd by the fires of Hell,
While thou, dear spirit, happy star,[5]
O'erlook'st the tumult from afar,
And smilest, knowing all is well.   20

128

The love that rose on stronger wings,
Unpalsied when he met with Death,
Is comrade of the lesser faith
That sees the course of human things.

No doubt vast eddies in the flood   5
Of onward time shall yet be made,
And throned races may degrade;[6]
Yet O ye mysteries of good,

9. Religious dogma and social order.
1. Does not refer to the three revolutions of 1789, 1830, and 1848 since the section was written, as Tennyson confirmed, before 1848. "'This may well be true, but Tennyson's memory in later years was often imperfect" (Shatto and Shaw), for there is no other way to explain "thrice."
2. The Revolution of 1830.
3. Compare 2 *Henry IV* III, i, line 31: "Uneasy lies the head that wears a crown."
4. Not, obviously, the "closing cycle" of 105, 7, but the cataclysmic collapse of the Western world or, perhaps, of all civilization. Although Tennyson probably derived his imagery from Revelation, this decription bears an uncanny similarity to modern conceptions of earth being struck by a ten-kilometer-wide object from outer space. See, for example, Paul Davies, *The Last Three Minutes* (1994).
5. Compare the end of Shelley's "Adonais" for Keats: "The soul of Adonais, like a star / Beacons from the abode where the Eternal are."
6. Races now highest and even those to come may degenerate. See "Locksley Hall Sixty Years After," lines

Wild Hours that fly with Hope and Fear,
   If all your office had to do   10
   With old results that look like new[7] —
If this were all your mission here,

To draw, to sheathe a useless sword,
   To fool the crowd with glorious lies,
   To cleave a creed in sects and cries,   15
To change the bearing of a word,

To shift an arbitrary power,
   To cramp the student at this desk,
   To make old bareness picturesque
And tuft with grass a feudal tower,   20

Why, then my scorn might well descend
   On you and yours. I see in part[8]
   That all, as in some piece of art,
Is toil coöperant to an end.[9]

129

Dear friend, far off, my lost desire,
   So far, so near in woe and weal,
   O loved the most, when most I feel
There is a lower and a higher;

Known and unknown, human, divine;   5
   Sweet human hand and lips and eye;
   Dear heavenly friend that canst not die,
Mine, mine, for ever, ever mine;

Strange friend, past, present, and to be;
   Loved deeplier, darklier understood;   10
   Behold, I dream a dream of good,
And mingle all the world with thee.

130

Thy voice is on the rolling air;
   I hear thee where the waters run;
   Thou standest in the rising sun,[1]
And in the setting thou art fair.

What art thou then? I cannot guess;   5
   But tho' I seem in star and flower

235–36. Tennyson's, and many of his contemporaries', conventional notions of "racial superiority" are often, as here, somewhat qualified by his tentativeness as to its permanence.
7. The idea is not that the past repeats itself in what seems new in the present, but that there really is progress through the cycles: what seems ("look like new"), then seems not, may be.
8. See 1 Corinthians 13:12: "For now we see through a glass, darkly; but then face to face: now I know in part; but then shall I know even as also I am known." One of the poet's favorite passages; compare "Crossing the Bar."
9. Compare "The Two Voices," lines 295–97.
1. Compare Revelation 19:17: "And I saw an angel standing in the sun; and he cried with a loud voice."

To feel thee some diffusive power,
I do not therefore love thee less.

My love involves the love before;
    My love is vaster passion now;   10
    Tho' mix'd with God and Nature thou,[2]
I seem to love thee more and more.

Far off thou art, but ever nigh;
    I have thee still, and rejoice;
    I prosper, circled with thy voice;   15
I shall not lose thee tho' I die.

131

O living will[3] that shalt endure
    When all that seems shall suffer shock,
    Rise in the spiritual rock,[4]
Flow thro' our deeds and make them pure,

That we may lift from out of dust,   5
    A voice as unto him that hears,
    A cry above the conquer'd years[5]
To one that with us works, and trust,

With faith that comes of self-control,
    The truths that never can be proved   10
    Until we close with all we loved,
And all we flow from, soul in soul.

[Epilogue]

O true and tried, so well and long,
    Demand not thou a marriage lay;
    In that it is thy marriage day
Is music more than any song.[6]

Nor have I felt so much of bliss   5
    Since first he[7] told me that he loved
    A daughter of our house, nor proved
Since that dark day a day like this;

2. This section hints at the idea, developed much later in "The Higher Pantheism," that the material universe may either be God himself or a projection of God.
3. Tennyson explained "as that which we know as Free-will, the higher and enduring part of man" (*Memoir* I, 319). Compare "Prologue," 4. "Free-will was undoubtedly, he said, the 'main miracle, apparently an act of self-limitation by the Infinite, and yet a revelation by Himself of Himself'" (*Memoir* I, 316–17).
4. 1 Corinthians 10:14: "And did all drink the same spiritual drink: for they drank of that spiritual Rock that followed them: and that Rock was Christ."
5. "The victor Hours" of 1, 4.
6. Addressed to Edmund Lushington, the "Epilogue" is an epithalamion celebrating the marriage on October 10, 1842, of Edmund Lushington and Tennyson's youngest sister, Cecilia (see 85 and notes). To Knowles, Tennyson said of *IM*: "It begins with a funeral and ends with a marriage—begins with death and ends in promise of a new life—a sort of Divine Comedy, cheerful at the close." "See also *Memoir* I, 304.
7. Hallam was to marry Emily.

Tho' I since then have number'd o'er
    Some thrice three years;[8] they went and came,   10
    Remade the blood and changed the frame,
And yet is love not less, but more;

No longer caring to embalm
    In dying songs a dead regret,
    But like a statue solid-set,   15
And moulded in colossal calm.

Regret is dead, but love is more
    Than in the summers that are flown,
    For I myself with these have grown
To something greater that before;[9]   20

Which makes appear the songs I made
    As echoes out of weaker times,
    As half but idle brawling rhymes,
The sport of random sun and shade.

But where is she, the bridal flower,   25
    That must be made a wife ere noon?
    She enters, glowing like the moon
Of Eden on its bridal bower.

On me she bends her blissful eyes
    And then on thee; they meet thy look   30
    And brighten like the start[1] that shook
Betwixt the palms of Paradise.

O, when her life was yet in bud,
    He too foretold the perfect rose.
    For thee she grew, for thee she grows   35
For ever, and as fair as good.

And thou art worthy, full of power;
    As gentle; liberal-minded, great,
    Consistent; wearing all that weight
Of learning[2] lightly like a flower.   40

But now set out: the noon is near,
    And I must give away[3] the bride;
    She fears not, or with thee beside
And me behind her, will not fear.

---

8. Confirms the composition date as 1842.
9. "This fulfills the promise of 1, 11. 3–4: 'men may rise on stepping-stones / Of their dead selves to higher things'" (Shatto and Shaw).
1. The stars shook when Jupiter approved the marriage of Thetis and Peleus.
2. Lushington was professor of Greek at Glasgow, from 1838 to 1875. He and Tennyson met at Trinity College, where Lushington also was a member of the Apostles.
3. Their father had died in 1831.

For I that danced her on my knee,   45
    That watch'd her on her nurse's arm,
    That shielded all her life from harm,
At last must part with her to thee;

Now waiting to be made a wife[4]
    Her feet, my darling, on the dead;[5]   50
    Their pensive tablets round her head,
And the most living words[6] of life

Breathed in her ear. The ring is on,
    The "Wilt thou?" answer'd, and again
    The "Wilt thou?" ask'd, till out of twain   55
Her sweet "I will" has made you one.

Now sign your names,[7] which shall be read,
    Mute symbols of a joyful morn,
    By village eyes as yet unborn.
The names are sign'd, and overhead   60

Begins the clash and clang that tells
    The joy to every wandering breeze;
    The blind wall rocks, and on the trees
The dead leaf trembles to the bells.

O happy hour, and happier hours   65
    Await them. Many a merry face
    Salutes them—maidens of the place,
That pelt us in the porch with flowers.

O happy hour, behold the bride
    With him to whom her hand I gave.   70
    They leave the porch, they pass the grave
That has to-day its sunny side.

To-day the grave is bright for me,
    For them the light of life increased,
    Who stay to share the morning feast,   75
Who rest to-night beside the sea.

Let all my genial spirits[8] advance
    To meet and greet a whiter sun[9]
    My drooping memory will not shun
The foaming grape of eastern France.   80

4. Tennyson's elder brother, the Reverend Charles Tennyson Turner, performed the ceremony (see 79).
5. The bride stands on the stone covering those buried in the church's chancel; the tablets on the walls
   above commemorate them.
6. Probably refers to the exchange of vows in the next stanza.
7. In the parish register.
8. Tennyson is clearly using the phrase in the Coleridgean-Wordsworthian sense—poetic powers, as in "Dejection: An Ode": "My genial spirits fail," the old adjectival use of *genius*.
9. Brighter days.

It circles round, and fancy plays.
  And hearts are warm'd and faces bloom,
  As drinking health to bride and groom
We wish them store of happy days.

Nor count me all to blame if I   85
  Conjecture of a stiller guest,
  Perchance, perchance, among the rest,
And, tho' in silence, wishing joy.

But they must go, the time draws on,
  And those white-favor'd horses wait: 90
  They rise, but linger; it is late;
Farewell, we kiss, and they are gone.

A shade falls on us like the dark
  From little cloudlets on the grass,
  But sweeps away as out we pass   95
To range the woods, to roam the park,[1]

Discussing how their courtship grew,
  And talk of others that are wed,
  And how she look'd, and what he said,
And back we come at fall of dew.   100

Again the feast, the speech, the glee,
  The shade of passing through, the wealth
  Of words and wit, the double health,
The crowning cup, the three-times-three,[2]

And last the dance;—till I retire.   105
  Dumb is that tower which spake so loud,
  And high in heaven the streaming cloud,
And on the downs a rising fire:[3]

And rise, O moon, from yonder down,
  Till over down and over dale   110
  All night the shining vapor sail
And pass the silent-lighted town,

The white faced halls, the glancing rills,
  And catch at every mountain head.
  And o'er the friths that branch and spread   115
Their sleeping silver thro' the hills;

And touch with shade the bridal doors,
  With tender gloom the roof, the wall;
  And breaking let the splendor fall
To spangle all the happy shores   120

1. Park House, the Lushington family home.
2. The cheer.
3. The northern lights.

By which they rest, and ocean sounds,
    And, star and system rolling past,
    A soul shall draw from out the vast
And strike his being into bounds[4]

And, moved thro' life of lower phase,[5]   125
    Result in man, be born and think,[6]
    And act and love, a closer link
Betwixt us and the crowning race

Of those, eye to eye, shall look
    On knowledge; under whose command   130
    Is Earth and Earth's, and in their hand
Is Nature like an open book;

No longer half-akin to brute,
    For all we thought and loved and did,
    And hoped, and suffer'd, is but seed   135
Of what in them is flower and fruit;

Where of the man that with me trod
    This planet was a noble type
    Appearing ere the times were ripe
That friend of mine who lives in God,   140

That God, which ever lives and loves,
    One God, one law, one element,
    And one far-off divine event,
To which the whole creation moves.

                                        1833–49; 1850

4. "The idea is that the individual soul emerges at conception from a general soul" (Shatto and Shaw). But Tennyson had rejected the notion that after death there is "Remerging in the general soul" (47, 1). See 120, 3 and notes: "But I was *born* to other things." Througout his life, even following the difficult acceptance of Darwin's theory concerning the physical evolution of man, Tennyson held fast to his faith that each individual soul was a special act of the Creator's.
5. Stages in the development of the human fetus appear to resemble lower forms of animal life, or in the more technical phrase: Ontogeny recapitulates phylogeny. See note to line 196 of "The Palace of Art."
6. "Of babies he would say: 'There is something gigantic about them. The wide-eyed wonder of a babe has a grandeur in it which as children they lose. They seem to me to be prophets of a mightier race'" (*Memoir* I, 369)—a remark that begs recollection of Wordsworth's "Mighty Prophet: Seer blest!" (*Intimations Ode*, line 116).

Poems 1850–1872

To the Queen[1]

Revered, beloved—O you that hold
    A nobler office upon earth
    Than arms, or power of brain, or birth
Could give the warrior kings of old,

Victoria,—since your Royal grace   5
    To one of less desert allows
    This laurel greener from the brows
Of him[2] that uttered nothing base;

And should your greatness, and the care
    That yokes with empire, yield you time   10
    To make demand of modern rhyme[3]
If aught of ancient worth be there;

Then-while a sweeter music wakes,
    And through wild March the throstle calls,
    Where all about your palace-walls   15
The sun-lit almond-blossom shakes—

Take, Madam, this poor book of song;
    For though the faults were thick as dust
    In vacant chambers, I could trust
Your kindness. May you rule us long,   20

And leave us rulers of your blood
    As noble till the latest day!
    May children of our children say,
'She wrought her people lasting good;

'Her court was pure; her life serene;   25
    God gave her peace; her land reposed;
    A thousand claims to reverence closed
In her as Mother, Wife, and Queen;

---

1. This was Tennyson's first publication as poet laureate. "On November 18th [1850] my father was appointed Poet Laureate, owing chiefly to Prince Albert's admiration for 'In Memoriam'" (*Memoir* I, 334). "The offer came as a complete surprise to him. . . . It must, therefore, be considered a curious and entertaining coincidence that, the night before the Royal letter reached him, he dreamed that Prince Albert came and kissed him on the cheek, and that he commented to himself in his dream, 'Very kind, but very German'" (*Alfred Tennyson*, p. 254).
2. Wordsworth, Tennyson's predecessor as poet laureate, 1843–50.
3. Compare *IM* 77, 1: "What hope is here for modern rhyme?"

'And statesmen at her council met
Who knew the seasons when to take   30
Occasion⁴ by the hand, and make
The bounds of freedom wider yet

'By shaping some august decree,
Which kept her throne unshaken still,
Broad-based upon her people's will,   35
And compassed by the inviolate sea.'

                                        March 1851

To E. L., on His Travels in Greece¹

Illyrian² woodlands, echoing falls
Of water, sheets of summer glass,
The long divine Peneïan pass,
The vast Akrokeraunian³ walls,

Tomohrit, Athos,⁴ all things fair,   5
With such a pencil, such a pen,
You shadow forth to distant men,
I read and felt that I was there.

And trust me while I turn'd the page,
And track'd you still on classic ground,   10
I grew in gladness till I found
My spirits in the golden age.

For me the torrent ever pour'd
And glisten'd—here and there alone
The broad-limb'd Gods at random thrown   15
By fountain-urns;—and Naiads⁵ oar'd

A glimmering shoulder under gloom
Of cavern pillars; on the swell
The silver lily heaved and fell;
And many a slope was rich in bloom,   20

From him that on the mountain lea
By dancing rivulets fed his flocks

4. "The topical allusion to the Great Exhibition in the Crystal Palace (1851) had lost its point by 1853" (Ricks). Perhaps, but most certainly not for the queen and her consort, for Prince Albert had been its most illustrious and influential supporter.
1. The poem is addressed to Edward Lear, best known for his nonsense books, who was a close friend of the Tennysons and had sent the poet a copy of his new travel book, *Journal of a Landscape Painter in Greece and Albania* (1851), to which the poem alludes.
2. Illyria was the ancient name for an area roughly equivalent to Albania.
3. Refers to the ancient fortress of Chimaera on the southern coast of Albania.
4. A mountain in northern Greece on the Aegean Sea. Tomohrit is a mountain in southern Albania.
5. Water nymphs in Greek mythology.

To him who sat upon the rocks
And fluted to the morning sea.

1853

Ode on the Death of the Duke of Wellington[1]

1

Bury the Great Duke
    With an empire's lamentation;
Let us bury the Great Duke
    To the noise of the mourning of a mighty nation;
Mourning when their leaders fall,   5
Warriors carry the warrior's pall,
And sorrow darkens hamlet and hall.

2

Where shall we lay[2] the man whom we deplore?
Here, in streaming London's central roar.
Let the sound of those he wrought for,   10
And the feet of those he fought for,
Echo round his bones for evermore.

3

Lead out the pageant: sad and slow,
As fits an universal woe,
Let the long, long procession go,   15
And let the sorrowing crowd about it grow,
And let the mournful martial music blow;
The last great Englishman is low.

4

Mourn, for to us he seems the last,
Remembering all his greatness in the past.   20
No more in soldier fashion will he greet
With lifted hand the gazer in the street.
O friends, our chief state-oracle is mute!
Mourn for the man of long-enduring blood,
The statesman-warrior, moderate, resolute,   25
Whole in himself, a common good.
Mourn for the man of amplest influence,
Yet clearest of ambitious crime,
Our greatest yet with least pretence,

1. The Duke of Wellington died on September 14, 1852; but the funeral was not held until November 18.
Tennyson had his poem ready for distribution on that day. For the first time speaking publicly as poet laureate, he found his performance almost universally condemned by the critics. Given the fact that the
poem *is* one of the very few first-rate pieces of occasional verse in the language, he was understandably,
depressed. "Strictly speaking, the *Ode on the Death of the Duke of Wellington* was not written as Poet
Laureate, since it was not requested by the Queen and had no official publication" (Martin's *Tennyson*,
p. 368). Although Tennyson had met the duke but once passing in the street, he had been a hero to Tennyson from early childhood.
2. The duke was buried in St. Paul's Cathedral in the center of London.

Great in council and great in war,   30
Foremost captain of his time,
Rich in saving common-sense,
And, as the greatest only are,
In his simplicity sublime.
O good gray head which all men knew,   35
O voice from which their omens all men drew,
O iron nerve to true occasion true,
O fallen at length that tower of strength
Which stood four-square to all the winds that blew!
Such was he whom we deplore.   40
The long self-sacrifice of life is o'er.
The great World-victor's victor[3] will be seen no more.

                                5
All is over and done.
Render thanks to the Giver,
England, for thy son.   45
Let the bell be toll'd.[4]
Render thanks to the Giver,
And render him to the mould.
Under the cross of gold[5]
That shines over city and river,   50
There he shall rest for ever
Among the wise and the bold.
Let the bell be toll'd,
And a reverent people behold
The towering car, the sable steeds.   55
Bright let it be with its blazon'd deeds,[6]
Dark in its funeral fold.
Let the bell be toll'd,
And a deeper knell in the heart be knoll'd;
And the sound of the sorrowing anthem roll'd   60
Thro' the dome of the golden cross;
And the volleying cannon thunder his loss;
He knew their voices of old.
For many a time in many a clime
His captain's-ear has heard them boom   65
Bellowing victory, bellowing doom.
When he with those deep voices wrought,
Guarding realms and kings from shame,
With those deep voices our dead captain taught
The tyrant, and asserts his claim   70
In that dread sound to the great name
Which he has worn so pure of blame,
In praise and in dispraise the same,

3. The conqueror of Napoleon at Waterloo in 1815.
4. "A special honour, since the Great Bell was tolled only for the Royal Family, the Bishop, the Dean, and the Lord Mayor" (Ricks). As exceptions in recent times, the triumvirate thus honored with a state funeral were Nelson, Wellington, and Churchill.
5. On top of St. Paul's.
6. Wellington's victories were emblazoned in gold on his bier.

A man of well-attemper'd frame.
O civic muse, to such a name,   75
To such a name for ages long,
To such a name,
Preserve a broad approach of fame,
And ever-echoing avenues of song!

6
"Who is he that cometh, like an honor'd guest,   80
With banner and with music, with soldier and with priest,
With a nation weeping, and breaking on my rest?" —
Mighty Seaman[7] this is he
Was great by land as thou by sea.
Thine island loves thee well, thou famous man,   85
The greatest sailor since our world began.
Now, to the roll of muffled drums,
To thee the greatest soldier comes;
For this is he
Was great by land as thou by sea.   90
His foes were thine; he kept us free;
O, give him welcome, this is he
Worthy of our gorgeous rites,
And worthy to be laid by thee;
For this is England's greatest son,   95
He that gain'd a hundred fights,
Nor ever lost an English gun;[8]
This is he that far away
Against the myriads of Assaye[9]
Clash'd with his fiery few and won;   100
And underneath another sun,
Warring on a later day,
Round affrighted Lisbon[1] drew
The treble works, the vast designs
Of his labor'd rampart-lines,   105
Where he greatly stood at bay,
Whence he issued forth anew,
And ever great and greater grew,
Beating from the wasted vines
Back to France her banded swarms,   110
Back to France with countless blows,
Till o'er the hills her eagles flew

7. Lord Nelson, the speaker above, whose series of naval victories during the Napoleonic Wars culminated
   with his triumph and death at Trafalgar in 1805.
8. Ricks observes that "Disraeli's speech on Wellington also mentions that he 'captured 3,000 cannon from
   the enemy, and never lost a single gun.'" During the Crimean War (1853–56) at the battle of the Alma,
   the Great Redoubt, held by the Russians, was evidently impregnable; but "the British saw, to their stu-
   pefaction, that the Russians, with frantic haste, were limbering up their guns and dragging them away.
   The Emperor Nicholas had given Prince Menschikoff an order that on no account whatsoever was a single gun to be lost, because he believed, incorrectly, that the Duke of Wellington had never lost a gun"
   (Cecil Woodham-Smith, The Reason Why, p. 184). The laureate's contribution to the myth was not without real military consequence.
9. In India, where, in 1803, Wellington defeated a far superior force.
1. From 1808 to 1814, the Iron Duke waged his Peninsular Campaign against the French from Spain, first
   in a holding action and then in a series of increasingly successful offensive strikes. His decisive victory at
   Vitoria in northern Spain (June 21, 1813) exposed France to invasion through the Pyrenees.

Beyond the Pyrenean pines,
Follow'd up in valley and glen
With blare of bugle, clamor of men.   115
Roll of cannon and clash of arms,
And England pouring on her foes.
Such a war had such a close.
Again their ravening eagle rose[2]
In anger, wheel'd on Europe-shadowing wings,   120
And barking for the thrones of kings;
Till one that sought but Duty's iron crown
On that loud Sabbath[3] shook the spoiler down;
A day of onsets of despair!
Dash'd on every rocky square,   125
Their surging charges foam'd themselves away;
Last, the Prussian[4] trumpet blew;
Thro' the long-tormented air
Heaven flash'd a sudden jubilant ray,[5]
And down we swept and charged and overthrew.   130
So great a soldier taught us there
What long-enduring hearts could do
In that world-earthquake, Waterloo!
Mighty Seaman, tender and true,
And pure as he from taint of craven guile,   135
O saviour of the silver-coasted isle,
O shaker of the Baltic and the Nile,[6]
If aught of things that here befall
Touch[7] a spirit among things divine,
If love of country move thee there at all,   140
Be glad, because his bones are laid by thine
And thro' the centuries let a people's voice
In full acclaim,
A people's voice,
The proof and echo of all human fame,   145
A people's voice, when they rejoice
At civic revel and pomp and game,
Attest their great commander's claim
With honor, honor, honor, honor to him,
Eternal honor to his name.   150

7

A people's voice! we are a people yet.
Tho' all men else their nobler dreams forget,
Confused by brainless mobs and lawless Powers,
Thank Him who isled us here, and roughly set
His Briton in blown seas and storming showers,   155

2. Napoleon, whose symbol was the eagle, returned from Elba in 1815 and reassembled much of his army.
3. The Battle of Waterloo was fought on Sunday, June 18, 1815.
4. The arrival of the Prussian army under Blücher decided the outcome.
5. "The setting sun glanced on this last charge of the English and Prussians" (Tennyson).
6. In 1798, at the mouth of the Nile, Nelson destroyed major elements of the French fleet through an original and daring maneuver by which he simultaneously sent his ships, broadsides firing, down both sides of the French line. In 1801 in the Baltic he neutralized the Danish fleet.
7. "Dwell on the word 'touch' and make it as long as 'can touch'" (Tennyson).

We have a voice with which to pay the debt
Of boundless love and reverence and regret
To those great men who fought, and kept it ours.
And keep it ours, O God, from brute control!
O Statesmen, guard us, guard the eye, the soul   160
Of Europe, keep our noble England whole,
And save the one true seed of freedom sown
Betwixt a people and their ancient throne,
That sober freedom out of which there springs
Our loyal passion for our temperate kings!   165
For, saving that, ye help to save mankind
Till public wrong be crumbled into dust,
And drill the raw world for the march of mind,
Till crowds at length be sane and crowns be just.
But wink no more in slothful overtrust.   170
Remember him who led your hosts;
He bade you guard the sacred coasts.
Your cannons moulder on the seawards wall;
His voice is silent in your council-hall
For ever; and whatever tempests lour   175
For ever silent; even if they broke
In thunder, silent; yet remember all
He spoke among you, and the Man who spoke;
Who never sold the truth to serve the hour,
Nor palter'd with Eternal God for power;   180
Who let the turbid streams of rumor flow
Thro' either babbling world of high and low;
Whose life was work, whose language rife
With rugged maxims hewn from life;
Who never spoke against a foe;   185
Whose eighty[8] winters freeze with one rebuke
All great self-seekers trampling on the right.
Truth-teller was our England's Alfred named;
Truth-lover was our English Duke;
Whatever record leap to light   190
He never shall be shamed.

8

Lo! the leader in these glorious wars
Now to glorious burial slowly borne,
Follow'd by the brave of other lands,
He, on whom from both her open hands   195
Lavish Honor shower'd all her stars,
And affluent Fortune emptied all her horn[9]
Yea, let all good things await
Him who cares not to be great
But as he saves or serves the state.   200
Not once or twice in our rough island-story

---

8. The duke was eighty-three when he died.
9. "These [lines 195–97] are full-vowelled lines to describe Fortune emptying her Cornucopia" (Tennyson).

The path of duty was the way to glory.[1]
He that walks it, only thirsting
For the right, and learns to deaden
Love of self, before his journey closes,   205
He shall find the stubborn thistle bursting
Into glossy purples, which outredden
All voluptuous garden-roses.
Not once or twice in our fair island-story
The path of duty was the way to glory.   210
He, that ever following her commands,
On with toil of heart and knees and hands,
Thro' the long gorge to the far light has won
His path upward, and prevail'd,
Shall find the toppling crags of Duty scaled   215
Are close upon the shining table-lands
To which our God Himself is moon and sun.
Such was he: his work is done.
But while the races of mankind endure
Let his great example stand   220
Colossal, seen of every land,
And keep the soldier firm, the statesman pure;
Till in all lands and thro' all human story
The path of duty be the way to glory.
And let the land whose hearths he saved from shame   225
For many and many an age proclaim
At civic revel and pomp and game,
And when the long-illumined cities flame,
Their ever-loyal iron leader's fame,
With honor, honor, honor, honor to him,   230
Eternal honor to his name.

9

Peace, his triumph will be sung
By some yet unmoulded tongue
Far on in summers that we shall not see.
Peace, it is a day of pain   235
For one about whose patriarchal knee
Let the little children clung.
O peace, it is a day of pain
For one upon whose hand and heart and brain
Once the weight and fate of Europe hung.   240
Ours the pain, be his the gain!
More than is of man's degree
Must be with us, watching here
At this, our great solemnity.
Whom we see not we revere;   245
We revere, and we refrain
From talk of battles loud and vain,
And brawling memories all too free

---

1. Contrast "The paths of glory lead but to the grave" from Gray's "Elegy Written in a Country Churchyard," line 36.

For such a wise humility
As befits a solemn fane: 250
We revere, and while we hear
The tides of Music's golden sea
Setting toward eternity,
Uplifted high in heart and hope are we,
Until we doubt not that for one so true 255
There must be other nobler work to do
Than when he fought at Waterloo,
And Victor he must ever be.
For tho' the Giant Ages heave the hill
And break the shore, and evermore 260
Make and break, and work their will,
Tho' world on world in myriad myriads roll
Round us, each with different powers,
And other forms of life than ours,
What know we greater than the soul? 265
On God and Godlike men we build our trust.
Hush, the Dead March[2] wails in the people's ears;
The dark crowd moves, and there are sobs and tears;
The black earth yawns; the mortal disappears;
Ashes to ashes, dust to dust; 270
He is gone who seem'd so great. —
Gone, but nothing can bereave him
Of the force he made his own
Being here, and we believe him
Something far advanced in State, 275
And that he wears a truer crown
Than any wreath that man can weave him.
Speak no more of his renown,
Lay your earthly fancies down,
And in the vast cathedral leave him, 280
God accept him, Christ receive him![3]

1852 (1855)

The Daisy

WRITTEN AT EDINBURGH

O love,[1] what hours were thine and mine,
In lands of palm and southern pine;
   In lands of palm, or orange-blossom,
Of olive, aloe, and maize and vine!

---

2. From Handel's *Saul*.
3. Romans 14:3: "God hath received him."
1. The poem is addressed to Tennyson's wife, Emily, who had been left behind at Richmond on a tour of
Yorkshire, and celebrates their belated wedding trip to Italy in the summer of 1851. The original meter,
involving a feminine ending in the third line of each stanza and an extra syllable in the fourth, Tennyson
called "a far-off echo of the Horatian Alcaic" (*Memoir* I, 341).

What Roman strength Turbia² show'd 5
In ruin, by the mountain road;
  How like a gem, beneath, the city
Of little Monaco, basking, glow'd!

How richly down the rocky dell
The torrent vineyard streaming fell 10
  To meet the sun and sunny waters,
That only heaved with a summer swell!

What slender campanili grew
By bays, the peacock's neck in hue;
  Where, here and there, on sandy beaches 15
A milky-bell'd amaryllis blew!

How young Columbus seem'd to rove,
Yet present in his natal grove,
  Now watching high on mountain cornice,
And steering, now, from a purple cove, 20

Now pacing mute by ocean's rim;
Till, in a narrow street and dim,
  I stay'd the wheels at Cogoletto,³
And drank, and loyally drank to him!

Nor knew we well what pleased us most; 25
Not the clipt palm of which they boast,
  But distant color, happy hamlet,
A moulder'd citadel on the coast,

Or tower, or high hill-convent, seen
A light amid its olives green; 30
  Or olive-hoary cape in ocean;
Or rosy blossom in hot ravine,

Where oleanders flush'd the bed
Of silent torrents, gravel-spread;
  And, crossing, oft we saw the glisten 35
Of ice, far up on a mountain head.

We loved that hall,⁴ tho' white and cold,
Those niched shapes of noble mould,
  A princely people's awful princes,
The grave, severe Genovese of old. 40

At Florence too what golden hours,
In those long galleries, were ours;

2. "In the Western Riviera" (Tennyson).
3. Assumed, perhaps wrongly, to be Columbus's birthplace.
4. In the Ducal Palace in Genoa, or possibly in the ancient Bank of St. George.

What drives about the fresh Cascine,
Or walks in Boboli's[5] ducal bowers!

In bright vignettes, and each complete,   45
Of tower or duomo, sunny-sweet,
    Or palace, how the city glitter'd,
Thro' cypress avenues, at our feet!

But when we crost the Lombard plain
Remember what a plague of rain;   50
    Of rain at Reggio, rain at Parma,
At Lodi rain, Piacenza rain.[6]

And stern and sad—so rare the smiles
Of sunlight—look'd the Lombard piles;
    Porch-pillars on the lion resting,   55
And sombre, old, colonnaded aisles.

O Milan, O the chanting quires,
The giant window's blazon'd fires,
    The height, the space, the gloom, the glory!
A mount of marble, a hundred spires![7]   60

I climb'd the roofs at break of day;
Sun-smitten Alps before me lay.
    I stood among the silent statues,
And statued pinnacles, mute as they.

How faintly-flush'd, how phantom-fair,   65
Was Monte Rosa,[8] hanging there
    A thousand shadowy-pencill'd valleys
And snowy dells in a golden air!

Remember how we came at last
To Como; shower and storm and blast   70
    Had blown the lake beyond his limit,
And all was flooded; and how we past

From Como, when the light was gray,
And in my head, for half the day,
    The rich Virgilian rustic measure   75
Of "Lari Maxume,"[9] all the way,

Like ballad-burthen music, kept,
As on the Lariano[1] crept

5. The Boboli Gardens are behind the Pitti Palace. Cascine is the park of Florence on the bank of the Arno.
6. The stanza alludes to towns in and around the Lombardy district in north-central Italy.
7. The great Gothic cathedral of Milan.
8. A mountain on the Swiss-Italian border; the highest point (over 15,000 feet) in the Pennine Alps.
9. "Larius the Greatest"; in the *Georgics*, Virgil's name for Lake Como, north of Milan.
1. A small boat.

To that fair port below the castle
Of Queen Theodolind,[2] where we slept;   80

Or hardly slept, but watch'd awake
A cypress in the moonlight shake,
    The moonlight touching o'er a terrace
One tall agavè[3] above the lake.

What more? we took our last adieu,   85
And up the snowy Splügen[4] drew;
    But ere we reach'd the highest summit
I pluck'd a daisy, I gave it you.

It told of England then to me,
And now it tells of Italy.   90
    O love, we two shall go no longer
To lands of summer across the sea,

So dear a life[5] your arms enfold
Whose crying is a cry for gold;
    Yet here to-night in this dark city,   95
When ill and weary, alone and cold,

I found, tho' crush'd to hard and dry,
This nursling of another sky
    Still in the little book you lent me,
And where you tenderly laid it by;   100

And I forgot the clouded Forth,[6]
The gloom that saddens heaven and earth,
    The bitter east, the misty summer
And gray metropolis of the North.[7]

Perchance to lull the throbs of pain,   105
Perchance to charm a vacant brain,
    Perchance to dream you still beside me,
My fancy fled to the South again.

                                        1853; 1855

---

2. The wife of a late-sixth-century ruler of the Lombards. "Fair port": Varenna.
3. Plants grown for ornament, fiber, and food. "A handsome tropical plant" (Ricks).
4. A pass across the Alps.
5. The poet's first son, Hallam, born August 11, 1852.
6. Edinburgh.
7. "A Scotch professor objected to this. So I asked him to call London if he liked the 'black metropolis of the south'" (Tennyson).

De Profundis[1]

The Two Greetings

1

Out of the deep, my child, out of the deep,
Where all that was to be, in all that was,
Whirl'd for a million æons thro' the vast
Waste dawn of multitudinous-eddying light—
Out of the deep, my child, out of the deep,   5
Thro' all this changing world of changeless law,
And every phase of ever-heightening life,
And nine long months of antenatal gloom,
With this last moon, this crescent—her dark orb
Touch'd with earth's light—thou comest, darling boy;   10
Our own; a babe in lineament and limb
Perfect, and prophet of the perfect man;
Whose face and form are hers and mine in one,
Indissolubly married like our love.
Live, and be happy in thyself, and serve   15
This mortal race thy kin so well that men
May bless thee as we bless thee, O young life
Breaking with laughter from the dark; and may
The fated channel where thy motion lives
Be prosperously shaped, and sway thy course   20
Along the years of haste and random youth
Unshatter'd; then full-current thro' full man;
And last in kindly curves, with gentlest fall,
By quiet fields, a slowly-dying power,
To that last deep where we and thou are still.   25

2

I

Out of the deep, my child, out of the deep,
From that great deep, before our world begins,
Whereon the Spirit of God moves as he will—
Out of the deep, my child, out of the deep,
From that true world[2] within the world we see,   30
Whereof our world is but the bounding shore—
Out of the deep, Spirit, out of the deep,
With this ninth moon, that sends the hidden sun
Down yon dark sea, thou comest, darling boy.

1. Begun after the birth of the poet's first son, Hallam, on August 11, 1852, the poem was not completed until much later. Toward the end of his life, Tennyson interpreted the poem for Mr. Ward, who wrote of the first section: "Life is viewed as we see it in the world, and as we know it by physical science." In the second greeting, "we gaze into that other deep—the world of spirit, the world of realities." Compare "The Passing of Arthur," lines 443–45, and *IM* Epilogue, lines 123–26: "A soul shall draw from out the vast / And strike his being into bounds, / And, moved thro' life of lower phase, / Result in man, be born and think."
2. "At times I have possessed the power of making my individuality as it were dissolve and fade away into boundless being, and this not a confused state but the clearest of the clearest, the surest of the surest, utterly beyond words, where death was an almost laughable impossibility, and the loss of personality, if so it were, seeming no alteration but the only true life" (Tennyson). See *IM* 95 and notes.

II

For in the world which is not ours They said,   35
"Let us make man," and that which should be man,
From that one light no man can look upon,
Drew to this shore lit by the suns and moons
And all the shadows. O dear Spirit, half-lost
In thine own shadow and this fleshly sign   40
That thou art thou—who wailest being born
And banish'd into mystery, and the pain
Of this divisible-indivisible world
Among the numerable-innumerable
Sun, sun, and sun, thro' finite-infinite space   45
In finite-infinite Time—our mortal veil
And shatter'd phantom of that infinite One,
Who made thee unconceivably Thyself
Out of His whole World-self and all in all—
Live thou! and of the grain and husk, the grape   50
And ivy-berry, choose; and still depart
From death to death thro' life and life, and find
Nearer and ever nearer Him, who wrought
Not matter, nor the finite-infinite,
But this main-miracle, that thou art thou,   55
With power on thine own act and on the world.

The Human Cry[3]

1

Hallowed be Thy name—Halleluiah!—
    Infinite Ideality!
    Immeasurable Reality!
    Infinite Personality   60
Hallowed be Thy name—Halleluiah!

2

We feel we are nothing—for all is Thou and in Thee;
We feel we are something—that also has come from Thee;
We know we are nothing—but Thou wilt help us to be.
Hallowed be Thy name—Halleluiah!   65

                                        1852ff.; 1880

To the Rev. F. D. Maurice[1]

Come, when no graver cares employ,
Godfather, come and see your boy;

---

3. This prayer, really a second poem published under the title "De Profundis," was designed to show the futility in our efforts to comprehend fundamental truths.
1. Maurice and Henry Hallam, Arthur's father, were the godfathers of Tennyson's first son, Hallam. At Cambridge, though before Tennyson's time, Maurice had been a founder of the Apostles. He was the moving force behind the Christian Socialist Movement and for his unorthodoxy had been ejected from his professorship at

Your presence will be sun in winter,
Making the little one leap for joy.

For, being of that honest few   5
Who give the Fiend himself his due,
    Should eighty thousand college-councils
Thunder "Anathema," friend, at you,

Should all our churchmen foam in spite
At you, so careful of the right,   10
    Yet one lay-heart would give you welcome —
Take it and come — to the Isle of Wight;[2]

Where, far from noise and smoke of town,
I watch the twilight falling brown
    All round a careless-order'd garden   15
Close to the ridge of a noble down.

You'll have no scandal while you dine,
But honest talk and wholesome wine,
    And only hear the magpie gossip
Garrulous under a roof of pine;   20

For groves of pine on either hand,
To break the blast of winter, stand,
    And further on, the hoary Channel
Tumbles a billow on chalk and sand;

Where, if below the milky steep   25
Some ship of battle slowly creep,
    And on thro' zones of light and shadow
Glimmer away to the lonely deep,

We might discuss the Northern sin
Which made a selfish war[3] begin,   30
    Dispute the claims, arrange the chances, —
Emperor, Ottoman, which shall win;

Or whether war's avenging rod
Shall lash all Europe into blood;
    Till you should turn to dearer matters,   35
Dear to the man that is dear to God, —

King's College. "Anathema" in line 8 is literally "accursed thing." According to Tennyson, Maurice had merely
pointed out that *eternal* in "eternal punishment" referred to the quality and not to the duration of punishment.
2. Tennyson leased Farringford on the Isle of Wight in 1853 and bought the house in 1856.
3. The Crimean War (1853–56) in which the English and French ostensibly sought to preserve the Ottoman Empire from Russian occupation. "The *Times* was against it, the Queen and the Prince Consort
were uncertain. But the people were intoxicated. Memories of past victories went to their heads, the
names of Waterloo and Trafalgar were on every lip. . . . Mr Disraeli's explanation did not seem much
more satisfactory [than Palmerston's]: he remarked that he thought we were going to war to prevent the
Emperor of all the Russias from protecting the Christian subjects of the sultan of Turkey" (Cecil Woodham-Smith, *The Reason Why*, p. 131). War was declared on March 28, 1854.

How best to help the slender store,
How mend the dwellings, of the poor,
How gain in life, as life advances,
Valor and charity more and more. 40

Come, Maurice, come; the lawn as yet
Is hoar with rime or spongy-wet,
But when the wreath of March has blossom'd,—
Crocus, anemone, violet,—

Or later, pay one visit here, 45
For those are few we hold as dear;
Nor pay but one, but come for many,
Many and many a happy year.

1854; 1855

The Charge of the Light Brigade[1]

1

Half a league, half a league,
Half a league onward,
All in the valley of Death
Rode the six hundred.
"Forward the Light Brigade! 5
Charge for the guns!" he said.
Into the valley of Death
Rode the six hundred.

2

"Forward, the Light Brigade!"
Was there a man dismay'd? 10
Not tho' the soldier knew
Some one had blunder'd.
Theirs not to make reply,
Theirs not to reason why,
Theirs but to do and die. 15
Into the valley of Death
Rode the six hundred.

1. Written on December 2, 1854, "in a few minutes, after reading the description in the *Times* in which occurred the phrase 'some one had blundered.' and this was the origin of the metre of his poem" (*Memoir* I, 381). *The Times* editorial (November 13) "in fact spoke of 'some hideous blunder.' "Tennyson also drew on the report (Nov. 14), where— as he says—'only 607 sabres are mentioned.' Tennyson wrote to Foster, 6 Dec.: 'Six is much better than seven hundred (as I think) metrically so keep it' (*Letters* II 101)" (Ricks).
   This disastrous engagement, probably the stupidest exploit in British military history, took place at Balaklava on October 25, during the initial phases of the Crimean War. Through a misinterpretation of orders, the light brigade charged headlong into entrenched Russian artillery. Of some 700 men, only 195 returned. Learning that the soldiers liked his poem, Tennyson had 1000 copies sent over for distribution among the troops. Cecil Woodham-Smith gives a splendid account of the engagement in *The Reason Why* (1953), which, to this day, remains the single, most readable account. Baring Temberton's *Battles of Crimean War* (1962) is also worth consulting.

3

Cannon to right of them,
Cannon to left of them,
Cannon in front of them   20
    Volley'd and thunder'd;
Storm'd at with shot and shell,
Boldly they rode and well,
Into the jaws of Death,
Into the mouth of hell   25
    Rode the six hundred.

4

Flash'd all their sabres bare,
Flash'd as they turn'd in air
Sabring the gunners there,
Charging an army, while   30
    All the world wonder'd.
Plunged in the battery-smoke
Right thro' the line they broke;
Cossack and Russian
Reel'd from the sabre-stroke   35
    Shatter'd and sunder'd.
Then they rode back, but not,
    Not the six hundred.

5

Cannon to right of them,
Cannon to left of them,   40
Cannon behind them
    Volley'd and thunder'd;
Storm'd at with shot and shell,
While horse and hero fell,
They that had fought so well   45
Came thro' the jaws of Death,
Back from the mouth of hell,
All that was left of them,
    Left of six hundred.

6

When can their glory fade?   50
O the wild charge they made!
    All the world wonder'd.
Honor the charge they made!
Honor the Light Brigade,
    Noble six hundred!   55

1854

MAUD

The so-called germ of *Maud* is the poem, "O that 'twere possible," (section IV of Part 2), which apparently was in existence before 1834. See *Memoir* I, 139. At the suggestion of his friend Sir John Simeon, who thought the earlier poem could be made more intelligible with a predecessor, Tennyson "wrote it; the second poem too required a predecessor; and thus the whole work was written, as it were, *backwards*" (Aubrey de Vere in *Memoir* I, 379). The poem was composed at Farringford on the Isle of Wight in about a year (it was finished in July 1855), but the divisions as we have them did not appear until the eleventh edition (1865). Although *Maud* was not favorably received by the critics, it was widely read and very remunerative. Gladstone, as did many others, faulted it for its seeming support of the Crimean War as panacea for disaffected youth; Browning, predictably, was enthusiastic in praise. Of more modern commentators, T. S. Eliot has appreciated the poem's "lyrical resourcefulness." During Tennyson's lifetime, it became well known that *Maud* was one of his favorites, a poem he particularly liked to read aloud. It was certainly with mixed emotions, however, that, when an old man, Tennyson forced himself to sit through a recitation of the entire work memorized by an American who had worked his way over to England on a cattle ship for that single purpose.

As in "Locksley Hall," many readers have supposed Tennyson was reflecting his own views through his speakers. It is true that he was sometimes morbidly concerned with hereditary insanity in his own family, more than once referring to the "black blood" of the Tennysons out of fear of his own susceptibility. It is likewise true that the poet's father was a disinherited eldest son always in financial hardships and had been, in effect, a suicide, though he settled for the lingering version through drink. But as the poet's grandson has observed, if some original in real life must be found, heroes "so idealistic, passionate and unstable, have more than a little reference to Frederick," the poet's older brother (*Alfred Tennyson*, p. 194). The hero of *Maud*, or more properly the Byronic antihero, is clearly unbalanced, indeed paranoiac, and in some ways prefigures those other angry young men of a century later. His neuroses, his obsession with violence and merciless introspection, are shared by protagonists of the "Spasmodic School," a group headed by Alexander Smith and Sydney Dobell whose poetry was in vogue during the 1850s and 1860s.

Tennyson called his poem "a little *Hamlet*" and explained to his son that it was

> the history of a morbid poetic soul, under the blighting influence of a recklessly speculative age. He is the heir of madness, an egotist with the makings of a cynic, raised to sanity by a pure and holy love which elevates his whole nature, passing from the height of triumph to the lowest depth of misery, driven into madness by the loss of her whom he has loved, and, when he has at length passed through the fiery furnace, and has recovered his reason, giving himself up to work for the good of mankind through the unselfishness born of his great passion. . . . "The pecularity of his poem," my father added, "is that different phases of passion in one person take the place of different characters." (*Memoir* I, 396)

In that last sentence surely lies the key to the proper reading of the poem.

If we are perhaps reluctant to grant the poet complete dramatic distance from his speaker, and authorship of such pieces as "The Charge of the Light Brigade" contributes to our reluctance, we should likewise not assert that the poem is an exercise in support of the Crimean War. Henry van Dyke recorded Tennyson as saying of his speaker: "He is wrong in thinking that war will transform the cheating tradesman into a great-souled hero, or that it will sweep away the dishonesties and lessen the miseries of humanity. The history of the Crimean War proves his error. But this very delusion is natural to him: it is in keeping with his morbid, melancholy, impulsive character to see a cure for the evils of peace in the horrors of war." Certainly we should also bear in mind the poet's own statement that a "Northern sin" had "made a selfish war begin" (see "To the Rev. F. D. Maurice," lines 30–31). In short, *Maud* should be read on its own terms, without undue stress on its autobiographical elements or historical context. Then it is what it appears to be: a splendidly executed psychological study.

Maud; A Monodrama

Part 1

I

1

I hate the dreadful hollow behind the little wood;
Its lips in the field above are dabbled with blood-red heath,[1]
The red-ribb'd ledges drip with a silent horror of blood,
And Echo there, whatever is ask'd her, answers "Death."

2

For there in the ghastly pit long since a body was found,   5
His who had given me life—O father! O God! was it well?—
Mangled, and flatten'd, and crush'd, and dinted into the ground;
There yet lies the rock that fell with him when he fell.

3

Did he fling himself down? who knows? for a vast speculation[2] had fail'd,
And ever he mutter'd and madden'd, and ever wann'd with despair,   10
And out he walk'd when the wind like a broken worldling wail'd,
And the flying gold of the ruin'd woodlands drove thro' the air.

4

I remember the time, for the roots of my hair were stirr'd
By a shuffled step, by a dead weight trail'd, by a whisper'd fright.
And my pulses closed their gates with a shock on my heart as I heard   15
The shrill-edged shriek of a mother divide the shuddering night.

5

Villainy somewhere! whose? One says, we are villains all.[3]
Not he! his honest fame should at least by me be maintained;
But that old man, now lord of the broad estate and the Hall,

1. "In calling heath 'blood'-red, the hero," according to Tennyson, "showed his extravagant fancy, which is already on the road to madness." "His suspicion that all the world is against him is as true to this nature as the mood when he is 'fantastically merry'" (*Memoir* I, 396). Today he would well qualify as a case study of a bipolar personality. In his note to Browning's "Porphyria's Lover" James F. Loucks observes "the projection of the speaker's mood onto nature anticipates Tennyson's *Maud* (1855), wherein the device—for which John Ruskin coined the perjorative term 'pathetic fallacy'—is employed extensively."
2. A venture, never specified, which had enriched Maud's father, the "old man" of line 19. "Usually understood as an allusion to Matthew Allen's scheme to make wood-carvings by steam-driven machine. Tennyson and his family invested £8000 [1840–41] in the project, but it collapsed two years later and the Tennysons lost all their money" (Shatto's *Tennyson's "Maud*," p. 164).
3. Paul Turner points out that his obsession to avenge his father's death is like Hamlet's, as is his conception of those around him: "We are arrant knaves all" (III, i, line 128). And "like Hamlet he is profoundly disgusted by himself and the whole human race, is haunted by a ghost, and kills the brother of the girl he loves in a duel" (*Tennyson*, p. 139).

Dropt off gorged from a scheme that had left us flaccid and drain'd.   20

6

Why do they prate of the blessings of peace? we have made them a curse,
Pickpockets, each hand lusting for all that is not its own;
And lust of gain, in the spirit of Cain, is it better or worse
Than the heart of the citizen hissing in war on his own hearthstone?

7

But these are the days of advance, the works of the men of mind,   25
When who but a fool would have faith in a tradesman's ware or his word?
Is it peace or war? Civil war, as I think and that of a kind
The viler, as underhand, not openly bearing the sword.

8

Sooner or later I too may passively take the print
Of the golden age—why not? I have neither hope nor trust;   30
May make my heart as a millstone, set my face as a flint,[4]
Cheat and be cheated, and die—who knows? we are ashes and dust.

9

Peace sitting under her olive, and slurring the days gone by,
When the poor are hovell'd and hustled together, each sex, like swine,
When only the ledger lives, and when only not all men lie;   35
Peace in her vineyard—yes!—but a company forges the wine.

10

And the vitriol madness flushes up in the ruffian's head,
Till the filthy by-lane rings to the yell of the trampled wife,
And chalk and alum and plaster are sold to the poor for bread,
And the spirit of murder works in the every means of life,   40

11

And Sleep must lie down arm'd, for the villainous centre-bits[5]
Grind on the wakeful ear in the hush of the moonless nights,
While another is cheating the sick of a few last gasps, as he sits
To pestle a poison'd poison behind his crimson lights.

12

When a Mammonite mother kills her babe for a burial fee,   45
And Timour[6] Mammon grins on a pile of children's bones,
Is it peace or war? better, war! loud war by land and by sea,
War with a thousand battles, and shaking a hundred thrones!

---

4. Ricks notes: "His heart is as firm as a stone: yea, as hard as a piece of the nether millstone" (Job 41:24).
5. A tool for boring holes, here used in burglary.
6. Tamerlane, the ruthless descendant of Genghis Khan, who ravaged Asia during the last part of the four-
   teenth century. At Sivas, Turkey, in 1400, he was supposed to have crushed a thousand children under
   the hoofs of his horses.

13

For I trust if an enemy's fleet came yonder round by the hill,
And the rushing battle-bolt sang from the three-decker out of the foam,   50
That the smooth-faced, snub-nosed rogue would leap from his counter
    and till,
And strike, if he could, were it but with his cheating yardwand, home.

14

What! am I raging alone as my father raged in his mood?
Must *I* too creep to the hollow and dash myself down and die
Rather than hold by the law that I made, nevermore to brood   55
On a horror of shatter'd limbs and a wretched swindler's lie?

15

Would there be sorrow for *me*? there was *love* in the passionate shriek,
Love for the silent thing that had made false haste to the grave —
Wrapt in a cloak, as I saw him, and thought he would rise and speak
And rave at the lie and the liar, ah God, as he used to rave.   60

16

I am sick of the Hall and the hill, I am sick of the moor and the main.
Why should I stay? can a sweeter chance ever come to me here?
O, having the nerves of motion as well as the nerves of pain,
Were it not wise if I fled from the place and the pit and the fear?

17

Workmen up at the Hall! — they are coming back from abroad;   65
The dark old place will be gilt by the touch of a millionaire
I have heard, I know not whence, of the singular beauty of Maud;
I play'd with the girl when a child; she promised then to be fair.

18

Maud, with her venturous climbings and tumbles and childish escapes,
Maud, the delight of the village, the ringing joy of the Hall,   70
Maud, with her sweet purse-mouth when my father dangled the grapes,
Maud, the beloved of my mother, the moon-faced darling of all, —

19

What is she now? My dreams are bad. She may bring me a curse.
No, there is fatter game on the moor; she will let me alone.
Thanks; for the fiend best knows whether woman or man be the worse   75
I will bury myself in myself, and the Devil may pipe to his own.[7]

---

7. Concerning Rosa Baring here and in line 79ff., see "Locksley Hall" and n. 1, p. 115. Of various excluded passages in manuscript versions of *Maud*, Ricks cogently observes: "Tennyson's indignation after losing Rosa Baring could not find a true place in *Maud*." *Indignation* may be too strong a word. They met in the autumn of 1832. "The depth of Tennyson's sensual feelings for Rosa may have been as exaggerated in the telling as his sense of rejection by her. . . . His love appears to have been more imaginary than actual, more dutiful than driving. What finally seems most persuasive is that in later years Rosa was quite unaware that Tennyson had ever entertained any particularly deep feelings for her." Furthermore, with reference to early poems perhaps addressed to her, "A clear indication that Tennyson realized how immature these poems were and how jejune his reactions to Rosa Baring is given by his plundering of them in 1854, when he was writing *Maud*. . . . The girl whom he [the speaker] is describing has never really existed, and the hero discovers that he has been using her as a mirror of his own neurotic prejudices, precisely as Tennyson had been doing with Rosa in real life" (Martin's *Tennyson*, pp. 218–20).

II

Long have I sigh'd for a calm; God grant I may find it at last!
It will never be broken by Maud; she has neither savor nor salt,
But a cold and clear-cut face, as I found when her carriage past,
Perfectly beautiful; let it be granted here; where is the fault?   80
All that I saw—for her eyes were downcast, not to be seen—
Faultily faultless, icily regular, splendidly null,
Dead perfection, no more,; nothing more, if it had not been
For a chance of travel, a paleness, an hour's defect of the rose,
Or an underlip, you may call it a little too ripe, too full,   85
Or the least little delicate aquiline curve in a sensitive nose,
From which I escaped heart-free, with the least little touch of spleen.

III

Cold and clear-cut face, why come you so cruelly meek,
Breaking a slumber in which all spleenful folly was drown'd?
Pale with the golden beam of an eyelash dead on the cheek,   90
Passionless, pale, cold face, star-sweet on a gloom profound;
Womanlike, taking revenge too deep for a transient wrong
Done but in thought to your beauty, and ever as pale as before
Growing and fading and growing upon me without a sound,
Luminous, gemlike, ghostlike, deathlike, half the night long   95
Growing and fading and growing, till I could bear it no more,
But arose, and all by myself in my own dark garden ground,
Listening now to the tide in its broad-flung shipwrecking roar,[8]
Now to the scream of a madden'd beach dragg'd down by the wave,
Walk'd in a wintry wind by a ghastly glimmer, and found   100
The shining daffodil dead, and Orion low in his grave.

IV

1

A million emeralds break from the ruby-budded lime
In the little grove where I sit—ah, wherefore cannot I be
Like things of the season gay, like the bountiful season bland,
When the far-off sail is blown by the breeze of a softer clime,   105
Half-lost in the liquid azure bloom of a crescent of sea,
The silent sapphire-spangled marriage ring of the land?

2

Below me, there, is the village, and looks how quiet and small
And yet bubbles o'er like a city, with gossip, scandal, and spite;
And Jack on his ale-house bench has as many lies as a Czar;[9]   110
And here on the landward side, by a red rock, glimmers the Hall;
And up in the high Hall-garden I see her pass like a light;
But sorrow seize me if ever that light be my leading star!

8. Tennyson commented that on the Isle of Wight "the roar can be heard nine miles away from the beach"
   (*Memoir* I, 402).
9. Nicholas I and Russian propaganda in conducting the Crimean War.

3

When have I bow'd[1] to her father, the wrinkled head of the race?
I met her to-day with her brother, but not to her brother I bow'd;   115
I bow'd to his lady-sister as she rode by on the moor,
But the fire of a foolish pride flash'd over her beautiful face.
O child, you wrong your beauty, believe it, in being so proud;
Your father has wealth well-gotten, and I am nameless and poor.

4

I keep but a man and a maid, ever ready to slander and steal;   120
I know it, and smile a hard-set smile, like a stoic, or like
A wiser epicurean, and let the world have its way.
For nature[2] is one with rapine, a harm no preacher can heal;
The Mayfly is torn by the swallow, the sparrow spear'd by the shrike,
And the whole little wood where I sit is a world of plunder and prey.[3]   125

5

We are puppets, Man in his pride, and Beauty fair in her flower;
Do we move ourselves, or are moved by an unseen hand at a game
That pushes us off from the board, and others ever succeed?
Ah yet, we cannot be kind to each other here for an hour;
We whisper, and hint, and chuckle, and grin at a brother's shame;   130

6

A monstrous eft[4] was of old the lord and master of earth,
For him did his high sun flame, and his river billowing ran,
And he felt himself in his force to be Nature's crowning race.
As nine months go to the shaping an infant ripe for his birth,
So many million of ages have gone to the making of man: 135
He now is first, but is he the last? is he not too base?[5]

7

The man of science himself is fonder of glory, and vain,
An eye well-practised in nature, a spirit bounded and poor;
The passionate heart of the poet is whirl'd into folly and vice.
I would not marvel at either, but keep a temperate brain;   140
For not to desire or admire, if a man could learn it, were more
Than to walk all day like the sultan of old in garden of spice.[6]

8

For the drift of the Maker is dark, and Isis[7] hid by the veil.
Who knows the ways of the world, how God will bring them about?
Our planet is one, the suns are many, the world is wide.   145

1. To have done so would have been to acknowledge his status gained through plunder of the poor.
2. Human as well as external nature.
3. Compare *IM* 56.
4. Literally, a newt, though Tennyson was thinking of "the great old lizards of geology." His note suggests he may have had Chambers's *Vestiges of Creation* (1844) in mind.
5. Like several sections of *IM*, this stanza is often cited in support of the claim that Tennyson anticipated Darwinism.
6. "Compare Song of Solomon, 4, 16: 'Blow upon my garden, that the spices thereof may flow out. Let my beloved come into his garden, and eat his pleasant fruits'" (Ricks).
7. The Egyptian goddess of fertility.

Shall I weep if a Poland fall? shall I shriek if a Hungary[8] fail?
Or an infant civilization be ruled with rod or with knout?
I have not made the world, and He that made it will guide.

9

Be mine a philosopher's life in the quiet woodland ways,
Where if I cannot be gay let a passionless peace be my lot,   150
Far-off from the clamor of liars belied in the hubbub of lies;
From the long-neck'd geese of the world that are ever hissing dis-praise
Because their natures are little, and, whether he heed it or not,
Where each man walks with his head in a cloud of poisonous flies.

10

And most of all would I flee from the cruel madness of love   155
The honey of poison-flowers and all the measureless ill.
Ah, Maud, you milk-white fawn, you are all unmeet for a wife.
Your mother is mute in her grave as her image in marble above;
Your father is ever in London, you wander about at your will;
You have but fed on the roses and lain in the lilies of life.   160

V

1

A voice by the cedar tree
In the meadow under the Hall!
She is singing an air that is known to me,
A passionate ballad gallant and gay,
A martial song like a trumpet's call!   165
Singing alone in the morning of life,
In the happy morning of life and of May,
Singing of men that in battle array,
Ready in heart and ready in hand,
March with banner and bugle and fife   170
To the death, for their native land.

2

Maud with her exquisite face,
And wild voice pealing up to the sunny sky,
And feet like sunny gems on an English green,
Maud in the light of her youth and her grace,   175
Singing of Death, and of Honor that cannot die,
Till I well could weep for a time so sordid and mean,
And myself so languid and base.

3

Silence, beautiful voice!
Be still, for you only trouble the mind   180
With a joy in which I cannot rejoice,
A glory I shall not find.
Still! I will hear you no more,

8. In 1849 the Hungarian uprising against Austria failed. In 1846 and again in 1848, Russia and Austria
   had partitioned and reduced Poland.

For your sweetness hardly leaves me a choice
But to move to the meadow and fall before   185
Her feet on the meadow grass, and adore,
Not her, who is neither courtly nor kind,
Not her, not her, but a voice.

VI

1

Morning arises stormy and pale,
No sun, but a wannish[9] glare   190
In fold upon fold of hueless cloud;
And the budded peaks of the wood, are bow'd,
Caught, and cuff'd by the gale:
I had fancied it would be fair.

2

Whom but Maud should I meet   195
Last night, when the sunset burn'd
On the blossom'd gable-ends
At the head of the village street,
Whom but Maud should I meet?
And she touch'd my hand with a smile so sweet,   200
She made me divine amends
For a courtesy not return'd.

3

And thus a delicate spark
Of glowing and growing light
Thro' the livelong hours of the dark   205
Kept itself warm in the heart of my dreams,
Ready to burst in a color'd flame;
Till at last, when the morning came
In a cloud, it faded, and seems
But an ashen-gray delight.   210

4

What if with her sunny hair,
And smile as sunny as cold,
She meant to weave me a snare
Of some coquettish deceit,
Cleopatra-like as of old   215
To entangle me when we met,
To have her lion roll in a silken net
And fawn at a victor's feet.

5

Ah, what shall I be at fifty
Should Nature keep me alive,   220
If I find the world so bitter

9. Ricks compares Keats's "Lamia" i, line 57: "wannish fire." Interestingly, the OED cites "Lamia" then
   Maud as the last two instances of the word's appearance.

When I am but twenty-five?
Yet, if she were not a cheat,
If Maud were all that she seem'd,
And her smile were all that I dream'd,   225
Then the world were not so bitter
But a smile could make it sweet.

6

What if, tho' her eye seem'd full
Of a kind intent to me,
What if that dandy-despot, he,   230
That jewell'd mass of millinery,
That oil'd and curl'd Assyrian bull[1]
Smelling of musk and of insolence,[2]
Her brother, from whom I keep aloof,
Who wants the finer politic sense   235
To mask, tho' but in his own behoof,
With a glassy smile his brutal scorn—
What if he had told her yestermorn
How prettily for his own sweet sake
A face of tenderness might be feign'd,   240
And a moist mirage in desert eyes,
That so, when the rotten hustings[3] shake
In another month to his brazen lies,
A wretched vote may be gain'd?

7

For a raven ever croaks, at my side,   245
Keep watch and ward, keep watch and ward,
Or thou wilt prove their tool.
Yea, too, myself from myself I guard,
For often a man's own angry pride
Is cap and bells for a fool.   250

8

Perhaps the smile and tender tone
Came out of her pitying womanhood,
For am I not, am I not, here alone
So many a summer since she died,
My mother, who was so gentle and good?   255
Living alone in an empty house,
Here half-hid in the gleaming wood,
Where I hear the dead at midday moan,
And the shrieking rush of the wainscot mouse,[4]
And my own sad name in corners cried,   260
When the shiver of dancing leaves is thrown

1. "With hair curled like that of the bulls on Assyrian sculpture" (Tennyson).
2. "The zeugma suggests *Paradise Lost*, I, 501–02: 'the Sons / Of Belial flown with insolence and wine'"
   (Ricks).
3. Platforms on which candidates for Parliament formerly stood for nomination, hence a place for making
   campaign speeches. The implication is of "rotten borough," an election district with only a few voters,
   hence an easy way to buy one's election to the House of Commons.
4. Compare "Mariana," lines 63–64: "the mouse / Behind the mouldering wainscot shriek'd."

About its echoing chambers wide,
Till a morbid hate and horror have grown
Of a world in which I have hardly mixt,
And a morbid eating lichen fixt　　　　　　　　　　265
On a heart half-turn'd to stone.

9

O heart of stone, are you flesh, and caught
By that you swore to withstand?
For what was it else within me wrought
But, I fear, the new strong wine of love,　　　　　　　270
That made my tongue so stammer and trip
When I saw the treasured splendor, her hand,
Come sliding out of her sacred glove,
And the sunlight broke from her lip?

10

I have play'd with her when a child;　　　　　　　275
She remembers it now we meet.
Ah, well, well, well, I *may* be beguiled
By some coquettish deceit.
Yet, if she were not a cheat,
If Maud were all that she seem'd,　　　　　　　280
And her smile had all that I dream'd,
Then the world were not so bitter
But a smile could make it sweet.

VII

1

Did I hear it half in a doze
Long since, I know not where?　　　　　　　285
Did I dream it an hour ago,
When asleep in this arm-chair?

2

Men were drinking together,
Drinking and talking of me:
"Well, if it prove a girl, the boy　　　　　　　290
Will have plenty; so let it be."[5]

3

Is it an echo of something
Read with a boy's delight,[6]
Viziers[7] nodding together　　　　　　　295
In some Arabian night?

---

5. "He remembers his father and her father talking just before the birth of Maud" (Tennyson). As Part 1, section XIX, 4, later clarifies, they have arranged a marriage if the child proves to be a girl. Implicitly, Maud's father has brought up the subject of a dowry, and the speaker's father's response is that in quotation marks.
6. Padden, in *Tennyson in Egypt*, as Ricks also notes, was among or the first to note that the reference is to *The Story of Nourredin Ali and Bedreddin Hassan* in the *Arabian Nights*. There, two brothers make a similar bargain and fight, and the children at last marry. As so often, confusions between fact and fiction are not the least of the protagonist's problems.
7. High executive officers in Muslim countries.

4

Strange, that I hear two men,
  Somewhere, talking of me:
"Well, if it prove a girl, my boy
  Will have plenty; so let it be."

VIII

She came to the village church,   300
  And sat by a pillar alone;
An angel watching an urn
  Wept over her, carved in stone;
And once, but once, she lifted her eyes,
  And suddenly, sweetly, strangely blush'd   305
To find they were met by my own;
  And suddenly, sweetly, my heart beat stronger
And thicker, until I heard no longer
  The snowy-banded, dilettante,
Delicate-handed priest intone;   310
  And thought, is it pride? and mused and sigh'd,
"No surely, now it cannot be pride."[8]

IX

I was walking a mile,
  More than a mile from the shore,
The sun look'd out with a smile   315
  Betwixt the cloud and the moor;
And riding at set of day
  Over the dark moor land,
Rapidly riding far away,
  She waved to me with her hand.   320
There were two[9] at her side,
  Something flash'd in the sun,
Down by the hill I saw them ride,
  In a moment they were gone;
Like a sudden spark   325
  Struck vainly in the night,
Then returns the dark
  With no more hope of light.

X

1

Sick, am I sick of a jealous dread?
  Was not one of the two at her side   330
This new-made lord, whose splendor plucks
  The slavish hat from the villager's head?
Whose old grandfather has lately died,
  Gone to a blacker pit, for whom
Grimy nakedness dragging his trucks   335

8. "It cannot be pride that she did not return his bow," alluding to lines 116–17 (Tennyson).
9. Maud's brother and her suitor, the "new-made lord" of line 332.

And laying his trams in a poison'd gloom
Wrought, till he crept from a gutted mine
Master of half a servile shire,
And left his coal all turn'd into gold
To a grandson, first of his noble line,   340
Rich in the grace all women desire,
Strong in the power that all men adore,
And simper and set their voices lower,
And soften as if to a girl, and hold
Awe-stricken breaths at a work divine,   345
Seeing his gewgaw[1] castle shine,
New as his title, built last year,
There amid perky larches and pine,
And over the sullen-purple moor—
Look at it—pricking a cockney ear.   350

2

What, has he found my jewel out?
For one of the two that rode at her side
Bound for the Hall, I am sure was he;
Bound for the Hall, and I think for a bride.
Blithe would her brother's acceptance be   355
Maud could be gracious too, no doubt,
To a lord, a captain, a padded shape,
A bought commission,[2] a waxen face,
A rabbit mouth that is ever agape—
Bought? what is it he cannot buy?   360
And therefore splenetic, personal, base,
A wounded thing with a rancorous cry,
At war with myself and a wretched race,
Sick, sick to the heart of life, am I.

3

Last week came one to the county town,   365
To preach our poor little army down,
And play the game of the despot kings,
Tho' the state has done it and thrice as well.
This broad-brimm'd hawker[3] of holy things,
Whose ear is cramm'd with his cotton, and rings   370
Even in dreams to the chink of his pence,
This huckster put down war! can he tell

1. Very likely a reference to Tennyson's estranged uncle, his disinherited father's favored younger brother. "The dining hall was spectacular in its dimensions, for it could seat 200. After such a beginning [in 1835] there was no reason to stop, and for the next decade Charles put all his energy and a great deal of his money into the rebuilding of Bayons" (Martin's *Tennyson*, p. 210). Blown up in a single day after World War II, this sham castle with drawbridge and moat, along with the change of name to d'Eyncourt, was symbolic of his fruitless quest for a title.
2. "The system of purchasing commissions, combined with the conferral of military appointments on men of social distinction, initiated a middle-class attack upon the aristocracy during the Crimean War" (Shatto's *Tennyson's "Maud,"* p. 186). For a full account, see Cecil Woodham-Smith's *The Reason Why* for the buying of commissions, the familial feud and bickerings between Lords Lucan and Cardigan before and during the war, an amusing yet horrifying charade given the military consequences.
3. The Quakers were identifiable by their "broad-brimm'd" hats. The *Westminster Review* said the figure was John Bright, who had vigorously opposed the Crimean War. Tennyson, only half-convincingly, denied the allegation, saying, "I did not know at the time that he was a Quaker" (*Memoir* 1, 403).

Whether war be a cause or a consequence?
Put down the passions that make earth hell!
Down with ambition, avarice, pride,   375
Jealousy, down! cut off from the mind
The bitter springs of anger and fear!
Down too, down at your own fireside,
With the evil tongue and the evil ear,
For each is at war with mankind!   380

4

I wish I could hear again
The chivalrous battle-song
That she warbled alone in her joy!
I might persuade myself then
She would not do herself this great wrong,   385
To take a wanton dissolute boy
For a man and leader of men.

5

Ah God, for a man with heart, head, hand,
Like some of the simple great ones gone
For ever and ever by,   390
One still strong man in a blatant land,
Whatever they call him—what care I?—
Aristocrat, democrat, autocrat—one
Who can rule and dare not lie!

6

And ah for a man to arise in me,   395
That the man I am may cease to be!

XI

1

O, let the solid ground
    Not fail beneath my feet
Before my life has found
    What some have found so sweet!   400
Then let come what come may,
What matter if I go mad,
I shall have had my day.

2

Let the sweet heavens endure,
    Not close and darken above me   405
Before I am quite quite sure
    That there is one to love me!
Then let come what come may
To a life that has been so sad,
I shall have had my day.   410

XII

1

Birds in the high Hall-garden
  When twilight was falling,
Maud, Maud, Maud, Maud,[4]
  They were crying and calling.

2

Where was Maud? in our wood;   415
  And I—who else?—was with her,
Gathering woodland lilies,
  Myriads blow together.

3

Birds in our wood sang
  Ringing thro' the valleys,   420
Maud is here, here, here
  In among the lilies.

4

I kiss'd her slender hand,
  She took the kiss sedately;
Maud is not seventeen,   425
  But she is tall and stately.

5

I to cry out on pride
  Who have won her favor!
O, Maud were sure of heaven
  If lowliness could save her!   430

6

I know the way she went
  Home with her maiden posy,
For her feet have touch'd the meadows
  And left the daisies rosy[5]

7

Birds in the high Hall-garden   435
  Were crying and calling to her,
Where is Maud, Maud, Maud?
  One is come to woo her.

8

Look, a horse at the door,
  And little King Charley[6] snarling!   440

---

4. "Like the rook's caw" (Tennyson). As with "here, here, here" (line 422): "Like the call of the little birds" (Tennyson).
5. "If you tread on the daisy," Tennyson pointed out of the English variety, "it turns up a rosy underside."
6. "A King Charles spaniel . . . it is used to imply the 'fawning' attitude of the Peace Society towards the Czar; here, merely as a favorite dog of ladies" (Shatto's *Tennyson's "Maud,"* p. 191).

Go back, my lord, across the moor,
  You are not her darling.

XIII[7]

1

Scorn'd, to be scorn'd by one that I scorn,
Is that a matter to make me fret?
That a calamity hard to be borne?   445
Well, he may live to hate me yet.
Fool that I am to be vext with his pride!
I past him, I was crossing his lands;
He stood on the path a little aside;
His face, as I grant, in spite of spite,   450
Has a broad-blown comeliness, red and white,
And six feet two, as I think, he stands;
But his essences turn'd the live air sick,
And barbarous opulence jewel-thick
Sunn'd itself on his breast and his hands.   455

2

Who shall call me ungentle, unfair?
I long'd so heartily then and there
To give him the grasp of fellowship;
But while I past he was humming an air,
Stopt, and then with a riding-whip   460
Leisurely tapping a glossy boot,
And curving a contumelious lip,
Gorgonized[8] me from head to foot
With a stony British stare.

3

Why sits he here in his father's chair?   465
That old man never comes to his place;
Shall I believe him ashamed to be seen?
For only once, in the village street,
Last year, I caught a glimpse of his face,
A gray old wolf and a lean.   470
Scarcely, now, would I call him a cheat;
For then, perhaps, as a child of deceit,
She might by a true descent be untrue;
And Maud is as true as Maud is sweet,
Tho' I fancy her sweetness only due   475
To the sweeter blood by the other side;
Her mother has been a thing complete,
However she came to be so allied.
And fair without, faithful within,

---

7. According to Knowles, Tennyson said: "A counter passion—passionate & furious." Also: "Morbidly prophetic. He sees Maud's brother, who will not recognize him" (Tennyson).
8. Medusa, one of the three Gorgon sisters, had a face so hideous that it turned to stone anyone who gazed directly on it.

Maud to him is nothing akin.   480
Some peculiar mystic grace
Made her only the child of her mother,
And heap'd the whole inherited sin
On that huge scapegoat of the race,
All, all upon the brother.   485

4

Peace, angry spirit, and let him be!⁹
Has not his sister smiled on me?

XIV

1

Maud has a garden of roses
And lilies on a lawn;
There she walks in her state   490
And tends upon bed and bower,
And thither I climb'd at dawn
And stood by her garden-gate.
A lion ramps at the top,
He is claspt by a passion-flower.   495

2

Maud's own little oak-room —
Which Maud, like a precious stone
Set in the heart of the carven gloom,
Lights with herself, when alone
She sits by her music and books   500
And her brother lingers late
With a roystering company — looks
Upon Maud's own garden-gate;
And I thought as I stood, if a hand, as white
As ocean-foam in the moon, were laid   505
On the hasp of the window, and my Delight
Had a sudden desire, like a glorous ghost, to glide,¹
Like a beam of the seventh heaven, down to my side,
There were but a step to be made.

3

The fancy flatter'd my mind,   510
And again seem'd overbold;
Now I thought that she cared for me,
Now I thought she was kind
Only because she was cold.

4

I heard no sound where I stood   515
But the rivulet on from the lawn

9. To Knowles Tennyson said: "He makes allowances for the man — Yet he is called a mere brute!"
1. "Alludes to the time when she did come out" (Tennyson to Knowles).

Running down to my own dark wood,
Or the voice of the long sea-wave as it swell'd
Now and then in the dim-gray dawn;
But I look'd, and round, all round the house I beheld   520
The death-white curtain drawn,
Felt a horror over me creep,
Prickle my skin and catch my breath,
Knew that the death-white curtain meant but sleep,
Yet I shudder'd and thought like a fool of the sleep of death.   525

XV

So dark a mind within me dwells,
    And I make myself such evil cheer,
That if I be dear to some one else,
    Then some one else may have much to fear;
But if I be dear to some one else,   530
    Then I should be to myself more dear.
Shall I not take care of all that I think,
Yea, even of wretched meat and drink,
If I be dear,
If I be dear to some one else?[2]   535

XVI

1

This lump of earth has left his estate
The lighter by the loss of his weight;
And so that he find what he went to seek,
And fulsome pleasure clog him, and drown
His heart in the gross mud-honey of town,   540
He may stay for a year who has gone for a week.
But this is the day when I must speak,
And I see my Oread[3] coming down,
O, this is the day!
O beautiful creature, what am I   545
That I dare to look her way?
Think I may hold dominion sweet,
Lord of the pulse that is lord of her breast,
And dream of her beauty with tender dread,
From the delicate Arab arch of her feet[4]   550
To the grace that, bright and light as the crest
Of a peacock, sits on her shining head,

2. "He begins with universal hatred of all things & gets more human by the influence of Maud" (Tennyson
to Knowles). Compare "Guinevere," lines 474–80:
    " . . . for indeed I knew
    Of no more subtle master under heaven
    Than is the maiden passion for a maid,
    Not only to keep down the base in man,
    But teach high thoughts, and amiable words
    And courtliness, and the desire of fame,
    And love of truth, and all that makes a man."
3. A mountain nymph. "She lives on the hill near him" (Tennyson to Knowles).
4. "Like the arched neck of an Arab horse" (Ricks).

And she knows it not—O, if she knew it,
To know her beauty might half undo it!
I know it the one bright thing to save   555
My yet young life in the wilds of Time,
Perhaps from madness, perhaps from crime,
Perhaps from a selfish grave.

                        2
What, if she be fasten'd to this fool lord,
Dare I bid her abide by her word?   560
Should I love her so well if she
Had given her word to a thing so low?
Shall I love her as well if she
Can break her word were it even for me?
I trust that it is not so.[5]   565

                        3
Catch not my breath, O clamorous heart,
Let not my tongue be a thrall to my eye,
For I must tell her before we part,
I must tell her, or die.

                        XVII

Go not, happy day,   570
    From the shining fields,
Go not, happy day,
    Till the maiden yields.
Rosy is the West,
    Rosy is the South,   575
Roses are her cheeks,
    And a rose her mouth.
When the happy Yes
    Falters from her lips,
Pass and blush the news   580
    Over glowing ships;
Over blowing seas,
    Over seas at rest,
Pass the happy new,
    Blush it thro' the West;   585
Till the red man dance
    By his red cedar-tree,
And the red man's babe
    Leap, beyond the sea.
Blush from West to East,   590
    Blush from East to West,
Till the West is East,
    Blush it thro' the West.
Rosy is the West,
    Rosy is the South,   595

5. Of this stanza, Tennyson told Knowles: "You see he is the most conscientious fellow—a perfect gentleman though semi-insane: he would not have been so, had he met with happiness."

Roses are her cheeks,
    And a rose her mouth.

XVIII[6]

1

I have led her home, my love, my only friend.
There is none like her, none.
And never yet so warmly ran my blood   600
And sweetly, on and on
Calming itself to the long-wish'd-for end,
Full to the banks, close on the promised good.

2

None like her, none.
Just now the dry-tounged laurel's pattering talk   605
Seem'd her light foot along the garden walk,
And shook my heart to think she comes once more.
But even then I heard her close the door;
The gates of heaven are closed, and she is gone.

3

There is none like her, none,   610
Nor will be when our summers have deceased.
O, art thou[7] sighing for Lebanon
In the long breeze that streams to thy delicious East,
Sighing for Lebanon,[8]
Dark cedar, tho' thy limbs have here increased,   615
Upon a pastoral slope as fair,
And looking to the South and fed
With honey'd rain and delicate air,
And haunted by the starry head
Of her whose gentle will has changed my fate,   620
And made my life a perfumed altar-flame;
And over whom thy darkness must have spread
With such delight as theirs of old, thy great
Forefathers of the thornless garden, there
Shadowing the snow-limb'd Even from whom she came?[9]   625

4

Here will I lie, while these long branches sway,
And you fair stars that crown a happy day
Go in and out as if at merry play,
Who am no more so all forlorn
As when it seem'd far better to be born   630
To labor and the mattock-harden'd hand

---

6. This whole section is an Epithalamion, perhaps the most successful effort of the kind since Spenser, from whom there are several echoes.
7. The cedar of Lebanon tree in Maud's garden. "Happy. The sigh in the cedar branches seems to chime in with his own yearning" (Tennyson).
8. Ricks cites Psalm 104:16: "The trees of the Lord are full of sap; the cedars of Lebanon, which he hath planted."
9. "Snow in contrast with the dark black cedars" (Tennyson to Knowles).

Than nursed at ease and brought to understand
A sad astrology,[1] the boundless plan
That makes you tyrants in your iron skies,
Innumerable, pitiless, passionless eyes,   635
Cold fires, yet with power to burn and brand
His nothingness into man.

                                   5
But now shine on, and what care I,
Who in this stormy gulf have found a pearl
The countercharm of space and hollow sky,   640
And do accept my madness, and would die
To save from some slight shame one simple girl? —

                                   6
Would die, for sullen-seeming Death may give
More life to Love than is or ever was
In our low world, where yet 't is sweet to live.   645
Let no one ask me how it came to pass;
It seems that I am happy, that to me
A livelier emerald twinkles in the grass,
A purer sapphire melts into the sea.

                                   7
Not die, but live a life of truest breath,[2]   650
And teach true life to fight with mortal wrongs.
O, why should Love, like men in drinking-songs,
Spice his fair banquet with the dust of death?
Make answer, Maud my bliss,
Maud made my Maud by that long loving kiss,   655
Life of my life, wilt thou not answer this?
"The dusky strand of Death inwoven here
With dear Love's tie, makes Love himself more dear."

                                   8
Is that enchanted moan only the swell
Of the long waves that roll in yonder bay?   660
And hark the clock within, the silver knell
Of twelve sweet hours that past in bridal white,
And died to live, long as my pulses play;
But now by this my love has closed her sight
And given false death[3] her hand, and stolen away   665
To dreamful wastes where footless fancies dwell
Among the fragments of the golden day.
May nothing there her maiden grace affright!
Dear heart, I feel with thee the drowsy spell.

1. "The *sad astrology* is modern astronomy, for of old astrology was thought to sympathise with and rule
   man's fate. The stars are 'cold fires,' for 'tho they emit light of the highest intensity, no perceptible
   warmth reaches us. His newer astrology describes them [line 677] as 'soft splendours'" (Tennyson).
2. "This is the central idea—the holy power of Love" (Tennyson). See "Vastness," lines 23–24: "Love for
   the maiden, crown'd with marriage, no regrets for aught that has been, / Household happiness, gracious
   children, debtless competence, golden mean."
3. Sleep.

My bride to be, my evermore delight,   670
My own heart's heart, my ownest own, farewell;
It is but for a little space I go.
And ye⁴ meanwhile far over moor and fell
Beat to the noiseless music of the night!
Has our whole earth gone nearer to the glow   675
Of your soft splendors that you look so bright?
I have climb'd nearer out of lonely hell.
Beat, happy stars, timing with things below,
Beat with my heart more blest than heart can tell,
Blest, but for some dark undercurrent woe   680
That seems to draw—but it shall not be so;
Let all be well, be well.⁵

XIX

1

Her brother is coming back to-night,
Breaking up my dream of delight.

2

My dream? do I dream of bliss?   685
I have walk'd a awake with Truth.
O, when did a morning shine
So rich in atonement as this
For my dark-dawning youth,
Darken'd watching a mother decline   690
And that dead man⁶ at her heart and mine;
For who was left to watch her but I?
Yet so did I let my freshness die.

3

I trust that I did not talk
To gentle Maud in our walk—   695
For often in lonely wanderings
I have cursed him even to lifeless things—
But I trust that I did not talk,
Not touch on her father's sin.
I am sure I did but speak   700
Of my mother's faded cheek
When it slowly grew so thin
That I felt she was slowly dying
Vext with lawyers and harrass'd with debt;
For how often I caught her with eyes all wet,   705
Shaking her head at her son and sighing
A world of trouble within!

4. The stars.
5. Compare *Hamlet* III, iii, line 72: The word "ominously echoes Claudius' 'all may be well' before praying to be forgiven for 'a brother's murder'" (Turner's *Tennyson*, p. 139).
6. The speaker's father.

47

And Maud too, Maud was moved
To speak of the mother she loved
As one scarce less forlorn,   710
Dying abroad and it seems apart
From him who had ceased to share her heart,
And ever mourning over the feud,
The household Fury sprinkled with blood
By which our houses are torn.   715
How strange was what she said,
When only Maud and the brother
Hung over her dying bed—
That Maud's dark father and mine
Had bound us one to the other,   720
Betrothed us over their wine,
On the day when Maud was born;
Seal'd her mine from her first sweet breath!
Mine, mine by a right, from birth till death!
Mine, mine—our fathers have sworn!   725

5

But the true blood spilt had in it a heat
To dissolve the precious seal on a bond,
That, if left uncancell'd, had been so sweet;
And none of us thought of a something beyond,
A desire that awoke in the heart of the child,   730
As it were a duty done to the tomb,
To be friends for her sake, to be reconciled;
And I was cursing them and my doom,
And letting a dangerous thought run wild
While often abroad in the fragrant gloom   735
Of foreign churches—I see her there,
Bright English lily, breathing a prayer
To be friends, to be reconciled!

6

But then what a flint is he!
Abroad, at Florence, at Rome,   740
I find whenever she touch'd on me
This brother had laugh'd her down,
And at last, when each came home,
He had darken'd into a frown,
Chid her, and forbid her to speak   745
To me, her friend of the years before;
And this was what had redden'd her cheek
When I bow'd to her on the moor.

7

Yet Maud, altho' not blind
To the faults of his heart and mind,   750

7. This stanza did not appear in the first edition of 1855. As noted earlier, this subsection clarifies the pledge
of marriage, about which the poem's first readers were justifiably confused.

I see she cannot but love him,
And says he is rough but kind,
And wishes me to approve him,
And tells me, when she lay
Sick once, with a fear of worse,   755
That he left his wine and horses and play,
Sat with her, read to her, night and day,
And tended her like a nurse.

8

Kind? but the death-bed desire
Spurn'd by this heir of the liar—   760
Rough but kind? yet I know
He has plotted against me in this,
That he plots sgainst me still.
Kind to Maud? that were not amiss.
Well, rough but kind; why, let it be so,   765
For shall not Maud have her will?

9

For, Maud, so tender and true,
As long as my life endures
I feel I shall owe you a debt
That I never can hope to pay;   770
And if ever I should forget
That I owe this debt to you
And for your sweet sake to yours,
O, then, what then shall I say?—
If ever I *should* forget,   775
May God make me more wretched
Than ever I have been yet!

10

So now I have sworn to bury
All this dead body of hate,
I feel so free and so clear   780
By the loss of that dead weight,
That I should grow light-hearted, I fear,
Fantastically merry,
But that her brother comes, like a blight
On my fresh hope, to the Hall to-night.   785

XX

1

Strange, that I felt so gay,
Strange, that I tried to-day
To beguile her melancholy;
The Sultan, as we name him—
She did not wish to blame him—   790
But he vext her and perplext her
With his wordly talk and folly.

Was it gentle to reprove her
For stealing out of view
From a little lazy lover   795
Who but claims her as his due?
Or for chilling his caresses
By the coldness of her manners,
Nay, the plainness of her dresses?
Now I know her but in two,   800
Nor can pronounce upon it
If one should ask me whether
The habit, hat, and feather,
Or the frock and gipsy bonnet
Be the neater and completer;   805
For nothing can be sweeter
Than maiden Maud in either.[8]

                                      2
But to-morrow, if we live,
Our ponderous squire will give
A grand political dinner   810
To half the squirelings near;
And Maud will wear her jewels,
And the bird of prey will hover,
And the titmouse hope to win her
With his chirrup at her ear.   815

                                      3
A grand political dinner
To the men of many acres
A gathering of the Tory,
A dinner and then a dance
For the maids and marriage-makers,   820
And every eye but mine will glance
At Maud in all her glory.

                                      4
For I am not invited,
But, with the Sultan's pardon,
I am all as well delighted,   825
For I know her own rose-garden,
And mean to linger in it
Till the dancing will be over;
And then, O, then, come out to me
For a minute, but for a minute,   830
Come out to your own true lover,[9]
That your true lover may see
Your glory also, and render

8. Clearly in his manic mood, the speaker is as clinically unbalanced here as he is in his paranoic depressed
   states. Tennyson seems to be playing on Herrick, especially "Upon Julia's Clothes" and "Delight in Disorder," lines 1–4: "A sweet disorder in the dress / Kindles in clothes a wantoness. / A lawn about the shoulders thrown / Into a fine distraction," a cavalier art a bit more in control of its giddiness than is the speaker.
9. Of lines 832–36, Tennyson told Knowles: "The verse should be read here as if it were prose—Nobody
   can read it naturally enough!"

All homage to his own darling,
Queen Maud in all her splendor.   835

XXI

Rivulet crossing my ground,
And bringing me down from the Hall
This garden-rose that I found,
Forgetful of Maud and me,
And lost in trouble and moving round   840
Here at the head of a tinkling fall,
And trying to pass to the sea;
O rivulet, born at the Hall,
My Maud has sent it by thee—
If I read her sweet will right—   845
On a blushing mission to me,
Saying in odor and color, "Ah, be
Among the roses to-night."

XXII[1]

1

Come into the garden, Maud,
    For the black bat, night, has flown,   850
Come into the garden, Maud,
    I am here at the gate alone;
And the woodbine spices are wafted abroad,
    And the musk of the rose is blown.

2

For a breeze of morning moves,   855
    And the planet of Love is on high,
Beginning to faint in the light that she loves
    On a bed of daffodil sky,
To faint in the light of the sun she loves,
    To faint in his light, and to die.   860

3

All night have the roses heard
    The flute, violin, bassoon;
All night has the casement jessamine stirr'd
    To the dancers dancing in tune;
Till a silence fell with the waking bird,   865
    And a hush with the setting moon.

4

I said to the lily, "There is but one,
    With whom she has heart to be gay.
When will the dancers leave her alone?
    She is weary of dance and play."   870

1. In rhythm and stanza form, similarities to Dryden's songs have long been noted. Ricks observes that J.
H. Mangles recorded in 1871 Tennyson's saying that "'Come into the garden, Maud' had, & was intended to have a taint of madness."

Now half to the setting moon are gone,
    And half to the rising day;
Low on the sand and loud on the stone
The last wheel echoes away.

5

I said to the rose, "The brief night goes   875
    In babble and revel and wine.
O young lord-lover, what sighs are those,
    For one that will never be thine?[2]
But mine, but mine," so I sware to the rose,
    "For ever and ever, mine."[3]   880

6

And the soul of the rose went into my blood,
    As the music clash'd in the hall;
And long by the garden lake I stood,
    For I heard your rivulet fall
From the lake to the meadow and on to the wood,   885
    Our wood, that is dearer than all;

7

From the meadow your walks have left so sweet
    That whenever a March-wind sighs
He sets the jewel-print of your feet
    In violets blue as your eyes,   890
To the woody hollows in which we meet
    And the valleys of Paradise.

8

The slender acacia would not shake
    One long milk-bloom on the tree;
The white lake-blossom fell into the lake   895
    As the pimpernel dozed on the lea;
But the rose was all night for your sake,
    Knowing your promise to me;
The lilies and roses were all awake,
    They sigh'd for the dawn and thee.   900

9

Queen rose of the rosebud garden of girls,
    Come hither, the dances are done,
In gloss of satin and glimmer of pearls,
    Queen lily and rose in one;
Shine out, little head, sunning over with curls,   905
    To the flowers, and be their sun.

---

2. "No reproach for the young lover—now that he feels successful" (Tennyson to Knowles).
3. Compare Robert Browning's "Porphyria's Lover," lines 36–38: "That moment she was mine, mine, fair, / Perfectly pure and good." Published 1836 and then appropriately titled *Madhouse Cells*; the speaker quite literally goes over the edge into insanity at this moment and strangles her with her own hair. In his precarious manic mode, Tennyson's speaker may, as well, be the most dangerous.

10

There has fallen a splendid tear
    From the passion-flower at the gate.
She is coming, my dove, my dear;
    She is coming, my life, my fate.   910
The red rose cries, "She is near, she is near;"
    And the white rose weeps, "She is late;"
The larkspur listens, "I hear, I hear;"
    And the lily whispers, "I wait."⁴

11

She is coming, my own, my sweet;   915
    Were it ever so airy a tread,
My heart would hear her and beat,
    Were it earth in an earthy bed;
My dust would hear her and beat,
    Had I lain for a century dead,   920
Would start and tremble under her feet,
    And blossom in purple and red.

Part 2

I

1

"The fault was mine, the fault was mine"—
Why am I sitting here⁵ so stunn'd and still,
Plucking the harmless wild-flower on the hill?—
It is this guilty hand!—
And there rises ever a passionate cry   5
From underneath in the darkening land—
What is it, that has been done?
O dawn of Eden bright over earth and sky,
The fires of hell brake out of thy rising sun,
The fires of hell and of hate;   10
For she, sweet soul, had hardly spoken a word,
When her brother ran in his rage to the gate,
He came with the babe-faced lord,
Heap'd on her terms of disgrace;
And while she wept, and I strove to be cool,   15
He fiercely gave me the lie,
Till I with as fierce an anger spoke,
And he struck me, madman, over the face,
Struck me before the languid fool,
Who was gaping and grinning by;   20
Struck for himself an evil stroke,
Wrought for his house an irredeemable woe.
For front to front in an hour we stood,

4. In his chapter "Of the Pathetic Fallacy" (*Modern Painters* Part IV, ch. 12) Ruskin quotes this stanza as an "exquisite" example of how the "fallacy" can be properly, i.e., consciously, used to project a deranged sensibility.
5. The precise time and place are not clear. The landscape and Tennyson's note to the section, "The Phantom (after the duel with Maud's brother)," suggest that the speaker is still in England and that only a short time has elapsed since the duel. In Part 2, section II, lines 49ff., he has crossed the Channel into Brittany.

And a million horrible bellowing echoes broke
From the red-ribb'd hollow the wood,   25
And thunder'd up into heaven the Christless code[6]
That must have life for a blow.
Ever and ever afresh they seem'd to grow.
Was it he lay there with a fading eye?
"The fault was mine," he whisper'd, "fly!"   30
Then glided out of the joyous wood
The ghastly Wraith[7] of one that I know,
And there rang on a sudden a passionate cry,
A cry for a brother's blood;
It will ring in my heart and my ears, till I die, till I die.   35

2[8]

Is it gone? my pulses beat—
What was it? a lying trick of the brain?
Yet I thought I saw her stand,
A shadow there at my feet,
High over the shadowy land.   40
It is gone; and the heavens fall in a gentle rain,
When they should burst and drown with deluging storms
The feeble vassals of wine and anger and lust,
The little hearts that know not how to forgive.
Arise, my God, and strike, for we hold Thee just,   45
Strike dead the whole weak race of venomous worms,
That sting each other here in the dust;
We are not worthy to live.

II

1

See what a lovely shell,[9]
Small and pure as a pearl,   50
Lying close to my foot,
Frail, but a work divine,
Made so fairily well
With delicate spire and whorl,
How exquisitely minute,   55
A miracle of design!

2

What is it? a learned man
Could give it a clumsy name.

6. The code of honor. Although there were strict laws against it, dueling was primarily engaged in by the
   aristocracy. By mid-century, however, it had become an anachronism.
7. Maud. A "wraith" is an apparition in a person's exact likeness that portends his or her imminent death. Maud
   soon dies, offstage. Throughout Part 2 we are receiving the distorted impressions of a speaker who is at first
   unbalanced, then quite literally mad. Sequence in time and unity of place are appropriately blurred.
8. Of this section Tennyson told Knowles: "It all has to be read like passionate prose."
9. "In Brittany. The shell undestroyed amid the storm perhaps symbolises to him his own first and highest
   nature preserved amid the storms of passion" (Tennyson). The lyric had been written in the 1830s. Turner
   believes these lines were likely provoked by "Lyell's remark (ii, 281): 'It sometimes appears extraordinary
   when we observe the violence of the breakers on our coast that many tender and fragile shells should in-
   habit the sea in the immediate vicinity of this turmoil'" (Tennyson, p. 134, also cited by Ricks).

Let him name it who can,
The beauty would be the same.   60

                                   3

The tiny cell is forlorn,
Void of the little living will
That made it stir on the shore.
Did he stand at the diamond door
Of his house in a rainbow frill?   65
Did he push, when he was uncurl'd,
A golden foot or a fairy horn
Thro' his water-world?

                                   4

Slight, to be crush'd with a tap
Of my finger-nail on the sand,   70
Small, but a work divine,
Frail, but of force to withstand,
Year upon year, the shock
Of cataract seas that snap
The three-decker's oaken spine   75
Athwart the ledges of rock,
Here on the Breton strand!

                                   5

Breton, not Briton; here
Like a shipwreck'd man on a coast
Of ancient fable and fear—   80
Plagued with a flitting to and fro,
A disease, a hard mechanic ghost
That never came from on high
Nor ever arose from below,
But only moves with the moving eye,   85
Flying along the land and the main—
Why should it look like Maud?
Am I to be overawed
By what I cannot but know
Is a juggle born of the brain?   90

                                   6

Back from the Breton coast,
Sick of a nameless fear,
Back to the dark sea-line
Looking, thinking of all I have lost;
An old song vexes my ear,   95
But that of Lamech[1] is mine.

                                   7

For years, a measureless ill,
For years, for ever, to part—

_____

1. "'I have slain a man to my wounding, and a young man to my hurt' *Genesis*, iv 23" (Tennyson).

But she, she would love me still;
And as long, O God, as she   100
Have a grain of love for me,
So long, no doubt, no doubt,
Shall I nurse in my dark heart,
However weary, a spark of will
Not to be trampled out.   105

                              8

Strange, that the mind, when fraught
With a passion so intense
One would think that it well
Might drown all life in the eye,—
That it should, by being so overwrought,   110
Suddenly strike on a sharper sense
For a shell, or a flower, little things
Which else would have been past by!
And now I remember, I,
When he lay dying there,   115
I noticed one of his many rings—
For he had many, poor worm—and thought,
It is his mother's hair.[2]

                              9

Who knows if he be dead?
Whether I need have fled?   120
Am I guilty of blood?
However this may be,
Comfort her, comfort her, all things good,
While I am over the sea!
Let me and my passionate love go by,   125
But speak to her all things holy and high,
Whatever happen to me!
Me and my harmful love go by;
But come to her waking, find her asleep,
Powers of the height, Powers of the deep,   130
And comfort her tho' I die!

                             III[3]

Courage, poor heart of stone!
I will not ask thee why
Thou canst not understand
That thou art left for ever alone;   135
Courage, poor stupid heart of stone!—
Or if I ask thee why,
Care not thou to reply:

---

2. Set in the ring under glass.
3. These nine lines were added for the edition of 1856 and tell us what we otherwise could only assume—
   that he has learned of Maud's death. "He felt himself going mad" (Tennyson). "Here he comes back to
   England and London" (Tennyson to Knowles).

She is but dead, and the time is at hand
When thou shalt more than die.[4]   140

IV

1

O that't were possible[5]
After long grief and pain
To find the arms of my true love
Round me once again!

2

When I was wont to meet her   145
In the silent woody places
By the home that gave me birth,
We stood tranced in long embraces
Mixt with kisses sweeter, sweeter
Than anything on earth.   150

3

A shadow flits before me,
Not thou, but like to thee.
Ah, Christ, that it were possible
For one short hour to see
The souls we loved, that they might tell us   155
What and where they be!

4

It leads me forth at evening,
It lightly winds and steals
In a cold white robe before me,
When all my spirit reels   160
At the shouts, the leagues of lights,
And the roaring of the wheels.

5

Half the night I waste in sighs,
Half in dreams I sorrow after
The delight of early skies;   165
In a wakeful doze I sorrow
For the hand, the lips, the eyes,
For the meeting of the morrow,
The delight of happy laughter,
The delight of low replies.   170

---

4. This phrase grimly and accurately anticipates the living hell of his forthcoming incarceration in a mad-
   house.
5. As noted in the headnote, the germ of *Maud*. "'O that 'twere possible' appeared first in the *Tribute*, 1837.
   Sir John Simeon years after begged me to weave a story round this poem, and so *Maud* came into being"
   (Tennyson). "The opening resembles the famous early sixteenth-century lyric: 'Westron winde, when wilt
   thou blow, / The smalle raine downe can raine? / Christ if my love were in my arms, / And I in my bed
   againe'" (Ricks).

6

'T is a morning pure and sweet,
And a dewy splendor falls
On the little flower that clings
To the turrets and the walls;
'T is a morning pure and sweet,   175
And the light and shadow fleet.
She is walking in the meadow,
And the woodland echo rings;
In a moment we shall meet.
She is singing in the meadow,   180
And the rivulet at her feet
Ripples on in light and shadow
To the ballad that she sings.

7

Do I hear her sing as of old,
My bird with the shining head,
My own dove with the tender eye?   185
But there rings on a sudden a passionate cry,[6]
There is some one dying or dead,
And a sullen thunder is roll'd;
For a tumult shakes the city,   190
And I wake, my dream is fled.
In the shuddering dawn, behold,
Without knowledge, without pity,
By the curtains of my bed
That abiding phantom cold!   195

8

Get thee hence, nor come again,
Mix not memory with doubt,
Pass, thou deathlike type of pain,
Pass and cease to move about!
'T is the blot upon the brain[7]   200
That *will* show itself without.

9

Then I rise, the eave-drops fall,
And the yellow vapors choke
The great city sounding wide;
The day comes, a dull red ball   205
Wrapt in drifts of lurid smoke
On the misty river-tide.

6. Of lines 187–90: "Perhaps the sound of a cab in the street suggests this cry of recollection" (Tennyson to Knowles).
7. Compare "If any vision should reveal / Thy likeness, I might count in vain / As but the canker of the brain," *IM* 92, 1 (noted by Ricks). That attention to allusion is apt, but one must bear in mind that "blot upon the brain" for Tennyson speaking in his elegy would not have had the implication it does here for his protagonist, where the phrase seems designed to alert the reader to the inevitability of revealed madness, "that *will* show itself without."

10

Thro' the hubbub of the market
I steal, a wasted frame;
It crosses here, it crosses there,   210
Thro' all that crowd confused and loud,
The shadow still the same;
And on my heavy eyelids
My anguish hangs like shame.

11

Alas for her that meet me,   215
That heard me softly call,
Came glimmering thro' the laurels
At the quiet evenfall,
In the garden by the turrets
Of the old manorial hall!   220

12

Would the happy spirit descend
From the realms of light and song,
In the chamber or the street,
As she looks among the blest,
Should I fear to greet my friend   225
Or to say "Forgive the wrong,"
Or to ask her, "Take me, sweet,
To the regions of thy rest"?

13

But the broad light glares and beats,
And the shadow flits and fleets   230
And will not let me be;
And I loathe the squares and streets,
And the faces that one meets,
Hearts with no love for me.
Always I long to creep   235
Into some still cavern deep,
There to weep, and weep, and weep
My whole soul out to thee.

V⁸

1

Dead, long dead,
Long dead!   240
And my heart is a handful of dust,
And the wheels go over my head,⁹

8. In section V the speaker has been consigned to an insane asylum and records in fragments some of his experience there.
9. Compare Part 1, section XXII, 11, where, in a rather different context, he also imagined he was buried. Lines 239–342 were directly the result of Tennyson's reading Edgar Allan Poe's tale "The Premature Burial," in which the narrator imagines himself buried alive. With Poe's story fresh in his thoughts, Tennyson said: "The whole of the stanzas where he is mad in Bedlam, from 'Dead, long dead' to 'Deeper, ever so little deeper,' were written in twenty minutes, and some mad doctor wrote to me that nothing since Shakespeare has been so good for madness as this" (Shatto's *Tennyson's "Maud,"* p. 209). See *Memoir* I, 398.

And my bones are shaken with pain,
For into a shallow grave they are thrust,
Only a yard beneath the street,   245
And the hoofs of the horses beat, beat,
The hoofs of the horses beat,
Beat into my scalp and my brain,
With never an end to the stream of passing feet,
Driving, hurrying, marrying, burying,   250
Clamor and rumble, and ringing and clatter;
And here beneath it is all as bad,
For I thought the dead had peace, but it is not so.
To have no peace in the grave, is that not sad?
But up and down and to and fro,   255
Ever about me the dead men go;
And then to hear a dead man chatter
Is enough to drive one mad.

                                    2
Wretchedest age, since Time began,
They cannot even bury a man;   260
And tho' we paid our tithes in the days that are gone,
Not a bell rung, not a prayer was read.
It is that which makes us loud in the world of the dead;
There is none that does his work, not one.
A touch of their office might have sufficed,   265
But the churchmen fain would kill their church,
As the churches have kill'd their Christ.

                                    3
See, there is one of us[1] sobbing,
No limit to his distress;
And another, a lord of all things, praying   270
To his own great self, as I guess;
And another, a stateman there, betraying
His party-secret, fool, to the press;
And yonder a vile physician, blabbing
The case of his patient—all for what?   275
To tickle the maggot born in an empty head,
And wheedle a world that loves him not,
For it is but a world of the dead.

                                    4
Nothing but idiot gabble!
For the prophecy given of old[2]   280
And then not understood,
Has come to pass as foretold;
Not let any man think for the public good,
But babble, merely for babble.
For I never whisper'd a private affair   285

---

1. Other corpses, that is, inmates of the madhouse.
2. Luke 12:3: "Therefore whatsover ye have spoken in darkness shall be heard in the light; and that which
   ye have spoken in the ear in closets shall be proclaimed upon the housetops."

Within the hearing of cat or mouse,
No, not to myself in the closet alone,
But I heard it shouted at once from the top of the house;
Everything came to be known.
Who told *him*[3] we were there?   290

5

Not that gray old wolf,[4] for he came not back
From the wilderness, full of wolves, where he used to lie;
He has gather'd the bones for his o'ergrown whelp to crack—
Crack them now for yourself, and howl, and die.[5]

6

Prophet, curse me the blabbing lip,   295
And curse me the British vermin, the rat;
I know not whether he came in the Hanover[6] ship,
But I know that he lies and listens mute
In an ancient mansion's crannies and holes.
Arsenic, arsenic, sure, would do it,   300
Except that now we poison our babes, poor souls!
It is all used up for that.

7

Tell him now: she is standing here at my head;
Not beautiful now, not even kind;
He may take her now; for she never speaks her mind,   305
But is ever the one thing silent here.
She is not *of* us, as I divine;
She comes from another stiller world of the dead,
Stiller, not fairer than mine.

8

But I know where a garden grows,   310
Fairer than aught in the world beside,
All made up of the lily and rose
That blow by night, when the season is good,
To the sound of dancing music and flutes:
It is only flowers, they had no fruits,   315
And I almost fear they are not roses, but blood;
For the keeper was one, so full of pride,
He linkt a dead man[7] there to a spectral bride;
For he, if had not been a Sultan of brutes,
Would he have that hole in his side?   320

9

But what will the old man say?
He laid a cruel snare in a pit

3. Maud's brother.
4. Maud's father.
5. "For his son is, he thinks, dead" (Tennyson).
6. In 1714 the House of Hanover succeeded to the British throne, and the Jacobites claimed they brought
   with them the so-called Norwegian rat.
7. The speaker himself. "The keeper": Maud's brother.

To catch a friend of mine one stormy day;
Yet now I could even weep to think of it;
For what will the old man say 325
When he comes to the second corpse[8] in the pit?

10

Friend, to be struck by the public foe,
Then to strike him and lay him low,
That were a public merit, far,
Whatever the Quaker holds, from sin; 330
But the red life split for a private blow—
I swear to you, lawful and lawless war
Are scarcely even akin.[9]

11

O me, why have they not buried me deep enough?
Is it kind to have made me a grave so rough, 335
Me, that was never a quiet sleeper?
Maybe still I am but half-dead;
Then I cannot be wholly dumb.
I will cry to the steps above my head
And somebody, surely, some kind heart will come 340
To bury me, bury me
Deeper, ever so little deeper.

Part 3

1

My life has crept so long[1] on a broken wing
Thro' cells of madness, haunts of horror and fear,
That I come to be grateful at last for a little thing.
My mood is changed, for it fell at a time of year
When the face of night is fair on the dewy downs, 5
And the shining daffodil dies,[2] and the Charioteer
And starry Gemini[3] hang like glorious crowns
Over Orion's grave low down in the west,
That like a silent lighting under the stars
She seem'd to divide in a dream from a band of the blest, 10
And spoke of a hope for the world in the coming wars—
"And in that hope, dear soul, let trouble have rest,
Knowing I tarry for thee," and pointed to Mars
As he glow'd like a ruddy shield on the Lion's[4] breast.

---

8. Maud's brother. The first corpse would be the speaker's father, whom he now assumes Maud's father murdered.
9. He feels he is getting a little too sensible in this remark" (Tennyson to Knowles).
1. The period of insanity having passed, the speaker is left "sane but shattered." Tennyson added that this part of the poem was "written when the cannon was heard booming from the battle-ships in the Solent before the Crimean War" (*Memoir* I, 405).
2. Late spring.
3. The twin stars Castor and Pollux. "The Charioteer" is the constellation Auriga midway between the North Star and the constellation of Orion.
4. Mars (the god of war) is now in the constellation of the Lion (the symbol of Britain).
   Of interest here is Hallam Tennyson's observation: "On the 16th of March 1854 my father was looking through his (Farrinford) study window at the planet Mars, 'as he glow'd like a ruddy shield on the Lion's heart,' and so determined to name his second son, who was born on that day, Lionel."

2

And it was but a dream, yet it yielded a dear delight   15
To have look'd tho' but in a dream, upon eyes so fair,
That had been in a weary world my one thing bright;
And it was but a dream, yet it lighten'd my despair
When I thought that a war would arise in defence of the right,
That an iron tyranny[5] now should bend or cease,   20
The glory of manhood stand on his ancient height,
Nor Britain's one sole God be the millionaire.
No more shall commerce be all in all, and Peace
Pipe on her pastoral hillock a languid note.
And watch her harvest ripen, her herd increase,   25
Nor the cannon-bullet rust on a slothful shore,
And the cobweb woven across the cannon's throat
Shall shake its threaded tears in the wind no more.

3

And as months ran on and rumor of battle grew,
"It is time, it is time, O passionate heart," said I,—   30
For I cleaved to a cause that I felt to be pure and true,—
"It is time, O passionate heart and morbid eye,
That old hysterical mock-disease should die."
And I stood on giant deck[6] and mixt my breath
With a loyal people shouting a battlecry,   35
Till I saw the dreary phantom[7] arise and fly
Far into the North, and battle, and seas of death.

4

Let it go or stay, so I wake to the higher aims
Of a land that has lost for a little her lust of gold,
And love of a peace that was full of wrongs and shames,   40
Horrible, hateful, monstrous, not to be told;
And hail once more to the banner of battle unroll'd!
Tho' many a light shall darken, and many shall weep
For those that are crush'd in the clash of jarring claims
Yet God's just wrath shall be wreak'd on a giant liar,[8]   45
And many a darkness into the light shall leap,
And shine in the sudden making of splendid names,
And noble thought be freer under the sun,
And the heart of a people beat with one desire;
For the peace, that I deem'd no peace, is over and done,   50
And now by the side of the Black[9] and the Baltic deep,

5. That of Czar Nicholas I of Russia.
6. Sailing off to the Crimea.
7. Throughout Part 2 he has been haunted by Maud's phantom, and now he finds the spirit exorcised as
   he seeks to lose himself in a cause larger than himself. Maud's spirit has, or as the speaker imagines,
   assumed dual identities: she is both the "ghastly Wraith" (Part 2, line 32) and "hard mechanic ghost"
   (line 82) or "from a band of the blest" (Part 3, line 10). As the former images imply, she there inevitably
   recalls to him his slaying of her brother, a bestial act, "the Christless code," engaged out of "fierce"
   rage. Compare *IM* 118: "Arise and fly / . . . Move upward, working out the beast, / And let the ape and
   tiger die." Also see Part 1, X, 6: "And ah for a man to arise in me, / That the man I am may cease to
   be."
8. Nicholas I.
9. The Black Sea.

And deathful-grinning mouths of the fortress, flames
The blood-red blossom of war with a heart of fire.

5

Let it flame or fade, and the war roll down like a wind,
We have proved we have hearts in a cause, we are noble still,   55
And myself have awaked, as it seems, to the better mind.
It is better to fight for the good than to rail at the ill;
I have felt with my native land, I am one with my kind,
I embrace the purpose of God, and the doom assign'd.[1]

1855 (1856); (1865)

In the Valley of Cauteretz[1]

All along the valley, stream that flashest white,
Deepening thy voice with the deepening of the night,
All along the valley, where thy waters flow,
I walk'd with one I loved two and thirty years ago.
All along the valley, while I walk'd to-day,   5
The two and thirty[2] years were a mist that rolls away;
For all along the valley, down thy rocky bed,
Thy living voice to me was as the voice of the dead,
And all along the valley, by rock and cave and tree,
The voice of the dead was a living voice to me.   10

1861; 1864

Milton

(ALCAICS)[1]

O mighty-mouth'd inventor of harmonies,
O skill'd to sing of Time or Eternity,
    God-gifted organ-voice of England,[2]
        Milton, a name to resound for ages;
Whose Titan angels, Gabriel, Abdiel,[3]   5

1. Nineteenth-century critics generally failed to distinguish between poet and speaker, and hence Part 3 was all too easily interpreted to show that Tennyson was a jingoist. Lucid, but nonetheless "shattered," the speaker is hardly one through whom Tennyson would elect to express his own views.
1. Tennyson revisited the Pyrenees in the summer of 1861, and his poem recalls his first visit there with Hallam in 1830. See the notes to "Œnone."
2. Actually one and thirty.
1. The Alcaic stanza, named for its reputed inventor, the Greek poet Alcaeus (c. 600 B.C.), is composed of two eleven-syllable lines followed by one of nine and one of ten syllables. As distinguished from English qualitative verse, in which the accent falls on stressed syllables, the classical quantitative verse places the accent on long vowels and short vowels when followed by two consonantal sounds. In commenting on this "experiment," Tennyson took care to distinguish between the Horatian Alcaic and the Greek Alcaic he imitates, which "had a much freer and lighter movement" (Memoir II, 11).
2. Compare Wordsworth's sonnet "London, 1802": "Milton! thou shouldst be living at this hour: / England hath need of thee." And "Thou hadst a voice whose sound was like the sea."
3. Archangels of Paradise Lost, respectively the guardian of Paradise and the one angel among Satan's rebels who remained constant to God.

Starr'd[4] from Jehovah's gorgeous armories,
Tower, as the deep-domed empyrean
Rings to the roar of an angel onset!
Me rather all that bowery loneliness,
The brooks of Eden mazily murmuring,   10
And bloom profuse and cedar arches
Charm, as a wanderer out in ocean,
Where some refulgent sunset of India
Streams o'er a rich ambrosial ocean isle,
And crimson-hued the stately palm-woods   15
Whisper in odorous heights of even.

1863

Enoch Arden[1]

Long lines of the cliff breaking have left a chasm;
And in the chasm are foam and yellow sands;
Beyond, red roofs about a narrow wharf
In cluster; then a moulder'd church; and higher
A long street climbs to one tall-tower'd mill;   5
And high in heaven behind it a gray down
With Danish barrows,[2] and a hazel-wood,
By autumn nutters haunted, flourishes
Green in a cuplike hollow of the down.
Here on this beach a hundred years ago,   10
Three children of three houses, Annie Lee,
The prettiest little damsel in the port,
And Philip Ray, the miller's only son,
And Enoch Arden, a rough sailor's lad
Made orphan by a winter shipwreck, play'd   15
Among the waste and lumber of the shore,
Hard coils of cordage, swarthy fishing-nets,
Anchors of rusty fluke, and boats updrawn;
And built their castles of dissolving sand
To watch them overflow'd, or following up   20

4. "Adorned, compare Pope, *Iliad*, i, 326: 'His Scepter star'd with golden Studs around'" (Ricks).
1. "'Enoch Arden' (like 'Aylmer's Field') is founded on a theme given me by the sculptor Woolner. I believe that this particular story came out of Suffolk, but something like the same story is told in Britanny"
(Tennyson, in *Memoir* II, 7). The tale was certainly influenced by Crabbe's story in verse, "The Parting
Hour" in *Tales* (1812), which Tennyson had been reading in 1859 and 1862. See also Genesis 5:24: "And
Enoch walked with God: and he was not; for God took him," among numerous following biblical allusions. "Enoch Arden" was immensely popular, was soon translated into most European languages, and
established Tennyson as "The Poet of the People."
    Apart from the many who heaped praise upon the poem just after its publication, Walter Bagehot was
almost alone in discerning its central failings: "So much has not often been made of selling fish. The
essence of ornate art is in this manner to accumulate round the typical object, everything which can be
said about it, every associated thought that can be connected with it." And he added, "A dirty sailor who
did *not* go home to his wife is not an agreeable being: a varnish must be put on him to make him shine."
One has only to think of *Maud*, which was by critics generally unappreciated, to be impressed again by
the truisms about the ephemerality of a poet's most popular poem. A reviewer of the volume for *Harper's
Magazine* (October 1864) unknowingly makes the point: "As his poems are the most striking illustration
of the fondness of the literary spirit of the age for the most gorgeous verbiage, so they are the most noble
examples of a luxuriant tendency constantly restrained and tempered by the truest taste."
2. Burial mounds, many of which predate the Danish invasions of the ninth century.

And flying the white breaker, daily left
The little footprint daily wash'd away.

A narrow cave ran in beneath the cliff;
In this the children play'd at keeping house.
Enoch was host one day, Philip the next,   25
While Annie still was mistress; but at times
Enoch would hold possession for a week:
"This is my house and this my little wife."
"Mine too," said Philip; "turn and turn about;"
When, if they quarrell'd, Enoch stronger-made   30
Was master. Then would Philip, his blue eyes
All flooded with the helpless wrath of tears,
Shriek out, "I hate you, Enoch," and at this
The little wife would weep for company,
And pray them not to quarrel for her sake,   35
And say she would be little wife to both.
    But when the dawn of rosy childhood past,
And the new warmth of life's ascending sun
Was felt by either, either fixt his heart
On that one girl; and Enoch spoke his love,   40
But Philip loved in silence; and the girl
Seem'd kinder unto Philip than to him;
But she loved Enoch, tho' she knew it not,
And would if ask'd deny it. Enoch set
A purpose evermore before his eyes,   45
To hoard all savings to the uttermost,
To purchase his own boat, and make a home
For Annie; and so prosper'd that at last
A luckier or a bolder fisherman,
A carefuller in peril, did not breathe   50
For leagues along that breaker-beaten coast
Than Enoch. Likewise had he served a year[3]
On board a merchantman, and made himself
Full sailor; and he thrice had pluck'd a life
From the dread sweep of the down-streaming seas,   55
And all men look'd upon him favorably.
And ere he touch'd his one-and-twentieth May
He purchased his own boat, and made a home
For Annie, neat and nestlike, halfway up
The narrow street that clamber'd toward the mill.   60

    Then, on a golden autumn eventide,
The younger people making holiday,
With bag and sack and basket, great and small,
Went nutting to the hazels. Philip stay'd —
His father lying sick and needing him —   65

---

3. Tennyson's wife had written FitzGerald for seafaring details; and in his response, evidently referring to one specific, he said: "There is no *apprentiship* to fishing: anyone takes anyone who comes handy; i.e. not along the coast, but out to the Dogger Bank, Scotland, Ireland etc. (for cod-fish); anyone *may* go who *can* get a berth." He also took this occasion in 1862 to say, "Ah! Alfred should never have left his old country with its Mablethorpe sea" (*Memoir* I, 515).

An hour behind; but as he climb'd the hill,
Just where the prone edge of the wood began
To feather toward the hollow, saw the pair,
Enoch and Annie, sitting hand-in-hand,
His large gray eyes and weather-beaten face   70
All-kindled by a still and sacred fire,
That burn'd as on an altar. Philip look'd,
And in their eyes and faces read his doom;
Then, as their faces drew together, groan'd,
And slipt aside, and like a wounded life   75
Crept down into the hollows of the wood;
There, while the rest were loud in merrymaking,
Had his dark hour unseen, and rose and past
Bearing a lifelong hunger in his heart.

So these were wed, and merrily rang the bells,   80
And merrily ran the years, seven happy years,
Seven happy years of health and competence,
And mutual love and honorable toil,
With children, first a daughter. In him woke,
With his first babe's first cry, the noble wish   85
To save all earnings to the uttermost,
And give his child a better bringing-up
Than his had been, or hers; a wish renew'd,
When two years after came a boy to be
The rosy idol of her solitudes,   90
While Enoch was abroad on wrathful seas,
Or often journeying landward; for in truth
Enoch's white horse, and Enoch's ocean-spoil
In ocean-smelling osier, and his face,
Rough-redden'd with a thousand winter gales,   95
Not only to the market-cross were known,
But in the leafy lanes behind the down,
Far as the portal-warding lion-whelp
And peacock yew-tree[4] of the lonely Hall,
Whose Friday fare was Enoch's ministering.[5]   100

Then came a change, as all things human change.
Ten miles to northward of the narrow port
Open'd a larger haven. Thither used
Enoch at times to go by land or sea;
And once when there, and clambering on a mast   105
In harbor, by mischance he slipt and fell.
A limb was broken when they lifted him;
And while he lay recovering there, his wife
Bore him another son, a sickly one.
Another hand crept too across his trade   110
Taking her bread and theirs; and on him fell,

4. "Cut in the form of a peacock" (Tennyson).
5. Bagehot, citing lines 91–100, observed: "Everyone knows that in himself Enoch could not have been
charming. People who sell fish about the country (and that is what he did, though Mr. Tennyson won't
speak out, and wraps it up) never are beautiful."

Altho' a grave and staid God-fearing man,
Yet lying thus inactive, doubt and gloom.
He seem'd, as in a nightmare of the night,
To see his children leading evermore   115
Low miserable lives of hand-to-mouth,
And her he loved a beggar. Then he pray'd,
"Save them from this, whatever comes to me."
And while he pray'd, the master of that ship
Enoch had served in, hearing his mischance,   120
Came, for he knew the man and valued him,
Reporting of his vessel China-bound,
And wanting yet a boatswain. Would he go?
There yet were many weeks before she sail'd,
Sail'd from this port. Would Enoch have the place?   125
And Enoch all at once assented to it,
Rejoicing at that answer to his prayer.

So now that shadow of mischance appear'd
No graver than as when some little cloud
Cuts off the fiery highway of the sun,   130
And isles a light[6] in the offing. Yet the wife —
When he was gone — the children — what to do?
Then Enoch lay long-pondering on his plans:
To sell the boat — and yet he loved her well —
How many a rough sea had he weather'd in her!   135
He knew her, as a horseman knows his horse —
And yet to sell her — then with what she brought
Buy goods and stores — set Annie forth in trade
With all that seamen needed or their wives —
So might she keep the house while he was gone.   140
Should he not trade himself out yonder? go
This voyage more than once? yea, twice or thrice —
As oft as needed — last, returning rich,
Become the master of a larger craft,
With fuller profits lead an easier life,   145
Have all his pretty young ones educated,
And pass his days in peace among his own.

Thus Enoch in his heart determined all;
Then moving homeward came on Annie pale,
Nursing the sickly babe, her latest-born.   150
Forward she started, with a happy cry,
And laid the feeble infant in his arms;
Whom Enoch took, and handled all his limbs,
Appraised his weight and fondled fatherlike,
But had no heart to break his purposes   155
To Annie, till the morrow, when he spoke.

6. "This line was made at Brighton, from the islands of light on the sea on a day of sunshine and clouds" (Tennyson).

Then first since Enoch's golden ring had girt
Her finger, Annie fought against his will;
Yet not with brawling opposition she,
But manifold entreaties, many a tear,   160
Many a sad kiss by day, by night, renew'd—
Sure that all evil would come out of it—
Besought him, supplicating, if he cared
For her or his dear children, not to go.
He not for his own self caring, but her,   165
Her and her children, let her plead in vain;
So grieving held his will, and bore it thro'.

For Enoch parted with his old sea-friend,
Bought Annie goods and stores, and set his hand
To fit their little streetward sitting-room   170
With shelf and corner for the goods and stores.
So all day long till Enoch's last at home,
Shaking their pretty cabin, hammer and axe,
Auger and saw, while Annie seem'd to hear
Her own death-scaffold raising, shrill'd and rang,   175
Till this was ended, and his careful hand,—
The space was narrow,—having order'd all
Almost as neat and close as Nature packs
Her blossom or her seedling, paused; and he,
Who needs would work for Annie to the last,   180
Ascending tired, heavily slept till morn.

And Enoch faced this morning of farewell
Brightly and boldly. All his Annie's fears,
Save as his Annie's, were a laughter to him.
Yet Enoch as a brave God-fearing man   185
Bow'd himself down, and in that mystery
Where God-in-man is one with man-in-God,
Pray'd for a blessing on his wife and babes,
Whatever came to him; and then he said:
"Annie, this voyage by the grace of God   190
Will bring fair weather yet to all of us.
Keep a clean hearth and a clear fire for me,
For I'll be back, my girl, before you know it,"
Then lightly rocking baby's cradle, "and he,
This pretty, puny, weakly little one,—   195
Nay—for I love him all the better for it—
God bless him, he shall sit upon my knees
And I will tell him tales of foreign parts,
And make him merry, when I come home again.
Come, Annie, come, cheer up before I go."   200
    Him running on thus hopefully she heard,
And almost hoped herself; but when he turn'd
The current of his talk to graver things
In sailor fashion roughly sermonizing
On providence and trust in heaven, she heard,   205
Heard and not heard him; as the village girl,

Who sets her pitcher underneath the spring,
Musing on him that used to fill it for her,
Hears and not hears, and lets it overflow.

At length she spoke: "O Enoch, you are wise;   210
And yet for all your wisdom well know I
That I shall look upon your face no more."[7]

"Well, then," said Enoch, "I shall look on yours.
Annie, the ship I sail in passes here" —
He named the day; — "get you a seaman's glass,   215
Spy out my face, and laugh at all your fears."

But when the last of those last moments came:
"Annie, my girl, cheer up, be comforted,
Look to the babes, and till I come again
Keep everything shipshape, for I must go.   220
And fear no more for me; or if you fear,
Cast all your cares on God; that anchor holds.
Is He not yonder in those uttermost
Parts of the morning? if I flee to these,
Can I go from Him? and the sea is His,   225
The sea is His; He made it."[8]
                              Enoch rose,
Cast his strong arms about his drooping wife,
And kiss'd his wonder-stricken little ones;
But for the third, the sickly one, who slept
After a night of feverous wakefulness,   230
When Annie would have raised him Enoch said,
"Wake him not, let him sleep; how should the child
Remember this?" and kiss'd him in his cot.
But Annie from her baby's forehead clipt
A tiny curl, and gave it; this he kept   235
Thro' all his future, but now hastily caught
His bundle, waved his hand, and went his way.

She, when the day that Enoch mention'd came,
Borrow'd a glass, but all in vain. Perhaps
She could not fix the glass to suit her eye;   240
Perhaps her eye was dim, hand tremulous;
She saw him not, and while he stood on deck
Waving, the moment and the vessel past.

Even to the last dip of the vanishing sail
She watch'd it, and departed weeping for him;   245
Then, tho' she mourn'd his absence as his grave,
Set her sad will no less to chime with his,

---

7. Acts 20:38: "Sorrowing most of all for the words which he spake, that they should see his face no more. And they accompanied him unto the ship" (noted by Ricks).
8. For lines 222–26, Ricks identifies the following: 1 Peter 5:7: "Casting all your care upon him; for he careth for you"; Hebrews 6:19: "Which hope we have as an anchor of the soul, both sure and steadfast"; Psalm 139:9: "If I take the wings of the morning, and dwell in the uttermost parts of the sea"; and Psalm 95:5: "The sea is his, and he made it."

But throve not in her trade, not being bred
To barter, nor compensating[9] the want
By shrewdness, neither capable of lies,   250
Nor asking overmuch and taking less,
And still foreboding "what would Enoch say?"
For more than once, in days of difficulty
And pressure, had she sold her wares for less
Than what she gave in buying what she sold.   255
She fail'd and sadden'd knowing it; and thus,
Expectant of that news which never came,
Gain'd for her own a scanty sustenance,
And lived a life of silent melancholy.

Now the third child was sickly-born and grew   260
Yet sicklier, tho' the mother cared for it
With all a mother's care, nevertheless,
Whether her business often call'd her from it,
Or thro' the want of what it needed most,
Or means to pay the voice who best could tell   265
What most it needed—howsoe'er it was,
After a lingering—ere she was aware,—
Like a caged bird escaping suddenly,
The little innocent soul flitted away.

In that same week when Annie buried it,   270
Philip's true heart, which hunger'd for her peace,—
Since Enoch left he had not look'd upon her,—
Smote him, as having kept aloof so long,
"Surely," said Philip, "I may see her now,
May be some little comfort;" therefore went,   275
Past thro' the solitary room in front,
Paused for a moment at an inner door,
Then struck it thrice, and, no one opening,
Enter'd, but Annie, seated with her grief,
Fresh from the burial of her little one,   280
Cared not to look on any human face,
But turn'd her own toward the wall and wept.
Then Philip standing up said falteringly,
"Annie, I came to ask a favor of you."

He spoke, the passion in her moan'd reply,   285
"Favor from one so sad and so forlorn
As I am!" half abash'd him; yet unask'd,
His bashfulness and tenderness at war,
He set himself beside her, saying to her:

"I came to speak to you of what he wish'd,   290
Enoch, your husband. I have ever said
You chose the best among us—a strong man;
For where he fixt his heart he set his hand

9. "Apparently the usual pronunciation till the mid-nineteenth century was *compénsating*" (Ricks).

To do the thing he will'd, and bore it thro'.
And wherefore did he go this weary way,   295
And leave you lonely? not to see the world—
For pleasure?—nay, but for the wherewithal
To give his babes a better bringing up
Than his had been, or yours; that was his wish.
And if he come again, vext will he be   300
To find the precious morning hours were lost.
And it would vex him even in his grave,
If he could know his babes were running wild
Like colts about the waste. So, Annie, now—
Have we not known each other all our lives?   305
I do beseech you by the love you bear
Him and his children not to say me nay—
For, if you will, when Enoch comes again
Why then he shall repay me—if you will,
Annie—for I am rich and well-to-do.   310
Now let me put the boy and girl to school;
This is the favor that I came to ask."

    Then Annie with her brows against the wall
Answer'd, "I cannot look you in the face;
I seem so foolish and so broken down.   315
When you came in my sorrow broke me down;
And now I think your kindness breaks me down.
But Enoch lives, that is borne in on me;
He will repay you. Money can be repaid,
Not kindness such as yours."

                          And Philip ask'd,   320
"Then you will let me, Annie?"

                          There she turn'd,
She rose, and fixt her swimming eyes upon him,
And dwelt a moment on his kindly face,
Then calling down a blessing on his head
Caught at his hand, and wrung it passionately,   325
And past into the little garth[1] beyond.
So lifted up in spirit he moved away.

    Then Philip put the boy and girl to school,
And bought them needful books, and every way,
Like one who does his duty by his own,   330
Made himself theirs, and tho' for Annie's sake,
Fearing the lazy gossip of the port,
He oft denied his heart his dearest wish,
And seldom crost her threshold, yet he sent
Gifts by the children, garden-herbs and fruit,   335
The late and early roses from his wall,
Or conies from the down, and now and then,

1. Garden.

With some pretext of fineness in the meal
To save the offence of charitable, flour
From his tall mill that whistled on the waste.   340

    But Philip did not fathom Annie's mind;
Scarce could the woman, when he came upon her,
Out of full heart and boundless gratitude
Light on a broken word to thank him with.
But Philip was her children's all-in-all;   345
From distant corners of the street they ran
To greet his hearty welcome heartily;
Lords of his house and of his mill were they,
Worried his passive ear with petty wrongs
Or pleasures, hung upon him, play'd with him   350
And call'd him Father Philip. Philip gain'd
As Enoch lost, for Enoch seem'd to them
Uncertain as a vision or a dream,
Faint as a figure seen in early dawn
Down at the far end of an avenue,   355
Going we know not where; and so ten years,
Since Enoch left his hearth and native land,
Fled forward, and no news of Enoch came.

    It chanced one evening Annie's children long'd
To go with others nutting to the wood,   360
And Annie would go with them; then they begg'd
For Father Philip, as they call'd him, too.
Him, like the working bee in blossom-dust,
Blanch'd with his mill, they found; and saying to him,
"Come with us, Father Philip," he denied;   365
But when the children pluck'd at him to go,
He laugh'd, and yielded readily to their wish,
For was not Annie with them? and they went.

    But after scaling half the weary down,
Just where the prone edge of the wood began   370
To feather toward the hollow, all her force
Fail'd her; and sighing, "Let me rest," she said.
So Philip rested with her well-content;
While all the younger ones with jubilant cries
Broke from their elders, and tumultuously   375
Down thro' the whitening² hazels made a plunge
To the bottom, and dispersed, and bent or broke
The lithe reluctant boughs to tear away
Their tawny clusters, crying to each other
And calling, here and there, about the wood.   380

    But Philip sitting at her side forgot
Her presence, and remember'd one dark hour
Here in this wood, when like a wounded life

---

2. "When the breeze blows, it turns upward the silvery under-part of the leaf" (Tennyson).

He crept into the shadow. At last he said,
Lifting his honest forehead, "Listen, Annie,   385
How merry they are down yonder in the wood.
Tired, Annie?" for she did not speak a word.
"Tired?" but her face had fallen upon her hands;
At which, as with a kind of anger in him,
"The ship was lost," he said, "the ship was lost!   390
No more of that! why should you kill yourself
And make them orphans quite?" And Annie said,
"I thought not of it; but—I know not why—
Their voices make me feel so solitary."

        Then Philip coming somewhat closer spoke: 395
"Annie, there is a thing upon my mind,
And it has been upon my mind so long
That, tho' I know not when it first came there,
I know that it will out at last. O Annie,
It is beyond all hope, against all chance,   400
That he who left you ten long years ago
Should still be living; well, then—let me speak.
I grieve to see you poor and wanting help;
I cannot help you as I wish to do
Unless—they say that women are so quick—   405
Perhaps you know what I would have you know—
I wish you for my wife. I fain would prove
A father to your children; I do think
They love me as a father; I am sure
That I love them as if they were mine own;   410
And I believe, if you were fast my wife,
That after all these sad uncertain years
We might be still as happy as God grants
To any of his creatures. Think upon it;
For I am well-to-do—no kin, no care,   415
No burthen, save my care for you and yours,
And we have known each other all our lives,
And I have loved you longer than you know."

        Then answer'd Annie—tenderly she spoke:
"You have been as God's good angel in our house.   420
God bless you for it, God reward you for it,
Philip, with something happier than myself.
Can one love twice? can you be ever loved
As Enoch was? what is it that you ask?"
"I am content," he answer'd, "to be loved   425
A little after Enoch." "O," she cried,
Scared as it were, "dear Philip, wait a while.
If Enoch comes—but Enoch will not come—
Yet wait a year, a year is not so long.
Surely, I shall be wiser in a year.   430
O, wait a little!" Philip sadly said,
"Annie, as I have waited all my life
I well may wait a little." "Nay," she cried,

"I am bound: you have my promise—in a year.
Will you not bide your year as I bide mine?"   435
And Philip answer'd, "I will bide my year."

    Here both were mute, till Philip glancing up
Beheld the dead flame of the fallen day
Pass from the Danish barrow overhead;
Then, fearing night and chill for Annie, rose   440
And sent his voice beneath him thro' the wood.
Up came the children laden with their spoil;
Then all descended to the port, and there
At Annie's door he paused and gave his hand,
Saying gently, "Annie, when I spoke to you,   445
That was your hour of weakness. I was wrong,
I am always bound to you, but you are free."
Then Annie weeping answer'd, "I am bound."

    She spoke; and in one moment as it were,
While yet she went about her household ways,   450
Even as she dwelt upon his latest words,
That he had loved her longer than she knew,
That autumn into autumn flash'd again,
And there he stood once more before her face,
Claiming her promise. "Is it a year?" she ask'd.   455
"Yes, if the nuts," he said, "be ripe again;
Come out and see." But she—she put him off—
So much to look to—such a change—a month—
Give her a month—she knew that she was bound—
A month—no more. Then Philip with his eyes   460
Full of that lifelong hunger, and his voice
Shaking a little like a drunkard's hand,
"Take your own time, Annie, take your own time."
And Annie could have wept for pity of him;
And yet she held him on delayingly   465
With many a scarce-believable excuse,
Trying his truth and his long-sufferance,
Till half another year had slipt away.

    By this the lazy gossips of the port,
Abhorrent of a calculation crost,   470
Began to chafe as at a personal wrong.
Some thought that Philip did but trifle with her;
Some that she but held off to draw him on;
And others laugh'd at her and Philip too,
As simple folk that knew not their own minds;   475
And one, in whom all evil fancies clung
Like serpent eggs together, laughingly
Would hint at worse in either. Her own son
Was silent, tho' he often look'd his wish;
But evermore the daughter prest upon her   480
To wed the man so dear to all them
And lift the household out of poverty,

And Philip's rosy face contracting grew
Careworn and wan; and all these things fell on her
Sharp as reproach.

                  At last one night it chanced   485
That Annie could not sleep, but earnestly
Pray'd for a sign,[3] "My Enoch, is he gone?"
Then compass'd round by the blind wall of night
Brook'd not the expectant terror of her heart,
Started from bed, and struck herself a light,   490
Then desperately seized the holy Book,
Suddenly set it wide to find a sign,
Suddenly put her finger on the text,
"Under the palm-tree."[4] That was nothing to her,
No meaning there; she closed the Book and slept.   495
When lo! her Enoch sitting on a height,
Under a palm-tree, over him the sun.
"He is gone," she thought, "he is happy, he is singing
Hosanna in the highest; yonder shines
The Sun of Righteousness, and these be palms   500
Whereof the happy people strowing cried
'Hosanna in the highest!'" Here she woke,
Resolved, sent for him and said wildly to him,
"There is no reason why we should not wed."
"Then for God's sake," he answer'd, "both our sakes,   505
So you will wed me, let it be at once."

    So these were wed, and merrily rang the bells,
Merrily rang the bells, and they were wed.
But never merrily beat Annie's heart.
A footstep seem'd to fall beside her path,   510
She knew not whence; a whisper on her ear,
She knew not what; nor loved she to be left
Alone at home, nor ventured out alone.
What ail'd her then that, ere she enter'd, often
Her hand dwelt lingeringly on the latch,   515
Fearing to enter? Philip thought he knew:
Such doubts and fears were common to her state,
Being with child; but when her child was born,
Then her new child was as herself renew'd,
Then the new mother came about her heart,   520
Then her good Philip was her all-in-all,
And that mysterious instinct wholly died.

    And where was Enoch? Prosperously sail'd
The ship "Good Fortune," tho' at setting forth
The Biscay, roughly ridging eastward, shook   525
And almost overwhelm'd her, yet unvext

3. Judges 6:17: "If now I have found grace in thy sight, then shew me a sign."
4. Judges 4:5. A method of divination in which the Bible is opened at random and the first passage blindly
   touched by the finger portends something of the future or reveals the unknown. The practice is known
   as *Sortes Virgilianae*, derived from similarly consulting the *Aeneid*.

She slipt across the summer of the world,[5]
Then after a long tumble about the Cape
And frequent interchange of foul and fair,
She passing thro' the summer world again,   530
The breath of heaven came continually
And sent her sweetly by the golden isles,
Till silent in her oriental haven.

There Enoch traded for himself, and bought
Quaint monsters for the market of those times,   535
A gilded dragon also for the babes.

Less lucky her home-voyage: at first indeed
Thro' many a fair sea-circle, day by day,
Scarce-rocking, her full-busted figure-head
Stared o'er the ripple feathering from her bows: 540
Then follow'd calms, and then winds variable,
Then baffling, a long course of them; and last
Storm, such as drove her under moonless heavens
Till hard upon the cry of "breakers" came
The crash of ruin, and loss of all   545
But Enoch and two others. Half the night,
Buoy'd upon floating tackle and broken spars,
These drifted, stranding on an isle at morn
Rich, but the loneliest in a lonely sea.

No want was there of human sustenance,   550
Soft fruitage, mighty nuts, and nourishing roots;
Nor save for pity was it hard to take
The helpless life so wild that it was tame.
There in a seaward-gazing mountain-gorge
They built, and thatch'd with leaves of palm, a hut,   555
Half hut, half native cavern. So the three,
Set in this Eden of all plenteousness,
Dwelt with eternal summer, ill-content.
For one, the youngest, hardly more than boy,
Hurt in that night of sudden ruin and wreck,   560
Lay lingering out a five-years' death-in-life.
They could not leave him. After he was gone,
The two remaining found a fallen stem;
And Enoch's comrade, careless of himself,
Fire-hollowing this in Indian fashion, fell   565
Sun-stricken, and that other lived alone.
In those two deaths he read God's warning "wait."

The mountain wooded to the peak, the lawns
And winding glades high up like ways to heaven,
The slender coco's drooping crown of plumes,   570
The lightning flash of insect and of bird,
The lustre of the long convolvuluses

5. "The Equator" (Tennyson).

That coil'd around the stately stems, and ran
Even to the limit of the land, the glows
And glories of the broad belt of the world,—   575
All these he saw; but what he fain had seen
He could not see, the kindly human face,
Nor ever hear a kindly voice, but heard
The myriad shriek of wheeling ocean-fowl,[6]
The league-long roller thundering on the reef,   580
The moving whisper of huge trees that branch'd
And blossom'd in the zenith, or the sweep
Of some precipitous rivulet to the wave,
As down the shore he ranged, or all day long
Sat often in the seaward-gazing gorge,   585
A shipwreck'd sailor, waiting for a sail.
No sail from day to day, but every day
The sunrise broken into scarlet shafts
Among the palms and ferns and precipices;
The blaze upon the waters to the east;   590
The blaze upon his island overhead;
The blaze upon the waters to the west;
Then the great stars that globed themselves in heaven,
The hollower-bellowing ocean, and again
The scarlet of sunrise—but no sail.   595

    There often as he watch'd or seem'd to watch,
So still the golden lizard on him paused,
A phantom made of many phantoms moved
Before him haunting him, or he himself
Moved haunting people, things, and places, known   600
Far in a darker isle beyond the line;
The babes, their babble, Annie, the small house,
The climbing street, the mill, the leafy lanes,
The peacock yew-tree and the lonely Hall,
The horse he drove, the boat he sold, the chill   605
November dawns and dewy-glooming[7] downs,
The gentle shower, the smell of dying leaves,
And the low moan of leaden-color'd seas.

    Once likewise, in the ringing of his ears,
Tho' faintly, merrily—far and far away—   610
He heard the pealing of his parish bells;[8]
Then, tho' he knew not wherefore, started up
Shuddering, and when the beauteous hateful isle
Return'd upon him, had not his poor heart
Spoken with That which being everywhere   615

6. "The cries of cormorants and albatrosses" (Ricks).
7. "Dewy and dark" (Tennyson).
8. "Mr. Kinglake told me that he had heard his own parish bells in the midst of an Eastern desert, not knowing at the time that it was Sunday, when they would have been ringing the bells at home; and added, 'I
might have had a ringing in my ears, and the imaginative memory did the rest'" (Tennyson). "My father
would say that there is nothing really supernatural, mechanically or otherwise, in Enoch Arden's hearing bells; tho' he most probably did intend the passage to tell upon the reader mystically" (Hallam Tennyson).

Lets none who speaks with Him seem all alone,
Surely the man had died of solitude.

    Thus over Enoch's early-silvering head
The sunny and rainy seasons came and went
Year after year. His hopes to see his own,   620
And pace the sacred old familiar fields,
Not yet had perish'd, when his lonely doom
Came suddenly to an end. Another ship—
She wanted water—blown by baffling winds,
Like the "Good Fortune," from her destined course,   625
Stay'd by this isle, not knowing where she lay;
For since the mate had seen at early dawn
Across a break on the mist-wreathen isle
The silent water slipping from the hills,
They sent a crew that landing burst away   630
In search of stream or fount, and fill'd the shores
With clamor. Downward from his mountain gorge
Stept the long-hair'd, long-bearded solitary,
Brown, looking hardly human, strangely clad,
Muttering and mumbling, idiot-like it seem'd,   635
With inarticulate rage, and making signs
They knew not what; and yet he led the way
To where the rivulets of sweet water ran,[9]
And ever as he mingled with the crew,
And heard them talking, his long-bounden tongue[1]   640
Was loosen'd, till he made them understand;
Whom, when their casks were fill'd, they took aboard.
And there the tale he utter'd brokenly,
Scarce-credited at first but more and more,
Amazed and melted all who listen'd to it;   645
And clothes they gave him and free passage home,
But oft he work'd among the rest and shook
His isolation from him. None of these
Came from his country, or could answer him,
If question'd, aught of what he cared to know.   650
And dull the voyage was with long delays,
The vessel scarce sea-worthy; but evermore
His fancy fled before the lazy wind
Returning, till beneath a clouded moon
He like a lover down thro' all hid blood   655
Drew in the dewy meadowy morning-breath
Of England, blown across her ghostly wall.[2]
And that same morning officers and men
Levied a kindly tax upon themselves,
Pitying the lonely man, and gave him it;   660
Then moving up the coast they landed him,
Even in that harbor whence he sail'd before.

9. Tennyson compares *Aeneid* I, line 167: "Within are fresh waters and seats in the living stone."
1. Ricks compares Luke 1:64: "And his mouth was opened immediately, and his tongue loosed, and he spake, and praised God."
2. The chalk cliffs on the southern coast.

There Enoch spoke no word to any one,
But homeward—home—what home? had he a home?—
His home, he walk'd. Bright was the afternoon,   665
Sunny but chill; till drawn thro' either chasm,
Where either haven open'd on the deeps,
Roll'd a sea-haze and whelm'd the world in gray,
Cut off the length of highway on before,
And left but narrow breadth to left and right   670
Of wither'd holt or tilth or pasturage.
On the nigh-naked tree the robin piped
Disconsolate, and thro' the dripping haze
The dead weight of the dead leaf bore it down.
Thicker the drizzle grew, deeper the gloom;   675
Last, as it seem'd, a great mist-blotted light[3]
Flared on him, and he came upon the place.

Then down the long street having slowly stolen,
His heart foreshadowing all calamity,
His eyes upon the stones, he reach'd the home   680
Where Annie lived and loved him, and his babes
In those far-off seven happy years were born;
But finding neither light nor murmur there—
A bill of sale gleam'd thro' the drizzle—crept
Still downward thinking, "dead or dead to me!"   685

Down to the pool and narrow wharf he went,
Seeking a tavern which of old he knew,
A front of timber-crost antiquity,
So propt, worm-eaten, ruinously old,
He thought it must have gone; but he was gone   690
Who kept it, and his widow Miriam Lane,
With daily-dwindling profits held the house;
A haunt of brawling seamen once, but now
Stiller, with yet a bed for wandering men.
There Enoch rested silent many days.   695

But Miriam Lane was good and garrulous,
Nor let him be, but often breaking in,
Told him, with other annals of the port,
Not knowing—Enoch was so brown, so bow'd,
So broken,—all the story of his house: 700
His baby's death, her growing poverty,
How Philip put her little ones to school,
And kept them in it, his long wooing her,
Her slow consent and marriage, and the birth
Of Philip's child; o'er his countenance,   705
No shadow past, nor motion. Any one,
Regarding, well had deem'd he felt the tale
Less than the teller; only when she closed,
"Enoch, poor man, was cast away and lost,"

3. "From Philip's house, the latest house to landward" (Tennyson).

He, shaking his gray head pathetically,   710
Repeated muttering, "cast away and lost;"
Again in deeper inward whispers, "lost!"

   But Enoch yearn'd to see her face again:
"If I might look on her sweet face again,
And know that she is happy." So the thought   715
Haunted and harass'd him, and drove him forth,
At evening when the dull November day
Was growing duller twilight, to the hill.
There he sat down gazing on all below;
There did a thousand memories roll upon him,   720
Unspeakable for sadness. By and by
The ruddy square of comfortable light,
Far-blazing from the rear of Philip's house,
Allured him, as the beacon-blaze allures
The bird of passage, till he madly strikes   725
Against it and beats out his weary life.

   For Philip's dwelling fronted on the street,
The latest house to landward; but behind,
With one small gate that open'd on the waste,
Flourish'd a little garden square and wall'd,   730
And in it throve an ancient evergreen,
A yew-tree, and all round it ran a walk
Of shingle, and a walk divided it.
But Enoch shunn'd the middle walk and stole
Up by the wall, behind the yew; and thence   735
That which he better might have shunn'd, if griefs
Like his have worse or better, Enoch saw.

   For cups and silver on the burnish'd board
Sparkled and shone; so genial was the hearth;
And on the right hand of the hearth he saw   740
Philip, the slighted suitor of old times,
Stout, rosy, with his babe across his knees;
And o'er her second father stoopt a girl,
A later but a loftier Annie Lee,
Fair-hair'd and tall, and from her lifted hand   745
Dangled a length of ribbon and a ring
To tempt the babe, who rear'd his creasy arms,
Caught at and ever miss'd it, and they laugh'd;
And on the left hand of the hearth he saw
The mother glancing often toward her babe,   750
But turning now and then to speak with him,
Her son, who stood beside her tall and strong,
And saying that which pleased him, for he smiled.

   Now when the dead man come to life beheld
His wife his wife no more, and saw the babe   755
Hers, yet not his, upon the father's knee,
And all the warmth, the peace, the happiness,

And his own children tall and beautiful,
And him, that other, reigning in his place,
Lord of his rights and of his children's love—   760
Then he, tho' Miriam Lane had told him all,
Because things seen are mightier than things heard,
Stagger'd and shook, holding the branch, and fear'd
To send abroad a shrill and terrible cry,
Which in one moment, like the blast of doom,   765
Would shatter all the happiness of the hearth.

He therefore turning softly like a thief,
Lest the harsh shingle should grate underfoot,
And feeling all along the garden-wall,
Lest he should swoon and tumble and be found,   770
Crept to the gate, and open'd it and closed,
As lightly as a sick man's chamber-door,
Behind him, and came out upon the waste.

And there he would have knelt, but that his knees
Were feeble, so that falling prone he dug   775
His fingers into the wet earth, and pray'd:

"Too hard to bear! why did they take me thence?
O God Almighty, blessed Saviour, Thou
That didst uphold me on my lonely isle,
Uphold me, Father, in my loneliness[4]   780
A little longer! aid me, give me strength
Not to tell, never to let her know.
Help me not to break in upon her peace.
My children too! must I not speak to these?
They know me not. I should betray myself.   785
Never! no father's kiss me—the girl
So like her mother, and the boy, my son."

There speech and thought and nature fail'd a little,
And he lay tranced; but when he rose and paced
Back toward his solitary home again,   790
All down the long and narrow street he went
Beating it in upon his weary brain,
As tho' it were the burthen of a song,
"Not to tell her, never to let her know."

He was not all unhappy. His resolve   795
Upbore him, and firm faith, and evermore
Prayer from a living source within the will,
And beating up thro' all the bitter world,
Like fountains of sweet water in the sea,
Kept him a living soul. "This miller's wife,"   800
He said to Miriam, "that you spoke about,
Has she no fear that her first husband lives?"

---

4. Psalm 145:14: "The Lord upholdeth all that fall, and raiseth up all those that be bowed down."

"Ay, ay, poor soul," said Miriam, "fear enow!
If you could tell her you had seen him dead,
Why, that would be her comfort;" and he thought,   805
"After the Lord has call'd me she shall know,
I wait His time;" and Enoch set himself,
Scorning an alms, to work whereby to live.
Almost to all things could he turn his hand.
Cooper he was and carpenter, and wrought   810
To make the boatmen fishing-nets, or help'd
At lading and unlading the tall barks
That brought the stinted commerce of those days,
Thus earn'd a scanty living for himself.
Yet since he did but labor for himself,   815
Work without hope,[5] there was not life in it
Whereby the man could live; and as the year
Roll'd itself round again to meet the day
When Enoch had return'd, a langour came
Upon him, gentle sickness, gradually   820
Weakening the man, till he could do no more,
But kept the house, his chair, and last his bed.
And Enoch bore his weakness cheerfully.
For sure no gladlier does the stranded wreck
See thro' the gray skirts of a lifting squall   825
The boat that bears the hope of life approach
To save the life despair'd of, than he saw
Death dawning on him, and the close of all.

        For thro' that dawning gleam'd a kindlier hope
On Enoch thinking, "after I am gone,   830
Then may she learn I loved her to the last."
He call'd aloud for Miriam Lane and said:
"Woman, I have a secret—only swear,
Before I tell you—swear upon the book
Not to reveal it, till you see me dead."   835
"Dead," clamor'd the good woman, "hear him talk!
I warrant, man, that we shall bring you round."
"Swear," added Enoch sternly, "on the book;"
And on the book, half-frighted, Miriam swore.
Then Enoch rolling his gray eyes upon her,   840
"Did you know Enoch Arden of this town?"
"Know him?" she said, "I knew him far away.
Ay, ay, I mind him coming down the street;
Held his head high, and cared for no man, he."
Slowly and sadly Enoch answer'd her: 845
"His head is low, and no man cares for him.
I think I have no three days more to live;
I am the man." At which the woman gave
A half-incredulous, half-hysterical cry:
"You Arden, you! nay,—sure he was a foot   850

5. Ricks compares Coleridge's "Work without Hope," lines 13–14: "Work without Hope draws nectar in a
sieve, / And Hope without an object cannot live," though the *work* referred to is rather of a different sort.

Higher than you be." Enoch said again:
"My God has bow'd me down to what I am;
My grief and solitude have broken me;
Nevertheless, know you that I am he
Who married—but that name has twice been changed—   855
I married her who married Philip Ray.
Sit, listen." Then he told her of his voyage,
His wreck, his lonely life, his coming back,
His gazing in on Annie, his resolve,
And how he kept it. As the woman heard,   860
Fast flow'd the current of her easy tears,
While in her heart she yearn'd incessantly
To rush abroad all around the little haven,
Proclaiming Enoch Arden and his woes;
But awed and promise-bounden she forbore,   865
Saying only, "See your bairns[6] before you go!
Eh, let me fetch 'em, Arden," and arose
Eager to bring them down, for Enoch hung
A moment on her words, but then replied:

"Woman, disturb me not now at the last,   870
But let me hold my purpose till I die.
Sit down again; mark me and understand,
While I have power to speak. I charge you now,
When you shall see her, tell her that I died
Blessing her, praying for her, loving her;   875
Save for the bar between us, loving her
As when she laid her head beside my own.
And tell my daughter Annie, whom I saw
So like her mother, that my latest breath
Was spent in blessing her and praying for her.   880
And tell my son that I died blessing him.
And say to Philip that I blest him too;
He never meant us anything but good.
But if my children care to see me dead,
Who hardly knew me living, let them come,   885
I am their father; but she must not come,
For my dead face would vex her after-life.
And now there is but one of all my blood
Who will embrace me in the world-to-be.
This hair is his, she cut it off and gave it,   890
And I have borne it with me all these years,
And thought to bear it with me to my grave;
But now my mind is changed, for I shall see him,
My babe in bliss. Wherefore when I am gone,
Take, give her this, for it may comfort her;   895
It will moreover be a token to her
That I am he."

---

6. Children, in dialects of Scotland and northern England.

He ceased; and Miriam Lane
Made such a voluble answer promising all,
That once again he roll'd his eyes upon her
Repeating all he wish'd, and once again   900
She promised.

Then the third night after this,
While Enoch slumber'd motionless and pale,
And Miriam watch'd and dozed at intervals,
There came so loud a calling of the sea[7]
That all the houses in the haven rang.   905
He woke, he rose, he spread his arms abroad,
Crying with a loud voice, "A sail! a sail!
I am saved;" and so fell back and spoke no more.

So past the strong heroic soul away.
And when they buried him the little port   910
Had seldom seen a costlier funeral.[8]

                                            1862; 1864

Northern Farmer[1]

Old Style

1

Wheer' asta beän saw long and meä liggin' 'ere aloän?[2]
Noorse?[3] thoort nowt o' a noorse; whoy, Doctor's abeän an' agoän;
Says that I moänt a naw[4] moor aäle, but I beänt a fool;
Git ma my aäle, fur I beänt a-gawin' to breäk my rule.

---

7. "'The calling of the sea,' a term used, I believe, chiefly in the western parts of England to signify a ground swell" (Tennyson).
8. To understandable criticism of the poem's close, Tennyson responded in a note: "The costly funeral is all that poor Annie could do for him after he was gone. This is entirely introduced for her sake, and, in my opinion, quite necessary to the perfection of the Poem and the simplicity of the narration." Arguing for the need of serious study of "Victorian sentimentality," Sir Charles Tennyson's questionings are particularly apt in regard to Enoch Arden: "Why did it happen & how bad is it? It affected I think all the best writers of the time (except perhaps Mat. Arnold?—???)." [Sir Charles Tennyson in a letter to me (Houghton Library, Harvard University).] With a clear distinction between sentiment and sentimentality in mind after reading Enoch Arden, no more devastating remark exists than that from a much younger, though contemporary poet: "A horrible thing has happened to me. I have begun to doubt Tennyson." Gerard Manley Hopkins (see Turner, English Literature: 1832–1890, p. 18).
1. Of this and the following poem Tennyson said: "The first is founded on the dying words of a farm-bailiff, as reported to me by a great uncle of mine when verging upon 80,—'God A'mighty little knows what He's about, a-taking me. An' Squire will be so mad an' all.' I conjectured the man from that one saying. . . . [The second poem] is likewise founded on a single sentence, 'When I canters my 'erse along the ramper (highway) I 'ears proputty, proputty, proputty.' I had been told that a rich farmer in our neighbourhood was in the habit of saying this. I never saw the man and know no more of him" (Memoir II, 9). Both these dramatic monologues in Lincolnshire dialect give a welcome but all too infrequent glimpse into Tennyson's sense of humor, like Keats's, seldom revealed in poems.
2. Where hast thou been so long and me lying here alone?
3. Nurse.
4. Must not have.

2

Doctors, they knaws nowt, fur a[5] says what's nawways true;   5
Naw soort o' koind o' use to saäy the things that a do.
I've 'ed my point o' aäle ivry noight sin' I beän 'ere.
An I've 'ed my quart ivry market-noight for foorty year.

3

Parson's a beän loikewoise, an' a sittin' ere o' my bed.
"The Amoighty's a taäkin o' you to' issén[6] my friend," a said,   10
An' a towd ma my sins, an' 's toithe were due[7] an' I gied it in hond;
I done moy duty boy 'um, as I 'a done boy the lond.

4

Larn'd ma' beä.[8] I reckons I' annot sa mooch to larn.
But a cast oop, thot a did, 'bout Bessy Marris's barne.[9]
Thaw a knaws I hallus voäted wi' Squoire an' choorch an' staäte,   15
An' i' the woost o' toimes I wur niver agin the raäte.[1]

5

An' I hallus coom'd to 's choorch afoor moy Sally wur deäd,
An' 'eärd 'um a bummin' awaäy loike a buzzard-clock[2] ower my 'eäd,
An' I niver knaw'd whot a meän'd but I thowt a 'ad summut to saäy,
An' I thowt a said whot a owt to 'a said, an' I coom'd awaäy.   20

6

Bessy Marris's barne! tha knaws she laäid it to meä.
Mowt a beän, mayhap, for she wur a bad un, sheä.
'Siver,[3] I kep 'um, I kep 'um, my lass, tha mun understood;
I done moy duty boy 'um, as I 'a done boy the lond.

7

But Parson a cooms an' a goäs, an' a says it eäsy an' freeä: 25
"The Amoighty's taäkin o' to you to 'issén, my friend," say 'eä.
I weänt saäy men be loiars, thaw summun[4] said it in 'aäste;
But 'e reäds wonn sarmin a weeäk, an' I' a stubb'd[5] Thurnaby waäste.

8

D'ya moind the waäste, my lass? naw, naw, tha was not born then;
Theer wur a boggle[6] in it, I often 'eärd 'um mysén;   30

5. He.
6. Himself. "You" is pronounced with the *ou* as in *hour*.
7. And he told me my sins, and his tithe was due.
8. Learned he may be.
9. But he brought up, that he did, about Bessy Marris's child.
1. Rate, i,e., poor-tax.
2. Cockchafer, a large destructive beetle. A story Tennyson liked to tell was about "a Lincolnshire farmer coming home on Sunday after a sermon about the endless fires of hell and talking to his wife—'Noä, Sally, it woän't do, noä constitootion cud stan' it.'" Another "was of a Lincolnshire minister praying for rain: 'O God, send us rain, and specially on John Stubbs' field in the middle marsh, and if Thou doest not know it, it has a big thorn-tree in the middle of it'" (*Memoir* II, 10).
3. Howsoever.
4. Someone, i.e., David: "I said in my haste, All men *are* liars" (Psalm 116:11).
5. Cleared, perhaps plowed.
6. Bogy or ghost.

Moäst loike a butter-bump,[7] fur I 'eärd 'um about an' about,
But I stubb'd 'um oop wi' the lot, an raäved an' rembled[8] 'um out.

9

Keäper's it wur; fo' they fun 'um theer a-laäid of 'is faäce[9]
Down i' the woild 'enemies[1] afor I com'd to the plaäce.
Noäks or Thimbleby—toäner[2] 'ed shot 'um deäd as a naäil.   35
Noäks wur 'ang'd for it oop at soize[3]—but git ma my aäle.

10

Dubbut[4] looök at the waäste; theer warn't not feeäd for a cow;
Nowt at all but bracken an' fuzz, an' looök at it now—
Warn't worth nowt a haäcre, an' now theer's lots o' feeäd,
Fourscoor yows[5] upon it, an' some on it down i' seeäd.[6]   40

11

Nobbut a bit[7] on it 's left, an' I meän'd to 'a stubb'd it at fall,
Done it ta-year[8] I meän'd, an' runn'd plow thruff it an' all,
If Godamoighty an' parson 'ud nobbut let ma aloän,—
Meä, wi' haäte hoonderd haäcre o' Squoire's, an' lond o' my oän.

12

Do Godamoighty knaw what a 's doing a-taäkin' o' meä?   45
I beänt wonn as saws[9] 'ere a beän an' yonder a peä;
An' Squoire 'ull be sa mad an' all—a' dear, a' dear!
And I 'a managed for Squoire coom Michaelmas thutty year.

13

A mowt 'a taäen owd Joänes, as 'ant not a aäpoth o' sense,[1]
Or a mowt 'a taäen young Robins—a niver mended a fence;   50
But Godamoighty a moost taäke meä an' taäke ma now,
Wi aäf the cows to cauve[2] an' Thurnaby hoälms[3] tu plow!

14

Looök 'ow quoloty[4] smoiles when they seeäs ma a passin' boy,
Says to thessén,[5] naw doubt, "What a man a beä sewer-loy!"[6]
Fur they knaws what I beän to Squoire sin' fust a coom'd to the 'All;   55
I done moy duty by Squoire an' I done moy duty boy hall.

7. A bittern or kind of heron, which makes loud booming noises during the mating season.
8. Tore up and threw away.
9. It was the gamekeeper's (ghost), for they found him there lying on his face.
1. Anemones.
2. One or the other.
3. Assizes or court trial
4. Do but.
5. Ewes. "Foursoor": i.e., fourscore; pronounced *ou* as in *hour.*
6. Clover.
7. Nought but a little.
8. This year.
9. I be not one that sows.
1. He might have taken old Jones, that hasn't a halfpenny-worth of sense.
2. Calve.
3. Low lands.
4. Quality or gentry.
5. Themselves.
6. Surely.

15

Squoire 's i' Lunnon, an' summun I reckons 'ull 'a to wroite,
For whoä 's to howd[7] the lond ater meä, thot muddles ma quoit;[8]
Sartin-sewer[9] I beä thot a weänt niver give it to Joänes,
Naw, nor a moänt to Robins—a niver rembles the stoäns.[1]   60

16

But summon 'ull come ater meä mayhap wi' 'is kittle o' steäm[2]
Huzzin' an' maäzin'[3] the blessed feälds wi' the divils oän teäm.
Sin mun doy I mun doy, thaw loife they says is sweet,
But sin' I mun doy I mun doy, for I couldn abeär to see it.

17

What atta stannin' theer fur, an' doesn bring ma the aäle?   65
Doctor's a 'toättler,[4] lass, an a 's hallus i' the owd taäle;[5]
I weänt breäk rules fur Doctor, a knaws naw moor nor a floy;[6]
Git ma my aäle, I tell tha, an' if I mun doy I mun doy.

1861; 1864

Northern Farmer

New Style

1

Dosn't thou 'ear my 'erse's[1] legs, as they canters awaäy?
Proputty,[2] proputty, proputty—that's what I 'ears 'em saäy.
Proputty, proputty, proputty—Sam, thou's an ass for thy païns;
Theer's moor sense i' one o' 'is legs, nor in all thy braïns.

2

Woä—theer 's a craw to pluck[3] wi' tha, Sam: yon 's parson's 'ouse—   5
Dosn't thou knaw that man mun be eäther a man or a mouse?
Time to think on it then; for thou 'll be twenty to weeäk.[4]
Proputty, proputty—woä then, woä—let ma 'ear mysén[5] speäk.

3

Me an' thy muther, Sammy, 'as beän a-talkin' o' thee;
Thou's beän talkin' to muther, an' she beä a-tellin it me.   10

7. Hold.
8. Quite.
9. Certain sure.
1. No, nor he must not (give the land) to Robbins—he never removes the stones.
2. The newfangled steam thresher.
3. Worrying and confusing.
4. Teetotaler.
5. And he's always in (telling) the same old tale.
6. Fly.
1. Horse's.
2. Property.
3. A crow to pluck, a dispute to settle.
4. This week.
5. Myself.

Thou'll not marry for munny—thou's sweet upo' parson's lass—
Noä—thou'll marry for luvv—an' we boäth on us thinks tha an ass.

4

Seeä'd her to-daäy goä by—Saäint's-daäy—they was ringing the bells.
She 's a beauty, thou thinks—an' soä is scoors o' gells,[6]
Them as 'as munny an' all—wot's a beauty?—the flower as blaws.   15
But propputty, propputty sticks, an' propputty, propputty graws.

5

Do'ant be stunt,[7] taäke time. I knaws what maäkes tha sa mad.
Warn't I craäzed fur the lasses mysén when I wur a lad?
But I knaw'd a Quaäker feller as often 'as towd[8] ma this:
"Doänt thou marry for munny, but goä wheer munny is!"   20

6

An' I went wheer munny war;[9] an' thy muther coom to 'and,
Wi' lots o' munny laaïd by, an' a nicetish bit o' land.
Maäybe she warn't a beauty—I niver giv it a thowt—
But warn't she as good to cuddle an' kiss as a lass 'ant nowt?[1]

7

Parson's las 'ant nowt, an' she weänt 'a nowt when 'e 's deäd,   25
Mun be a guvness, lad, or summut, and addle[2] her breäd.
Why? fur 'e 's nobbut[3] a curate, an' weänt niver get hissén clear,
An' 'e maäde the bed as 'e ligs[4] on afoor 'e comm'd to the shere.[5]

8

An' thin 'e comm'd to the parish wi' lots o' Varsity debt,
Stook to his taail they did, an' 'e 'ant got shut on[6] 'em yet.   30
An' 'e ligs on 'is back i' the grip[7] wi' noän to lend 'im a shove,
Woorse nor a far-welter'd yowe;[8] fur, Sammy, 'e married fur luvv.

9

Luvv? what's luvv? thou can luvv thy lass an' 'er munny too,
Maäkin' 'em goä togither, as they 've good right to do.
Couldn I luvv thy muther b' y cause o' 'er munny laaïd by?   35
Naäy—fur I luvv'd 'er a vast sight moor fur it; reäson why.

6. Scores of girls.
7. Stubborn.
8. Told.
9. "It was also reported of the wife of this worthy that, when she entered the *salle á manger* of a sea bathing-
   place, she slapt her pockets and said, 'When I married I brought him £5000 on each shoulder'" (*Memoir* II, 9).
1. Has nothing.
2. Earn.
3. Nothing but.
4. Lies.
5. Shire.
6. Clear of.
7. Ditch.
8. Ewe lying on her back.

10

Ay, an' thy muther says thou wants to marry the lass,
Cooms of a gentleman burn;[9] an' we boäth on us thinks tha an ass.
Woä then, proputty, wiltha?[1]—an ass as near as mays nowth[2]
Woä then, wiltha? dangtha!—the bees is as fell as owt.[3]   40

11

Breäk me a bit o' the esh for his 'eäd,[4] lad, out o' the fence!
Gentleman burn! what's gentleman burn? is it shillins an' pence?
Proputty, proputty's ivrything 'ere, an' Sammy, I 'm blest
If it is n't the saäme oop yonder, fur them as 'as it 's the best.

12

Tis 'n them as 'as munny as breäks into 'ouses an' steäls,   45
Them as 'as coäts to their backs an' taäkes their regular meäls.
Noä, but it 's them as niver knaws wheer a meäl 's to be 'ad.
Taäke my word for it, Sammy, the poor in a loomp is bad.

13

Them or thir feythers, tha sees, mun 'a beän a laäzy lot,
Fur work mun 'a gone to the gittin' whiniver munny was got.   50
Feyther 'ad ammost nowt; leästways 's munny was 'id.
But 'e tued an' moil'd issén deäd,[5] an' 'e died a good un, 'e did.

14

Looök thou theer wheer Wrigglesby beck[6] cooms out by the 'll!
Feyther run oop to the farm, an' I runs oop to the mill;
An' I 'll run oop to the brig,[7] an' that thou 'll live to see;   55
And if thou marries a good un I 'll leäve the land to thee.

15

Thim's my noätions, Sammy, wheerby I meäns to stick;
But if thou marries a bad un, I 'll leäve the land to Dick.—
Com oop, proputty, proputty—that's what I 'ears 'im saäy—
Proputty, proputty, proputty—canter an' canter awaäy.   60

1865; 1869

"Flower in the Crannied Wall"[1]

Flower in the crannied wall,
I pluck you out of the crannies

9. Born.
1. Wilt thou.
2. Makes nothing.
3. The flies are as fierce as anything.
4. An ash branch to keep the flies off the horse's head.
5. But he toiled and drudged himself to death.
6. Brook.
7. Bridge.
1. "The flower was plucked out of a wall at 'Wagoners Wells,' near Haslemere" (Tennyson). Perhaps a dim echo of Herbert's "The Flower," line 21: "Thy word is all, if we could spell," the poem similarly has Blakean understones and compatibilities with Buddhist thought.

I hold you here, root and all, in my hand,
Little flower—but *if* I could understand
What you are, root and all, and all in all,   5
I should know what God and man is.

1869

The Higher Pantheism[1]

The sun, the moon, the stars, the seas, the hills and the plains,—
Are not these, O Soul, the Vision of Him who reigns?

Is not the Vision He, tho' He be not that which He seems?
Dreams are true while they last, and do we not live in dreams?

Earth, these solid stars, this weight of body and limb,   5
Are they not sign and symbol of thy division from Him?

Dark is the world to thee; thyself art the reason why,
For is He not all but thou, that hast power to feel "I am I"?

Glory about thee, without thee; and thou fulfillest thy doom,
Making Him broken gleams and a stifled spendor and gloom.   10

Speak to Him, thou, for He hears, and Spirit with Spirit can meet—
Closer is He than breathing, and nearer than hands and feet.

God is law, say the wise; O Soul, and let us rejoice,
For if He thunder by law the thunder is yet His voice.

Law is God, say some; no God at all, says the fool,[2]   15
For all we have power to see is a straight staff bent in a pool;

And the ear of man cannot hear, and the eye of man cannot see;
But if we could see and hear, this Vision—were it not He?

1867; 1869

1. The "lower," or old, pantheism proposes that God is identified with nature and has no existence outside the natural world. Tennyson's version insists that the spirit is the only reality there is. From his earliest poetry through *IM*, he had been working toward an articulation of this philosophy. (See *The Devil and the Lady* 2, 1, lines 40–57 and n. 9, p. 8; also *IM* 130.) Swinburne's savage but funny parody begins: "One, who is not, we see: but one, whom we see not, is; / Surely this is not that: but that is assuredly this." It ends with the devastating couplet: "God, whom we see not, is: and God, who is not, we see; / Fiddle, we know, is diddle: and diddle, we take it, is dee."
2. Among several less direct biblical allusions, Ricks notes Psalm 14:1 here: "The fool hath said in his heart, There is no God."

In the Garden at Swainston[1]

Nightingales warbled without,
  Within was weeping for thee;
Shadows of three dead men
  Walk'd in the walks with me,
Shadows of three dead men, and thou wast one of the three.   5
Nightingales sang in his woods,
  The Master was far away;
Nightingales warbled and sang
  Of a passion that lasts but a day;
Still in the house in his coffin the Prince of courtesy lay.   10
Two dead men have I known
  In courtesy like to thee;
Two dead men[2] have I loved
  With a love that ever will be;
Three dead men have I loved, and thou art last of the three.   15

1870; 1874

IDYLLS OF THE KING

Few poems, if any, have been so widely acclaimed and then so thoroughly maligned as Tennyson's *Idylls of the King*, his most ambitious work. When Tennyson's star was at its height, the praises heaped on his poem obscured its defects; when appreciation of him reached its lowest, during the first third of the twentieth century, the often niggling criticism of the *Idylls* made a general appraisal of the poet's achievements impossible. Writing in 1872, Swinburne, who disparagingly called the poem "The Morte d'Albert, or Idylls of the Prince Consort," was perhaps the first clearly to perceive that Tennyson's greatest enemies were "those of his own household," the close circle of friends who indiscriminately took every utterance as prophecy from the Bard. But in the reaction against Tennyson and those who had inflated his reputation, even Swinburne would have been surprised to discover how right he had been.

With varying degrees of intensity, Tennyson worked on his *Idylls* for some forty years, and therein lies an obvious cause of the poem's problems of coherence. In 1859 he published four *Idylls*: "Enid" (later divided into two parts), "Vivien," "Elaine," and "Guinevere." His purpose here was simply to contrast true and false love, and any thematic relationship to the first-written of the idylls, the "Morte d'Arthur" (1833), was negligible. In 1869 he published "The Coming of Arthur," "Pelleas and Ettarre," "The Holy Grail," and "The Passing of Arthur," which was based on the earlier "Morte d'Arthur." The motivating impulse behind these poems,

---

1. Swainston was Sir John Simeon's home on the Isle of Wight, near Tennyson's Farringford. Sir John (see headnote to *Maud*) had been one of the poet's closest friends; he died suddenly and unexpectedly in Switzerland. The moving account of the poem's composition deserves repeating in full: "He [Tennyson] arrived sometime before the procession was due to leave the house, and asked his old friend's eldest son if he could give him a pipe of his father's and one of his cloaks and hats. 'Come for me yourself,' he added, 'when it is time to start, and do not send a servant.' When the moment arrived young Simeon went to fetch the poet. He found him, stretched at full length on the ground, wearing the hat and cloak and smoking the pipe. The tears were streaming down his face, and in his hand was a scrap of paper on which he had roughly jotted down the beautiful lines 'In the Garden at Swainston.'" (*Alfred Tennyson*, p. 389).
2. Arthur Hallam and Henry Lushington.

and what later would be the central concern in the whole work, was to show the rise and fall of a society and to suggest symbolically and allegorically a pertinence to the age in which he lived. As Marion Shaw has aptly observed in "Tennyson's Dark Continent," after 1859 the poem "was progressively expanded into an imperial dream and elegy." Even more pointed is C. Y. Lang's statement: "The real subject of this great poem is the British Empire." The project was laudable, although one suspects that the Arthurian legends, chiefly derived from Malory, never could fully lend themselves to such an ambitious design.

A more immediate obstacle lay ahead—how to bring together two essentially irreconcilable sets of poems. He wrote "The Last Tournament" in 1871 and "Gareth and Lynette" in 1872; he published "Balin and Balan" in 1885 and divided "Enid" in 1888. But only extensive rewriting and rigorous cutting could have produced the coherence and structure necessary to the strict demands of the "Epic" he initially wished his poem to be. And even then, as just noted, there is reason to believe that the source material could not sustain the larger purpose, or what Tennyson preferred to call the "parabolic drift in the poem" (*Memoir* II, 127). What we have, to put it most simply, is a long poem in which the sum of the twelve parts is more than the whole.

Criticism on the *Idylls* is all but endless, while criticism on the criticism has sometimes led to the neglect of the poem. Jerome H. Buckley's restorative appraisal of the *Idylls* in his *Tennyson: The Growth of a Poet* remains (as it was in 1960) an informative, balanced commentary of a poem that, more recently, has become a focus for "anti-colonialist" criticism. It was hugely popular throughout the long history of its publications (see the following chronologies for more complete information on composition and publication dates), but even at the outset hostile voices were to be heard. Of the first four *Idylls*, Carlyle was one of the few who spoke derogatively; he saw an "inward perfection of vacancy" and sarcastically observed, "The lollipops were so Superlative." Matthew Arnold elaborated: "The real truth is that Tennyson, with all his temperament and artistic skill, is deficient in intellectual power." Of all the charges brought against the poem and the poet, this is the most serious and most frequently encountered in subsequent criticism. Before one too readily agrees, however, one could do worse than ponder the complexities of the problem to which Tennyson addressed his poem. In his *Science and the Modern World* (1925), Alfred North Whitehead wrote: "This history of thought in the eighteenth and nineteenth centuries is governed by the fact that the world had got hold of a general idea which it could neither live with nor live without." The idea is the mechanistic theory of nature or the theory of scientific materialism.

The shortcoming of the *Idylls* is not, as is so frequently maintained, that Tennyson avoided facing the consequences of materialistic thought because he lacked the intellectual equipment, but that the poem offers no working alternative to it. To support his belief in the spiritual, Tennyson could not get beyond his statement in the "Prologue" to *In Memoriam*, "By faith and faith alone, embrace, / Believing where we cannot prove." It would be up to later thinkers like William James and Whitehead to attempt to articulate a substitute for materialistic philosophies. But "even though mechanistic doctrines of the nineteenth century came to be repudiated," Douglas Bush has written, "the new and more fluid conceptions were not much more reassuring, and the staggering fact of immensity or infinity has remained a part of the modern consciousness." The achievement of *Idylls of the King* is simply that it offered a repudiation. Those who look to *In Memoriam*, particularly to the notion expressed there "That mind and soul, according well, / May make one music as before," and from that point of departure conclude that Tennyson looked to the past for the harmony the modern world so conspicuously lacked, must also acknowledge that *Idylls* does diagnose the plights of modern life. King Arthur, in the dominant metaphor of the poem, sees that all his realm "Reels back into the beast and is no more." Our sophistication is not such that we can ignore, except at our peril, the implications of "The darkness of that battle in the west / Where all of high and holy dies away."

Idylls of the King: A Chronology

ORDER OF POEMS	ORDER OF FIRST PUBLICATION*
"Dedication"	"Merlin and Vivien" ("Nimuë"), 1857, in trial copies privately printed
1. "The Coming of Arthur"	
2. "Gareth and Lynette"	"Geraint and Enid" ("Enid"), 1857
3. "The Marriage of Geraint"	"Guinevere," 1859
4. "Geraint and Enid"	"Elaine," 1859
5. "Balin and Balan"	"Dedication," 1862
6. "Merlin and Vivien"	"The Holy Grail," 1869 (dated 1870)
7. "Lancelot and Elaine"	
8. "The Holy Grail"	"The Coming of Arthur," 1869 (dated 1870)
9. "Pelleas and Ettarre"	"Pelleas and Ettarre," 1869 (dated 1870)
10. "The Last Tournament"	
11. "Guinevere"	"The Passing of Arthur," 1869 (dated 1870) ("Morte d'Arthur" published 1842)
12. "The Passing of Arthur"	
"To the Queen"	"The Last Tournament," 1871
	"Gareth and Lynette," 1872
	"To the Queen," 1873
	"Balin and Balan," 1885
	"Geraint and Enid": "Enid" divided in 1888 into two idylls— "The Marriage of Geraint" and "Geraint and Enid" (see 3 and 4 in lefthand column)

---

* The original titles of the poems are given in parentheses.

ORDER OF COMPOSITION

"Morte d'Arthur" composed 1833–35 (published 1842)
"Merlin and Vivien" ("Nimuë") started end of 1855; rough draft January 1856; completed March 1856
"Geraint and Enid" ("Enid") started April 1856; worked on intensively September 1856; completed October 1856
"Guinevere" started July 1857; completed January 1858; finishing touches added March 1858
"Lancelot and Elaine" ("Elaine") conceived March 1858; mostly written winter 1858–59; completed end of February 1859
"Dedication" (Prince Albert died December 18, 1861) set in type by January 9, 1862
"The Holy Grail" started March 1868; re-started September 1868; completed November 1868
"The Coming of Arthur" worked on winter 1868–69; completed end of February 1869
"Pelleas and Ettarre" well under way May 1869; completed September 1869
"The Passing of Arthur" ("Morte d'Arthur"): introduction and conclusion added to "Morte d'Arthur" September 1869
"The Last Tournament" started April 1871; completed May 1871
"Gareth and Lynette" started October 1869; worked on for a year; picked up again November 1871; completed summer 1872
"To the Queen" composed toward end of 1872
"Balin and Balan" composed during later part of 1872 and early 1873; completed 1874 (140 lines added to opening of "Merlin and Vivien" 1874)

FROM IDYLLS OF THE KING

Dedication[1]

These to His Memory—since he held them dear,
Perchance as finding there unconsciously
Some image of himself—I dedicate,
I dedicate, I consecrate with tears—
These Idylls.[2]

And indeed he seems to me   5
Scarce other than my king's ideal knight,[3]
Who reverenced his conscience as his king;

1. To Prince Albert, husband of Queen Victoria, who died in December 1861. He had particularly liked the four *Idylls* published in 1859, and at his request Tennyson had sent him an autographed copy.
2. Tennyson used two *l*'s to distinguish them from his "English Idyls" concerning rural domestic life. "Tennyson pronounced the word with an I as in 'idle'" (Ricks).
3. "The first reading, 'my own ideal knight,' was altered because Leslie Stephen and others called King Arthur a portrait of the Prince Consort" (Hallam Tennyson). See "To the Queen," line 38 and n. 6, p. 522.

Whose glory was, redressing human wrong;
Who spake no slander, no, nor listen'd to it;
Who loved one only and who clave to her[4]—   10
Her—over all whose realms to their last isle,
Commingled with the gloom of imminent war,[5]
The shadow of his loss drew like eclipse,
Darkening the world. We have lost him; he is gone.
We know him now; all narrow jealousies   15
Are silent, and we see him as he moved,
How modest, kindly, all-accomplish'd, wise,
With what sublime repression of himself,
And in what limits, and how tenderly;
Not swaying to this faction or to that;   20
Not making his high place the lawless perch
Of wing'd ambitions, nor a vantage-ground
For pleasure; but thro' all this tract of years
Wearing the white flower of a blameless life,
Before a thousand peering littlenesses,   25
In that fierce light which beats upon a throne
And blackens every blot; for where is he
Who dares foreshadow for an only son
A lovelier life, a more unstain'd, than his?
Or how should England dreaming of *his* sons   30
Hope more for these than some inheritance
Of such a life, a heart, a mind as thine,
Thou noble Father of her Kings to be,
Laborious for her people and her poor—
Voice in the rich dawn of an ampler day—   35
Far-sighted summoner of War and Waste
To fruitful strifes and rivalries of peace[6]—
Sweet nature gilded by the gracious gleam
Of letters, dear to Science, dear to Art,
Dear to thy land[7] and ours, a Prince indeed,   40
Beyond all titles, and a household name,
Hereafter, thro' all times, Albert the Good.

    Break not, O woman's-heart, but still endure;
Break not, for thou art royal, but endure,
Remembering all the beauty of that star   45
Which shone so close beside thee that ye made
One light together, but has past and leaves
The Crown a lonely splendor.

               May all love,
His love, unseen but felt, o'ershadow[8] thee,

4. Paraphrased from "Guinevere," lines 465–72, where King Arthur summarizes the ideals of the Round Table.
5. Alludes to the *Trent* affair, in which two Confederate commissioners were taken off the British ship *Trent* by a Federal man-of-war. "The Queen and the Prince Consort," according to Tennyson's note, "were said to have averted war by their modification of a dispatch."
6. According to Hallam Tennyson, these words refer to Prince Albert's efforts in planning the International Exhibitions of 1851 and 1862.
7. Albert's native land was Saxe Comburg, in Germany.
8. Citing the *OED*, Ricks notes the word means "protect."

The love of all thy sons encompass thee,   50
The love of all thy daughters cherish thee,
The love of all thy people comfort thee,
Till God's love set thee at his side again!

                                                              1862

Flos Regum Arthurus.
— JOSEPH OF EXETER[9]

The Coming of Arthur[1]

Leodogran, the king of Cameliard,[2]
Had one fair daughter, and none other child;
And she was fairest of all flesh on earth,
Guinevere, and in her his one delight.

For many a petty king ere Arthur came   5
Ruled in this isle and, ever-waging war
Each upon other, wasted all the land;
And still from time to time the heathen host
Swarm'd over-seas, and harried what was left.
And so there grew great tracts of wilderness,   10
Wherein the beast was ever more and more,
But man was less and less, till Arthur came.
For first Aurelius lived and fought and died,
And after him King Uther[3] fought and died,
But either fail'd to make the kingdom one.   15
And after these King Arthur for a space,
And thro' the puissance of his Table round,[4]
Drew all their petty princedoms[5] under him,
Their king and head, and made a realm and reign'd.

And thus the land of Cameliard was waste,   20
Thick with wet woods, and many a beast therein,
And none or few to scare or chase the beast;

9. "Arthur, the flower of kings." Joseph of Exeter was a medieval English poet who wrote epic verse in em-
ulation of Virgil.
1. "The vision of Arthur as I have drawn him came upon me when, little more than a boy, I first lighted
upon Malory. . . . The coming of Arthur is on the night of the New Year; when he is wedded 'the world
is white with May'; on a summer night the vision of the Holy Grail appears; and the 'Last Tournament'
is in the 'yellowing autumn-tide.' Guinevere flees through the mists of autumn, and Arthur's death takes
place at midnight in mid-winter. The form of the Coming of Arthur and of the Passing is purposely more
archaic than that of the other Idylls. The blank verse throughout each of the twelve Idylls varies according to the subject" (Tennyson).
   Within the ellipsis above: "The time came that was chosen, then Arthur was born. So soon as he came
on earth, elves took him; they enchanted the child with magic most strong, they gave him might to be
the best of all knights; they gave him another thing, that he should be a rich king; they gave him the third,
that he should live long; they gave to him, the child, virtues most good, so that he was most generous of
all men alive: This the elves gave him, and thus the child thrived" (Tennyson, citing Malory, as rendered
by Ricks).
2. Sometimes located as far north as Scotland or, as probable here, in south Wales.
3. Aurelius's brother and, by some accounts, Arthur's father.
4. "A table called King Arthur's is kept at Winchester. It was supposed to symbolize the world, being flat
and round" (Tennyson).
5. "The several petty princedoms were under one head, the 'pendragon'" (Tennyson).

So that wild dog and wolf and boar and bear
Came night and day, and rooted in the fields,
And wallow'd in the gardens of the King.   25
And ever and anon the wolf would steal
The children and devour, but now and then,
Her own brood lost or dead, lent her fierce teat
To human sucklings; and the children, housed
In her foul den, there at their meat would growl,   30
And mock their foster-mother on four feet,[6]
Till, straighten'd, they grew up to wolf-like men,
Worse than the wolves. And King Leodogran
Groan'd for the Roman legions here again
And Cæsar's eagle. Then his brother king,   35
Urien,[7] assail'd him; last a heathen horde,
Reddening the sun with smoke and earth with blood,
And on the spike that split the mother's heart
Spitting the child, brake on him, till, amazed,
He knew not whither he should turn for aid.   40

   But—for he heard of Arthur newly crown'd,
Tho' not without an uproar made by those
Who cried, "He is not Uther's son"—the King
Sent to him, saying, "Arise, and help us thou!
For here between the man and beast we die."   45

   And Arthur yet had done no deed of arms,
But heard the call and came; and Guinevere
Stood by the castle walls to watch him pass;
But since he neither wore on helm or shield
The golden symbol[8] of his kinglihood,   50
But rode a simple knight among his knights,
And many of these in richer arms than he,
She saw him not, or mark'd not, it she saw,
One among many, tho' his face was bare.
But Arthur, looking downward as he past,   55
Felt the light of her eyes into his life
Smite on the sudden, yet rode on, and pitch'd
His tents beside the forest. Then he drave
The heathen,[9] after, slew the beast, and fell'd
The forest, letting in the sun, and made   60
Broad pathways for the hunter and the knight,
And so return'd.

                        For a while he linger'd there,
A doubt that ever smoulder'd in the hearts
Of those great lords and barons of his realm
Flash'd forth and into war, for most of these,   65
Colleaguing with a score of petty kings,

6. "Imitate the wolf by going on four feet" (Tennyson).
7. "King of North Wales" (Tennyson).
8. "The golden dragon" (Tennyson).
9. "Angles, Jutes, and Saxons" (Tennyson).

Made head against him, crying: "Who is he
That he should rule us? who hath proven him
King Uther's son? for lo! we look at him,
And find nor face nor bearing, limbs nor voice,   70
Are like to those of Uther whom we knew.
This is the son of Gorloïs, not the King;
This is the son of Anton, not the King."

And Arthur, passing thence to battle, felt
Travail, and throes and agonies of the life,   75
Desiring to be join'd with Guinevere,
And thinking as he rode: "Her father said
That there between the man and beast they die.
Shall I not lift her from this land of beasts
Up to my throne and side by side with me?   80
What happiness to reign a lonely king,
Vext—O ye stars that shudder over me,
O earth that soundest hollow under me,
Vext with waste dreams? for saving I be join'd
To her that is the fairest under heaven,   85
I seem as nothing in the mighty world,
And cannot will my will nor work my work
Wholly, nor make myself in mine own realm
Victor and lord. But were I join'd with her,
Then might we live together as one life,   90
And reigning with one will in everything
Have power on this dark land to lighten it,
And power on this dead world to make it live."[1]

Thereafter—as he speaks who tells the tale—
When Arthur reach'd a field of battle bright   95
With pitch'd pavilions of his foe, the world
Was all so clear about him that he saw
The smallest rock far on the faintest hill,
And even in high day the morning star.[2]
So when the King had set his banner broad,[3]   100
At once from either side, with trumpet-blast,
And shouts, and clarions shrilling unto blood,
The long-lanced battle let their horses run.
And now the barons and the kings prevail'd,
And now the King, as here and there that war   105
Went swaying; but the Powers who walk the world
Made lightnings and great thunders over him,
And dazed all eyes, till Arthur by main might,
And mightier of his hands with every blow,
And leading all his knighthood threw the kings,   110

---

1. On the simplest allegorical level, Arthur represents the spirit and Guinevere the flesh. "The whole," Tennyson said, "is the dream of man coming into practical life and ruined by one sin. Birth is a mystery and death is a mystery, and in the midst lies the tableland of life, and its struggles and performances. It is not the history of one man or of one generation but of a whole cycle of generations" (Memoir II, 127).
2. Compare "Armageddon," lines 171ff., for an interesting early parallel to this mode of vision.
3. A fusion of: "And in the name of our God we will set up our banners" (Psalm 20:5) and "with scutchins gilt and banners broad displayd" (Faerie Queen IV, iii, line 5) (noted by Gray).

Carádos, Urien, Cradlemont of Wales,
Claudius, and Clariance of Northumberland,
The King Brandagoras of Latangor,
With Anguisant of Erin, Morganore,
And Lot of Orkney.[4] Then, before a voice   115
As dreadful as the shout of one who sees
To one who sins, and deems himself alone
And all the world asleep, they swerved and brake
Flying, and Arthur[5] call'd to stay the brands
That hack'd among the flyers, "Ho! they yield!"   120
So like a painted battle the war stood
Silenced, the living quiet as the dead,
And in the heart of Arthur joy was lord.
He laugh'd upon his warrior[6] whom he loved
And honor'd most. "Thou dost not doubt me King,   125
So well thine arm hath wrought for me today."
"Sir and my liege," he cried, "the fire of God
Descends upon thee in the battle-field.
I know thee for my King!" Whereat the two,
For each had warded either in the fight,   130
Sware on the field of death a deathless love.
And Arthur said, "Man's world is God in man;[7]
Let chance what will, I trust thee to the death."

    Then quickly from the foughten field he sent
Ulfius, and Brastias, and Bedivere,   135
His new-made knights, to King Leodogran,
Saying, "If I in aught have served thee well,
Give me thy daughter Guinevere to wife."

    Whom when he heard, Leodogran in heart
Debating—"How should I that am a king,   140
However much he holp me at my need,
Give my one daughter saving to a king,
And a king's son?"—lifted his voice, and call'd
A hoary man, his chamberlain, to whom
He trusted all things, and of him required   145
His counsel: "Knowest thou aught of Arthur's birth?"

    Then spake the hoary chamberlain and said:
"Sir King, there be but two old men that know;
And each is twice as sold as I; and one
Is Merlin, the wise man that ever served   150
King Uther thro' his magic art, and one
Is Merlin's master—so they call him—Bleys,
Who taught him magic; but the scholar ran
Before the master, and so far that Bleys

4. This list of conquered kings is from Malory, whom Tennyson follows quite closely in this idyll.
5. Contrast "The Last Tournament," lines 466–76, in which Arthur's commands go unheeded. One of the
    themes throughout the *Idylls* is the growing failure of communication and its consequences.
6. Lancelot.
7. A central precept on which the order of knights is founded and, in the poem's design, any social organi-
    zation.

Laid magic by, and sat him down, and wrote   155
All things and whatsoever Merlin did
In one great annal-book, where after-years
Will learn the secret of our Arthur's birth."

    To whom the King Leodogran replied:
"O friend, had I been holpen half as well   160
By this King Arthur as by thee to-day,
Then beast and man had had their share of me;
But summon here before us yet once more
Ulfius, and Brastias, and Bedivere."

    Then, when they came before him, the king said: 165
"I have seen the cuckoo chased by lesser fowl,
And reason in the chase; but wherefore now
Do these your lords stir up the heat of war,
Some calling Arthur born of Gorloïs,
Others of Anton? Tell me, ye yourselves,   170
Hold ye this Arthur for King Uther's son?"

    And Ulfius and Brastias answer'd, "Ay."
Then Bedivere, the first of all his knights
Knighted by Arthur at his crowning, spake —
For bold in heart and act and word was he,   175
Whenever slander breathed against the King —

    "Sir, there be many rumors on this head;
For there be those who hate him in their hearts,
Call him baseborn, and since his ways are sweet,
And theirs are bestial, hold him less than man;   180
And there be those who deem him more than man,
And dream he dropt from heaven. But my belief
In all this matter — so ye care to learn —
Sir, for ye know that in King Uther's time
The prince and warrior Gorloïs, he that held   185
Tintagil castle by the Cornish sea,
Was wedded with a winsome wife, Ygerne.
And daughters had she borne him, — one whereof,
Lot's wife, the Queen of Orkney,[8] Bellicent,
Hath ever like a loyal sister cleaved   190
To Arthur, — but a son she had not borne.
And Uther cast upon her eyes of love;
But she, a stainless wife to Gorloïs,
So loathed the bright dishonor of his love
That Gorloïs and King Uther went to war,   195
And overthrown was Gorloïs and slain.
Then Uther in his wrath and heat beseiged
Ygerne within Tintagil, where her men,
Seeing the mighty swarm about their walls,
Left her and fled, and Uther enter'd in,   200

---

8. "The kingdom of Orkney and Lothian composed the North and East of Scotland" (Tennyson).

And there was none to call to but himself.
So, compass'd by the power of the king,
Enforced she was to wed him in her tears,
And with a shameful swiftness; afterward
Not many moons, King Uther died himself,   205
Moaning and wailing for an heir to rule
After him, lest the realm should go to wrack.
And that same night, the night of the new year,
By reason of the bitterness and grief
That vext his mother, all before his time   210
Was Arthur born, and all as soon as born
Deliver'd at a secret postern-gate
To Merlin, to be holden far apart
Until his hour should come, because the lords
Of that fierce day were as the lords of this,   215
Wild beasts, and surely would have torn the child
Piecemeal among them, had they known; for each
But sought to rule for his own self and hand,
And many hated Uther for the sake
Of Gorloïs. Wherefore Merlin took the child,   220
And gave him to Sir Anton, an old knight
And ancient friend of Uther; and his wife
Nursed the young prince, and rear'd him with her own;
And no man knew. And ever since the lords
Have foughten like wild beasts among themselves,   225
So that the realm has gone to wrack; but now,
This year, when Merlin—for his bour had come—
Brought Arthur forth, and set him in the hall,
Proclaiming, 'Here is Uther's heir, your king,'
A hundred voices cried: 'Away with him!   230
No king of ours! a son of Gorloïs he,
Or else the child of Anton, and no king,
Or else baseborn.' Yet Merlin thro' his craft,
And while the people clamor'd for a king,[9]
Had Arthur crown'd; but after, the great lords   235
Banded, and so brake out in open war."

    Then while the king debated with himself
If Arthur were the child of shamefulness,
Or born the son of Gorloïs after death,
Or Uther's son and born before his time.   240
Or whether there were truth in anything
Said by these three, there came to Cameliard,
With Gawain and young Modred, her two sons,
Lot's wife, the Queen of Orkney, Bellicent;
Whom as he could, not as he would, the king   245
Made feast for, saying, as they sat at meat:
"A doubtful throne is ice on summer seas.
Ye come from Arthur's court. Victor his men
Report him! Yea, but ye—think ye this king—

9. "Wherefore all the commons cried at once, 'We will have Arthur unto our king' (Malory, Bk. i)" (Tennyson).

So many those that hate him, and so strong, 250
So few his knights, however brave they be—
Hath body[1] enow to hold his foemen down?"

"O King," she cried, "and I will tell thee: few,
Few, but all brave, all of one mind with him;
For I was near him when the savage yells 255
Of Uther's peerage died, and Arthur sat
Crowned on the daïs, and his warriors cried,
'Be thou the king, and we will work thy will
Who love thee.' Then the King in low deep tones,
And simple words of great authority, 260
Bound them by so strait vows to his own self
That when they rose, knighted from kneeling, some
Were pale as at the passing of a ghost,
Some flush'd, and others dazed, as one who wakes
Half-blinded at the coming of a light. 265

"But when he spake, and cheer'd his Table Round
With large, divine, and comfortable words,
Beyond my tongue to tell thee—I beheld
From eye to eye thro' all their Order flash
A momentary likeness of the King; 270
And ere it left their faces, thro' the cross
And those around it and the Crucified,
Down from the casement over Arthur smote
Flame-color, vert, and azure, in three rays,
One falling upon each of three fair queens[2] 275
Who stood in silence near his throne, the friends
Of Arthur, gazing on him, tall, with bright
Sweet faces, who will help him at his need.

"And there I saw mage Merlin, whose vast wit
And hundred winters are but as the hands 280
Of loyal vassals toiling for their liege.

"And near him stood the Lady of the Lake,[3]
Who knows a subtler magic than his own—
Clothed in white samite, mystic, wonderful.
She gave the King his huge cross-hilted sword, 285
Whereby to drive the heathen out. A mist
Of incense curl'd about her, and her face
Wellnigh was hidden in the minster gloom;
But there was heard among the holy hymns
A voice as of the waters,[4] for she dwells 290
Down in a deep—calm, whatsoever storms

1. "Strength" (Tennyson).
2. They may represent Faith, Hope, and Charity. To those who offered that interpretation, Tennyson responded: "They are right, and they are not right. They mean that and they do not. They are three of the noblest of women. They are also those three Graces, but they are much more. I hate to be tied down to say, 'This means that'" (Memoir II, 127). They reappear in "The Passing of Arthur," line 366.
3. "The Lady of the Lake in the old legends is the Church" (Tennyson).
4. "Compare 'I heard a voice from heaven, as the voice of many waters' (Rev. xiv.2)" (Tennyson).

May shake the world—and when the surface rolls,
Hath power to walk the waters like our Lord.

"There likewise I beheld Excalibur[5]
Before him at his crowning borne, the sword   295
That rose from out the bosom of the lake,
And Arthur row'd across and took it—rich
With jewels, elfin Urim,[6] on the hilt,
Bewildering heart and eye—the blade so bright
That men are blinded by it—on one side,   300
Graven in the oldest tongue of all this world,
'Take me,' but turn the blade and ye shall see,
And written in the speech ye speak yourself,
'Cast me away!' And sad was Arthur's face
Taking it, but old Merlin counsell'd him,   305
'Take thou and strike! the time to cast away[7]
Is yet far-off.' So this great brand the king
Took, and by this will beat his foemen down."

Thereat Leodogran rejoiced, but thought
To sift his doubtings to the last, and ask'd   310
Fixing full eyes of question on her face,
"The swallow and the swift are near akin,
But thou art closer to this noble prince,
Being his own dear sister;" and she said,
"Daughter of Gorloïs and Ygerne am I;"   315
"And therefore Arthur's sister?" ask'd the king.
She answer'd, "These be secret things," and sign'd
To those two sons to pass, and let them be.
And Gawain went, and breaking into song
Sprang out, and follow'd by his flying hair   320
Ran like a colt, and leapt at all he saw;
But Modred laid his ear beside the doors,
And there half-heard—the same that afterward
Struck for the throne, and striking found his doom.

And then the Queen made answer: "What know I?   325
For dark my mother was in eyes and hair,
And dark in hair and eyes am I; and dark
Was Gorloïs; yea, and dark was Uther too,
Wellnigh to blackness; but this king is fair
Beyond the race of Britons and of men.   330
Moreover, always in my mind I hear
A cry from out the dawning of my life,
A mother weeping, and I hear her say,
'O that ye had some brother, pretty one,
To guard thee on the rough ways of the world.'"   335

5. "Said to mean 'cut-steel'. In the Romance of Merlin the sword bore the following description: 'Ich am y-
   hote Escalabore / Unto a king a fair tresore', and it is added: 'On Inglis is this writing / Kerve steel and
   yren and all thing'" (Tennyson).
6. Refers to precious stones, which the Jewish high priests took to be symbols of revelation. See Exodus
   28:30: "And thou shalt put in the breastplate of judgment the Urim and the Thummim."
7. "'A time to get, and a time to lose; a time to keep, and a time to cast away,' Ecclesiastes, 3:6" (Ricks).

"Ay," said the king, "and hear ye such a cry?
But when did Arthur chance upon thee first?"

"O King!" she cried, "and I will tell thee true.
He found me first when yet a little maid.
Beaten I had been for a little fault   340
Whereof I was not guilty; and out I ran
And flung myself down on a bank of heath,
And hated this fair world and all therein,
And wept, and wish'd that I were dead; and he—
I know not whether of himself he came,   345
Or brought by Merlin, who, they say, can walk
Unseen at pleasure—he was at my side,
And spake sweet words, and comforted my heart,
And dried my tears, being a child with me.
And many a time he came, and evermore   350
As I grew greater grew with me; and sad
At times he seem'd, and sad with him was I,
Stern too at times, and then I loved him not,
But sweet again, and then I loved him well.
And now of late I see him less and less,   355
But those first days had golden hours for me,
For then I surely thought he would be king.

"But let me tell thee now another tale:
For Bleys, our Merlin's master, as they say,
Died but of late, and sent his cry to me,   360
To hear him speak before he left his life.
Shrunk like a fairy changeling lay the mage;[8]
And when I enter'd told me that himself
And Merlin ever served about the king,
Uther, before he died; and on the night   365
When Uther in Tintagil past away
Moaning and wailing for an heir, the two
Left the still king, and passing forth to breathe,
Then from the castle gateway by the chasm
Descending thro' the dismal night—a night   370
In which the bounds of heaven and earth were lost—
Beheld, so high upon the dreary deeps
It seem'd in heaven, a ship, the shape thereof
A dragon wing'd, and all from stem to stern
Bright with a shining people on the decks,   375
And gone as soon as seen. And then the two
Dropt to the cove, and watch'd the great sea fall,
Wave after the wave, each mightier than the last,
Till last, a ninth one,[9] gathering half the deep
And full of voices, slowly rose and plunged   380
Roaring, and all the wave was in a flame;

8. An archaic form of *magus*, a magician. "Changeling": the elves the fairies substituted for the human children they stole could supposedly be recognized by their shrivelled appearance.
9. "Every ninth wave is supposed by the Welsh bards to be larger than those that go before" (Hallam Tennyson).

And down the wave and in the flame was borne
A naked babe, and rode to Merlin's feet,
Who stoopt and caught the babe, and cried, 'The King!
Here is an heir for Uther!' And the fringe   385
Of that great breaker, sweeping up the strand,
Lash'd at the wizard as he spake the word,
And all at once all round him rose in fire,
So that the child and he were clothed in fire.
And presently thereafter follow'd calm,   390
Free sky and stars. 'And this same child,' he said,
'Is he who reigns; nor could I part in peace
Till this were told.' And saying this the seer
Went thro' the strait and dreadful pass of death,
Not ever to be question'd any more   395
Save on the further side; but when I met
Merlin, and ask'd him if these things were truth —
The shining dragon and the naked child
Descending in the glory of the seas —
He laugh'd as is his wont, and answer'd me   400
In riddling triplets of old time, and said: —

          "'Rain, rain, and sun!¹ a rainbow in the sky!
          A young man will be wiser by and by;
          An old man's wit may wander ere he die.

          "'Rain, rain, and sun! a rainbow on the lea!   405
          And truth is this to me, and that to thee;
          And truth or clothed or naked let it be.

          "'Rain, sun, and rain! and the free blossom blows;
          Sun, rain, and sun! and where is he who knows?
          From the great deep to the great deep he goes.'   410

     "So Merlin riddling anger'd me; but thou
Fear not to give this King thine only child,
Guinevere; so great bards of him will sing
Hereafter, and dark sayings from of old
Ranging and ringing thro' the minds of men,   415
And echo'd by old folk beside their fires
For comfort after their wage-work is done,
Speak of the King; and Merlin in our time
Hath spoken also, not in jest, and sworn
Tho' men may wound him that he will not die,   420
But pass, again to come, and then or now
Utterly smite the heathen underfoot,
Till these and all men hail him for their king."²

1. "The truth appears in different guise to different persons — either (1) with spiritual significance as a rainbow in the sky, or as (2) with earthly significance as a rainbow on the lea in the dewy grass" (Hallam Tennyson). "The one fact is that man comes from the great deep and returns to it. This is an echo of the
   triads of the Welsh bards" (Tennyson). See "De Profundis" 2, line 1: "Out of the deep, my child, out of
   the deep, / From that great deep, before our world began."
2. Ricks notes Malory, xxi, 7: "Some men yet say, in many parts of England, that king Arthur is not dead;
   but, by the will of our Lord Jesu Christ, into another place: and men say, that he will come again, and
   he shall win the holy cross."

She spake and King Leodogran rejoiced,
But musing "Shall I answer yea or nay?"   425
Doubted, and drowsed, nodded and slept, and saw,
Dreaming, a slope of land that ever grew,
Field after field, up to a height, the peak
Haze-hidden, and thereon a phantom king,
Now looming, and now lost; and on the slope   430
The sword rose, the hind fell, the herd was driven,
Fire glimpsed; and all the land from roof and rick,
In drifts of smoke before a rolling wind,
Stream'd to the peak, and mingled with the haze
And made it thicker; while the phantom king   435
Sent out at times a voice; and here or there
Stood one who pointed toward the voice, the rest
Slew on and burnt, crying, "No king of ours,
No son of Uther, and no king of ours;"
Till with a wink his dream was changed, the haze   440
Descended, and the solid earth became
As nothing, but the King stood out in heaven,
Crown'd. And Leodogran awoke, and sent
Ulfius, and Brastias, and Bedivere,
Back to the court of Arthur answering yea.   445

    Then Arthur charged his warrior whom he loved
And honor'd most, Sir Lancelot, to ride forth
And bring the Queen, and watch'd him from the gates;
And Lancelot past away among the flowers—
For then was latter April—and return'd   450
Among the flowers, in May, with Guinevere.
To whom arrived, by Dubric[3] the high saint,
Chief of the church in Britain, and before
The stateliest of her altar-shrines,[4] the King
That morn was married, while in stainless white,   455
The fair beginners of a nobler time,[5]
And glorying in their vows and him, his knights
Stood round him, and rejoicing in his joy.
Far shone the fields of May thro' open door,
The sacred altar blossom'd white with May,   460
The sun of May descended on their King,
They gazed on all earth's beauty in their Queen,
Roll'd incense, and there past along the hymns
A voice as of the waters, while the two
Sware at the shrine of Christ a deathless love.   465
And Arthur said, "Behold, thy doom is mine.
Let chance what will, I love thee to the death!"
To whom the Queen replied with drooping eyes,
"King and my lord, I love thee to the death!"
And holy Dubric spread his hands and spake: 470

---

3. "Archbishop of Caerleon. His crozier is said to be at St David's" (Tennyson).
4. "According to Malory, the Church of St Stephen at Camelot" (Tennyson).
5. Throughout the *Idylls* Tennyson does attempt to preserve a consistency of color symbolism and seasonal motif. See n. 1, p. 379.

"Reign ye, and live and love, and make the world
Other, and may thy Queen be one with thee,
And all this Order of thy Table Round
Fulfil the boundless purpose of their King!"[6]

So Dubric said; but when they left the shrine   475
Great lords from Rome[7] before the portal stood,
In scornful stillness gazing as they past;
Then while they paced a city all on fire
With sun and cloth of gold, the trumpets blew,
And Arthur's knighthood sang before the King: —   480

"Blow trumpet, for the world is white with May![8]
Blow trumpet, the long night hath roll'd away!
Blow thro' the living world—'Let the King reign!'

"Shall Rome or Heathen rule in Arthur's realm?
Flash brand and lance, fall battle-axe upon helm,   485
Fall battle-axe, and flash brand! Let the King reign!

"Strike for the King and live! his knights have heard
That God hath told the King a secret word.
Fall battle-axe, and flash brand! Let the King reign!

"Blow trumpet! he will lift us from the dust.   490
Blow trumpet! live the strength, and die the lust!
Clang battle-axe, and clash brand! Let the King reign!

"Strike for the King and die! and if thou diest,
The King is king, and ever wills the highest.
Clang battle-axe, and clash brand! Let the King reign!   495

"Blow, for our Sun is mighty in his May!
Blow, for our Sun is mightier day by day!
Clang battle-axe, and clash brand! Let the King reign!

"The King will follow Christ,[9] and we the King,
In whom high God hath breathed a secret thing.   500
Fall battle-axe, and clash brand! Let the King reign!"

So sang the knighthood, moving to their hall.
There at the banquet those great lords from Rome,
The slowly-fading mistress of the world,
Strode in and claim'd their tribute as of yore.   505

6. The question of the king's reality, as that of any ideal, is met with increasing skepticism in the later idylls
   as the dissolution of the Order approaches. Leodogran's acknowledgment of the king, in what amounts
   to the acceptance of divine revelation, signifies the health of the society in its early stages. Tennyson said
   he meant the king to be "mystic and no mere British Prince" (quoted in Buckley's *Tennyson*, p. 176).
   From the outset and to this day, Tennyson has been faulted for stressing "ideal manhood" at the expense
   of projecting the king having human qualities.
7. "Because Rome had been the Lord of Britain" (Tennyson).
8. "My father wrote to my mother that this Viking song, a pendant to Merlin's song, 'rings like a grand
   music.' This and Leodogran's dream give the drift and grip of the poem, which describes the aspirations
   and ambitions of Arthur and his knights, doomed to downfall—the hints of coming doom being heard
   throughout" (Hallam Tennyson, and see *Memoir* II, 117).
9. "'Be ye followers of me, even as I also am of Christ,' I *Corinthians*, 11:1" (Ricks).

But Arthur spake: "Behold, for these have sworn
To wage my wars, and worship me their King;
The old order changeth, yielding place to new,
And we that fight for our fair father Christ,
Seeing that ye be grown too weak and old   510
To drive the heathen from your Roman wall,[1]
No tribute will we pay." So those great lords
Drew back in wrath, and Arthur strove with Rome.

    And Arthur and his knighthood for a space
Were all one will, and thro' that strength the King   515
Drew in the petty princedoms under him,
Fought, and in twelve great battles overcame
The heathen hordes, and made a realm and reign'd.

                                                          1869

Following "The Coming of Arthur" are three idylls, "Gareth and Lynette," "The Marriage of Geraint," and "Geraint and Enid," in which the poet's purpose is to show how hardships and obstacles may be overcome while the founding principles of the Order are fresh and believable. In the first, Gareth, the youngest son of Bellicent, is eager to set forth for Camelot to seek his fame and fortune. To prove his knighthood, Arthur assigns him a quest. Into a land green with promise, he sets out with Lynette as guide to free her sister imprisoned in the Castle Perilous. Lynette, bitter at having the task entrusted to an untried youth, is more difficult to win than the several battles, but knight and lady are finally united. In the second and third idylls, roles are reversed. Geraint, through a series of adventures in which the obstacles are far more formidable than those Gareth encountered, first wins Enid and then, in the next idyll, tests his blameless wife's fidelity in every conceivable manner. Like Spenser's Red Cross Knight, Geraint is besieged with self-doubts, and the wastelands he must traverse are as much a psychological condition within himself. Many readers, with some justification, have found the two Geraint idylls tediously drawn out, but they do manage to stress the viability of the Order while it strives to maintain its ideals.

    "Geraint and Enid" is the last idyll to end happily, and it concludes what can be conveniently thought of as a tripartite division of the poem into sets of four idylls. In the middle group, seeds of discontent have been sown; rumors of Guinevere's adulterous relationship with Lancelot are generally bruited about. The sequence begins with "Balin and Balan." The idyll opens on a note of discord, and the leisurely pace of the Geraint idylls gives way to a relentless rush of events that bring two brother knights to their deaths. Their identities hidden, the two brothers slay each other in an argument over the Queen's faithfulness, "brainless bulls / Dead for one heifer," as Vivien cynically puts it. "Merlin and Vivien" follows and carries the process of disintegration closer to the center of Arthur's court. In the allegorical scheme, intellect, wisdom, and age prove unable to resist the sensuality personified by Vivien.

    Given my druthers, I most certainly would have included these four idylls here, but the familiar exigencies of space and economics took inexorable precedence. I am somewhat mollified, however, by Sir Charles Tennyson's remark in a letter to me (April 28, 1972): "I applaud your abstinence from *partial* quotation—the four omissions from the Idylls are easily defensible" (Houghton Library, Harvard). Nonetheless, I would particularly alert users of this volume to the significance of

----

1. "A line of forts built by Agricola betwixt the Firth of Forth and the Clyde, forty miles long" (Tennyson).

"Balin and Balan," wherein, as Hallam Tennyson long ago observed: "Loyal natures are wrought to anger and madness against the world." For Tennyson, throughout his life, there was no more central theme in his work than his fear for our species' survival should violence and aggression hold sway, that civilization could, as in his poem, reel back into the beast and be no more. The depth of Tennyson's prescience can clearly be measured with two quotations: "Unless we can use our intelligence to control our aggression, there is not much chance for the human race" (Stephen Hawking, *Black Holes and Baby Universes*, p. 137); "If we become even slightly more violent, shortsighted, ignorant, and selfish than we are now, almost certainly we will have no future" (Carl Sagan, *Pale Blue Dot*, p. 397) [editor's note].

Merlin and Vivien[1]

A storm was coming, but the winds were still,
And in the wild woods of Broceliande;[2]
Before an oak, so hollow, huge, and old
It look'd a tower of ivied masonwork,
At Merlin's feet the wily Vivien lay.   5

For he that always bare in bitter grudge[3]
The slights of Arthur and his Table, Mark
The Cornish King, had heard a wandering voice,
A minstrel of Caerleon[4] by strong storm
Blown into shelter at Tintagil, say   10
That out of naked knight-like purity
Sir Lancelot worshipt no unmarried girl,
But the great Queen herself, fought in her name,
Sware by her—vows like theirs that high in heaven
Love most, but neither marry nor are given   15
In marriage, angels of our Lord's report.

He ceased, and then—for Vivien sweetly said—
She sat beside the banquet nearest Mark,—
"And is the fair example follow'd, sir,
In Arthur's household?"—answer'd innocently: 20

"Ay, by some few—ay, truly—youths that hold
It more beseems the perfect virgin knight
To worship woman as true wife beyond
All hopes of gaining, than as maiden girl.
They place their pride in Lancelot and the Queen.   25
So passionate for an utter purity
Beyond the limit of their bond are these,

1. "For the name of Vivien my father is indebted to the old *Romance of Merlin*. . . . 'Some even among the highest intellects become the slaves of the evil which is at first half disdained' [Tennyson]. My father created the character of Vivien with care—as the evil genius of the Round Table— who in her lustfulness of the flesh could not believe in anything either good or great. . . . [Although founded on a short passage from Malory], the story of the poem of *Merlin and Vivien* is essentially original" (Hallam Tennyson).
2. "The forest in Broceliand in Brittany near St Malo" (Tennyson).
3. Lines 6–147 were added in 1874.
4. In Monmouthshire in Wales, where reputedly Arthur may frequently have held court.

For Arthur bound them not to singleness.
Brave hearts and clean! and yet—God guide them!—young."

Then Mark was half in heart to hurl his cup 30
Straight at the speaker, but forbore. He rose
To leave the hall, and, Vivien following him,
Turn'd to her: "Here are snakes within the grass;
And you methinks, O Vivien, save ye fear
The monkish manhood, and the mask of pure 35
Worn by this court, can stir them till they sting."

And Vivien answer'd, smiling scornfully:
"Why fear? because that foster'd at *thy* court
I savor of thy—virtues? fear them? no,
As love, if love be perfect, casts out fear, 40
So hate, if hate be perfect, casts out fear.
My father died in battle against the King,
My mother on his corpse in open field;
She bore me there, for born from death was I
Among the dead and sown upon the wind— 45
And then on thee! and shown the truth betimes,
That old true filth, and bottom of the well,
Where Truth is hidden. Gracious lessons thine,
And maxims of the mud! 'This Arthur pure!
Great Nature thro' the flesh herself hath made 50
Gives him the lie! There is no being pure,⁵
My Cherub; saith not Holy Writ the same?'—
If I were Arthur, I would have thy blood.
Thy blessing, stainless King! I bring thee back,
When I have ferreted out their burrowings, 55
The hearts of all this Order in mine hand—
Ay—so that fate and craft and folly close,
Perchance, one curl of Arthur's golden beard.
To me this narrow grizzled fork of thine
Is cleaner-fashion'd—Well, I loved thee first; 60
That warps the wit."

Loud laugh'd the graceless Mark.
But Vivien, into Camelot stealing, lodged
Low in the city, and on a festal day
When Guinevere was crossing the great hall
Cast herself down, knelt to the Queen, and wail'd. 65
"Why kneel ye there? What evil have ye wrought?
Rise!" and the damsel bidden rise arose
And stood with folded hands and downward eyes
Of glancing corner and all meekly said:
"None wrought, but suffer'd much, an orphan maid! 70
My father died in battle for thy King,
My mother on his corpse—in open field,

5. Job 25:4: "How then can man be justified with God? or how can he be clean that is born of a woman?" Ricks notes Proverbs 20:9: "Who can say, I have made my heart clean, I am pure from my sin?"

The sad sea-sounding wastes of Lyonnesse—
Poor wretch—no friend!—and now by Mark the king,
For that small charm of feature mine, pursued—   75
If any such be mine—I fly to thee.
Save, save me thou! Woman of women—thine
The wreath of beauty, thine the crown of power,
Be thine the balm of pity, O heaven's own white
Earth-angel, stainless bride of stainless King—   80
Help, for he follows! take me to thyself!
O yield me shelter for mine innocency
Among thy maidens!"

                    Here her slow sweet eyes
Fear-tremulous, but humbly hopeful, rose
Fixt on her hearer's while the Queen who stood   85
All glittering like May sunshine on May leaves
In green and gold, and plumed with green replied:
"Peace child! of over-praise and over-blame
We choose the last. Our noble Arthur, him
Ye scarce can overpraise, will hear and know.   90
Nay—we believe all evil of thy Mark—
Well, we shall test thee farther; but this hour
We ride a-hawking with Sir Lancelot.
He hath given us a fair falcon which he train'd;
We go to prove it. Bide ye here the while."   95

          She past; and Vivien murmur'd after, "Go!
I bide the while." Then thro' the portal-arch
Peering askance, and muttering brokenwise,
As one that labors with an evil dream,
Beheld the Queen and Lancelot get to horse.   100

          "Is that the Lancelot? goodly—ay, but gaunt;
Courteous—amends for gauntness—takes her hand—
That glance of theirs, but for the street, had been
A clinging kiss—how hand lingers in hand!
Let go at last!—they ride away—to hawk   105
For waterfowl. Royaller game is mine.
For such a supersensual bond
As that gray cricket[6] chirpt of at our hearth—
Touch flax with flame—a glance will serve—the liars!
Ah little rat that borest in the dyke   110
Thy hole by night to let the boundless deep
Down upon far-off cities while they dance—
Or dream—of thee they dream'd not—nor of me
These—ay, but each of either; ride, and dream
The mortal dream that never yet was mine—   115
Ride, ride and dream until ye wake—to me!"[7]
Then, narrow court and lubber King, farewell

6. The "minstrel of Caerleon," line 9.
7. "The only real bit of feeling, and the only pathetic line which Vivien speaks" (Tennyson).

For Lancelot will be gracious to the rat,
And our wise Queen, if knowing that I know,
Will hate, loathe, fear—but honor me the more."   120

　　Yet while they rode together down the plain,
Their talk was all of training, terms of art,
Diet and seeling,[8] jesses, leash and lure.
"She is too noble," he said, to check at pies,[9]
Nor will she rake:[1] there is no basenesss in her."   125
Here when the Queen demanded as by chance,
"Know ye the stranger woman?" "Let her be,"
Said Lancelot, and unhooded casting off
The goodly falcon free; she tower'd;[2] her bells,
Tone under tone, shrill'd; and they lifted up   130
Their eager faces, wondering at the strength,
Boldness, and royal knighthood of the bird,
Who pounced her quarry and slew it. Many a time
As once—of old—among the flowers—they rode.

　　But Vivien half-forgotten of the Queen   135
Among her damsels broidering sat, heard, watch'd,
And whisper'd. Thro' the peaceful court she crept
And whisper'd; then, as Arthur in the highest
Leaven'd the world, so Vivien in the lowest,
Arriving at a time of golden rest,   140
And sowing one ill hint from ear to ear,
While all the heathen lay at Arthur's feet,
And no quest came, but all was joust and play,
Leaven'd his hall. They heard and let her be.

　　Thereafter, as an enemy that has left   145
Death in the living waters[3] and withdrawn,
The wily Vivien stole from Arthur's court.

　　She hated all the knights, and heard in thought
Their lavish comment when her name was named.
For once, when Arthur walking all alone,   150
Vext at a rumor issued from herself
Of some corruption crept among his knights,
Had met her, Vivien, being greeted fair,
Would fain have wrought upon his cloudly mood
With reverent eyes mock-loyal, shaken voice,   155
And flutter'd adoration, and at last
With dark sweet hints of some who prized him more
Than who should prize him most; at which the King
Had gazed upon her blankly and gone by.
But one had watch'd, and had not held his peace;   160

---

8. Straps of leather attached to the legs. "Seeling": part of the taming process of a young hawk, in which its
　eyelids are partly stitched together.
9. Fly at magpies instead of pursuing the game bird.
1. Fly off at other unintended game.
2. "Soared" (Tennyson).
3. "Poisoned the wells" (Tennyson).

It made the laughter of an afternoon
That Vivien should attempt the blameless King.
And after that, she set herself to gain
Him, the most famous man of all those times,
Merlin, who knew the range of all their arts,   165
Had built the King his havens, ships, and halls,
Was also bard, and knew the starry heavens;
The people call'd him wizard; whom at first
She play'd about with slight and sprightly talk,
And vivid smiles, and faintly-venom'd points   170
Of slander, glancing here and grazing there;
And yielding to his kindlier moods, the seer
Would watch her at her petulance and play,
Even when they seem'd unlovable, and laugh
As those that watch a kitten. Thus he grew   175
Tolerant of what he half disdain'd, and she,
Perceiving that she was but half disdain'd,
Began to break her sports with graver fits,
Turn red or pale, would often when they met
Sigh fully, or all-silent gaze upon him   180
With such a fixt devotion that the old man,
Tho' doubtful, felt the flattery, and at times
Would flatter his own wish in age for love,
And half believe her true; for thus at times
He waver'd, but that other clung to him,   185
Fixt in her will, and so the seasons went.

     Then fell on Merlin a great melancholy;
He walk'd with dreams and darkness, and he found
A doom that ever poised itself to fall,
An ever-moaning battle in the mist,   190
World-war of dying flesh against the life,
Death in all life and lying in all love,
The meanest having power upon the highest,
And the high purpose broken by the worm.[4]

     So leaving Arthur's court he gain'd the beach,   195
There found a little boat and stept into it;
And Vivien follow'd, but he mark'd her not.
She took the helm and he the sail; the boat
Drave with a sudden wind across the deeps,
And, touching Breton sands, they disembark'd.   200
And then she follow'd Merlin all the way,
Even to the wild woods of Broceliande.
For Merlin once had told her of a charm,
The which if any wrought on any one

---

4. Lines 188–98 were added in 1873. "The vision of the battle at the end" (Tennyson). As a premonition of the last great battle in the west, they are an obvious attempt at making a link between idylls. Here, and often in the later idylls, Tennyson's notion of the final catastrophe, along with his cyclical view of history, remind us of Yeats. "The meanest having power upon the highest," a condition dramatized fully in the ironic ceremony of innocence in "The Last Tournament," finds a parallel expression in Yeats's "The Second Coming": "Everywhere / The ceremony of innocence is drowned; / The best lack all conviction, while the worst / Are full of passionate intensity."

With woven paces and with waving arms, 205
The man so wrought on ever seem'd to lie
Closed in the four walls of a hollow tower,
From which was no escape for evermore;
And none could find that man for evermore,
Nor could he see but him who wrought the charm 210
Coming and going, and he lay as dead
And lost to life and use and name and fame.
And Vivien ever sought to work the charm
Upon the great enchanter of the time,
As fancying that her glory would be great 215
According to his greatness whom she quench'd.

There lay she all her length and kiss'd his feet,
As if in deepest reverence and in love.
A twist of gold was round her hair; a robe
Of samite without price, that more exprest 220
Than hid her, clung about her lissome limbs,
In color like the satin-shining palm
On sallows in the windy gleams of March.
And while she kiss'd them, crying, "Trample me,
Dear feet, that I have follow'd thro' the world, 225
And I will pay you worship; tread me down
And I will kiss you for it;" he was mute.
So dark a forethought roll'd about his brain,
As on a dull day in an ocean cave[5]
The blind wave feeling round his long sea-hall 230
In silence; wherefore, when she lifted up
A face of sad appeal, and spake and said,
"O Merlin, do ye love me?" and again,
"O Merlin, do ye love me?" and once more,
"Great Master, do ye love me?" he was mute. 235
And lissome Vivien, holding by his heel,
Writhed toward him, slided up his knee and sat,
Behind his ankle twined her hollow feet
Together, curved an arm about his neck,
Clung like a snake;[6] and letting her left hand 240
Droop from his mighty shoulder, as a leaf,
Made with her right a comb of pearl to part
The lists of such a beard as youth gone out
Had left in ashes. Then he spoke and said,
Not looking at her, "Who are wise in love 245
Love most, say least," and Vivien answer'd quick:
"I saw the little elf-god eyeless once
In Arthur's arras hall at Camelot;
But neither eyes nor tongue—O stupid child!

5. "This simile is taken from what I saw in the Caves of Ballybunion" (Tennyson).
6. It was specifically passages such as this that prompted Swinburne to say the theme of the *Idylls* was "rather a case for the divorce-court than for poetry." He particularly objected to this idyll: "The Vivien of Mr. Tennyson's idyl seems to me, to speak frankly, about the most base and repulsive person ever set forth in serious literature. . . . It is the utterly ignoble quality of Vivien which makes her so unspeakably repulsive and unfit for artistic treatment." To the contrary, Tennyson arguably was rather successful at drawing just the portrait he had in mind.

Yet you are wise who say it; let me think   250
Silence is wisdom. I am silent then,
And ask no kiss;" then adding all at once,
"And lo, I clothe myself with wisdom," drew
The vast and shaggy mantle of his beard
Across her neck and bosom to her knee,   255
And call'd herself a gilded summer fly
Caught in a great old tyrant spider's web,
Who meant to eat her up in that wild wood
Without one word. So Vivien call'd herself,
But rather seem'd a lovely baleful star   260
Veil'd in gray vapor; till he sadly smiled:
"To what request for what strange boon," he said,
"Are these your pretty tricks and fooleries,
O Vivien, the preamble? yet my thanks,
For these have broken up my melancholy."   265

      And Vivien answer'd smiling saucily:
"What, O my Master, have ye found your voice?
I bid the stranger welcome. Thanks at last!
But yesterday you never open'd lip,
Except indeed to drink. No cup had we;   270
In mine own lady palms I cull'd the spring
That gather'd trickling dropwise from the cleft,
And made a pretty cup of both my hands
And offer'd you it kneeling. Then you drank
And knew no more, nor gave me one poor word;   275
O, no more thanks than might a goat have given
With no more sign of reverence than a beard.
And when we halted at that other well,
And I was faint to swooning, and you lay
Foot-gilt with all the blossom-dust of those   280
Deep meadows we had traversed, did you know
That Vivien bathed your feet before her own?[7]
And yet no thanks; and all thro' this wild wood
And all this morning when I fondled you.
Boon, ay, there was a boon, one not so strange—   285
How had I wrong'd you? surely ye are wise,
But such a silence is more wise than kind."

      And Merlin lock'd his hand in hers and said:
"O, did ye never lie upon the shore,
And watch the curl'd white of the coming wave   290
Glass'd in the slippery sand before it breaks?
Even such a wave, but not so pleasurable,
Dark in the glass of some presageful mood,
Had I for three days seen, ready to fall.

---

7. See John 13:15–16, where Jesus washes the feet of his disciples; and Luke 7:37–38 "And behold, a woman
in the city, which was a sinner . . . stood at his feet behind him, weeping, and began to wash his feet with
tears, and did wipe them with the hair of her head, and kissed his feet, and anointed them with ointment"
(both noted by Rosenberg).

And then I rose and fled from Arthur's court   295
To break the mood. You follow'd me unask'd;
And when I look'd, and saw you following still,
My mind involved yourself the nearest thing
In that mind-mist—for shall I tell you truth?
You seem'd that wave about to break upon me   300
And sweep me from my hold upon the world,
My use and name and fame. Your pardon, child.
Your pretty sports have brighten'd all again.
And ask your boon, for boon I owe you thrice,
Once for wrong done you by confusion, next   305
For thanks it seems till now neglected, last
For these your dainty gambols; wherefore ask,
And take this boon so strange and not so strange."

        And Vivien answer'd smiling mournfully:
"O, not so strange as my long asking it,   310
Not yet so strange as you yourself are strange,
Nor half so strange as that dark mood of yours.
I ever fear'd ye were not wholly mine;
And see, yourself have own'd ye did me wrong.
The people call you prophet; let it be;   315
But not of those that can expound themselves.
Take Vivien for expounder; she will call
That three-days-long presageful gloom of yours
No presage, but the same mistrustful mood
That makes you seem less noble than yourself,   320
Whenever I have ask'd this very boon,
Now ask'd again; for see you not, dear love,
That such a mood as that which lately gloom'd
Your fancy when ye saw me following you
Must make me fear still more you are not mine,   325
Must make me yearn still more to prove you mine,
And make me wish still more to learn this charm
Of woven paces and of waving hands,
As proof of trust. O Merlin, teach it me!
The charm so taught will charm us both to rest.   330
For, grant me some slight power upon your fate,
I, feeling that you felt me worthy trust,
Should rest and let you rest, knowing you mine.
And therefore be as great as ye are named,
Not muffled round with selfish reticence.   335
How hard you look and how denyingly!
O, if you think this wickedness in me,
That I should prove it on you unawares,
That makes me passing wrathful; then our bond
Had best be loosed for ever; but think or not,   340
By Heaven that hears, I tell you the clean truth,
As clean as blood of babes, as white as milk!
O Merlin, may this earth, if ever I,
If these unwitty wandering wits of mine,
Even in the jumbled rubbish of a dream,   345

Have tript on such conjectural treachery—
May this hard earth cleave to the nadir hell
Down, down, and close again and nip me flat,
If I be such a traitress! Yield my boon,
Till which I scarce can yield you all I am;   350
And grant my re-reiterated wish,
The great proof of your love; because I think,
However wise, ye hardly know me yet."

    And Merlin loosed his hand from hers and said:
"I never was less wise, however wise,   355
Too curious Vivien, tho' you talk of trust,
Than when I told you first of such a charm.
Yea, if ye talk of trust I tell you this,
Too much I trusted when I told you that,
And stirr'd this vice in you which ruin'd man   360
Thro' woman the first hour; for howsoe'er
In children a great curiousness be well,
Who have to learn themselves and all the world,
In you, that are no child, for still I find
Your face is practised when I spell the lines,   365
I call it,—well, I will not call it vice;
But since you name yourself the summer fly,
I well could wish a cobweb for the gnat
That settles beaten back, and beaten back
Settles, till one could yield for weariness.   370
But since I will not yield to give you power
Upon my life and use and name and fame,
Why will ye never ask some other boon?
Yea, by God's rood, I trusted you too much!"
    And Vivien, like the tenderest-hearted maid   375
That ever bided tryst at village stile,
Made answer, either eyelid wet with tears:
"Nay, Master, be not wrathful with your maid;
Caress her, let her feel herself forgiven
Who feels no heart to ask another boon.   380
I think ye hardly know the tender rhyme
Of 'trust me not at all or all in all.'
I heard the great Sir Lancelot sing it once,
And it shall answer for me. Listen to it.

        "'In love, if love be love, if love be ours,   385
    Faith and unfaith can ne'er be equal powers:
    Unfaith in aught is want of faith in all.

        "'It is the little rift within the lute,
    That by and by will make the music mute,
    And ever widening slowly silence all.   390

        "'The little rift within the lover's lute,
    Or little pitted speck in garner'd fruit,
    That rotting inward slowly moulders all.

"'It is not worth the keeping; let it go:
But shall it? answer, darling, answer, no.   395
And trust me not at all or all in all.'

"O master, do ye love my tender rhyme?"

And Merlin look'd and half believed her true,
So tender was her voice, so fair her face,
So sweetly gleam'd her eyes behind her tears   400
Like sunlight on the plain behind a shower;[8]
And yet he answer'd half indignantly:

"Far other was the song[9] that once I heard
By this huge oak, sung nearly where we sit;
For here we met, some ten or twelve of us,   405
To chase a creature that was current then
In these wild woods, the hart with golden horns.
It was the time when first the question rose
About the founding of a Table Round,
That was to be, for love of God and men   410
And noble deeds, the flower of all the world;
And each incited each to noble deeds.
And while we waited, one, the youngest of us,
We could not keep him silent, out he flash'd,
And into such a song, such fire for fame,   415
Such trumpet-blowings in it, coming down
To such a stern and iron-clashing close,
That when he stopt we long'd to hurl together,
And should have done it, but the beauteous beast
Scared by the noise upstarted at our feet,   420
And like a silver shadow slipt away
Thro' the dim land. And all day long we rode
Thro' the dim land against a rushing wind,
That glorious roundel echoing in our ears,
And chased the flashes of his golden horns   425
Until they vanish'd by the fairy well
That laughs at iron—as our warriors did—
Where children cast their pins and nails, and cry,
'Laugh, little well!' but touch it with a sword,
It buzzes fiercely round the point; and there   430
We lost him—such a noble song was that.
But, Vivien, when you sang me that sweet rhyme,
I felt as tho' you knew this cursed charm,
Were proving it on me, and that I lay
And felt them slowly ebbing, name and fame."   435

And Vivien answer'd smiling mournfully:
"O, mine have ebb'd away for evermore,
And all thro' following you to this wild wood,
Because I saw you sad, to comfort you.

8. "As seen from a hill in Yorkshire" (Tennyson).
9. "The song about the clang of battle-axes, etc., in the *Coming of Arthur* [lines 484ff.]" (Tennyson).

Lo now, what hearts have men! they never mount   440
As high as woman in her selfless mood.
And touching fame, howe'er ye scorn my song,
Take one verse more—the lady speaks it—this:

    "'My name, once mine, now thine, is closelier mine,
    For fame, could fame be mine, that fame were thine,   445
    And shame, could shame be thine, that shame were mine.
    So trust me not at all or all in all.'

    "Says she not well? and there is more—this rhyme
Is like the fair pearl-necklace of the Queen,
That burst in dancing and the pearls were spilt;   450
Some lost, some stolen, some as relics kept;
But nevermore the same two sister pearls
Ran down the silken thread to kiss each other
On her white neck—so is it with this rhyme.
It lives dispersedly in many hands,   455
And every minstrel sings it differently;
Yet is there one true line, the pearl of pearls:
"Man dreams of fame while woman wakes to love.'
Yea! love, tho' love were of the grossest, carves
A portion from the solid present, eats   460
And uses, careless of the rest; but fame,
The fame that follows death is nothing to us;
And what is fame in life but half-disfame
And counterchanged with darkness? ye yourself
Know well that envy calls you devil's son,   465
And since ye seem the master of all art,
They fain would make you master of all vice."

    And Merlin lock'd his hand in hers and said:
"I once was looking for a magic weed,
And found a fair young squire who sat alone,   470
Had carved himself a knightly shield of wood,
And then was painting on it fancied arms,
Azure, an eagle rising or, the sun
In dexter chief;[1] the scroll, 'I follow fame.'
And speaking not, but leaning over him,   475
I took his brush and blotted out the bird,
And made a gardener putting in a graff,
With this for motto, 'Rather use than fame.'
You should have seen him blush; but afterwards
He made a stalwart knight. O Vivien,   480
For you, methinks you think you love me well;
For me, I love you somewhat. Rest; and Love
Should have some rest and pleasure in himself,
Not ever be too curious for a boon,
Too prurient for a proof against the grain   485
Of him ye say ye love. But Fame with men,
Being but ampler means to serve mankind,

1. A representation of a coat of arms on the upper part of the shield to the bearer's right.

Should have small rest or pleasure in herself,
But work as vassal to the larger love
That dwarfs the petty love of one to one. 490
Use gave me fame at first, and fame again
Increasing gave me use. Lo, there my boon!
What other? for men sought to prove me vile,
Because I fain had given them greater wits;
And then did envy call me devil's son. 495
The sick weak beast, seeking to help herself
By striking at her better, miss'd, and brought
Her own claw back, and wounded her own heart.
Sweet were the days when I was all unknown,
But when my name was lifted up the storm 500
Brake on the mountain and I cared not for it.
Right well know I that fame is half-disfame,
Yet needs must work my work. That other fame,
To one at least who hath not children vague,
The cackle of the unborn about the grave, 505
I cared not for it. A single misty star,[2]
Which is the second in a line of stars
That seem a sword beneath a belt of three,
I never gazed upon it but I dreamt
Of some vast charm concluded in that star 510
To make fame nothing. Wherefore, if I fear,
Giving you power upon me thro' this charm,
That you might play me falsely, having power,
However well ye think ye love me now—
As sons of kings loving in pupilage 515
Have turn'd to tyrants when they came to power—
I rather dread the loss of use than fame;
If you—and not so much from wickedness,
As some wild turn of anger, or a mood
Of overstrain'd affection, it may be, 520
To keep me all to your own self,—or else
A sudden spurt of woman's jealousy,—
Should try this charm on whom ye say ye love."

And Vivien answer'd smiling as in wrath:
"Have I not sworn? I am not trusted. Good! 525
Well, hide it, hide it; I shall find it out,
And being found take heed of Vivien.
A woman and not trusted, doubtless I
Might feel some sudden turn of anger born
Of your misfaith; and your fine epithet 530
Is accurate too, for this full love of mine
Without the full heart back may merit well
Your term of overstrain'd. So used as I,
My daily wonder is, I love at all.
And as to woman's jealousy, O, why not? 535

2. "When this was written," Tennyson noted, "some astronomers fancied that this nebula in Orion was the vastest object in the universe—a firmament of suns too far away to be resolved into stars by the telescope, and yet so huge as to be seen by the naked eye."

O, to what end, except a jealous one,
And one to make me jealous if I love,
Was this fair charm inverted by yourself?
I well believe that all about this world
Ye cage a buxom captive here and there,   540
Closed in the four walls of a hollow tower
From which is no escape for evermore."

   Then the great master merrily answer'd her:
"Full many a love in loving youth was mine;
I needed then no charm to keep them mine   545
But youth and love; and that full heart of yours
Whereof ye prattle, may now assure you mine;
So live uncharm'd. For those who wrought it first,
The wrist is parted from the hand that waved,
The feet unmortised from their anklebones   550
Who paced it, ages back—but will ye hear
The legend as in guerdon for your rhyme?

   "There lived a king in the most eastern East,[3]
Less old than I, yet older, for my blood
Hath earnest in it of far springs to be.   555
A tawny pirate anchor'd in his port,
Whose bark had plunder'd twenty nameless isles;
And passing one, at the high peep of dawn,
He saw two cities in a thousand boats
All fighting for a woman on the sea.   560
And pushing his back craft among them all,
He lightly scatter'd theirs and brought her off,
With loss of half his people arrow-slain;
A maid so smooth, so white, so wonderful,
They said a light came from her when she moved.   565
And since the pirate would not yield her up,
The king impaled him for his piracy,
Then made her queen. But those isle-nurtured eyes
Waged such unwilling tho' successful war
On all the youth, they sicken'd; councils thinn'd,   570
And armies waned, for magnet-like she drew
The rustiest iron of old fighters' hearts;
And beasts themselves would worship, camels knelt
Unbidden, and the brutes of mountain back
That carry kings in castles bow'd black knees   575
Of homage, ringing with their serpent hands,
To make her smile, her golden ankle-bells.
What wonder, being jealous, that he sent
His horns of proclamation out thro' all
The hundred under-kingdoms that he sway'd   580
To find a wizard who might teach the king
Some charm which, being wought upon the queen,
Might keep her all his own. To such a one

3. Of lines, 553–97 Tennyson noted: "People have tried to discover this legend, but there is no legend of
the kind that I know of."

He promised more than ever king has given,
A league of mountain full of golden mines,   585
A province with a hundred miles of coast,
A palace and a princess, all for him;
But on all those who tried and fail'd the king
Pronounced a dismal sentence, meaning by it
To keep the list low and pretenders back,   590
Or, like a king, not to be trifled with—
Their heads should moulder on the city gates.
And many tried and fail'd, because the charm
Of nature in her overbore their own;
And many a wizard brow bleach'd on the walls,   595
And many weeks a troop of carrion crows
Hung like a cloud above the gateway towers."

   And Vivien breaking in upon him, said:
"I sit and gather honey; yet, methinks,
Thy tongue has tript a little; ask thyself.   600
The lady never made *unwilling* war
With those fine eyes; she had her pleasure in it,
And made her good man jealous with good cause.
And lived there neither dame nor damsel then
Wroth at a lover's loss? were all as tame,   605
I mean, as noble, as their queen was fair?
Not one to flirt a venom at her eyes,
Or pinch a murderous dust into her drink,
Or make her paler with a poison'd rose?
Well, those were not our days—but did they find   610
A wizard? Tell me, was he like to thee?"

   She ceased, and made her lithe arm round his neck
Tighten, and then drew back, and let her eyes
Speak for her, glowing on him, like a bride's
On her new lord, her own, the first of men.   615

   He answer'd laughing: "Nay, not like to me.[4]
At last they found—his foragers for charms—
A little glassy-headed hairless man,
Who lived alone in a great wild on grass,
Read but one book, and ever reading grew   620
So grated down and filed away with thought,
So lean his eyes were monstrous; while the skin
Clung but to crate and basket, ribs and spine.
And since he kept his mind on one sole aim,
Nor ever touch'd fierce wine, nor tasted flesh,   625
Nor own'd a sensual wish, to him the wall
That sunders ghosts and shadow-casting men
Became a crystal, and he saw them thro' it,
And heard their voices talk behind the wall,
And learnt their elemental secrets, powers   630

---

4. Of lines 616–48: "Nor is this a legend to be found" (Tennyson).

And forces; often o'er the sun's bright eye
Drew the vast eyelid of an inky cloud,
And lash'd[5] it at the base with slanting storm;
Or in the noon of mist and driving rain,
When the lake whiten'd and the pinewood roar'd,   635
And the cairn'd mountain was a shadow, sunn'd
The world to peace again. Here was the man;
And so by force they dragg'd him to the king.
And then he taught the king to charm the queen
In such-wise that no man could see her more,   640
Nor saw she save the king, who wrought the charm,
Coming and going, and she lay as dead,
And lost all use of life. But when the king
Made proffer of the league of golden mines,
The province with a hundred miles of coast,   645
The palace and the princess, that old man
Went back to his old wild, and lived on grass,
And vanish'd and his book came down to me."

     And Vivien answer'd smiling saucily:
"Ye have the book; the charm is written in it.   650
Good! take my counsel, let me know it at once;
For keep it like a puzzle chest in chest,
With each chest lock'd and padlock'd thirty fold,
And whelm all this beneath as vast a mound
As after furious battle turfs the slain   655
On some wild down above the windy deep,
I yet should strike upon a sudden means
To dig, pick, open, find and read the charm;
Then, if I tried it, who should blame me then?"

     And smiling as a master smiles at one   660
That is not of his school, nor any school
But that where blind and naked Ignorance
Delivers brawling judgments, unashamed,
On all things all day long, he answer'd her:

     "Thou read the book,[6] my pretty Vivien!   665
O, ay, it is but twenty pages long,
But every page having an ample marge,
And every marge enclosing in the midst
A square of text that looks a little blot,
The text no larger than the limbs of fleas;   670
And every square of text an awful charm,
Writ in a language that has long gone by,
So long that mountains have arisen since
With cities on their flanks—thou read the book!
And every margin scribbled, crost, and cramm'd   675

5. "Like an eyelash" (Tennyson).
6. "The text is the English Constitution. 'None can read the text, not even I'—and this is the literal truth,
   for the English Constitution (unlike the American, for example) is 'the whole body of common and statu-
   tory law of the realm' plus 'the knowledge of the working of the government'" (Lang, Tennyson's Pscho-
   drama, pp. 11–12).

With comment, densest condensation, hard
To mind and eye; but the long sleepless nights
Of my long life have made it easy to me.
And none can read the text, not even I;
And none can read the comment but myself;   680
And in the comment did I find the charm.
O, the results are simple; a mere child
Might use it to the harm of any one,
And never could undo it. Ask no more;
For tho' you should not prove it upon me,   685
But keep that oath ye sware, ye might, perchance,
Assay it on some one of the Table Round,
And all because ye dream they babble of you."

   And Vivien, frowning in true anger, said:
"What dare the full-fed liars say of me?   690
They ride abroad redressing human wrongs!
They sit with knife in meat and wine in horn.
They bound to holy vows of chastity!
Were I not woman, I could tell a tale.
But you are man, you well can understand   695
The shame that cannot be explain'd for shame.
Not one of all the drove should touch me—swine!"

   Then answer'd Merlin careless of her words:
"You breathe but accusation vast and vague,
Spleen-born, I think, and proofless. If ye know,   700
Set up the charge ye know, to stand or fall!"

   And Vivien answer'd frowning wrathfully:
"O, ay, what say ye to Sir Valence, him
Whose kinsman left him watcher o'er his wife
And two fair babes, and went to distant lands,   705
Was one year gone, and on returning found
Not two but three? there lay the reckling,[7] one
But one hour old! What said the happy sire?
A seven-months' babe had been a truer gift.
Those twelve sweet moons confused his fatherhood."   710

   Then answer'd Merlin: "Nay, I know the tale.
Sir Valence wedded with an outland dame;
Some cause had kept him sunder'd from his wife.
One child they had; it lived with her; she died.
His kinsman travelling on his own affair   715
Was charged by Valence to bring home the child.
He brought, not found it therefore; take the truth."

   "O, ay," said Vivien, "over-true a tale!
What say ye then to sweet Sir Sagramore,
That ardent man? 'To pluck the flower in season,'   720

7. The runt in a litter of puppies, hence a weakling infant.

So says the song, 'I trow it is no treason.'
O Master, shall we call him over-quick
To crop his own sweet rose before the hour?"

    And Merlin answer'd: "Over-quick art thou
To catch a loathly plume fallen from the wing   725
Of that foul bird of rapine whose whole prey
Is man's good name. He never wrong'd his bride.
I know the tale. An angry gust of wind
Puff'd out his torch among the myriad-room'd
And many-corridor'd complexities   730
Of Arthur's palace. Then he found a door,
And darkling felt the sculptured ornament
That wreathen round it made it seem his own,
And wearied out made for the couch and slept,
A stainless man beside a stainless maid;   735
And either slept, nor knew of other there,
Till high the dawn piercing the royal rose
In Arthur's casement glimmer'd chastely down,
Blushing upon them blushing, and at once
He rose without a word and parted from her.   740
But when the thing was blazed about the court,
The brute world howling forced them into bonds,
And as it chanced they are happy, being pure."

    "O, ay," said Vivien, "that were likely too!
What say ye then to fair Sir Percivale   745
And of the horrid foulness that he wrought,
The saintly youth, the spotless lamb of Christ,
Or some black wether of Saint Satan's fold?
What, in the precincts of the chapel-yard,
Among the knightly brasses of the graves,   750
And by the cold Hic Jacets[8] of the dead!"

    And Merlin answer'd careless of her charge:
"A sober man is Percivale and pure,
But once in life was fluster'd with new wine,
Then paced for coolness in the chapel-yard,   755
Where one of Satan's shepherdesses caught
And meant to stamp him with her master's mark.
And that he sinn'd is not believable;
For, look upon his face!—but if he sinn'd,
The sin that practice burns into the blood,   760
And not the one dark hour which brings remorse,
Will brand us, after, of whose fold we be;
Or else were he, the holy king[9] whose hymns
Are chanted in the minster, worse than all.
But is your spleen froth'd out, or have ye more?"   765

8. The "here lies" beginning the epitaphs on tomb stones.
9. "David" (Tennyson).

And Vivien answer'd frowning yet in wrath:
"O, ay; what say ye to Sir Lancelot, friend,
Traitor or true? that commerce with the Queen,
I ask you, is it clamor'd by the child,
Or whisper'd in the corner? do ye know it?" 770

To which he answer'd sadly: "Yea, I know it.
Sir Lancelot went ambassador, at first,
To fetch her, and she watch'd him from her walls.
A rumor runs, she took him for the king,
So fixt her fancy on him; let them be. 775
But have ye no one word of loyal praise
For Arthur, blameless king and stainless man?"

She answer'd with a low and chuckling laugh:
"Man! is he man at all, who knows and winks?
Sees what his fair bride is and does, and winks? 780
By which the good King means to blind himself,
And blinds himself and all the Table Round
To all the foulness that they work. Myself
Could call him—were it not for womanhood—
The pretty, popular name such manhood earns, 785
Could call him the main cause of all their crime,
Yea, were he not crown'd king, coward and fool."

Then Merlin to his own heart, loathing, said:
"O true and tender! O my liege and King!
O selfless man and stainless gentleman, 790
Who wouldst against thine own eye-witness fain
Have all men true and leal, all women pure!
How, in the mouths of base interpreters,
From over-fineness not intelligible
To things with every sense as false and foul 795
As the poach'd[1] filth that floods the middle street.
Is thy white blamelessness accounted blame!"

But Vivien, deeming Merlin overborne
By instance, recommenced, and let her tongue
Rage like a fire among the noblest names, 800
Polluting, and imputing her whole self,
Defaming and defacing, till she left
Not even Lancelot brave nor Galahad clean.
Her words had issue other than she will'd.
He dragg'd his eyebrow bushes down, and made 805
A snowy pent-house for his hollow eyes,[2]
And mutter'd in himself: "Tell her the charm!
So, if she had it, would she rail on me
To snare the next, and if she have it not
So will she rail. What did the wanton say? 810
'Not mount as high!' we scarce can sink as low;

1. An uncommon dictionary definition: "To make (land) muddy or broken up by trampling."
2. Ricks compares Coleridge, *The Raven*, line 5: "His brow, like a pent-house, hung over his eyes."

For men at most differ as heaven and earth,
But women, worst and best, as heaven and hell.
I know the Table Round, my friends of old;
All brave, and many generous, and some chaste.   815
She cloaks the scar of some repulse with lies.
I well believe she tempted them and fail'd,
Being so bitter; for fine plots may fail,
Tho' harlots paint their talk as well as face
With colors of the heart that are not theirs.   820
I will not let her know; nine tithes of times
Face-flatterer and backbiter are the same.
And they, sweet soul, that most impute a crime
Are pronest to it, and impute themselves,
Wanting the mental range, or low desire   825
Not to feel lowest makes them level all;
Yea, they would pare the mountain to the plain,
To leave an equal baseness; and in this
Are harlots like the crowd that if they find
Some stain or blemish in a name of note,   830
Not grieving that their greatest are so small,
Inflate themselves with some insane delight,
And judge all nature from her feet of clay,
Without the will to lift their eyes, and see
Her godlike head crown'd with spiritual fire,   835
And touching other worlds. I am weary of her."

     He spoke in words part heard, in whispers part,
Half-suffocated in the hoary fell
And many-winter'd fleece of throat and chin.
But Vivien, gathering somewhat of his mood,   840
And hearing "harlot" mutter'd twice or thrice,
Leapt from her session[3] on his lap, and stood
Stiff as a viper frozen; loathsome sight,
How from the rosy lips of life and love
Flash'd the bare-grinning skeleton of death!   845
White was her cheek; sharp breaths of anger puff'd
Her fairy nostril out; her hand half-clench'd
Went faltering sideways downward to her belt,
And feeling. Had she found a dagger there—
For in a wink the false love turns to hate—   850
She would have stabb'd him; but she found it not.
His eye was calm, and suddenly she took
To bitter weeping, like a beaten child,
A long, long weeping, not consolable.
Then her false voice made way, broken with sobs: 855

     "O crueller than was ever told in tale
Or sung in song! O vainly lavish'd love!
O, cruel there was nothing wild or strange,
Or seeming shameful—for what shame in love,

---

3. In the archaic sense, the act of sitting or posture of being seated.

So love be true, and not as yours is?—nothing   860
Poor Vivien had not done to win his trust
Who call'd her what he call'd her—all her crime,
All—all—the wish to prove him wholly hers."

    She mused a little, and then clapt her hands
Together with a wailing shriek, and said: 865
"Stabb'd through the heart's affections to the heart!
Seethed like the kid in its own mother's milk![4]
Kill'd with a word than a life of blows!
I thought that he was gentle, being great;
O God, that I had loved a smaller man!   870
I should have found in him a greater heart.
O, I, that flattering my true passion, saw
The knights, the court, the King, dark in your light,
Who loved to make men darker than they are,
Because of that high pleasure which I had   875
To seat you sole upon my pedestal
Of worship—I am answer'd, and henceforth
The course of life that seem'd so flowery to me
With you for guide and master, only you,
Becomes the sea-cliff pathway broken short,   880
And ending in a ruin—nothing left
But into some low cave to crawl, and there,
If the wolf spare me, weep my life away,
Kill'd with unutterable unkindliness."

    She paused, she turn'd away, she hung her head,   885
The snake of gold slid from her hair, the braid
Slipt and uncoil'd itself, she wept afresh,
And the dark wood grew darker toward the storm
In silence, while his anger slowly died
Within him, till he let his wisdom go   890
For ease of heart, and half believed her true;
Call'd her to shelter in the hollow oak,
"Come from the storm," and having no reply,
Gazed at the heaving shoulder and the face
Hand-hidden, as for utmost grief or shame;   895
Then thrice essay'd, by tenderest-touching terms,
To sleek her ruffled peace of mind, in vain.
At last she let herself be conquer'd by him,
And as the cageling newly flown returns,
The seeming-injured simple hearted thing   900
Came to her old perch back, and settled there.
There while she sat, half-falling from his knees,
Half-nestled at his heart, and since he saw
The slow tear creep from her closed eyelid yet,
About her, more in kindness than in love,   905
The gentle wizard cast a shielding arm.
But she dislink'd herself at once and rose,

4. Exodus 23:19 and 34:26: "Thou shalt not seethe a kid in his mother's milk."

Her arms upon her breast across, and stood,
A virtuous gentlewoman deeply wrong'd,
Upright and flush'd before him; then she said: 910

"There must be now no passages of love
Betwixt us twain henceforward evermore;
Since, if I be what I am grossly call'd,
What should be granted which your own gross heart
Would reckon worth the taking? I will go.   915
In truth, but one thing now—better have died
Thrice than have ask'd it once—could make me stay—
That proof of trust—so often ask'd in vain!
How justly, after that vile term of yours,
I find with grief! I might believe you then,   920
Who knows? once more. Lo! what was once to me
Mere matter of the fancy, now hath grown
The vast necessity of heart and life.
Farewell; think gently of me, for I fear
My fate or folly, passing gayer youth   925
For one so old, must be to love thee still.
But ere I leave thee let me swear once more
That if I schemed against thy peace in this,
May yon just heaven, that darkens o'er me, send
One flash that, missing all things else, may make   930
My scheming brain a cinder, if I lie."

    Scarce had she ceased, when out of heaven a bolt—
For now the storm was close above them—struck,
Furrowing a giant oak, and javelining
With darted spikes and splinters of the wood   935
The dark earth round. He raised his eyes and saw
The tree that shone white-listed[5] thro' the gloom.
But Vivien, fearing heaven had heard her oath,
And dazzled by the livid-flickering fork,
And deafen'd with the stammering cracks and claps   940
That follow'd, flying back and crying out,
"O Merlin, tho' you do not love me, save,
Yet save me!" clung to him and hugg'd him close;
And call'd him dear protector in her fright,
Nor yet forgot her practice in her fright,   945
But wrought upon his mood and hugg'd him close.
The pale blood of the wizard at her touch
Took gayer colors, like an opal warm'd.
She blamed herself for telling hearsay tales;
She shook from fear, and for her fault she wept   950
Of petulancy; she call'd him lord and liege,
Her seer, her bard, her silver star of eve,
Her God, her Merlin, the one passionate love
Of her whole life; and overhead
Bellow'd the tempest, and the rotten branch   955

5. "Striped with white" (Tennyson).

Snapt in the rushing of the river-rain
Above them; and in change of glare and gloom
Her eyes and neck glittering went and came;
Till now the storm; its burst of passion spent,
Moaning and calling out of other lands,   960
Had left the ravaged woodland yet once more
To peace; and what should not have been had been,
For Merlin, overtalk'd and overworn,
Had yielded, told her all the charm, and slept.

Then, in one moment, she put forth the charm   965
Of woven paces and of waving hands,
And in the hollow oak he lay as dead,
And lost to life and use and name and fame.

Then crying, "I have made his glory mine,"
And shrieking out, "O fool!" the harlot leapt   970
Adown the forest, and the thicket closed
Behind her, and the forest echo'd "fool."

                                        1855–56; 1859

Lancelot and Elaine[1]

Elaine the fair, Elaine the lovable,
Elaine, the lily maid of Astolat,[2]
High in her chamber up a tower to the east
Guarded the sacred shield of Lancelot;
Which first she placed where morning's earliest ray   5
Might strike it, and awake her with the gleam;
Then fearing rust or soilure fashion'd for it
A case of silk, and braided thereupon
All the devices blazon'd on the shield
In their own tinct, and added, of her wit,   10

1. Although the primary source is Malory, the legend or versions of it had been in Tennyson's mind for many years. Compare "The Lady of Shalott," and n. 1, p. 41, in which Tennyson claims he did not know of Malory's Elaine in 1832. One cannot be certain just when he became familiar with Malory's account. He does say, "The vision of Arthur as I have drawn him had come upon me when, little more than a boy, I first lighted upon Malory" (*Memoir* II, 128), implying, perhaps, only partial familiarity.
  In contrast to "Merlin and Vivien," numerous passages of this idyll are direct quotations from or close paraphrases of Malory. Among his notes to the poem, Christopher Ricks reproduces in ample detail the more relevant parts, opening with: "The source is Malory xviii 9–20, beginning: 'This old baron had a daughter at that time, that was called the fair maid of Astolat, and ever she beheld sir Launcelot wonderfully; and she cast such a love unto sir Launcelot, that she could not withdraw her love, wherefore she died; and her name was Elaine la Blaunch.'"
  Tennyson's brief note in the *Eversley* edition surely gives us the key to the place he felt this idyll had in the whole: "The tenderest of all natures sinks under the blight, that which is of the highest in her working her doom." As in "Balin and Balan," then much closer to the top in "Merlin and Vivien," the point is that corruption at the highest levels of any society or civil orders takes its toll first, and manifests itself dramatically, in the quotidian world, albeit a chivalric, allegorical rendering of "the banality of evil." For the poet is acutely aware that the Hobbsian world of presocial man is indeed one of "continual fear and danger of violent death; and the life of man, solitary, poor, nasty, brutish and short." We have seen those adjectives come alive in the preceding two idylls; here the focus seems to be on "poor" and "short." Edward Engleberg ("The Beast Image in Tennyson's *Idylls of the King*," *ELH*, 1955) was among the first to recognize the centrality of this motif.
2. The town of Guilford, in Surrey, according to Malory.

A border fantasy of branch and flower,
And yellow-throated nestling in the nest.
Nor rested thus content, but day by day,
Leaving her household and good father, climb'd
That eastern tower, and entering barr'd her door,   15
Stript off the case, and read the naked shield,
Now guess'd a hidden meaning in his arms,
Now made a pretty history to herself
Of every dint a sword had beaten in it,
And every scratch a lance had made upon it,   20
Conjecturing when and where: this cut is fresh,
That ten years back; this dealt him at Caerlyle,[3]
That at Caerleon—this at Camelot[4]—
And ah, God's mercy, what a stroke was there!
And here a thrust that might have kill'd, but God   25
Broke the strong lance, and roll'd his enemy down,
And saved him: so she lived in fantasy.

How came the lily maid by that good shield
Of Lancelot, she that knew not even his name?
He left it with her, when he rode to tilt   30
For the great diamond in the diamond jousts,
Which Arthur had ordain'd, and by that name
Had named them, since a diamond was the prize.

For Arthur, long before they crown'd him king,
Roving the trackless realms of Lyonnesse,[5]   35
Had found a glen, gray boulder and black tarn.
A horror lived about the tarn, and clave
Like its own mists to all the mountain side;
For here two brothers,[6] one a king, had met
And fought together, but their names were lost;   40
And each had slain his brother at a blow;
And down they fell and made the glen abhorr'd.
And there they lay till all their bones were bleach'd,
And lichen'd into color with crags.
And he that once was king had on a crown,   45
Of diamonds, one in front and four aside.
And Arthur came, and laboring up the pass,
All in a misty moonshine, unawares
Had trodden that crown'd skeleton, and the skull
Brake from the nape, and from the skull the crown   50
Roll'd into light, and turning on its rims
Fled like a glittering rivulet to the tarn.
And down the shingly scaur[7] he plunged, and caught,

---

3. Carlisle, in Cumberland.
4. Arthur's capital has been variously located in Somersetshire, Winchester, and Wales. Caerleon (see line 9 in "Merlin and Vivien") was in Wales.
5. "A land that is said to have streched between Land's End and Scilly, and to have contained some of Cornwall as well" (Tennyson).
6. As Ricks notes, "This episode [lines 39–55] is not in Malory."
7. A variant of scar; a precipitous bank.

And set it on his head, and in his heart
Heard murmurs, 'Lo, thou likewise shalt be king.'   55

Thereafter, when a king, he had the gems
Pluck'd from the crown, and show'd them to his knights
Saying: "These jewels, whereupon I chanced
Divinely, are the kingdom's, not the King's—
For public use. Henceforward let there be   60
Once every year, a joust for one of these;
For so by nine years' proof we needs must learn
Which is our mightiest, and ourselves shall grow
In use of arms and manhood, till we drive
The heathen,[8] who, some say, shall rule the land   65
Hereafter, which God hinder!' Thus he spoke.
And eight years past, eight jousts had been, and still
Had Lancelot won the diamond of the year,
With purpose to present them to the Queen
When all were won; but, meaning all at once   70
To snare her royal fancy with a boon
Worth half her realm, had never spoken word.

Now for the central diamond and the last
And largest, Arthur, holding then his court
Hard on the river nigh the place which now   75
Is this world's hugest,[9] let proclaim a joust
At Camelot, and when the time drew nigh
Spake—for she had been sick—to Guinevere:
'Are you so sick, my Queen, you cannot move
To these fair jousts?' 'Yea, lord,' she said, 'ye know it.'   80
'Then will ye miss,' he answer'd, 'the great deeds
Of Lancelot, and his prowess in the lists,
A sight ye love to look on.' And the Queen
Lifted her eyes, and they dwelt languidly
On Lancelot, where he stood beside the King.   85
He, thinking that he read her meaning there,
'Stay with me, I am sick; my love is more
Than many diamonds,' yielded; and a heart
Love-loyal to the least wish of the Queen—
However much he yearn'd to make complete,   90
The tale[1] of diamonds for his destined boon—
Urged him to speak against the truth, and say,
'Sir King, mine ancient wound is hardly whole,
And lets[2] me from the saddle;' and the King
Glanced first at him, then her, and went his way.   95
No sooner gone than suddenly she began:

'To blame, my lord Sir Lancelot, much to blame!
Why go ye not to these fair jousts? the knights

8. Angles, Saxons, and Jutes (see "The Coming of Arthur," line 59).
9. London.
1. "Tally" (Ricks).
2. "Hinders" (Ricks).

Are half of them our enemies, and the crowd
Will murmur, "Lo the shameless ones, who take   100
Their pastime now the trustful King is gone!'"
Then Lancelot, vext at having lied in vain:
'Are ye so wise? ye were not once so wise,
My Queen, that summer when ye loved me first.
Then of the crowd ye took no more account   105
Than of the myriad cricket of the mead,
When its own voice clings to each blade of grass,
And every voice is nothing. As to knights,
Them surely can I silence with all ease.
But now my loyal worship is allow'd   110
Of all men; many a bard, without offence,
Has link'd our names together in his lay,
Lancelot, the flower of bravery, Guinevere,
The pearl of beauty; and our knights at feast
Have pledged us in this union, while the King   115
Would listen smiling. How then? is there more?
Has Arthur spoken aught? or would yourself,
Now weary of my service and devoir,[3]
Henceforth be truer to your faultless lord?'

She broke into a little scornful laugh: 120
'Arthur, my lord, Arthur, the faultless King,
That passionate perfection, my good lord—
But who can gaze upon the sun in heaven?
He never spake word of reproach to me,
He never had a glimpse of mine untruth,   125
He cares not for me. Only here to-day
There gleamed a vague suspicion in his eyes;
Some meddling rogue has tampered with him—else
Rapt in this fancy of his Table Round,
And swearing men to vows impossible.   130
To make them like himself; but, friend, to me
He is all fault who hath no fault at all.
For who loves me must have a touch of earth;
The low sun makes the color.[4] I am yours,
Not Arthur's, as ye know, save by the bond.   135
And therefore hear my words: go to the jousts;
The tiny-trumpeting gnat can break our dream
When sweetest; and the vermin voices here
May buzz so loud—we scorn them, but they sting.'
Then answer'd Lancelot, the chief of knights: 140
'And with what face, after my pretext made,
Shall I appear, O Queen, at Camelot, I
Before a king who honors his own word
As if it were his God's?'

'Yea,' said the Queen,
'A moral child without the craft to rule,   145

---

3. Duty.
4. "The colors of sunrise and sunset" (Ricks).

Else had he not lost me; but listen to me,
If I must find you wit. We hear it said
That men go down before your spear at a touch,
But knowing you are Lancelot; your great name,
This conquers. Hide it therefore; go unknown.   150
Win! by this kiss you will; and our true King
Will then allow your pretext, O my knight,
As all for glory; for to speak him true,
Ye know right well, how meek soe'er he seem,
No keener hunter after glory breathes.   155
He loves it in his knights more than himself;
They prove to him his work. Win and return.'

    Then got Sir Lancelot suddenly to horse,
Wroth at himself. Not willing to be known,
He left the barren-beaten thoroughfare,   160
Chose the green path that show'd the rarer foot,
And there among the solitary downs,
Full often lost in fancy, lost his way;
Till as he traced a faintly-shadow'd track,
That all in loops and links among the dales   165
Ran to the Castle of Astolat, he saw
Fired from the west, far on a hill, the towers.
Thither he made, and blew the gateway horn.
Then came an old, dumb, myriad-wrinkle man,
Who let him into lodging and disarm'd.   170
And Lancelot marvell'd at the wordless man;
And issuing the Lord of Astolat
With two strong sons, Sir Torre and Sir Lavaine,
Moving to meet him in the castle court;
And close behind them stept the lily maid   175
Elaine, his daughter; mother of the house
There was not. Some light jest among them rose
With laughter dying as the great knight
Approach'd them; then the Lord of Astolat:
'Whence comest thou, my guest, and by what name[5]   180
Livest between the lips? for by thy state
And presence I might guess thee chief of those,
After the King, who eat in Arthur's halls.
Him have I seen; the rest, his Table Round,
Known as they are, to me they are unknown.'   185
    Then answer'd Lancelot, the chief of knights:
'Known am I, and of Arthur's hall, and known,
What I by mere mischance have brought, my shield.
But since I go to joust as one unknown
At Camelot for the diamond, ask me not;   190
Hereafter ye shall know me—and the shield—
I pray you lend me one, if such you have,
Blank, or at least with some device not mine.'

---

5. Compare Queen Arete to Odysseus, "Who art thou among men and from whence?" (*Odyssey* VII, lines 237ff.), and *Odyssey* III, lines 79ff. and VII, lines 239ff. (Eve Adler). As Ricks notes, referring to *Aeneid* XII, line 235, "an epic formula."

Then said the Lord of Astolat: 'Here is Torre's:
Hurt in his first tilt was my son, Sir Torre,   195
And so, God wot, his shield is blank enough.
His ye can have.' Then added plain Sir Torre,
'Yea, since I cannot use it, ye may have it.'
Here laugh'd the father saying: 'Fie, Sir Churl,
Is that an answer for a noble knight?   200
Allow him! but Lavaine, my younger here,
He is so full of lustihood, he will ride,
Joust for it, and win, and bring it in an hour,
And set it in this damsel's golden hair,
To make her thrice as wilful as before.'   205

'Nay, father, nay, good father, shame me not
Before this noble knight,' said young Lavaine,
'For nothing. Surely I but play'd on Torre,
He seem'd so sullen, vext he could not go;
A jest, no more! for, knight, the maiden dreamt   210
That some one put this diamond in her hand,
And that it was too slippery to be held,
And slipt and fell into some pool or stream,[6]
The castle-well, belike; and then I said
That *if* I went and *if* I fought and won it—   215
But all was jest and joke among ourselves—
Then must she keep it safelier. All was jest.
But, father, give me leave, an if he will,
To ride to Camelot with this noble knight.
Win shall I not, but do my best to win;   220
Young as I am, yet would I do my best.'

'So ye will grace me,' answer'd Lancelot,
Smiling a moment, "with your fellowship
O'er these waste downs whereon I lost myself,
Then were I glad of you as guide and friend;   225
And you shall win this diamond,—as I hear,
It is a fair large diamond,—if ye may,
And yield it to this maiden, if ye will.'
'A fair large diamond,' added plain Sir Torre,
'Such be for queens, and not for simple maids.'   230
Then she, who held her eyes upon the ground,
Elaine, and heard her name so tost about,
Flush'd slightly at the slight disparagement
Before the stranger knight, who, looking at her,
Full courtly, yet not falsely, thus return'd: 235
'If what is fair but for what is fair,
And only queens are to be counted so,
Rash were my judgment then, who deem this maid
Might wear as fair a jewel as is on earth,
Not violating the bond of like to like.'   240

---

6. "A vision prophetic of Guinevere hurling the diamonds into the Thames" (Tennyson).

He spoke and ceased; the lily maid Elaine,
Won by the mellow voice before she look'd,
Lifted her eyes and read his lineaments.
The great and guilty love he bare the Queen,
In battle with the love he bare his lord,   245
Had marr'd his face, and mark'd it ere his time.
Another sinning on such heights with one,
The flower of all the west and all the world,
Had been the sleeker for it; but in him
His mood was often like a fiend, and rose   250
And drove him into wastes and solitudes
For agony, who was yet a living soul.
Marr'd he was, he seem'd the goodliest man
That ever among ladies ate in hall,
And noblest, when she lifted up her eyes.[7]   255
However marr'd, of more than twice her years,
Seam'd with an ancient sword-cut on the cheek,
And bruised and bronzed, she lifted up her eyes
And loved him, with that love which was her doom.

    Then the great knight, the darling of the court,   260
Loved of the loveliest, into that rude hall
Stept with all grace, and not with half disdain
Hid under grace, as in a smaller time,
But kindly man moving among his kind;
Whom they with meats and vintage of their best   265
And talk and minstrel melody entertain'd,
And much they ask'd of court and Table Round,
And ever well and readily answer'd he;
But Lancelot, when they glanced at Guinevere,
Suddenly speaking of the wordless man,   270
Heard from the baron that, ten years before,
The heathen caught and reft him of his tongue.
'He learnt and warn'd me of their fierce design
Against my house, and him they caught and maim'd;
But I, my sons, and little daughter fled   275
From bonds or death, and dwelt among the woods
By the great river in a boatman's hut.
Dull days were those, till our good Arthur broke
The Pagan yet once more on Badon hill.'[8]

---

7. Gray among others notes Tennyson's uses of biblical expressions to convey expectation, e.g., Genesis 13:10: "And Lot lifted up his eyes."
8. The last of the twelve battles against the Angles and Saxons. Tennyson took the list that follows from Bohn's translation of Nennius's *Historia Britonum* (c. 796): "Thus it was that the magnanimous Arthur, with all the kings and military force of Britain, fought against the Saxons. And though there were many more noble than himself, yet he was twelve times chosen their commander, and was as often conqueror. The first battle in which he was engaged was at the mouth of the river Glem. The second, third, fourth, and fifth were on another river, by the Britons called Duglas, in the region Linuis. The sixth on the river Bassas. The seventh in the wood Celidon, which the Britons call Cat Coit Celidon. The eighth was near Gurnion Castle, where Arthur bore the image of the Holy Virgin, mother of God, upon his shoulders, and through the power of our Lord Jesus Christ, and the holy Mary, put the Saxons to flight, and pursued them the whole day with great slaughter. The ninth was at the City of Legion, which is called Caerleon. The tenth was on the banks of the river Trat Treuroit. The eleventh was on the mountain Breguoin, which we call Cat Bregion. The twelfth was a most severe contest, when Arthur penetrated to the hill of Badon. In this engagement, nine hundred and forty fell by his hand alone, no one but the Lord affording him assistance. In all these engagements the Britons were successful. For no strength can avail against the will of the Almighty."

'O, there, great lord, doubtless,' Lavaine said, rapt   280
By all the sweet and sudden passion of youth
Toward greatness in its elder, 'you have fought.
O, tell us—for we live apart—you know
Of Arthur's glorious wars.' And Lancelot spoke
And answer'd him at full, as having been   285
With Arthur in the fight which all day long
Rang by the white mouth of the violent Glem;
And in the four loud battles by the shore
Of Duglas; that on Bassa; then the war
That thunder'd in and out the gloomy skirts   290
Of Celidon the forest; and again
By Castle Gurnion, where the glorious King
Had on his cuirass[9] worn our Lady's Head,
Carved of one emerald centred in a sun
Of silver rays, that lighten'd as he breathed;   295
And at Caerloeon had he help'd his lord,
When the strong neighings of the wild White Horse[1]
Set every gilded parapet shuddering;
And up in Agned-Cathregonion too,
And down the waste sand-shores of Trath Treroit,   300
Where many a heathen fell; 'and on the mount
Of Badon I myself beheld the King
Charge at the head of all his Table Round,
And all his legions crying Christ and him,
And break them; and I saw him, after, stand   305
High on a heap of slain, from spur to plume
Red as the rising sun with heathen blood,
And seeing me, with a great voice he cried,
"They are broken, they are broken!" for the King,
However mild he seems at home, nor cares   310
For triumph in our mimic wars, the jousts—
For if his own knight casts him down, he laughs,
Saying his knights are better men than he—
Yet in this heathen war the fire of God
Fills him. I never saw his like; there lives   315
No greater leader.'

                    While he utter'd this,
Low to her own heart said the lily maid,
'Save your great self, fair lord;' and when he fell
From talk of war to traits of pleasantry—
Being mirthful he, but in a stately kind—   320
She still took note that when the living smile
Died from his lips, across him came a cloud
Of melancholy severe, from which again,
Whenever in her hovering to and fro
The lily maid had striven to make cheer,   325
There brake a sudden-beaming tenderness
Of manners and of nature; and she thought

9. Breastplate.
1. The emblem of the English or Saxons. The dragon was the the emblem of the Britons.

That all was nature, all, perchance, for her.
And all night long his face before her lived,
As when a painter, poring on a face,   330
Divinely thro' all hindrance finds the man
Behind it, and so paints him that his face,
The shape and color of a mind and life,
Lives for his children, ever at its best
And fullest; so the face before her lived,   335
Dark-splendid, speaking in the silence, full
Of noble things, and held her from her sleep,
Till rathe² she rose, half-cheated in the thought
She needs must bid farewell to sweet Lavaine.
First as in fear, step after step, she stole   340
Down the long tower-stairs,³ hesitating.
Anon, she heard Sir Lancelot cry in the court,
'This shield, my friend, where is it?' and Lavaine
Past inward, as she came from out the tower.
There to his proud horse Lancelot turn'd, and smooth'd   345
The glossy shoulder, humming to himself.
Half-envious of the flattering hand, she drew
Nearer and stood. He look'd, and, more amazed
Than if seven men had set upon him, saw
The maiden standing in the dewy light.   350
He had not dream'd she was so beautiful.
Then came on him a sort of sacred fear,
For silent, tho' he greeted her, she stood
Rapt on his face as if it were a god's.
Suddenly flash'd on her a wild desire   355
That he should wear her favor at the tilt.
She braved a riotous heart in asking for it.
'Fair lord, whose name I know not—noble it is,
I well believe, the noblest—will you wear
My favor at this tourney?' 'Nay,' said he,   360
'Fair lady, since I never yet have worn
Favor of any lady in the lists.
Such is my wont, as those who know me know.'
'Yea, so,' she answer'd; 'then in wearing mine
Needs must be lesser likelihood, noble lord,   365
That those who know should know you.' And he turn'd
Her counsel up and down within his mind,
And found it true, and answer'd: 'True, my child.
Well, I will wear it; fetch it out to me.
What is it?' and she told him, 'A red sleeve   370
Broider'd with pearls,' and brought it. Then he bound
Her token on his helmet, with a smile
Saying, 'I never yet have done so much
For any maiden living,' and the blood
Sprang to her face and fill'd her with delight;   375

2. "Early" (Tennyson).
3. "'Stairs' is to be read as a monosyllable, with a pause after it" (Tennyson). Spedding wrote: "The art with which A. T. has represented Elaine's action by the slow and lingering movement, the sudden arrest, and the hesitating advance of the meter, has been altogether lost on some critics" (Hallam Tennyson).

But left her all the paler when Lavaine
Returning brought the yet-unblazon'd shield,
His brother's, which he gave to Lancelot,
Who parted with his own to fair Elaine:
'Do me this grace, my child, to have my shield   380
In keeping till I come.' 'A grace to me,'
She answer'd, 'twice to-day. I am your squire!'
Whereat Lavaine said laughing: 'Lily maid,
For fear our people call you lily maid
In earnest, let me bring your color back;   385
Once, twice, and thrice. Now get you hence to bed;'
So kiss'd her, and Sir Lancelot his own hand,
And thus they moved away. She staid a minute,
Then made a sudden step to the gate, and there—
Her bright hair blown about the serious face   390
Yet rosy-kindled with her brother's kiss—
Paused by the gateway, standing near the shield
In silence, while she watch'd their arms far-off
Sparkle, until they dipt below the downs.
Then to her tower she climb'd, and took the shield,   395
There kept it, and so lived in fantasy.

    Meanwhile the new companions past away
Far o'er the long backs of the bushless downs,
To where Sir Lancelot knew there lived a knight
Not far from Camelot, now for forty years   400
A hermit, who had pray'd, labor'd and pray'd,
And ever laboring had scoop'd himself
In the white rock a chapel and a hall
On massive columns, like a shore-cliff cave,
And cells and chambers. All were fair and dry;   405
The green light from the meadows underneath
Struck up and lived along the milky roofs;
And in the meadows tremulous aspen-trees
And poplars made a noise of falling showers.
And thither wending there that night they bode.   410

    But when the next day broke from underground,
And shot red fire and shadows thro' the cave,
They rose, heard mass, broke fast, and rode away.
Then Lancelot saying, 'Hear, but hold my name
Hidden, you ride with Lancelot of the Lake,'   415
Abash'd Lavaine, whose instant reverence,
Dearer to true young hearts than their own praise,
But left him leave to stammer, 'Is it indeed?'
And after muttering, 'The great Lancelot,'
At last he got his breath and answer'd: 'One,   420
One have I seen—that other, our liege lord,
The dread Pendragon,[4] Britain's King of kings,

---

4. The title, denoting chief leader, given to ancient British or Welsh kings. The word is derived from the Welsh *pen*, "head," and the Latin *draco*, "dragon." The title, according to Geoffrey of Monmouth, originated with Arthur's father, Uther Pendragon, who first carried the standard into battle.

Of whom the people talk mysteriously.
He will be there—then were I stricken blind
That minute, I might say that I had seen.'   425

    So spake Lavaine, and when they reach'd the lists
By Camelot in the meadow, let his eyes
Run thro' the peopled gallery which half round
Lay like a rainbow fallen upon the grass,
Until they found the clear-faced King, who sat   430
Robed in red samite, easily to be known,
Since to his crown the golden dragon clung,
And down his robe the dragon writhed in gold,
And from the carven-work behind him crept
Two dragons gilded, sloping down to make   435
Arms for his chair, while all the rest of them
Thro' knots and loops and folds innumerable
Fled ever thro' the woodwork, till they found
The new design wherein they lost themselves,
Yet with all ease, so tender was the work;   440
And, in the costly canopy o'er him set,
Blazed the last diamond of the nameless king.

    Then Lancelot answer'd young Lavaine and said:
'Me you call great; mine is the firmer seat,
The truer lance; but there is many a youth   445
Now crescent, who will come to all I am
And overcome it; and in me there dwells
No greatness, save it be some far-off touch
Of greatness to know well I am not great.[5]
There is the man.' And Lavaine gaped upon him   450
As on a thing miraculous, and anon
The trumpets blew; and then did either side,
They that assail'd, and they that held the lists,
Set lance in rest, strike spur, suddenly move,
Meet in the midst, and there so furiously   455
Shock that a man far-off might well perceive,
If any man that day were left afield,
The hard earth shake, and a low thunder of arms.
And Lancelot bode a little, till he saw
Which were the weaker; then he hurl'd into it   460
Against the stronger. Little need to speak
Of Lancelot in his glory! King, duke, earl,
Count, baron—whom he smote, he overthew.

    But in the field were Lancelot's kith and kin,
Ranged with the Table Round that held the lists,   465
Strong men, and wrathful that a stranger knight
Should do and almost overdo the deeds
Of Lancelot; and one said to the other, 'Lo!

5. "When I wrote that, I was thinking of Wordsworth and myself" (*Tennyson and His Friends*, p. 210). All but certainly, he was thinking of the last two lines in Wordsworth's sonnet "Afterthought": "Through love, through hope, and faith's transcendant dower, / We feel that we are greater than we know."

What is he? I do not mean the force alone—
The grace and versatility of the man!   470
Is it not Lancelot?' 'When has Lancelot worn
Favor of any lady in the lists?
Not such his wont, as we that know him know.'
'How then? who then?' a fury seized them all,
A fiery family passion for the name   475
Of Lancelot, and a glory one with theirs.
They couch'd their spears and prick'd their steeds, and thus,
Their plumes driven backward by the wind they made
In moving, all together down upon him
Bare, as a wild wave in the wide North Sea,   480
Green-glimmering toward the summit, bears, with all
Its stormy crests that smoke against the skies,[6]
Down on a bark, and overbears the bark
And him that helms it; so they overbore
Sir Lancelot and his charger, and a spear   485
Down-glancing lamed the charger, and a spear
Prick'd sharply his own cuirass, and the head
Pierced thro' his side, and there snapt and remain'd.

    Then Sir Lavaine did well and worshipfully.
He bore a knight of old repute to the earth,   490
And brought his horse to Lancelot where he lay.
He up the side, sweating with agony, got,
But thought to do while he might yet endure,
And being lustily holpen by the rest,
His party,—tho' it seem'd half-miracle   495
To those he fought with,—drave his kith and kin,
And all the Table Round that held the lists,
Back to the barrier; then the trumpets blew
Proclaiming his the prize who wore the sleeve
Of scarlet and the pearls; and all the knights,   500
His party, cried, 'Advance and take thy prize
The diamond;' but he answer'd: 'Diamond me
No diamonds! for God's love, a little air!
Prize me no prizes, for my prize is death!
Hence will I, and I charge you, follow me not.'   505

    He spoke, and vanish'd suddenly from the field
With young Lavaine into the poplar grove.
There from his charger down he slid, and sat,
Gasping to Sir Lavaine, 'Draw the lance-head.'
'Ah, my sweet lord Sir Lancelot,' said Lavaine,   510
'I dread me, if I draw it, you will die.'
But he, 'I die already with it; draw—
Draw,'—and Lavaine drew, and Sir Lancelot gave
A marvellous great shriek and ghastly groan,

---

6. "Seen on a voyage of mine to Norway" (Tennyson). Hallam Tennyson quotes a letter (July 24, 1858) from
   his father to his mother: "The green sea looking like a mountainous country, far-off waves with foam at
   the top looking like snowy mountains bounding the scene; one great wave, green-shining, past with all
   its crests smoking high up beside the vessel."

And half his blood burst forth, and down he sank   515
For the pure pain, and wholly swoon'd away.
Then came the hermit out and bare him in,
There stanch'd his wound; and there, in daily doubt
Whether to live or die, for many a week
Hid from the wild world's rumor by the grove   520
Of poplars with their noise of falling showers,
And ever-tremulous aspen-trees, he lay.

But on that day when Lancelot fled the lists,
His party, knights of utmost North and West,
Lords of waste marshes, kings of desolate isles,   525
Came round their great Pendragon, saying to him,
'Lo, Sire, our knight, thro' whom we won the day,
Hath gone sore wounded, and hath left his prize
Untaken, crying that his prize is death.'
'Heaven hinder,' said the King, 'that such an one,   530
So great a knight as we have seen to-day—
He seem'd to me another Lancelot—
Yea, twenty times I thought him Lancelot—
He must not pass uncared for. Wherefore rise,
O Gawain, and ride forth and find the knight.   535
Wounded and wearied, needs must he be near.
I charge you that you get at once to horse.
And, knights and kings, there breathes not one of you
Will deem this prize of ours is rashly given;
His prowess was too wondrous. We will do him   540
No customary honor; since the knight
Came not to us, of us to claim the prize,
Ourselves will send it after. Rise and take
This diamond, and deliver it, and return,
And bring us where he is, and how he fares,   545
And cease not from your quest until ye find.'

So saying, from the carven flower above,
To which it made a restless heart, he took
And gave the diamond. Then from where he sat
At Arthur's right, with smiling face arose,   550
With smiling face and frowning heart, a prince
In the mid might and flourish of his May,
Gawain, surnamed the Courteous, fair and strong,
And after Lancelot, Tristram, and Geraint,
And Gareth, a good knight, but therewithal   555
Sir Modred's brother, and the child of Lot,
Nor often loyal to his word,[7] and now
Wroth that the King's command to sally forth

7. In the older traditions, as in *Sir Gawain and the Green Knight*, Gawain is the knight of perfect courtesy; he was also probably the original hero of the Grail quest. Although Malory somewhat downgraded him, Gawain was still one of the most outstanding of the Round Table knights, whose loyalty was beyond question. In Malory, Sir Launcelot unknowingly kills Gawain's brother; Gawain forces Launcelot into a challenge, is mortally wounded, and later, from his deathbed, writes Launcelot a letter of reconciliation. But throughout Tennyson's poem, Gawain is a villainous figure, a self-serving opportunist like Tristram.

In quest of whom he knew not, made him leave
The banquet and concourse of knights and kings.   560

So all in wrath he got to horse and went;
While Arthur to the banquet, dark in mood,
Past, thinking, 'Is it Lancelot who hath come
Despite the wound he spake of, all for gain
Of glory, and hath added wound to wound,   565
And ridden away to die?' So fear'd the King,
And, after two day's tarriance there, return'd.
Then when he saw the Queen, embracing ask'd,
'Love, are you yet so sick?' 'Nay, lord,' she said.
'And where is Lancelot?' Then the Queen amazed,   570
'Was he not with you? won he not your prize?'
'Nay, but one like him.' 'Why, that like was he.'
And when the King demanded how she knew,
Said: 'Lord, no sooner had ye parted from us
Than Lancelot told me of a common talk   575
That men went down before his spear at a touch,
But knowing he was Lancelot; his great name
Conquer'd; and therefore would he hide his name
From all men, even the King, and to this end
Had made the pretext of a hindering wound,   580
That he might joust unknown of all, and learn
If his old prowess were in aught decay'd;
And added, "Our true Arthur, when he learns,
Will well allow my pretext, as for gain
Of purer glory."'

Then replied the King: 585
'Far lovelier in our Lancelot had it been,
In lieu of idly dallying with the truth,
To have trusted me as he hath trusted thee.
Surely his King and most familiar friend
Might well have kept his secret. True, indeed,   590
Albeit I know my knights fantastical,
So fine a fear in our large Lancelot
Must needs have moved my laughter; now remains
But little cause for laughter. His own kin—
Ill news, my Queen, for all who love him, this!—   595
His kith and kin, not knowing, set upon him;
So that he went sore wounded from the field.
Yet good news too; for goodly hopes are mine
That Lancelot is no more a lonely heart.
He wore, against his wont, upon his helm   600
A sleeve of scarlet, broider'd with great pearls,
Some gentle maiden's gift.'

Yea, lord,' she said,
'Thy hopes are mine,' and saying that, she choked,
And sharply turn'd about to hide her face,
Past to her chamber, and there flung herself   605

Down on the great King's couch, and writh'd upon it,
And clench'd her fingers till they bit the palm,
And shriek'd out 'Traitor!' to the unhearing wall,
Then flash'd into wild tears, and rose again,
And moved about her palace, proud and pale.   610

   Gawain the while thro' all the region round
Rode with his diamond, wearied of the quest,
Touch'd at all points except the poplar grove,
And came at last, tho' late, to Astolat;
Whom glittering in enamell'd arms the maid   615
Glanced at, and cried, 'What news from Camelot, lord?
What of the knight with the red sleeve?' 'He won.'
'I knew it,' she said. 'But parted from the jousts
Hurt in the side;' whereat she caught her breath.
Thro' her own side she felt the sharp lance go.   620
Thereon she smote her hand; wellnigh she swoon'd.
And, while he gazed wonderingly at her, came
The Lord of Astolat out, to whom the prince
Reported who he was, and on what quest
Sent, that he bore the prize and could not find   625
The victor, but had ridden a random round
To seek him, and had wearied of the search.
To whom the Lord of Astolat: 'Bide with us,
And ride no more at random, noble prince!
Here was the knight, and here he left a shield;   630
This will he send or come for. Furthermore
Our son is with him; we shall hear anon,
Needs must we hear.' To this the courteous prince
Accorded with his wonted courtesy,
Courtesy with a touch of traitor in it,   635
And staid; and cast his eyes on fair Elaine;
Where could be found face daintier? then her shape
From forehead down to foot, perfect—again
From foot to forehead exquisitely turn'd.
'Well—if I bide, lo! this wild flower for me!'   640
And oft they met among the garden yews,
And there he set himself to play upon her
With sallying wit, free flashes from a height
Above her, graces of the court, and songs,
Sighs, and low smiles, and golden eloquence   645
And amorous adulation, till the maid
Rebell'd against it, saying to him: 'Prince,
O loyal nephew of our noble King,
Why ask you not to see the shield he left,
Whence you might learn his name? Why slight your King,   650
And lose the quest he sent you on, and prove
No surer than our falcon yesterday,
Who lost the hern we slipt her at, and went
To all the winds?' 'Nay, by mine head,' said he,
'I lose it, as we lose the lark in heaven,   655
O damsel, in the light of your blue eyes;

But an ye will it let me see the shield.'
And when the shield was brought, and Gawain saw
Sir Lancelot's azure lions, crown'd with gold,
Ramp in the field,[8] he smote his thigh, and mock'd: 660
'Right was the King! our Lancelot that true man!'
'And right was I,' she answer'd merrily, 'I,
Who dream'd my knight the greatest knight of all.'
'And if I dream'd,' said Gawain, 'that you love
This greatest knight, your pardon! lo, ye know it!   665
Speak therefore; shall I waste myself in vain?'
Full simple was her answer: 'What know I?
My brethren have been all my fellowship;
And I, when often they have talk'd of love,
Wish'd it had been my mother, for they talk'd,   670
Meseem'd, of what they knew not; so myself—
I know not if I know what true love is,
But if I know, then, if I love not him,
I know there is none other I can love.'
'Yea, by God's death,' said he, 'ye love him well,   675
But would not, knew ye what all others know,
And whom he loves.' 'So be it,' cried Elaine,
And lifted her fair face and moved away;
But he pursued her, calling, "Stay a little!
One golden minute's grace! he wore your sleeve.   680
Would he break faith with one I may not name?
Must our true man change like a leaf at last?
Nay—like enow. Why then, far be it from me
To cross our mighty Lancelot in his loves!
And, damsel, for I deem you know full well   685
Where your great knight is hidden, let me leave
My quest with you; the diamond[9] also—here!
For if you love, it will be sweet to give it;
And if he love, it will be sweet to have it
From your own hand; and whether he love or not,   690
A diamond is a diamond. Fare you well
A thousand times!—a thousand times farewell!
Yet, if he love, and his love hold, we two
May meet at court hereafter! there, I think,
So ye will learn the courtesies of the court,   695
We two shall know each other.'

                              Then he gave,
And slightly kiss'd the hand to which he gave,
The diamond, and all wearied of the quest
Leapt on his horse, and carolling as he went
A true-love ballad, lightly rode away.   700

     Thence to the court he past; there told the King
What the King knew, 'Sir Lancelot is the knight.'

8. "Surface of the shield" (Ricks).
9. As Ricks notes: "The leaving of the diamond and the king's anger with Gawain (ll. 710–13) are additions to Malory."

And added, 'Sire, my liege, so much I learnt,
But fail'd to find him, tho' I rode all round
The region; but I lighted on the maid   705
Whose sleeve he wore. She loves him; and to her,
Deeming our courtesy is the truest law,
I gave the diamond. She will render it;
For by mine head she knows his hiding-place.'

    The seldom-frowning King frown'd, and replied,   710
'Too courteous truly! ye shall go no more
On quest of mine, seeing that ye forget
Obedience is the courtesy due to kings.'

    He spake and parted. Wroth, but all in awe,
For twenty strokes of the blood, without a word,   715
Linger'd that other, staring after him;
Then shook his hair, strode off, and buzz'd abroad
About the maid of Astolat, and her love.
All ears were prick'd at once, all tongues were loosed:
'The maid of Astolat loves Sir Lancelot,   720
Sir Lancelot loves the maid of Astolat.'
Some read the King's face, some the Queen's, and all
Had marvel what the maid might be, but most
Predoom'd her as unworthy. One old dame
Came suddenly on the Queen with the sharp news.   725
She, that had heard the noise of it before,
But sorrowing Lancelot should have stoop'd so low,
Marr'd her friend's aim with pale tranquillity.
So ran the tale like fire about the court,
Fire in dry stubble a nine-days' wonder flared;   730
Till even the knights at banquet twice or thrice
Forgot to drink to Lancelot and the Queen,
And pledging Lancelot and the lily maid
Smiled at each other, while the Queen, who sat
With lips severely placid, felt the knot   735
Climb in her throat, and with her feet unseen
Crush'd the wild passion out against the floor
Beneath the banquet, where the meats became
As wormwood and she hated all who pledged.

    But far away the maid in Astolat,   740
Her guiltless rival, she that ever kept
The one-day-seen Sir Lancelot in her heart,
Crept to her father, while he mused alone,
Sat on his knee, stroked his gray face and said:
'Father, you call me wilful, and the fault   745
Is yours who let me have my will, and now,
Sweet father, will you let me lose my wits?'
'Nay,' said he, 'surely.' 'Wherefore, let me hence,'
She answer'd, 'and find out our dear Lavaine.
'Ye will not lose your wits for dear Lavaine.   750
Bide,' answer'd he: 'we needs must hear anon

Of him, and of that other.' 'Ay,' she said,
'And of that other, for I needs must hence
And find that other, wheresoe'er he be,
And with mine own hand give his diamond to him,   755
Lest I be found as faithless in the quest
As yon proud prince who left the quest to me.
Sweet father, I behold him in my dreams
Gaunt as it were the skeleton of himself,
Death-pale, for the lack of gentle maiden's aid.   760
The gentler-born the maiden, the more bound,
My father, to be sweet and serviceable
To noble knights in sickness, as ye know,
When these have worn their tokens. Let me hence,
I pray you.' Then her father nodding said: 765
'Ay, ay, the diamond. Wit ye well, my child,
Right fain were I to learn this knight were whole,
Being our greatest. Yea, and you must give it—
And sure I think this fruit is hung too high
For any mouth to gape for save a queen's—   770
Nay, I mean nothing; so then, get you gone,
Being so very wilful you must go.'

      Lightly, her suit allow'd, she slipt away,
And while she made her ready for her ride
Her father's latest word humm'd in her ear,   775
'Being so very wilful you must go,'
And changed itself and echo'd in her heart,
'Being so very wilful you must die.'
But she was happy enough and shook it off,
As we shake off the bee that buzzes at us;   780
And in her heart she answer'd it and said,
'What matter, so I help him back to life?'
Then far away with good Sir Torre for guide
Rode o'er the long backs of the bushless downs
To Camelot, and before the city-gates   785
Came on her brother with a happy face
Making a roan horse caper and curvet[1]
For pleasure all about a field of flowers;
Whom when she saw, 'Lavaine,' she cried, 'Lavaine,
How fares my lord Sir Lancelot?' He amazed,   790
'Torre and Elaine! why here? Sir Lancelot!
How know ye my lord's name is Lancelot?'
But when the maid had told him all her tale,
Then turn'd Sir Torre, and being in his moods
Left them, and under the strange-statued gate,   795
Where Arthur's wars were render'd mystically,
Past up the still rich city to his kin,
His own far blood,[2] which dwelt at Camelot;

---

1. A curvet is a leap in which the horse's forelegs are raised together and the hindlegs are raised up with a
   spring before the front legs touch the ground.
2. Distant relations.

And her, Lavaine across the poplar grove
Led to the caves. There first she saw the casque   800
Of Lancelot on the wall; her scarlet sleeve,
Tho' carved and cut, and half the pearls away,
Stream'd from it still; and in her heart she laugh'd,
Because he had not loosed it from his helm,
But meant once more perchance to tourney in it.   805
And when they gain'd the cell wherein he slept,
His battle-writhen arms and mighty hands
Lay naked on the wolf-skin, and a dream
Of dragging down his enemy made them move.
Then she that saw him lying unsleek; unshorn,   810
Gaunt as it were the skeleton of himself,
Utter'd a little tender dolorous cry.
The sound not wonted in a place so still
Woke the sick knight, and while he roll'd his eyes
Yet blank from sleep, she started to him, saying,   815
'Your prize the diamond sent you by the King.'
His eyes glisten'd; she fancied, 'Is it for me?'
And when the maid had told him all the tale
Of king and prince, the diamond sent, the quest
Assign'd to her not worthy of it, she knelt   820
Full lowly by the corners of his bed,
And laid the diamond in his open hand.
Her face was near, and as we kiss the child
That does the task assign'd, he kiss'd her face.
At once she slipt like water to the floor.   825
'Alas,' he said, 'your ride hath wearied you.
Rest must you have.' 'No rest for me,' she said;
'Nay, for near you, fair lord, I am at rest.'
What might she mean by that? his large black eyes,
Yet larger thro' his leanness, dwelt upon her,   830
Till all her heart's sad secret blazed itself
In the heart's colors on her simple face;
And Lancelot look'd and was perplext in mind,
And being weak in body said no more,
But did not love the color; woman's love,   835
Save one, he not regarded, and so turn'd
Sighing, and feign'd a sleep until he slept.

     Then rose Elaine and glided thro' the fields,
And past beneath the weirdly-sculptured gates
Far up the dim rich city to her kin;   840
There bode the night, but woke with dawn, and past
Down thro' the dim rich city to the fields,
Thence to the cave. So day by day she past
In either twilight ghost-like to and fro
Gliding, and every day she tended him,   845
And likewise many a night; and Lancelot
Would, tho' he call'd his wound a little hurt
Whereof he should be quickly whole, at times
Brain-feverous in his heat and agony, seem

Uncourteous, even he. But the meek maid   850
Sweetly forbore him ever, being to him
Meeker than any child to a rough nurse,
Milder than any mother to a sick child,
And never woman yet, since man's first fall,
Did kindlier unto man, but her deep love   855
Upbore her; till the hermit, skill'd in all
The simples and the sciences of that time,
Told him that her fine care had saved his life.
And the sick man forgot her simple blush,
Would call her friend and sister, sweet Elaine,   860
Would listen for her coming and regret
Her parting step, and held her tenderly,
And loved her with all love except the love
Of man and woman when they love their best,
Closest and sweetest, and had died the death   865
In any knightly fashion for her sake.
And peradventure had he seen her first
She might have made this and that other world
Another world for the sick man; but now
The shackles of an old love straiten'd him,   870
His honor rooted in dishonor stood,
And faith unfaithful kept him falsely true.

　　Yet the great knight in his mid-sickness made
Full many a holy vow and pure resolve.
These, as but born of sickness, could not live;   875
For when the blood ran lustier in him again,
Full often the bright image of one face,
Making a treacherous quiet in his heart,
Dispersed his resolution like a cloud.
Then if the maiden, while that ghostly grace[3]   880
Beam'd on his fancy, spoke, he answer'd not,
Or short and coldly, and she knew right well
What the rough sickness meant, but what this meant
She knew not, and the sorrow dimm'd her sight,
And drave her ere her time across the fields   885
Far into the rich city, where alone
She murmur'd, 'Vain, in vain! it cannot be.
He will not love me. How then? must I die?'
Then as a little helpless innocent bird,[4]
That has but one plain passage of few notes,   890
Will sing the simple passage o'er and o'er
For all an April morning, till the ear
Wearies to hear it, so the simple maid
Went half the night repeating, 'Must I die?'
And now to right she turn'd, and now to left,   895
And found no ease in turning or in rest;

3. "Vision of Guinevere" (Tennyson).
4. "Chaffinch" (Tennyson).

And 'Him or death,' she mutter'd, 'death or him,'
Again and like a burthen, 'Him or death.'

    But when Sir Lancelot's deadly hurt was whole,
To Astolat returning rode the three.   900
There morn by morn, arraying her sweet self
In that wherein she deem'd she look'd her best,
She came before Sir Lancelot, for she thought,
'If I be loved, these are my festal robes,
If not, the victim's flowers before he fall.'   905
And Lancelot ever prest upon the maid
That she should ask some goodly gift of him
For her own self or hers: 'and do not shun
To speak the wish most near to your true heart;
Such service have ye done me that I make   910
My will of yours, and prince and lord am I
In mine own land, and what I will I can.'
Then like a ghost she lifted up her face,
But like a ghost without the power to speak.
And Lancelot saw that she withheld her wish,   915
And bode among them yet a little space
Till he should learn it; and one morn it chanced
He found her in among the garden yews,
And said, 'Delay no longer, speak your wish,
Seeing I go to-day.' Then out she brake: 920
'Going? and we shall never see you more.
And I must die for want of one bold word.'
'Speak; that I live to hear,' he said, 'Is yours.'
Then suddenly and passionately she spoke:
'I have gone mad. I love you; let me die.'   925
'Ah, sister,' answer'd Lancelot, 'what is this?'
And innocently extending her white arms,
'Your love,' she said, 'your love—to be your wife.'
And Lancelot answer'd, 'Had I chosen to wed,
I had been wedded earlier, sweet Elaine;   930
But now there never will be wife of mine.'
'No, no,' she cried, 'I care not to be wife,
But to be with you still, to see your face,
To serve you, and to follow you thro' the world.'
And Lancelot answer'd: 'Nay, the world, the world,   935
All ear and eye, with such a stupid heart
To interpret ear and eye, and such a tongue
To blare its own interpretation—nay,
Full ill then should I quit your brother's love,
And your good father's kindness.' And she said,   940
'Not to be with you, not to see your face—
Alas, for me then, my good days are done!'
'Nay, noble maid,' he answer'd, 'ten times nay!
This is not love, but love's first flash in youth,
Most common; yea, I know it of mine own self,   945
And you yourself will smile at your own self
Hereafter, when you yield your flower of life

To one more fitly yours, not thrice your age.
And then will I, for true you are and sweet
Beyond mine old belief in womanhood,   950
More specially should your good knight be poor,
Endow you with broad land and territory
Even to the half my realm beyond the seas,
So that would make you happy; futhermore,
Even to the death, as tho' ye were my blood,   955
In all your quarrels will I be your knight.
This will I do, dear damsel, for your sake,
And more than this I cannot.'

               While he spoke
She neither blush'd nor shook, but deathly-pale
Stood grasping what was nearest, then replied,   960
'Of all this will I nothing,' and so fell,
And thus they bore her swooning to her tower.

    Then spake, to whom thro' those black walls of yew
Their talk had pierced, her father: 'Ay, a flash,
I fear me, that will strike my blossom dead.   965
Too courteous are ye, fair Lord Lancelot.
I pray you, use some rough discourtesy
To blunt or break her passion.'

               Lancelot said,
'That were against me; what I can I will;'
And there that day remain'd, and toward even   970
Sent for his shield. Full meekly rose the maid,
Stript off the case, and gave the naked shield;
Then, when she heard his horse upon the stones,
Unclasping flung the casement back, and look'd
Down on his helm, from which her sleeve had gone.   975
And Lancelot knew the little clinking sound;
And she by tact of love was well aware
That Lancelot knew that she was looking at him.
And yet be glanced not up, nor waved his hand,
Nor bade farewell, but sadly rode away.   980
This was the one discourtesy that he used.

    So in her tower alone the maiden sat.
His very shield was gone; only the case,
Her own poor work, her empty labor, left.
But still she heard him, still his picture form'd   985
And grew between her and the pictured wall.
Then came her father, saying in low tones,
'Have comfort,' whom she greeted quietly.
Then came her brethren saying, 'Peace to thee,
Sweet sister,' whom she answer'd with all calm.   990
But when they left her to herself again,
Death, like a friend's voice from a distant field
Approaching thro' the darkness, call'd; the owls

Wailing had power upon her, and she mixt
Her fancies with the sallow-rifted glooms 995
Of evening and the moanings of the wind.

And in those days she made a little song,
And call'd her song 'The Song of Love and Death,'
And sang it; sweetly could she make and sing.

'Sweet is true love tho' given in vain, in vain; 1000
And sweet is death who puts an end to pain.
I know not which is sweeter, no, not I.

'Love, art thou sweet? then bitter death must be.
Love, thou are bitter, sweet is death to me.
O Love, if death be sweeter, let me die. 1005

'Sweet love, that seems not made to fade away;
Sweet death, that seem to make us loveless clay;
I know not which is sweeter, ne, not I.

'I fain would follow love, if that could be,
I needs must follow death, who calls for me; 1010
Call and I follow, I follow! let me die.'

High with last line scaled her voice, and this,
All in a fiery dawning wild with wind
That shook her tower, the brothers heard, and thought
With shuddering, 'Hark the Phantom[5] of the house 1015
That ever shrieks before a death,' and call'd
The father, and all three in hurry and fear
Ran to her, and lo! the blood-red light of dawn
Flared on her face, she shrilling, 'Let me die!'

As when we dwell upon a word we know, 1020
Repeating, till the word we know so well
Becomes a wonder, and we know not why,
So dwelt the father on her face, and thought,
Is this Elaine?' till back the maiden fell,
Then gave a languid hand to each, and lay, 1025
Speaking a still good-morrow with her eyes.
At last she said: 'Sweet brothers, yester-night
I seem'd a curious little maid again,
As happy as when we dwelt among the woods,
And when ye used to take me with the flood 1030
Up the great river in the boatman's boat.
Only ye would not pass beyond the cape
That has the poplar on it; there ye fixt
Your limit, oft returning with the tide.
And yet I cried because ye would not pass 1035
Beyond it, and far up the shining flood

---

5. In Irish and Scottish folklore the banshee, a female spirit whose wailings under the windows of a house signal a family member's approaching death.

Until we found the palace of the King.
And yet ye would not; but this night I dream'd
That I was all alone upon the flood,
And then I said, "Now shall I have my will;"   1040
And there I woke, but still the wish remain'd.
So let me hence that I may pass at last
Beyond the poplar and far up the flood,
Until I find the palace of the King.
There will I enter in among them all,   1045
And no man there will dare to mock at me;
But there the fine Gawain will wonder at me,
And there the great Sir Lancelot muse at me;
Gawain, who bade a thousand farewells to me,
Lancelot, who coldly went, nor bade me one.   1050
And there the King will know me and my love,
And there the Queen herself will pity me,
And all the gentle court will welcome me,
And after my long voyage I shall rest!'

    'Peace,' said her father, 'O my child, ye seem   1055
Light-headed, for what force is yours to go
So far, being sick? and wherefore would ye look
On this proud fellow again, who scorns us all?'

    Then the rough Torre began to heave and move,
And bluster into stormy sobs and say: 1060
'I never loved him; an I meet with him,
I care not howsoever great he be,
Then will I strike at him and strike him down.
Give me good fortune, I will strike him dead,
For this discomfort he hath done the house.'   1065

    To whom the gentle sister made reply:
'Fret not yourself, dear brother, nor be wroth,
Seeing it is no more Sir Lancelot's fault
Not to love me than it is mine to love
Him of all men who seems to me the highest.'   1070

    'Highest?' the father answer'd, echoing 'highest?' —
He meant to break the passion in her — 'nay,
Daughter, I know not what you call the highest;
But this I know, for all the people know it,
He loves the Queen, and in an open shame,   1075
And she returns his love in open shame,
If this be high, what is it to be low?'
    Then spake the lily maid of Astolat:
'Sweet father, all too faint and sick am I
For anger. These are slanders, never yet   1080
Was noble man but made ignoble talk.[6]
He makes no friend who never made a foe.

6. "The noblest are ever subject to calumny" (Tennyson).

But now it is my glory to have loved
One peerless, without stain; so let me pass,
My father, howsoe'er I seem to you,   1085
Not all unhappy, having loved God's best
And greatest, tho' my love had no return.
Yet, seeing you desire your child to live,
Thanks, but you work against your own desire,
For if I could believe the things you say   1090
I should but die the sooner; wherefore cease,
Sweet father, and bid call the ghostly man[7]
Hither, and let me shrive me clean and die.'

        So when the ghostly man had come and gone,
She, with a face bright as for sin forgiven,   1095
Besought Lavaine to write as she devised
A letter, word for word; and when he ask'd,
'Is it for Lancelot, is it for my dear lord?
Then will I bear it gladly;' she replied,
'For Lancelot and the Queen and all the world,   1100
But I myself must bear it.' Then he wrote
The letter she devised; which being writ
And folded, 'O sweet father, tender and true,
Deny me not,' she said—'ye never yet
Denied my fancies—this, however strange,   1105
My latest. Lay the letter in my hand
A little ere I die, and close the hand
Upon it; I shall guard it even in death.
And when the heat has gone from out my heart,
Then take the little bed on which I died   1110
For Lancelot's love, and deck it like the Queen's
For richness, and me also like the Queen
In all I have of rich, and lay me on it.
And let there be prepared a chariot-bier
To take me to the river, and a barge   1115
Be ready on the river, clothed in black.
I go in state to court, to meet the Queen.
There surely I shall speak for mine own self,
And none of you can speak for me so well.
And therefore let our dumb old man alone   1120
Go with me, he can steer and row, and he
Will guide me to that palace, to the doors.'

        She ceased. Her father promised; whereupon
She grew so cheerful that they deem'd her death
Was rather in the fantasy than the blood.   1125
But ten slow mornings past, and on the eleventh
Her father laid the letter in her hand,
And closed the hand upon it, and she died.
So that day there was dole in Astolat.

7. A priest.

But when the next sun brake from underground,   1130
Then, those two brethren slowly with bent brows
Accompanying, the sad chariot-bier
Past like a shadow thro' the field, that shone
Full-summer, to that stream whereon the barge,
Pall'd all its length in blackest samite, lay.   1135
There sat the lifelong creature of the house,
Loyal, the dumb old servitor, on deck,
Winking his eyes, and twisted all his face.
So those two brethren from the chariot took
And on the black decks laid her in her bed,   1140
Set in her hand a lily, o'er her hung
The silken case with braided blazonings,
And kiss'd her quiet brows, and saying to her,
'Sister, farewell forever,' and again,
'Farewell, sweet sister,' parted all in tears.   1145
Then rose the dumb old servitor, and the dead,
Oar'd by the dumb, went upward with the flood—
In her right hand the lily, in her left
The letter—all her bright hair streaming down—
And all the coverlid was cloth of gold   1150
Drawn to her waist, and she herself in white
All but her face, and that clear-featured face
Was lovely, for she did not seem as dead,
But fast asleep, and lay as tho' she smiled.

That day Sir Lancelot at the palace craved   1155
Audience of Guinevere, to give at last
The price of half a realm, his costly gift,
Hard-won and hardly won with bruise and blow,
With deaths of others, and almost his own,
The nine-years-fought-for diamonds; for he saw   1160
One of her house, and sent him to the Queen
Bearing his wish, whereto the Queen agreed
With such and so unmoved a majesty
She might have seem'd her statue, but that he,
Low-drooping till he wellnigh kiss'd her feet   1165
For loyal awe, saw with a sidelong eye
The shadow of some piece of pointed lace,
In the Queen's shadow, vibrate on the walls,
And parted, laughing in his courtly heart.

All in an oriel[8] on the summer side,   1170
Vine-clad, of Arthur's palace toward the stream,
They met, and Lancelot kneeling utter'd: 'Queen,
Lady, my liege, in whom I have my joy,
Take, what I had not won except for you,
These jewels, and make me happy, making them   1175
An armlet for the roundest arm on earth,
Or necklace for a neck to which the swan's

___

8. A room or recess with a bay window, usually in an upper story.

Is tawnier than her cygnet's.[9] These are words;
Your beauty is your beauty, and I sin
In speaking, yet O, grant my worship of it   1180
Words, as we grant grief tears. Such sin in words
Perchance, we both can pardon; but my Queen,
I hear of rumors flying thro' your court.[1]
Our bond, as not the bond of man and wife,
Should have in it an absoluter trust   1185
To make up that defect: let rumors be.
When did not rumors fly? these, as I trust
That you trust me in your own nobleness,
I may not well believe that you believe.'

    While thus he spoke, half turn'd away, the Queen   1190
Brake from the vast oriel-embowering vine
Leaf after leaf, and tore, and cast them off,
Till all the place whereon she stood was green;
Then, when he ceased, in one cold passive hand
Received at once and laid aside the gems   1195
There on a table near her, and replied:

    'It may be I am quicker of belief
Than you believe me, Lancelot of the Lake.
Our bond is not the bond of man and wife.
This good is in it, whatsoe'er of ill,   1200
It can be broken easier. I for you
This many a year have done despite and wrong
To one whom ever in my heart of hearts
I did acknowledge nobler. What are these?
Diamonds for me! they had been thrice their worth   1205
Being your gift, had you not lost your own.
To loyal hearts the value of all gifts
Must vary as the giver's. Not for me!
For her! for your new fancy. Only this
Grant me, I pray you; have your joys apart.   1210
I doubt not that, however changed, you keep
So much of what is graceful; and myself
Would shun to break those bounds of courtesy
In which as Arthur's Queen I move and rule,
So cannot speak my mind. An end to this!   1215
A strange one! yet I take it with Amen.
So pray you, add my diamonds to her pearls;
Deck her with these, tell her, she shines me down:
An amlet for an arm to which the Queen's
Is haggard, or a necklace for a neck   1220
O, as much fairer—as a faith once fair
Was richer than these diamonds—hers not mine—
Nay, by the mother of our Lord himself,

9. An elaborate piece of flattery playing on a reversal of the fact that a cygnet, or young swan, has a yellow-ish down, in contrast to the adult's pure white.
1. "Rumours of his love for Elaine" (Tennyson).

Or hers or mine, mine now to work my will —
She shall not have them.'

                    Saying which she seized,   1225
And, thro' the casement standing wide for heat,
Flung them, and down they flash'd, and smote the stream.
Then from the smitten surface flash'd, as it were,
Diamonds to meet them, and they past away.
Then while Sir Lancelot leant, in half disdain   1230
At love, life, all things, on the window ledge,
Close underneath his eyes, and right across
Where these had fallen, slowly past the barge
Whereon the lily maid of Astolat
Lay smiling, like a star in blackest night.   1235

    But the wild Queen, who saw not, burst away
To weep and wail in secret; and the barge,
On to the palace-doorway sliding, paused.
There two stood arm'd, and kept the door; to whom,
All up the marble stair, tier over tier,   1240
Were added mouths that gaped, and eyes that ask'd,
'What is it?' but that oarsman's haggard face,
As hard and still as is the face that men
Shape to their fancy's eye from broken rocks
On some cliff-side, appall'd them, and they said: 1245
'He is enchanted, cannot speak — and she,
Look how she sleeps — the Fairy Queen, so fair!
Yea, but how pale! what are they? flesh and blood?
Or come to take the King to Fairyland?
For some do hold our Arthur cannot die,   1250
But that he passes into Fairyland.'

    While thus they babbled of the King, the King
Came girt with knights. Then turn'd the tongueless man
From the half-face to the full eye, and rose
And pointed to the damsel and the doors.   1255
So Arthur bade the meek Sir Percivale
And pure Sir Galahad to uplift the maid;
And reverently they bore her into hall.
Then came the fine Gawain and wonder'd at her,
And Lancelot later came and mused at her,   1260
And last the Queen herself, and pitied her;
But Arthur spied the letter in her hand,
Stoopt, took, brake seal, and read it; this was all:

    'Most noble lord, Sir Lancelot of the Lake,
I, sometime call'd the maid of Astolat,   1265
Come, for you left me taking no farewell,
Hither, to take my last farewell of you.
I loved you, and my love had no return,
And therefore my true love has been my death.
And therefore to our Lady Guinevere,   1270

And to all other ladies, I make moan:
Pray for my soul, and yield me burial.
Pray for my soul thou too, Sir Lancelot,
As thou art a knight peerless.'

                   Thus he read;
And ever in the reading lords and dames   1275
Wept, looking often from his face who read
To hers which lay so silent, and at times,
So touch'd were they, half-thinking that her lips
Who had devised the letter moved again.
    Then freely spoke Sir Lancelot to them all: 1280
'My lord liege Arthur, and all ye that hear,
Know that for this most gentle maiden's death
Right heavy am I; for good she was and true,
But loved me with a love beyond all love
In women, whomsoever I have known.   1285
Yet to be loved makes not to love again;
Not at my years, however it hold in youth.
I swear by truth and knighthood that I gave
No cause, not willingly, for such a love.
To this I call my friends in testimony,   1290
Her brethren, and her father, who himself
Besought me to be plain and blunt, and use,
To break her passion, some discourtesy
Against my nature; what I could, I did.
I left her and I bade her no farewell;   1295
Tho', had I dreamt the damsel would have died,
I might have put my wits to some rough use,
And help'd her from herself.'

                   Then said the Queen—
Sea was her wrath, yet working after storm:
'Ye might at least have done her so much grace,   1300
Fair lord, as would have help'd her from her death.'
He raised his head, their eyes met and hers fell,
He adding: 'Queen, she would not be content
Save that I wedded her, which could not be.
Then might she follow me thro' the world, she ask'd;   1305
It could not be. I told her that her love
Was but the flash of youth, would darken down,
To rise hereafter in a stiller flame
Toward one more worthy of her—then would I,
More specially were he she wedded poor,   1310
Estate them with large land and territory
In mine own realm beyond the narrow seas,
To keep them in all joyance. More than this
I could not; this she would not, and she died.'
    He pausing, Arthur answer'd: 'O my knight,   1315
It will be to thy worship, as my knight,
And mine, as head of all our Table Round,
To see that she be buried worshipfully.'

So toward that shrine which then in all the realm[2]
Was richest, Arthur leading, slowly went   1320
The marshall'd Order of their Table Round,
And Lancelot sad beyond his wont, to see
The maiden buried, not as one unknown,
Nor meanly, but with gorgeous obsequies,
And mass, and rolling music, like a queen.   1325
And when the knights had laid her comely head
Low in the dust of half-forgotten kings,
Then Arthur spake among them: 'Let her tomb
Be costly, and her image thereupon,
And let the shield of Lancelot at her feet   1330
Be carven, and her lily in her hand.
And let the story of her dolorous voyage
For all true hearts be blazon'd on her tomb
In letters gold and azure!' which was wrought
Thereafter; but when now the lords and dames   1335
And people, from the high door streaming, brake
Disorderly, as homeward each, the Queen,
Who mark'd Sir Lancelot where he moved apart,
Drew near, and sigh'd in passing, 'Lancelot,
Forgive me; mine was jealousy in love.'   1340
He answer'd with his eyes upon the ground,
'That is love's curse; pass on, my Queen, forgiven.'
But Arthur, who beheld his cloudy brows,
Approach'd him, and with full affection said:

'Lancelot, my Lancelot, thou in whom I have   1345
Most joy and most affiance, for I know
What thou hast been in battle by my side,
And many a time have watch'd thee at the tilt
Strike down the lusty and long practised knight
And let the younger and unskill'd go by   1350
To win his honor and to make his name,
And loved thy courtesies and thee, a man
Made to be loved; but now I would to God,
Seeing the homeless trouble in thine eyes,
Thou couldst have loved this maiden, shaped, it seems,   1355
By God for thee alone, and from her face,
If one may judge the living by the dead,
Delicately pure and marvellously fair,
Who might have brought thee, now a lonely man
Wifeless and heirless, noble issue, sons   1360
Born to the glory of thy name and fame,
My knight, the great Sir Lancelot of the Lake.'

Then answer'd Lancelot: 'Fair she was, my King,
Pure, as you ever wish your knights to be.
To doubt her fairness were to want an eye,   1365
To doubt her pureness were to want a heart—

2. "This passage [lines 1319–27] and the 'tower-stair' [lines 341ff.] are among the best blank verse in *Lancelot and Elaine*, I think" (Tennyson).

Yea, to be loved, if what is worthy love
Could bind him, but free love will not be bound.'

'Free love, so bound, were freest,' said the King.
'Let love be free; free love is for the best.   1370
And, after heaven, on our dull side of death,
What should be best, if not so pure a love
Clothed in so pure a loveliness? yet thee
She fail'd to bind, tho' being, as I think,
Unbound as yet, and gentle, as I know.'   1375

And Lancelot answer'd nothing, but he went,
And at the inrunning of a little brook
Sat by the river in a cove, and watch'd
The high reed wave, and lifted up his eyes
And saw the barge that brought her moving down,   1380
Far-off, a blot upon the stream, and said
Low in himself: 'Ah, simple heart and sweet,
Ye loved me, damsel, surely with a love
Far tenderer than my Queen's. Pray for thy soul?
Ay, that will I. Farewell too—now at last—   1385
Farewell, fair lily. "Jealousy in love?"
Not rather dead love's harsh heir, jealous pride?
Queen, if I grant the jealousy as of love,
May not your crescent fear for name and fame
Speak, as it waxes, of a love that wanes?   1390
Why did the King dwell on my name to me?
Mine own shames me, seeming a reproach,
Lancelot, whom the Lady of the Lake
Caught from his mother's arms—the wondrous one
Who passes thro' the vision of the night—   1395
She chanted snatches of mysterious hymns
Heard on the winding waters, eve and morn
She kiss'd me saying, "Thou art fair, my child,
As a king's son," and often in her arms
She bare me, pacing on the dusky mere.   1400
Would she had drown'd me in it, where'er it be!
For what am I? what profits me my name
Of greatest knight? I fought for it, and have it.
Pleasure to have it, none; to lose it, pain;
Now grown a part of me; but what use in it?   1405
To make men worse by making my sin known?
Or sin seem less, the sinner seeming great?
Alas for Arthur's greatest knight, a man
Not after Arthur's heart! I needs must break
These bonds that so defame me. Not without   1410
She wills it—would I, if she will'd it? nay,
Who knows? but if I would not, then may God,
I pray him, send a sudden angel down
To seize me by the hair and bear me far,
And fling me deep in that forgotten mere,   1415
Among the tumbled fragments of the hills.'

So groan'd Sir Lancelot in remorseful pain,
Not knowing he should die a holy man.[3]

1859

The Holy Grail[1]

From noiseful arms, acts of prowess done
In tournament or tilt, Sir Percivale
Whom Arthur and his knighthood call'd the Pure,
Had past into the silent life of prayer,
Praise, fast, and alms; and leaving for the cowl   5
The helmet in an abbey far away
From Camelot, there, and not long after, died.

And one, a fellow-monk among the rest,
Ambrosius, loved him much beyond the rest,
And honor'd him, and wrought into his heart   10
A way by love that waken'd love within,
To answer that which came; and as they sat
Beneath a world-old yew-tree, darkening half
The cloisters, on a gustful April morn
That puff'd the swaying branches into smoke[2]   15
Above them, ere the summer when he died,
The monk Ambrosius question'd Percivale:

3. "I asked my father why he did not write an Idyll 'How Sir Lancelot came unto the hermitage, and how he took the habit unto him; how he went to Almesbury and found Queen Guinevere dead, whom they brought to Glastonbury; and how Sir Lancelot died a holy man'; and he answered, 'Because it could not be done better than by Malory.' My father loved his own great imaginative knight, the Lancelot of the *Idylls*" (Hallam Tennyson).
1. One of several reasons Tennyson gave for pausing in the production of the *Idylls* after 1859 was: "I doubt whether such a subject as the San Graal could be handled in these days without incurring a charge of irreverence. It would be too much like playing with sacred things" (*Memoir* II, 126). Although perhaps this is a valid excuse for procrastination, more likely he simply had been unable to devise a plan to incorporate the four earlier idylls. "The Holly Grail" was the first written of the new poems and became the central idyll in the work. It clearly shows the direction in which his thoughts are tending. The focus has moved from the relatively simplistic allegorical concern with true and false love to the much more complex matters of spiritualism and materialism. Indeed, the subject of the Grail poem, showing that an excessively zealous pursuit after spiritual truth can be as destructive to social order as an indulgence in the materialistic qualities of life, suggests that Tennyson was a step ahead of himself in articulating his conception. For not until the following two idylls, "Pelleas and Ettarre" and "The Last Tournament," which were written later, does he seek to dramatize fully the consequences of a materialistic philosophy.
    Among other of Tennyson's most important comments on *The Holy Grail*, he notes: "Faith declines, religion in many turns from practical goodness to the quest after the supernatural and marvelous and selfish religious excitement. Few are those for whom the quest is a source of spiritual strength." He told his son: "At twenty-four I meant to write an epic or a drama of King Arthur, and I thought that I should take twenty years about the work. They will now say that I have been forty years about it. *The Holy Grail* is one of the most imaginative of my poems. I have expressed there my strong feeling as to the Reality of the Unseen. The end, where the king speaks of his work and of his visions, is intended to be the summing up of all in the highest note by the highest of men." From a letter sent him by Knowles, Hallam Tennyson records: "He always told me that he had from the beginning meant to make Arthur something more and other than a mystic or historic king, but that he had changed his mind from his original meaning. In 1869 he gave me a memorandum written in his own hand which he told me was then thirty or forty years old. He said that in those early days (about 1830) the poem was to be a sort of allegory of the Church, but that now King Arthur was to stand in a symbolic way for the Soul, and his Knights for the human passions which the Soul was to order and subdue."
    In Christian medieval legends, of which there are many, the Grail was the cup from which Christ drank at the Last Supper or the container in which Joseph of Arimathea caught some of the crucified Christ's blood; or it was one and the same vessel.
2. "The pollen in Spring, which, blown abroad by the wind, looks like smoke" (Tennyson). Tennyson refers readers to *IM* 39.

"O brother, I have seen this yew-tree smoke,
Spring after spring, for half a hundred years;
For never have I known the world without,   20
Nor ever stray'd beyond the pale. But thee,
When first thou camest—such a courtesy
Spake thro' the limbs and in the voice—I knew
For one of those who eat in Arthur's hall;
For good ye are and bad, and like to coins,   25
Some true, some light, but every one of you
Stamp'd with the image of the King; and now
Tell me, what drove thee from the Table Round,
My brother? was it earthly passion crost?"

   "Nay," said the knight; "for no such passion mine.   30
But the sweet vision of the Holy Grail
Drove me from all vainglories, rivalries,
And earthly heats that spring and sparkle out
Among us in the jousts, while women watch
Who wins, who falls, and waste the spiritual strength   35
Within us, better offer'd up to heaven."
   To whom the monk: "The Holy Grail!—I trust
We are green in Heaven's eyes; but here too much
We moulder—as to things without I mean—
Yet one of your own knights, a guest of ours,   40
Told us of this in our refectory,
But spake with such a sadness and so low
We heard not half of what he said. What is it?
The phantom of a cup that comes and goes?"

   "Nay, monk! what phantom?" answer'd Percivale.   45
"The cup, the cup itself, from which our Lord
Drank at the last sad supper with his own.
This, from the blessed land of Aromat[3]
After the day of darkness, when the dead
Went wandering o'er Moriah[4]—the good saint,   50
Arimathæan Joseph, journeying brought
To Glastonbury,[5] where the winter thorn
Blossoms at Christmas, mindful of our Lord.
And there awhile it bode; and if a man
Could touch or see it, he was heal'd at once,   55
By faith, of all his ills. But then the times
Grew to such evil that the holy cup
Was caught away to heaven, and disappear'd."

   To whom the monk: "From our old books I know
That Joseph came of old to Glastonbury,   60
And there the heathen Prince, Arviragus,[6]

---

3. Poetic variation of *Arimathea*. In Tennyson's note: "Used for Arimathea, the home of Joseph of Arimathea, who, according to the legend, received in the Grail the blood that flowed from our Lord's side."
4. A mountain near Jerusalem.
5. An ancient town in Somerset where Joseph is said to have established the first Christian church in England. There, supposedly, he planted his staff, from which sprouted the winter thorn.
6. In legend, the son of Cymbeline. His refusal to pay tribute supposedly precipitated another Roman invasion.

Gave him an isle of marsh whereon to build;
And there he built with wattles from the marsh
A little lonely church in days of yore,
For so they say, these books of ours, but seem   65
Mute of this miracle, far as I have read.
But who first saw the holy thing to-day?"

    "A woman," answer'd Percivale, "a nun,
And one no further off in blood from me
Than sister; and if ever holy maid   70
With knees of adoration wore the stone,
A holy maid; tho' never maiden glow'd,
But that was in her earlier maidenhood,
With such a fervent flame of human love,
Which, being rudely blunted, glanced and shot   75
Only to holy things; to prayer and praise
She gave herself, to fast and alms. And yet,
Nun as she was, the scandal of the Court,
Sin against Arthur and the Table Round,
And the strange sound of an adulterous race,   80
Across the iron grating of her cell
Beat, and she pray'd and fasted all the more.

    "And he to whom she told her sins, or what
Her all but utter whiteness held for sin,
A man wellnigh a hundred winters old,   85
Spake often with her of the Holy Grail,
A legend handed down thro' five or six,
And each of these a hundred winters old,
From our Lord's time. And when King Arthur made
His Table Round,[7] and all men's hearts became   90
Clean for a season, surely he had thought
That now the Holy Grail would come again;
But sin broke out. Ah, Christ, that it would come,
And heal the world of all their wickedness!
'O Father! ask'd the maiden, 'might it come   95
To me by prayer and fasting?' 'Nay,' said he,
'I know not, for thy heart is pure as snow.'
And so she pray'd and fasted, till the sun
Shone, and the wind blew, thro' her, and I thought
She might have risen and floated when I saw her.   100

    "For on a day she sent to speak with me.
And when she came to speak, behold her eyes
Beyond my knowing of them, beautiful,
Beyond all knowing of them, wonderful,
Beautiful in the light of holiness!   105
And 'O my brother Percivale,' she said,
'Sweet brother, I have seen the Holy Grail;

---

7. According to Malory, it seated 150 knights in a circle to avoid arguments over precedence. Merlin made
    it for Uther, who gave it to Leodogran, king of Cameliard (see "The Coming of Arthur"), who in turn
    gave it to Arthur when he married his daughter Guinevere—an account Tennyson omits.

For, waked at dead of night, I heard a sound
As of a silver horn from o'er the hills
Blown, and I thought, "It is not Arthur's use   110
To hunt by moonlight." And the slender sound
As from a distance beyond distance grew
Coming upon me—O never harp nor horn,
Nor aught we blow with breath, or touch with hand,
Was like that music as it came; and then   115
Stream'd thro' my cell a cold and silver beam,
And down the long beam stole the Holy Grail,
Rose-red with beatings in it, as if alive,
Till all the white walls of my cell were dyed
With rosy colors leaping on the wall;   120
And then the music faded, and the Grail
Past, and the beam decay'd, and from the walls
The rosy quiverings died into the night.
So now the Holy Thing is here again
Among us, brother, fast thou too and pray,   125
And tell thy brother knights to fast and pray,
That so perchance the vision may be seen
By thee and those, and all the world be heal'd.'

      "Then leaving the pale nun, I spake of this
To all men; and myself fasted and pray'd   130
Always, and many among us many a week
Fasted and pray'd even to the uttermost,
Expectant of the wonder that would be.

      "And one there was among us, ever moved
Among us in white armor, Galahad.   135
'God make thee good as thou art beautiful!'
Said Arthur, when he dubb'd him knight, and none
In so young youth was ever made a knight
Till Galahad; and this Galahad, when he heard
My sister's vision, fill'd me with amaze;   140
His eyes became so like her own, they seem'd
Hers, and himself her brother more than I.

      "Sister or brother none had he; but some
Call'd him a son of Lancelot,[8] and some said
Begotten by enchantment—chatterers they,   145
Like birds of passage piping up and down,
That gape for flies—we know not whence they come;
For when was Lancelot wanderingly lewd?

      "But she, the wan sweet maiden, shore away
Clean from her forehead all that wealth of hair   150
Which made a silken mat-work for her feet;
And out of this she plaited broad and long
A strong sword-belt, and wove with silver thread

8. In Malory, Launcelot dallies with several ladies; and Galahad, the last descendant of Joseph of Arimathea, is his illegitimate son by princess Elaine (not the lily maid of Astolat).

And crimson in the belt a strange device,
A crimson grail within a silver beam;   155
And saw the bright boy-knight, and bound it on him,
Saying: 'My knight, my love, my knight of heaven,
O thou, my love, whose love is one with mine,
I, maiden, round thee, maiden, bind my belt.
Go forth, for thou shalt see what I have seen,   160
And break thro' all, till one will crown thee king
Far in the spiritual city;'[9] and as she spake
She sent the deathless passion in her eyes
Thro' him, and made him hers, and laid her mind
On him, and he believed in her belief.   165

    "Then came a year of miracle. O brother,
In our great hall there stood a vacant chair,
Fashion'd by Merlin ere he past away,
And carven with strange figures; and in and out
The figures, like a serpent, ran a scroll   170
Of letters in a tongue no man could read.
And Merlin call'd it 'the Siege Perilous',[1]
Perilous for good and ill; 'for there,' he said,
'No man could sit but he should lose himself.'
And once by misadvertence Merlin sat   175
In his own chair, and so was lost;[2] but he,
Galahad, when he heard of Merlin's doom,
Cried, 'If I lose myself, I save myself!'

    "Then on a summer night it came to pass,
While the great banquet lay along the hall,   180
That Galahad would sit down in Merlin's chair.

    "And all at once, as there we sat, we heard
A cracking and a riving of the roofs,
And rending, and a blast, and overhead
Thunder and in the thunder was a cry.   185
And in the blast there smote along the hall
A beam of light seven times more clear than day;
And down the long beam stole the Holy Grail
All over cover'd with a luminous cloud,
And none might see who bare it, and it past.   190
But every knight beheld his fellow's face
As in a glory, and all the knights arose,
And staring each at other like dumb men
Stood, till I found a voice and sware a vow.

    "I sware a vow before them all, that I,   195
Because I had not seen the Grail, would ride

---

9. Ricks records G. C. Macaulay's note: "In the Grail legends 'the spiritual city' is the city of Sarras, where
   Joseph of Arimathaea converted King Evelac."
1. The vacant chair at the Round Table reserved for the knight who was destined to achieve the quest of
   the Grail. Tennyson said it "stands for the spiritual imagination."
2. Not according to Tennyson's "Merlin and Vivien" or Malory.

A twelvemonth and a day in quest of it,
Until I found and saw it, as the nun
My sister saw it; and Galahad sware the vow,
And good Sir Bors, our Lancelot's cousin, sware,   200
And Lancelot sware, and many among the knights,
And Gawain sware, and louder than the rest.'

    Then spake the monk Ambrosius, asking him,
"What said the King? Did Arthur take the vow?"

    "Nay, for my lord," said Percivale, "the King,   205
Was not in hall; for early that same day,
Scaped thro' a cavern from a bandit hold,
An outraged maiden sprang into the hall
Crying on help; for all her shining hair
Was smear'd with earth, and either milky arm   210
Red-rent with hooks of bramble, and all she wore
Torn as a sail that leaves the rope is torn
In tempest. So the King arose and went
To smoke the scandalous hive of those wild bees
That made such honey in his realm. Howbeit   215
Some little of this marvel he too saw,
Returning o'er the plain that then began
To darken under Camelot; whence the King
Look'd up, calling aloud, 'Lo, there! the roofs
Of our great hall are roll'd in thunder-smoke!   220
Pray heaven, they be not smitten by the bolt!'
For dear to Arthur was that hall of ours,
As having there so oft with all his knights
Feasted, and as the stateliest under heaven.

    "O brother, had you known our mighty hall,   225
Which Merlin built for Arthur long ago!
For all the sacred mount of Camelot,[3]
And all the dim rich city, roof by roof,
Tower after tower, spire beyond spire,
By grove, and garden-lawn, and rushing brook,   230
Climbs to the mighty hall that Merlin built.
And four great zones[4] of sculpture, set betwixt
With many a mystic symbol, gird the hall;
And in the lowest beasts are slaying men,

3. Of his "city of shadowy palaces," Tennyson said it is "everywhere symbolic of the gradual growth of
human beliefs and institutions, and of the spiritual development of man" (*Memoir* II, 127). Its decay, as
described later in this idyll, obviously symbolizes the reverse.
4. The four zones represent human progress from bestiality to realization of the spiritual ideal. Throughout
the *Idylls* Tennyson's use of the beast metaphor is, in part, a reflection of his continuing interest in Darwinism. But whereas earlier, in *IM* for example, he had conceived of progress toward the "one far-off divine event" as essentially linear, the *Idylls* stress the cyclical nature of history, with no guarantees that the
human race will ever achieve an earthly utopia.
    Toward the end of his life, Tennyson increasingly believed in the necessity for human intervention to
achieve ethical progress for our species, or, as T. H. Huxley would put it in "Evolution and Ethics" (written the year after the poet's death): "Social progress means a checking of the cosmic process at every step
and the substitution for it of another, which may be called the ethical process; the end of which is not
the survival of those who may happen to be the fittest, in respect of the whole of the conditions which
obtain, but of those who are ethically the best."

And in the second men are slaying beasts,   235
And on the third are warriors, perfect men,
And on the fourth are men with growing wings,
And over all one statue in the mould
Of Arthur, made by Merlin, with a crown,
And peak'd wings pointed to the Northern Star.   240
And eastward fronts the statue, and the crown
And both the wings are made of gold, and flame
At sunrise till the people in far fields,
Wasted so often by the heathen hordes,
Behold it, crying 'We have still a king.'   245

      "And, brother had you known our hall within,
Broader and higher than any in all the lands!
Where twelve great windows blazon Arthur's wars,[5]
And all the light that falls upon the board
Streams thro' the twelve great battles of our King.   250
Nay, one there is, and at the eastern end,
Wealthy with wandering lines of mount and mere,
Where Arthur finds the brand Excalibur.
And also one to the west, and counter to it,
And blank; and who shall blazon it? when and how? —   255
O, there, perchance, when all our wars are done,
The brand Excalibur will be cast away!

      So to this hall full quickly rode the King,
In horror lest the work by Merlin wrought,
Dreamlike, should on the sudden vanish, wrapt   260
In unremorseful folds of rolling fire.[6]
And in he rode, and up I glanced, and saw
The golden dragon sparkling over all;
And many of those who burnt the hold, their arms
Hack'd, and their foreheads grimed with smoke and sear'd,   265
Follow'd and in among bright faces, ours,
Full of the vision, prest; and then the King
Spake to me, being nearest, 'Percivale,' —
Because the hall was all in tumult—some
Vowing, and some protesting, — 'what is this?'   270

      "O brother, when I told him what had chanced,
My sister's vision and the rest, his face
Darken'd, as I have seen it more than once,
When some brave deed seem'd to be done in vain,
Darken; and 'Woe is me, my knights,' he cried,   275
'Had I been here, ye had not sworn the vow.'
Bold was mine answer, 'Had thyself been here,
My King, thou wouldst have sworn.' 'Yea, yea,' said he,
'Art thou so bold and hast not seen the Grail?'

5. See "Launcelot and Elaine," lines 279ff. and n. 8, p. 419.
6. "This line gives onomatopoeically the 'unremorseful flames'" (Tennyson).

"'Nay, lord, I heard the sound, I saw the light,   280
But since I did not see the holy thing,
I sware a vow to follow it till I saw.'

"Then when he ask'd us, knight by knight, if any
Had seen it, all their answers were as one:
'Nay, lord, and therefore have we sworn our vows.'   285

"'Lo, now,' said Arthur, 'have ye seen a cloud?
What go ye into the wilderness to see?'[7]

"Then Galahad on the sudden, and in a voice
Shrilling along the hall to Arthur, call'd,
'But I, Sir Arthur, saw the Holy Grail,   290
I saw the Holy Grail and heard a cry—
"O Galahad, and O Galahad, follow me!"'"

"'Ah, Galahad, Galahad,' said the King, 'for such
As thou art is the vision, not for these.[8]
Thy holy nun and thou have seen a sign—   295
Holier is none, my Percivale, than she—
A sign to maim this Order which I made.
But ye that follow but the leader's bell,'—
Brother, the King was hard upon his knights,—
'Taliessin'[9] is our fullest throat of song,   300
And one hath sung and all the dumb will sing.
Lancelot is Lancelot, and hath overborne
Five knights at once, and every younger knight,
Unproven, holds himself as Lancelot,
Till overborne by one, he learns—and ye,   305
What are ye? Galahads?—no, nor Percivales'—
For thus it pleased the King to range me close
After Sir Galahad;—'nay,' said he, 'but men
With strength and will to right the wrong'd, of power
To lay the sudden heads of violence flat,   310
Knights that in twelve great battles splash'd and dyed
The strong White Horse[1] in his own heathen blood—
But one hath seen, and all the blind will see.
Go, since your vows are sacred, being made.
Yet—for ye know the cries of all my realm   315
Pass thro' this hall—how often, O my knights,
Your places being vacant at my side,
This chance of noble deeds will come and go
Unchallenged, while ye follow wandering fires
Lost in the quagmire! Many of you, yea most,   320

7. See Matthew 11:7: "What went ye out into the wilderness to see? A reed shaken with the wind?"
8. As given in the headnote to this poem, Tennyson said: "Faith declines, religion in many turns from practical goodness to the quest after the spiritual and marvellous and selfish religious excitement. Few are
those for whom the quest is a source of spiritual strength." In his note, specifically to lines 293–94, Tennyson said: "The king thought that most men ought to do the duty that lies closest to them, and that to
few only is given the spiritual enthusiasm. Those who have it not ought not to affect it."
9. A Welsh bard of the sixth century.
1. The Saxons' emblem.

Return no more. Ye think I show myself
Too dark a prophet. Come now, let us meet
The morrow morn once more in one full field
Of gracious pastime, that once more the King,
Before ye leave him for this quest, may count   325
The yet-unbroken strength of all his knights,
Rejoicing in that Order which he made.'

    "So when the sun broke next from underground,
All the great Table of our Arthur closed
And clash'd in such a tourney and so full,   330
So many lances broken—never yet
Had Camelot seen the like since Arthur came;
And I myself and Galahad, for a strength
Was in us from the vision, overthrew
So many knights that all the people cried,   335
And almost burst the barriers in their heat,
Shouting, 'Sir Galahad and Sir Percivale!'

    "But when the next day brake from underground—
O brother, had you known our Camelot,
Built by old kings, age after age, so old   340
The King himself had fears that it would fall,
So strange, and rich, and dim; for where the roofs
Totter'd toward each other in the sky,
Met foreheads all along the street of those
Who watch'd us pass; and lower, and where the long   345
Rich galleries, lady-laden, weigh'd the necks
Of dragons clinging to the crazy walls,
Thicker than drops from thunder, showers of flowers
Fell as we past; and men and boys astride
On wyvern,[2] lion, dragon, griffin, swan,   350
At all the corners, named us each by name,
Calling 'God speed!' but in the ways below
The knights and ladies wept, and rich and poor
Wept, and the King himself could hardly speak
For grief, and all in middle street the Queen,   355
Who rode by Lancelot, wail'd and shriek'd aloud,
'This madness has come on us for our sins.'
So to the Gate of the Three Queens[3] we came,
Where Arthur's wars are render'd mystically,
And thence departed every one his way.   360

    "And I was lifted up in heart, and thought
Of all my late-shown prowess in the lists,
How my strong lance had beaten down the knights,
So many and famous names; and never yet
Had heaven appear'd so blue, nor earth so green,   365
For all my blood danced in me, and I knew
That I should light upon the Holy Grail.

2. "Two legged dragon. Old French *wivre*, viper" (Tennyson); the griffin is half lion and half eagle.
3. See "The Coming of Arthur," line 275 and n. 2, p. 385.

"Thereafter, the dark warning of our King,
That most of us would follow wandering fires,
Came like a driving gloom across my mind.   370
Then every evil word I had spoken once,
And every evil thought I had thought of old,
And every evil deed I ever did,
Awoke and cried, 'This quest is not for thee.'
And lifting up mine eyes, I found myself   375
Alone, and in a land of sand and thorns,
And I was thirsty even unto death;
And I, too, cried, 'This quest is not for thee.'

"And on I rode, and when I thought my thirst
Would slay me, saw deep lawns, and then a brook,   380
With one sharp rapid, where the crisping white
Play'd ever back upon the sloping wave
And took both ear and eye; and o'er the brook
Were apple-trees, and apples by the brook
Fallen, and on the lawns. 'I will rest here,'   385
I said, 'I am not worthy of the quest;'
But even while I drank the brook, and ate
The goodly apples, all these things at once
Fell into dust, and I was left alone
And thirsting in a land of sand and thorns.[4]   390

"And then behold a woman at a door
Spinning; and fair the house whereby she sat.
And kind the woman's eyes and innocent,
And all her bearing gracious; and she rose
Opening her arms to meet me, as who should say,   395
'Rest here;' but when I touch'd her, lo! she, too,
Fell into dust and nothing, and the house
Became no better than a broken shed,
And in it a dead babe; and also this
Fell into dust, and I was left alone.   400

"And on I rode, and greater was my thirst.
Then flash'd a yellow gleam across the world,
And where it smote the plowshare in the field
The plowman left his plowing and fell down
Before it; where it glitter'd on her pail   405

---

4. "The gratification of sensual appetite brings Percivale no content" (Tennyson). Of the following episodes,
   sequentially Tennyson notes: "Nor does wifely love and the love of the family"; "Nor does wealth, which
   is worshipt by labour"; "Nor does glory"; "Nor does Fame." Compare "Guinevere," lines 472–80:
   To love one maiden only, cleave to her,
   And worship her by years of noble deeds,
   Until they won her; for indeed I knew
   Of no more subtle master under heaven
   Than is the maiden passion for a maid,
   Not only to keep down the base in man,
   But teach high thoughts, and amiable words
   And courtliness, and the desire of fame,
   And love of truth, and all that makes a man.
   Michael Timko remarks: "Tennyson stresses the unit of the family, sees it as a microcosm of the nation
   and the universe, and is willing to wait, seeing hope in the future" (*Carlyle and Tennyson*, p. 67).

The milkmaid left her milking and fell down
Before it, and I knew not why, but thought
'The sun is rising,' tho' the sun had risen.
Then was I ware of one that on me moved
In golden armor with a crown of gold   410
About a casque all jewels, and his horse
In golden armor jewelled everywhere;
And on the splendor came, flashing me blind,
And seem'd to me the lord of all the world,
Being so huge. But when I thought he meant   415
To crush me, moving on me, lo! he, too,
Open'd his arms to embrace me as he came,
And up I went and touch'd him, and he, too,
Fell into dust, and I was left alone
And wearying in a land of sand and thorns.   420

    "And I rode on and found a mighty hill,
And on the top a city wall'd; the spires
Prick'd with incredible pinnacles into heaven.
And by the gateway stirr'd a crowd; and these
Cried to me climbing, 'Welcome, Percivale!   425
Thou mightiest and thou purest among men!'
And glad was I and clomb, but found at top
No man, nor any voice. And thence I past
Far thro' a ruinous city, and I saw
That man had once dwelt there; but there I found   430
Only one man of an exceeding age.
'Where is that goodly company,' said I,
'That so cried out upon me?' and he had
Scarce any voice to answer, and yet gasp'd,
'Whence and what art thou?' and even as he spoke   435
Fell into dust and disappear'd, and I
Was left alone once more and cried in grief,
'Lo, if I find the Holy Grail itself
And touch it, it will crumble into dust!'

    "And thence I dropt into a lowly vale,   440
Low as the hill was high, and where the vale
Was lowest found a chapel, and thereby
A holy hermit in a hermitage,
To whom I told my phantoms, and he said:
    "'O son, thou hast not true humility,   445
The highest virtue, mother of them all;
For when the Lord of all things made Himself
Naked of glory for His mortal change,
"Take thou my robe," she said, "for all is thine,"
And all her form shone forth with sudden light   450
So that the angels were amazed, and she
Follow'd Him down, and like a flying star
Led on the gray-hair'd wisdom of the east.[5]

---

5. "The Magi" (Tennyson).

But her thou hast not known; for what is this
Thou thoughtest of thy prowess and thy sins?   455
Thou hast not lost thyself to save thyself
As Galahad.' When the hermit made an end,
In silver armor suddenly Galahad shone
Before us, and against the chapel door
Laid lance and enter'd, and we knelt in prayer.   460
And there the hermit slaked my burning thirst,
And at the sacring⁶ of the mass I saw
The holy elements alone; but he,
'Say ye no more? I, Galahad, saw the Grail,
The Holy Grail, descend upon the shrine.   465
I saw the fiery face as of a child
That smote itself into the bread and went;
And hither am I come; and never yet
Hath what thy sister taught me first to see,
This holy thing, fail'd from my side, nor come   470
Cover'd, but moving with me night and day,
Fainter by day, but always in the night
Blood-red, and sliding down the blacken'd marsh
Blood-red, and on the naked mountain top
Blood-red, and in the sleeping mere below   475
Blood-red. And in the strength of this I rode,
Shattering all evil customs everywhere,
And past thro' Pagan realms, and made them mine,
And clash'd with Pagan hordes, and bore them down,
And broke thro' all, and in the strength of this   480
Come victor. But my time is hard at hand,
And hence I go, and one will crown me king
Far in the spiritual city; and come thou, too,
For thou shalt see the vision when I go.'

"While thus he spake, his eye, dwelling on mine,   485
Drew me, with power upon me, till I grew
One with him, to believe as he believed.
Then, when the day began to wane, we went.

"There rose a hill that none but man could climb,
Scarr'd with a hundred wintry watercourses—   490
Storm at the top, and when we gain'd it, storm⁷
Round us and death; for every moment glanced
His silver arms and gloom'd, so quick and thick
The lightnings here and there to left and right
Struck, till the dry old trunks about us, dead,   495
Yea, rotten with a hundred years of death,
Sprang into fire. And at the base we found
On either hand, as far as eye could see,
A great black swamp and of an evil smell,
Part black, part whiten'd with the bones of men,   500
Not to be crost, save that some ancient king

6. "Consecration" (Tennyson).
7. "It was a time of storm when men could imagine miracles, and so storm is emphasized" (Tennyson).

Had built a way, where, link'd with many a bridge,
A thousand piers ran into the great Sea.
And Galahad fled along them bridge by bridge,
And every bridge as quickly as he crost   505
Sprang into fire and vanish'd, tho' I yearn'd
To follow; and thrice above him all the heavens
Open'd and blazed with thunder such as seem'd
Shoutings of all the sons of God.[8] And first
At once I saw him far on the great Sea,   510
In silver-shining armor starry-clear;
And o'er his head the Holy Vessel hung
Clothed in white samite or a luminous cloud.
And with exceeding swiftness ran the boat,
If boat it were—I saw not whence it came.   515
And when the heavens open'd and blazed again
Roaring, I saw him like a silver star—
And had he set the sail, or had the boat
Become a living creature clad with wings?
And o'er his head the Holy Vessel hung   520
Redder than any rose, a joy to me,
For now I knew the veil had been withdrawn.
Then in a moment when they blazed again
Opening, I saw the least of little stars
Down on the waste, and straight beyond the star   525
I saw the spiritual city and all her spires
And gateways in a glory like one pearl—
No larger, tho' the goal of all the saints—
Strike from the sea; and from the star there shot
A rose-red sparkle to the city, and there   530
Dwelt, and I knew it was the Holy Grail,
Which never eyes on earth again shall see.
Then fell the floods of heaven drowning the deep,
And how my feet recrost the deathful ridge
No memory in me lives; but that I touch'd   535
The chapel-doors at dawn I know, and thence
Taking my war-horse from the holy man,
Glad that no phantom vext me more, return'd
To whence I came, the gate of Arthur's wars."

"O brother," ask'd Ambrosius,—"for in sooth   540
These ancient books—and they would win thee—teem,
Only I find not there this Holy Grail,
With miracles and marvels like to these,
Not all unlike; which oftentime I read,
Who read but on my breviary with ease,   545
Till my head swims, and then go forth and pass
Down to the little thorpe that lies so close,
And almost plaster'd like a martin's nest
To these old walls—and mingle with our folk;
And knowing every honest face of theirs   550

---

8. Job 38:7: "When the morning stars sang together, and all the sons of God shouted for joy?"

As well as ever shepherd knew his sheep,
And every homely secret in their hearts,
Delight myself with gossip and old wives,
And ills and aches, and teethings, lyings-in,
And mirthful sayings, children of the place,   555
That have no meaning half a league away;
Or lulling random squabbles when they rise,
Chafferings and chatterings at the market-cross,
Rejoice, small man, in this small world of mine,
Yea, even in their hens and in their eggs—   560
O brother, saving this Sir Galahad,
Came ye on none but phantoms in your quest,
No man, no woman?"

         Then Sir Percivale:
"All men, to one so bound by such a vow,
And women were as phantoms. O, my brother,   565
Why wilt thou shame me to confess to thee
How far I falter'd from my quest and vow?
For after I had lain so many nights,
A bed-mate of the snail and eft and snake,
In grass and burdock, I was changed to wan   570
And meagre, and the vision had not come;
And then I chanced upon a goodly town
With one great dwelling in the middle of it.
Thither I made, and there was I disarm'd
By maidens each as fair as any flower;   575
But when they led me into hall, behold,
The princess of that castle was the one,
Brother, and that one only, who had ever
Made my heart leap; for when I moved of old
A slender page about her father's hall,   580
And she a slender maiden, all my heart
Went after her with longing, yet we twain
Had never kiss'd a kiss or vow'd a vow.
And now I came upon her once again,
And one had wedded her, and he was dead,   585
And all his land and wealth and state were hers.
And while I tarried, every day she set
A banquet richer than the day before
By me, for all her longing and her will
Was toward me as of old; till one fair morn,   590
I walking to and fro beside a stream
That flash'd across her orchard underneath
Her castle-walls, she stole upon my walk,
And calling me the greatest of all knights,
Embraced me, and so kiss'd me the first time,   595
And gave herself and all her wealth to me.
Then I remember'd Arthur's warning word,
That most of us would follow wandering fires,
And the quest faded in my heart. Anon,
The heads of all her people drew to me,   600

With supplication both of knees and tongue:
'We have heard of thee; thou art our greatest knight,
Our Lady says it, and we well believe.
Wed thou our Lady, and rule over us,
And thou shalt be as Arthur in our land.'   605
O me, my brother! but one night my vow
Burnt me within, so that I rose and fled,
But wail'd and wept, and hated mine own self,
And even the holy quest, and all but her;
Then after I was join'd with Galahad   610
Cared not for her nor anything upon earth."

    Then said the monk: "Poor men, when yule is cold,
Must be content to sit by little fires.
And this am I, so that ye care for me
Ever so little; yea, and blest be heaven   615
That brought thee here to this poor house of ours
Where all the brethren are so hard, to warm
My cold heart with a friend; but O the pity
To find thine own first love once more—to hold,
Hold her a wealthy bride within thine arms,   620
Or all but hold, and then—cast her aside,
Foregoing all her sweetness, like a weed!
For we that want the warmth of double life,
We that are plagued with dreams of something sweet
Beyond all sweetness in a life so rich,—   625
Ah, blessed Lord, I speak too earthly-wise,
Seeing I never stray'd beyond the cell,
But live like an old badger in his earth,
With earth about him everywhere, despite
All fast and penance. Saw ye none beside,   630
None of your knights?"

              "Yea, so," said Percivale:
"One night my pathway swerving east, I saw
The pelican on the casque of our Sir Bors
All in the middle of the rising moon,
And toward him spurr'd, and hail'd him, and he me,   635
And each made joy of either. Then he ask'd:
'Where is he? hast thou seen him—Lancelot?—Once,'
Said good Sir Bors, 'he dash'd across me—mad,
And maddening what he rode; and when I cried,
"Ridest thou then so hotly on a quest   640
So holy?" Lancelot shouted, "Stay me not!
I have been the sluggard, and I ride apace,
For now there is a lion in the way!"
So vanish'd.'

      "Then Sir Bors had ridden on
Softly, and sorrowing for our Lancelot,   645
Because his former madness, once the talk
And scandal of our table, had return'd;

For Lancelot's kith and kin so worship him
That ill to him is ill to them, to Bors
Beyond the rest. He well had been content   650
Not to have seen, so Lancelot might have seen,
The Holy Cup of healing; and, indeed,
Being so clouded with his grief and love,
Small heart was his after the holy quest.
If God would send the vision, well; if not,   655
The quest and he were in the hands of Heaven.

        "And then, with small adventure met, Sir Bors
Rode to the lonest tract of all the realm,
And found a people there among their crags,
Our race and blood, a remnant that were left   660
Paynim amid their circles, and the stones⁹
They pitch up straight to heaven; and their wise men
Were strong in that old magic which can trace
The wandering of the stars, and scoff'd at him
And this high quest as at a simple thing,   665
Told him he follow'd—almost Arthur's words—
A mocking fire: 'what other fire than he¹
Whereby the blood beats, and the blossom blows,
And the sea rolls, and all the world is warm'd?'
And when his answer chafed them, the rough crowd,   670
Hearing he had a difference with their priests,
Seized him, and bound and plunged him into a cell
Of great piled stones; and lying bounden there
In darkness thro' innumerable hours
He heard the hollow-ringing heavens sweep   675
Over him till by miracle—what else?—
Heavy as it was, a great stone slipt and fell,
Such as no wind could move; and thro' the gap
Glimmer'd the streaming scud. Then came a night
Still as the day was loud, and thro' the gap   680
The seven clear stars² of Arthur's Table Round—
For, brother, so one night, because they roll
Thro' such a round in heaven, we named the stars,
Rejoicing in ourselves and in our King—
And these, like bright eyes of familiar friends,   685
In on him shone: 'And then to me, to me,'
Said good Sir Bors, 'beyond all hope of mine,
Who scarce had pray'd or ask'd it for myself—
Across the seven clear stars—O grace to me!—
In color like the fingers of a hand   690
Before a burning taper, the sweet Grail

9. "The temples and upright stones of the Druidic religion" (Tennyson). Their mysterious astrologic rites
   were held in the stone circles, the most famous remains of which are at Stonehenge. The Ring of Brodgar
   and the Standing Stones of Stenness in the Orkneys attest to their prevalence. "Paynim" is archaic for
   pagan or heathen.
1. The sun. Of "A mocking fire," Tennyson noted: "The sun-worshippers that were said to dwell on Lyonnesse scoffed at Percival."
2. "The Great Bear" (Tennyson).

Glided and past,[3] and close upon it peal'd
A sharp quick thunder.' Afterwards, a maid,
Who kept our holy faith among her kin
In secret, entering, loosed and let him go."   695

    To whom the monk: "And I remember now
That pelican on the casque. Sir Bors it was
Who spake so low and sadly at our board,
And mighty reverent at our grace was he;
A square-set man and honest, and his eyes,   700
An outdoor sign of all the warmth within,
Smiled with his lips—a smile beneath a cloud,
But heaven had meant it for a sunny one.
Ay, ay, Sir Bors, who else? But when ye reach'd
The city, found ye all your knights return'd,   705
Or was there sooth in Arthur's prophecy,
Tell me, and what said each, and what the King?"

    Then answer'd Percivale: "And that can I,
Brother, and truly; since the living words
Of so great men as Lancelot and our King   710
Pass not from door to door and out again,
But sit within the house. O, when we reach'd
The city, our horses stumbling as they trode
On heaps of ruin, hornless unicorns,
Crack'd basilisks, and splinter'd cockatrices,   715
And shatter'd talbots,[4] which had left the stones
Raw that they fell from, brought us to the hall.

    "And there sat Arthur on the dais-throne,
And those that had gone out upon the quest,
Wasted and worn, and but a tithe of them,   720
And those that had not, stood before the King,
Who, when he saw me, rose and bade me hail,
Saying: 'A welfare in thine eyes reproves
Our fear of some disastrous chance for thee
On hill or plain, at sea or flooding ford.   725
So fierce a gale made havoc here of late
Among the strange devices of our kings,
Yea, shook this newer, stronger hall of ours,
And from the statue Merlin moulded for us
Half-wrench'd a golden wing; but now—the quest,   730
This vision—hast thou seen the Holy Cup
That Joseph brought of old to Glastonbury?'

    "So when I told him all thyself hast heard,
Ambrosius, and my fresh but fixt resolve
To pass away into the quiet life,   735

---

3. "It might have been a meteor" (Tennyson).
4. "Heraldic dogs." "Basilisks": "the fabulous crown'd serpent whose look killed." "Cockatrices": "in heraldry, winged snakes" (all Tennyson).

He answer'd not, but, sharply turning, ask'd
Of Gawain, 'Gawain, was this quest for thee?'

"'Nay, lord,' said Gawain, 'not for such as I.
Therefore I communed with a saintly man,
Who made me sure the quest was not for me;   740
For I was much a-wearied of the quest,
But found a silk pavilion in a field,
And merry maidens in it; and then this gale
Tore my pavilion from the tenting-pin,
And blew my merry maidens all about   745
With all discomfort; yea, and but for this,
My twelvemonth and a day were pleasant to me.'

"He ceased; and Arthur turn'd to whom at first
He saw not, for Sir Bors, on entering, push'd
Athwart the throng to Lancelot, caught his hand,   750
Held it, and there, half-hidden by him, stood,
Until the King espied him, saying to him,
'Hail, Bors! if ever loyal man and true
Could see it, thou hast seen the Grail;' and Bors,
'Ask me not, for I may not speak of it;   755
I saw it;' and the tears were in his eyes.

"Then there remain'd but Lancelot, for the rest
Spake but of sundry perils in the storm.
Perhaps, like him of Cana⁵ in Holy Writ,
Our Arthur kept his best until the last;   760
'Thou, too, my Lancelot,' ask'd the King, 'my friend,
Our mightiest, hath this quest avail'd for thee?'

"'Our mightiest!' answer'd Lancelot, with a groan;
'O King!'—and when he paused methought I spied
A dying fire of madness in his eyes—   765
'O King, my friend, if friend of thine I be,
Happier are those that welter in their sin,
Swine in the mud, that cannot see for slime,
Slime of the ditch; but in me lived a sin
So strange, of such a kind, that all of pure,   770
Noble, and knightly in me twined and clung
Round that one sin, until the wholesome flower
And poisonous grew together, each as each,
Not to be pluck'd asunder; and when thy knights
Sware, I sware with them only in the hope   775
That could I touch or see the Holy Grail
They might be pluck'd asunder. Then I spake
To one most holy saint, who wept and said
That, save they could be pluck'd asunder, all
My quest were but in vain; to whom I vow'd   780
That I would work according as he will'd.

5. The first of Christ's miracles was the changing of water to wine at the marriage in Cana of Galilee. The governor of the feast praised the bridegroom for serving the best wine last. See John 2:1–11.

And forth I went, and while I yearn'd and strove
To tear the twain asunder in my heart,
My madness came upon me as of old,
And whipt me into waste fields far away.   785
There was I beaten down by little men,
Mean knights, to whom the moving of my sword
And shadow of my spear had been enow
To scare them from me once; and then I came
All in my folly to the naked shore,   790
Wide flats, where nothing but coarse grasses grew;
But such a blast, my King, began to blow,
So loud a blast along the shore and sea,
Ye could not hear the waters for the blast,
Tho' heapt in mounds and ridges all the sea   795
Drove like a cataract, and all the sand
Swept like a river, and the clouded heavens
Were shaken with the motion and the sound.
And blackening in the sea-foam sway'd a boat,
Half-swallow'd in it, anchor'd with a chain;   800
And in my madness to myself I said,
"I will embark and I will lose myself,
And in the great sea wash away my sin."
I burst the chain, I sprang into the boat.
Seven days I drove along the dreary deep,   805
And with me drove the moon and all the stars;
And the wind fell, and on the seventh night
I heard the shingle grinding in the surge,
And felt the boat shock earth, and looking up,
Behold, the enchanted towers of Carbonek[6]   810
A castle like a rock upon a rock,
With chasm-like portals open to the sea,
And steps that met the breaker! There was none
Stood near it but a lion on each side
That kept the entry, and the moon was full.   815
Then from the boat I leapt, and up the stairs,
There drew my sword. With sudden-flaring manes
Those two great beasts rose upright like a man,
Each gript a shoulder, and I stood between,
And, when I would have smitten them, heard a voice,   820
"Doubt not, go forward; if thou doubt, the beasts
Will tear thee piecemeal." Then with violence
The sword was dash'd from out my hand, and fell.
And up into the sounding hall I past;
But nothing in the sounding hall I saw,   825
No bench nor table, painting on the wall
Or shield of knight, only the rounded moon
Thro' the tall oriel[7] on the rolling sea.
But always in the quiet house I heard,

---

6. Malory located the Grail there.
7. Bay window. Of "only the rounded moon / Thro' the tall oriel on the rolling sea," Hallam Tennyson said:
"My father was fond of quoting these lines for the beauty of the sound. 'The lark' in the tower toward the rising sun symbolizes Hope."

Clear as a lark, high o'er me as a lark,   830
A sweet voice singing in the topmost tower
To the eastward. Up I climb'd a thousand steps
With pain; as in a dream I seem'd to climb
For ever; at the last I reach'd a door,
A light was in the crannies, and I heard,   835
"Glory and joy and honor to our Lord
And to the holy Vessel of the Grail!"
Then in my madness I essay'd the door;
It gave, an thro' a stormy glare, a heat
As from a seven-times-heated furnace, I,   840
Blasted and burnt, and blinded as I was,
With such a fierceness that I swoon'd away—
O, yet methought I saw the Holy Grail,
All pall'd in crimson samite, and around
Great angels, awful shapes, and wings and eyes!   845
And but for all my madness and my sin,
And then my swooning, I had sworn I saw
That which I saw; but what I saw was veil'd
And cover'd, and this quest was not for me.'

    "So speaking, and here ceasing, Lancelot left   850
The hall long silent, till Sir Gawain—nay,
Brother, I need not tell thee foolish words,—
A reckless and irreverent knight was he,
Now bolden'd by the silence of his King,—
Well, I will tell thee: 'O King, my liege,' he said,   855
'Hath Gawain fail'd in any quest of thine?
When have I stinted stroke in foughten field?
But as for thine, my good friend Percivale,
Thy holy nun and thou have driven men mad,
Yea, made our mightiest madder than our least.   860
But by mine eyes and by mine ears I swear,
I will be deafer than the blue-eyed cat,[8]
And thrice as blind as any noonday owl,
To holy virgins in their ecstasies,
Henceforward.'

                "'Deafer,' said the blameless King,   865
'Gawain, and blinder unto holy things,
Hope not to make thyself by idle vows,
Being too blind to have desire to see.
But if indeed there came a sign from heaven,
Blessed are Bors, Lancelot, and Percivale,   870
For these have seen according to their sight.
For every fiery prophet in old times,
And all the sacred madness of the bard,
When God made music thro' them, could but speak

---

8. "Cf. Darwin's *The Origin of Species*, ch. i.: 'Thus cats which are entirely white and have blue eyes are generally deaf; but it has lately been pointed out by Mr. Tait that this is confined to the males'" (Hallam Tennyson).

His music by the framework and the chord;   875
And as ye saw it ye have spoken truth.

"'Nay—but thou errest, Lancelot; never yet
Could all the true and noble in knight and man
Twine round one sin, whatever it might be,
With such a closeness but apart there grew,   880
Save that he were the swine thou spakest of,
Some root of knighthood and pure nobleness;
Whereto see thou, that it may bear its flower.

"'And spake I not too truly, O my knights?
Was I too dark a prophet when I said   885
To those who went upon the Holy Quest,
That most of them would follow wandering fires,
Lost in the quagmire?—lost to me and gone,
And left me gazing at a barren board,
And a lean Order—scarce return'd a tithe—   890
And out of those to whom the vision came
My greatest hardly will believe he saw.
Another hath beheld it afar off,
And, leaving human wrongs to right themselves,
Cares but to pass into the silent life.   895
And one hath had the vision face to face,
And now his chair desires him here in vain,
However they may crown him otherwhere.

"'And some among you held that if the King
Had seen the sight he would have sworn the vow.   900
Not easily, seeing that the King must guard
That which he rules, and is but as the hind
To whom a space of land is given to plow,
Who may not wander from the allotted field
Before his work be done, but being done,   905
Let visions of the night or of the day
Come as they will; and many a time they come,
Until this earth he walks on seems not earth,
This light that strikes his eyeball is not light,
This air that smites his forehead is not air   910
But vision—yea, his very hand and foot—
In moments when he feels he cannot die,
And knows himself no vision to himself,
Nor the high God a vision,[9] nor that One
Who rose again. Ye have seen what ye have seen.'   915

"So spake the King; I knew not all he meant."

                                                                        1869

---

9. "I have expressed there my strong feelings as to the Reality of the Unseen. The end, where the king speaks
of his work and of his visions, is intended to be the summing up of all in the highest note by the highest
of human men. These three lines [912–14] in Arthur's speech are the (spiritually) central lines of the
Idylls" (Memoir II, 90).

Pelleas and Ettarre[1]

King Arthur made new knights to fill the gap
Left by the Holy Quest; and as he sat
In hall at old Caerleon, the high doors
Were softly sunder'd, and thro' these a youth,
Pelleas, and the sweet smell of the fields   5
Past, and the sunshine came along with him.

"Make me thy knight, because I know, Sir King,
All that belongs to knighthood, and I love."
Such was his cry; for having heard the King
Had let proclaim a tournament—the prize   10
A golden circlet and a knightly sword,
Full fain had Pelleas for his lady won
The golden circlet, for himself the sword.
And there were those who knew him near the King,
And promised for him; and Arthur made him knight.   15

And this new knight, Sir Pelleas of the Isles—
But lately come to his inheritance,
And lord of many a barren isle was he—
Riding at noon, a day or twain before,
Across the forest call'd of Dean,[2] to find   20
Caerleon and the King, had felt the sun
Beat like a strong knight on his helm and reel'd
Almost to falling from his horse, but saw
Near him a mound of even-sloping side
Whereon a hundred stately beeches grew,   25
And here and there great hollies under them;
But for a mile all round was open space
And fern and heath. And slowly Pelleas drew
To that dim day, then, binding his good horse
To a tree, cast himself down; and as he lay   30
At random looking over the brown earth
Thro' that green-glooming twilight of the grove,
It seem'd to Pelleas that the fern without
Burnt as a living fire of emeralds,[3]
So that his eyes were dazzled looking at it.   35
Then o'er it crost the dimness of a cloud
Floating, and once the shadow of a bird

1. "Gareth and Lynette," which Tennyson started writing almost immediately after finishing "Pelleas and
Ettarre," seems deliberately designed to contrast the fortunes of two young knights. Whereas Gareth's
idealism prevails and wins him Lynette, Pelleas's similar qualities cannot possibly sustain him when faced
with Ettarre's lascivious conduct. Although Tennyson had been praised more than once in the last century for never penning a line that could bring a blush to the cheeks of an English maiden, one can only
postulate a rather unimaginative reading of this idyll by critic and maiden alike.
2. Dating from ancient times, an extensive tract of country in Gloucestershire.
3. "Seen as I lay in the New Forest" (Tennyson). "This whole passage is descriptive of the New Forest,
which he called 'the finest bit of old England left, the most peculiar'" (Hallam Tennyson). Echoing
popular sentiment at the time, his son also says: "Almost the saddest of the Idylls. The breaking of the
storm."

Flying, and then a fawn; and his eyes closed.
And since he loved all maidens, but no maid
In special, half-awake he whisper'd: "Where?   40
O, where? I love thee, tho' I know thee not.
For fair thou art and pure as Guinevere,
And I will make thee with my spear and sword
As famous—O my Queen, my Guinevere,
For I will be thine Arthur when we meet."   45

    Suddenly waken'd with a sound of talk
And laughter at the limit of the wood,
And glancing thro' the hoary boles, he saw,
Strange as to some old prophet might have seem'd
A vision hovering on a sea of fire,   50
Damsels in divers colors like the cloud
Of sunset and sunrise, and all of them
On horses, and the horses richly trapt
Breast-high in that bright line of bracken stood;
And all the damsels talk'd confusedly,   55
And one was pointing this way and one that,
Because the way was lost.

                 And Pelleas rose,
And loosed his horse, and led him to the light.
There she that seem'd the chief among them said:
"In happy time behold our pilot-star!   60
Youth, we are damsels-errant,[4] and we ride,
Arm'd as ye see, to tilt against the knights
There at Caerleon, but have lost our way.
To right? to left? straight forward? back again?
Which? tell us quickly."

               Pelleas gazing thought,   65
"Is Guinevere herself so beautiful?"
For large her violet eyes look'd, and her bloom
A rosy dawn kindled in stainless heavens,
And round her limbs, mature in womanhood;
And slender was her hand and small her shape;   70
And but for those large eyes, the haunts of scorn,
She might have seem'd a toy to trifle with,
And pass and care no more. But while he gazed
The beauty of her flesh abash'd the boy,
As tho' it were the beauty of her soul;   75

4. Gray compares *Faerie Queen* II, i, XIX. Defending the reputation and honor of the Redcrosse Knight, Guyon says:
    A right good knight, and trew of word ywis:
    I present was, and can it witnesse well,
    When arms he swore, and streight did enterpris
    Th' adventure of the Errant Damozell;
    In which he hath great glory wonne, as I heare tell.
The passage is noteworthy, because it shows, through contrast, the difference between the effects of false and true rumor.

For as the base man, judging of the good,
Puts his own baseness in him by default
Of will and nature, so did Pelleas lend
All the young beauty of his own soul to hers,
Believing her, and when she spake to him   80
Stammer'd, and could not make her a reply.
For out of the waste islands had he come,
Where saving his own sisters he had known
Scarce any but the women of his isles,
Rough wives, that laugh'd and scream'd against the gulls,   85
Makers of nets, and living from the sea.

    Then with a slow smile turn'd the lady round
And look'd upon her people; and, as when
A stone is flung into some sleeping tarn
The circle widens till it lip the marge,   90
Spread the slow smile thro' all her company.
Three knights were thereamong, and they too smiled,
Scorning him; for the lady was Ettarre,
And she was a great lady in her land.

    Again she said: "O wild and of the woods,   95
Knowest thou not the fashion of our speech?
Or have the Heavens but given thee a fair face,
Lacking a tongue?"

              "O damsel," answer'd he,
"I woke from dreams, and coming out of gloom
Was dazzled by the sudden light, and crave   100
Pardon; but will ye to Caerleon? I
Go likewise; shall I lead you to the King?"

    "Lead then," she said; and thro' the woods they went.
And while they rode, the meaning in his eyes,
His tenderness of manner, and chaste awe,   105
His broken utterances and bashfulness,
Were all a burthen to her, and in her heart
She mutter'd, "I have lighted on a fool,
Raw, yet so stale!" But since her mind was bent
On hearing, after trumpet blown, her name   110
And title, "Queen of Beauty," in the lists
Cried—and beholding him so strong she thought
That peradventure he will fight for me,
And win the circlet—therefore flatter'd him,
Being so gracious that he wellnigh deem'd   115
His wish by hers was echo'd; and her knights
And all her damsels too were gracious to him,
For she was a great lady.

              And when they reach'd
Caerleon, ere they past to lodging, she,
Taking his hand, "O the strong hand," she said,   120

"See! look at mine! but wilt thou fight for me,
And win this fine circlet, Pelleas,
That I may love thee?"

                              Then his helpless heart
Leapt, and he cried, "Ay! wilt thou if I win?"
"Ay, that will I," she answer'd, and she laugh'd,   125
And straitly nipt the hand, and flung it from her;
Then glanced askew at those three knights of hers,
Till all her ladies laugh'd along with her.

    "O happy world," thought Pelleas, "all, meseems,
Are happy; I the happiest of them all!"   130
Nor slept that night for pleasure in his blood,
And green wood-ways, and eyes among the leaves;
Then being on the morrow knighted, sware
To love one only. And as he came away,
The men who met him rounded on their heels   135
And wonder'd after him, because his face
Shone like the countenance of a priest of old
Against the flame about a sacrifice
Kindled by fire from heaven; so glad was he.

    Then Arthur made vast banquets, and strange knights   140
From the four winds came in; and each one sat,
Tho' served with choice from air, land, stream, and sea,
Oft in mid-banquet measuring with his eyes
His neighbor's make and might; and Pelleas look'd
Noble among the noble, for he dream'd   145
His lady loved him, and he knew himself
Loved of the King; and him his new-made knight
Worshipt, whose lightest whisper moved him more
Than all the ranged reasons of the world.

    Then blush'd and brake the morning of the jousts,   150
And this was call'd "The Tournament of Youth;"
For Arthur, loving his young knight, withheld
His older and his mightier from the lists,
That Pelleas might obtain his lady's love,
According to her promise, and remain   155
Lord of the tourney. And Arthur had the jousts
Down in the flat field by the shore of Usk
Holden; the gilded parapets were crown'd
With faces, and the great tower fill'd with eyes
Up to the summit, and the trumpets blew.   160
There all day long Sir Pelleas kept the field
With honor; so by that strong hand of his
The sword and golden circlet were achieved.

    Then rang the shout his lady loved; the heat
Of pride and glory fired her face, her eye   165
Sparkled; she caught the circlet from his lance,

And there before the people crown'd herself.
So for the last time she was gracious to him.

Then at Caerleon for a space—her look
Bright for all others, cloudier on her knight—   170
Linger'd Ettarre; and, seeing Pelleas droop,
Said Guinevere, "We marvel at thee much,
O damsel, wearing this unsunny face
To him who won thee glory!" And she said,
"Had ye not held your Lancelot in your bower,   175
My Queen, he had not won." Whereat the Queen,
As one whose foot is bitten by an ant,
Glanced down upon her, turn'd and went her way.[5]

But after, when her damsels, and herself,
And those three knights all set their faces home,   180
Sir Pelleas follow'd. She that saw him cried:
"Damsels—and yet I should be shamed to say it—
I cannot bide Sir Baby.[6] Keep him back
Among yourselves. Would rather that we had
Some rough old knight who knew the worldly way,   185
Albeit grizzlier than a bear, to ride
And jest with! Take him to you, keep him off,
And pamper him with papmeat, if ye will,
Old milky fables of the wolf and sheep,
Such as the wholesome mothers tell their boys.   190
Nay, should ye try him with a merry one
To find his mettle, good; and if he fly us,
Small matter! let him." This her damsels heard,
And, mindful of her small and cruel hand,
They, closing round him thro' the journey home,   195
Acted her hest,[7] and always from her side
Restrain'd him with all manner of device,
So that he could not come to speech with her.
And when she gain'd her castle, upsprang the bridge,
Down rang the grate of iron thro' the groove,   200
And he was left alone in open field.

"These be the ways of ladies," Pelleas thought,
"To those who love them, trials of our faith.
Yea, let her prove me to the uttermost,
For loyal to the uttermost am I."   205
So made his moan, and, darkness falling, sought
A priory not far off, there lodged, but rose
With morning every day, and, moist or dry,
Full-arm'd upon his charger all day long
Sat by the walls, and no one open'd to him.   210

---

5. A significant exchange in that the queen is openly confronted with what previously had been only rumor.
6. Malory's language is particularly explicit: "But she was so proud that she had scorn of him, and said, 'That she would never love him, though he would die for her.'"
7. Archaic for behest or bidding.

And this persistence turn'd her scorn to wrath.
Then, calling her three knights, she charged them, "Out!
And drive him from the walls." And out they came,
But Pelleas overthrew them as they dash'd
Against him one by one; and these return'd,   215
But still he kept his watch beneath the wall.

Thereon her wrath became a hate; and once,
A week beyond, while walking on the walls
With her three knights, she pointed downward, "Look,
He haunts me—I cannot breathe—besieges me!   220
Down! strike him! put my hate into your strokes,
And drive him from my walls." And down they went,
And Pelleas overthrew them one by one;
And from the tower above him cried Ettarre,
"Bind him, and bring him in."

                                            He heard her voice;   225
Then let the strong hand, which had overthrown
Her minion-knights, by those he overthrew
Be bounded straight, and so they brought him in.

Then when he came before Ettarre, the sight
Of her rich beauty made him at one glance   230
More bondsman in his heart than in his bonds.
Yet with good cheer he spake: "Behold me, lady,
A prisoner, and the vassal of thy will;
And if thou keep me in thy donjon here,
Content am I so that I see thy face   235
But once a day; for I have sworn my vows,
And thou hast given thy promise, and I know
That all these pains are trials of my faith,
And that thyself, when thou hast seen me strain'd
And sifted to the utmost, wilt at length   240
Yield me thy love and know me for thy knight."

Then she began to rail so bitterly,
With all her damsels, he was stricken mute,
But, when she mock'd his vows and the great King,
Lighted on words: "For pity of thine own self,   245
Peace, lady, peace; is he not thine and mine?"
"Thou fool," she said, "I never heard his voice
But long'd to break away. Unbind him now,
And thrust him out of doors; for save he be
Fool to the midmost marrow of his bones,   250
He will return no more." And those, her three,
Laugh'd, and unbound, and thrust him from the gate.

And after this, a week beyond, again
She call'd them, saying: "There he watches yet,
There like a dog before his master's door!   255
Kick'd, he returns; do ye not hate him, ye?

Ye know yourselves; how can ye bide at peace,
Affronted with his fulsome innocence?
Are ye but creatures of the board and bed.
No men, to strike? Fall on him all at once,   260
And if ye slay him I reck not; if ye fail,
Give ye the slave mine order to be bound,
Bind him as heretofore, and bring him in.
It may be ye shall slay him in his bonds."

　　She spake, and at her will they couch'd their spears,   265
Three against one; and Gawain passing by,
Bound upon solitary adventure, saw
Low down beneath the shadow of those towers
A villainy, three to one; and thro' his heart
The fire of honor and all noble deeds   270
Flash'd, and he call'd, "I strike upon thy side—
The caitiffs!" "Nay," said Pelleas, "but forbear;
He needs no aid who doth his lady's will."

　　So Gawain, looking at the villainy done,
Forbore, but in his heat and eagerness   275
Trembled and quiver'd, as the dog, withheld
A moment from the vermin that he sees
Before him, shivers ere he springs and kills.

　　And Pelleas overthrew them, one to three;
And they rose up, and bound, and brought him in.   280
Then first her anger, leaving Pelleas, burn'd
Full on her knights in many an evil name
Of craven, weakling, and thrice-beaten hound:
"Yet, take him, ye that scarce are fit to touch,
Far less to bind, your victor, and thrust him out,   285
And let who will release him from his bonds.
And if he comes again"—there she brake short;
And Pelleas answer'd: "Lady, for indeed
I loved you and I deem'd you beautiful,
I cannot brook to see your beauty marr'd   290
Thro' evil spite; and if ye love me not,
I cannot bear to dream you so forsworn.
I had liefer ye were worthy of my love
Than to be loved again of you—farewell.
And tho' ye kill my hope, not yet my love,   295
Vex not yourself; ye will not see me more."

　　While thus he spake, she gazed upon the man
Of princely bearing, tho' in bonds, and thought:
"Why have I push'd him from me? this man loves,
If love there be; yet him I loved not. Why?   300
I deem'd him fool? yea, so? or that in him
A something—was it nobler than myself?—
Seem'd my reproach? He is not of my kind.
He could not love me, did he know me well.

Nay, let him go—and quickly." And her knights   305
Laugh'd not, but thrust him bounden out of door.

   Forth sprang Gawain, and loosed him from his bonds,
And flung them o'er the walls; and afterward,
Shaking his hands, as from a lazar's rag,
"Faith of my body," he said, "and art thou not—   310
Yea thou art he, whom late our Arthur made
Knight of his table; yea, and he that won
The circlet? wherefore hast thou so defamed
Thy brotherhood in me and all the rest
As let these caitiffs on thee work their will?"   315

   And Pelleas answer'd: "O, their wills are hers
For whom I won the circlet; and mine, hers,
Thus to be bounden, so to see her face,
Marr'd tho' it be with spite and mockery now,
Other than when I found her in the woods;   320
And tho' she hath me bounden but in spite,
And all to flout me, when they bring me in,
Let me be bounden, I shall see her face;
Else must I die thro' mine unhappiness."

   And Gawain answer'd kindly tho' in scorn: 325
"Why, let my lady bind me if she will,
And let my lady beat me if she will;
But an she send her delegate to thrall
These fighting hands of mine—Christ kill me then
But I will slice him handless by the wrist,   330
And let my lady sear the stump for him,
Howl as he may! But hold me for your friend.
Come, ye know nothing; here I pledge my troth,
Yea, by the honor of the Table Round,
I will be leal[8] to thee and work thy work,   335
And tame thy jailing princess to thine hand.
Lend me thine horse and arms, and I will say
That I have slain thee. She will let me in
To hear the manner of thy fight and fall;
Then, when I come within her counsels, then   340
From prime to vespers will I chant thy praise
As prowest[9] knight and truest lover, more
Than any have sung thee living, till she long
To have thee back in lusty life again,
Not to be bound, save by white bonds and warm,   345
Dearer than freedom. Wherefore now thy horse
And armor; let me go; be comforted.
Give me three days to melt her fancy, and hope
The third night hence will bring thee news of gold."

8. Loyal.
9. "Noblest" (Tennyson).

Then Pelleas lent his horse and all his arms,   350
Saving the goodly sword, his prize, and took
Gawain's, and said, "Betray me not, but help—
Art thou not he whom men call light-of-love?"

"Ay," said Gawain, "for women be so light;"
Then bounded forward to the castle walls,   355
And raised a bugle hanging from his neck,
And winded it, and that so musically
That all the old echoes hidden in the wall
Rang out like hollow woods at huntingtide.

Up ran a score of damsels to the tower;   360
"Avaunt," they cried, "our lady loves thee not!"
But Gawain lifting up his vizor said:
"Gawain am I, Gawain of Arthur's court,
And I have slain this Pelleas whom ye hate.
Behold his horse and armor. Open gates,   365
And I will make you merry."

                                    And down they ran,
Her damsels, crying to their lady, "Lo!
Pelleas is dead—he told us—he that hath
His horse and armor; will ye let him in?
He slew him! Gawain, Gawain of the court,   370
Sir Gawain—there he waits below the wall,
Blowing his bugle as who should say him nay."

And so, leave given, straight on thro' open door
Rode Gawain, whom she greeted courteously.
"Dead, is it so?" she ask'd. "Ay, ay," said he,   375
"And oft in dying cried upon your name."
"Pity on him," she answer'd, "a good knight,
But never let me bide one hour at peace."
"Ay," thought Gawain, "and you be fair enow;
But I to your dead man have given my troth,   380
That whom ye loathe, him will I make you love."

So those three days, aimless about the land,
Lost in a doubt, Pelleas wandering
Waited, until the third night brought a moon
With promise of large light on woods and ways.   385

Hot was the night and silent; but a sound
Of Gawain ever coming, and this lay—
Which Pelleas had heard sung before the Queen,
And seen her sadden listening—vext his heart,
And marr'd his rest—"A worm within the rose."   390

    "A rose, but one, none other rose had I,
    A rose, one rose, and this was wondrous fair,
    One rose, a rose that gladden'd earth and sky,

One rose, my rose, that sweeten'd all mine air—
I cared not for the thorns; the thorns were there.   395

"One rose, a rose to gather by and by,
One rose, a rose, to gather and to wear,
No rose but one—what other rose had I?
One rose, my rose; a rose that will not die,—
He dies who loves it,—if the worm be there."   400

This tender rhyme, and evermore the doubt,
"Why lingers Gawain with his golden news?"
So shook him that he could not rest, but rode
Ere midnight to her walls, and bound his horse
Hard by the gates. Wide open were the gates,   405
And no watch kept; and in thro' these he past,
And heard but his own steps, and his own heart
Beating, for nothing moved but his own self
And his own shadow. Then he crost the court,
And spied not any light in hall or bower,   410
But saw the postern portal also wide
Yawning; and up a slope of garden, all
Of roses white and red, and brambles mixt
And overgrowing them, went on, and found,
Here too, all hush'd below the mellow moon,   415
Save that one rivulet from a tiny cave
Came lightening downward, and so split itself
Among the roses and was lost again.

Then was he ware of three pavilions rear'd
Above the bushes, gilden-peakt. In one,   420
Red after revel, droned her lurdane[1] knights
Slumbering, and their three squires across their feet;
In one, their malice on the placid lip
Frozen by sweet sleep, four of her damsels lay;
And in the third, the circlet of the jousts   425
Bound on her brow, were Gawain and Ettarre.

Back, as a hand that pushes thro' the leaf
To find a nest and feels a snake, he drew;
Back, as a coward slinks from what he fears
To cope with, or a traitor proven, or hound   430
Beaten, did Pelleas in an utter shame
Creep with his shadow thro' the court again,
Fingering at his sword-handle until he stood
There on the castle-bridge once more, and thought,
"I will go back, and slay them where they lie."   435

And so went back, and seeing them yet in sleep
Said, "Ye, that so dishallow the holy sleep,
Your sleep is death," and drew the sword, and thought,

---

1. "From old French *lourdin*, heavy" (Tennyson). *OED* defines as "worthless, ill-bred, lazy," the last cita-
tion here.

"What! slay a sleeping knight? the King hath bound
And sworn me to this brotherhood;" again, 440
"Alas that ever a knight should be so false!"
Then turn'd, and so return'd, and groaning laid
The naked sword athwart their naked throats,
There left it, and them sleeping; and she lay,
The circlet of the tourney round her brows, 445
And the sword of the tourney across her throat.[2]

And forth he past, and mounting on his horse
Stared at her towers that, larger than themselves
In their own darkness, throng'd into the moon;
Then crush'd the saddle with his thighs, and clench'd 450
His hands, and madden'd with himself and moan'd:

"Would they have risen against me in their blood
At the last day? I might have answer'd them
Even before high God. O towers so strong,
Huge, solid, would that even while I gaze 455
The crack of earthquake shivering to your base
Split you, and hell burst up your harlot roofs
Bellowing, and charr'd you thro' and thro' within,
Black as the harlot's heart—hollow as a skull!
Let the fierce east scream thro' your eyelet-holes, 460
And whirl the dust of harlots round and round
In dung and nettles! hiss, snake—I saw him there—
Let the fox bark, let the wolf yell! Who yells
Here in the still sweet summer night but I—
I, the poor Pelleas whom she call'd her fool 465
Fool, beast—he, she, or I? myself most fool;
Beast too, as lacking human wit—disgraced,
Dishonor'd all for trial of true love—
Love?—we be all alike; only the King
Hath made us fools and liars. O noble vows! 470
O great and sane and simple race of brutes
That own no lust because they have no law!
For why should I have loved her to my shame?
I loathe her, as I loved her to my shame.
I never loved her, I but lusted for her— 475
Away!"—
He dash'd the rowel into his horse,
And bounded forth and vanish'd thro' the night.

Then she, that felt the cold touch on her throat,
Awaking knew the sword, and turn'd herself
To Gawain: "Liar, for thou hast not slain 480
This Pelleas! here he stood, and might have slain
Me and thyself." And he that tells the tale
Says that her ever-veering fancy turn'd
To Pelleas, as the one true knight on earth

2. "The line gives the quiver of the sword across their throats" (Tennyson).

And only lover; and thro' her love her life   485
Wasted and pined, desiring him in vain.

But he by wild and way, for half the night,
And over hard and soft, striking the sod
From out the soft, the spark from off the hard,
Rode till the star above the wakening sun,   490
Beside that tower where Percivale was cowl'd,
Glanced from the rosy forehead of the dawn.
For so the words were flash'd into his heart
He knew not whence or wherefore: "O sweet star,
Pure on the virgin forehead of the dawn!"   495
And there he would have wept, but felt his eyes
Harder and drier than a fountain bed
In summer. Thither came the village girls
And linger'd talking, and they come no more
Till the sweet heavens have fill'd it from the heights   500
Again with living waters in the change
Of seasons. Hard his eyes, harder his heart
Seem'd; but so weary were his limbs that he,
Gasping, "Of Arthur's hall am I, but here,
Here let me rest and die," cast himself down,   505
And gulf'd his griefs in inmost sleep; so lay,
Till shaken by a dream, that Gawain fired
The hall of Merlin, and the morning star
Reel'd in the smoke, brake into flame, and fell.

He woke, and being ware of some one nigh,   510
Sent hands upon him, as to tear him, crying,
"False! and I held thee pure as Guinevere."

But Percivale stood near him and replied,
"Am I but false as Guinevere is pure?
Or art thou mazed with dreams? or being one   515
Of our free-spoken Table hast not heard
That Lancelot"—there he check'd himself and paused.

Then fared it with Sir Pelleas as with one
Who gets a wound in battle, and the sword
That made it plunges thro' the wound again,   520
And pricks it deeper; and he shrank and wail'd,
"Is the Queen false?" and Percivale was mute.
"Have any of our Round Table held their vows?"
And Percivale made answer not a word.
Is the King true?" "The King!" said Percivale.   525
"Why, then let men couple at once with wolves.
What! art thou mad?"

                              But Pelleas, leaping up,
Ran thro' the doors and vaulted on his horse
And fled. Small pity upon his horse had he,
Or on himself, or any, and when he met   530

A cripple, one that held a hand for alms—
Hunch'd as he was, and like an old dwarf elm
That turns its back on the salt blast, the boy
Paused not, but overrode him, shouting, "False,
And false with Gawain!" and so left him bruised   535
And batter'd, and fled on, and hill and wood
Went ever streaming by him till the gloom
That follows on the turning of the world
Darken'd the common path. He twitch'd the reins,
And made his beast, that better knew it, swerve   540
Now off it and now on; but when he saw
High up in heaven the hall that Merlin built,
Blackening against the dead-green stripes of even,
"Black nest of rats," he groan'd, "ye build too high."

    Not long thereafter from the city gates   545
Issued Sir Lancelot riding airily,
Warm with a gracious parting from the Queen,
Peace at his heart, and gazing at a star
And marvelling what it was; on whom the boy,
Across the silent seeded meadow-grass   550
Borne, clash'd; and Lancelot, saying, "What name hast thou
That ridest here so blindly and so hard?"
"No name, no name," he shouted, "a scourge am I
To lash the treasons of the Table Round."
"Yea, but thy name?" "I have many names," he cried: 555
"I am wrath and shame and hate and evil fame,
And like a poisonous wind I pass to blast
And blaze the crime of Lancelot and the Queen."
"First over me," said Lancelot, "shalt thou pass."
"Fight therefore," yell'd the youth, and either Knight   560
Drew back a space, and when they closed, at once
The weary steed of Pelleas floundering flung
His rider, who call'd out from the dark field,
"Thou art false as hell; slay me, I have no sword."
Then Lancelot, "Yea, between thy lips—and sharp;   565
But here will I disedge it by thy death."
"Slay then," he shriek'd, "my will is to be slain,"
And Lancelot, with his heel upon the fallen,
Rolling his eyes, a moment stood, then spake:
"Rise, weakling; I am Lancelot; say thy say."   570

    And Lancelot slowly rode his war-horse back
To Camelot, and Sir Pelleas in brief while
Caught his unbroken limbs from the dark field,
And follow'd to the city. It chanced that both
Brake into hall together, worn and pale.   575
There with her knights and dames was Guinevere.
Full wonderingly she gazed on Lancelot
So soon return'd, and then on Pelleas, him
Who had not greeted her, but cast himself
Down on a bench, hard-breathing. "Have ye fought?"   580

She ask'd of Lancelot. "Ay, my Queen," he said.
"And thou hast overthrown him?" "Ay, my Queen."
Then she, turning to Pelleas, "O young knight,
Hath the great heart of knighthood in thee fail'd
So far thou canst not bide, unfrowardly,   585
A fall from *him*?" Then, for he answer'd not,
"Or hast thou other griefs? If I, the Queen,
May help them, loose thy tongue, and let me know."
But Pelleas lifted up an eye so fierce
She quail'd; and he, hissing "I have no sword,"   590
Sprang from the door into the dark. The Queen
Look'd hard upon her lover, he on her,
And each foresaw the dolorous day to be;
And all talk died, as in a grove all song
Beneath the shadow of some bird of prey.   595
Then a long silence came upon the hall,
And Modred thought, "The time is hard at hand."

                                                          1869

The Last Tournament

Dagonet,[1] the fool, whom Gawain in his mood.
Had made mock-knight of Arthur's Table Round,
At Camelot, high above the yellowing woods,
Danced like a wither'd leaf before the hall.
And toward him from the hall, with harp in hand,   5

And from the crown thereof a carcanet[2]
Of ruby swaying to and fro, the prize
Of Tristram in the jousts of yesterday,
Came Tristram, saying, "Why skip ye so, Sir Fool?"
    For Arthur and Sir Lancelot riding once   10
Far down beneath a winding wall of rock
Heard a child wail. A stump of oak half-dead,
From roots like some black coil of carven snakes,
Clutch'd at the crag, and started thro' mid air
Bearing an eagle's nest; and thro' the tree   15
Rush'd ever a rainy wind, and thro' the wind
Pierced ever a child's cry; and crag and tree
Scaling, Sir Lancelot from the perilous nest,
This ruby necklace thrice around her neck,
And all unscarr'd from beak or talon, brought   20
A maiden babe, which Arthur pitying took,
Then gave it to his Queen to rear. The Queen,

---

1. Although he appears in Malory, the fool is largely of Tennyson's invention. "The bare outline of the story
and of the vengeance of Mark is taken from Malory; my father often referred with pleasure to his creation of the half-humorous, half-pathetic fool Dagonet" (Hallam Tennyson). The fool in *King Lear* may
have, in part, been present in Tennyson's mind, although there is no direct evidence of that.
2. A necklace. The following story of its origin was apparently derived from a legendary incident in the life
of King Alfred.

But coldly acquiescing, in her white arms
Received, and after loved it tenderly,
And named it Nestling; so forgot herself 25
A moment, and her cares; till that young life
Being smitten in mid heaven with mortal cold
Past from her, and in time the carcanet
Vext her with plaintive memories of the child.
So she, delivering it to Arthur, said 30
"Take thou the jewels of this dead innocence,
And make them, as thou wilt, a tourney-prize."

    To whom the King: "Peace to thine eagle-borne
Dead nestling, and this honor after death,
Following thy will! but, O my Queen, I muse 35
Why ye not wear on arm, or neck, or zone
Those diamonds that I rescued from the tarn,[3]
And Lancelot won, methought, for thee to wear."

    "Would rather you had let them fall," she cried;
"Plunge and be lost—ill-fated as they were, 40
A bitterness to me!—ye look amazed,
Not knowing they were lost as soon as given—
Slid from my hands when I was leaning out
Above the river—that unhappy child[4]
Past in her barge; but rosier luck will go 45
With these rich jewels, seeing that they came
Not from the skeleton of a brother-slayer,
But the sweet body of a maiden babe.
Perchance—who knows?—the purest of thy knights
May win them for the purest of my maids." 50

    She ended, and the cry of a great jousts
With trumpet-blowings ran on all the ways
From Camelot in among the faded fields
To furthest towers; and everywhere the knights
Arm'd for a day of glory before the King. 55

    But on the hither side of that loud morn
Into the hall stagger'd, his visage ribb'd
From ear to ear with dogwhip-weals,[5] his nose
Bridge-broken, one eye out, and one hand off,
And one with shatter'd fingers dangling lame, 60
A churl, to whom indignantly the King:

    "My churl, for whom Christ died, what evil beast
Hath drawn his claws athwart thy face? or fiend?
Man was it who marr'd heaven's image in thee thus?"

3. See "Lancelot and Elaine," lines 34ff.
4. Elaine.
5. Ridges raised on the flesh from lashing.

Then, sputtering thro' the hedge of splinter'd teeth,   65
Yet strangers to the tongue, and with blunt stump[6]
Pitch-blacken'd sawing the air, said the maim'd churl:

"He took them and he drave them to his tower—
Some hold he was a table-knight of thine—
A hundred goodly ones—the Red Knight,[7] he—   70
Lord, I was tending swine, and the Red Knight
Brake in upon me and drave them to his tower;
And when I call'd upon thy name as one
That doest right by gentle and by churl,
Maim'd me and maul'd, and would outright have slain,   75
Save that he sware me to a message, saying:
"Tell thou the King and all his liars that I
Have founded my Round Table in the North,
And whatsoever his own knights have sworn
My knights have sworn the counter to it—and say   80
My tower is full of harlots, like his court,
But mine are worthier, seeing they profess
To be none other than themselves—and say
My knights are all adulterers like his own,
But mine are truer, seeing they profess   85
To be none other; and say his hour is come,
The heathen are upon him, his long lance
Broken, and his Excalibur a straw.'"

Then Arthur turn'd to Kay the seneschal:
"Take thou my churl, and tend him curiously   90
Like a king's heir, till all his hurts be whole.
The heathen—but that ever-climbing wave,
Hurl'd back again so often in empty foam,
Hath lain for years at rest—and renegades,
Thieves, bandits, leavings of confusion, whom   95
The wholesome realm is purged of otherwhere,
Friends, thro' your manhood and your fealty,—now
Make their last head like Satan in the North.[8]
My younger knights, new-made, in whom your flower
Waits to be solid fruit of golden deeds,   100
Move with me toward their quelling, which achieved,
The loneliest ways are safe from shore to shore.
But thou, Sir Lancelot, sitting in my place
Enchair'd to-morrow, arbitrate the field;
For wherefore shouldst thou care to mingle with it,   105
Only to yield my Queen her own again?
Speak, Lancelot, thou art silent; is it well?"

Thereto Sir Lancelot answer'd: "It is well;
Yet better if the King abide, and leave

6. "'Blunt stump' where the hand had been cut off and the stump had been pitched." "Tongue": "rough"
(both Tennyson).
7. Tennyson said he is Pelleas, though here and later the text never makes the identity clear.
8. Satan mustered his rebellious forces in the north of Heaven. See Isaiah 14:12–14.

The leading of his younger knights to me. 110
Else, for the King has will'd it, it is well."

Then Arthur rose and Lancelot follow'd him,
And while they stood without the doors, the King
Turn'd to him saying: "Is it then so well?
Or mine the blame that oft I seem as he 115
Of whom was written, 'A sound is in his ears'?
The foot that loiters, bidden go, — the glance
That only seems half-loyal to command, —
A manner somewhat fallen from reverence —
Or have I dream'd the bearing of our knights 120
Tells of manhood ever less and lower?
Or whence the fear lest this my realm, uprear'd
By noble deeds at one with noble vows,
From flat confusion and brute violences,
Reel back into the beast, and be no more?" 125

He spoke, and taking all his younger knights,
Down the slope city rode, and sharply turn'd
North by the gate. In her high bower the Queen,
Working a tapestry, lifted up her head,
Watch'd her lord pass, and knew not that she sigh'd 130
Then ran across her memory the strange rhyme
Of bygone Merlin, "Where is he who knows?
From the great deep to the great deep he goes.[9]

But when the morning of a tournament,
By these in earnest those in mockery call'd 135
The Tournament of the Dead Innocence,
Brake with a wet wind blowing, Lancelot,
Round whose sick head all night, like birds of prey,
The words of Arthur flying shriek'd, arose,
And down a streetway hung with folds of pure 140
White samite, and by fountains running wine,
Where children sat in white with cups of gold,
Moved to the lists, and there, with slow sad steps
Ascending, fill'd his double-dragon'd chair.
He glanced and saw the stately galleries, 145
Dame, damsel, each thro' worship of their Queen
White-robed in honor of the stainless child,
And some with scatter'd jewels, like a bank
Of maiden snow mingled with sparks of fire.
He look'd but once, and vail'd[1] his eyes again. 150

The sudden trumpet sounded as in a dream
To ears but half-awaked, then one low roll
Of Autumn[2] thunder, and the jousts began;

9. From Merlin's song in "The Coming of Arthur," lines 409–10. See "De Profundis," line 25: "To that last deep where we and thou art still."
1. "Drooped" (Tennyson), hence lowered, not veiled.
2. "The autumn of the Round Table" (Tennyson).

And ever the wind blew, and yellowing leaf,
And gloom and gleam, and shower and shorn plume   155
Went down it. Sighing weariedly, as one
Who sits and gazes on a faded fire,
When all the goodlier guests are past away,
Sat their great umpire looking o'er the lists.
He saw the laws that ruled the tournament   160
Broken, but spake not; once, a knight cast down
Before his throne of arbitration cursed
The dead babe and the follies of the King;
And once the laces of a helmet crack'd,
And show'd him, like a vermin in its hole,   165
Modred, a narrow face. Anon he heard
The voice that billow'd round the barriers roar
An ocean-sounding welcome to one knight,
But newly-enter'd, taller than the rest,
And armor'd all in forest green, whereon   170
There tript a hundred tiny silver deer,
And wearing but a holly-spray for crest,
With ever-scattering berries, and on shield
A spear, a harp, a bugle—Tristram[3]—late
From over-seas in Brittany return'd   175
And marriage with a princess of that realm
Isolt the White—Sir Tristram[4] of the Woods—
Whom Lancelot knew, had held sometime with pain
His own against him, and now yearn'd to shake
The burthen off his heart in one full shock   180
With Tristram even to death. His strong hands gript
And dinted the gilt dragons right and left,
Until he groan'd for wrath—so many of those
That ware their ladies' colors on the casque
Drew from before Sir Tristram to the bounds,   185
And there with gibes and flickering mockeries
Stood, while he mutter'd, "Craven crests! O shame!
What faith have these in whom they sware to love?
The glory of our Round Table is no more."
    So Tristram won, and Lancelot gave, the gems,   190
Not speaking other word than, "Hast thou won?
Art thou the purest, brother?[5] See, the hand
Wherewith thou takest this is red!" to whom
Tristram, half plagued by Lancelot's languorous mood,
Made answer: "Ay, but wherefore toss me this   195
Like a dry bone cast to some hungry hound?
Let be thy fair Queen's fantasy. Strength of heart
And might of limb, but mainly use and skill,
Are winners in this pastime of our King.

3. "He was a harper and a hunter" (Tennyson).
4. With Tristram, as with Gawain, Tennyson has drastically altered personalities to suit his own purposes. The chief exponent of free love, Tristram becomes a cynical materialist whose affair with Mark's wife is meant to parallel the Lancelot-Guinevere-Arthur triangle. In Malory, Tristram was a knight of the Round Table second only to Launcelot, and in legends generally Tristram was the quintessence of the romantic lover.
5. "Because the Queen had said: 'The purest of thy knights / May use them for the purest of my maids'" (Tennyson).

My hand—belike the lance hath dript upon it—   200
No blood of mine, I trow; but O chief knight,
Right arm of Arthur in the battle-field,
Great brother, thou nor I have made the world;
Be happy in thy fair Queen as I in mine."

And Tristram round the gallery made his horse   205
Caracole;[6] then bow'd his homage, bluntly saying,
"Fair damsels, each to him who worships each
Sole Queen of Beauty and of love, behold
This day my Queen of Beauty is not here."
And most of these were mute, some anger'd, one   210
Murmuring, "All courtesy is dead," and one,
"The glory of our Round Table is no more."[7]

Then fell thick rain, plume droopt and mantle clung,
And pettish cries awoke, and the wan day
Went glooming down in wet and weariness;   215
But under her black brows a swarthy one
Laugh'd shrilly, crying: "Praise the patient saints,
Our one white day of Innocence hath past,
Tho' somewhat draggled at the skirt. So be it.
The snowdrop only, flowering thro' the year,[8]   220
Would make the world as blank as winter-tide.
Come—let us gladden their sad eyes, our Queen's
And Lancelot's, at this night's solemnity
With all the kindlier colors of the field."

So dame and damsel glitter'd at the feast   225
Variously gay; for he[9] that tells the tale
Liken'd them, saying, as when an hour of cold
Falls on the mountain in midsummer snows,[1]
And all the purple slopes of mountain flowers
Pass under white, till the warm hour returns   230
With veer of wind and all are flowers again,
So dame and damsel cast the simple white,
And glowing in all colors, the live grass,
Rose-campion, bluebell, kingcup, poppy, glanced
About the revels, and with mirth so loud   235
Beyond all use, that, half-amazed, the Queen,
And wroth at Tristram and the lawless jousts,
Brake up their sports, then slowly to her bower
Parted, and in her bosom pain was lord.

And little Dagonet on the morrow morn   240
High over all the yellowing autumn-tide,

---

6. In horsemanship, to execute half-turns to the right or left.
7. Of lines 205–12: "It was the law to give the prize to some lady on the field, but the laws are broken, and
   Tristram the courteous has lost his courtesy, for the great sin of Lancelot was sapping the Round Table"
   (Tennyson).
8. "Because they were dressed in white" (Tennyson)
9. Tennyson himself.
1. "Seen by me at Müreen Switzerland" (Tennyson).

Danced liked a wither'd leaf before the hall.
Then Tristram saying, "Why skip ye so, Sir Fool?"
Wheel'd round on either heel, Dagonet replied.
"Belike for lack of wiser company;   245
Or being fool, and seeing too much wit
Makes the world rotten, why, belike I skip
To know myself the wisest knight of all."
"Ay, fool," said Tristram, "but 't is eating dry
To dance without a catch, a roundelay   250
To dance to." Then he twangled on his harp,
And while he twangled little Dagonet stood
Quiet as any water-sodden log
Stay'd in the wandering warble of a brook,
But when the twangling ended, skipt again;   255
And being ask'd, "Why skipt ye not, Sir Fool?"
Made answer, "I had liefer twenty years
Skip to the broken music of my brains
Than any broken music thou canst make."
Then Tristram, waiting for the quip to come,   260
"Good now, what music have I broken, fool?"
And little Dagonet, skipping, "Arthur, the King's;
For when thou playest that air with Queen Isolt,
Thou makest broken music with thy bride.
Her daintier namesake[2] down in Britanny—   265
And so thou breakest Arthur's music too."
"Save for that broken music in thy brains,
Sir Fool," said Tristram, "I would break thy head.
Fool, I came late, the heathen wars were o'er,
The life had flown, we sware but by the shell[3]   270
I am but a fool to reason with a fool—
Come, thou art crabb'd and sour; but lean me down,
Sir Dagonet, one of thy long asses' ears,
And harken if my music be not true.

        "'Free love—free field—we love but while we may.   275
        The woods are hush'd, their music is no more;
        The leaf is dead, the yearning past away.
        New leaf, new life—the days of frost are o'er;
        New life, new love, to suit the newer day;
        New loves are sweet as those that went before   280
        Free love—free field—we love but while we may.'

    "Ye might have moved slow-measure to my tune,
Not stood stock-still. I made it in the woods,
And heard it ring as true as tested gold."

    But Dagonet with one foot poised in his hand: 285
"Friend, did ye mark that fountain yesterday,
Made to run wine?—but this had run itself
All out like a long life to a sour end—

---

2. "Isolt of the White Hands" (Tennyson).
3. "Husk" (Tennyson).

And them that round it sat with golden cups
To hand the wine to whosever came—   290
The twelve small damosels white as Innocence,
In honor of poor Innocence the babe,
Who left the gems which Innocence the Queen
Lent to the King, and Innocence the King
Gave for a prize—and one of those white slips   295
Handed her cup and piped, the pretty one,
'Drink, drink, Sir Fool,' and thereupon I drank,
Spat—pish—the cup was gold, the draught was mud."

        And Tristram: "Was it muddier than thy gibes?
Is all the laughter gone dead out of thee—   300
Not marking how the knighthood mock thee, fool—
"Fear God: honor the King—his one true knight—
Sole follower of the vows'—for here be they
Who knew thee swine enow before I came,
Smuttier than blasted grain. But when the King   305
Had made thee fool, thy vanity so shot up
It frighted all free fool from out thy heart;
Which left thee less than fool, and less than swine,
A naked aught—yet swine I hold thee still,
For I have flung thee pearls and find thee swine."   310

        And little Dagonet mincing with his feet:
"Knight, an ye fling those rubies round my neck
In lieu of hers, I'll hold thou hast some touch
Of music, since I care not for thy pearls.
Swine? I have wallow'd, I have wash'd—the world   315
Is flesh and shadow—I have had my day.
The dirty nurse, Experience, in her kind
Hath foul'd me—an I wallow'd, then I wash'd—
I have had my day and my philosophies—
And thank the Lord I am King Arthur's fool.   320
Swine, say ye? swine, goats, asses, rams, and geese
Troop'd round a Paynim harper[4] once, who thrumm'd
On such a wire as musically as thou
Some such fine song—but never a king's fool."

        And Tristram, "Then were swine, goats, asses, geese   325
The wiser fools, seeing thy Paynim bard
Had such a mastery of his mystery
That he could harp his wife up out of hell."

        Then Dagonet, turning on the ball of his foot,
"And whither harp'st thou thine? down! and thyself   330
Down! and two more; a helpful harper thou,
That harpest downward! Dost thou know the star
We call the Harp of Arthur[5] up in heaven?"

4. "Orpheus" (Tennyson). "Paynim": pagan.
5. Lyra, a northern constellation.

    And Tristram, "Ay, Sir Fool, for when our King
Was victor wellnigh day by day, the knights,   335
Glorying in each new glory, set his name
High on all hills and in the signs of heaven."

    And Dagonet answer'd: "Ay, and when the land
Was freed, and the Queen false, ye set yourself
To babble about him, all to show your wit—   340
And whether he were king by courtesy,
Or king by right—and so went harping down
The black king's[6] highway, got so far and grew
So witty that ye play'd at ducks and drakes
With Arthur's vows on the great lake of fire.   345
Tuwhoo! do ye see it? do ye see the star?"[7]

    "Nay, fool," said Tristram, "not in open day."
And Dagonet: "Nay, nor will; I see it and hear.
It makes a silent music up in heaven,
And I and Arthur and the angels hear,   350
And then we skip," "Lo, fool," he said, "ye talk
Fool's treason; is the King thy brother fool?"
Then little Dagonet clapt his hands and shrill'd:
"Ay, ay, my brother fool, the king of fools!
Conceits himself as God that he can make   355
Figs out of thistles, silk from bristles, milk
From burning spurge,[8] honey from hornet-combs,
And men from beasts—Long live the king of fools!"

    And down the city Dagonet danced away;
But thro' the slowly-mellowing avenues   360
And solitary passes of the wood
Rode Tristram toward Lyonnesse and the west.
Before him fled the face of Queen Isolt

    With ruby-circled neck, but evermore
Past, as a rustle or twitter in the wood   365
Made dull his inner, keen his outer eye[9]
For all that walk'd, or crept, or perch'd, or flew.
Anon the face, as, when a gust hath blown,
Unruffling waters re-collect the shape
Of one that in them sees himself, return'd;   370
But at the slot or fewmets[1] of a deer
Or even a fallen feather, vanish'd again.

    So on for all that day from lawn to lawn
Thro' many a league-long bower he rode. At length
A lodge of intertwisted beechen-boughs,   375

6. The devil's. "Enter ye in at the straight gate, and broad is the way, that leadeth to destruction"(Matthew 7:13).
7. Either the constellation Lyra, or perhaps Vega, the first magnitude and brightest star in it.
8. A shrublike plant that contains an acrid, milky juice.
9. "The hunter's eye" (Tennyson).
1. Droppings. "Slot": a footprint or tracks.

Furze-cramm'd and bracken-rooft, the which himself
Built for a summer day with Queen Isolt
Against a shower, dark in the golden grove
Appearing, sent his fancy back to where
She lived a moon in that low lodge with him;   380
Till Mark her lord had past, the Cornish King,
With six or seven, when Tristram was away,
And snatch'd her thence, yet, dreading worse than shame
Her warrior Tristram, spake not any word,
But bode his hour, devising wretchedness.   385

      And now that desert lodge to Tristram lookt
So sweet that, halting, in he past and sank
Down on a drift of foliage random-blown;
But could not rest for musing how to smooth
And sleek his marriage over to the queen.   390
Perchance in lone Tintagil far from all
The tonguesters of the court she had not heard.
But then what folly had sent him over-seas
After she left him lonely here? a name?
Was it the name of one in Brittany,   395
Isolt, the daughter of the king? "Isolt
Of the White Hands" they call'd her: the sweet name
Allured him first, and then the maid herself,
Who served him well with those white hands of hers,[2]
And loved him well, until himself had thought   400
He loved her also, wedded easily,
But left her all as easily, and return'd.
The black-blue Irish hair and Irish eyes
Had drawn him home—what marvel? then he laid
His brows upon the drifted leaf and dream'd.   405

      He seem'd to pace the strand of Brittany
Between Isolt of Britain and his bride,
And show'd them both the ruby-chain, and both
Began to struggle for it, till his queen
Graspt it so hard that all her hand was red.   410
Then cried the Breton, "Look, her hand is red!
These be no rubies, this is frozen blood,
And melts within her hand—her hand is hot
With ill desires, but this I gave thee, look,
Is all as cool and white as any flower."   415
Follow'd a rush of eagle's wings, and then
A whimpering of the spirit of the child,
Because the twain had spoil'd her carcanet.

2. She had cured Tristram of a wound from a poisoned arrow. Previously Tristram had been healed of another wound by Isolt of Ireland. When he told King Mark of her beauty, he sent Tristram to bring her for his wife. On the return voyage, they unknowingly drank in each other's presence the love philtre reserved for Isolt's first meeting with Mark. In Malory, the effects of the philtre wear off by the time Tristram marries Isolt of Brittany; in other versions, its effect is permanent.

He dream'd; but Arthur with a hundred spears
Rode far, till o'er the illimitable reed,   420
And many a glancing plash and sallowy[3] isle,
The wide-wing'd sunset of the misty marsh
Glared on a huge machicolated[4] tower
That stood with open doors, whereout was roll'd
A roar of riot, as from men secure   425
Amid their marshes, ruffians at their ease
Among their harlot-brides, an evil song.
"Lo there," said one of Arthur's youth, for there,
High on a grim dead tree before the tower,
A goodly brother of the Table Round   430
Swung by the neck; and on the boughs a shield
Showing a shower of blood in a field noir,
And therebeside a horn, inflamed the knights
At that dishonor done the gilded spur,
Till each would clash the shield and blow the horn.   435
But Arthur waved them back. Alone he rode.
Then at the dry harsh roar of the great horn,
That sent the face of all the marsh aloft
An ever upward-rushing storm and cloud
Of shriek and plume, the Red Knight heard, and all,   440
Even to tipmost lance and topmost helm,
In blood-red armor sallying, howl'd to the King:

"The teeth of Hell flay bare and gnash thee flat! —
Lo! art thou not that eunuch-hearted king
Who fain had clipt free manhood from the world —   445
The woman-worshipper? Yea, God's curse, and I,
Slain was the brother of my paramour
By a knight of thine, and I that heard her whine
And snivel, being eunuch-hearted too.
Sware by the scorpion-worm[5] that twists in hell   450
And stings itself to everlasting death,
To hang whatever knight of thine I fought
And tumbled. Art thou king? — Look to thy life!"

He ended. Arthur knew the voice; the face
Wellnigh was helmet-hidden, and the name[6]   455
Went wandering somewhere darkling in his mind.
And Arthur deign'd not use of word or sword,
But let the drunkard, as he stretch'd from horse
To strike him, overbalancing his bulk,
Down from the causeway heavily to the swamp   460
Fall, as the crest of some slow-arching wave,[7]
Heard in dead night along that table-shore,
Drops flat, and after the great waters break

3. "Having willows" (Ricks).
4. A tower with openings between the corbels, the supports for a projecting parapet, through which molten
   lead, stones, etc., were dropped upon assailants.
5. In legend, the scorpion, when surrounded by fire, stings itself to death.
6. "Pelleas" (Tennyson).
7. As I have heard and seen the sea on the shore of Mablethorpe" (Tennyson).

Whitening for half a league, and thin themselves,
Far over sands marbled with moon and cloud,   465
From less and less to nothing; thus he fell
Head-heavy. Then the knights, who watch'd him, roar'd
And shouted and leapt down upon the fallen,
There trampled out his face from being known,
And sank his head in mire, and slimed themselves;   470
Nor heard the King for their own cries, but sprang
Thro' open doors, and swording right and left
Men, women, on their sudden faces, hurl'd
The tables over and the wines, and slew
Till all the rafters rang with woman-yells,   475
And all the pavement stream'd with massacre.[8]
Then, echoing yell with yell, they fired the tower,
Which half that autumn night, like the live North;[9]
Red-pulsing up thro' Alioth and Alcor,[1]
Made all above it, and a hundred meres   480
About it, as the water Moab[2] saw
Come round by the east, and out beyond them flush'd
The long low dune and lazy-plunging sea.

So all the ways were safe from shore to shore,
But in the heart of Arthur pain was lord.   485

Then, out of Tristram waking, the red dream
Fled with a shout, and that low lodge return'd,
Mid-forest, and the wind among the boughs.
He whistled his good war-horse left to graze
Among the forest greens, vaulted upon him,   490
And rode beneath an ever-showering leaf,
Till one lone woman, weeping near a cross,
Stay'd him. "Why weep ye?" "Lord," she said, "my man
Hath left me or is dead;" whereon he thought—
"What, if she[3] hate me now? I would not this.   495
What, if she love me still? I would not that.
I know not what I would"—but said to her,
"Yet weep not thou, lest, if thy mate return,
He find thy favor changed and love thee not"—
Then pressing day by day thro' Lyonnesse   500
Last in a roky hollow, belling,[4] heard
The hounds of Mark, and felt the goodly hounds
Yelp at his heart,[5] but, turning, past and gain'd
Tintagil,[6] half in sea and high on land,
A crown of towers.

8. Contrast "The Coming of Arthur," lines 119ff.
9. The northern lights.
1. "Two stars in the Great Bear" (Tennyson).
2. Alludes to the Moabites, who saw water as red as blood. See II Kings 3:22.
3. His wife, Isolt.
4. Baying in unison, like chiming bells. "Roky": misty, foggy.
5. Either a premonition of approaching doom or, since Tristram was a famous hunter, a momentary diver-
   sion.
6. The ruins of the castle by the Cornish Sea are still visible. See *Memoir* II, 340–41, for Tennyson's last
   visit there.

                           Down in a casement sat,   505
A low sea-sunset glorying round her hair
And glossy-throated grace, Isolt the queen.
And when she heard the feet of Tristram grind
The spiring stone[7] that scaled about her tower,
Flush'd, started, met him at the doors, and there   510
Belted his body with her white embrace,
Crying aloud: "Not Mark—not Mark, my soul!
The footstep flutter'd me at first—not he!
Catlike thro' his own castle steals my Mark,
But warrior-wise thou stridest thro' his halls   515
Who hates thee, as I him—even to the death.
My soul, I felt my hatred for my Mark
Quicken within me, and knew that thou wert nigh."
To whom Sir Tristram smiling, "I am here;
Let be thy Mark, seeing he is not thine."   520

    And drawing somewhat backward she replied:
"Can he be wrong'd who is not even his own,
But save for dread of thee had beaten me,
Scratch'd, bitten, blinded, marr'd me somehow—Mark?
What rights are his that dare not strike for them?   525
Not lift a hand—not, tho' he found me thus!
But harken! have ye met him? hence he went
To-day for three days' hunting—as he said—
And so returns belike within an hour.
Mark's way, my soul!—but eat not thou with Mark,   530
Because he hates thee even more than fears,
Nor drink; and when thou passest any wood
Close vizor, lest an arrow from the bush
Should leave me all alone with Mark and hell.
My God, the measure of my hate for Mark   535
Is as the measure of my love for thee!"

    So, pluck'd one way by hate and one by love,
Drain'd of her force, again she sat, and spake
To Tristram, as he knelt before her, saying:
"O hunter, and O blower of the horn,   540
Harper, and thou hast been a rover too,
For, ere I mated with my shambling king,
Ye twain had fallen out about the bride
Of one—his name is out of me—the prize,
If prize she were—what marvel?—she could see—   545
Thine, friend; and ever since my craven seeks
To wreck thee villainously—but, O Sir Knight,
What dame or damsel have ye kneel'd to last?"

    And Tristram, "Last to my Queen Paramount,
Here now to my queen paramount of love   550
And loveliness—ay, lovelier than when first

---

7. "Winding stone staircase" (Tennyson).

Her light fell on our rough Lyonnesse,
Sailing from Ireland."⁸

              Softly laugh'd Isolt:
"Flatter me not, for hath not our great Queen
My dole of beauty trebled?" and he said: 555
"Her beauty is her beauty, and thine thine,
And thine is more to me — soft, gracious, kind —
Save when thy Mark is kindled on thy lips
Most gracious; but she, haughty, even to him,
Lancelot, for I have seen him wan enow   560
To make one doubt if ever the great Queen
Have yielded him her love."

              To whom Isolt:
"Ah, then, false hunter and false harper, thou
Who brakest thro' the scruple of my bond,
Calling me thy white hind, and saying to me   565
That Guinevere had sinn'd against the highest,
And I — misyoked with such a want of man —
That I could hardly sin against the lowest."

     He answer'd: "O my soul, be comforted!
If this be sweet, to sin in leading-strings,   570
If here be comfort, and if ours be sin,
Crown'd warrant had we for the crowning sin
That made us happy; but how ye greet me — fear
And fault and doubt — no word of that fond tale —
Thy deep heart-yearnings, thy sweet memories   575
Of Tristram in that year he was away."

     And, saddening on the sudden, spake Isolt:
"I had forgotten all in my strong joy
To see thee — yearnings? — ay! for, hour by hour,
Here in the never-ended afternoon,   580
O, sweeter than all memories of thee,
Deeper than any yearning after thee
Seem'd those far-rolling, westward-smiling seas,
Watch'd from this tower. Isolt of Britain dash'd
Before Isolt of Brittany on the strand,   585
Would that have chill'd her bride-kiss? Wedded her?
Fought in her father's battles? wounded there?
The King was all fulfill'd with gratefulness,
And she, my namesake of the hands, that heal'd
Thy hurt and heart with unguent and caress —   590
Well — can I wish her any huger wrong
Than having known thee? her too hast thou left
To pine and waste in those sweet memories.

8. "Tristram had told his uncle Mark of the beauty of Isolt, when he saw her in Ireland, so Mark demanded
her hand in marriage, which he obtained. Then Mark sent Tristram to fetch her as in my *Idylls* Arthur
sent Lancelot for Guinevere" (Tennyson).

O, were I not my Mark's, by whom all men
Are noble, I should hate thee more than love."   595

    And Tristram, fondling her light hands, replied:
"Grace, queen, for being loved; she loved me well.
Did I love her? the name at least I loved.
Isolt?—I fought his battles, for Isolt!
The night was dark; the true star set. Isolt!   600
The name was ruler of the dark—Isolt?
Care not for her! patient, and prayerful, meek,
Pale-blooded, she will yield herself to God."

    And Isolt answer'd: "Yea, and why not I?
Mine is the larger need, who am not meek;   605
Pale-blooded, prayerful. Let me tell thee now.
Here one black, mute midsummer night I sat,
Lonely, but musing on thee, wondering where,
Murmuring a light song I had heard thee sing,
And once or twice I spake thy name aloud   610
Then flash'd a levin-brand;[9] and near me stood,
In fuming sulphur blue and green, a fiend—
Mark's way to steal behind one in the dark—
For here was Mark: 'He has wedded her,' he said,
Not said, but hiss'd it; then this crown of towers   615
So shook to such a roar of all the sky,
That there in utter dark I swoon'd away,
And woke again in utter dark, and cried,
'I will flee hence and give myself to God'—
And thou wert lying in thy new leman's[1] arms."   620

    Then Tristram, ever dallying with her hand,
"May God be with thee, sweet, when old and gray,
And past desire!" a saying that anger'd her.
"'May God be with thee, sweet, when thou art old,
And sweet no more to me!' I need Him now.   625
For when had Lancelot utter'd aught so gross
Even to the swineherd's malkin in the mast?[2]
The greater man the greater courtesy.
Far other was the Tristram, Arthur's knight!
But thou, thro' ever harrying thy wild beasts—   630
Save that to touch a harp, tilt with a lance
Becomes thee well—art grown wild beast thyself.
How darest thou, if lover, push me even
In fancy from thy side, and set me far
In the gray distance, half a life away.   635
Her to be loved no more? Unsay it, unswear!
Flatter me rather, seeing me so weak,
Broken with Mark and hate and solitude,
Thy marriage and mine own, that I should suck

9. Flash of lightning.
1. Lover's.
2. "Slut among the beech nuts" (Tennyson).

Lies like sweet wines. Lie to me; I believe.   640
Will ye not lie? not swear, as there ye kneel,
And solemnly as when ye sware to him,
The man of men, our King—My God, the power
Was once in vows when men believed the King!
They lied not then who sware, and thro' their vows   645
The King prevailing made his realm—I say,
Swear to me thou wilt love me even when old,
Gray-hair'd, and past desire, and in despair."

      Then Tristram, pacing moodily up and down:
"Vows! did you keep the vow you made to Mark   650
More than I mine? Lied, say ye? Nay, but learnt,
The vow that binds too strictly snaps itself—
My knighthood taught me this—ay, being snapt—
We run more counter to the soul thereof
Than had we never sworn. I swear no more.   655
I swore to the great King, and am forsworn.
For once—even to the height—I honor'd him.
'Man, is he man at all?' methought, when first
I rode from our rough Lyonnesse, and beheld
That victor of the Pagan throned in hall—   660
His hair, a sun that ray'd from off a brow
Like hill-snow high in heaven, the steel-blue eyes,
The golden beard that clothed his lips with light—
Moreover, that weird legend of his birth,
With Merlin's mystic babble about his end   665
Amazed me; then, his foot was on a stool
Shaped as a dragon; he seem'd to me no man,
But Michael trampling Satan; so I sware,
Being amazed. But this went by—The vows!
O, ay—the wholesome madness of an hour—   670
They served their use, their time; for every knight
Believed himself a greater than himself,[3]
And every follower eyed him as a God;
Till he, being lifted up beyond himself,
Did mightier deeds than elsewise he had done,   675
And so the realm was made.[4] But then their vows—
First mainly thro' that sullying of our Queen—
Began to gall the knighthood, asking whence
Had Arthur right to bind them to himself?
Dropt down from heaven? wash'd up from out the deep?   680
They fail'd to trace him thro' the flesh and blood
Of our old kings. Whence then? a doubtful lord
To bind them by inviolable vows,
Which flesh and blood perforce would violate;
For feel this arm of mine—the tide within   685

3. "When the man had an ideal before him" (Tennyson).
4. "My father felt strongly that only under the inspiration of ideals, and with his 'sword bathed in heaven,' can a man combat the cynical indifference, the intellectual selfishness, the sloth of will, the utilitarian materialism of a transition age" (*Memoir* II, 129). Tristram manifests all these negative qualities.

Red with free chase and heather-scented air,
Pulsing full man. Can Arthur make me pure
As any maiden child? lock up my tongue
From uttering freely what I freely hear?
Bind me to one? The wide world laughs at it.   690
And worldling of the world am I, and know
The ptarmigan[5] that whitens ere his hour
Woos his own end; we are not angels here
Nor shall be. Vows—I am woodman of the woods,
And hear the garnet-headed yaffingale[6]   695
Mock them—my soul, we love but while we may;
And therefore is my love so large for thee,
Seeing it is not bounded save by love."

    Here ending, he moved toward her, and she said:
"Good, an I turn'd away my love for thee   700
To some one thrice as courteous as thyself—
For courtesy wins woman all as well
As valor may, but he that closes both
Is perfect, he is Lancelot—taller indeed,
Rosier and comelier, thou—but say I loved   705
This knightliest of all knights, and cast thee back
Thine own small saw, 'We love but while we may,'
Well then, what answer?"

                           He that while she spake,
Mindful of what he brought to adorn her with,
The jewels, had let one finger lightly touch   710
The warm white apple of her throat, replied,
"Press this a little closer, sweet, until—
Come, I am hunger'd and half-anger'd—meat,
Wine, wine—and I will love thee to the death,
And out beyond into the dream to come."   715

    So then, when both were brought to full accord,
She rose, and set before all he will'd;
And after these had comforted the blood
With meats and wines, and satiated their hearts—
Now talking of their woodland paradise,   720
The deer, the dews, the fern, the founts, the lawns;
Now mocking at the much ungainliness,
And craven shifts, and long crane legs of Mark—
Then Tristram laughing caught the harp and sang:

        "Ay, ay, O, ay—the winds that bend the brier!   725
        A star in heaven, a star within the mere![7]
        Ay, ay, O, ay—a star was my desire,
        And one was far apart and one was near.

5. A bird of the grouse family whose feathers change from brown to white for camouflage in winter. "Seen
   by me in the Museum at Christiania in Norway" (Tennyson).
6. "Old word, and still provincial for the green wood-pecker (so called from its laughter). In Sussex 'yaffel'"
   (Tennyson).
7. "Like an old Gaelic song—the two stars symbolic of the two Isolts" (Tennyson).

Ay, ay, O, ay—the winds that bow the grass!
And one was water and one star was fire,   730
And one will ever shine and one will pass.
Ay, ay, O, ay—the winds that move the mere!"

Then in the light's last glimmer Tristram show'd
And swung the ruby carcanet. She cried,
"The collar of some Order, which our King   735
Hath newly founded, all for thee, my soul,
For thee, to yield thee grace beyond thy peers."

"Not so, my queen," he said, "but the red fruit
Grown on a magic oak-tree in mid-heaven,
And won by Tristram as a tourney-prize,   740
And hither brought by Tristram for his last
Love-offering and peace-offering unto thee."

He spoke, he turn'd, then, flinging round her neck,
Claspt it, and cried, "Thine Order, O my queen!"
But, while he bow'd to kiss the jewell'd throat,   745
Out of the dark, just as the lips had touch'd,
Behind him rose a shadow and a shriek—
"Mark's way," said Mark, and clove him thro' the brain.

That night came Arthur home, and while he climb'd,
All in a death-dumb autumn-dripping gloom,   750
The stairway to the hall, and look'd and saw
The great Queen's bower was dark,—about his feet
A voice clung sobbing till he question'd it,
"What art thou?" and the voice about his feet
Sent up an answer, sobbing, "I am thy fool,   755
And I shall never make thee smile again."

1871

Guinevere[1]

Queen Guinevere had fled the court, and sat
There in the holy house at Almesbury[2]
Weeping, none with her save a little maid,
A novice. One low light betwixt them burn'd
Blurr'd by the creeping mist, for all abroad,   5

1. As Hallam Tennyson notes, his father said he had written "Guinevere" in "about a fortnight." The idyll as a whole draws very little on Malory or any other source except the poet's imagination. Guinevere has learned that King Arthur, along with the rest of his knights, has been slain, and she has stolen away taking five ladies with her. Acknowledging that the story is "largely original," the poet's son cites the following passage from Malory as its foundation:
    And so shee went to Almesbury, and there shee let make herself a nunne and ware white cloathes and blacke. And great pennance shee tooke as ever did sinfull lady in this land: and never creature could make her merry, but lived in fastings, prayers, and almes deedes, that all manner of people mervailed how vertuously shee eas changed. Now leave wee Queene Guenever in Almesbury, that was a nunne in white cloathes and blacke; and there she was abbesse and ruler, as reason would.
2. "Near Stonehenge, now Amesbury" (Tennyson).

Beneath a moon unseen albeit at full,
The white mist, like a face-cloth to the face,
Clung to the dead earth, and the land was still.

    For hither had she fled, her cause of flight
Sir Modred;[3] he that like a subtle beast   10
Lay couchant with his eyes upon the throne,
Ready to spring, waiting a chance. For this
He chill'd the popular praises of the King
With silent smiles of slow disparagement;
And tamper'd with the Lords of the White Horse,   15
Heathen, the brood by Hengist[4] left; and sought
To make disruption in the Table Round
Of Arthur, and to splinter it into feuds
Serving his traitorous end; and all his aims
Were sharpen'd by strong hate for Lancelot.   20

    For thus it chanced one morn when all the court,
Green-suited, but with plumes that mock'd the may,[5]
Had been—their wont—a-maying and return'd,
That Modred still in green, all ear and eye,
Climb'd to the high top of the garden-wall   25
To spy some secret scandal if he might,
And saw the Queen who sat betwixt her best
Enid and lissome Vivien, of her court
The wiliest and the worst; and more than this
He saw not, for Sir Lancelot passing by   30
Spied where he couch'd, and as the gardener's hand
Picks from the colewort[6] a green caterpillar,
So from the high wall and the flowering grove
Of grasses Lancelot pluck'd him by the heel,
And cast him as a worm upon the way;   35
But when he knew the prince tho' marr'd with dust,
He, reverencing king's blood in a bad man,
Made such excuses as he might, and these
Full knightly without scorn. For in those days
No knight of Arthur's noblest dealt in scorn;   40
But, if a man were halt,[7] or hunch'd, in him
By those who God had made full-limb'd and tall,
Scorn was allow'd as part of his defect,
And he was answer'd softly by the King
And all his Table. So Sir Lancelot holp   45
To raise the prince, who rising twice or thrice

---

3. In Malory, Sir Mordred usurps the throne and attempts to marry Guinevere while the king is off fighting in France. Upon Arthur's return, they mortally wound each other. Although Modred makes several brief appearances in the *Idylls*, Tennyson never attempts to develop his character fully. He is a minor villain whose chief function is to expose Guinevere's liaison with Lancelot.
4. Hengist and his brother Horsa, according to Geoffrey of Monmouth's *History of the Kings of Britain*, were Jute invaders of England (c. 449). Hengist was said to have ruled the kingdom of Kent until 488. The Saxons' emblem was the White Horse.
5. I.e., as white as hawthorn blossoms.
6. Cabbage.
7. Crippled.

Full sharply smote his knees, and smiled, and went;
But, ever after, the small violence done
Rankled in him and ruffled all his heart,
As the sharp wind that ruffles all day long   50
A little bitter pool about a stone
On the bare coast.

             But when Sir Lancelot told
This matter to the Queen, at first she laugh'd
Lightly, to think of Modred's dusty fall,
Then shudder'd, as the village wife who cries,   55
"I shudder, some one steps across my grave;"
Then laugh'd again, but faintlier, for indeed
She half-foresaw that he, the subtle beast,
Would track her guilt until he found, and hers
Would be for evermore a name of scorn.   60
Henceforward rarely could she front in hall,
Or elsewhere, Modred's narrow foxy face,
Heart-hiding smile, and gray persistent eye.
Henceforward too, the Powers that tend the soul,
To help it from the death that cannot die,   65
And save it even in extremes, began
To vex and plague her. Many a time for hours,
Beside the placid breathings of the King,
In the dead night, grim faces came and went
Before her, or a vague spiritual fear—   70
Like to some doubtful noise of creaking doors,
Heard by the watcher in a haunted house,
That keeps the rust of murder on the walls—
Held her awake; or if she slept she dream'd
An awful dream, for then she seem'd to stand   75
On some vast plain before a setting sun,
And from the sun there swiftly made at her
A ghastly something, and its shadow flew
Before it till it touch'd her, and she turn'd—
When lo! her own, that broadening from her feet,   80
And blackening, swallow'd all the land, and in it
Far cities burnt, and with a cry she woke.
And all this trouble did not pass but grew,
Till even the clear face of the guileless King,
And trustful courtesies of household life,   85
Became her bane; and at the last she said:
"O Lancelot, get thee hence to thine own land,
For if thou tarry we shall meet again,
And if we meet again some evil chance
Will make the smouldering scandal break and blaze 90
Before the people and our lord the King."
And Lancelot ever promised, but remain'd,
And still they met and met. Again she said,
"O Lancelot, if thou love me get thee hence."
And then they were agreed upon a night—   95
When the good King should not be there—to meet

And part for ever. Vivien, lurking, heard.
She told Sir Modred. Passion-pale they met
And greeted. Hands in hands, and eye to eye,
Low on the border of her couch they sat   100
Stammering and staring. It was their last hour,
A madness of farewells. And Modred brought
His creatures to the basement of the tower
For testimony; and crying with full voice,
"Traitor, come out, ye are trapt at last," aroused   105
Lancelot, who rushing outward lionlike
Leapt on him, and hurl'd him headlong, and he fell
Stunn'd, and his creatures took and bare him off,
And all was still. Then she, "The end is come,
And I am shamed for ever;" and he said: 110
"Mine be the shame, mine was the sin; but rise,
And fly to my strong castle over-seas.
There will I hide thee till my life shall end,
There hold thee with my life against the world."
She answer'd: "Lancelot, wilt thou hold me so?   115
Nay, friend, for we have taken our farewells.
Would God that thou couldst hide me from myself!
Mine is the shame, for I was wife, and thou
Unwedded; yet rise now, and let us fly,
For I will draw me into sanctuary,   120
And bide my doom." So Lancelot got her horse,
Set her thereon, and mounted on his own,
And then they rode to the divided way,
There kiss'd and parted weeping; for he past,
Love-loyal to the least wish of the Queen,   125
Back to his land; but she to Almesbury
Fled all night long by glimmering waste and weald,
And heard the spirits of the waste and weald
Moan as she fled, or thought she heard them moan.
And in herself she moan'd, "Too late, too late!"   130
Till in the cold wind that foreruns the morn,
A blot in heaven, the raven, flying high,
Croak'd, and she thought, "He spies a field of death;
For now the heathen of the Northern Sea,
Lured by the crimes and frailties of the court,   135
Begin to slay the folk and spoil the land."
     And when she came to Almesbury she spake
There to the nuns, and said, "Mine enemies
Pursue me, but, O peaceful Sisterhood,
Receive and yield me sanctuary, nor ask   140
Her name to whom ye yield it till her time
To tell you;" and her beauty, grace, and power
Wrought as a charm upon them, and they spared
To ask it.

        So the stately Queen abode
For many a week, unknown, among the nuns,   145
Nor with them mix'd, nor told her name, nor sought,

Wrapt in her grief, for housel[8] or for shrift
But communed only with the little maid,
Who pleased her with a babbling heedlessness
Which often lured her from herself; but now,   150
This night, a rumor wildly blown about
Came that Sir Modred had usurp'd the realm
And leagued him with the heathen, while the King
Was waging war on Lancelot. Then she thought,
"With what a hate the people and the king   155
Must hate me," and bow'd down upon her hand
Silent, until the little maid, who brook'd
No silence, brake it, uttering "Late! so late!
What hour, I wonder now?" and when she drew
No answer, by and by began to hum   160
An air the nuns had taught her: "Late, so late!"
Which when she heard, the Queen look'd up, and said,
"O maiden, if indeed ye list to sing,
Sing, and unbind my heart that I may weep."
Whereat full willingly sang the little maid.   165

        "Late, late, so late! and dark the night and chill!
        Late, late, so late! but we can enter still.
        Too late, too late! ye cannot enter now.

        "No light had we; for that we do repent,
        And learning this, the bridegroom will relent.   170
        Too late, too late! ye cannot enter now.

        "No light! so late! and dark and chill the night!
        O, let us in, that we may find the light!
        Too late, too late! ye cannot enter now.

        "Have we not heard the bridegroom is so sweet?   175
        O, let us in, tho' late, to kiss his feet!
        No, no, too late! ye cannot enter now."[9]

    So sang the novice,[1] while full passionately,
Her head upon her hands, remembering
Her thought when first she came, wept the sad Queen.   180
Then said the little novice prattling to her:

    "O pray you, noble lady, weep no more:
But let my words—the words of one so small,
Who knowing nothing knows but to obey,
And if I do not there is penance given—   185
Comfort your sorrows, for they do not flow
From evil done; right sure am I of that,
Who see your tender grace and stateliness.
But weigh your sorrows with our lord the King's,

8. Confession. "Housel": "Anglo-Saxon *husel*, the Eucharist" (Tennyson).
9. See the parable of the wise and foolish virgins (Matthew 25).
1. There is something to be said for Littledale's observation that "the child's talk that follows is a recapitulation
   of the story of the Coming of Arthur, as it may be supposed to have settled itself in the popular imagination."

And weighing find them less; for gone is he   190
To wage grim war against Sir Lancelot there,
Round that strong castle where he holds the Queen;
And Modred whom he left in charge of all,
The traitor—Ah, sweet lady, the King's grief
For his own self, and his own Queen, and realm,   195
Must needs be thrice as great as any of ours!
For me, I thank the saints, I am not great;
For if there ever come a grief to me
I cry my cry in silence, and have done;
None knows it, and my tears have brought me good.   200
But even were the griefs of little ones
As great as those of great ones, yet this grief
Is added to the griefs the great must bear,
That, howsoever much they desire
Silence, they cannot weep behind a cloud;   205
As even here they talk at Almesbury
About the good King and his wicked Queen,
And were I such a King with such a Queen,
Well might I wish to veil her wickedness,
But were I such a King it could not be."   210

    Then to her own sad heart mutter'd the Queen,
"Will the child kill me with her innocent talk?"
But openly she answer'd, "Must not I
If this false traitor have displaced his lord,
Grieve with the common grief of all the realm?"   215

    "Yea," said the maid, "this all is woman's grief,
That *she* is woman, whose disloyal life
Hath wrought confusion in the Table Round
Which good King Arthur founded, years ago,
With signs and miracles and wonders, there   220
At Camelot, ere the coming of the Queen."

    Then thought the Queen within herself again,
"Will the child kill me with her foolish prate?"
But openly she spake and said to her,
"O little maid, shut in by nunnery walls,   225
What canst thou know of Kings and Tables Round,
Or what of signs and wonders, but the signs
And simple miracles of thy nunnery?"

    To whom the little novice garrulously:
"Yea, but I know; the land was full of signs   230
And wonders ere the coming of the Queen.
So said my father, and himself was knight
Of the great Table—at the founding of it,
And rode thereto from Lyonnesse; and he said
That as he rode, an hour or maybe twain   235
After the sunset, down the coast, he heard
Strange music, and he paused, and turning—there,

All down the lonely coast of Lyonnesse,
Each with a beacon-star upon his head,
And with a wild sea-light about his feet,   240
He saw them—headland after headland flame
Far on into the rich heart of the west.
And in the light the white mermaiden swam,
And strong man-breasted things stood from the the sea,
And sent a deep sea-voice thro' all the land,   245
To which the little elves of chasm and cleft
Made answer, sounding like a distant horn.
So said my father—yea, and furthermore,
Next morning, while he past the dim-lit woods
Himself beheld three spirits mad with joy   250
Come dashing down on a tall wayside flower,
That shook beneath them as the thistle shakes
When three gray linnets wrangle for the seed.
And still at evenings on before his horse
The flickering fairy-circle wheel'd and broke   255
Flying, and link'd again, and wheel'd and broke
Flying, for all the land was full of life.
And when at last he came to Camelot,
A wreath of airy dancers hand-in-hand
Swung round the lighted lantern of the hall;   260
And in the hall itself was such a feast
As never man had a dream'd; for every knight
Had whatsoever meat he long'd for served
By hands unseen; and even as he said
Down in the cellars merry bloated things   265
Shoulder'd the spigot,[2] straddling on the butts
While the wine ran; so glad were spirits and men
Before the coming of the sinful Queen."

   Then spake the Queen and somewhat bitterly,
"Were they so glad? ill prophets were they all,   270
Spirits and men. Could none of them foresee,
Not even thy wise father with his signs
And wonders, what has fallen upon the realm?"

   To whom the novice garrulously again:
"Yea, one, a bard, of whom my father said,   275
Full many a noble war-song had he sung,
Even in the presence of an enemy's fleet,
Between the steep cliff and the coming wave;
And many a mystic lay of life and death
Had chanted on the smoky mountain-tops,   280
When round him bent the spirits of the hills
With all their dewy hair blown back like flame.
So said my father—and that night the bard
Sang Arthur's glorious wars, and sang the King
As wellnigh more than man, and rail'd at those   285

2. "The bung" (Tennyson); the stopper for the mouth of the cask or butt.

Who call'd him the false son of Gorloïs.[3]
For there was no man knew from whence he came;
But after tempest, when the long wave broke
All down the thundering shores of Bude and Bos,[4]
There came a day as still as heaven, and then   290
They found a naked child upon the sands
Of dark Tintagil by the Cornish sea,
And that was Arthur, and they foster'd him
Till he by miracle was approven King;
And that his grave should be a mystery   295
From all men, like his birth; and could he find
A woman in her womanhood as great
As he was in his manhood, then, he sang,
The twain together well might change the world.
But even in the middle of his song   300
He falter'd, and his hand fell from the harp,
And pale he turn'd, and reel'd, and would have fallen,
But that they stay'd him up; nor would he tell
His vision; but what doubt that he foresaw
This evil work of Lancelot and the Queen?"   305

    Then thought the Queen, "Lo! they have set her on,
Our simple-seeming abbess and her nuns,
To play upon me," and bow'd her head nor spake.
Whereat the novice crying, with clasp'd hands,
Shame on her own garrulity garrulously,   310
Said the good nuns would check her gadding[5] tongue
Full often, "and, sweet lady, if I seem
To vex an ear too sad to listen to me,
Unmannerly, with prattling and the tales
Which my good father told me, check me too   315
Nor let me shame my father's memory, one
Of noblest manners, tho' himself would say
Sir Lancelot had the noblest; and he died,
Kill'd in a tilt, come next, five summers back,
And left me; but of others who remain,   320
And of the two first-famed for courtesy—
And pray you check me if I ask amiss—
But pray you, which had noblest, while you moved
Among them, Lancelot or our lord the King?"

    Then the pale Queen look'd up and answer'd her: 325
"Sir Lancelot, as became a noble knight,
Was gracious to all ladies, and the same
In open battle or the tilting-field
Forbore his own advantage, and the King
In open battle or the tilting-field   330
Forbore his own advantage, and these two
Were the most nobly-manner'd men of all;

3. See "The Coming of Arthur," lines 67–73, for the beginning of the extensive discussion about Arthur's origins.
4. Areas of Cornwall, north of Tintagil, as Tennyson noted.
5. Rambling.

For manners are not idle, but the fruit
Of loyal nature and of noble mind."

"Yea," said the maid, "be manners such fair fruit?						335
Then Lancelot's needs must be a thousand fold
Less noble, being as all rumor runs,
The most disloyal friend in all the world."

To which a mournful answer made the Queen:
"O, closed about by narrowing nunnery-walls,						340
What knowest thou of the world and all its lights
And shadows, all the wealth and all the woe?
If ever Lancelot, that most noble knight,
Were for one hour less noble than himself,
Pray for him that he scape the doom of fire,						345
And weep for her who drew him to his doom."

"Yea," said the little novice, "I pray for both;
But I should all as soon believe that his,
Sir Lancelot's, were as noble as the King's,
As I could think, sweet lady, yours would be						350
Such as they are, were you the sinful Queen."

So she, like many another babbler, hurt
Whom she would soothe, and harm'd where she would heal;
For here a sudden flush of wrathful heat
Fired all the pale face of the Queen, who cried:						355
"Such as thou art be never maiden more
For ever! thou their tool, set on to plague
And play upon and harry me, petty spy
And traitress!" When that storm of anger brake
From Guinevere, aghast the maiden rose,						360
White as her veil, and stood before the Queen
As tremulously as foam upon the beach
Stands in a wind, ready to break and fly,
And when the Queen had added, "Get thee hence!"
Fled frighted. Then that other left alone						365
Sigh'd, and began to gather heart again,
Saying in herself: "The simple, fearful child
Meant nothing, but my own too-fearful guilt,
Simpler than any child, betrays itself.
But help me, Heaven, for surely I repent!						370
For what is true repentance but in thought—
Not even in inmost thought to think again
The sins that made the past so pleasant to us?
And I have sworn never to see him more,
To see him more."

And even in saying this,						375
Her memory from old habit of the mind
Went slipping back upon the golden days
In which she saw him first, when Lancelot came,

Reputed the best knight and goodliest man,
Ambassador, to yield her to his lord   380
Arthur, and led her forth, and far ahead
Of his and her retinue moving, they,
Rapt in sweet talk or lively, all on love
And sport and tilts and pleasure,—for the time
Was may-time, and as yet no sin was dream'd,—   385
Rode under groves that look'd a paradise
Of blossom, over sheets of hyacinth
That seem'd the heavens[6] upbreaking thro' the earth,
And on from hill to hill, and every day
Beheld at noon in some delicious dale   390
The silk pavilions of King Arthur raised
For brief repast or afternoon repose
By couriers gone before; and on again,
Till yet once more ere set of sun they saw
The Dragon of the great Pendragonship,[7]   395
That crown'd the state pavilion of the King,
Blaze by the rushing brook or silent well.

But when the Queen immersed in such a trance,
And moving thro' the past unconsciously,
Came to the point where first she saw the King   400
Ride toward her from the city, sigh'd to find
Her journey done, glanced at him, thought him cold,
High, self-contain'd, and passionless, not like him,
"Not like my Lancelot"—while she brooded thus
And grew half-guilty in her thoughts again,   405
There rode an armed warrior to the doors.
A murmuring whisper thro' the nunnery ran,
Then on a sudden a cry, "The King!" She sat
Stiff-stricken, listening; but when armed feet
Thro' the long gallery from the outer doors   410
Rang coming, prone from off her seat she fell,
And grovell'd with her face against the floor.
There with her milk-white arms and shadowy hair
She made her face a darkness from the King,
And in the darkness heard his armed feet   415
Pause by her; then came silence, then a voice,
Monotonous and hollow like a ghost's
Denouncing judgment, but, tho' changed, the King's:

"Liest here so low, the child of one
I honor'd, happy, dead before thy shame?   420
Well is it that no child is born of thee.
The children born of thee are sword and fire,
Red ruin, and the breaking up of laws,

---

6. "This simile was made from the hyacinths in the Wilderness at Farringford" (Hallam Tennyson).
7. "The headship of the tribes who had confederated against the Lords of the White Horse. 'Pendragon':
   not a dactyl, as some make it, but Pén–drágon" (Tennyson). See "Lancelot and Elaine," line 422, and n.
   4, p. 422.

The craft of kindred and the godless hosts
Of heathen swarming o'er the Northern Sea;   425
Whom I, while yet Sir Lancelot, my right arm,
The mightiest of my knights, abode with me,
Have everywhere about this land of Christ
In twelve great battles ruining overthrown.
And knowest thou now from whence I come—from him,   430
From waging bitter war with him; and he,
That did not shun to smite me in worse way,
Had yet that grace of courtesy in him left,
He spared to lift his hand against the King
Who made him knight. But many a knight was slain;   435
And many more and all his kith and kin
Clave to him, and abode in his own land.
And many more when Modred raised revolt,
Forgetful of their troth and fealty, clave
To Modred, and a remnant stays with me.   440
And of this remnant will I leave a part,
True men who love me still, for whom I live,
To guard thee in the wild hour coming on,
Lest but a hair of his low head be harm'd.
Fear not; thou shalt be guarded till my death.   445
Howbeit I know, if ancient prophecies
Have err'd not, that I march to meet my doom.
Thou hast not made my life so sweet to me,
That I the King should greatly care to live;
For thou has spoilt the purpose of my life.   450
Bear with me for the last time while I show,
Even for thy sake, the sin which thou hast sinn'd.
For when the Roman left us, and their law
Relax'd its hold upon us, and the ways
Were fill'd with rapine, here and there a deed   455
Of prowess done redress'd a random wrong.
But I was first of all the kings who drew
The knighthood-errant of this realm and all
The realms together under me, their Head,
In that fair Order of my Table Round,   460
A glorious company, the flower of men,
To serve as model for the mighty world,
And be the fair beginning of a time.
I made them lay their hands in mine and swear
To reverence the King, as if he were   465
Their conscience, and their conscience as their King,
To break the heathen and uphold the Christ,
To ride abroad redressing human wrongs,
To speak no slander, no, nor listen to it,
To honor his own word as if his God's,   470
To lead sweet lives in purest chastity,
To love one maiden only, cleave to her,
And worship her by years of noble deeds,
Until they won her; for indeed I knew
Of no more subtle master under heaven   475

Than is the maiden passion for a maid,
Not only to keep down the base in man,
But teach high thought, and amiable words
And courtliness, and the desire of fame,
And love of truth, and all that makes a man.   480
And all this throve before I wedded thee,
Believing, 'Lo, mine helpmate, one to feel
My purpose and rejoicing in my joy!'
Then came thy shameful sin with Lancelot;
Then came the sin of Tristram and Isolt;   485
Then others, following these my mightiest knights,
And drawing foul ensample from fair names,
Sinn'd also, till the loathsome opposite
Of all my heart had destined did obtain,
And all thro' thee! so that this life of mine   490
I guard as God's high gift from scathe and wrong,
Not greatly care to lose; but rather think
How sad it were for Arthur, should he live,
To sit once more within his lonely hall,
And miss the wonted number of my knights,   495
And miss to hear high talk of noble deeds
As in the golden days before thy sin.
For which of us who might be left could speak
Of the pure heart, nor seem to glance at thee?
And in thy bowers of Camelot or of Usk   500
Thy shadow still would glide from room to room,
And I should evermore be vext with thee
In hanging robe or vacant ornament,
Or ghostly footfall echoing on the stair.
For think not, tho' thou wouldst not love thy lord,   505
Thy lord has wholly lost his love for thee.
I am not made of so slight elements.
Yet must I leave thee, woman, to thy shame.
I hold that man the worst of public foes
Who either for his own or children's sake,   510
To save his blood from scandal, lets the wife
Whom he knows false abide and rule the house:
For being thro' his cowardice allow'd
Her station, taken everywhere for pure,
She like a new disease, unknown to men,   515
Creeps, no precaution used, among the crowd,
Makes wicked lightnings of her eyes, and saps
The fealty of our friends, and stirs the pulse
With devil's leaps, and poisons half the young.
Worst of the worst were that man he that reigns!   520
Better the King's waste hearth and aching heart
Than thou reseated in thy place of light,
The mockery of my people and their bane!"

    He paused, and in the pause she crept an inch
Nearer, and laid her hands about his feet.   525
Far off a solitary trumpet blew.

Then waiting by the doors the war-horse neigh'd
As at a friend's voice, and he spake again:

    "Yet think not that I come to urge thy crimes;
I did not come to curse thee, Guinevere,   530
I, whose vast pity almost makes me die
To see thee, laying there thy golden head,
My pride in happier summers, at my feet.
The wrath of which forced my thoughts on that fierce law,
The doom of treason and the flaming death,[8]   535
When first I learnt thee hidden here,—is past.
The pang—which, while I weigh'd thy heart with one
Too wholly true to dream untruth in thee,
Made my tears burn—is also past—in part.
And all is past, the sin is sinn'd, and I,   540
Lo, I forgive thee, as Eternal God
Forgives! do thou for thine own soul the rest.
But how to take last leave of all I loved?
O golden hair, with which I used to play
Not knowing! O imperial-moulded form,   545
And beauty such as never woman wore,
Until it came a kingdom's curse with thee—
I cannot touch thy lips, they are not mine,
But Lancelot's; nay, they never were the King's.
I cannot take thy hand; that too is flesh,   550
And in the flesh thou hast sinn'd; and mine own flesh,
Here looking down on thine polluted, cries,
'I loathe thee;' yet not less, O Guinevere,
For I was ever virgin save for thee,
My love thro' flesh hath wrought into my life   555
So far that my doom is, I love thee still.
Let no man dream but that I love thee still.
Perchance, and so thou purify thy soul,
And so thou lean on our fair father Christ,
Hereafter in that world where all are pure   560
We two may meet before high God, and thou
Wilt spring to me, and claim me thine, and know
I am thine husband—not a smaller soul,
Nor Lancelot, nor another. Leave me that,
I charge thee, my last hope. Now must I hence.   565
Thro' the thick night I hear the trumpet blow.
They summon me their King to lead mine hosts
Far down to that great battle in the west,
Where I must strike against the man they call
My sister's son—no kin of mine, who leagues   570
With Lords of the White Horse, heathen, and knights,
Traitors—and strike him dead, and meet myself
Death, or I know not what mysterious doom.
And thou remaining here wilt learn the event;

---

8. In Malory, Guinevere is condemned by Arthur to be burnt at the stake and is rescued by Lancelot at the last minute.

But hither shall I never come again.   575
Never lie by thy side, see thee no more—
Farewell!"

    And while she grovell'd at his feet,[9]
She felt the King's breath wander o'er her neck,
And in the darkness o'er her fallen head
Perceived the waving of his hands that blest.   580

    Then, listening till those armed steps were gone,
Rose the pale Queen, and in her anguish found
The casement: "peradventure," so she thought,
"If I might see his face, and not be seen."
And lo, he sat on horseback at the door!   585
And near him the sad nuns with each a light
Stood, and he gave them charge about the Queen,
To guard and foster her for evermore.
And while she spake to these his helm was lower'd,
To which for crest the golden dragon clung   590
Of Britain; so she did not see the face,
Which then was as an angel's,[1] but she saw,
Wet with the mists and smitten by the lights,
The Dragon of the great Pendragonship
Blaze, making all the night a steam of fire.   595
And even then he turn'd; and more and more
The moony vapor rolling round the King,
Who seem'd the phantom of a giant in it,
Enwound him fold by fold, and made him gray
And grayer, till himself became as mist   600
Before her, moving ghostlike to his doom[2]

    Then she stretch'd out her arms and cried aloud,
"O Arthur!" there her voice brake suddenly,
Then—as a stream that spouting from a cliff
Fails in mid air, but gathering at the base   605
Re-makes itself, and flashes down the vale—
Went on in passionate utterance:
                  "Gone—my lord!
Gone thro' my sin to slay and to be slain!
And he forgave me, and I could not speak.
Farewell? I should have answer'd his farewell.   610
His mercy choked me. Gone, my lord the King,
My own true lord! how dare I call him mine?
The shadow of another cleaves to me,
And makes me one pollution. He, the King,

---

9. The queen's posture and Arthur's conduct toward her have often been used in arguments to show the
   king's priggishness. Although perhaps he does uncomfortably resemble our stereotyped notion of the Victorian patriarch indignant over his wife's infidelity, there is no convincing alternative offered to explain
   how Tennyson should have conducted the scene.
1. Of Stephen: "And all that sat in the council, looking stedfastly on him, saw his face as it had been the
   face of an angel" (Acts 6:15).
2. In part accounting for the pause in writing the *Idylls*, Tennyson said of these lines: "I could hardly light
   upon a finer close than that ghost-like passing away of the King" (*Memoir* II, 126).

Call'd me polluted. Shall I kill myself? 615
What help in that? I cannot kill my sin,
If soul be soul, nor can I kill my shame;
No, nor by living can I live it down.
The days will grow to weeks, the weeks to months,
The months will add themselves and make the years, 620
The years will roll into the centuries,
And mine will ever be a name of scorn.
I must not dwell on that defeat of fame.
Let the world be; that is but of the world—
What else? what hope? I think there was a hope, 625
Except he mock'd me when he spake of hope;
His hope he call'd it; but he never mocks,
For mockery is the fume of little hearts.
And blessed be the King, who hath forgiven
My wickedness to him, and left me hope 630
That in mine own heart I can live down sin
And be his mate hereafter in the heavens
Before high God! Ah great and gentle lord,
Who wast, as is the conscience of a saint
Among his warring senses, to thy knights— 635
To whom my false voluptuous pride, that took
Full easily all impressions from below,
Would not look up, or half-despised the height
To which I would not or I could not climb—
I thought I could not breathe in that fine air, 640
That pure severity of perfect light—
I yearn'd for warmth and color which I found
In Lancelot—now I see thee what thou art,
Thou art the highest and most human too,
Not Lancelot, nor another. Is there none 645
Will tell the King I love him tho' so late?
Now—ere he goes to the great battle? none!
Myself must tell him in that purer life,
But now it were too daring. Ah my God,
What might I not have made of thy fair world, 650
Had I but loved thy highest creature here?
It was my duty to have loved the highest;
It surely was my profit had I known;
It would have been my pleasure had I seen.
We needs must love the highest when we see it, 655
Not Lancelot, nor another."
                              Here her hand
Grasp'd made her vail[3] her eyes. She look'd and saw
The novice, weeping, suppliant, and said to her,
"Yea, little maid, for am I not forgiven?"
Then glancing up beheld the holy nuns 660
All round her, weeping; and her heart was loosed
Within her, and she wept with these and said:

3. Lower.

"Ye know me then, that wicked one, who broke
The vast design and purpose of the King.
O, shut me round with narrowing nunnery-walls,   665
Meek maidens, from the voices crying, 'Shame!'
I must not scorn myself; he loves me still.
Let no one dream but that he loves me still.
So let me, if you do not shudder at me,
Nor shun to call me sister, dwell with you;   670
Wear black and white, and be a nun like you,
Fast with your fasts, not feasting with your feasts;
Grieve with your griefs, not grieving at your joys,
But not rejoicing; mingle with your rites;
Pray and be pray'd for; lie before your shrines;   675
Do each low office of your holy house;
Walk your dim cloister, and distribute dole
To poor sick people, richer in His eyes
Who ransom'd us, and haler too than I;
And treat their loathsome hurts and heal mine own;   680
And so wear out in alms-deed and in prayer
The sombre close of that voluptuous day
Which wrought the ruin of my lord the King."

  She said. They took her to themselves; and she
Still hoping, fearing "Is it yet too later?"   685
Dwelt with them, till in time their abbess died.
Then she, for her good deeds and her pure life,
And for the power of ministration in her,
And likewise for the high rank she had borne,
Was chosen abbess, there, and abbess, lived   690
For three brief years, and there, an abbess, past
To where beyond these voices there is peace.

                                                    1859

The Passing of Arthur[1]

That story which the bold Sir Bedivere,
First made and latest left of all the knights,
Told, when the man was no more than a voice
In the white winter of his age, to those
With whom he dwelt, new faces, other minds.   5

  For on their march to westward, Bedivere,
Who slowly paced among the slumbering host,
Heard in his tent the moanings of the King:

1. The first-written of the *Idylls*, the earlier "Morte d'Arthur" (see "The Epic") was expanded by adding an introduction (lines 1–169) and a conclusion (lines 441–69) for publication in 1869. "The form of the 'Coming of Arthur' and of the 'Passing,'" Tennyson said, "is purposely more archaic than that of the other 'Idylls,'" adding elsewhere that they "are simpler and more severe in style, as dealing with the awfulness of Birth and Death" (*Memoir* II, 133, and I, 483 n.). Quoting his father on the early "Morte d'Arthur," Hallam Tennyson introduces this idyll: "The temporary triumph of evil, the confusion of moral order, closing in the Great Battle of the West."

"I found Him in the shining of the stars,
I mark'd Him in the flowering of His fields,   10
But in His ways with men I find Him not.
I waged His wars, and now I pass and die.
O me! for why is all around us here
As if some lesser god² had made the world,
But had not force to shape it as he would,   15
Till the High God behold it from beyond,
And enter it, and make it beautiful?
Or else as if the world were wholly fair,
But that these eyes of men are dense and dim,
And have not power to see it as it is—   20
Perchance, because we see not to the close;—
For I, being simple, thought to work His will,
And have but stricken with the sword in vain,
And all whereon I lean'd in wife and friend
Is traitor to my peace, and all my realm   25
Reels back into the beast, and is no more.³
My God, thou hast forgotten me in my death!⁴
Nay—God my Christ—I pass but shall nor die."
   Then, ere that last weird battle in the west,
There came on Arthur sleeping, Gawain kill'd   30
In Lancelot's war, the ghost of Gawain blown
Along a wandering wind, and past his ear
Went shrilling: "Hollow, hollow all delight!
Hail, King! to-morrow thou shalt pass away.
Farewell! there is an isle of rest for thee.   35
And I am blown along a wandering wind,⁵
And hollow, hollow, hollow all delight!"
And fainter onward, like wild birds that change
Their season in the night and wail their way
From cloud to cloud, down the long wind the dream   40
Shrill'd; but in going mingled with dim cries
Far in the moonlit haze among the hills,
As of some lonely city sack'd by night,
When all is lost, and wife and child with wail
Pass to new lords; and Arthur woke and call'd: 45
"Who spake? A dream. O, light upon the wind,
Thine, Gawain, was the voice—are these dim cries

2. "Cf. the demiurge of Plato, and the gnostic belief that lesser powers created the world" (Tennyson).
3. Before, and for some time after the publication of *The Origin of Species* (1859), Tennyson, as did many
   of his contemporaries, subscribed to the variously called "myth of evolution" or "sentimental evolution."
   In brief, they misconstrued Darwin's theory as giving scientific authority to the notion that the human
   race was on a linear path to the "one far-off divine event, / To which the whole creation moves" celebrated at the close of *IM*. As forms of life "progressed" from the simple to the increasingly complex, so
   there seemed to be a corrollary to the human species, of which Hallam "was a noble type / Appearing
   ere the times were ripe," prefiguring a future, more perfect "race." In this one line, "Reels back into the
   beast, and is no more," composed two years before the publication of *The Descent of Man* (1871), Tennyson strongly registers his doubts of any guaranteed future perfectability of our species. As T. H. Huxley would put the matter later in "Evolution and Ethics" (1893): "We also know modern speculative
   optimism, with its perfectability of the species, reign of peace, and lion and lamb transformation scenes;
   but one does not hear so much of it as one did forty years ago." See "Locksley Hall Sixty Years After," line
   148: "Have we risen from out the beast, then back into the beast again?"
4. Matthew 27:46 and Psalm 22:1: "My God, my God, why hast thou forsaken me?" (noted by Ricks).
5. Tennyson compares *Aeneid* VI, lines 740–41: "Some are hung stretched out to the empty winds."

Thine? or doth all that haunts the waste and wild
Mourn, knowing it will go along with me?"

This heard the bold Sir Bedivere and spake: 50
"O me, my King, let pass whatever will,
Elves, and the harmless glamour of the field;[6]
But in their stead thy name and glory cling
To all high places like a golden cloud
For ever; but as yet thou shall not pass.   55
Light was Gawain in life, and light in death
Is Gawain, for the ghost[7] is as the man;
And care not thou for dreams from him, but rise —
I hear the steps of Modred in the west,
And with him many of thy people, and knights   60
Once thine, whom thou hast loved, but grosser grown
Than heathen, spitting at their vows and thee.
Right well in heart they know thee for the King.
Arise, go forth and conquer as of old."

Then spake King Arthur to Sir Bedivere: 65
"Far other is this battle in the west
Whereto we move than when we strove in youth,
And brake the petty kings, and fought with Rome,
Or thrust the heathen from the Roman wall,
And shook him thro' the north. Ill doom is mine   70
To war against my people and my knights.
The king who fights his people fights himself.
And they my knights, who loved me once, the stroke
That strikes them dead is as my death to me.
Yet let us hence, and find or feel a way   75
Thro' this blind haze which, ever since I saw
One[8] lying in the dust at Almesbury,
Hath folded in the passes of the world."

Then rose the King and moved his host by night,
And ever push'd Sir Modred, league by league,   80
Back to the sunset bound of Lyonnesse[9] —
A land of old upheaven from the abyss
By fire, to sink into the abyss again;
Where fragments of forgotten peoples[1] dwelt,
And the long mountains ended in a coast   85
Of ever-shifting sand, and far away
The phantom circle of a moaning sea.
There the pursuer could pursue no more,
And he that fled no further fly the King;
And there, that day when the great light of heaven   90
Burn'd at his lowest in the rolling year,[2]

6. "The legends which cluster round the King's name" (Tennyson).
7. "The spirit" (Tennyson).
8. Guinevere.
9. In fable, the land that sank into the sea. See "Lancelot and Elaine," line 35 and n. 5 p. 414.
1. "Perhaps old Celts" (Tennyson).
2. "The winter solstice" (Tennyson).

On the waste sand by the waste sea they closed.
Nor ever yet had Arthur fought a fight
Like this last, dim, weird battle of the west.[3]
A death-white mist slept over sand and sea,   95
Whereof the chill, to him who breathed it, drew
Down with his blood, till all his heart was cold
With formless fear; and even on Arthur fell
Confusion, since he saw not whom he fought.
For friend and foe were shadows in the mist,   100
And friend slew friend not knowing whom he slew;
And some had visions out of golden youth,
And some beheld the faces of old ghosts
Look in upon the battle; and in the mist
Was many a noble deed, many a base,   105
And chance and craft and strength in single fights,
And ever and anon with host to host
Shocks, and the splintering spear, the hard mail hewn,
Shield-breakings, and the clash of brands, the crash
Of battle-axes on shatter'd helms, and shrieks   110
After the Christ, of those who falling down
Look'd up for heaven, and only saw the mist;
And shouts of heathen and the traitor knights,
Oaths, insult, filth, and monstrous blasphemies,[4]
Sweat, writhings, anguish, laboring of the lungs   115
In that close mist, and cryings for the light,
Moans of the dying, and voices of the dead.

 Last, as by some one death-bed after wail
Of suffering, silence follows, or thro' death
Or death-like swoon, thus over all that shore,   120
Save for some whisper of the seething seas,
A dead hush fell; but when the dolorous day
Grew drearier toward twilight falling, came
A bitter wind, clear from the north, and blew
The mist aside, and with that wind the tide   125
Rose, and the pale King glanced across the field
Of battle. But no man moving there;
Nor any cry of Christian heard thereon,
Nor yet of heathen; only the wan wave
Brake in among dead faces, to and fro   130
Swaying the helpless hands, and up and down
Tumbling the hollow helmets of the fallen,
And shiver'd brands that once had fought with Rome,
And rolling far along the gloomy shores
The voice of days of old and days to be.[5]   135

---

3. "A Vision of Death" (Tennyson).
4. Tennyson compares Revelation 16:21: "And men blasphemed God," after the battle of Armageddon.
5. "This grim battle in the mist contrasts with Arthur's glorious battle in the *Coming of Arthur*, fought on a bright day when 'he saw the smallest rock far on the faintest hill'" (Tennyson). Compare the end of Arnold's "Dover Beach": "And we are here as on a darkling plain / Swept with confused alarms of struggle and flight, / Where ignorant armies clash by night" (ca. 1851).

Then spake King Arthur to Sir Bedivere,
And whiter than the mist that all day long
Had held the field of battle was the King:

"Hearest thou this great voice that shakes the world,
And wastes the narrow realm whereon we move,   140
And beats upon the faces of the dead,
My dead, as tho' they had not died for me? —
O Bedivere, for on my heart hath fallen
Confusion, till I know not what I am,
Nor whence I am, nor whether I be king;   145
Behold, I seem but king among the dead."

Then spoke the bold Sir Bedivere: "My King!
King everywhere! and so the dead have kings,
There also will I worship thee as king.
Yet still thy life is whole, and still I live   150
Who love thee; but who hates thee, he that brought
The heathen back among us, yonder stands,
Modred, unharm'd, the traitor of thine house."

Then spake the King: "My house hath been my doom.
But call not thou this traitor of my house   155
Who hath but dwelt beneath one roof with me.
My house are rather they who sware my vows,
Yea, even while they brake them, own'd me king.
And well for thee, saying in my dark hour,
When all the purport of my throne hath fail'd,   160
That quick or dead thou holdest me for king.
King am I, whatsoever be their cry;
And one last act of kinghood shalt thou see
Yet, ere I pass." And uttering this the King
Made at the man. Then Modred smote his liege   165
Hard on that helm which many a heathen sword
Had beaten thin; while Arthur at one blow,
Striking the last stroke with Excalibur,
Slew him, and, all but slain himself, he fell.

So all day long the noise of battle roll'd   170
Among the mountains by the winter sea,
Until King Arthur's Table, man by man,
Had fallen in Lyonnesse about their lord,
King Arthur; then, because his wound was deep,
The bold Sir Bedivere uplifted him,   175
And bore him to a chapel nigh the field,
A broken chancel with a broken cross,
That stood on a dark strait of barren land.
On one side lay the Ocean, and on one
Lay a great water, and the moon was full.   180

Then spake King Arthur to Sir Bedivere:
"The sequel of to-day unsolders all

The goodliest fellowship of famous knights
Whereof this world holds record. Such a sleep
They sleep—the men I loved. I think that we   185
Shall never more, at any future time,
Delight our souls with talk of knightly deeds,
Walking about the gardens and the halls
Of Camelot, as in the days that were.
I perish by this people which I made,—   190
Tho' Merlin sware that I should come again
To rule once more—but let what will be be,
I am so deeply smitten thro' the helm
That without help I cannot last till morn.
Thou therefore take my brand Excalibur,   195
Which was my pride; for thou rememberest how
In those old days, on summer noon, an arm
Rose up from out the bosom of the lake,
Clothed in white samite, mystic, wonderful,
Holding the sword—and how I row'd across   200
And took it, and have worn it, like a king;
And, wheresoever I am sung or told
In aftertime, this also shall be known.
But now delay not; take Excalibur,
And fling him far into the middle mere;   205
Watch what thou seest, and lightly[6] bring me word."

    To him replied the bold Sir Bedivere:
"It is not meet, Sir King, to leave thee thus,
Aidless, alone, and smitten thro' the helm—
A little thing may harm a wounded man;   210
Yet I thy hest will all perform at full,
Watch what I see, and lightly bring thee word."

    So saying, from the ruin'd shrine he stept,
And in the moon athwart the place of tombs,
Where lay the mighty bones of ancient men,   215
Old knights, and over them the sea-wind sang
Shrill, chill, with flakes of foam. He, stepping down
By zigzag paths and juts of pointed rock,
Came on the shining levels of the lake.

    There drew he forth the brand Excalibur,   220
And o'er him, drawing it, the winter moon,
Brightening the skirts of a long cloud, ran forth
And sparkled keen with frost againts the hilt;
For all the haft twinkled with diamond sparks,
Myriads of topaz-lights, and jacinth[7]-work   225
Of subtlest jewellery. He gazed so long
That both his eyes were dazzled as he stood,
This way and that dividing the swift mind,

6. Quickly.
7. In ancient usage, a gem of blue color, probably the sapphire. In modern use it is a reddish orange gem.
    "Haft": hilt.

In act to throw; but at the last it seem'd
Better to leave Excalibur conceal'd   230
There in the many-knotted water-flags,
That whistled stiff and dry about the marge.
So strode he back slow to the wounded King.

   Then spake King Arthur to Sir Bedivere:
"Hast thou perform'd my mission which I gave?   235
What is it thou hast seen? or what hast heard?"

   And answer made the bold sir Bedivere:
"I heard the ripple washing in the reeds,
And the wild water lapping on the crag."

   To whom replied King Arthur, faint and pale: 240
"Thou hast betray'd thy nature and thy name,
Not rendering true answer, as beseem'd
Thy fealty, nor like a noble knight;
For surer sign had follow'd, either hand,
Or voice, or else a motion of the mere.   245
This is a shameful thing for men to lie.
Yet now, I charge thee, quickly go again,
As thou art lief⁸ and dear, and do the thing
I bade thee, watch, and lightly bring me word."

   Then went Sir Bedivere the second time   250
Across the ridge, and paced beside the mere,
Counting the dewy pebbles, fixt in thought;
But when he saw the wonder of the hilt,
How curiously and strangely chased, he smote
His palms together, and he cried aloud: 255

   "And if indeed I cast the brand away,
Surely a precious things, one worthy note,
Should thus be lost for ever from the earth,
Which might have pleased the eyes of many men.
What good should follow this, if this were done?   260
What harm, undone? Deep harm to disobey,
Seeing obedience is the bond of rule.
Were it well to obey then, if a king demand
An act unprofitable, against himself?
The King is sick, and knows not what he does.   265
What record or what relic of my lord
Should be to aftertime, but empty breath
And rumors of a doubt? But were this kept,
Stored in some treasure-house of mighty kings,
Some one might show it at a joust of arms,   270
Saying: 'King Arthur's sword, Excalibur,
Wrought by the lonely Maiden of the Lake.
Nine years she wrought it, sitting in the deeps

8. Beloved.

Upon the hidden bases of the hills.'
So might some old man speak in the aftertime   275
To all the people, wining reverence.
But now much honor and much fame were lost."

    So spake he, clouded with his own conceit,
And hid Excalibur the second time,
And so strode back slow to the wounded King.   280

    Then spoke King Arthur, breathing heavily:
"What is it thou hast seen? or what hast heard?"

    And answer made the bold Sir Bedivere:
"I heard the water lapping on the crag,
And the long ripple washing in the reeds."   285

    To whom replied King Arthur, much in wrath:
"Ah miserable, and unkind, untrue,
Unknightly, traitor-heated! Woe is me!
Authority forgets a dying king,
Laid widow'd of the power in his eye   290
That bow'd the will. I see thee what thou art,
For thou, the latest-left of all my knights,
In whom should meet the offices of all,
Thou wouldst betray me for the precious hilt;
Either from lust of gold, or like a girl   295
Valuing the giddy pleasure of the eyes.
Yet, for a man may fail in duty twice,
And the third time may prosper, get thee hence;
But, if thou spare to fling Excalibur,
I will arise and slay thee with my hands."   300

    Then quickly rose Sir Bedivere, and ran,
And, leaping down the ridges lightly, plunged
Among the bulrush beds, and clutch'd the sword,
And strongly wheel'd and threw it. The great brand
Made lightnings in the splendor of the moon,   305
And flashing round and round, and whirl'd in an arch,[9]
Shot like a streamer[1] of the northern morn,
Seen where the moving isles[2] of winter shock
By night, with noises of the Northern sea.
So flash'd and fell the brand Excalibur;   310
But ere he dipt the surface, rose an arm
Clothed in white samite, mystic, wonderful,
And caught him by the hilt, and brandish'd him
Three times, and drew him under in the mere.
And lightly went the other to the King.   315

---

9. Of the line, Tennyson notes: "The extra syllable gives the rush of the sword as it is whirled in parabolic curve."
1. "The Aurora Borealis" (Tennyson).
2. "Icebergs" (Tennyson).

Then spoke King Arthur, drawing thicker breath:[3]
"Now see I by thine eyes that this is done.
Speak out; what is it thou hast heard, or seen?"

And answer made the bold Sir Bedivere:
"Sir King, I closed mine eyelids, lest the gems   320
Should blind my purpose, for I never saw,
Nor shall see, here or elsewhere, till I die,
Not tho' I live three lives of mortal men,
So great a miracle as yonder hilt.
Then with both hands I flung him, wheeling him;   325
But when I look'd again, behold an arm,
Clothed in white samite, mystic, wonderful,
That caught him by the hilt, and brandish'd him
Three times, and drew him under in the mere."

And answer made King Arthur, breathing hard: 330
"My end draws nigh; 't is time that I were gone.
Make broad thy shoulders to receive my weight,
And bear me to the margin; yet I fear
My wound hath taken cold, and I shall die."

So saying, from the pavement he half rose,   335
Slowly, with pain, reclining on his arm,
And looking wistfully with wide blue eyes
As in a picture. Him Sir Bedivere
Remorsefully regarded thro' his tears,
And would have spoken, but he found not words;   340
Then took with care, and kneeling on one knee,
O'er both his shoulders drew the languid hands,
And rising bore him thro' the place of tombs.

But, as he walk'd, King Arthur panted hard,
Like one that feels a nightmare on his bed   345
When all the house is mute. So sigh'd the King,
Muttering and murmuring at his ear, "Quick, quick!
I fear it is too late, and I shall die."
But the other swiftly strode from ridge to ridge,
Clothed with his breath, and looking, as he walk'd,   350
Larger than human on the frozen hills.
He heard the deep behind him, and a cry
Before. His own throught drove him like a goad.
Dry clash'd his harness in the icy caves
And barren chasms, and all to left and right   355
The bare black cliff clang'd round him, as he based
His feet on juts of slippery crag that rang
Sharp-smitten with the dint of armed heels—
And on a sudden, lo, the level lake,
And the long glories of the winter moon!   360

---

3. "Breathing more heavily" (Tennyson).

Then saw they how there hove a dusky barge,
Dark as a funeral scarf from stem to stern,
Beneath them; and descending they were ware
That all the decks were dense with stately forms,
Black-stoled, black-hooded, like a dream—by these   365
Three queens[4] with crowns of gold—and from them rose
A cry that shiver'd to the tingling stars,
And, as it were one voice, an agony
Of lamentation, like a wind that shrills
All night in a waste land, where no one comes,   370
Or hath come, since the making of the world.

Then murmur'd Arthur, "Place me in the barge."
So to the barge they came. There those three queens
Put forth their hands, and took the King, and wept.
But she that rose the tallest of them all   375
And fairest laid his head upon her lap,
And loosed the shatter'd casque,[5] and chafed his hands,
And call'd him by his name, complaining loud,
And dropping bitter tears against a brow
Striped with dark blood; for all his face was white   380
And colorless, and like the wither'd moon[6]
Smote by the fresh beam of the springing east;
And all his greaves and cuisses[7] dash'd with drops
Of onset;[8] and the light and lustrous curls—
That made his forehead like a rising sun   385
High from the dais-throne—were parch'd with dust,
Or, clotted into points and hanging loose,
Mixt with the knightly growth that fringed his lips.
So like a shatter'd column lay the King;
Not like that Arthur who, with lance in rest,   390
From spur to plume a star of tournament,
Shot thro' the lists at Camelot, and charged
Before the eyes of ladies and of kings.

Then loudly cried the bold Sir Bedivere:
"Ah! my Lord Arthur, whither shall I go?   395
Where shall I hide my forehead and my eyes?
For now I see the true old times are dead,
When every morning brought a noble chance,
And every chance brought out a noble knight.
Such times have been not since the light[9] that led   400
The holy Elders with the gift of myrrh.
But now the whole Round Table is dissolved
Which was an image of the mighty world;
And I, the last, go forth companionless,

---

4. They may represent Faith, Hope, and Charity. See "The Coming of Arthur," line 275 and n. 2, p. 385.
5. Helmet.
6. "When smitten by the rising sun" (Tennyson).
7. Guards for protecting the front of the thighs. "Greaves": armor for the shins.
8. Blood from the battle.
9. The star of Bethlehem.

And the days darken round me, and the years,   405
Among new men, strange faces, other minds."

    And slowly answer'd Arthur from the barge:
"The old order changeth yielding place to new,
And God fulfils himself in many ways,
Lest one good custom should corrupt the world.   410
Comfort thyself; what comforth is in me?
I have lived my life, and that which I have done
May He within himself make pure! but thou,
If thou shouldst never see my face again,
Pray for my soul. More things are wrought by prayer   415
Than this world dreams of. Wherefore, let thy voice
Rise like a fountain for me night and day.
For what are men better than sheep or goats
That nourish a blind life within the brain,
If, knowing God, they lift not hands of prayer   420
Both for themselves and those who call them friend?
For so the whole round earth is every way
Bound by gold chains about the feet of God.
But now farewell. I am going a long way
With these thou seest—if indeed I go—   425
For all my mind is clouded with a doubt—
To the island-valley of Avilion;[1]
Where falls not hail, or rain, or any snow,
Nor ever wind blows loudly; but it lies
Deep-meadow'd, happy, fair with orchard lawns   430
And bowery hollows crown'd with summer sea,
Where I will heal me of my grievous wound."

    So said he, and the barge with oar and sail
Moved from the brink, like some full-breasted swan
That, fluting a wild carol ere her death,   435
Ruffles her pure cold plume, and takes the flood
With swarthy webs. Long stood Sir Bedivere
Revolving many memories, till the hull
Look'd one black dot against the verge of dawn,
And on the mere the wailing died away.   440

    But when that moan had past for evermore,
The stillness of the dead world's winter dawn
Amazed him, and he groan'd, "The King is gone."
And therewithal came on him the weird rhyme,
"From the great deep to the great deep he goes."[2]   445

    Whereat he slowly turn'd and slowly clomb
The last hard footstep of that iron crag,
Thence mark'd the black hull moving yet, and cried:
"He passes to be king among the dead,

---

1. In Celtic mythology, Avalon was the Island of Blessed Souls, an earthly paradise in the Western seas.
2. "See Merlin's song in *The Coming of Arthur*" (Tennyson).

And after healing of his grievous wound   450
He comes again; but—if he come no more—
O me, be yon dark queens in yon black boat,
Who shriek'd and wail'd, the three whereat we gazed
On that high day, when, clothed with living light,
They stood before his throne in silence, friends   455
Of Arthur, who should help him at his need?"

Then from the dawn it seem'd there came, but faint[3]
As from beyond the limit of the world,
Like the last echo born of a great cry,
Sounds, as if some fair city were one voice   460
Around a king returning from his wars.

Thereat once more he moved about, and clomb
Even to the highest he could climb, and saw,
Straning his eyes beneath an arch of hand,
Or thought he saw, the speck that bare the King,   465
Down that long water opening on the deep
Somewhere far off, pass on and on, and go
From less to less and vanish into light[4]
And the new sun rose bringing the new year.

1833–35; 1842 (1869)

To the Queen

O loyal to the royal in thyself,
And loyal to thy land, as this to thee—
Bear witness, that rememberable day,[1]
When, pale as yet and fever-worn, the Prince
Who scarce had pluck'd his flickering life again   5
From halfway down the shadow of the grave
Past with thee thro' thy people and their love,
And London roll'd one tide of joy thro' all
Her trebled millions, and loud leagues of man
And welcome! witness, too, the silent cry,   10
The prayer of many a race and creed, and clime—
Thunderless lightnings[2] striking under sea
From sunset and sunrise of all thy realm,

3. "From (the dawn) the East, whence have sprung all the great religions of the world. A triumph of welcome is given to him who has proved himself 'more than conqueror'" (Tennyson).
4. "The purpose of the individual man may fail for a time, but his work cannot die" (Tennyson). Hallam Tennyson says that to this his father would add: "*There are two beliefs I have always held—that there is Someone who knows—God watching over all,—and that Death is not the end-all of Man's existence.*" Tennyson cites Malory: "Yet somme say in many partyes of Englond that King Arthur is not deed, But had by the wylle of our Lord Jhesu in to another place, and men say that he shal come ageyn and he shal wynne the holy crosse." From Layamon's *Brut*, Tennyson quotes: "And afterwards I will come (again) to my kingdom and dwell with the Britons with much joy."
1. "When the Queen and the Prince of Wales went to the thanksgiving at St. Paul's (after the Prince's dangerous illness) in Feb. 1872" (Tennyson).
2. Messages by transatlantic cable (first dependable transmissions, 1866).

And that true North,[3] whereof we lately heard
A strain to shame us, "Keep you to yourselves;   15
So loyal is too costly! friends—your love
Is but a burthen; loose the bond, and go."
Is this the tone of empire? here the faith
That made us rulers? this, indeed, her voice
And meaning whom the roar of Hougoumont[4]   20
Left mightiest of all peoples under heaven?
What shock has fool'd her since, that she should speak
So feebly? wealthier—wealthier—hour by hour!
The voice of Britain, or a sinking land,
Some third-rate isle half-lost among her seas?   25
There rang her voice, when the full city peal'd
Thee and thy Prince! The loyal to their crown
Are loyal to their own far sons, who love
Our ocean-empire with her boundless homes
For ever-broadening England, and her throne   30
In our vast Orient, and one isle, one isle,
That knows not her own greatness; if she knows
And dreads it we are fallen.—But thou, my Queen,
Not for itself, but thro' thy living love
For one[5] to whom I made it o'er his grave   35
Sacred, accept this old imperpect tale,
New-old, and shadowing Sense at war with Soul,
Ideal manhood closed in real man[6]
Rather than that gray king[7] whose name, a ghost,
Streams like a cloud, man-shaped, from mountain peak,   40
And cleaves to cairn and cromlech[8] still; or him
Of Geoffrey's book, or him of Malleor's,[9] one
Touch'd by the adulterous finger of a time
That hover'd between war and wantonness,
And crownings and dethronements. Take withal   45
Thy poet's blessing, and his trust that Heaven
Will blow the tempest in the distance back
From thine and ours; for some are scared, who mark,
Or wisely or unwisely, signs of storm,
Waverings of every vane with every wind,   50
And wordy trucklings to the transient hour,
And fierce or careless looseners of the faith,
And Softness breeding scorn of simple life,
Or Cowardice, the child of lust for gold,

---

3. "Canada. A leading London journal had written advocating that Canada should sever her connection with Great Britain, as she was 'too costly': hence these lines" (Tennyson).
4. "Waterloo" (Tennyson). In the battle of Waterloo, this castle or fortified chateau had been the key to the British position; it was successfully defended against severe attack.
5. Prince Albert, to whom the *Idylls* were dedicated in 1862.
6. This line was inserted in 1891 as Tennyson's last correction, because, according to his son, he felt that "he had not made the real humanity of the king sufficiently clear in his epilogue" (*Memoir* II, 129).
7. "The legendary Arthur from whom many mountains, hills, and cairns throughout Great Britain are named" (Hallam Tennyson).
8. An ancient structure consisting of a large flat stone resting horizontally on three or more upright stones. "Cairn": a pyramid of stones raised as a memorial or landmark.
9. Geoffrey of Monmouth's *History of the Kings of Britain* (c. 1137). "Malory's name is given as Maleorye, Maleore, and Malleor" (Tennyson).

Or Labor, with a groan and not a voice,   55
Or Art with poisonous honey stolen from France,
And that which knows, but careful for itself,
And that which knows not, ruling that which knows
To its own harm. The goal of this great world
Lies beyond sight; yet—if our slowly-grown   60
And crowd'd Republic's crowning common-sense,
That sav'd her many times, not fail—their fears
Are morning shadows[1] huger than the shapes
That cast them, not those gloomier which forego[2]
The darkness of that battle in the west   65
Where all of high and holy dies away.

                                                      1872

---

1. The epilogue's optimism certainly jars with the grim allegorical implications of the last idylls.
2. Precede.

From *Poems* (1872–1892)

The Revenge[1]

A *Ballad of the Fleet*

1

At Flores in the Azores Sir Richard Grenville lay,
And a pinnace, like a flutter'd bird, came flying from far away:[2]
"Spanish ships of war at sea! we have sighted fifty-three!"
Then sware Lord Thomas Howard: "'Fore God I am no coward;
But I cannot meet them here, for my ships are out of gear,   5
And the half my men are sick. I must fly, but follow quick.
We are six ships of the line; can we fight with fifty-three?"

2

Then spake Sir Richard Grenville: "I know you are no coward;
You fly them for a moment to fight with them again.
But I've ninety men and more that are lying sick ashore.   10
I should count myself the coward if I left them, my Lord Howard,
To these Inquisition dogs and the devildoms of Spain."

3

So Lord Howard past away with five ships of war that day,
Till he melted like a cloud in the silent summer heaven;
But Sir Richard bore in hand all his sick men from the land   15
Very carefully and slow,
Men of Bideford[3] in Devon,
And we laid them on the ballast down below;
For we brought them all aboard,

---

1. Both the ship and Sir Richard Grenville had been famous before the engagement that was to immortalize them. In 1588 Drake had commanded the *Revenge* against the Spanish Armada, and in 1585 Grenville, under Sir Walter Raleigh, had led the first colonizing expedition to Roanoke Island, Virginia. In 1591 Lord Howard was sent to the Azores with sixteen ships to intercept Spanish treasure-vessels returning from the West Indies. A Spanish fleet of fifty-three warships was sent out against Howard, who escaped with five ships, but Grenville remained to take his sick men aboard. In the battle, Grenville alone attempted to run through the entire Spanish fleet and surrendered after fifteen hours, when he had been mortally wounded and his ship's complement had been reduced to only twenty able-bodied men.
   Tennyson had wanted to write a poem about the *Revenge* since 1852, when he read J. A. Froude's article "England's Forgotten Worthies" in the July issue of the *Westminster Review*. Although it described the action of a single ship, the story, Froude said, had struck a "deeper terror into the hearts of the Spanish people" than the fate of the Armada (*Memoir* II, 251). But not until 1877, when Tennyson saw Edward Arber's reprint of all available information about the *Revenge*, was he moved or did he feel sufficiently knowledgeable to write his poem. (See *Alfred Tennyson*, p. 438.) The ballad was instantly popular, but perhaps the sweetest praise of all came from Carlyle, who had found little enough to his liking in Tennyson's poetry after 1842: "Eh! Alfred, you have got the grip of it," he said after the poet read him the poem (*Memoir* II, 234).
2. From the coast of Portugal, where the earl of Cumberland had sighted the enemy fleet.
3. "Granville was from Bideford" (Ricks).

An they blest him in their pain, that they were not left to Spain,   20
To the thumb-screw and the stake, for the glory of the Lord.

4

He had only a hundred seamen to work the ship and to fight,
And he sailed away from Flores till the Spaniard came in sight,
With his huge sea-castles heaving upon the weather bow.
"Shall we fight or shall we fly?   25
Good Sir Richard, tell us now,
For to fight is but to die!
There'll be little of us left by the time this sun be set."
And Sir Richard said again: "We be all good English men.
Let us bang these dogs of Seville, the children of the devil,   30
For I never turn'd my back upon Don or devil yet."

5

Sir Richard spoke and he laugh'd and we roar'd a hurrah, and so
The little Revenge ran on sheer into the heart of the foe,
With her hundred fighters on deck, and her ninety sick below;
For half of their fleet to the right and half to the left were seen,   35
And the little Revenge ran on thro' the long sea-lane between.

6

Thousands of their soldiers look'd down from their decks and laugh'd,
Thousands of their seamen made mock at the mad little craft
Running on and on, till delay'd
By their mountain-like San Philip that, of fifteen hundred tons,   40
And up-shadowing high above us with her yawning tiers of guns,
Took the breath from our sails, and we stay'd.

7

And while now the great San Philip hung above us like a cloud
Whence the thunderbolt will fall
Long and loud,   45
Four galleons drew away
From the Spanish fleet that day,
And two upon the larboard and two upon the starboard lay,
And the battle-thunder broke from them all.

8

But anon the great San Philip, she bethought herself and went,   50
Having that within her womb that had left her ill content;
And the rest they came aboard us, and they fought us hand to hand,
For a dozen times they came with their pikes and musqueteers,
And a dozen times we shook' em off as a dog that shakes his ears
When he leaps from the water to the land.   55

9

An the sun went down, and the stars came out far above the summer sea,
But never a moment ceased the fight of the one and the fifty-three.
Ship after ship, the whole night long, their high-built galleons came,
Ship after ship, the whole night long, with her battle-thunder and flame;

Ship after ship, the whole night long, drew back with her dead and
　　her shame　　　　　　　　　　　　　　　　　　　　　　　　　60
For some were sunk and many were shatter'd, and so could fight us no
　　more—
God of battles, was ever a battle like this in the world before?

10

For he said, "Fight on! fight on!"
Tho' his vessel was all but a wreck;
And it chanced that, when half of the short summer night was gone,　　65
With a grisly wound to be drest he had left the deck,
But a bullet struck him that was dressing it suddenly dead,
And himself he was wounded again in the side and the head,
And he said, "Fight on! fight on!"

11

And the night went down, and the sun smiled out far over the summer sea,　70
And the Spanish fleet with broken sides lay round us all in a ring;
But they dared not touch us again, for they fear'd that we still could sting,
So they watch'd what the end would be.
And we had not fought them in vain,
But in perilous plight were we.　　　　　　　　　　　　　　　　75
Seeing forty of our poor hundred were slain,
And half of the rest of us maim'd for life
In the crash of the cannonades and the desperate strife;
And the sick men down in the hold were most of them stark and cold,
And the pikes were all broken or bent, and the powder was all of it spent;　80
And the masts and the rigging were lying over the side;
But Sir Richard cried in his English pride:
"We have fought such a fight for a day and a night
As may never be fought again!
We have won great glory, my men!　　　　　　　　　　　　　　85
And a day less or more
At sea or ashore,
We die—does it matter when?
Sink me the ship, Master Gunner—sink her, split her in twain.[4]
Fall into the hands of God, not into the hands of Spain!"　　　　　90

12

And the gunner said, "Ay, ay," but the seamen made reply:
"We have children, we have wives,
And the Lord hath spared our lives.
We will make the Spaniard promise, if we yield, to let us go;
We shall live to fight again and to strike another blow."　　　　　95
And the lion there lay dying, and they yielded to the foe.

4. According to Sir Walter Raleigh's account, Grenville "commanded the master gunner, whom he knew
to be a most resolute man, to split and sink the ship, that thereby nothing might remain of glory in victory to the Spaniards, seeing in so many hours they were not able to take her, having had fifteen hours'
time, fifteen thousand men, and fifty-three sail of men of war to perform it withal" (*Memoir* II, 251).

13
And the stately Spanish men to their flagship[5] bore him then,
Where they laid him by the mast, old Sir Richard caught at last,
And they praised him to his face with their courtly foreign grace;
But he rose upon their decks, and he cried: 100
"I have fought for Queen and Faith like a valiant man and true;
I have only done my duty as a man is bound to do.
With a joyful spirit I Sir Richard Grenville die!"
And he fell upon their decks, and he died.

14
And they stared at the dead that had been so valiant and true,   105
And had holden the power and glory of Spain so cheap
That he dared her with one little ship and his English few;
Was he devil or man? He was devil for aught they knew,
But they sank his body with honor down into the deep,
And they mann'd the Revenge with a swarthier alien crew,   110
And away she sail'd with her loss and long'd for her own;
When a wind from the lands[6] they had ruin'd awoke from sleep,
And the water began to heave and the weather to moan,
And or ever that evening ended a great gale blew,
And a wave like the wave that is raised by an earthquake grew,   115
Till it smote on their hulls and their sails and their masts and their flags,
And the whole sea plunged and fell on the shot-shatter'd navy of Spain,
And the little Revenge herself went down by the island crags
To be lost evermore in the main.

1878

Battle of Brunanburh[1]

1
Athelstan King,
Lord among Earls,
Bracelet-bestower and
Baron of Barons,
He with his brother,   5
Edmund Atheling,
Gaining a lifelong
Glory in battle,
Slew with the sword-edge

5. The *San Pablo*.
6. "West Indies" (Tennyson).
1. A translation from the Anglo-Saxon, printed in 1880 with the following prefatory note: "Constantinus, King of the Scots, after having sworn allegiance to Athelstan, allied himself with the Danes of Ireland under Anlaf, and invading England, was defeated by Athelstan and his brother Edmund with great slaughter at Brunanburh in the year 937." (Tennyson). "I have more or less availed myself of my son's prose translation of this poem in the 'Contemporary Review' (November, 1876)" (Tennyson). "The tenth-century Old English poem is one of a group of panegyrics on royalty, using an earlier style both in metre and diction. Tennyson's is in general a close translation. His metre is unrhymed dactylics and trochaics" (Ricks). "In rendering this Old English war-song into modern language and alliterative rhythm I have made free use of the dactylic beat. I suppose that the original was chanted to a slow, swinging recitative" (Tennyson).

There by Brunanburh,   10
Brake the shield-wall,
Hew'd the linden-wood,[2]
Hack'd the battle-shield,
Sons of Edward with hammer'd brands.

2

Theirs was a greatness   15
Got from their grandsires—
Theirs that so often in
Strife with their enemies
Struck for their hoards and their hearts and their homes.

3

Bow'd the spoiler,   20
Bent the Scotsman,
Fell the ship-crews
Doom'd to the death.
All the field with blood of the fighters
Flow'd, from when first the great   25
Sun-star of morning-tide,
Lamp of the Lord God
Lord everlasting,
Glode over earth till the glorious creature
Sank to his setting.   30

4

There lay many a man
Marr'd by the javelin,
Men of the Northland
Shot over shield.
There was the Scotsman   35
Weary of war.

5

We the West-Saxons,
Long as the daylight
Lasted, in companies
Troubled the track of the host that we hated;   40
Grimly with swords that were sharp from the grindstone,
Fiercely we hack'd at the flyers before us.

6

Mighty the Mercian[3]
Hard was his hand-play,
Sparing not any of   45
Those that with Anlaf,
Warriors over the
Weltering waters

2. "Shields of lindenwood" (Tennyson).
3. Mercia was the ancient Anglican kingdom in central England and included London.

Borne in the bark's-bosom,
Drew to this island—   50
Doom'd to the death.

7

Five youngs kings put asleep by the sword-stroke,
Seven strong earls of the army of Anlaf
Fell on the war-field, numberless numbers,
Shipmen and Scotsmen.   55

8

Then the Norse leader—
Dire was his need of it,
Few were his following—
Fled to his war-ship;
Fleeted his vessel to sea with the king in it,   60
Saving his life on the fallow flood.

9

Also the crafty one,
Constantinus,
Crept to his North again,
Hoar-headed hero!   65

10

Slender warrant had
He to be proud of
The welcome of war-knives[4]—
He that was reft of his
Folk and his friends that had   70
Fallen in conflict,
Leaving his son too
Lost in the carnage,
Mangled to morsels,
A youngster in war!   75

11

Slender reason had
He to be glad of
The clash of the war-glaive—
Traitor and trickster
And spurner of treaties—   80
He nor had Anlaf
With armies so broken
A reason for bragging
That they had the better
In perils of battle   85
On places of slaughter—
The struggle of standards,
The rush of the javelins,

---

4. "Literally 'fellowship or meeting of . . .', a keening for battle" (Ricks).

The crash of the charges,[5]
The wielding of weapons—   90
The play that they play'd with
The children of Edward.

12

Then with their nail'd prows
Parted the Norsemen, a
Blood-redden'd relic of   95
Javelins over
The jarring breaker, the deep-sea billow,
Shaping their way toward Dyflen[6] again,
Shamed in their souls.

13

Also the brethren,   100
King and Atheling,
Each in his glory,
Went to his own in his own West-Saxon-land,
Glad of the war.

14

Many a carcase they left to be carrion,   105
Many a livid one, many a sallow-skin—
Left for the white-tail'd eagle to tear it, and
Left for the horny-nibb'd raven to rend it, and
Gave to the garbaging war-hawk to gorge it, and
That gray beast, the wolf of the weald.   110

15

Never had huger
Slaughter of heroes
Slain by the sword-edge—
Such as old writers
Have writ of in histories—   115
Hapt in this isle, since
Up from the East hither
Saxon and Angle from
Over the broad billow
Broke into Britain with   120
Haughty war-workers who
Harried the Welshman, when
Earls that were lured by the
Hunger of glory gat
Hold of the land.   125

1880

---

5. "Lit. 'the gathering of men'" (Tennyson). "Rush": literally, "meeting" (Ricks).
6. "Dublin" (Tennyson).

Rizpah[1]

17—

1

Wailing, wailing, wailing, the wind over land and sea—
And Willy's voice in the wind, "O mother, come out to me!"
Why should he call me to-night, when he knows that I cannot go?
For the downs are as bright as day, and the full moon stares at the snow.

2

We should be seen, my dear; they would spy us out of the town.   5
The loud black nights for us, and the storm rushing over the down,
When I cannot see my own hand, but am led by the creak of the chain,
And grovel and grope for my son till I find myself drenched with the rain.

3

Anything fallen again? nay—what was there left to fall?
I have taken them home, I have number'd the bones, I have hidden them
    all.   10
What am I saying? and what are *you*? do you come as a spy?
Falls? what falls? who knows? As the tree falls so must it lie.[2]

4

Who let her in? how long has she been? you—what have you heard?
Why did you sit so quiet? you never have spoken a word.
O—to pray with me—yes—a lady—none of their spies—   15
But the night has crept into my heart, and begun to darken my eyes.

5

Ah—you, that have lived so soft, what should *you* know of the night,
The blast and the burning shame and the bitter frost and the fright?
I have done it, while you were asleep—you were only made for the day.
I have gather'd my baby together—and now you may go your way.   20

6

Nay—for it's kind of you, madam, to sit by an old dying wife.
But say nothing hard of my boy, I have only an hour of life.
I kiss'd my boy in the prison, before he went out to die.

---

1. Tennyson founded his poem on an incident "related in some penny magazine called *Old Brighton*." For the account, see *Memoir* II, 249–51. The late-eighteenth-century tale involved two young men, Rooke and Howell, who robbed a mail coach and, according to the justice of the day, were hanged on the spot where the crime was committed. As was customary, their chained bodies were left on the gallows to rot. Rooke's old mother collected her son's bones as they dropped from the decaying flesh and finally buried them in Old Shoreham Churchyard's hallowed ground, denied to executed criminals. Although Tennyson first titled his poem "Bones," before publication he took his title from 2 Samuel, 21:8–11. Rizpah's two sons were hanged by the Gibeonites, and she stood guard over their bodies warding off birds and beasts.
   Tennyson cast his poem as a dramatic monologue spoken by the dying old mother from her hospital bed to a rather dense, visiting charity worker. Swinburne, whose response to *Idylls of the King* had seldom been less than vicious, pleaded that language failed him in expressing the depth of his feelings about "Rizpah." If it alone survived of all the poet's work, he said, it would be "proof positive . . . that in the author of this single poem a truly great poet had been born." The statement indirectly reminds us that Tennyson was seventy when he wrote the poem.
2. Ecclesiastes 11:3: "In the place where the tree falleth, there it shall be."

"They dared me to do it," he said, and he never has told me a lie.
I whipt him for robbing an orchard once when he was but a child—   25
"The farmer dared me to do it," he said; he was always so wild—
And idle—and could n't be idle—my Willy—he never could rest.
The King should have made him a soldier, he would have been one of his
      best.

7

But he lived with a lot of wild mates, and they never would let him be good;
They swore that he dare not rob the mail, and he swore that he would;   30
And he took no life, but he took one purse, and when all was done
He flung it among his fellows—"I'll none of it," said my son.

8

I came into court to the judge and the lawyers. I told them my tale,
God's own truth—but they kill'd him, they kill'd him for robbing the mail.
They hang'd him in chains for a show—we had always borne a good
      name—   35
To be hang'd for a thief—and then put away—is n't that enough shame?
Dust to dust—low down—let us hide! but they set him, so high
That all the ships of the world could stare at him, passing by.
God 'ill pardon the hell-black raven and horrible fowls of the air,
But not the black heart of the lawyer who kill'd him and hang'd him there.   40

9

And the jailer forced me away. I had bid him my last good-bye;
They had fasten'd the door of his cell. "O mother!" I heard him cry.
I could n't get back tho' I tried, he had something further to say,
And now I never shall know it. The jailer forced me away.

10

Then since I could n't but hear that cry of my boy that was dead,   45
They seized me and shut me up: they fasten'd me down on my bed.
"Mother, O mother!"—he call'd in the dark to me year after year—
They beat me for that, they beat me—you know that I could n't but hear;
And then at the last they found I had grown so stupid and still
They let me abroad again—but the creatures had worked their will.   50

11

Flesh of my flesh was gone, but bone of my bone was left[3]—
I stole them all from the lawyers—and you, will you call it a theft?—
My baby, the bones that had suck'd me, the bones that had laughed and had
      cried—
Theirs? O, no! they are mine—not theirs—they had moved in my side.

12

Do you think I was scared by the bones? I kiss'd 'em, I buried 'em all—   55
I can't dig deep, I am old—in the night by the churchyard wall.
My Willy 'ill rise up whole when the trumpet of judgment 'ill sound,
But I charge you never to say that I laid him in holy ground.

3. Genesis 2:23: "And Adam said, This is now bone of my bones, and flesh of my flesh."

13

They would scratch him up—they would hang him again on the cursed
    tree.[4]
Sin? O, yes, we are sinners, I know—let all that be,   60
And read me a Bible verse of the Lord's goodwill toward men—
"Full of compassion and mercy, the Lord"[5]—let me hear it again;
"Full of compassion and mercy—long-suffering." Yes, O, yes!
For the lawyer is born but to murder—the Saviour lives but to bless.
He 'll never put on the black cap[6] except for the worst of the worst,   65
And the first may be last—I have heard it in church—and the last may be
    first.[7]
Suffering—O, long-suffering—yes, as the Lord must know,
Year after year in the mist and the wind and the shower and the snow.

14

Heard, have you? what? they have told you he never repented his sin.
How do they know it? are *they* his mother? are *you* of his kin?   70
Heard! have you ever heard, when the storm on the downs began,
The wind that 'ill wail like a child and the sea that 'ill moan like a man?

15

Election, Election, and Reprobation[8]—it 's all very well.
But I go to-night to my boy, and I shall not find him in hell.
For I cared so much for my boy that the Lord has look'd into my care,   75
And He means me I'm sure to be happy with Willy, I know not where.

16

And if *he* be lost—but to save *my* soul, that is all your desire—
Do you think that I care for *my* soul if my boy be gone to the fire?
I have been with God in the dark—go, go, you may leave me alone—
You never have borne a child—you are just as hard as a stone.   80

17

Madam, I beg your pardon! I think that you mean to be kind,
But I cannot hear what you say for my Willy's voice in the wind—
The snow and the sky so bright—he used but to call in the dark,
And he calls to me now from the church and not from the gibbet—for hark!
Nay—you can hear it yourself—it is coming—shaking the walls—   85
Willy—the moon 's in a cloud—Good-night. I am going. He calls.

                                                                          1880

4. Deuteronomy 21:22–23: "And if a man have committed a sin worthy of death, and he be to be put to
   death, and thou hang him on a tree: His body shall not remain all night upon the tree, but thou shalt in
   any wise bury him that day; (for he that is hanged is accursed of God)" (noted by Adler and Ricks).
5. Psalm 86:15: "But thou, O Lord, art a God full of compassion, and gracious, longsuffering, and plen-
   teous in mercy and truth."
6. Put on by the judge when he passed the death sentence.
7. See Matthew 19:30: "But many that are first, shall be last; and the last shall be first." Adler and Ricks cite
   Mark 10:31: "But many that are first, shall be last; and the last first."
8. Alludes to the Calvinistic doctrine of predestination; regardless of the apparent quality of one's life, people have been damned or saved even before the world was created.

"Frater Ave Atque Vale"[1]

Row us out from Desenzano,[2] to your Sirmione row!
So they row'd, and there we landed—"O venusta Sirmio!"[3]
There to me thro' all the groves of olive in the summer glow,
There beneath the Roman ruin where the purple flowers grow,
Came that "Ave atque Vale" of the Poet's hopeless woe,   5
Tenderest of Roman poets nineteen hundred years ago,
"Frater Ave atque Vale"—as we wander'd to and fro
Gazing at the Lydian laughter of the Garda Lake below
Sweet Catullus's all-but-island,[4] olive-silvery Sirmio!

1880; 1883

Despair[1]

1

Is it you,[2] that preach'd in the chapel there looking over the sand?
Follow'd us too that night, and dogg'd us, and drew me to land?

2

What did I feel that night? You are curious. How should I tell?
Does it matter so much what I felt? You rescued me—yet—was it well
That you came unwish'd for, uncall'd, between me and the deep and my
        doom,   5
Three days since, three more dark days of the Godless gloom
Of a life without sun, without health, without hope, without any delight
In anything here upon earth? but, ah, God! that night, that night
When the rolling eyes of the lighthouse there on the fatal neck
Of land running out into rock—they had saved many hundreds from
        wreck—   10
Glared on our way toward death, I remember I thought, as we past,
Does it matter how many they saved? we are all of us wreck'd at last—

1. The death of Tennyson's brother Charles in April 1879 was foremost in the poet's mind during the summer of 1880 while visiting Sirmione, the peninsula in Lake Garda where Catullus (c. 87–54 B.C.) had maintained his country villa. The words of the title, "Brother, hail and farewell," are from Catullus's elegiac lament for his brother (see IM 57, 4, and note).
2. A town at the southern end of Lake Garda, about three miles from Sirmione.
3. "O lovely Sirmione."
4. I.e., the peninsula.
1. When the poem was published in 1881, Tennyson included the following prefatory note: "A man and his wife having lost faith in a God, and hope of a life to come, and being utterly miserable in this, resolve to end themselves by drowning. The woman is drowned, but the man is rescued by a minister of the sect he had abandoned." At the end of his poem he wrote: "In my boyhood I came across the Calvinist Creed, and assuredly however unfathomable the mystery, if one cannot believe in the freedom of the human will as of the Divine, life is hardly worth having" (*Memoir* I, 317). (See Tennyson's early poem "Remorse" and notes.) Predictably, the poem provoked vigorous protest, from both free-thinkers and Evangelicals. (See *Alfred Tennyson*, pp. 460–61.) Although by no means as clever as Browning's "Caliban upon Setebos" (1864) in its attack on Calvinist dogma, the poem is nonetheless important to an understanding of the late Tennyson. His deepening pessimism occasionally led him into hectorings against the dark times he saw resulting from widespread acceptance of materialistic doctrines. In "Despair" as in "Locksley Hall Sixty Years After," the speakers' views and the poet's are very close.
2. The Calvinist minister.

'Do you fear?' and there came thro' the roar of the breaker a whisper, a breath,
'Fear? am I not with you? I am frighted at life, not death.'

3
And the suns of the limitless universe sparkled and shone in the sky,   15
Flashing with fires as of God, but we knew that their light was a lie—
Bright as with deathless hope—but, however they sparkled and shone,
The dark little worlds running round them were worlds of woe like our
    own—
No soul in the heaven above, no soul on the earth below,
A fiery scroll written over with lamentation and woe.[3]   20

4
See, we were nursed in the drear nightfold of your fatalist creed,
And we turn'd to the growing dawn, we had hoped for a dawn indeed,
When the light of a sun that was coming would scatter the ghosts of the past,
And the cramping creeds that had madden'd the peoples would vanish at last,
And we broke away from the Christ, our human brother and friend,   25
For He spoke, or it seem'd that He spoke, of a hell without help, without end.

5
Hoped for a dawn, and it came, but the promise had faded away;
We had past from a cheerless night to the glare of a drearier day;
He is only a cloud and a smoke who was once a pillar of fire,
The guess of a worm in the dust and the shadow of its desire—   30
Of a worm as it writhes in a world of the weak trodden down by the strong;
Of a dying worm in a world, all massacre, murder, and wrong.[4]

6
O, we poor orphans of nothing—alone on that lonely shore—
Born of the brainless Nature who knew not that which she bore!
Trusting no longer that earthly flower would be heavenly fruit—   35
Come from the brute, poor souls—no souls—and to die with the brute[5]—

7
Nay, but I am not claiming your pity; I know you of old—
Small pity for those that have ranged from the narrow warmth of your fold,
Where you bawl'd the dark side of your faith and a God of eternal rage,
Till you flung us back on ourselves, and the human heart, and the Age.   40

8
But pity—the Pagan held it a vice—was in her and in me,
Helpless, taking the place of the pitying God that should be!
Pity for all that aches in the grasp of an idiot power,
And pity for our own selves on an earth that bore not a flower;
Pity for all that suffers on land or in air or the deep,   45
And pity for our own selves till we long'd for eternal sleep.

---

3. Ezekiel 2:9–10: "A roll of a book . . . and there was written therein lamentations, and mourning, and woe" (noted by Ricks).
4. Compare *Maud* 1, IV, 4, lines 120ff. Job 25:6: "How much less man, that is a worm: and the son of man, which is a worm."
5. Compare *IM* 56.

9

'Lightly step over the sands! the waters—you hear them call!
Life with its anguish, and horrors, and errors—away with it all!'
And she laid her hand in my own—she was always loyal and sweet—
Till the points of the foam in the dusk came playing about our feet.   50
There was a strong sea-current would sweep us out to the main.
'Ah, God!' tho' I felt as I spoke I was taking the name in vain—
'Ah, God!' and we turn'd to each other, we kiss'd, we embraced, she and I,
Knowing the love we were used to believe everlasting would die.
We had read their know-nothing[6] books, and we lean'd to the darker
        side—   55
Ah God, should we find Him, perhaps, perhaps, if we died, if we died;
We never had found Him on earth,[7] this earth is a fatherless hell—
'Dear love, for ever and ever, for ever and ever farewell!'
Never a cry so desolate, not since the world began,
Never a kiss so sad, no, not since the coming of man!   60

10

But the blind wave cast me ashore, and you saved me, a valueless life.
Not a grain of gratitude mine! You have parted the man from the wife.
I am left alone on the land, she is all alone in the sea;
If a curse meant aught, I would curse you for not having let me be.

11

Visions of youth—for my brain was drunk with the water, it seems;   65
I had past into perfect quiet at length out of pleasant dreams,
And the transient trouble of drowning—what was it when match'd with the
        pains
Of the hellish heat of a wretched life rushing back thro' the veins?

12

Why should I live? one son had forged on his father and fled,
And if I believed in a God, I would thank Him, the other is dead,   70
And there was a baby-girl, that had never look'd on the light;
Happiest she of us all, for she past from the night to the night.

13

But the crime, if a crime, of her eldest-born, her glory, her boast,
Struck hard at the tender heart of the mother, and broke it almost;
Tho', glory and shame dying out for ever in endless time,   75
Does it matter so much whether crown'd for a virtue, or hang'd for a crime?

14

And ruin'd by *him*, by *him*, I stood there, naked, amazed[8]
In a world of arrogant opulence, fear'd myself turning crazed,

6. A popular cheapening of Huxley's coined word *agnostic*, to define one who believes no proof of God's existence is possible but does not deny the possibility of God's existence. "'Suggested by Prof. Huxley at a party held previous to the formation of the now defunct Metaphysical Society, at Mr. James Knowles's house on Clapham Common, one evening in 1869, in my hearing. He took it from St. Paul's mention of the altar to "the Unknown God."' R. M. Hutton in letter 13 Mar. 1881" (OED).
7. See IM 124.
8. Of lines 77–79 and 30–32, "all the details here suggest *Maud*" (Ricks).

And I would not be mock'd in a mad-house! and she, the delicate wife,
With a grief that could only be cured, if cured, by the surgeon's knife,— 80

15

Why should we bear with an hour of torture, a moment of pain,
If every man die for ever, if all his griefs are in vain,
And the homeless planet at length will be wheel'd thro' the silence of space,
Motherless evermore of an ever-vanishing race,
When the worm shall have writhed its last, and its last brother-worm will have
 fled 85
From the dead fossil skull that is left in the rocks of an earth that is dead?

16

Have I crazed myself over their horrible infidel writings? O, yes,
For these are the new dark ages, you see, of the popular press,
When the bat comes out of his cave, and the owls are whooping at noon,
And Doubt is the lord of this dunghill and crows to the sun and the moon, 90
Till the sun and the moon of our science are both of them turn'd into
 blood,[9]
And Hope will have broken her heart, running after a shadow of good;
For their knowing and know-nothing books are scatter'd from hand to hand—
We have knelt in your know-all chapel too, looking over the sand.

17

What! I should call on that Infinite Love that has served us so well? 95
Infinite cruelty rather that made everlasting hell,
Made us, foreknew us, foredoom'd us, and does what he will with his own;
Better our dead brute mother who never has heard us groan![1]

18

Hell? if the souls of men were immortal, as men have been told,
The lecher would cleave to his lusts, and the miser would yearn for his
 gold, 100
And so there were hell for ever! but were there a God, as you say,
His love would have power over hell till it utterly vanish'd away.

19

Ah, yet—I have had some glimmer, at times, in my gloomiest woe,
Of a God behind all—after all—the great God, for aught that I know;
But the God of love and of hell together—they cannot be thought, 105
If there be such a God, may the Great God curse him and bring him to
 nought!

20

Blasphemy! whose is the fault? is it mine? for why would you save
A madman to vex you with wretched words, who is best in his grave?
Blasphemy! ay, why not, being damn'd beyond hope of grace?
O, would I were yonder with her, and away from your faith and your face! 110

9. "'The sun shall be turned into darkness, and the moon into blood, before the great and the terrible day
 of the Lord come,' *Joel*, 2:31" (Ricks).
1. "Combining *Romans*, 8:29: 'For whom he did foreknow, he also did predestinate'; and *Matthew*, 20:15:
 'Is it not lawful for me to do what I will with mine own?'" (Ricks).

Blasphemy! true! I have scared you pale with my scandalous talk,
But the blasphemy to *my* mind lies all in the way that you walk.

21

Hence! she is gone! can I stay? can I breathe divorced from the past?
You needs must have good lynx-eyes if I do not escape you at last.
Our orthodox coroner doubtless will find it a felo-de-se,[2]   115
And the stake and the cross-road, fool, if you will, does it matter to me?[3]

1881

To Virgil[1]

Written at the Request of the Mantuans for the Nineteenth Centenary of Virgil's Death

1

Roman Virgil, thou that singest Ilion's lofty temples robed in fire,

Ilion falling, Rome arising, wars, and filial faith, and Dido's pyre;[2]

2

Landscape-lover, lord of language more than he[3] that sang the "Works and
    Days,"

All the chosen coin of fancy flashing out from many a golden phrase;

3

Thou that singest wheat and woodland, tilth and vineyard, hive and horse
    and herd;   5

All the charm of all the Muses often flowering in a lonely word;

4

Poet of the happy Tityrus[4] piping underneath his beechen bowers;

Poet of the poet-satyr whom[5] the laughing shepherd bound with flowers;

---

2. "A case in which the verdict 'felo de se' is appropriate; self-murder, suicide," *OED*, 2.
3. Suicides were customarily denied a Christian burial in hallowed ground and buried at a crossroads with
   a stake driven through the heart.
1. Virgil, to whom Tennyson had always looked as the master artist, was born on a farm near Mantua in 70
   B.C. and died in 19 B.C., making this celebration of the nineteenth centenary a year late. Ricks quotes Trapp
   for pointing out that "the lay-out of the manuscript poem differs from all the published versions, which print
   it in ten numbered stanzas of two lines each, broken at the caesura, so that they look like twice two . . .
   Tennyson clearly intended it as a single unit of twenty long trochaic lines, rhyming in couplets."
2. The allusions are to *Aeneid*, the burning of Troy (Ilion), and Dido's suicide after Aeneas abondoned her
   in Carthage.
3. Hesiod, the eighth-century B.C. Greek poet whose *Works and Days* contained moral maxims and pre-
   cepts on farming, which anticipated Virgil's *Georgics*.
4. *Eclogue* I, line 1: "You, Tityrus, lie under your spreading beech's covert."
5. Silenus, *Eclogue* VI, line 19, whom "They cast into fetters made from his own garlands."

5
Chanter of the Pollio,[6] glorying in the blissful years again to be,

Summers of the snakeless meadow, unlaborious earth and oarless sea;[7]   10

6
Thou that seest Universal Nature moved by Universal Mind;[8]

Thou majestic in thy sadness at the doubtful doom of human kind;[9]

7
Light among the vanish'd ages; star that gildest yet this phantom shore;

Golden branch[1] amid the shadows, kings and realms that pass to rise no
        more;

8
Now thy Forum roars no longer, fallen every purple Cæsar's[2] dome—   15

Tho' thine ocean-roll of rhythm sound forever of Imperial Rome—

9
Now the Rome of slaves hath perish'd, and the Rome of freemen holds her
        place,

I, from out the Northern Island sunder'd once from all the human race,[3]

10
I salute thee, Mantovano,[4] I that loved thee since my day began,

Wielder of the stateliest measure ever moulded by the lips of man.   20

1882

---

6. Virgil's patron, mentioned in *Eclogue* IV, in which the prophecy of a golden age has been frequently
   read as anticipating Christ's birth.
7. *Eclogue* IV: "But for thee, child, shall the earth untilled pour forth, as her first pretty gifts, straggling ivy
   with foxglove everywhere" and "even the trader shall quit the sea" (noted by Ricks).
8. Ricks notes *Aeneid* VI, line 727: "mind sways the mass."
9. *Aeneid* I, line 462: "There are tears for misfortune and mortal sorrows touch the heart" (Ricks).
1. The Golden Bough, with which Aeneas gained access to the underworld, *Aeneid* VI, lines 206ff. By analogy, Virgil himself in his poem giving us access to the mysterious underworld.
2. "Horace's *Odes*, I, xxxv, 12: *purpurei tyranni*" (Ricks).
3. *Eclogue* I, line 67: "And the Britons, wholly sundered from all the world" (Hallam Tennyson).
4. "Mantuan, cf. Dante, *Purgatorio* VI, 74 (Hallam Tennyson), which allows Tennyson to join Dante in
   venerating Virgil" (Ricks).

The Dead Prophet[1]

182–

1

Dead!
And the Muses cried with a stormy cry,
'Send them no more, for evermore
Let the people die.'

2

Dead!   5
'Is it *he* then brought so low?'
And a careless people flock'd from the fields
With a purse to pay for the show.

3

Dead, who had served his time,
Was one of the people's kings,   10
Had labor'd in lifting them out of slime,
And showing them, souls have wings!

4

Dumb on the winter heath he lay.
His friends had stript him bare,
And roll'd his nakedness everyway   15
That all the crowd might stare.

5

A storm-worn signpost not to be read,
And a tree with a moulder'd nest
On its barkless bones, stood stark by the dead;
And behind him, low in the West,   20

6

With shifting ladders of shadow and light,
And blurr'd in color and form,

---

1. Although the date "182–" has led to speculation, Tennyson said his poem was "about no particular prophet." As his much earlier poem "To ———, After Reading a Life and Letters" may have been in response to the publication of Keats's correspondence with Fanny Brawne, so "The Dead Prophet" may have been prompted by Froude's disclosure of the bickerings in the private life of Jane and Thomas Carlyle. "I am sure that Froude is wrong," Tennyson said. "I saw a great deal of them. They were always 'chaffing' one another, and they could not have done that if they had got on so 'badly together' as Froude thinks." Tennyson always believed a writer's work should stand for his life (see *Memoir* II, 165), and a measure of his dread of biography is given in his son's remark that, when writing "The Dead Prophet," the poet chanted:
    While I live the OWLS!
    When I die the GHOULS!!

The sun hung over the gates of night,
    And glared at a coming storm.

7

Then glided a vulturous beldam forth,   25
    That on dumb death had thriven;
They call'd her 'Reverence' here upon earth,
    And 'The Curse of the Prophet' in heaven.

8

She knelt—'We worship him'—all but wept—
    'So great, so noble, was he!'   30
She clear'd her sight, she arose, she swept
    The dust of earth from her knee.

9

'Great! for he spoke and the people heard,
    And his eloquence caught like a flame
From zone to zone of the world, till his word   35
    Had won him a noble name.

10

'Noble! he sung, and the sweet sound ran
    Thro' palace and cottage door,
For he touch'd on the whole sad planet of man,
    The kings and the rich and the poor;   40

11

'And he sung not alone of an old sun set,
    But a sun coming up in his youth!
Great and noble—O, yes—but yet—
    For man is a lover of truth,

12

'And bound to follow, wherever she go   45
    Stark-naked, and up or down,
Thro' her high hill-passes of stainless snow,
    Or the foulest sewer of the town—

13

'Noble and great—O, ay—but then,
    Tho' a prophet should have his due,   50
Was he noblier-fashion'd than other men?
    Shall we see to it, I and you?

14

'For since he would sit on a prophet's seat,
    As a lord of the human soul,
We needs must scan him from head to feet,   55
    Were it but for a wart or a mole?'

15

His wife and his child stood by him in tears,
　　But she—she push'd them aside.
'Tho' a name may last for a thousand years,
　　Yet a truth is a truth,' she cried　　　　　　　　　　60

16

And she that had haunted his pathway still,
　　Had often truckled and cower'd
When he rose in his wrath, and had yielded her will
　　To the master, as overpower'd,

17

She tumbled his helpless corpse about.　　　　　　65
　　'Small blemish upon the skin!
But I think we know what is fair without
　　Is often as foul within.'

18

She crouch'd, she tore him part from part,
　　And out of his body she drew　　　　　　　　70
The red 'blood-eagle'[2] of liver and heart;
　　She held them up to the view;

19

She gabbled, as she groped in the dead,
　　And all the people were pleased;
'See, what a little heart,' she said,　　　　　　　75
　　'And the liver is half-diseased!'

20

She tore the prophet after death,
　　And the people paid her well.
Lightnings flicker'd along the heath;
　　One shriek'd, 'The fires of hell!'　　　　　　80

1885

The Ancient Sage[1]

A thousand summers ere the time of Christ,
From out his ancient city came a Seer[2]

2. "Old Viking term for lungs, liver, etc., when torn by the conqueror out of the body of the conquered" (Tennyson).
1. A synthesis of Tennyson's lifelong concern with the problems of faith, free will, immortality, and mysticism, "The Ancient Sage" embodies nearly all of the poet's more idealistic assumptions about life and death. "The whole poem," he said, "is very personal. The passages about 'Faith' and the 'Passion of the Past' were more especially my own personal feelings. This 'Passion of the Past' I used to feel when a boy" (*Memoir* II, 319). Tennyson had been reading of Lao-tse, a seventh-century B.C. Chinese philosopher, and noted that the poem expressed "what I might have believed about the deeper problems of life 'A thousand summers ere the birth of Christ.'" "My father considered this one of his best later poems" (Hallam Tennyson).
2. Lao-tse's name means "Old Philosopher."

Whom one that loved and honor'd him, and yet
Was no disciple, richly garb'd, but worn
From wasteful living, follow'd—in his hand   5
A scroll of verse—till that old man before
A cavern whence an affluent fountain pour'd
From darkness into daylight, turn'd and spoke:
    "This wealth of waters might but seem to draw
From yon dark cave, but, son, the source is higher,   10
Yon summit half-a-league in air—and higher
The cloud that hides it—higher still the heavens
Whereby the cloud was moulded, and whereout
The cloud descended. Force is from the heights.
I am wearied of our city, son, and go   15
To spend my one last year among the hills.
What hast thou there? Some death-song for the Ghouls
To make their banquet relish? let me read.

        "'How far thro' all the bloom and brake
        That nightingale is heard!   20
        What power but the bird's could make
        This music in the bird?
        How summer-bright are yonder skies,
        And earth as fair in hue!
        And yet what sign of aught that lies   25
        Behind the green and blue?
        But man to-day is fancy's fool
        As man hath ever been.
        The nameless Power, of Powers that rule
        Were never heard or seen.'   30

If thou wouldst hear the Nameless, and wilt dive
Into the temple-cave of thine own self,[3]
There, brooding by the central altar, thou
Mayst haply learn the Nameless hath a voice,
By which thou wilt abide, if thou be wise,   35
As if thou knewest, tho' thou canst not know;
For Knowledge[4] is the swallow on the lake
That sees and stirs the surface-shadow there
But never yet hath dipt into the abysm,
The abysm of all abysms, beneath, within   40
The blue of sky and sea, the green of earth,
And in the million-millionth of a grain
Which cleft and cleft again for evermore,
And ever vanishing, never vanishes,
To me, my son, more mystic than myself,   45
Or even than the Nameless is to me.
    "And when thou sendest thy free soul thro' heaven,
Nor understandest bound nor boundlessness,
Thou seest the Nameless of the hundred names.
    "And if the Nameless should withdraw from all   50

3. Compare *IM* 124, 4.
4. Compare *IM* "Prologue."

Thy frailty counts most real, all thy world
Might vanish like thy shadow in the dark.

  "'And since—from when this earth began—
   The Nameless never came
   Among us, never spake with man,   55
   And never named the Name'—

Thou canst not prove the Nameless, O my son,
Nor canst thou prove the world thou movest in,
Thou canst not prove that thou art body alone,
Nor canst thou prove that thou art spirit alone,   60
Nor canst thou prove that thou art both in one.
Thou canst not prove thou art immortal, no,
Nor yet that thou art mortal—nay, my son,
Thou canst not prove that I, who speak with thee,
Am not thyself in converse with thyself,   65
For nothing worthy proving can be proven,
Nor yet disproven.[5] Wherefore thou be wise,
Cleave ever to the sunnier side of doubt,
And cling to Faith beyond the forms of Faith!
She reels not in the storm of warring words,   70
She brightens at the clash of 'Yes' and 'No,'
She sees the best that glimmers thro' the worst,
She feels the sun is hid but for a night,
She spies the summer thro' the winter bud,
She tastes the fruit before the blossom falls,   75
She hears the lark within the songless egg,
She finds the fountain where they wail'd 'Mirage!'

  "'What Power? aught akin to Mind,
   The mind in me and you?
  Or power as of the Gods gone blind   80
   Who see not what they do?'

But some in yonder city hold, my son,
That none but gods could build this house of ours,
So beautiful, vast, various,[6] so beyond
All work of man, yet, like all work of man,   85
A beauty with defect—till That which knows,
And is not known, but felt thro' what we feel
Within ourselves is highest, shall descend
On this half-deed, and shape it at the last
According to the Highest in the Highest.   90

  "'What Power but the Years that make
   And break the vase of clay,
  And stir the sleeping earth, and wake
   The bloom that fades away?
  What rulers but the Days and Hours   95
   That cancel weal with woe,

---

5. Essentially the same reasoning was used in "The Two Voices" to defeat the arguments of the negative voice.
6. Ricks compares Arnold's "Dover Beach," line 32: The world "so various, so beautiful."

And wind the front of youth with flowers,
And cap our age with snow?'

The days and hours are ever glancing by,
And seem to flicker past thro' sun and shade,   100
Or short, or long, as Pleasure leads, or Pain,
But with the Nameless is nor day nor hour;
Tho' we, thin minds, who creep from thought to thought,
Break into 'Thens' and 'Whens' the Eternal Now—
This double seeming of the single world!—   105
My words are like the babblings in a dream
Of nightmare, when the babblings break the dream.
But thou be wise in this dream-world of ours,
Nor take thy dial for thy deity,
But make the passing shadow serve thy will.   110

        "'The years that made the stripling wise
            Undo their work again,
        And leave him, blind of heart and eyes,
            The last and least of men;
        Who clings to earth, and once would dare   115
            Hell-heat or Arctic cold,
        And now one breath of cooler air
            Would loose him from his hold.
        His winter chills him to the root,
            He withers marrow and mind;   120
        The kernel of the shrivell'd fruit
            Is jutting thro' the rind;
        The tiger spasms tear his chest,
            The palsy wags his head;
        The wife, the sons, who love him best   125
            Would fain that he were dead;
        The griefs by which he once was wrung
            Were never worth the while'—

Who knows? or whether this earth-narrow life
Be yet but yolk, and forming in the shell?   130

        "'The shaft of scorn that once had stung
            But wakes a dotard smile.'

The placid gleam of sunset after storm!

        "'The statesman's brain that sway'd the past
            Is feebler than his knees;   135
        The passive sailor wrecks at last
            In ever-silent seas;
        The warrior hath forgot his arms,
            The learned all his lore;
        The changing market frets or charms   140
            The merchant's hope no more:
        The prophet's beacon burn'd in vain,
            And now is lost in cloud;
        The plowman passes, bent with pain,

To mix with what he plow'd;[7] 145
The poet whom his age would quote
As heir of endless fame —
He knows not even the book he wrote,
Not even his own name.
For man has overlived his day, 150
And, darkening in the light,
Scarce feels the senses break away
To mix with ancient Night.'

The shell must break before the bird can fly.

"'The years that when my youth began 155
Had set the lily and rose
By all my ways where'er they ran,
Have ended mortal foes;
My rose of love for ever gone,
My lily of truth and trust — 160
They made her lily and rose in one,
And changed her into dust.
O rose-tree planted in my grief,
And growing on her tomb,
Her dust is greening in your leaf, 165
Her blood is in your bloom.
O slender lily waving there,
And laughing back the light,
In vain you tell me "Earth is fair"
When all is dark as night.' 170

My son, the world is dark with griefs and graves,
So dark that men cry out against the heavens.
Who knows but that the darkness is in man?
The doors of Night may be the gates of Light;
For wert thou born or blind or deaf, and then 175
Suddenly heal'd, how wouldst thou glory in all
The splendors and the voices of the world!
And we, the poor earth's dying race, and yet
No phantoms, watching from a phantom shore
Await the last and largest sense to make 180
The phantom walls of this illusion fade,
And show us that the world is wholly fair.

"'But vain the tears for darken'd years
As laughter over wine,
And vain the laughter as the tears, 185
O brother, mine or thine,
For all that laugh, and all that weep
And all that breathe are one

---

7. Ricks compares the opening of "Tithonus": "Man comes and tills the field and lies beneath." Compare
the opening stanza of Gray's "Elegy Written in a Country Churchyard":
    The curfew tolls the knell of parting day,
        The lowing herd wind slowly o'er the lea,
    The plowman homeward plods his weary way,
        And leaves the world to darkness and to me.

Slight ripple on the boundless deep
  That moves, and all is gone.'   190

But that one ripple on the boundless deep
Feels that the deep is boundless, and itself
For ever changing form, but evermore
One with the boundless motion of the deep.

    "'Yet wine and laughter, friends! and set   195
      The lamps alight, and call
    For golden music, and forget
      The darkness of the pall.'

If utter darkness closed the day, my son—
But earth's dark forehead flings athwart the heavens   200
Her shadow crown'd with stars—and yonder—out
To northward—some that never set, but pass
From sight and night to lose themselves in day.
I hate the black negation of the bier,[8]
And wish the dead, as happier than ourselves   205
And higher, having climb'd one step beyond
Our village miseries, might be borne in white
To burial or to burning, hymn'd from hence
With songs in praise of death, and crown'd with flowers!

    "'O worms and maggots of to-day   210
      Without their hope of wings!'"

But louder than thy rhyme the silent Word
Of that world-prophet in the heart of man.

    "'Tho' some have gleams, or so they say,
      Of more than mortal things.'   215

To-day? but what of yesterday? for oft
On me, when boy, there came what then I call'd,
Who knew no books and no philosophies,
In my boy-phrase, 'The Passion of the Past.'[9]
The first gray streak of earliest summer-dawn,   220
The last long stripe of waning crimson gloom,
As if the late and early were but one—
A height, a broken grange, a grove, a flower
Had murmurs, 'Lost and gone, and lost and gone!'
A breath, a whisper—some divine farewell[1]—   225
Desolate sweetness—far and far away—
What had he loved, what had he lost, the boy?
I know not, and I speak of what has been.

---

8. Upon his mother's death in 1865, Tennyson said: "We all of us hate the pompous funeral we have to join in, black plumes, black coaches and nonsense. We should like all to go in white and gold rather" (*Memoir* II, 18–19).
9. "This Passion of the Past I used to feel when a boy" (Tennyson), as noted above.
1. Compare "Tears, Idle Tears": "Tears from the depth of some divine despair . . . And thinking of the days that are no more."

"And more, my son! for more than once when I
Sat all alone, revolving in myself   230
The word that is the symbol of myself,
The mortal limit of the Self was loosed,
And past into the Nameless, as a cloud
Melts into heaven. I touch'd my limbs, the limbs
Were strange, not mine—and yet no shade of doubt,   235
But utter clearness, and thro' loss of self
The gain of such large life as match'd with ours
Were sun to spark—unshadowable in words,
Themselves but shadows of a shadow-world.[2]

   "'And idle gleams will come and go,   240
    But still the clouds remain;'

The clouds themselves are children of the Sun.

   "'And Night and Shadow rule below
    When only Day should reign.'

And Day and Night are children of the Sun,   245
And idle gleams to thee are light to me.
Some say, the Light was father of the Night,
And some, the Night was father of the Light,
No night, no day!—I touch thy world again—
No ill, no good! such counter-terms, my son,   250
Are border-races, holding each its own
By endless war. But night enough is there
In yon dark city. Get thee back; and since
The key to that weird casket, which for thee
But holds a skull, is neither thine nor mine,   255
But in the hand of what is more than man,
Or in man's hand when man is more than man,
Let be thy wail, and help thy fellow-men,
And make thy gold thy vassal, not thy king,
And fling free alms into the beggar's bowl,   260
And send the day into the darken'd heart;
Nor list for guerdon in the voice of men,
A dying echo from a falling wall;
Nor care—for Hunger hath the evil eye—
To vex the noon with fiery gems, or fold   265
Thy presence in the silk of sumptuous looms;

2. "This is also a personal experience which I have had more than once" (Tennyson). "My most passionate desire is to have a clearer and fuller vision of God. The soul seems to me one with God, how I cannot tell. . . . A kind of waking trance I have frequently had, quite up from boyhood, when I have been all alone. This has generally come upon me thro' repeating my own name two or three times to myself silently, till all at once, as it were out of the intensity of the consciousness of individuality, the individuality itself seemed to dissolve and fade away into boundless being, and this is not a confused state, but the clearest of the clearest (*Memoir* I, 319–20).

"There are moments," he said, "when the flesh is nothing to me, when I feel and know the flesh to be the vision, God and the Spiritual the only real and true. Depend upon it, the Spiritual *is* the real: it belongs to one more than the hand and the foot. You may tell me that my hand and my foot are only imaginary symbols of my existence, I could believe you; but you never, never can convince me that the *I* is not an eternal Reality, and that the Spiritual is not the true and real part of me" (*Memoir* II, 90). See also *IM* 95; and King Arthur's speech in "The Holy Grail," lines 906–15.

Nor roll thy viands on a luscious tongue,
Nor drown thyself with flies in honeyed wine;
Nor thou be rageful, like a handled bee,
And lose thy life by usage of thy sting;   270
Nor harm an adder thro' the lust for harm,
Nor make a snail's horn shrink for wantonness.
And more—think well! Do-well will follow thought,
And in the fatal sequence of this world
An evil thought may soil thy children's blood;   275
But curb the beast would cast thee in the mire,[3]
And leave the hot swamp of voluptuousness,
A cloud between the Nameless and thyself,
And lay thine uphill shoulder to the wheel,
And climb the Mount of Blessing, whence, if thou   280
Look higher, then—perchance—thou mayest—beyond
A hundred ever-rising mountain lines,
And past the range of Night and Shadow—see
The high-heaven dawn of more than mortal day
Strike on the Mount of Vision![4]
　　　　　　　　So, farewell."   285

　　　　　　　　　　　　　　　　　　　　1885

Vastness[1]

1
Many a hearth upon our dark globe sighs after many a vanish'd face.
Many a planet by many a sun may roll with the dust of a vanish'd race.

2
Raving politics, never at rest—as this poor earth's pale history runs,—
What is it all but a trouble of ants in the gleam of a million million of suns?

3
Lies upon this side, lies upon that side, truthless violence mourn'd by the
　　wise,   5
Thousands of voices drowning his own in a popular torrent of lies upon lies;

3. Throughout the later *Idylls of the King* the use of the beast metaphor expresses Tennyson's preoccupation with scientific materialism and its consequences following acceptance of the Darwinian hypothesis. Although the application of the metaphor underwent little change from the 1840s, the ideas informing it were not static. One may notice that in the late poems the city, which earlier had been rendered as the locus of all that is high and holy, is no longer the corrective metaphor it once was. Tennyson toward the end of his life adopts a Dickensian view of the city.
4. Compare 2 Peter 1:18–19: "The holy mount . . . as unto a light that shineth in a dark place" (Ricks).
1. Although "The Ancient Sage" expresses the poet's optimistic beliefs, "Vastness" shows the mood of delusion more characteristic of his last years. In an attempt at objectivity lacking in "Locksley Hall, Sixty Years After," he asks yet once more the question that had so deeply concerned him throughout his life: "Hast thou made all this for naught! Is all this trouble of life worth undergoing if we only end in our own corpse-coffins at last? If you allow a God, and God allows this strong instinct and universal yearning for another life, surely that is in a measure a presumption of its truth" (*Memoir* I, 321).

4

Stately purposes, valor in battle, glorious annals of army and fleet,
Death for the right cause, death for the wrong cause, trumpets of victory,
    groans of defeat;

5

Innocence seethed in her mother's milk,[2] and Charity setting the martyr
    aflame
Thraldom who walks with the banner of Freedom, and recks not to ruin a
    realm in her name   10

6

Faith at the zenith, or all but lost in the gloom of doubts that darken the
    schools;
Craft with a bunch of all-heal[3] in her hand, follow'd up by her vassal legion
    of fools;

7

Trade flying over a thousand seas with her spice and her vintage, her silk
    and her corn;
Desolate offing, sailorless harbors, famishing populace, wharves forlorn;

8

Star of the morning, Hope in the sunrise; gloom of the evening, Life at a
    close;   15
Pleasure who flaunts on her wide downway with her flying robe and her
    poison'd rose;

9

Pain, that has crawl'd from the corpse of Pleasure, a worm which writhes all
    day, and at night
Stirs up again in the heart of the sleeper, and stings him back to the curse of
    the light;

10

Wealth with his wines and his wedded harlots; honest Poverty, bare to the
    bone;
Opulent Avarice, lean as Poverty; Flattery gilding the rift in a throne;   20

11

Fame blowing out from her golden trumpet a jubilant challenge to Time
    and to Fate;
Slander, her shadow, sowing the nettle on all the laurell'd graves of the great;

12

Love for the maiden, crown'd with marriage, no regrets for aught that has been,
Household happiness, gracious children, debtless competence, golden mean;

2. Exodus 34:26: "Thou shalt not seethe a kid in his mother's milk."
3. An herb for all maladies, generally associated with rustics' remedies.

13

National hatreds of whole generations, and pigmy spites of the village
   spire;   25
Vows that will last to the last death-ruckle, and vows that are snapt in a
   moment of fire;

14

He that has lived for the lust of the minute, and died in the doing it, flesh
   without mind;
He that has nail'd all flesh to the Cross, till Self died out in the love of his kind;

15

Spring and Summer and Autumn and Winter, and all these old revolutions
   of earth;
All new-old revolutions of Empire—change of the tide—what is all of it
   worth?   30

16

What the philosophies, all the sciences, poesy, varying voices of prayer,
All that is noblest, all that is basest, all that is filthy with all that is fair?

17

What is it all, if we all of us end but in being our own corpse-coffins at last?
Swallow'd in Vastness, lost in Silence, drown'd in the deeps of a meaningless
   Past?

18

What but a murmur of gnats in the gloom, or a moment's anger of bees in
   their hive?—   35
Peace, let it be! for I loved him, and love him for ever: the dead are not
   dead but alive.[4]

1885

Locksley Hall Sixty Years After[1]

Late, my grandson! half the morning have I paced these sandly tracts,
Watch'd again the hollow ridges roaring into cataracts,

4. Tennyson glossed: "The last line means 'What matters anything in this world without faith in the immortality of the soul and of Love?'" The "him" is usually taken to be Arthur Hallam; but as Jerome Buckley has convincingly argued from earlier drafts that mention a brother, the reference is probably to
Charles. See *Tennyson*, pp. 231–32. Responding to Buckley, Ricks re-asserts the claim for Hallam, citing *IM* 9: "My friend, the brother of my love . . . / More than my brothers are to me." As is rather likely,
the identity will remain obscure forever; Tennyson variously loved them both to the mystery-depths as
with closest friends: "Loved deeplier, darklier understood" (*IM* 129, 3). Perhaps "Darkling I listen," Keats
to his unknowable nightingale, is enough to settle upon?
1. Contrary to Tennyson's assertion that he had written "a dramatic poem, and the Dramatis Personae are
imaginary," the views of the speaker are very close to the poet's own. Published forty-four years after
"Locksley Hall," the sequel thunders forth the opinions of an old man looking back in disillusionment
at his youthful optimism and faith in progress. "It seemed to my father," Hallam noted, "that the two
Locksley Halls were likely to be in the future two of the most historically interesting of his poems, as descriptive of the tone of the age at two distinct periods of his life."
    Tennyson went to some length to dissociate himself from the speaker. "My father said that the old man
in the second 'Locksley Hall' had a stronger faith in God and in human goodness than he had had in

Wander'd back to living boyhood while I heard the curlews call,
I myself so close on death, and death itself in Locksley Hall.

So—your happy suit was blasted—she the faultless, the divine;   5
And you liken—boyish babble—this boy-love of yours with mine.

I myself have often babbled doubtless of a foolish past;
Babble, babble; our old England may go down in babble at last.

'Curse him!' curse your fellow-victim? call him dotard in your rage?
Eyes that lured a doting boyhood well might fool a dotard's age.   10

Jilted for a wealthier! wealthier? yet perhaps she was not wise;
I remember how you kiss'd the miniature with those sweet eyes.

In the hall there hangs a painting—Amy's arms about my neck—
Happy children in a sunbeam sitting on the ribs of wreck.

In my life there was a picture, she that clasp'd my neck had flown;   15
I was left within the shadow sitting on the wreck alone.[2]

Yours has been a slighter ailment, will you sicken for her sake?
You, not you! your modern amorist is of easier, earthlier make.

Amy loved me, Amy fail'd me, Amy was a timid child;
But your Judith—but your worldling—*she* had never driven me wild.   20

She that holds the diamond necklace dearer than the golden ring,
She that finds a winter sunset[3] fairer than a morn of spring.

She that in her heart is brooding on his briefer lease of life,
While she vows 'till death shall part us,' she the would-be-widow wife.

She the worldling born of worldlings—father, mother—be content,   25
Even the homely farm can teach us there is something in descent.

Yonder in that chapel, slowly sinking now into the ground,
Lies the warrior, my forefather, with his feet upon the hound.

Cross'd![4] for once he sail'd the sea to crush the Moslem in his pride;
Dead the warrior, dead his glory, dead the cause in which he died.   30

---

his youth"—a point, particularly the latter, that is difficult to discover in the poem itself. His son continued: "But he had also endeavored to give the moods of despondency which are caused by the decreased energy of life," a point not difficult to discover (*Memoir* II, 329). Tennyson wrote to Charles Esmarch (*Letters* III, 366–67, April 18, 1888): "I must object and strongly to the statement in your preface that *I* am the hero in either poem. I never had a cousin Amy. Locksley Hall is an entirely imagined edifice. My grandsons are little boys. I am not white-haired, I never had a gray hair in my head. The whole thing is a dramatic impersonation, but I find in almost all modern criticism this absurd tendency to personalities. Some of my thoughts *may* come out in the poem, but am I therefore the hero? *There is not one touch of autobiography in it from end to end*" (see also *Memoir* II, 331). The protest is perhaps simply too much; it's the speaker's tone, rather than the tone of the age, that forges the link.
2. Lines 13–16, Tennyson said, "were the nucleus of the poem, and were written fifty years ago."
3. I.e., marriage to the older man.
4. The statue's crossed feet indicate that he had been a crusader.

Yet how often I and Amy in the mouldering aisle have stood,
Gazing for one pensive moment on that founder of our blood.

There again I stood to-day, and where of old we knelt in prayer,
Close beneath the casement crimson with the shield of Locksley—there,

All in white Italian marble, looking still as if she smiled,   35
Lies my Amy dead in childbirth, dead the mother, dead the child.

Dead—and sixty years ago, and dead her aged husband now—
I, this old white-headed dreamer, stoopt and kiss'd her marble brow.

Gone the fires of youth, the follies, furies, curses, passionate tears,
Gone like fires and floods and earthquakes of the planet's dawning years.   40

Fires that shook me once, but now to silent ashes fallen away.
Cold upon the dead volcano sleeps the gleam of dying day.[5]

Gone the tyrant[6] of my youth, and mute below the chancel stones,
All his virtues—I forgive them—black in white[7] above his bones.

Gone the comrades of my bivouac, some in fight against the foe,   45
Some thro' age and slow diseases, gone as all on earth will go.

Gone with whom for forty years my life in golden sequence ran,
She with all the charm of woman, she with all the breadth of man,[8]

Strong in will and rich in wisdom, Edith, yet so lowly-sweet,
Woman to her inmost heart, and woman to her tender feet,   50

Very woman of very woman, nurse of ailing body and mind,
She that link'd again the broken chain that bound me to my kind.

Here to-day was Amy with me, while I wander'd down the coast,
Near us Edith's holy shadow, smiling at the slighter ghost.

Gone our sailor son thy father, Leonard early lost at sea;   55
Thou alone, my boy, or Amy's kin and mine art left to me.

Gone thy tender-natured mother, wearying to be left alone,
Pining for the stronger heart that once had beat beside her own.

Truth, for truth is truth, he worshipt, being true as he was brave;
Good, for good is good, he follow'd, yet he look'd beyond the grave,[9]   60

5. "My father always quoted this line as the most imaginative in the poem" (Hallam Tennyson).
6. The "selfish uncle" (see "Locksley Hall," line 156), whose ward he became after his father's death.
7. The inscription, lettered in black, has been carved in a white stone slab. "Half a century after his grandfather's death Tennyson still resented his grandfather and the tablet to his memory so deeply that [here]
   he refers to the tomb in Tealby Church" (Martin's *Tennyson*, p. 213).
8. In manuscript the line read, "As our greatest is man-woman, so was she the woman-man" (noted by
   Ricks). "What he called 'the man-woman' in Christ, the union of tenderness and strength" (*Memoir* I,
   326). Compare *IM* and Hallam, 109, 5.
9. This couplet and lines 71–72 were written in April 1886, just after Tennyson learned that his son Lionel
   had died while returning home from India.

Wiser there than you, that crowning barren Death as lord of all,
Deem this over-tragic drama's closing curtain is the pall!

Beautiful was death in him, who saw the death, but kept the deck,
Saving women and their babes, and sinking with the sinking wreck,

Gone for ever! Ever? no—for since our dying race began,   65
Ever, ever, and for ever was the leading light of man.
Those that in barbarian burials kill'd the slave, and slew the wife
Felt within themselves the sacred passion of the second life.

Indian warriors dream of ampler hunting grounds beyond the night;
Even the black Australian dying hopes he shall return, a white.   70

Truth for truth, and good for good! The good, the true, the pure, the just—
Take the charm 'For ever' from them, and they crumble into dust.

Gone the cry of 'Forward, Forward,' lost within a growing gloom;
Lost, or only heard in silence from the silence of a tomb.

Half the marvels of my morning, triumphs over time and space,   75
Staled by frequence, shrunk by usage into commonest commonplace!

'Forward' rang the voices then, and of the many mine was one.
Let us hush this cry of 'Forward' till ten thousand years have gone.

Far among the vanish'd races, old Assyrian kings would flay
Captives whom they caught in battle—iron-hearted victors they.   80

Ages after, while in Asia, he that led the wild Moguls,
Timur[1] built his ghastly tower of eighty thousand human skulls;

Then, and here in Edward's time,[2] an age of noblest English names,
Christian conquerors took and flung the conquer'd Christian into flames.

Love your enemy, bless your haters, said the Greatest of the great;   85
Christian love among the Churches look'd the twin of heathen hate.

From the golden alms of Blessing man had coin'd himself a curse:
Rome of Cæsar, Rome of Peter, which was crueller? which was worse?

France had shown a light to all men, preach'd a Gospel, all men's good;
Celtic Demos rose a Demon, shriek'd and slaked the light with blood.[3] 90

Hope was ever on her mountain, watching till the day begun—
Crown'd with sunlight—over darkness—from the still unrisen sun.

---

1. Tamerlane (1336–1405), whose Asian conquests resulted in several massive slaughters.
2. Alludes to the reign of Edward VI (1547–53), when the Catholics were persecuted; his successor, Bloody Mary (1553–58), persecuted the Protestants.
3. Alludes to the French Revolution of 1789 and the Reign of Terror in 1793–94. "Demos": common people.

Have we grown at last beyond the passion of the primal clan?
'Kill your enemy, for you hate him,' still, 'your enemy' was a man.

Have we sunk below them? peasants maim[4] the helpless horse, and drive   95
Innocent cattle under thatch, and burn the kindlier brutes alive.
Brutes, the brutes are not your wrongers—burnt at midnight, found at
    morn,
Twisted hard in mortal agony with their offspring, born-unborn,

Clinging to the silent mother! Are we devils? are we men?
Sweet Saint Francis[5] of Assisi, would that he were here again,   100

He that in his Catholic wholeness used to call the very flowers
Sisters, brothers—and the beasts—whose pains are hardly less than ours!

Chaos, Cosmos! Cosmos, Chaos! who can tell how all will end?
Read the wide world's annals, you, and take their wisdom for your friend.

Hope the best, but hold the present fatal daughter of the Past,   105
Shape your heart to front the hour, but dream not that the hour will last.

Ay, if dynamite and revolver leave you courage to be wise—
When was age so cramm'd with menace? madness? written, spoken lies?

Envy wears the mask of Love, and, laughing sober fact to scorn,
Cries to weakest as to strongest, 'Ye are equals, equal-born.'   110

Equal-born? O, yes, if yonder hill be level with the flat.
Charm us, orator, till the lion look no larger than the cat,

Till the cat thro' that mirage of overheated language loom
Larger than the lion,—Demos end in working its own doom.

Russia burst our Indian barrier,[6] shall we fight her? shall we yield?   115
Pause! before you sound the trumpet, hear the voices from the field.

Those three hundred millions under one Imperial sceptre now,
Shall we hold them? shall we loose them? take the suffrage of the plow.[7]

Nay, but these would feel and follow Truth if only you and you,
Rivals of realm-ruining party, when you speak were wholly true.   120

---

4. "The modern Irish cruelties" (Tennyson), alluding to the uprisings in the 1880s over Home Rule. From
the queen's private journal and her meeting with Tennyson in 1883: "He spoke of Ireland, and the
wickedness of ill-using poor animals: 'I am afraid I think the world is darkened; I dare say it will brighten
again'" (Memoir II, 457).
5. Chiefly known for his tenderness toward all living creatures.
6. The Panjdeh incident of 1885 involved another of Russia's periodic attempts to gain entry into India
through Afghanistan, which the British regarded as a buffer zone.
7. I.e., let the farm laborer's vote (a right granted by Parliament in 1884) decide the fate of India, which
had become part of the Empire in 1877.

Plowmen, shepherds,[8] have I found, and more than once, and still could
    find,
Sons of God,[9] and kings of men in utter nobleness of mind,

Truthful, trustful, looking upward to the practised hustings-liar,[1]
So the higher wields the lower, while the lower is the higher.

Here and there a cotter's babe is royal-born by right divine;				125
Here and there my lord is lower than his oxen or his swine.

Chaos, Cosmos! Cosmos, Chaos! once again the sickening game;
Freedom, free to slay herself, and dying while they shout her name.

Step by step we gain'd a freedom known to Europe, known to all;
Step by step we rose to greatness,—thro' the tonguesters we may fall.		130

You that woo the Voices[2]—tell them 'old' experience is a fool,'
Teach your flatter'd kings that only those who cannot read can rule.

Pluck the mighty from their seat, but set no meek ones in their place;
Pillory Wisdom in your markets, pelt your offal at her face.

Tumble Nature heel o'er head, and, yelling with the yelling street,		135
Set the feet above the brain and swear the brain is in the feet.

Bring the old dark ages back without the faith, without the hope,
Break the State, the Church, the Throne, and roll their ruins down the slope.

Authors—essayist, atheist, novelist, realist, rhymester, play your part,
Paint the mortal shame of nature with the living hues of art.			140

Rip your brothers' vices open, strip your own foul passions bare;
Down with Reticence, down with Reverence—forward—naked—let them
    stare.

Feed the budding rose of boyhood with the drainage of your sewer;
Send the drain into the fountain, lest the stream should issue pure.

Set the maiden fancies wallowing in the troughs of Zolaism,[3]—			145
Forward, forward, ay, and backward, downward too into the abysm!

Do your best to charm the worst, to lower the rising race of men;
Have we risen from out the beast, then back into the beast again?[4]

8. "The three following verses show that the hero does not (as has been said) by any means dislike the
   democracy" (Tennyson).
9. "Compare *John*, 1:12–13: 'But as many as received him, to them gave he power to become the sons of
   god, even to them that believe on his Name: Which were born, not of blood, nor of the will of the flesh,
   nor of the will of man, but of God'" (Ricks).
1. A lying political campaigner.
2. Votes.
3. The popularity of Émile Zola, whose naturalistic novels such as *Nana* (1880) dealt openly with prosti-
   tution and dissipation, was to Tennyson symptomatic of England's susceptibility to the cultural decadence he had long associated with France.
4. Compare, "All my realm / Reels back into the beast," "The Passing of Arthur," lines 25–26 and notes.

Only 'dust to dust' for me that sicken at your lawless din,
Dust in wholesome old-world dust before the newer world begin.   150

Heated am I? you—you wonder—well, it scarce becomes mine age—
Patience! let the dying actor mouth his last upon the stage.

Cries of unprogressive dotage ere the dotard fall asleep?
Noises or a current narrowing, not the music of a deep?

Ay, for doubtless I am old, and think gray thoughts, for I am gray;   155
After all the stormy changes shall we find a changeless May?

After madness, after massacre, Jacobinism and Jacquerie;[5]
Some diviner force to guide us thro' the days I shall not see?

When the schemes and all the systems, kingdoms and republics fall,
Something kindlier, higher, holier—all for each and each for all?   160

All the full-brain, half-brain races, led by Justice, Love, and Truth;
All the millions one at length with all the visions of my youth?

All diseases quench'd by Science, no man halt, or deaf, or blind;
Stronger ever born of weaker, lustier body, larger mind?

Earth at last a warless world, a single race, a single tongue—   165
I have seen her far away—for is not Earth as yet so young?—

Every tiger madness muzzled, every serpent passion kill'd,
Every grim ravine a garden, every blazing desert till'd,

Robed in universal harvest up to either pole she smiles,
Universal ocean softly washing all her warless isles.   170

Warless? when her tens are thousands, and her thousands millions, then—
All her harvest all too narrow—who can fancy warless men?

Warless? war will die out late then. Will it ever? late or soon?
Can it, till this outworn earth be dead as yon dead world the moon?

Dead the new astronomy calls her.—On this day and at this hour,   175
In this gap between the sandhills, whence you see the Locksley tower,

Here we met, our latest meeting—Amy—sixty years ago—
She and I—the moon was falling greenish thro' a rosy glow.[6]

Just above the gateway tower, and even where you see her now—
Here we stood and claspt each other, swore the seeming-deathless vow.—   180

---

5. "Originally a revolt in 1358 against the Picardy nobles; and afterwards applied to insurrections of the
   mob. This and the eight following verses show that he is not a pessimist, I think" (Tennyson). "Jacobinism": the Jacobins were originally liberal members of the National Assembly (1789) and became increasingly radical and played a major role in the Reign of Terror.
6. "The tints at twilight were due to the eruption of Krakatoa in August 1883" (Ricks).

Dead, but how her living glory lights the hall, the dune, the grass!
Yet the moonlight is the sunlight, and the sun himself will pass.

Venus near her! smiling downward at this earlier earth of ours,
Closer on the sun, perhaps a world of never fading flowers.

Hesper, whom the poet[7] call'd the Bringer home of all good things—   185
All good things may move in Hesper, perfect peoples, perfect kings.

Hesper—Venus—were we native to that splendor or in Mars,
We should see the globe we groan in, fairest of their evening stars.

Could we dream of wars and carnage, craft and madness, lust and spite,
Roaring London, raving Paris, in that point of peaceful light?   190

Might we not in glancing heavenward on a star so silver-fair,
Yearn, and clasp the bands and murmur, 'Would to God that we were there'?

Forward, backward, backward, forward, in the immeasurable sea,
Sway'd by vaster ebbs and flows than can be known to you or me.

All the suns—are these but symbols of innumerable man,   195
Man or Mind that sees a shadow of the planner or the plan?

Is there evil but on earth? or pain in every peopled sphere?
Well, be grateful for the sounding watchword 'Evolution' here,

Evolution ever climbing after some ideal good.
And Reversion ever dragging Evolution[8] in the mud.   200

What are men that He should heed us? cried the king[9] of sacred song;
Insects of an hour, that hourly work their brother insect wrong,

While the silent heavens roll, and suns along their fiery way,
All their planets whirling round them, flash a million miles a day.

Many an æon moulded earth before her highest, man, was born,   205
Many an æon too may pass when earth is manless and forlorn,

Earth so huge, and yet so bounded—pools of salt, and plots of land—
Shallow skin of green and azure—chains of mountain, grains of sand!

Only That which made us meant us to be mightier by and by,
Set the sphere of all the boundless heavens within the human eye,   210

---

7. Sappho, in the line, "Oh, Hesperus! Thou bringest all things home."
8. Even before publication of Darwin's *Origin of Species* (1859), the idea of evolution seemed to promise
    scientific support to the popular notion of society's inevitable progress toward an earthly utopia (see
    "Locksley Hall," lines 119ff.). But as the real implications of the Darwinian hypothesis were assimilated
    during the 1870s and 1880s—notably, that the process involved almost incredibly long periods of time
    and that survival of the ethically best in human terms had nothing to do with natural laws—the "myth
    of Evolution" gradually lost its adherents.
9. David. See Psalm 8:4.

Sent the shadow of Himself, the boundless, thro' the human soul;
Boundless inward in the atom, boundless outward in the Whole.

   . . . .

Here is Locksley Hall, my grandson, here the lion-guarded gate.
Not to-night in Locksley Hall—to-morrow—you, you come so late.

Wreck'd—your train—or all but wreck'd? a shatter'd wheel? a vicious boy!   215
Good, this forward, you that preach it, is it well to wish you joy?

Is it well that while we range with Science, glorying in the Time,
City children soak and blacken soul and sense in city slime?

There among the glooming alleys Progress halts on palsied feet,
Crime and hunger cast our maidens by the thousand on the street.   220

There the master scrimps his haggard sempstress of her daily bread,
There a single sordid attic holds the living and the dead.

There the smouldering fire of fever creeps across the rotted floor,
And the crowded couch of incest in the warrens of the poor.[1]

Nay, your pardon, cry your 'Forward,' yours are hope and youth, but I—   225
Eighty winters leave the dog too lame to follow with the cry,

Lame and old, and past his time, and passing now into the night;
Yet I would the rising race were half as eager for the light.

Light the fading gleam of even? light the glimmer of the dawn?
Aged eyes may take the growing glimmer for the gleam withdrawn.   230

Far away beyond her myriad coming changes earth will be
Something other than the wildest modern guess of you and me.

Earth may reach her earthly-worst, or if she gain her earthly-best,
Would she find her human offspring this ideal man at rest?

Forward then, but still remember how the course of Time will swerve,   235
Crook and turn upon itself in many a backward streaming curve.

Not the Hall to-night, my grandson! Death and Silence hold their own.
Leave the master[2] in the first dark hour of his last sleep alone.

Worthier soul was he than I am, sound and honest, rustic Squire,
Kindly landlord, boon companion—youthful jealousy is a liar.   240

---

1. Throughout most of his life, Tennyson's associations with the city were predominately positive. Here, as in much of the late poetry, he reverts to a Dickensian view of the city as a product of the bad effects of the Industrial Revolution. His four-line poem "Beautiful City" (1889) sarcastically captures some of the bitterness:
    Beautiful city, the centre and crater of European confusion,
    O you with your passionate shriek for the rights of an equal humanity,
    How often your Re-volution has proven but E-volution
    Roll'd again back on itself in the tides of a civic insanity!
2. Amy's husband and the speaker's rival, maligned in the first "Locksley Hall."

Cast the poison from your bosom, oust the madness from your brain.
Let the trampled serpent show you that you have not lived in vain.

Youthful youth and age are scholars yet but in the lower school,
Nor is he the wisest man who never proved himself a fool.

Yonder lies our young sea-village—Art and Greece are less and less: 245
Science grows and Beauty dwindles—roofs of slated hideousness!

There is one old hostel left us where they swing the Locksley shield,
Till the peasant cow shall butt the 'lion passant' from his field.[3]

Poor old Heraldry, poor old History, poor old Poetry, passing hence,
In the common deluge drowning old political common-sense!   250

Poor old voice of eighty crying after voices that have fled!
All I loved are vanish'd voices, all my steps are on the dead.

All the world is ghost to me, and as the phantom disappears,
Forward far and far from here is all the hope of eighty years.
                . . . .
In this hostel—I remember—I repent it o'er his grave—   255
Like a clown—by chance he met me—I refused the hand he gave.

From that casement where the trailer mantles all the mouldering bricks—
I was then in early boyhood, Edith but a child of six—

While I shelter'd in this archway from a day of driving showers—
Peept the winsome face of Edith like a flower among the flowers.   260

Here to-night! the Hall to-morrow, when they toll the chapel bell!
Shall I hear in one dark room a wailing, 'I have loved thee well'?

Then a peal that shakes the portal—one has come to claim his bride,
Her that shrank, and put me from her, shriek'd, and started from my side—

Silent echoes! You, my Leonard, use and not abuse your day,   265
Move among your people, know them, follow him who led the way,

Strove for sixty widow'd years to help his homelier brother men,
Served the poor, and built the cottage, raised the school, and drain'd the
    fen.

Hears he now the voice that wrong'd him? who shall swear it cannot be?
Earth would never touch her worst, were one in fifty such as he.   270

Ere she gain her heavenly-best, a God must mingle with the game.
Nay, there may be those about us whom we neither see nor name,

---

3. The surface of the Locksley shield, on which the coat-of-arms showed a "lion passant." In heraldry, a beast facing and walking toward the viewer's left with one front leg raised.

Felt within us as ourselves, the Powers of Good, the Powers of Ill,
Strowing balm, or shedding poison in the fountains of the will.

Follow you the star that lights a desert pathway, yours or mine,   275
Forward, till you see the Highest Human Nature is divine.

Follow Light, and do the Right—for man can half-control his doom—
Till you find the deathless Angel[4] seated in the vacant tomb.

Forward, let the stormy moment fly and mingle with the past.
I that loathed have come to love him. Love will conquer at the last.   280

Gone at eighty, mine own age, and I and you will bear the pall;
Then I leave thee lord and master, latest lord of Locksley Hall.

1886

Demeter and Persephone[1]

(In Enna)

Faint as a climate-changing bird that flies
All night across the darkness, and at dawn
Falls on the threshold of her native land,
And can no more, thou camest, O my child,
Led upward by the God[2] of ghosts and dreams,   5
Who laid thee at Eleusis,[3] dazed and dumb
With passing thro' at once from state to state,
Until I brought thee hither, that the day,
When here thy hands let fall the gather'd flower,
Might break thro' clouded memories once again   10
On thy lost self. A sudden nightingale
Saw thee, and flash'd into a frolic of song
And welcome, and a gleam as of the moon,
When first she peers along the tremulous deep,
Fled wavering o'er thy face, and chased away   15

4. The angel who rolled away the stone from Christ's tomb. See Matthew 28:1–7.
1. From boyhood Tennyson had shown interest in this myth, and indeed his earliest extant poem is his "Translation from Claudian's 'Proserpine.'" At the request of his son for a poem about Demeter, he said: "I will write it, but when I write an antique like this I must put it into a frame—something modern about it. It is no use giving a mere *réchauffé* of old legends" (*Memoir* II, 364). The illusive "something modern" is, however, never obtrusive, as it often is in *Idylls of the King*, and adds an enriching complexity to the poem. Robert Stange has provocatively said: "Since the story of Persephone is a myth of generation, the poet includes in his treatment of it not only the fertility of the soil and the creation of new life, but his definition of the attributes of the artist—imperial, disimpassioned, who moves between divided and distinguished worlds."
    Among Tennyson's sources were the Homeric *Hymn to Demeter* and Ovid's *Metamorphoses*. The earth goddess Demeter abandons her care of the crops while vainly searching for her daughter Persephone, who, when gathering flowers in the field of Enna, had been carried off by Dis, or Pluto, to be queen of Hades. To ensure the resumption of nature's productivity, Zeus finally arranges to have Persephone returned to her mother for nine months of every year. Sir James Frazer in *The Golden Bough* (the first volume of which appeared in 1890) observes that the origin of the myth was clearly an attempt to account for the seasonal cycles.
2. Hermes or Mercury, the messenger of the gods, whose staff is entwined with serpents (line 25)
3. A town near Athens where Demeter was worshiped.

That shadow of a likeness to the king
Of shadows, thy dark mate. Persephone!
Queen of the dead no more—my child! Thine eyes
Again were human-godlike, and the Sun
Burst from a swimming fleece of winter gray,   20
And robed thee in his day from head to feet—
"Mother!" and I was folded in thine arms.

    Child, those imperial, disimpassion'd eyes
Awed even me at first, thy mother—eyes
That oft had seen the serpent-wanded power   25
Draw downward into Hades with his drift
Of flickering spectres, lighted from below
By the red race of fiercy Phlegethon;[4]
But when before have Gods or men beheld
The Life that had descended re-arise,   30
And lighted from above him by the Sun?
So mighty was the mother's childless cry,
A cry that rang thro' Hades, Earth, and Heaven!

    So in this pleasant vale we stand again,
The field of Enna,[5] now once more ablaze   35
With flowers that brighten as thy footstep falls,
All flowers—but for one black blur of earth
Left by that closing chasm, thro' which the car
Of dark Aïdoneus[6] rising rapt thee hence.
And here, my child, tho' folded in thine arms,   40
I feel the deathless heart of motherhood
Within me shudder, lest the naked glebe
Should yawn once more into the gulf, and thence
The shrilly whinnyings of the team of Hell,
Ascending, pierce the glad and songful air,   45
And all at once their arch'd necks, midnight-maned,
Jet upward thro' the midday blossom. No!
For, see, thy foot has touch'd it; all the space
Of blank earth-baldness clothes itself afresh,
And breaks into the crocus-purple hour   50
That saw thee vanish.

             Child, when thou wert gone,
I envied human wives, and nested birds,
Yea, the cubb'd lioness; went in search of thee
Thro' many a palace, many a cot, and gave
Thy breast[7] to ailing infants in the night,   55
And set the mother waking in a maze
To find her sick one whole; and forth again
Among the wail of midnight winds, and cried,

---

4. In Hades, the river of fire.
5. Compare *Paradise Lost* IV, lines 268–72: "Not that fair field of Enna, where Proserpin gathering flowers, / Herself a fairer flower, by gloomy Dis / Was gathered, which cost Ceres all that pain / To seek her through the world." Stange notes similar echoes in the poem's opening lines.
6. Dis or Pluto.
7. Demeter's breast, which had suckled Persephone.

"Where is my loved one? Wherefore do ye wail?"
And out from all the night an answer shrill'd,   60
"We know not, and we know not why we wail."
I climb'd on all the cliffs of all the seas,
And ask'd the waves that moan about the world,
"Where? do ye make your moaning for my child?"
And round from all the world the voices came,   65
"We know not, and we know not why we moan."
"Where?" and I stared from every eagle-peak,[8]
I thridded[9] the black heart of all the woods,
I peer'd thro' tomb and cave, and in the storms
Of autumn swept across the city, and heard   70
The murmur of their temples chanting me,
Me, me, the desolate mother! "Where?" —and turn'd,
And fled by many a waste, forlorn of man,
And grieved for man thro' all my grief for thee,—
The jungle rooted in his shatter'd hearth,   75
The serpent coil'd about his broken shaft,
The scorpion crawling over naked skulls;—
I saw the tiger in the ruin'd fane
Spring from his fallen God, but trace of thee
I saw not; and far on, and, following out   80
A league of labyrinthine darkness, came
On three gray heads[1] beneath a gleaming rift.
"Where?" and I heard one voice from all the three,
"We know not, for we spin the lives of men,
And not of Gods, and know not why we spin!   85
There is a Fate beyond us."[2] Nothing knew.

        Last as the likeness of a dying man,
Without his knowledge, from him flits to warn
A far-off friendship that he comes no more,
So he, the God of dreams, who heard my cry,   90
Drew from thyself the likeness of thyself
Without thy knowledge, and thy shadow past
Before me, crying, "The Bright one in the highest
Is brother of the Dark one in the lowest,
And Bright and Dark have sworn that I, the child   95
Of thee, the great Earth-Mother, thee, the Power
That lifts her buried life from gloom to bloom,
Should be for ever and for evermore
The Bride of Darkness."

                So the Shadow wail'd.
Then I, Earth-Goddess, cursed the Gods of heaven.   100
I would not mingle with their feasts; to me
Their nectar smack'd of hemlock on the lips,

8. "'Stared,' 'eagle,' 'peak' suggest Keats, 'On First Looking into Chapman's Homer'" (Ricks).
9. Threaded.
1. The Fates.
2. Tennyson compares Virgil, *Eclogues* IV, lines 46–47: "'Ages such as these glide on!' cried to their spin-
dles the Fates, voicing in unison the fixed will of Destiny!"

Their rich ambrosia tasted aconite.[3]
That man, that only lives and loves an hour,
Seem'd nobler than their hard eternities.   105
My quick tears kill'd the flower, my ravings hush'd
The bird, and lost in utter grief I fail'd
To send my life thro' olive-yard and vine
And golden-grain, my gift to helpless man.
Rain-rotten died the wheat, the barley-spears   110
Were hollow-husk'd, the leaf fell, and the Sun,
Pale at my grief, drew down before his time
Sickening, and Ætna kept her winter snow.

Then He,[4] the brother of this Darkness, He
Who still is highest, glancing from his height   115
On earth a fruitless fallow, when he miss'd
The wonted steam of sacrifice, the praise
And prayer of men, decreed that thou shouldst dwell
For nine white moons of each whole year with me,
Three dark ones in the shadow with thy king.   120

Once more the reaper in the gleam of dawn
Will see me by the landmark far away,
Blessing his field, or seated in the dusk
Of even, by the lonely threshing-floor,
Rejoicing in the harvest and the grange.[5]   125

Yet I, Earth-Goddess, am but ill-content
With them who still are highest. Those gray heads,
What meant they by their "Fate beyond the Fates"
But younger kindlier Gods to bear us down,[6]
As we bore down the Gods before us? Gods,   130
To quench, not hurl the thunderbolt, to stay,
Not spread the plague, the famine, Gods indeed,
To send the noon into the night and break
The sunless halls of Hades into Heaven?
Till thy dark lord accept and love the Sun,   135
And all the Shadow die into the Light,[7]
When thou shalt dwell the whole bright year with me,
And souls of men, who grew beyond their race,
And made themselves as Gods against the fear
Of Death and Hell; and thou that hast from men,   140
As Queen of Death, that worship which is Fear,
Henceforth, as having risen from out the dead,
Shalt ever send thy life along with mine
From buried grain thro' springing blade, and bless
Their garner'd autumn also, reap with me,   145
Earth-mother, in the harvest hymns of Earth

3. A deadly poison.
4. Zeus.
5. Perhaps an echo from Keats's "To Autumn": "Who hath not seen thee oft amid thy store? / Sometimes
   whoever seeks abroad may find / Thee sitting careless on a granary floor" (also picked up by Ricks).
6. "Recalls Aeschylus' *Prometheus Bound*" (Hallam Tennyson).
7. A line Tennyson cited as reflecting the "modern frame" (*Memoir* II, 364).

The worship which is Love, and see no more
The Stone, the Wheel,[8] the dimly-glimmering lawns
Of that Elysium, all the hateful fires
Of torment, and the shadowy warrior glide   150
Along the silent field of Asphodel.[9]

                                                       1886; 1889

To Ulysses[1]

1

Ulysses, much-experienced man,
    Whose eyes have known this globe of ours,
    Her tribes of men, and trees, and flowers,
From Corrientes[2] to Japan,

2

To you that bask below the Line,   5
    I soaking here in winter wet—
    The century's three strong eights have met
To drag me down to seventy-nine.

3

In summer if I reach my day—
    To you, yet young, who breathe the balm   10
    Of summer-winters by the palm
And orange grove of Paraguay,

4

I, tolerant of the colder time,
    Who love the winter woods, to trace
    On paler heavens the branching grace   15
Of leafless elm, or naked lime,

5

And see my cedar green, and there
    My giant ilex[3] keeping leaf
    When frost is keen and days are brief—
Or marvel how in English air   20

6

My yucca, which no winter quells,
    Altho' the months have scarce begun,

8. The stone of Sisyphus and Ixion's wheel, Greek conceptions of eternal torment.
9. The immortal flowers that covered the Elysian fields. Compare "Ulysses," lines 63–64: "It may be we
  shall touch the Happy Isles, / And see the great Achilles, whom we knew."
1. Addressed to W. G. Palgrave, whose varied career as soldier, Jesuit priest, missionary, and diplomat justifies his identification with Ulysses. "Ulysses was the title of a volume of Palgrave's essays. He died at
  Monte Video before seeing my poem" (Tennyson). In November, however, the poet had read the poem
  to Palgrave's brother, F. T. Palgrave (the justly famous editor of The Golden Treasury), whom he had
  known since the early 1860s (Memoir II, 507). The notes in quotation marks are Tennyson's.
2. Capital of an Argentine province of the same name.
3. An evergreen oak.

Has push'd toward our faintest sun
A spike of half-accomplish'd bells—

7

Or watch the waving pine which here   25
    The warrior[4] of Caprera set,
    A name that earth will not forget
Till earth has roll'd her latest year—

8

I, once half-crazed for larger light
    On broader zones beyond the foam,   30
    But chaining fancy now at home
Among the quarried downs of Wight,

9

Not less would yield full thanks to you
    For your rich gift, your tale of lands
    I know not,[5] your Arabian sands;   35
Your cane, your palm, tree-fern, bamboo,

10

The wealth of tropic bower and brake;
    Your Oriental Eden-isles[6]
    Where man, nor only Nature smiles;
Your wonder of the boiling lake;[7]   40

11

Phra-Chai, the Shadow of the Best[8]
    Phra-bat[9] the step; your Pontic coast;
    Crag-cloister[1] Anatolian Ghost;[2]
Hong-Kong;[3] Karnac,[4] and all the rest;

12

Thro' which I follow'd line by line   45
    Your leading hand, and came, my friend,
    To prize your various book, and send
A gift of slenderer value, mine.

1889

---

4. Garibaldi, the Italian patriot, who visited Tennyson at Farringford in 1864 and planted the "waving pine."
See *Memoir* II, 1–4. "Garibaldi said to me alluding to his barren island, 'I wish I had your trees.'"
5. "The Tale of Nejd." Palgrave published his *Narrative of a Year's Journey through Central and Eastern Arabia* in 1865.
6. "The Philippines." Compare "Locksley Hall," line 164: "summer isles of Eden." "Palgrave may have been thinking of this (he was certainly thinking of 'the Lotos-Eaters' when he called the Philippines 'isles of Eden, lotus-lands'). Tennyson, as it were, returns the compliment" (Ricks).
7. "In Dominica."
8. "The Shadow of the Lord. Certain obscure markings on a rock in Siam, which express the image of Buddha to the Buddhist more or less distinctly according to his faith and his moral worth."
9. "The footstep of the Lord on another rock."
1. "The monastery of Sumelas."
2. "Anatolian spectre stories."
3. "The Three Cities" (the title of Palgrave's chapter on Hong Kong), cited by Ricks.
4. "Travels in Egypt."

To Mary Boyle[1]

With the Following Poem

[*The Progress of Spring*]

1

'Spring-flowers'! While you still delay to take
    Your leave of town,
Our elm-tree's ruddy-hearted blossom-flake
    Is fluttering down.

2

Be truer to your promise. There! I heard   5
    Our cuckoo call.
Be needle to the magnet of your word,
    Nor wait, till all

3

Our vernal bloom from every vale and plain
    And garden pass,   10
And all the gold from each laburnum chain
    Drop to the grass.

4

Is memory with your Marian[2] gone to rest,
    Dead with the dead?
For ere she left us, when we met, you prest   15
    My hand, and said

5

'I come with your spring-flowers.' You came not, friend;
    My birds would sing,
You heard not. Take then this spring-flower I send,
    This song of spring,   20

6

Found yesterday—forgotten mine own rhyme
    By mine old self,
As I shall be forgotten by old Time,
    Laid on the shelf—

7

A rhyme that flower'd betwixt the whitening sloe   25
    And kingcup blaze,
And more than half a hundred years ago,
    In rick-fire days,[3]

---

1. Tennyson first met Mary Boyle, the aunt of Hallam Tennyson's wife, in 1882 (see *Memoir* II, 294) and dedicated to her "The Progress of Spring," a rediscovered piece written in the 1830s, not included in this book.
2. "Lady Marian Alfred" (Tennyson). She died February 9, 1888.
3. The early 1830s, when farmers burned their haystacks and sometimes their barns in protest against their landlords.

8

When Dives loathed the times, and paced his land
    In fear of worse,   30
And sanguine Lazarus felt a vacant hand
    Fill with *his* purse.[4]

9

For lowly minds were madden'd to the height
    By tonguester tricks,
And once—I well remember that red night   35
    When thirty ricks,

10

All flaming, made an English homestead hell—
    These hands of mine
Have helpt to pass a bucket from the well
    Along the line,   40

11

When this bare dome had not begun to gleam
    Thro' youthful curls,
And you were then a lover's fairy dream,
    His girl of girls;

12

And you, that now are lonely, and with Grief   45
    Sit face to face,
Might find a flickering glimmer of relief
    In change of place.

13

What use to brood? This life of mingled pains
    And joys to me,   50
Despite of every Faith and Creed, remains
    The Mystery.

14

Let golden youth bewail the friend, the wife,
    For ever gone,
He dreams of that long walk thro' desert life   55
    Without the one.

15

The silver year should cease to mourn and sigh—
    Not long to wait—
So close are we, dear Mary, you and I
    To that dim gate.   60

16

Take, read! and be the faults your Poet makes
    Or many or few,

4. For the parable of the rich man (Dives) and Lazarus see Luke 16:19–31.

He rests content, if his young music wakes
    A wish in you

17

To change our dark Queen-city, all her realm   65
    Of sound and smoke,
For his clear heaven, and these few lanes of elm
    And whispering oak.

1889

Far—Far—Away[1]

(For Music)

What sight so lured him thro' the fields he knew
As where earth's green stole into heaven's own hue,
            Far—far—away?

What sound was dearest in his native dells?
The mellow lin-lan-lone of evening bells   5
            Far—far—away?

What vague world-whisper, mystic pain or joy,
Thro' those three words would haunt him when a boy,
            Far—far—away?

A whisper from his dawn of life? a breath   10
From some fair dawn beyond the doors of death
            Far—far—away?

Far, far, how far? from o'er the gates of birth,
The faint horizons, all the bounds, of earth,
            Far—far—away?   15

What charm in words, a charm no words could give?
O dying words, can Music make you live
            Far—far—away?

1889

---

1. "Before I could read I was in the habit on a stormy day of spreading my arms to the wind and crying out, 'I hear a voice that's speaking in the wind,' and the words 'far, far away' had always a strange charm for me." In September 1888, Tennyson was seriously ill; according to his doctor "he had been as near death as a man could be without dying" (*Memoir* II, 508). Hallam adds to his father's note: "He said that he had wonderful thoughts about God and the Universe, and felt as if looking into the other world." This and the following poem are attempts to express these thoughts.

By an Evolutionist[1]

The Lord let the house of a brute to the soul of a man,
  And the man said, 'Am I your debtor?'
And the Lord—'Not yet; but make it as clean as you can,
  And then I will let you a better.'

1

If my body come from brutes, my soul uncertain or a fable,   5
  Why not bask[2] amid the senses while the sun of morning shines,
I, the finer brute[3] rejoicing in my hounds, and in my stable,
  Youth and health, and birth and wealth, and choice of women and of
    wines?[4]

2

What hast thou done for me, grim Old Age, save breaking my bones on the
    rack?
  Would I had past in the morning that looks so bright from afar!   10

Old Age

Done for thee? starved the wild beast that was linkt with thee eighty years
    back.
  Less weight now for the ladder-of-heaven that hangs on a star.

I

If my body come from brutes, tho' somewhat finer than their own,
  I am heir, and this my kingdom. Shall the royal voice be mute?
No, but if the rebel subject seek to drag me from the throne,   15
  Hold the sceptre, Human Soul, and rule thy province of the brute.

II

I have climb'd to the snows of Age, and I gaze at a field in the Past,
  Where I sank with the body at times in the sloughs of a low desire,
But I hear no yelp of the beast, and the Man is quiet at last,
  As he stands on the heights of his life with a glimpse of a height that is
    higher.   20

1889

---

1. Although nowhere in Tennyson does one find any direct reference to the transmutation of species, he generally accepts the theory that man evolved from some lower form of life. Tennyson reacted strongly, however, against those who, he felt, "exaggerated Darwinism" —i.e., used the hypothesis to deny the existence of God and the immortality of the soul.
2. Compare *IM* 35, 6: "And bask'd and batten'd in the woods."
3. Compare *IM* 118, 7: "Arise and fly / The reeling Faun, the sensual feast; / Move upward, working out the beast, / And let the ape and tiger die."
4. Ricks compares "Vastness," line 19: "Wealth with his wines and his wedded Harlots."

Parnassus[1]

Exegi monumentum . . .
Quod non . . .
Possit diruere . . .
          . . . innumerabilis
Annorum series et fuga temporum.
                                            —HORACE

1

What be those crown'd forms high over the sacred fountain?[2]
Bards, that the mighty Muses have raised to the heights of the mountain,
And over the flight of the Ages! O Goddesses, help me up thither!
Lightning may shrivel the laurel of Cæsar, but mine would not wither.
Steep is the mountain, but you, will help me to overcome it,   5
And stand with my head in the zenith, and roll my voice from the summit,
Sounding for ever and ever thro' Earth and her listening nations,
And mixt with the great sphere-music of stars and of constellations.

2

What be those two shapes high over the sacred fountain,
Taller than all the Muses, and huger than all the mountain?   10
On those two known peaks they stand ever spreading and heightening;
Poet, that evergreen laurel is blasted by more than lightning!
Look, in their deep double shadow the crown'd ones all disappearing!
Sing like a bird and be happy, nor hope for a deathless hearing!
"Sounding for ever and ever?" pass on! the sight confuses—   15
These are Astronomy and Geology, terrible Muses!

3

If the lips were touch'd with fire from off a pure Pierian[3] altar,
Tho' their music here be mortal need the singer greatly care?
Other songs for other worlds! the fire within him would not falter;
Let the golden Iliad vanish, Homer here is Homer there.   20

1889

Merlin and the Gleam[1]

O young Mariner,
You from the haven
Under the sea-cliff,
You that are watching

---

1. The epigraph from Horace, *Odes* III, xxx, lines 1–5, means: "I have constructed a monument which the passage of uncounted years cannot destroy." For most of his mature life, Tennyson had been struggling with the "terrible Muses" of astronomy and geology, concepts of infinite space and measureless time that forced on the Victorian mind such a difficult revaluation of the human condition. "Norman Lockyer visited him in October 1890, and said of my father: 'His mind in *saturated* with astronomy'" (Hallam Tennyson).
2. The fountain on Mount Parnassus sacred to the Muses.
3. Of Pieria in Thessaly, the reputed home of the Muses.
1. "'The Gleam,'" Tennyson noted, "signifies in my poem the higher poetic imagination." Although he conceived the poem as a poetic autobiography, he takes some license with chronology.

The gray Magician   5
With eyes of wonder,
I am Merlin,
And *I* am dying,
I am Merlin
Who follow the Gleam.   10

2

Mighty the Wizard
Who found me at sunrise
Sleeping, and woke me
And learn'd me Magic!
Great the Master,   15
And sweet the Magic,
When over the valley,
In early summers,
Over the mountain,
On human faces,   20
And all around me,
Moving to melody,[2]
Floated the Gleam.

3

Once at the croak of a Raven[3] who crost it
A barbarous people,   25
Blind to the magic
And deaf to the melody,
Snarl'd at and cursed me,
A demon vext me,
The light retreated,   30
The landskip darken'd,
The melody deaden'd,
The Master whisper'd,
"Follow the Gleam."

4

Then to the melody,[4]   35
Over a wilderness
Gliding, and glancing at
Elf of the woodland,
Gnome of the cavern,
Griffin and Giant,   40

2. Perhaps alludes to the poetry of the 1830 and 1832 volumes, much of which was composed from his impressions in and around the Somersby countryside.
3. Hallam says his father meant "the harsh voices of those who were unsympathetic." One thinks first of John Wilson Croker's nasty review in 1833 and also of John Wilson's (Christopher North's) hostile response in 1832. In a not wholly successful effort to reconcile the rest of the poem with the actual course of the poet's career, Sir Charles Tennyson believes the reference is to "the family troubles which followed Dr. Tennyson's death in 1831" and the several attempts of Tennyson's grandfather "to divert Alfred from his determination to devote himself to poetry" (*Alfred Tennyson*, p. 517 n).
4. According to Sir Charles's assumption about the "Raven," sections 4, 5, and 6 would refer to "the poet's development during the years of closest friendship with Arthur Hallam (1832 and 1833)." Possibly section 4 describes the "romantic" poems of 1842. Section 5 would then refer to the English Idyls first published in 1842, as the almost inescapable allusions to the rural domestic life pictured in them would suggest.

And dancing of Fairies
In desolate hollows,
And wraiths of the mountain,
And rolling of dragons
By warble of water, 45
Or cataract music
Of falling torrents,
Flitted the Gleam.

5

Down from the mountain
And over the level, 50
And streaming and shining on
Silent river,
Silvery willow,
Pasture and plowland,
Innocent maidens, 55
Garrulous children,
Homestead and harvest,
Reaper and gleaner,
And rough-ruddy faces
Of lowly labor, 60
Slided the Gleam—

6

Then, with a melody
Stronger and statelier,
Led me at length
To the city and palace 65
Of Arthur the King;[5]
Touch'd at the golden
Cross of the churches,
Flash'd on the tournament,
Flicker'd and bicker'd 70
From helmet to helmet,
And last on the forehead
Of Arthur the blameless
Rested the Gleam.

7[6]

Clouds and darkness 75
Closed upon Camelot;
Arthur had vanish'd
I knew not whither,
The king who loved me,
And cannot die; 80

5. The "Morte d'Arthur" was written between 1833 and 1835, first appearing in the 1842 volumes. Although it would have been a violation of the rigid chronological interpretation, Tennyson may have had the whole of *Idylls of the King* in mind.
6. This section obviously looks back to Hallam's death and the composition of the elegies for *IM* (1833–50; published 1850). The identification of Arthur Hallam with King Arthur strongly suggests that Tennyson did not feel himself constrained to follow a literal sequence of events.

For out of the darkness
Silent and slowly
The Gleam, that had waned to a wintry glimmer
On icy fallow
And faded forest,   85
Drew to the valley
Named of the shadow,
And slowly brightening
Out of the glimmer,
And slowly moving again to a melody   90
Yearningly tender,
Fell on the shadow.
No longer a shadow,
But clothed with the Gleam.

8[7]

And broader and brighter   95
The Gleam flying onward,
Wed to the Melody,
Sang thro' the world;
And slower and fainter,
Old and weary,   100
But eager to follow,
I saw, whenever
In passing it glanced upon
Hamlet or city,
That under the Crosses   105
The dead man's garden,
The mortal hillock,
Would break into blossom;
And so to the land's
Last limit I came[8] —   110
And can no longer,
But die rejoicing,
For thro' the Magic
Of Him the Mighty,
Who taught me in childhood,   115
There on the border
Of boundless Ocean,
And all but in Heaven
Hovers the Gleam.[9]

9

Not of the sunlight,   120
Not of the moonlight,

---

7. This and the following section express the poet's final acceptance of death as he comes to terms with the achievements of his literary life. He reasserts a faith and idealism seldom so unequivocally embraced in the late poems.
8. Referring to lines 95–110: "He faced death . . . with an added sense of the awe and mystery of the Infinite" (Hallam Tennyson).
9. "This is the reading of the poet's riddle as he gave it to me. He thought that *Merlin and the Gleam* would probably be enough of biography for those friends who urged him to write about himself" (Hallam Tennyson).

Not of the starlight!
O young Mariner,
Down to the haven,
Call your companions,   125
Launch your vessel
And crowd your canvas,
And, ere it vanishes
Over the margin,
After it, follow it,   130
Follow the Gleam.

                                                          1889

The Oak[1]

Live thy Life,
    Young and old,
Like yon oak,
Bright in spring,
    Living gold;   5

Summer-rich
    Then; and then
Autumn-changed,
Soberer-hued
    Gold again.   10

All his leaves
    Fallen at length,
Look, he stands,
Trunk and bough,
    Naked strength.   15

                                                          1889

June Bracken and Heather

TO ———[1]

There on the top of the down,
The wild heather round me and over me June's high blue,
When I look'd at the bracken so bright and the heather so brown,
I thought to myself I would offer this book to you,
This, and my love together,   5

1. Tennyson liked to think his poem could be called "clean cut like a Greek epigram" (*Memoir* II, 366); and indeed it does show elements of the best in his late style: spare and sharply focused. "The allusion is to the gold of the young oak leaves in spring, and to the autumal gold of the fading leaves (at Aldworth)" (Hallam Tennyson).
1. Written in June 1891 to Tennyson's wife, Emily (born July 9, 1813), and serving as the dedication to her of his last volume of poems.

To you that are seventy-seven,
With a faith as clear as the heights of the June-blue heaven,
And a fancy as summer-new
As the green of the bracken amid the gloom of the heather.

1892

The Dawn[1]

You are but children.
— EGYPTIAN PRIEST TO SOLON

1
Red of the Dawn!
Screams of a babe in the red-hot palms of a Moloch[2] of Tyre,
    Man with his brotherless dinner on man in the tropical wood,
    Priests in the name of the Lord passing souls thro' fire to the fire,
Head-hunters and boats of Dahomey[3] that float upon human blood!   5

2
Red of the Dawn!
Godless fury of peoples, and Christless frolic of kings,
    And the bolt of war dashing down upon cities and blazing farms,
    For Babylon was a child new-born, and Rome was a babe in arms,
And London and Paris and all the rest are as yet but in leading-strings.   10

3
Dawn not Day,
While scandal is mouthing a bloodless name at *her* cannibal feast,
    And rake-ruin'd bodies and souls go down in a common wreck,
    And the Press of a thousand cities is prized for it smells of the beast,
Or easily violates virgin Truth for a coin or a cheque.   15

4
Dawn not Day!
Is it Shame, so few should have climb'd from the dens in the level below,
    Men, with a heart and a soul, no slaves of a four-footed will?
    But if twenty million of summers[4] are stored in the sunlight still,
We are far from the noon of man, there is time, for the race to grow.   20

1. This and the following two poems fairly represent Tennyson's thoughts at the end of this life on the future of the human race. Resigned, insofar as possible, to the implications of geological time and the all but limitless space of the new astronomy, he clings with guarded optimism to the hope that our species may eventually resolve its human problems.
2. A Canaanite idol to whom children, especially the first-born, were sacrificed as burnt offerings.
3. In a conversation (ca. 1869–70), Tennyson said: "On the occasion of a king in Dahomey enough women victims are killed to float a small canoe (with their blood)" (Sir Charles Tennyson, *Twentieth Century*, p. clxv.) Ricks observes that Tennyson owned a copy (*Lincoln*) of Sir Richard Burton's book about this West African country, *A Mission to Gelele, King of Dahome* (1864), which discusses sceptically the "report that the king floated a canoe and paddled himself in a tank full of human blood."
4. Scientists of the time, particularly those of the stature of Lord Kelvin (1824–1907), were unaware that the sun was powered by nuclear processes, allowing for the hundreds of millions of years of relatively constant temperatures on earth necessary for evolution. The "facts'" then current, that the sun burned much faster through conventional combustion, gave Darwin and Huxley a lot of trouble, for they had no other explanation.

5

Red of the Dawn!
Is it turning a fainter red? so be it, but when shall we lay
   The Ghost of the Brute that is walking and haunting us yet, and be free?
   In a hundred, a thousand winters? Ah, what will *our* children be,
The men of a hundred thousand, a million summers away?   25

1892

The Making of Man

Where is one that, born of woman,[1] altogether can escape
From the lower world within him, moods of tiger, or of ape?[2]
   Man as yet is being made, and ere the crowning Age of ages,
Shall not æon after æon pass and touch him into shape?

All about him shadow still, but, while the races flower and fade,   5
Prophet-eyes may catch a glory slowly gaining on the shade,
   Till the peoples all are one, and all their voices blend in choric
Hallelujah to the Maker 'It is finish'd.[3] Man is made.'

1892

God and the Universe

1

Will my tiny spark of being wholly vanish in your deeps and heights?
Must my day be dark by reason, O ye Heavens, of your boundless nights,
Rush of Suns, and roll of systems,[1] and your fiery clash of meteorites?

2

'Spirit, nearing yon dark portal at the limit of thy human state,
Fear not thou the hidden purpose of that Power which alone is great,   5
Not the myriad world, His shadow, nor the silent Opener of the Gate.'[2]

1892

The Silent Voices[1]

When the dumb Hour, clothed in black,
Brings the Dreams about my bed,

---

1. Job 14:1: "Man that is born of woman is of few days, and full of trouble."
2. Compare *IM* 118, 7: "And let the ape and tiger die."
3. John 19:30: "When Jesus therefore had received the vinegar, he said, It is finished: and he bowed his head, and gave up the ghost."
1. Compare *IM*, "Epilogue," line 122: "star and system rolling past."
2. "As he was dying on Oct. 5th, 1982, he exclaimed: 'I have opened it'" (Hallam Tennyson).
1. Set to music by Tennyson's wife, this and "Crossing the Bar" were the two anthems sung at the poet's funeral in Westminster Abbey. See *Memoir* II, 430.

Call me not so often back,
Silent Voices of the dead,
Toward the lowland ways behind me,   5
And the sunlight that is gone!
Call me rather, silent voices,
Forward to the starry track
Glimmering up the heights beyond me
On, and always on!   10

1892

Crossing the Bar[1]

Sunset and evening star,
   And one clear call for me!
And may there be no moaning of the bar,
   When I put out to sea,

But such a tide as moving seems asleep,   5
   Too full for sound and foam,
When that which drew from out the boundless deep[2]
   Turns again home.

Twilight and evening bell,
   And after that the dark!   10
And may there be no sadness of farewell,
   When I embark;

For tho' from out our bourne[3] of Time and Place
   The flood may bear me far,
I hope to see my Pilot face to face[4]   15
   When I have crost the bar.

1889

1. Written after a serious illness while crossing the Solent from Aldworth to Farringford on the Isle of Wight,
the poem, Tennyson said, "came in a moment." In answer to the questions about the Pilot's presence,
why he should remain on board when the ship reaches open sea or why the speaker only sees him then,
Tennyson explained: "The Pilot has been on board all the while, but in the dark I have not seen him."
He is, he said, "that Divine and Unseen Who is always guiding us" (*Memoir* II, 367).
    Nurse Durham, who had cared for the poet throughout his near fatal illness, "scolded him sharply for
[grumbling], saying that instead of complaining he ought to write a hymn or something to show his gratitude for his marvelous recovery." In the jocular style bonding them and remembering her admonition,
he said: "Will this do for you, old woman?" and recited the poem. "It seemed to her that he had written
his own death song. Without a word, she turned and ran from the room" (*Alfred Tennyson*, pp. 511–15),
perhaps as fine a critic as any on what Hallam Tennyson said: "That is one of the most beautiful poems
ever written."
    A few days before he died, Tennyson instructed his son to "put 'Crossing the Bar' at the end of all edi-
tions of my poems"— a request all editors have honored.
2. Compare *IM* "Epilogue," lines 122–24: "A soul shall draw from out the vast / And strike his being into
bounds" and "De Profundis," line 25: "To that last deep where we and thou art still" and "The Passing
of Arthur," line 445: "From the great deep to the great deep he goes."
3. See *Hamlet* III, i, lines 79–80: speaking of death, "from whose bourn / No traveller returns."
4. 1 Corinthians 13:12: "For now we see through a glass, darkly; but then face to face."

CONTEXTS

ARTHUR HENRY HALLAM

On Some of the Characteristics of Modern Poetry, and on the Lyrical Poems of Alfred Tennyson[†]

When Mr. Wordsworth, in his celebrated Preface to the "Lyrical Ballads," asserted that immediate or rapid popularity was not the test of poetry, great was the consternation and clamour among those farmers of public favour, the established critics. Never had so audacious an attack been made upon their undoubted privileges and hereditary charter of oppression. * * * They could not put down Mr. Wordsworth by clamour, or prevent his doctrine, once uttered, and enforced by his example, from awakening the minds of men, and giving a fresh impulse to art. It was the truth, and it prevailed; not only against the exasperation of that hydra, the Reading Public, whose vanity was hurt, and the blustering of its keepers, whose delusion was exposed, but even against the false glosses and narrow apprehensions of the Wordsworthians themselves. It is the madness of all who loosen some great principle, long buried under a snowheap of custom and superstition, to imagine that they can restrain its operation, or circumscribe it by their purposes. But the right of private judgment was stronger than the will of Luther; and even the genius of Wordsworth cannot expand itself to the full periphery of poetic art.

It is not true, as his exclusive admirers would have it, that the highest species of poetry is the reflective: it is a gross fallacy, that, because certain opinions are acute or profound, the expression of them by the imagination must be eminently beautiful. Whenever the mind of the artist suffers itself to be occupied, during its periods of creation, by any other predominant motive than the desire of beauty, the result is false in art. Now there is undoubtedly no reason, why he may not find beauty in those moods of emotion, which arise from the combinations of reflective thought, and it is possible that he may delineate these with fidelity, and not be led astray by any suggestions of an unpoetical mood. But, though possible, it is hardly probable: for a man, whose reveries take a reasoning turn, and who is accustomed to measure his ideas by their logical relations rather than the congruity of the sentiments to which they refer, will be apt to mistake the pleasure he has in knowing a thing to be true, for the pleasure he would have in knowing it to be beautiful, and so will pile his thoughts in a rhetorical battery, that they may convince, instead of letting them glow in the natural course of contemplation, that they may enrapture. It would not be difficult to shew, by reference to the most admired poems of Wordsworth, that he is frequently chargeable with this error, and that much has been said by him which is good as philosophy, powerful as rhetoric, but false as poetry. Perhaps this very distortion of the truth did more in the peculiar juncture of our literary affairs to enlarge and liberalize the genius of our age, than could have been effected by a less sectarian temper. However this may be, a new school of reformers soon began to attract attention, who, professing the same independence

---

In the following commentaries, including those in the "Criticism" section, the footnotes of the originals have been retained, with additional notes by the present editor marked [*Editor*].

† From the *Englishman's Magazine*, I (August 1831), pp. 616–28.

of immediate favour, took their stand on a different region of Parnassus from that occupied by the Lakers, and one, in our opinion, much less liable to perturbing currents of air from ungenial climates. We shall not hesitate to express our conviction, that the Cockney school (as it was termed in derision, from a cursory view of its accidental circumstances) contained more genuine inspiration, and adhered more speedily to that portion of truth which it embraced, than any *form* of art that has existed in this country since the day of Milton. Their *caposetta* was Mr. Leigh Hunt, who did little more than point the way, and was diverted from his aim by a thousand personal predilections and political habits of thought. But he was followed by two men of a very superior make; men who were born poets, lived poets, and went poets to their untimely graves. Shelley and Keats were, indeed, of opposite genius; that of the one was vast, impetuous, and sublime: the other seemed to be "fed with honey-dew," and to have "drunk the milk of Paradise." Even the softness of Shelley comes out in bold, rapid, comprehensive strokes; he has no patience for minute beauties, unless they can be massed into a general effect of grandeur. On the other hand, the tenderness of Keats cannot sustain a lofty flight; he does not generalize or allegorize Nature; his imagination works with few symbols, and reposes willingly on what is given freely. Yet in this formal opposition of character there is, it seems to us, a ground-work of similarity sufficient for the purposes of classification, and constituting a remarkable point in the progress of literature. They are both poets of sensation rather than reflection. Susceptible of the slightest impulse from external nature, their fine organs trembled into emotion at colours, and sounds, and movements, unperceived or unregarded by duller temperaments. Rich and clear were their perceptions of visible forms; full and deep their feelings of music. So vivid was the delight attending the simple exertions of eye and ear, that it became mingled more and more with their trains of active thought, and tended to absorb their whole being into the energy of sense. Other poets *seek* for images to illustrate their conceptions; these men had no need to seek; they lived in a world of images; for the most important and extensive portion of their life consisted in those emotions, which are immediately conversant with sensation. Like the hero of Goethe's novel, they would hardly have been affected by what are called the pathetic parts of a book; but the *merely beautiful* passages, "those from which the spirit of the author looks clearly and mildly forth," would have melted them to tears. Hence they are not descriptive; they are picturesque. They are not smooth and *negatively* harmonious; they are full of deep and varied melodies. This powerful tendency of imagination to a life of immediate sympathy with the external universe, is not nearly so liable to false views of art as the opposite disposition of purely intellectual contemplation. For where beauty is constantly passing before "that inward eye, which is the bliss of solitude;" where the soul seeks it as a perpetual and necessary refreshment to the sources of activity and intuition; where all the other sacred ideas of our nature, the idea of good, the idea of perfection, the idea of truth, are habitually contemplated through the medium of this predominant mood, so that they assume its colour, and are subject to its peculiar laws—there is little danger that the ruling passion of the whole mind will cease to direct its creative operations, or the energetic principle of love for the beautiful sink, even for a brief period, to the level of a mere notion in the understanding. We do not deny that it is, on other accounts, dangerous for frail humanity to linger with fond attachment in the vicinity of sense. Minds of this description are especially liable to moral temptations, and upon them, more than any, it is incumbent to remember that their mission as men, which they share with all their fellow-beings, is of infinitely higher interest than their mission as artists, which they possess by rare and exclusive privilege. But it is obvious that, critically speaking, such temptations are of slight moment. Not the gross and evident passions of our nature, but the elevated and less separable desires are the dangerous enemies which misguide the poetic spirit in its attempts at self-cultivation. That delicate sense of fitness, which grows with the growth of artist feelings, and strengthens with their strength, until it acquires a celerity and weight of decision hardly inferior to the correspondent judgments of conscience, is weakened by every indulgence of heterogeneous aspirations, however pure they may be, however lofty, however suitable to human nature. We are therefore decidedly of opinion that the heights and depths of art are most within the reach of those who have received from Nature the "fearful and wonderful" constitution we have described, whose poetry is a sort of magic, producing a number of impressions too multiplied, too minute, and too diversified to allow of our tracing them to their causes, because just such was the effect, even so boundless, and so bewildering, produced on their imaginations by the real appearance of Nature. These things being so, our friends of the new school had evidently much reason to recur to the maxim laid down by Mr. Wordsworth, and to appeal from the immediate judgments of lettered or unlettered contemporaries to the decision of a more equitable posterity. How should they be popular, whose senses told them a richer and ampler tale than most men could understand, and who constantly expressed, because they constantly felt, sentiments of exquisite pleasure or pain, which most men were not permitted to experience? The public very naturally derided them as visionaries, and gibbeted *in terrorem* those inaccuracies of diction, occasioned sometimes by the speed of their conceptions, sometimes by the inadequacy of language to their peculiar conditions of thought. But, it may be asked, does not this line of argument prove too much? Does it not prove that there is a barrier between these poets and all other persons, so strong and immoveable, that, as has been said of the Supreme Essence, we must be themselves before we can understand them in the least? Not only are they not liable to sudden and vulgar estimation, but the lapse of ages, it seems, will not consolidate their fame, nor the suffrages of the wise few produce any impression, however remote or slowly matured, on the judgments of the incapacitated many. We answer, this is not the import of our argument. Undoubtedly the true poet addresses himself, in all his conceptions, to the common nature of us all. Art is a lofty tree, and may shoot up far beyond our grasp, but its roots are in daily life and experience. Every bosom contains the elements of those complex emotions which the artist feels, and every head can, to a certain extent, go over in itself the process of their combination, so as to understand his expressions and sympathize with his state. But this requires exertion; more or less, indeed, according to the difference of occasion, but always some degree of exertion. For since the emotions of the poet, during composition, follow a regular law of association, it follows that to accompany their progress up to the harmonious prospect of the whole, and to perceive the proper dependence of every step on that which preceded, it is absolutely necessary *to start from the same point*, i.e., clearly to apprehend that leading sentiment in the poet's mind, by their conformity to which the host of suggestions are arranged. Now this requisite exertion is not willingly made by the large majority of readers. It is so easy to judge capriciously, and according to indolent impulse! For very many, therefore, it has become *morally* impossible to attain the author's point of vision, on account of their habits, or their prejudices, or their circumstances; but it is never *physically* impossible, because nature has placed in every man the simple elements, of which art is the sublimation. Since then this demand on the reader for activity, when he wants to peruse his author in a luxurious passiveness, is the very thing that moves his bile, it is obvious that those writers will be always most popular, who require the least degree of exertion. Hence, whatever is mixed up with art, and appears under its semblance, is always more favourably regarded than art free and unalloyed. Hence, half the fashionable poems in the world are mere rhetoric, and half the remainder are perhaps not liked by the generality for their substantial merits. Hence, likewise, of the really pure compositions those are most universally agreeable, which take for their primary subject the *usual* passions of the heart, and deal with them in a simple state, without applying the transforming powers of high imagination. Love, friendship, ambition, religion, &e., are matters of daily experience, even amongst imaginative tempers. The forces of association, therefore, are ready to work in these directions, and little effort of will is necessary to follow the artist. For the same reason such subjects often excite a partial power of composition, which is no sign of a truly poetic organization. We are very far from wishing to depreciate this class of poems, whose influence is so extensive, and communicates so refined a pleasure. We contend only that the facility with which its impressions are communicated, is no proof of its elevation as a form of art, but rather the contrary. What then, some may be ready to exclaim, is the pleasure derived by most men from Shakespeare, or Dante, or Homer, entirely false and factitious? If these are really masters of their art, must not the energy required of the ordinary intellegences, that come in contact with their mighty genius, be the greatest possible? How comes it then that they are popular? Shall we not say, after all, that the difference is in the power of the author, not in the tenor of his meditations? Those eminent spirits find no difficulty in conveying to common apprehension their lofty sense, and profound observation of Nature. They keep no aristocratic state, apart from the sentiments of society at large; they speak to the hearts of all, and by the magnetic force of their conceptions elevate inferior intellects into a higher and purer atmosphere. The truth contained in this objection is undoubtedly important; geniuses of the most universal order, and assigned by destiny to the most propitious eras of a nation's literary developement, have a clearer and larger access to the minds of their compatriots, that can ever be open to those who are circumscribed by less fortunate circumstances. In the youthful periods of any literature there is an expansive and communicative tendency in mind, which produces unreservedness of communion, and reciprocity of vigour between different orders of intelligence. Without abandoning the ground which has always been defended by the partizans of Mr. Wordsworth, who declare with perfect truth that the number of real admirers of what is really admirable in Shakespeare and Milton are much fewer than the number of apparent admirers might lead one to imagine, we may safely assert that the intense thoughts set in circulation by those "orbs of song," and their noble satellites, "in great Eliza's golden time," did not fail to awaken a proportionable intensity in the natures of numberless auditors. Some might feel feebly, some strongly; the effect would vary according to the character of the recipient; but upon none was the stirring influence entirely unimpressive. The knowledge and power thus imbibed, became a part of national existence; it was ours as Englishmen; and amid the flux of generations and customs we retain unimpaired this privilege of intercourse with greatness. But the age in which we live comes late in our national progress. That first raciness, and juvenile vigour of literature, when nature "wantoned as in her prime, and played at will her virgin fancies," is gone, never to return. Since that day we have undergone a period of degradation. "Every handicraftsman has worn the mark of Poesy." It would be tedious to repeat the tale, so often related, of French contagion, and the heresies of the Popian school. With the close of the last century came an era of reaction, an era of painful struggle, to bring our overcivilised condition of thought into union with the fresh productive spirit that brightened the morning of our literature. But repentance is unlike innocence: the laborious endeavour to restore has more complicated methods of action, than the freedom of untainted nature. Those different powers of poetic disposition, the energies of Sensitive,[1] of Reflective, of Passionate Emotion, which in former times were intermingled, and derived from mutual support an extensive empire over the feelings of men, were now restrained within separate spheres of agency. The whole system no longer worked harmoniously, and by intrinsic harmony acquired external freedom; but there arose a violent and unusual action in the several component functions, each for itself, all striving to reproduce the regular power which the whole had once enjoyed. Hence the melancholy, which so evidently characterises the spirit of modern poetry; hence that return of the mind upon itself, and the habit of seeking relief in idiosyncracies rather than community of interest. In the old times the poetic impulse went along with the general impulse of the nation; in these, it is a reaction against it, a check acting for conservation against a propulsion towards change. We have indeed seen it urged in some of our fashionable publications, that the diffusion of poetry must necessarily be in the direct ratio of the diffusion of machinery, because a highly civilized people must have new objects of interest, and thus a new field will be opened to description. But this notable argument forgets that against this *objective* amelioration may be set the decrease of *subjective* power, arising from a prevalence of social activity, and a continual absorption of the higher feelings into the palpable interests of ordinary life. The French Revolution may be a finer theme than the war of Troy; but it does not so evidently follow that Homer is to find his superior. Our inference, therefore, from this change in the relative position of artists to the rest of the community is, that modern poetry, in proportion to its depth and truth, is likely to have little immediate authority over public opinion. Admirers it will have; sects consequently it will form; and these strong undercurrents will in time sensibly affect the principal stream. Those writers, whose genius, though great, is not strictly and essentially poetic, become mediators between the votaries of art and the careless cravers for excitement.[2] Art herself, less manifestly glorious than in her periods of undisputed supremacy, retains her essential prerogatives, and forgets not to raise up chosen spirits, who may minister to her state, and vindicate her title.

1. We are aware that this is not the right word, being appropriated by common use to a different signification. Those who think the caution given by Cæsar should not stand in the way of urgent occasion, may substitute "sensuous," a word in use amongst our elder divines, and revived by a few bold writers in our own time.
2. May we not compare them to the bright, but unsubstantial clouds which, in still evenings, girdle the sides of lofty mountains, and seem to form a natural connexion between the lowly vallies, spread out beneath, and those isolated peaks above, that hold the "last parley with the setting sun?"

One of this faithful Islam, a poet in the truest and highest sense, we are anxious to present to our readers. He has yet written little, and published less; but in these "preludes of a loftier strain," we recognise the inspiring god. Mr. Tennyson belongs decidedly to the class we have already described as Poets of Sensation. He sees all the forms of nature with the *"eruditus oculus,"* and his ear has a fairy fineness. There is a strange earnestness in his worship of beauty, which throws a charm over his impassioned song, more easily felt than described, and not to be escaped by those who have once felt it. We think he has more definiteness, and soundness of general conception, than the late Mr. Keats, and is much more free from blemishes of diction, and hasty capriccios of fancy. He has also this advantage over that poet, and his friend Shelley, that he comes before the public, unconnected with any political party, or peculiar system of opinions. Nevertheless, true to the theory we have stated, we believe his participation in their characteristic excellencies is sufficient to secure him a share in their unpopularity. The volume of "Poems, chiefly Lyrical," does not contain above 154 pages; but it shews us much more of the character of its parent mind, than many books we have known of much larger compass, and more boastful pretensions. The features of original genius are clearly and strongly marked. The author imitates nobody; we recognise the spirit of his age, but not the individual form of this or that writer. His thoughts bear no more resemblance to Byron or Scott, Shelley or Coleridge, than to Homer or Calderon, Ferdusi or Calidas. We have remarked five distinctive excellencies of his own manner. First, his luxuriance of imagination, and at the same time his control over it. Secondly, his power of embodying himself in ideal characters, or rather moods of character, with such extreme accuracy of adjustment, that the circumstances of the narration seem to have a natural correspondence with the predominant feeling, and, as it were, to be evolved from it by assimilative force. Thirdly, his vivid, picturesque delineation of objects, and the peculiar skill with which he holds all of them *fused*, to borrow a metaphor from science, in a medium of strong emotion. Fourthly, the variety of his lyrical measures, and exquisite modulation of harmonious words and cadences to the swell and fall of the feelings expressed. Fifthly, the elevated habits of thought, *implied* in these compositions, and imparting a mellow soberness of tone, more impressive, to our minds, than if the author had drawn up a set of opinions in verse, and sought to instruct the understanding, rather than to communicate the love of beauty to the heart. We shall proceed to give our readers some specimens in illustration of these remarks, and, if possible, we will give them entire; for no poet can fairly be judged of by fragments, least of all a poet, like Mr. Tennyson, whose mind conceives nothing isolated, nothing abrupt, but every part with reference to some other part, and in subservience to the idea of the whole.

"Recollections of the Arabian Nights!" What a delightful, endearing title! How we pity those to whom it calls up no reminiscence of early enjoyment, no sentiment of kindliness as towards one who sings a song they have loved, or mentions with affection a departed friend! But let nobody expect a multifarious enumeration of Viziers, Barmecides, Fireworshippers, and Cadis; trees that sing, horses that fly, and Goules that eat rice pudding! Our author knows what he is about: he has, with great judgment, selected our old acquaintance, "the good Haroun Alraschid," as the most prominent object of our childish interest, and with him has called up one of those luxurious garden scenes, the account of which, in plain prose, used to make our mouths water for sherbet, since luckily we were too young to think much about Zobeide! We think this poem will be the favourite among Mr. Tennyson's admirers; perhaps upon the whole it is our own; at least we find ourselves recurring to it oftener than to any other, and every time we read it, we feel the freshness of its beauty increase. * * *

Criticism will sound but poorly after this; yet we cannot give silent votes. The first stanza, we beg leave to observe, places us at once in the position of feeling, which the poem requires. This scene is before us, around us; we cannot mistake its localities, or blind ourselves to its colours. That happy ductility of childhood returns for the moment; "true Mussulmans are we, and sworn," and yet there is a latent knowledge, which heightens the pleasure, that to our change from really childish thought we owe the capacities by which we enjoy the recollection. As the poem proceeds, all is in perfect keeping. There is a solemn distinctness in every image, a majesty of slow motion in every cadence, that aids the illusion of thought, and steadies its contemplation of the complete picture. Originality of observation seems to cost nothing to our author's liberal genius; he lavishes images of exquisite accuracy and elaborate splendour, as a common writer throws about metaphysical truisms, and exhausted tropes. Amidst all the varied luxuriance of the sensations described, we are never permitted to lose sight of the idea which gives unity to this variety, and by the recurrence of which, as a sort of mysterious influence, at the close of every stanza, the mind is wrought up, with consummate art, to the final disclosure. This poem is a perfect gallery of pictures; and the concise boldness, with which in a few words an object is clearly painted, is sometimes (see the 6th stanza) majestic as Milton, sometimes (see the 12th) sublime as Æschylus. We have not, however, so far forgot our vocation as critics, that we would leave without notice the slight faults which adhere to this precious work. In the 8th stanza, we doubt the propriety of using the bold compound "black-green," at least in such close vicinity to "gold-green:" nor is it perfectly clear by the term, although indicated by the context, that "diamond plots" relates to shape rather than colour. We are perhaps very stupid, but "vivid stars unrayed" does not convey to us a very precise notion. "Rosaries of scented thorn," in the 10th stanza, is, we believe, an entirely unauthorized use of the word. Would our author translate "biferique rosaria Pæsti."—"And rosaries of Pæstum, twice in bloom?" To the beautiful 13th stanza, we are sorry to find any objection: but even the bewitching loveliness of that "Persian girl" shall not prevent our performing the rigid duty we have undertaken, and we must hint to Mr. Tennyson, that "redolent" is no synonyme for "fragrant." Bees may be redolent of honey: spring may be "redolent of youth and love," but the absolute use of the word has, we fear, neither in Latin nor English, any better authority than the monastic epitaph on Fair Rosamond. "Hic jacet in tombâ Rosa Mundi, non Rosa Munda, non redolet, sed olet, quæ redolere solet."

We are disposed to agree with Mr. Coleridge, when he says "no adequate compensation can be made for the mischief a writer does by confounding the distinct senses of words." At the same time our feelings in this instance rebel strongly in behalf of "redolent;" for the melody of the passage, as it stands, is beyond the possibility of improvement, and unless he should chance to light upon a word very nearly resembling this in consonants and vowels, we can hardly quarrel with Mr. Tennyson if, in spite of our judgment, he retains the offender in his service.

One word more, before we have done, and it shall be a word of praise. The language of this book, with one or two rare exceptions, is thorough and sterling English. A little more respect, perhaps, was due to the *"jus et norma loquendi,"* but we are inclined to consider as venial a fault arising from generous enthusiasm for the principles of sound analogy, and for that Saxon element, which constitutes the intrinsic freedom and nervousness of our native tongue. We see no signs in what Mr. Tennyson has written of the Quixotic spirit which has led some persons to desire the reduction of English to a single form, by excluding nearly the whole of Latin and Roman derivatives. Ours is necessarily a compound language; as such alone it can flourish and increase; nor will the author of the poems we have extracted be likely to barter for a barren appearance of symmetrical structure that fertility of expression, and variety of harmony, which "the speech, that Shakespeare spoke," derived from the sources of southern phraseology.

In presenting this young poet to the public, as one not studious of instant popularity, nor likely to obtain it, we may be thought to play the part of a fashionable lady, who deludes her refractory mate into doing what she chooses, by pretending to wish the exact contrary, or of a cunning pedagogue, who practises a similar manœuvre on some self-willed Flibbertigibbet of the schoolroom. But the supposition would do us wrong. We have spoken in good faith, commending this volume to feeling hearts and imaginative tempers, not to the stupid readers, or the voracious readers, or the malignant readers, or the readers after dinner! We confess, indeed, we never knew an instance in which the theoretical abjurers of popularity have shewn themselves very reluctant to admit its actual advances; so much virtue is not, perhaps, in human nature; and if the world should take a fancy to buy up these poems, in order to be revenged on the ENGLISHMAN'S MAGAZINE, who knows whether even we might not disappoint its malice by a cheerful adaptation of our theory to "existing circumstances?"

JOHN WILSON ["CHRISTOPHER NORTH"]

Tennyson's Poems[†]

* * *

But we are getting into the clouds, and our wish is to keep jogging along the turnpike road. So let all this pass for an introduction to our Article—and let us abruptly join company with the gentleman whose name stands at the head of it, Mr Alfred Tennyson, of whom the world, we presume, yet knows but little or

---

† From *Blackwood's Edinburgh Magazine*, XXXI (May 1832), pp. 721–41. Understandably enough, Tennyson was acutely sensitive to Wilson's gratuitous hostility, not only for his pompous dismissal of many of his poems, but particularly for his offensive ridicule of Hallam's review. Even Hallam could not persuade his friend not to publish a retaliatory squib in the 1832 poems:

To Christopher North

You did late review my lays,
    Crusty Christopher;
You did mingle blame and praise,
    Rusty Christopher.

When I learnt from whom it came,
I forgave you all the blame,

nothing, whom his friends call a Phoenix, but who, we hope, will not be dissatisfied with us, should we designate him merely a Swan.

One of the saddest misfortunes that can befall a young poet, is to be the Pet of a Coterie; and the very saddest of all, if in Cockneydom. Such has been the unlucky lot of Alfred Tennyson. He has been elevated to the throne of Little Britain, and sonnets were showered over his coronation from the most remote regions of his empire, even from Hampstead Hill. Eulogies more elaborate than the architecture of the costliest gingerbread, have been built up into panegyrical piles, in commemoration of the Birth-day; and 'twould be a pity indeed with one's crutch to smash the gilt battlements, white too with sugar as with frost, and begemmed with comfits. The besetting sin of all periodical criticism, and now-a-days there is no other, is boundless extravagance of praise; but none splash it on like the trowel-men who have been bedaubing Mr Tennyson. There is something wrong, however, with the compost. It won't stick; unseemly cracks deform the surface; it falls off piece by piece ere it has dried in the sun, or it hardens into blotches; and the worshippers have but discoloured and disfigured their Idol. The worst of it is, that they make the Bespattered not only feel, but look ridiculous; he seems as absurd as an Image in a tea-garden; and, bedizened with faded and fantastic garlands, the public cough on being told he is a Poet, for he has such more the appearance of a post.

The Englishman's Magazine ought not to have died; for it threatened to be a very pleasant periodical. An Essay [1] "on the Genius of Alfred Tennyson," sent it to the grave. The superhuman—nay, supernatural—pomposity of that one paper, incapacitated the whole work for living one day longer in this unceremonious world. The solemnity with which the critic approached the object of his adoration, and the sanctity with which he laid his offerings on the shrine, were too much for our irreligious age. The Essay "on the genius of Alfred Tennyson," awoke a general guffaw, and it expired in convulsions. Yet the Essay was exceedingly well-written —as well as if it had been "on the Genius of Sir Isaac Newton." Therein lay the mistake. Sir Isaac discovered the law of gravitation; Alfred had but written some pretty verses, and mankind were not prepared to set him among the stars. But that he has genius is proved by his being at this moment alive; for had he not, he must have breathed his last under that critique. The spirit of life must indeed be strong within him; for he has outlived a narcotic dose administered to him by a crazy charlatan in the Westminster,[2] and after that he may sleep in safety with a pan of charcoal.

But the Old Man must see justice done to this ingenious lad, and save him from his worst enemies, his friends. Never are we so happy—nay, 'tis now almost our only happiness—as when scattering flowers in the sunshine that falls

---

Musty Christopher;
I could *not* forgive the praise,
Fusty Christopher.

Hallam took the high ground in the whole proceedings: "I suppose one ought to feel very savage at being attacked," he wrote to his friend, "but somehow I feel much more amused" (*Memoir* I, 84). Tennyson indeed regretted not listening to his friend's advice. In a letter to John Wilson (April 26, 1834) he begged not to be held accountable for complicities with Mr. John Lake to get his own book published: "hew me piecemeal, cut me up in any way you will, exhaust all your world of fun and fancy upon me but do not suspect me—though I may have done, written, said foolish things not excepting a silly squib to Christopher North. . . . I would rather request you if you do not object to meeting me on such dirty grounds, to shake hands over the puddle he has made" (*Letters* I, 109) [*Editor*].
1. Hallam's review [*Editor*].
2. Alludes to a panegyrical review of *Poems, Chiefly Lyrical* in the *Westminster Review*, XIV (January 1831), pp. 210–24, probably by William Johnson Fox [*Editor*].

from the yet unclouded sky on the green path prepared by gracious Nature for the feet of enthusiastic youth. Yet we scatter them not in too lavish profusion; and we take care that the young poet shall see, along with the shadow of the spirit that cheers him on, that, too, of the accompanying crutch. Were we not afraid that our style might be thought to wax too figurative, we should say that Alfred is a promising plant; and that the day may come when, beneath sun and shower, his genius may grow up and expand into a stately tree, embowering a solemn shade within its wide circumference, while the daylight lies gorgeously on its crest, seen from afar in glory—itself a grove.

But that day will never come, if he hearken not to our advice, and, as far as his own nature will permit, regulate by it the movements of his genius. This may perhaps appear, at first sight or hearing, not a little unreasonable on our part; but not so, if Alfred will but lay our words to heart, and meditate on their spirit. We desire to see him prosper; and we predict fame as the fruit of obedience. If he disobey, he assuredly goes to oblivion.

* * *

Shakspeare—Spenser—Milton—Wordsworth—Coleridge—The Ettrick Shepherd—Allan Cunninghame, and some others, have loved, and been beloved by mermaidens, sirens, sea and land fairies, and revealed to the eyes of us who live in the thick atmosphere of this "dim spot which men call earth," all the beautiful wonders of subterranean and submarine climes—and of the climes of Nowhere, lovelier than them all. It pains us to think, that with such names we cannot yet rank that of Alfred Tennyson. We shall soon see that he possesses feeling, fancy, imagination, genius. But in the preternatural lies not the sphere in which he excels. Much disappointed were we to find him weak where we expected him strong; yet we are willing to believe that his failure has been from "affectations." In place of trusting to the natural flow of his own fancies, he has followed some vague abstract idea, thin and delusive, which has escaped in mere words—words—words—. Yet the Young Tailor in the Westminster thinks he could take the measure of the merman, and even make a riding-habit for the sirens to wear on gala days, when disposed for "some horseback." 'Tis indeed a jewel of a Snip. His protégee has indited two feeble and fantastic strains entitled "Nothing will Die," "All things will Die." And them, Parsnip Junior, without the fear of the shears before his eyes, compares with L'Allegro and Il Penseroso of Milton, saying that in Alfred's "there is not less truth, and perhaps more refined observation!" That comes of sitting from childhood cross-legged on a board beneath a skylight.

The Young Tailor can with difficulty keep his seat with delight, when talking of Mr Tennyson's descriptions of the sea. "'Tis barbarous," quoth he, "to break such a piece of coral for a specimen;" and would fain cabbage the whole lump, with the view of placing it among other rarities, such as bits of Derbyshire spar and a brace of mandarins, on the chimney-piece of the shew-parlour in which he notches the dimensions of his visitors. So fired is his imagination, that he beholds in a shred of green fustian a swatch of the multitudinous sea; and on tearing a skreed, thinks he hears him roaring. But Mr Tennyson should speak of the sea so as to rouse the souls of sailors, rather than the soles of tailors—the enthusiasm of the deck, rather than the board. Unfortunately, he seems never to have seen a ship, or, if he did, to have forgotten it. The vessel in which the landlubbers were drifting, when the Sea-Fairies salute them with a song, must have been an old tub of a thing, unfit even for a transport. Such a jib! In the cut of her mainsail you smoke the old table-cloth. To be solemn—Alfred Tennyson is as poor on the sea as Barry Cornwall—and, of course, calls him a serpent. They both write like people who, on venturing upon the world of waters in a bathing machine, would ensure their lives by a cork-jacket. Barry swims on the surface of the Great Deep like a feather; Alfred dives less after the fashion of a duck than a bell; but the one sees few lights, the other few shadows, that are not seen just as well by an oyster-dredger. But the soul of the true sea-poet doth undergo a sea-change, soon as he sees Blue Peter; and is off in the gig,

> While bending back, away they pull,
> With measured strokes most beautiful—

There goes the Commodore!

"Our author having the secret of the transmigration of the soul," passes, like Indur, into the bodies of various animals, and

> Three will I mention dearer than the rest,

the Swan, the Grashopper, and the Owl. The Swan is dying; and as we remember hearing Hartley Coleridge praise the lines, they must be fine; though their full meaning be to us like the moon "hid in her vacant interlunar cave." But Hartley, who is like the river Wye, a wanderer through the woods, is aye haunted with visions of the beautiful; and let Alfred console himself by the reflection, for the absent sympathy of Christopher. As for the Grashopper, Alfred, in that green grig, is for a while merry as a cricket, and chirps and chirrups, though with less meaning, with more monotony, than that hearth-loving insect, who is never so happy, you know, as when in the neighbourhood of a baker's oven. He says to himself as Tithon, though he disclaims that patronymic,

> Thou art a mailed warrior, in youth and strength complete.

a line liable to two faults; first, absurdity, and, second, theft; for the mind is unprepared for the exaggeration of a grashopper into a Templar; and Wordsworth, looking at a beetle through the wonder-working glass of a wizard, beheld

> A mailed angel on a battle-day.

But Tennyson out-Wordsworths Wordsworth, and pursues the knight, surnamed Longshanks, into the fields of chivalry.

> Arm'd cap-a-pie,
> Full pain to see;
> Unknowing fear,
> Undreading loss,
> A gallant cavalier,
> *Sans peur et sans reproche,*
> In sunlight and in shadow,
> THE BAYARD OF THE MEADOW!!

Conceived and executed in the spirit of the celebrated imitation— "Dilly—dilly Duckling! Come and be killed!" But Alfred is greatest as an Owl.

SONG. — THE OWL.

> When the cats run home and light is come,
> And dew is cold upon the ground,

And the far-off stream is dumb,
    And the whirring sail goes round,
    And the whirring sail goes round;
        Alone and warming his five wits,
        The white owl in the belfry sits.

When merry milkmaids click the latch,
    And rarely smells the new mown hay,
And the cock hath sung beneath the thatch
    Twice or thrice his roundelay:
    Twice or thrice his roundelay:
        Alone and warming his five wits,
        The white owl in the belfry sits.

SECOND SONG. — TO THE SAME

Thy tuwhits are lulled, I wot,
    Thy tuwhoos of yesternight,
Which upon the dark afloat,
    So took echo with delight,
    So took echo with delight,
        That her voice untuneful grown,
        Wears all day a fainter tone.

I would mock thy chant anew;
    But I cannot mimic it,
Not a whit of thy tuwhoo,
    Thee to woo to thy tuwhit,
    Thee to woo to thy tuwhit,
        With a lengthened loud halloo,
        Tuwhoo, tuwhit, tuwhit, tuwhoo-o-o.

All that he wants is to be shot, stuffed, and stuck into a glass-case, to be made immortal in a museum.

But, mercy on us! Alfred becomes a—Kraken! Leviathan, "wallowing unwieldy, enormous in his gait," he despises, as we would a minnow; his huge ambition will not suffer him to be "very like a whale;" he must be a—Kraken. And such a Kraken, too, as would have astounded Pontoppidan.

※　※　※

Our critique is near its conclusion; and in correcting it for press, we see that its whole merit, which is great, consists in the extracts, which are "beautiful exceedingly." Perhaps, in the first part of our article, we may have exaggerated Mr Tennyson's unfrequent silliness, for we are apt to be carried away by the whim of the moment, and in our humorous moods, many things wear a queer look to our aged eyes, which fill young pupils with tears; but we feel assured that in the second part we have not exaggerated his strength—that we have done no more than justice to his fine faculties—and that the millions who delight in Maga[3] will, with one voice, confirm our judgment—that Alfred Tennyson is a poet.

3. I.e., *Blackwood's Edinburgh Magazine* [Editor].

But, though it might be a mistake of ours, were we to say that he has much to learn, it can be no mistake to say that he has not a little to unlearn, and more to bring into practice, before his genius can achieve its destined triumphs. A puerile partiality for particular forms of expression, nay, modes of spelling and of pronunciation, may be easily overlooked in one whom *we* must look on as yet a mere body; but if he carry it with him, and indulge it in manhood, why it will make him seem silly as his sheep; and should he continue to bleat so when his head and beard are as grey as ours, he will be truly a laughable old ram, and the ewes will care no more for him than if he were a wether.

* * *

JOHN WILSON CROKER

Poems by Alfred Tennyson[†]

This is, as some of his marginal notes intimate, Mr. Tennyson's second[1] appearance. By some strange chance we have never seen his first publication, which, if it at all resembles its younger brother, must be by this time so popular that any notice of it on our part would seem idle and presumptuous; but we gladly seize this opportunity of repairing an unintentional neglect, and of introducing to the admiration of our more sequestered readers a new prodigy of genius — another and a brighter star of that galaxy or *milky way* of poetry of which the lamented Keats[2] was the harbinger; and let us take this occasion to sing our palinode on the subject of 'Endymion.' We certainly did not discover in that poem the same degree of merit that its more clear-sighted and prophetic admirers did. We did not foresee the unbounded popularity which has carried it through we know not how many editions; which has placed it on every table; and, what is still more unequivocal, familiarized it in every mouth. All this splendour of fame, however, though we had not the sagacity to anticipate, we have the candour to acknowledge; and we request that the publisher of the new and beautiful edition of Keats's works now in the press, with graphic illustrations by Calcott and Turner, will do us the favour and the justice to notice our conversion in his prolegomena.

Warned by our former mishap, wiser by experience, and improved, as we hope, in taste, we have to offer Mr. Tennyson our tribute of unmingled approbation, and it is very agreeable to us, as well as to our readers, that our present task will be little more than the selection, for their delight, of a few specimens of Mr. Tennyson's singular genius, and the venturing to point out, now and then, the peculiar brilliancy of some of the gems that irradiate his poetical crown. * * *

† From *Quarterly Review*, XLIX (April 1833), pp. 81–96.
1. Refers to the 1832 poems. Although "younger brother" is metaphorical, were a reader familiar with *Poems by Two Brothers*, Tennyson's first publication, he might first assume the reference was to one of Tennyson's older brothers, Frederick or Charles [*Editor*].
2. Utterly sarcastic. J. G. Lockhart, in an infamous series of articles, "On the Cockney School of Poetry," published anonymously in *Blackwood's Magazine* (1817–18), was out to attack Leigh Hunt in particular. J. W. Croker's review of Keats's *Endymion* in *The Quarterly* (April 1818) picked up on the theme and savaged Keats so severely that Shelley, in his pastoral elegy *Adonais* on Keats's death, believed (wrongly) that Croker had driven Keats to an early death, deriding the "calm, settled, imperturbable driveling idiocy of 'Endymion.'" For the flavor, and to suggest what Tennyson was up against: "Mr. Hunt is a small poet, but he is a clever man. Mr. Keats is a still smaller poet, and he is only a boy of pretty abilities, which he has done everything in his power to destroy." "Still smaller poet" is a double-entendre, a snipe at Keats's height, just over five feet [*Editor*].

The 'Lotuseaters'[3]—a kind of classical opium-eaters— are Ulysses and his crew. They land on the 'charmèd island,' and eat of the 'charmèd root,' and then they sing—

'Long enough the winedark wave our weary bark did carry.
This is lovelier and sweeter,
Men of Ithaca, this is meeter,
In the hollow rosy vale to tarry,
Like a dreamy Lotuseater—a delicious Lotuseater!
We will eat the Lotus, sweet
As the yellow honeycomb;
In the valley some, and some
On the ancient heights divine,
And no more roam,
On the loud hoar foam,
To the melancholy home,
At the limits of the brine,
The little isle of Ithaca, beneath the day's decline.'—p. 116.

Our readers will, we think, agree that this is admirably characteristic, and that the singers of this song must have made pretty free with the intoxicating fruit. How they got home you must read in Homer:—Mr. Tennyson—himself, we presume, a dreamy lotus-eater, a delicious lotus-eater—leaves them in full song.

Next comes another class of poems,—Visions. The first is the 'Palace of Art,' or a fine house, in which the poet *dreams* that he sees a very fine collection of well-known pictures. An ordinary versifier would, no doubt, have followed the old routine, and dully described himself as walking into the Louvre, or Buckingham Palace, and there seeing certain masterpieces of painting:—a true poet dreams it. We have not room to hang many of these *chefs-d'œuvre*, but for a few we must find space.—'The Madonna'—

'The maid mother by a crucifix,
In yellow pastures sunny warm,
Beneath branch work of costly sardonyx
Sat smiling—*babe in arm.*'— p. 72.

The use of this latter, apparently, colloquial phrase is a deep stroke of art. The form of expression is always used to express an habitual and characteristic action. A knight is described '*lance in rest*'—a dragoon, '*sword in hand*'—so, as the idea of the Virgin is inseparably connected with her child, Mr. Tennyson reverently describes her conventional position—'*babe in arm.*'

His gallery of illustrious portraits is thus admirably arranged:—The Madonna—Ganymede—St. Cecilia—Europa—Deep-haired Milton—Shakspeare—Grim Dante—Michael Angelo—Luther—Lord Bacon—Cervantes—Calderon—King David—'the Halicarnassëan' (*quœre*, which of them?)—Alfred, (not Alfred Tennyson, though no doubt in any other man's gallery *he* would have had a place) and finally—

'Isaïah, with fierce Ezekiel,
Swarth Moses by the Coptic sea,

---

3. Here Croker is playing petty games with Tennyson's spelling of "lotos-eater," and again just below, with lotus-eater for 'Lotuseaters' [*Editor*].

Plato, *Petrarca*, Livy, and Raphaël,
And eastern Confutzee!'

We can hardly suspect the very original mind of Mr. Tennyson to have har-
boured any recollections of that celebrated Doric idyll, 'The groves of Blarney,'
but certainly there is a strong likeness between Mr. Tennyson's list of pictures
and the Blarney collection of statues—

'Statues growing that noble place in,
All heathen goddesses most rare,
Homer, Plutarch, and Nebuchadnezzar,
All standing naked in the open air!'

In this poem we first observed a stroke of art (repeated afterwards) which we
think very ingenious. No one who has ever written verse but must have felt the
pain of erasing some happy line, some striking stanza, which, however excellent in itself, did not exactly suit the place for which it was destined. How curiously does an author mould and remould the plastic verse in order to fit in the
favourite thought; and when he finds that he cannot introduce it, as Corporal
Trim says, *any how*, with what reluctance does he at last reject the intractable,
but still cherished offspring of his brain! Mr. Tennyson manages this delicate
matter in a new and better way; he says, with great candour and simplicity, 'If
this poem were not already too long, I *should have added* the following stanzas,'
and *then he adds them,* (p. 84;)—or, 'the following lines are manifestly super-
fluous, as a part of the text, but they may be allowed to stand as a separate poem,'
(p. 121,) *which they do;*—or, 'I intended to have added something on statuary,
but I found it very difficult;'— (he had, moreover, as we have seen, been anticipated in this line by the Blarney poet)—'but I had finished the statues of *Eli-
jah* and *Olympias*—judge whether I have succeeded,' (p. 73)—and then we
have these two statues. This is certainly the most ingenious device that has ever
come under our observation, for reconciling the rigour of criticism with the indulgence of parental partiality. It is economical too, and to the reader prof-
itable, as by these means

'We lose no drop of the immortal man.'

The other vision is 'A Dream of Fair Women,' in which the heroines of all
ages—some, indeed, that belong to the times of 'heathen goddesses most
rare'—pass before his view. We have not time to notice them all, but the second, whom we take to be Iphigenia, touches the heart with a stroke of nature
more powerful than even the veil that the Grecian painter threw over the head
of her father.

————'dimly I could descry
The stern blackbearded kings with wolfish eyes,
Watching to see me die.
The tall masts quivered as they lay afloat;
The temples, and the people, and the shore;
One drew a sharp knife through my tender throat—
Slowly,—and *nothing more!*'

What touching simplicity—what pathetic resignation—he cut my throat —
'*nothing more!*' One might indeed ask, 'what *more*' she would have?

But we must hasten on; and to tranquillize the reader's mind after the last affecting scene, shall notice the only two pieces of a lighter strain which the volume affords. The first is elegant and playful; it is a description of the author's study, which he affectionately calls his *Darling Room*.

> 'O darling room, my heart's delight;
> Dear room, the apple of my sight;
> With thy two couches, soft and white,
> There is no room so exqui*site*;
> No little room so warm and bright,
> Wherein to read, wherein to write.'

We entreat our readers to note how, even in this little trifle, the singular taste and genius of Mr. Tennyson break forth. In such a dear *little* room a narrow-minded scribbler would have been content with *one* sofa, and that one he would probably have covered with black mohair, or red cloth, or a good striped chintz; how infinitely more characteristic is white dimity!—'tis as it were a type of the purity of the poet's mind.   * * *

The second of the lighter pieces, and the last with which we shall delight our readers, is a severe retaliation on the editor of the Edinburgh Magazine, who, it seems, had not treated the first volume of Mr. Tennyson with the same respect that we have, we trust, evinced for the second.

> 'TO CHRISTOPHER NORTH.
> You did late review my lays,
>   Crusty Christopher;
> You did mingle blame and praise,
>   Rusty Christopher.
>
> When I learnt from whom it came
> I forgave you all the blame,
>   Musty Christopher;
> I could *not* forgive the praise,
>   Fusty Christopher.'—p. 153.

Was there ever anything so genteelly turned—so terse—so sharp —and the point so stinging and *so true*?

* * *

JOHN STUART MILL

Tennyson's Poems[†]

* * *

Of all the capacities of a poet, that which seems to have arisen earliest in Mr. Tennyson, and in which he most excels, is that of scene-painting, in the higher sense of the term: not the mere power of producing that rather vapid species of

---

† From *London Review*, I (July 1835), pp. 402–24. "Early in 1835 Spedding sent him news that J. S. Mill intended writing favorably of him in the *London Review*, but he could not bear the thought even of a friendly criticism of his published work. 'It is the last thing I wish for,' he replied, 'and I would that you

composition usually termed descriptive poetry—for there is not in these volumes one passage of pure description; but the power of *creating* scenery, in keeping with some state of human feeling; so fitted to it as to be the embodied symbol of it, and to summon up the state of feeling itself, with a force not to be surpassed by anything but reality. Our first specimen, selected from the earlier of the two volumes, will illustrate chiefly this quality of Mr. Tennyson's productions. We do not anticipate that this little poem will be equally relished at first by all lovers of poetry: and, indeed, if it were, its merit could be but of the humblest kind; for sentiments and imagery which can be received at once, and with equal ease, into every mind, must necessarily be trite. Nevertheless, we do not hesitate to quote it at full length. The subject is Mariana, the Mariana of "Measure for Measure," living deserted and in solitude in the "moated grange." The ideas which these two words suggest, impregnated with the feelings of the supposed inhabitant, have given rise to the following picture: [Mill here reproduced the text of "Mariana."]

In the one peculiar and rare quality which we intended to illustrate by it, this poem appears to us to be preeminent. We do not, indeed, defend all the expressions in it, some of which seem to have been extorted from the author by the tyranny of rhyme; and we might find much more to say against the poem, if we insisted upon judging it by a wrong standard. The nominal subject excites anticipations which the poem does not even attempt to fulfil. The humblest poet who is a poet at all, could make more than is here made of the situation of a maiden abandoned by her lover. But that was not Mr. Tennyson's idea. The love-story is secondary in his mind. The words, "he cometh not," are almost the only words which allude to it at all. To place ourselves at the right point of view, we must drop the conception of Shakespeare's Mariana, and retain only that of a "moated grange," and a solitary dweller within it, forgotten by mankind. And now see whether poetic imagery ever conveyed a more intense conception of such a place, or of the feeling of such an inmate. From the very first line, the rust of age and the solitude of desertion are on the whole picture. Words surely never excited a more vivid feeling of physical and spiritual dreariness: and not dreariness alone—for that might be felt under many other circumstances of solitude—but the dreariness which speaks not merely of being far from human converse and sympathy, but of being *deserted* by it.

* * *

If every one approached poetry in the spirit in which it ought to be approached, willing to feel it first and examine it afterwards, we should not premise another word. But there is a class of readers (a class, too, on whose verdict the early success of a young poet mainly depends), who dare not enjoy until

---

or some other who may be friends of Mill would hint as much to him. I do not wish to be draggged again in any shape before the reading public at present, particularly on the score of my old poems" (*Alfred Tennyson*, p. 154). "So far as his poetry was concerned, the year brought no improvement in his position. J. S. Mill's admirable article, which appeared in June, was offset by the appearance at about the same time of Coleridge's *Table Talk*, containing the expression of regret that young Alfred Tennyson had begun writing verse without well knowing what meter was" (*Alfred Tennyson*, p. 161). "By the time 'Christopher Norths's' last reference had appeared [he had taken an offhand fling at Tennyson in April 1833 for the epigram directed at him] he had to wait more than two years for the first favorable review of real consequence, that by John Stuart Mill in the *London Review* in 1835, and by then he was so tender that he wished only to remain unnoticed, even by an approving critic" (Martin's *Tennyson*, pp. 172–73), which gives more than a hint for the reasons behind the so-called ten-year silence. For Tennyson did not venture into print again until 1842 [*Editor*].

they have felt satisfied themselves that they have a warrant for enjoying; who
read a poem with the critical understanding first, and only when they are convinced that it is right to be delighted, are willing to give their spontaneous feelings fair play. The consequence is that they lose the general effect, while they
higgle about the details, and never place themselves in the position in which,
even with their mere understandings, they can estimate the poem as a whole.
For the benefit of such readers, we tell them beforehand, that this is a tale of enchantment, and that they will never enter into the spirit of it unless they surrender their imagination to the guidance of the poet, with the same easy
credulity with which they would read the "Arabian Nights," or what this story
more resembles, the tales of magic of the Middle Ages.

Though the agency is supernatural, the scenery, as will be perceived, belongs
to the actual world. No reader of any imagination will complain, that the precise nature of the enchantment is left in mystery.

* * *

In powers of narrative and scene-painting combined, this poem must be
ranked among the very first of its class. The delineation of outward objects, as
in the greater number of Mr. Tennyson's poems, is, not picturesque, but (if we
may use the term) statuesque; with brilliancy of colour superadded. The forms
are not as in painting, of unequal degrees of definiteness; the tints do not melt
gradually into each other, but each individual object stands out in bold relief,
with a clear decided outline. This statue-like precision and distinctness few
artists have been able to give to so essentially vague a language as that of words:
but if once this difficulty be got over, scene-painting by words has a wider range
than either painting or sculpture; for it can represent (as the reader must have
seen in the foregoing poem), not only with the vividness and strength of the one,
but with the clearness and definiteness of the other, objects in motion. Along
with all this there is in the poem all that power of making a few touches do the
whole work, which excites our admiration in Coleridge. Every line suggests so
much more than it says, that much may be left unsaid: the concentration, which
is the soul of narrative, is obtained without the sacrifice of reality and life.
Where the march of the story requires that the mind shall pause, details are
specified; where rapidity is necessary, they are all brought before us at a flash.
Except that the versification is less exquisite, the "Lady of Shallot" is entitled to
a place by the side of "The Ancient Mariner" and "Christabel."

* * *

The poems which we have quoted from Mr. Tennyson prove incontestably
that he possesses, in an eminent degree, the natural endowment of a poet—the
poetic temperament. And it appears clearly not only from a comparison of the
two volumes, but of different poems in the same volume, that, with him, the
other element of poetic excellence—intellectual culture—is advancing both
steadily and rapidly; that he is not destined like so many others, to be remem-
bered for what he might have done, rather than for what he did; that he will not
remain a poet of mere temperament, but is ripening into a true artist. Mr. Tennyson may not be conscious of the wide difference in maturity of intellect,
which is apparent in his various poems. Though he now writes from greater fulness and clearness of thought, it by no means follows that he has learnt to de-

tect the absence of those qualities in some of his earlier effusions. Indeed, he himself in one of the most beautiful poems of his first volume (though, as a work of art, very imperfect), the "Ode to Memory," confesses a parental predilection for the "first born" of his genius. But to us it is evident, not only that his second volume differs from his first as early manhood from youth, but that the various poems of the first volume belong to different, and even distant stages of intellectual development;—distant, not perhaps in years—for a mind like Mr. Tennyson's advances rapidly—but corresponding to very different states of the intellectual powers, both in respect of their strength and of their proportions.

From the very first, like all writers of his natural gifts, he luxuriates in sensuous imagery; his nominal subject sometimes lies buried in a heap of it. From the first, too, we see his intellect, with every successive dgree of strength, struggling upwards to shape this sensuous imagery to a spiritual meaning, to bring the materials which sense supplies, and fancy summons up, under the command of a central and controlling thought or feeling. We have seen by the poem of "Mariana" with what success he could occasionally do this, even in the period which answers to his first volume; but that volume contains various instances in which he has attempted the same thing and failed.

* * *

Some of the smaller poems have a fault which in any but a very juvenile production would be the worse fault of all: they are altogether without meaning: none, at least, that can be discerned in them by persons otherwise competent judges of poetry; if the author had any meaning, he has not been able to express it. Such, for instance are the two songs on the Owl; such, also, are the verses headed "The How and the Why," in the first volume, and the lines on "To-day and Yesterday," in the second. In the former of these productions Mr. Tennyson aimed at shadowing forth the vague aspirations to a knowledge beyond the reach of man—the yearnings for a solution of all questions, soluble or insoluble, which concern our nature and destiny—the impatience under the insufficiency of the human faculties to penetrate the secret of our being here, and being what we are—which are natural in a certain state of the human mind; if this was what he sought to typify, he has only proved that he knows not the feeling—that he has neither experienced it, nor realized it in imagination. The questions which a Faust calls upon earth and heaven, and all powers supernal and infernal, to resolve for him, are not the ridiculous ones which Mr. Tennyson asks himself in these verses.

But enough of faults which the poet has almost entirely thrown off merely by the natural expansion of his intellect. We have alluded to them chiefly to show how rapidly progressive that intellect has been. There are traces, we think, of a continuance of the same progression throughout the second as well as the first volume.

In the art of painting a picture to the inward eye, the improvement is not so conspicuous as in other qualities; so high a degree of excellence having been already attained in the first volume. Besides the poems which we have quoted, we may refer, in that volume, to those entitled, "Recollections of the Arabian Nights," "The Dying Swan," "The Kraken," "The Sleeping Beauty," the beautiful poems (songs they are called, but are not), "In the glooming light," and "A spirit haunts the year's last hours," are (like the "Mariana") not mere pictures, but states of emotion, embodied in sensuous imagery. From these, however, to the command over the materials of outward sense for the purpose of bodying forth states of feeling, evinced by some of the poems in the second volume, especially "The Lady of Shallot" and "The Lotos Eaters," there is a considerable distance; and Mr. Tennyson seems, as he proceeded to have raised his aims still higher, to have aspired to render his poems not only vivid representations of spiritual states, but symbolical of spiritual truths. His longest poem, "The Palace of Art," is an attempt of this sort. As such we do not think it wholly successful, though rich in beauties of detail; but we deem it of the most favourable augury for Mr. Tennyson's future achievements, since it proves a continually increasing endeavour towards the highest excellence, and a constantly rising standard of it.

We predict, that as Mr. Tennyson advances in general spiritual culture, these higher aims will become more and more predominant in his writings, that he will strive more and more deligently, and, even without striving, will be more and more impelled by the natural tendencies of an expanding character, towards what has been described as the highest object of poetry, "to incorporate the everlasting reason of man in forms visible to his sense, and suitable to it." For the fulfilment of this exalted purpose, what we have already seen of him authorizes us to foretell with confidence that powers of execution will not fail him; it rests with himself to see that his powers of thought may keep pace with them. To render his poetic endowment the means of giving impressiveness to important truths, he must by continual study and meditation strengthen his intellect for the discrimination of such truths; he must see that his theory of life and the world be no chimera of the brain, but the well-grounded result of solid and mature thinking;—he must cultivate, and with no half-devotion, philosophy as well as poetry.

* * *

JOHN STERLING

Poems by Alfred Tennyson[†]

What poetry might be in our time and land, if a man of the highest powers and most complete cultivation exercised the art among us, will be hard to say until after the fact of such a man's existence. Waiting for this desirable event, we may at least see that poetry, to be for us what it has sometimes been among

† From *Quarterly Review*, LXX (September 1842), pp. 385–416. Although the publication of *Poems* in 1842 initially received little notice from the so-called professional critics, Tennyson had slowly been gathering "enthusiasm from a small but steadily increasing band of admirers including Carlyle, Dickens, Rogers and Edward FitzGerald" (*Alfred Tennyson*, p. 192). Five years before Hallam and Tennyson were elected to the Apostles, John Sterling along with F. D. Maurice (see Tennyson's poem "To the Rev. F. D. Maurice") were the prime movers in elevating that society to political prominence. As its leader, Sterling was the one who had been particularly attracted to General Torrijos, getting the organization "directly and even dangerously involved in the Spanish revolutionary movement." See the poems "In the Valley of Cauteretz" and "Œnone" and notes for Hallam's and Tennyson's participation. The appearance of Sterling's article in the *Quarterly* "nearly caused Croker to sever his connections with the review" (*Alfred Tennyson*, p. 195; also pp. 68–93). Sterling died of consumption at thirty-eight, but he had been the one most responsible for keeping the poet in close contact with London's rising political and literary figures, including Carlyle, Macready, Landor, and many former Apostles from the undergraduate days at Cambridge [*Editor*].

mankind, must wear a new form, and probably comprise elements hardly found in our recent writings, and impossible in former ones.

Of verses, indeed, of every sort but the excellent there is no want: almost all, however, so helpless in skill, so faint in meaning, that one might almost fancy the authors wrote metre from mere incapacity of expressing themselves at all in prose—as boys at school sometimes make nonsense-verses before they can construct a rational sentence. Yet it is plain that even our magazine stanzas, album sonnets, and rhymes in corners of newspapers aim at the forms of emotion, and use some of the words in which men of genius have symbolized profound thoughts. The whole, indeed, is generally a lump of blunder and imbecility, but in the midst there is often some turn of cadence, some attempt at an epithet of more significance and beauty than perhaps a much finer mind would have hit on a hundred years ago. The crowds of stammering children are yet the offspring of an age that would fain teach them—if it knew how—a richer, clearer language than they can learn to speak.

It is hard in this state of things not to conceive that the time, among us at least, is an essentially unpoetic one—one which, whatever may be the worth of its feelings, finds no utterance for them in melodious words.

* * * Now, strangely as our time is racked and torn, haunted by ghosts, and errant in search of lost realities, poor in genuine culture, incoherent among its own chief elements, untrained to social facility and epicurean quiet, yet unable to unite its means in pursuit of any lofty blessing, half-sick, half-dreaming, and whole confused—he would be not only misanthropic, but ignorant, who should maintain it to be a poor, dull, and altogether helpless age, and not rather one full of great though conflicting energies, seething with high feelings, and struggling towards the light with piercing though still hooded eyes. The fierce, too often mad force, that wars itself away among the labouring poor, the manifold skill and talent and unwearied patience of the middle classes, and the still unshaken solidity of domestic life among them—these are facts open to all, though by none perhaps sufficiently estimated. And over and among all society the wealth of our richer people is gathered and diffused as it has never been before anywhere else, shaping itself into a thousand arts of luxury, a million modes of social pleasure, which the moralist may have much to object against, but which the poet, had we a truly great one now rising among us, would well know how to employ for his own purposes.

Then, too, if we reflect that the empire and nation seated here as in its centre, and at home so moving and multifarious, spreads its dominions all round the globe, daily sending forth its children to mix in the life of every race of man, seek adventures in every climate, and fit themselves to every form of polity, or it to them— whereafter they return in body, or at least reflect their mental influences among us—it cannot be in point of diversity and meaning that Britain disappoints any one capable of handling what it supplies.

* * *

Little therefore as is all that has been done towards the poetic representation of our time—even in the looser and readier form of prose romance—

it is hard to suppose that it is incapable of such treatment. The still unadulterated purity of home among large circles of the nation presents an endless abundance of the feelings and characters, the want of which nothing else in existence can supply even to a poet. And these soft and steady lights strike an observer all the more from the restless activity and freedom of social ambition, the shifting changes of station, and the wealth gathered on one hard and spent on the other with a intenseness and amplitude of will to which there is at least nothing now comparable among mankind. The power of self-subjection combined with almost boundless liberty, indeed necessitated by it, and the habit of self-denial with wealth beyond all calculation—these are indubitable facts in modern England. But while recognised as facts, how far do they still remain from that development as thoughts which philosophy desires, or that vividness as images which is the aim of poetry! It is easy to say that the severity of conscience in the best minds checks all play of fancy, and the fierceness of the outward struggle for power and riches absorbs the energies that would otherwise exert themselves in shapeful melody. But had we minds full of the idea and the strength requisite for such work, they would find in this huge, harassed, and luxurious national existence the nourishment, not the poison, of creative art. The death-struggle of commercial and political rivalry, the brooding doubt and remorse, the gas-jet flame of faith irradiating its own coal-mine darkness—in a word, our overwrought materialism fevered by its own excess into spiritual dreams—all this might serve the purposes of a bold imagination, no less than the creed of the antipoetic Puritans became poetry in the mind of Milton, and all bigotries, superstitions, and gore-dyed horrors were flames that kindled steady light in Shakespeare's humane and meditative song.

* * *

In thus pointing to the problem which poetry now holds out, and maintaining that it has been but partially solved by our most illustrious writers, there is no design of setting up an unattainable standard, and then blaming any one in particular for inevitably falling short of it. Out of an age so diversified and as yet so unshapely, he who draws forth any graceful and expressive forms is well entitled to high praise. Turning into fixed beauty any part of the shifting and mingled matter of our time, he does what in itself is very difficult, and affords very valuable help to all his future fellow-labourers. If he has not given us back our age as a whole transmuted into crystalline clearness and lustre, a work accomplished only by a few of the greatest minds under the happiest circumstances for their art, yet we scarce know to whom we should be equally grateful as to him who has enriched us with any shapes of lasting loveliness 'won from the vague and formless infinite.'

Mr. Tennyson has done more of this kind than almost any one that has appeared among us during the last twenty years. And in such a task of alchemy a really successful experiment, even on a small scale, is of great worth compared with the thousands of fruitless efforts or pretences on the largest plan, which are daily clamouring for all men's admiration of their nothingness.

* * *

JAMES SPEDDING

Tennyson's Poems[†]

* * * The decade during which Mr Tennyson has remained silent has wrought a great improvement. The handling in his later pieces is much lighter and freer; the interest deeper and purer;— there is more humanity with less imagery and drapery; a closer adherence to truth; a greater reliance for effect upon the simplicity of nature. Moral and spiritual traits of character are more dwelt upon, in place of external scenery and circumstance. He addresses himself more to the heart, and less to the ear and eye. This change, which is felt in its results throughout the second volume, may in the latter half of the first be traced in its process. The poems originally published in 1832, are many of them largely altered; generally with great judgment, and always with a view to strip off redundancies— to make the expression simpler and clearer, to substitute thought for imagery, and substance for shadow. * * * All that is of true and lasting worth in poetry, must have its root in a sound view of human life and the condition of man in the world; a just feeling with regard to the things in which we are all concerned. Where this is not, the most consummate art can produce nothing which men will long care for—where it is, the rudest will never want audience, for then nothing is trivial—the most ordinary incidents of daily life are invested with an interest as deep as the springs of emotion in the heart—as deep as pity, and love, and fear, and awe. In this requisite Mr Tennyson will not be found wanting. The human soul, in its infinite variety of moods and trials, is his favourite haunt; nor can he dwell long upon any subject, however apparently remote from the scenes and objects of modern sympathy, without touching some string which brings it within the range of our common life. His moral views, whether directly or indirectly conveyed, are healthy, manly, and simple; and the truth and delicacy of his sentiments is attested by the depth of the pathos which he can evoke from the commonest incidents, told in the simplest manner, yet deriving all their interest from the manner of telling. * * * There are four poems in which Mr Tennyson has expressly treated of certain morbid states of the mind; and from these we may gather, not indeed his creed, but some hints concerning his moral theory of life and its issues, and of that which constitutes a sound condition of the soul. These are the 'Palace of Art,' the 'St Simeon Stylites,' the 'Two Voices,' and the 'Vision of Sin.' The 'Palace of Art' represents allegorically the condition of a mind which, in the love of beauty and the triumphant consciousness of knowledge and intellectual supremacy, in the intense enjoyment of its own power and glory has lost sight of its relation to man and to God.

---

† From *Edinburgh Review*, LXXVII (April 1843), pp. 373–91. Spedding was Tennyson's lifelong friend, since their undergraduate days together at Cambridge and among the Apostles. He was a first-rate literary critic, who devoted his whole life to a biography of Francis Bacon and editions of his works. By Hallam, Tennyson, and FitzGerald, among others, he was much beloved and respected: "His bald, dome-like forehead and sobriety of demeanour were the theme of endless jokes among them, while at the same time they looked up to him as the wisest man of their generation" (*Alfred Tennyson*, p. 71). His reputed "sobriety," however, is much qualified by the delight one takes in reading through his marginal notes on the Trinity manuscript of *IM*, in which he reveals not only his dry wit but an unrestrained familiarity to jot down just what he thinks. See *IM* 75 and notes and especially the notes to section 78. Tennyson's confidence in, respect for, and love of the man were well placed. (See the poet's poem "To J. S" on the untimely death of Spedding's younger brother) [*Editor*].

* * *

As the 'Palace of Art' represents the pride of voluptuous enjoyment in its no-blest form, the 'St Simeon Stylites' represents the pride of asceticism in its basest. To shadow forth dramatically the faith, the feelings, and the hopes, which support the man who, being taught that the rewards of another life will be proportioned to the misery voluntarily undergone in this, is best on qualify-ing himself for the best place—appears to be the design, or the running idea, of the poem. It is done with great force and effect; and, as far as we can guess, with great fidelity to nature. Of this, however, we must confess that we are not com-petent judges. Holding, as we do, that all self-torment inflicted for its own sake—all mortification beyond what is necessary to keep the powers of self-com-mand and self-restraint in exercise, and the lower parts of our nature in due sub-jection to the higher—is a thing unblest; and that the man who thinks to propitiate God by degrading his image and making his temple loathsome, must have his whole heart out of tune, and be in the right way to the wrong place—we must confess that we cannot so expand our human sympathy as to reach the case of St Simeon. We notice the poem for the light it throws on Mr Tennyson's feeling with regard to this disease of the mind; which, if we collect it rightly—(for, as the saint has all the talk to himself, it cannot of course be conveyed di-rectly)—is, that selfishness, sensuality, and carnal pride, are really at the bottom of it; and this, however paradoxical it may appear, we believe to be quite true.

In the 'Two Voices' we have a history of the agitations, the suggestions, and counter-suggestions, of a mind sunk in hopeless despondency, and meditating self-destruction; together with the manner of its recovery to a more healthy con-dition. Though not one of the most perfect, it is one of the most remarkable of Mr Tennyson's productions. An analysis of the arguments urged on either side, would present nothing very new or striking; and in point of poetical manage-ment—though rising occasionally into passages of great power and beauty, and though indicating throughout a subtle and comprehensive intellect, well fitted for handling such questions—it appears to us to be too long drawn out, and too full of a certain tender and passionate eloquence, hardly compatible with that dreary and barren misery in which the mind is supposed to be languishing. The dry and severe style with which the poem begins, should have been kept up, we think, through the greater portion of the dialogue, especially on the part of the 'dull and bitter' voice, which sustains the character of a tempting Mephistophe-les. These, however, are points of minute criticism, into which we have not room to enter. What we are at present concerned with, is the moral bearing of the poem. The disease is familiar; but where are we to look for the remedy? Many persons would have thought it enough to administer a little religious con-solation to the diseased mind; but unfortunately despondency is no more like ignorance than atrophy is like hunger; and as the most nutritious food will not nourish the latter, so the most comfortable doctrine will not refresh the former. Not the want of consoling topics, but the incapacity to receive consolation, con-stitutes the disease. Others would have been content to give the bad voice the worst of the argument; but, unhappily, all moral reasoning must ultimately rest on the internal evidence of the moral sense: and where this is disordered, the most unquestionable logic can conclude nothing, because it is the first princi-ples which are at issue;—the *major* is not admitted. Mr Tennyson's treatment of the case is more scientific. We quote it, not indeed as new or original,—(it has been anticipated, and may perhaps have been suggested, by Mr Wordsworth, in the memorable passage at the close of the fourth book of the 'Excursion,') — but for the soundness of the philosophy, and the poetic beauty of the handling. The dialogue ends, (as such a dialogue, if truly reported, must always do,) leaving every thing unsettled, and nothing concluded. * * *

The 'Vision of Sin' touches upon a more awful subject than any of these; — the end, here and hereafter, of the merely sensual man: —

> 'I had a vision when the night was late:
> A youth came riding toward a palace-gate.
> He rode a horse with wings, that would have flown,
> But that his heavy rider kept him down.
> And from the palace came a child of sin,
> And took him by the curls, and led him in.'

Then follows a passage of great lyrical power, representing, under the figure of Music, the gradual yielding up of the soul to sensual excitement, in its successive stages of languor, luxury, agitation, madness, and triumph: —

> 'Till, kill'd with some luxurious agony,
> The nerve-dissolving melody
> Flutter'd headlong from the sky.'

This is the sensual life to which the youth is supposed to be given up. Meantime, the inevitable, irrevocable judgment comes slowly on, — not without due token and warning, but without regard: —

> 'And then I look'd up toward a mountain-tract,
> That girt the region with high cliff and lawn:
> I saw that every morning, far withdrawn
> Beyond the darkness and the cataract,
> God made Himself an awful rose of dawn,
> Unheeded: and detaching, fold by fold,
> From those still heights, and, slowly drawing near,
> A vapour heavy, hueless, formless, cold,
> Came floating on for many a month and year,
> Unheeded; and I thought I would have spoken,
> And warn'd that madman ere it grew too late:
> But, as in dreams, I could not. Mine was broken,
> When that cold vapour touch'd the palace-gate,
> And link'd again. I saw within my head
> A grey and gap-tooth'd man as lean as death,
> Who slowly rode across a wither'd heath,
> And lighted at a ruin'd inn————'

This is the youth, the winged steed, and the palace—the warm blood, the mounting spirit, and the lustful body—now chilled, jaded, and ruined; the cup of pleasure drained to the dregs; the senses exhausted of their power to enjoy, the spirit of its wish to aspire: nothing left but 'loathing, craving, and rottenness.'[1] His mental and moral state is developed in a song, or rather a lyric speech, too long to quote; and of which, without quoting, we cannot attempt to convey an idea;—a ghastly picture (lightened only by a seasoning of wild in-

1. Berkeley.

human humour) of misery and mockery, impotent malice and impenitent regret; 'languid enjoyment of evil with utter incapacity to 'good.'[2] Such is his end
on earth. But the end of all?

> 'The voice grew faint: there came a further change;
> Again arose the mystic mountain-range:
> Below were men and horses pierced with worms,
> And slowly quickening into lower forms;
> By shards and scurf of salt, and scum of dross,
> Old plash of rains and refuse patch'd with moss.
> Then some one said. "Behold! it was a crime
> Of sense avenged by sense that wore with time."
> Another said, "The crime of sense became
> The crime of malice, and is equal blame."
> And one: "He had not wholly quench'd his power;
> A little grain of conscience made him sour."
> At last I heard a voice upon the slope
> Cry to the summit—"Is there any hope!"
> To which an answer peal'd from that high land,
> But in a tongue no man could understand;
> And on the glimmering limit, far-withdrawn,
> God made Himself an awful rose of dawn.'

Into the final mysteries of judgment and of mercy let no man presume to en-
quire further. Enough for us to know what for us is evil. Be the rest left to Him
with whom nothing is impossible!

We have dwelt longer on these four poems than either their prominence or
their relative poetic merit would have led us to do; because, though they may
not show the author's art in its most perfect or most attractive form, they show
the depth from which it springs; they show that it is no trick of these versifying
times—born of a superficial sensibility to beauty and a turn for setting to music
the current doctrines and fashionable feelings of the day; but a genuine growth
of nature, having its root deep in the pensive heart —a heart accustomed to
meditate earnestly, and feel truly, upon the prime duties and interests of man.

We cannot conclude without reminding Mr Tennyson, that highly as we
value the Poems which he has produced, we cannot accept them as a satisfactory account of the gifts which they show that he possesses; any more than we
could take a painter's collection of *studies* for a picture, in place of the picture
itself. Powers are displayed in these volumes, adequate, if we do not deceive ourselves, to the production of a great work; at least we should find it difficult to say
which of the requisite powers is wanting. But they are displayed in fragments
and snatches, having no connexion, and therefore deriving no light or fresh interest the one from the other. By this their effective value is incalculably di-
minished. Take the very best scenes in Shakspeare—detach them from the
context— and suppose all the rest to have perished, or never to have been written—where would be the evidence of the power which created Lear and Hamlet? Yet, perhaps, not one of those scenes could have been produced by a man
who was not capable of producing the whole. If Mr Tennyson can find a subject large enough[3] to take the entire impress of his mind, and energy persever-

2. Lamb.
3. Spedding had the best of reasons to be "convinced" that Tennyson "may produce a work" of huge significance; he was among the very few who were privy to the largely completed elegies that would be-

ing enough to work it faithfully out as one whole, we are convinced that he may produce a work, which, though occupying no larger space than the contents of these volumes, shall as much exceed them in value, as a series of quantities multiplied into each other exceeds in value the same series simply added together.

JAMES KNOWLES

A Personal Reminiscence[†]

If in the following pages I can contribute a few touches to the portrait of Lord Tennyson which his contemporaries alone can paint, my object in writing them will be accomplished. Of Tennyson the Poet his Poems will remain a 'monument more lasting than brass' to the remotest future. But of the man himself 'in his habit as he lived' the likeness can only be portrayed by those who knew him personally, and only now, while their memory of him is fresh, and before it passes away with them into oblivion. What would the world not give for such a picture of Shakespeare by his friends as may now be made of Tennyson?

In a letter of his which lies before me he draws a distinction between personal things which may be told of a man before and after his death, and complains of the neglect of that distinction during his life. He recognised that after death a Memoir of him was inevitable, and left the charge of it in its fulness to his son. What follow are but slight contributions towards any such complete biography, for only upon the few occasions which are here recorded did I make any note in writing of all Tennyson's talk heard and enjoyed for nearly thirty years. His own words I have printed always in italics.

More than thirty years ago I had the happiness of making his acquaintance. I was about to publish a little book on King Arthur, chiefly compiled from Sir Thomas Malory, and, as a stranger, had written to ask leave to dedicate it to him—a leave which was directly granted.

For some time afterwards I knew him merely by correspondence, but being in the Isle of Wight one autumn I called to thank him personally for what he had written to me, and then first saw him face to face. I found him even kinder than his letters, and from that time our acquaintance grew gradually closer until it became intimate.

Before long he asked me to become his architect for the new house he proposed to build near Haslemere ('Aldworth' as it was finally called), and the consultations and calculations which naturally followed as to his way of living, the

come *IM*, for he was reading and making notes on them during November 1842. Obviously completely trusted with the confidence, Spedding must have derived a great deal of pleasure while penning this conclusion to his article [*Editor*].

† From *The Nineteenth Century*, XXXIII (January 1893), pp. 164–88. Tennyson met Knowles in the summer of 1866, although the young architect had, with literary ambition in mind, dedicated in 1862 a volume of Arthurian stories to the laureate. It was Knowles who built "Aldworth," Tennyson's new, second country home (named for the village of Emily Tennyson's ancestors) on the condition that no fee would be accepted. The foundation stone, for what was often described as a miniature castle, was laid on Shakespeare's birthday, April 23, 1868. The initial relationship between the two was a mutually advantageous one — Knowles had literary aspirations; Tennyson got a splendid pile and his first bathroom with running water. Carlyle, who could spot upstart ambition when he saw it, despised Knowles, calling him "Tennyson's bricklayer" (Martin's *Tennyson*, p. 471). Yet, with gradually easing tensions between them, Knowles and Tennyson remained on good terms until the poet's death some twenty-five years later [*Editor*].

plans, and the cost of building, led to much business confidence. This presently extended to the field of his own business transactions with his publishers, and from these in time to confidences about his Work and Art; until at length he came to tell me of Poems not yet in being, but contemplated, and to talk about them and show me their progress.

Then, and for many years after, under his roof or under mine, it was my great privilege to see and know him intimately; and the more he was known the more impressive were his greatness, tenderness, and truth. The simplicity, sensitiveness, freshness, and almost divine insight of a child were joined in him, as in no other man, to the dignity, sagacity, humour, and knowledge of age at its noblest. An immense sanity underlay the whole—the perfection of common-sense— and over all was the perpetual glamour of supreme genius.

Affectation was so alien from him that he spoke and acted exactly as he felt and thought everywhere and about everything. This at times would perplex and bewilder strangers. The shy were frightened at it; the affected took it for affectation (for, as he was fond of saying, 'every man imputes himself'), the rough for roughness, the bears for bearishness; whereas it was but simple straightforward honesty, and as such of the deepest interest to all who could watch and learn in it the ways of Nature with her greatest men.

The little affectations and insincerities of life so troubled him, and his natural shyness, increased by his disabling short sight, so fought with his innate courtesy to all, that general society was always an effort and a burden to him. His fame increased the trouble, and he often told me how he wished he could have had all the money which his books had made without the notoriety. Even a single stranger was, as such and at first, always a trial to him, and his instinctive desire was to hide as much of himself as possible from observation until he found his companion sympathetic. Then he expanded as a flower does in the sunshine, and he never hoarded or kept back any of the profuse riches and splendour of his mind. When Frederick Robertson of Brighton—the great preacher, who had written much and admirably about his poems, and for whom he had a high regard—first called upon him, 'I felt,' said Tennyson, 'as if he had come to pluck out the heart of my mystery—so I talked to him about nothing but beer.' He could not help it; it was impossible for him to wear his heart upon his sleeve.

The shortness of his sight, which was extreme, tormented him always. When he was looking at any object he seemed to be smelling it. He said that he had 'never seen the two pointers of the Great Bear except as two intersecting circles, like the first proposition in Euclid,' and at my first visit to him he warned me, as I left, to come up and speak to him wherever I next met him, 'for if not,' he said, 'I shouldn't know you though I rubbed against you in the street.' His hearing, on the other hand, was exceptionally keen, and he held it as a sort of compensation for his blurred sight; he could hear 'the shriek of a bat,' which he always said was the test of a quick ear. Its real compensation, however, was in the quickness of his mental vision, which made more out of the imperfect indications of his bodily eyes than most men with perfect sight would see. I remember his telling me (in explanation of a passage in 'Maud')—'If you tread on daisies they turn up underfoot and get rosy.' He could read a man through and through in a flash even from his face, and it was wonderful to hear him sum up a complex character in some single phrase. He told me that he was once travelling with an unknown person whose countenance he caught but for an instant from behind a newspaper, but whom he set down, from that flying glimpse, as a rogue. To his surprise he turned out to be somebody of the highest local standing and repute, but he nevertheless held by his impression and in the end was justified for presently the man fled from justice and the country, leaving hundreds ruined who had trusted him.

His judgment of men was the more terrible because so naturally charitable and tender. Seldom, if ever, did he carry beyond words his anger even with those who had gravely injured him. '*I eat my heart with silent rage at* ———' he said one day of such a one. How different in this from Carlyle, whose open rage with mankind was so glaring! '*Ha! ye don't know,*' he cried out to me one day, '*ye don't know what d———d beasts men are.*' Tennyson, quite otherwise, had the tenderest thought and hope for all men individually, however much he loathed that 'many-headed beast' the mob. '*I feel ashamed to see misery and guilt,*' he said as he came out from going over Wandsworth Gaol; '*I can't look it in the face.*' Yet he had no love for milksops. '*The only fault of So-and-so,*' he said, '*is that he has no fault at all.*'

It was touching to see his playfulness with children, and how he would win them from their nervousness of his big voice and rather awful presence. I have seen him hopping about on the floor like a great bird, enveloped in his big cloak and flapping hat, in a game of pursuing a little band of them until they shrieked with laughter. It reminded me of a scene in his Cambridge days which he had described to me when he, '*Charles Tennyson, Spedding, and Thompson of Trinity, danced a quadrille together in the upper room of a house opposite the "Bull."*' There was a great abundance of playfulness under the grimness of his exterior, and as to humour, that was all-pervading and flavoured every day with salt. It was habitual with him, and seemed a sort of counteraction and relief to the intense solemnity of his also habitual gaze at life in its deeper aspects, which else would almost have overwhelmed him with awe. He had a marvellous fund of good stories which he loved to recount after dinner and over his 'bottle of port.' In later life he gave up the port, but not the stories. He used to say there ought to be collection of the hundred best ones in the world chosen from different countries so as to show the national diversities, and he would give illustrations of such, declaring that for true and piercing wit the French beat all the others. Could they have been reported *verbatim* as he gave them, they would have been models of English prose. More serious narratives he told thrillingly—one especially of how his own father escaped from Russia as a young man after an incautious speech about the recent murder of the Emperor Paul; how he wandered for months in the Crimea, where 'the wild people of the country came about him' and explained to him that twice a year only, at uncertain times, a courier passed through the place blowing a horn before him, and that then was his only chance of safety; how he lay waiting and which was as unlike ordinary prose as possible, sang the terrible war song, until the little attic at Farringford melted out of sight and one *saw* the far-off fields of early Britain, thronged with the maddened warriors of the maddened queen, and heard the clashing of the brands upon the shields, and the cries which

Roar'd as when the rolling breakers boom and blanch on the precipices.

The image of some ancient bard rose up before one as he might have sung the story by the watch-fires of an army the day before a battle. It was perhaps from some such association of ideas that his name among his intimates became 'The Bard'—a way of recognising in one word and in ordinary talk his mingled characters of Singer, Poet, and Prophet.

When building Aldworth he desired to have, whenever the room was finally decorated, the following names of his six favourite poets carved and painted on the six stone shields which I had designed as part of the chimney-piece in his study, and in front of which he always sat and smoked—namely, *Shakespeare, Chaucer, Milton, Wordsworth, Dante, and Goethe.*

He used to say 'Keats, *if he had lived, would have been the greatest of all of us;*' he considered Goethe '*the greatest artist of the nineteenth century, and Scott its greatest man of letters;*' and he said of Swinburne, '*He's a tube through which all things blow into music.*' He said '*Wordsworth would have been much finer if he had written much less,*' and he told Browning in my presence that '*if he got rid of two-thirds, the remaining third would be much finer.*' After saying that, and when Browning had left us, he enlarged on the imperative necessity of restraint in art. '*It is necessary to respect the limits,*' he said; '*an artist is one who recognises bounds to his work as a necessity, and does not overflow illimitably to all extent about a matter. I soon found that if I meant to make any mark at all it must be by shortness, for all the men before me had been so diffuse, and all the big things had been done. To get the workmanship as nearly perfect as possible is the best chance for going down the stream of time. A small vessel on fine lines is likely to float further than a great raft.*'

Once, as we stood looking at Aldworth just after its completion, he turned to me and said, '*You will live longer than I shall. That house will last five hundred years.*' I answered him, 'I think the English language will last longer.'

Another frequent subject of his talk was the criticism on his own work, *when unfavorable.* All the mass of eulogy he took comparatively little notice of, but he never could forget an unfriendly word, even from the most obscure and insignificant and unknown quarter. He was hurt by it as a sensitive child might be hurt by the cross look of a passing stranger; or rather as a supersensitive skin is hurt by the sting of an invisible midge. He knew it was a weakness in him, and could be laughed out of it for a time, but it soon returned upon him, and had given him from his early youth exaggerated vexation. When remonstrated with for the Hogarth's perspective he thus made, he would grimly smile and say, '*Oh yes, I know. I'm black-blooded like all the Tennysons—I remember everything that has been said against me, and forget all the rest.*' It was his temperament, and showed itself in other matters besides criticism. For instance, the last time I went with him to the oculist, he was most heartily reassured about his eyes by the great expert after a careful and detailed inspection. But as we left the door he turned to me and said with utter gloom, '*No man shall persuade me that I'm not going blind.*' Few things were more delightful than to help chase away such clouds and see and feel the sunshine come out again, responsive to the call of cheerfulness. To one who had so cheered him he said: '*You certainly are a jolly good fellow, you do encourage me so much.*' And at another time: '*I'm very glad to have known you. It has been a sort of lift in my life.*' The clouds would gather on him most in the solitude of the country, and he often told me it was needful for him to come from time to time to London to rub the rust from off him. It must be added that so soon as ever the rust was rubbed off he hastened to be back among the woods and hills.

CRITICISM

EVE KOSOFSKY SEDGWICK

Tennyson's *Princess:* One Bride for Seven Brothers[†]

It has seemed easiest for critical consensus to interest itself in the Gothic on "private" terms and in mainstream Victorian fictions on "public" terms; but just as the psychological harrowings of the Gothic are meaningful only as moves in a public discourse of power allocation, so the overtly public, ideological work of writers like Tennyson, Thackeray, and Eliot needs to be explicated in the supposedly intrapsychic terms of desire and phobia to make even its political outlines clear. *The Princess* in particular claims to be a major public statement, in a new form, about the history and meaning of femininity; but male homosocial desire, homophobia, and even the Gothic psychology of the "uncanny" are ultimately the structuring terms of its politics—and of its generic standing as well.

To generalize: it was the peculiar genius of Tennyson to light on the tired, moderate, unconscious ideologies of his time and class, and by the force of his investment in them, and his gorgeous lyric gift, to make them sound frothing-at-the-mouth mad.

Tennyson applied this genius with a regal impartiality that makes him seem like a Christmas present to the twentieth-century student of ideology, but made him something less reassuring to many of his contemporaries. We have suggested that the whole point of ideology is to negotiate invisibly between contradictory elements in the status quo, concealing the very existence of contradictions in the present by, for instance, recasting them in diachronic terms as a historical narrative of origins. For a writer as fervent, as credulous, and as conflicted as Tennyson to get interested in one of these functional myths was potentially subversive to a degree that, and in a way that, Tennyson himself was the last to perceive. Where he did perceive it, it was most often as a formal struggle with structural or stylistic incoherence in his work. These formal struggles, however, also answered to the enabling incoherences in his society's account of itself.

If *Henry Esmond* is an ahistorical diagram of bourgeois femininity disguised as an account of historical change, *The Princess* is in some respects the opposite. Its myth of the origin of modern female subordination is presented firmly *as* myth, in a deliberately a-chronic space of "Persian" fairy tale. On the other hand, the relation of the myth to its almost aggressively topical framing narrative is so strongly and variously emphasized that the poem seems to compel the reader to search for ways of reinserting the myth into the history. The mythic narrative is sparked by a young woman's speculation about the male homosocial discourse from which she is excluded: "—what kind of tales did men tell men, / She wonder'd, by themselves?"[1] Its substance, as well, is about the enforcement of women's relegation within the framework of male homosocial exchange. Some effects of uncanniness re-

† From Eve Kosofsky Sedgwick, *Between Men: English Literature and Male Homosocial Desire* (New York: Columbia University Press). Copyright 1985 by Columbia University Press. Reprinted by permission of the publisher.
1. Alfred, Lord Tennyson, *The Princess: A Medley,* in *The Poems of Tennyson,* ed. Christopher Ricks (London: Longman, 1969), 749 (Prologue, 11.193–94). Further citations are incorporated in the text, and designated by section and line numbers.

sult from this magnetic superposition of related tales—along with more explicable historic and generic torsions.

The "mythic" central narrative begins with the astonishing vision of a feminist separatist community, and ends with one of the age's definitive articulations of the cult of the angel in the house. The loving construction of a female world, centered on a female university, looking back on a new female history and forward to a newly empowered future; and then the zestful destruction of that world root and branch, the erasure of its learning and ideals and the evisceration of its institutions—both are the achievements of Tennyson's genius for ideological investment.

One important feature of the myth porpounded in *The Princess*'s inner narrative is that it traces the origin of nineteenth-century bourgeois gender arrangements directly back to the feudal aristocracy. Even there, however, the angel in the house does not seem to be new; for the Prince describes his ideal of womanhood as coming directly from his own mother, and describes it in terms that any middlebrow Victorian would have recognized:

>   one
> Not learned, save in gracious household ways,
> Not perfect, nay, but full of tender wants,
> No Angel, but a dearer being, all dipt
> In Angel instincts, breathing Paradise,
> Interpreter between the Gods and men,
> Who look'd all native to her place, and yet
> On tiptoe seem'd to touch upon a sphere
> Too gross to tread, and all male minds perforce
> Sway'd to her from their orbits as they moved,
> And girdled her with music. Happy he
> With such a mother!
>   (VII. 298–309)

Toward this destiny (presented as both idealized past and paradisal future) Ida, too, is being propelled. At the same time, it is significant that this nostalgic portrait of the Prince's mother is not arrived at until the last pages of the poem; for the poem until then at least gestures at a critique of the aristocratic feudal family that, if not thorough or consistent, is nevertheless part of its purpose. Although the mother who is its product is a good old angelic mother, the family that has created her is the bad old baronial family:

> My mother was as mild as any saint,
>   • • •
> But my good father thought a king a king;
> He cared not for the affection of the house;
> He held his sceptre like a pedant's wand
> To lash offence, and with long arms and hands
> Reach'd out, and pick'd offenders from the mass
> For judgment.
>   (I. 22–29)

The old king thinks his son is lily-livered as a wooer.

> "Tut, you know them not, the girls.
>   • • •

Man is the hunter; woman is his game:
The sleek and shining creatures of the chase,
We hunt them for the beauty of their skins;
They love us for it, and we ride them down.
Wheedling and siding with them! Out! for shame!
Boy, there's no rose that's half so dear to them
As he that does the thing they dare not do,
Breathing and sounding beauteous battle, comes
With the air of the trumpet round him, and leaps in
Among the women, snares them by the score
Flatter'd and fluster'd, wins, tho' dashed with death
He reddens what he kisses: thus I won
Your mother, a good mother, a good wife,
Worth winning"

(V. 144–60)

The Prince is an authentic liberal. His tactic in response to his father here is to present Princess Ida's feminism as a mirror-image extreme of his father's crudely patriarchal style, and himself as forging a new dialectic between them, arriving at the moderating terms of a compromise. To Ida, "'Blame not thyself too much,' I said, 'nor blame / Too much the sons of men and barbarous laws'" (VII. 239–40). As we see when Ida is forced to turn into a version of the Prince's mother, however, far from forging a new order or a new dialectic he is merely finding for himself a more advantageous place within the old one. Finding one, or preserving it: since one way of describing the Prince's erotic strategy is that, while maintaining the strict division of power and privilege between male and female, he favors (and permits to himself) a less exclusive assignment of "masculine" and "feminine" personal traits between men and women, in order that, as an "effeminized" man, he may be permitted to retain the privileged status of baby (*within* a rigidly divided family) along with the implicit empowerment of maleness. (The privileged avenue from a baby's need to a woman's sacrifice is one of the most repetitively enforced convictions in this inner narrative, and most especially in the lyrics.) In short, the Prince's strategy for achieving his sexual ends in battle differs from his father's only in a minor, stylistic detail: he gets what he wants by losing the battle, not by winning it.

The meaningfulness of the concept of fighting *against* a man *for* the hand of a woman can barely be made to seem problematical to him, however. And in general, the Prince's erotic perceptions are entirely shaped by the structure of the male traffic in women—the use of women by men as exchangeable objects, as counters of value, for the primary purpose of cementing relationships with other men. For instance, it never for one instant occurs to him to take seriously Ida's argument that an engagement contracted for reasons of state, by her father, without her consent, when she was eight years old, is not a reason why the entire course of her life should be oriented around the desires of a particular man. Similarly, as in Tennyson's own life, the giving of a sister in marriage to cement the love of the brother for another man is central in this narrative. Although romantic love is exalted in the Prince's view, as it is not in his father's, nevertheless its tendency in the mythic narrative must always be to ratify and enforce the male traffic in women, not to subvert it.

This emphasis on a chivalric code in which women are "priveleged" as the passive, exalted objects of men's intercourse with men, is part of the point of drawing a genealogy straight from the Victorian bourgeois family to the medievalistic courtly tradition. To cast the narrative in terms of a "Prince" and a "Princess" is both a conventional, transparent fairytale device, and a tendentious reading of history that accomplishes several simplifying purposes. First, it permits a view of the Victorian middle-class family that denies any relation between its structure and its economic functions. By making the persistence and decadence of a stylized aristocratic family look like a sufficient explanation for contemporary middle-class arrangements, it renders economic need invisible and hides from the middle-class audience both its historical ties to the working class and also the degree to which, while nominally the new empowered class or new aristocracy, most of the middle class itself functions on a wage system for males and a system of domestic servitude for females. Even though the fit between the structure of the ideologically normative family and the needs of capital for certain forms of labor-power is anything but seamless, nevertheless the new middle-class family reflects these imperatives in its structure at least as strongly as it reflects internal contradictions left over from the aristocratic family of feudal times. Thus, the appeal to high chivalry obscures the contemporary situation by glamorizing and in fact dehistoricizing it.

As we will see, though, the mock-heraldry of tracing the bourgeois family back to aristocratic origins in feudal society is not the only ideologically useful way of legitimating it. The *Adam Bede* model, the genealogy through the yeoman and artisan classes, has its uses as well; for instance, instead of excluding work and the facts of economic necessity, it incorporates them centrally, but in a form (individual artisanship evolving into a guildlike system of workshop production) that both affirms some of the features of modern industrial discipline (such as the exclusion of women) and conceals its discontinuity from more individualistic modes of work.

Why then is Tennyson's defense of contemporary social arrangements in *The Princess* cast in the archaizing, aristocratic mold? It is through this question, I think, that we can move to a consideration of the fascinating frame narrative of the poem. For the poem takes place in a very particular England of the present (i.e., 1847), an England that, with Tennysonian daring, seems almost to represent a simple projection into the present of the inner narrative's fantasy of a feudal past. Like *Wives and Daughters, The Princess* begins on a great estate, on the day of the year on which it is opened up to the tenantry and neighborhood:

> Thither flock'd at noon
> His tenants, wife and child, and thither half
> The neighbouring borough with their Institute
> Of which he was the patron. I was there
> From college, visiting the son, . . .
>   . . . with others of our set,
> Five others: we were seven at Vivian-place.
>
> (Prologue 3–9)

As these lines suggest, *The Princess* is unlike *Wives and Daughters* in locating its point of view among those who might be at Vivian-place even on a normal, non-open-house day; it is also different from any Gaskell novel in viewing all the activities of the neighborhood, *including* the industry-oriented sciences of the Institute, as firmly and intelligibly set within a context of aristocratic patronage. In fact, with a characteristic earnest bravado, Tennyson goes out of his way to underline the apparent incongruity of the juxtaposition of on the one hand ancient privilege and connoisseurship, and on the other hand modern science; like a small-scale exposition of arts and industry, the open grounds of Vivian-place are dotted for the day with "a little clockwork steamer," "a dozen angry model [engines] jett[ing] steam," "a petty railway," a miniature telegraph system where "flash'd a saucy message to and fro Between the mimic stations," and so forth, displayed along with the permanent family museum of geological specimens, Greek marbles, family armor from Agincourt and Ascalon, and trophies of empire from China, Malaya, and Ireland (Prologue 73–80, 13–24). The assertion that science, or technology, is the legitimate offspring of patronage and connoisseurship, that all these pursuits are harmonious, disinterested, and nationally unifying, that the raison d'etre of the great landowners is to execute most impartially a national consensus in favor of these obvious desiderata—the frame narrative assumes these propositions with a confidence that is almost assaultive.

Along with the breathtaking ellipsis with which *class* conflict is omitted from Tennyson's England, the aristocratic-oriented view of progress-as-patronage affects the *gender* politics of the poem, as well. The feminism presented in Princess Ida's part of the poem is a recognizable, searching, and, in its own terms, radical feminism. Some of the elements of it that are taught or practiced at the University include separatism, Lesbian love, a re-vision in female-centered terms of Western history, mythology, and art, a critique of Romantic love and the male traffic in women, and a critique of the specular rationalism of Western medical science. How is it possible for this elaborately imagined and riveting edifice to crumble at a mere male touch? What conceptual flaw has been built into it that allows it to hold the imagination so fully on its own terms, and yet to melt so readily into the poem's annihilatingly reactionary conclusion?

I am suggesting, of course, that its weakness is precisely the poem's vision of social change as something that occurs from the top down. For Princess Ida's relation to the University and in fact to the whole progress of feminism in the mythical southern kingdom is only an intensification of Sir Walter's relation to "progress" among his tenants: she is the founder, the benefactor, the theorist, the historian, and the beau ideal of a movement whose disinterested purpose is to liberate *them*, to educate *them*, "Disyoke their necks from custom, and assert / None lordlier than themselves. . . ." (II. 127–28). Ida's main feeling about actual living women is impatience, a sense of anger and incredulity that she cannot liberate them and their perceptions in a single heroic gesture:

> for women, up till this,
> Cramped under worse than South-sea-isle-taboo,
> Dwarfs of the gynaeceum, fail so far
> In high desire, they know not, cannot guess
> How much their welfare is a passion to us.
> If we could give them surer, quicker proof—
> Oh if our end were less achievable
> By slow approaches, than by single act
> Of immolation, any phase of death,
> We were as prompt to spring against the pikes,
> Or down the fiery gulf as talk of it,
> To compass our dear sisters' liberties.
> (III. 260–72)

618   EVE KOSOFSKY SEDGWICK

In an imaginative world where even a genuinely shared interest can be embodied and institutionalized only in the form of *noblesse oblige*, it is not surprising that a merely personal snag, encountered by the crucial person,
succeeds effortlessly in unraveling the entire fabric. A top-down politics of the
privileged, sacrificial, enlightened few making decisions for the brutalized, unconscious many will necessarily be an object of manipulation (from inside or
outside), of late-blooming self-interest on the part of the leaders, of anomie and
sabotage on the part of the led. A feminism based on this particular nostalgia
will be without faith or fortitude, a sisterhood waiting to be subverted.

Part of the oddity of Tennyson's poem, however, is that the ideological structure that permits him in the inner narrative to tumble the feminist community
down like a house of cards, is the same one whose value and durability for class
relations he is blandly asserting, in the frame narrative. It may be this that
caused his contemporaries to view the poem as a whole with such unease, an
unease which however both he and they persisted in describing as formal or
generic.

Tennyson describes the male narrator as being caught between the different
formal and *tonal* demands of his male and female listeners:

> And I, betwixt them both, to please them both,
> And yet to give the story as it rose,
> I moved as in a strange diagonal,
> And maybe neither pleased myself nor them.
> (Conclusion 25–29)

Indeed, like the slippages of political argument, the formal and generic slippages between frame and inner narratives are very striking, and do catch up and
dramatize the issues of class and gender, as well. For instance, the status of the
inner narrative as collective myth, as a necessary ideological invention, is un-
derlined by the indeterminacy about its authorship. During the Vivian-place
party, the telling of the story, like a woman, is passed from hand to hand among
the young men. The identification is directly made between the collectiveness
of the male involvement in women and in storytelling: the idea of storytelling
had started with an earlier Christmas reading-party of the seven young men
from the University, where, Walter tells his sister Lilia,

> Here is proof that you [women] were miss'd: . . .
> We [men] did but talk you over, pledge you all
> In wassail . . .
> —play'd
> Charades and riddles as at Christmas here, . . .
> And often told a tale from mouth to mouth.
> (Prologue 175–79)

It is to initiate and place the Vivian-place women in the context of this pro-
ceeding that the inner story in *The Princess* is begun. Walter jokes of it as an occasion for making a gift of his sister to his friend—" 'Take Lilia, then, for
heroine' clamour'd he, / . . .'and be you / The Prince to win her!'" (Prologue
217–19). The story is to be a "Seven-headed monster," of which each male narrator will "be hero in his turn! / Seven and yet one, like shadows in a dream"
(Prologue 221–22).

As we have seen, the interior of the "Seven-headed monster" story, the belly of the beast, is no less structured by the male exchange of women than the circumstances of its conception had been. But there is more unexpected and off-centered, thematic echo between inside and out, as well. The odd comparison of the male narrative communion to that of "shadows in a dream," almost unintelligible in its immediate context, leaps to salience in relation to one of the most notoriously puzzling features of the internal narrative. The Prince inherits from his family, perhaps through a sorcerer's curse, a kind of intermittent catalepsy,

> weird seizures, Heaven Knows what:
> On a sudden in the midst of men and day,
> And while I walk'd and talk'd as heretofore,
> I seem'd to move among a world of ghosts,
> And feel myself the shadow of a dream.
> (I. 14–18)

This fugue state is described throughout the poem with the words "shadow" and "dream," and most often simply "shadow of a dream."

> While I listen'd, came
> On a sudden the weird seizure and the doubt:
> I seem'd to move among a world of ghosts;
> The Princess with her monstrous woman-guard,
> The jest and earnest working side by side,
> The cataract and the tumult and the kings
> Were shadows; and the long fantastic night
> With all its doings had and had not been,
> And all things were and were not.
> (IV. 537–45)

The link between the seizures and the "seven and yet one" narrative frame does not disappear from the poem: one of the fugue states, for instance, corresponds to one of the moments when the narrative voice is being passed from one male storyteller to another. Its link to the use of sisters to cement emotional and property relations between men also recurs. Psyche, one of the Princess's companions, is the sister of Florian, a companion of the Prince's whom he considers "my other heart, / And almost my half-self, for still we moved / Together, twinn'd as horse's ear and eye" (I.54–56). Cyril, the Prince's other companion, falls in love with Psyche—and he asks,

> What think you of it, Florian? do I chase
> The substance or the shadow? will it hold?
> I have no sorcerer's malison on me,
> No ghostly hauntings like his Highness. I
> Flatter myself that always everywhere
> I know the substance when I see it. Well,
> Are castles shadows? Three of them? Is she
> The sweet proprietress a shadow? If not,
> Shall those three castles patch my tatter'd coat?
> For dear are those three castles to my wants,
> And dear is sister Psyche to my heart. . . .
> (II. 386–96)

Real estate can give body and substance to the shadowy bonds—of women, of words, of collective though hierarchical identification with a Prince—that link the interests of men.

I have no programmatic reading to offer of the meaning and placement of the Prince's cataleptic seizures. Surely, however, they are best described as a wearing-thin of the enabling veil of opacity that separates the seven male narrators from the one male speaker. The collective and contradictory eros and need of their investment in him—and through him, in each other— seem to fray away at his own illusion of discrete existence. Is the Prince a single person, or merely an arbitrarily chosen chord from the overarching, transhistorical, transindividual circuit of male entitlement and exchange? He himself is incapable of knowing.

In *Great Expectations*, Pip is subject to fuguelike states rather like the Prince's. The most notable is the one that occurs during Orlick's murderous attack on him at the lime-kiln:

> He drank again, and became more ferocious. I saw by his tilting of the bottle that there was no great quantity left in it. I distinctly understood that he was working himself up with its contents, to make an end of me. I knew that every drop it held, was a drop of my life. I knew that when I was changed into a part of the vapour that had crept towards me but a little while before, like my own warning ghost, he would . . . make all haste to the town, and be seen slouching about there, drinking at the ale-houses. My rapid mind pursued him to the town, made a picture of the street with him in it, and contrasted its lights and life with the lonely marsh and the white vapour creeping over it, into which I should have dissolved.
>
> It was not only that I could have summed up years and years and years while he said a dozen words, but that what he did say presented pictures to me, and not mere words. In the excited and exalted state of my brain, I could not think of a place without seeing it, or of persons without seeing them. It is impossible to over-state the vividness of these images, and yet I was so intent, all the time, upon him himself . . . that I knew of the slightest action of his fingers.[2]

For Pip, as (I am suggesting) for the Prince in Tennyson's poem, the psychologically presented fugue state involves, not an author's overidentification with his character, but a character's momentary inability to extricate himself from his author. Pip's sudden, uncharacteristic power of imagination and psychic investiture—as in his later delirium in which "I was a brick in the house wall, and yet entreating to be released from the giddy place where the builders had set me . . . I was a steel beam of a vast engine, clashing and whirling over a gulf yet . . . I implored in my own person to have the engine stopped and my part in it hammered off" (ch. 57)—is disturbing *to him*, and resembles nothing so much as Dickens' own most characteristic powers, as a personality, as a hypnotist, and of course as a novelist. This abrupt, short-lived, deeply disruptive fusion of authorial consciousness with a character's consciousness occurs in both works under three combined pressures. These are:

> First, a difficult *generic* schema of male identifications, narrators, personae;

---

2. Charles Dickens, *Great Expectations*, ed. Angus Calder (Harmondsworth: Penguin, 1965) 437–38 (ch. 53). Further citations are incorporated in the text and designated by chapter number.

Second, a stressed *thematic* foregrounding of the male homosocial bond; Third, undecidable confusions between singular and plural identity.

I have mentioned that the collectiveness of male entitlement is not incompatible with, but in fact inextricable from, its hierarchical structure. This fact, too, has formal as well as political importance in *The Princess*. Even though, among the seven young men, young Walter Vivian is surely the one who is closest to the Prince in power and privilege, it is instead the nameless narrator of the frame narrative—the visiting friend, a young poet—who takes responsibility for having put the Prince's narrative into its final form. Thus some of the political shape of this poem might be attributed to its being an argument on behalf of an aristocratic ideology, aimed at an aristocratic as well as a bourgeois audience, but embodied through a speaker whose relation to patronage is not that of the patron but of the patronized. In addition, the confusion—or division—of genre in *The Princess* has an even more direct and explicit link to the division of gender; for the narrative, feminist content and all, is attributed entirely to the young men, while the ravishing lyrics that intersperse the narrative, often at an odd or even subversive angle to what is manifestly supposed to be going on, are supposed to be entirely the work of women in the group: "the women sang/Between the rougher voices of the men,/Like linnets in the pauses of the wind" (Prologue 236–38). Certainly it is among the ironies of this passionate and confused myth of the sexes, that it has come to be valued and anthologized almost exclusively on the basis of its lyrics, its self-proclaimed "women's work." Perhaps in the eyes of those who actually enjoyed hegemonic privilege, a mere poet could in that age *not* be trusted with the job of articulating a justification for them, however ready he felt himself for the task. Perhaps in their view, if not in Tennyson's, poet's work and women's work fell in the same ornamental, angelic, and negligible class.

T. S. ELIOT

In Memoriam†

Tennyson is a great poet, for reasons that are perfectly clear. He has three qualities which are seldom found together except in the greatest poets: abundance, variety, and complete competence. We therefore cannot appreciate his work unless we read a good deal of it. We may not admire his aims: but whatever he sets out to do, he succeeds in doing, with a mastery which gives us the sense of confidence that is one of the major pleasures of poetry. His variety of metrical accomplishment is astonishing. Without making the mistake of trying to write Latin verse in English, he knew everything about Latin versification that an English poet could use; and he said of himself that he thought he knew the quantity of the sounds of every English word except perhaps *scissors*. He had the finest ear of any English poet since Milton. He was the master of Swin-

† From T. S. Eliot, *Selected Essays of T. S. Eliot*, New Edition (New York: Harcourt Brace Jovanovich, Inc.; London: Faber and Ltd., 1932), pp. 286–95. Copyright 1932, 1936, 1950 by Harcourt Brace Jovanovich, Inc.; renewed, 1960, 1964 by T. S. Eliot. Reprinted by permission of the publishers.

burne; and the versification of Swinburne, himself a classical scholar, is often crude and sometimes cheap, in comparison with Tennyson's. Tennyson extended very widely the range of active metrical forms in English: in *Maud* alone the variety is prodigious. But innovation in metric is not to be measured solely by the width of the deviation from accepted pratice. It is a matter of the historical situation: at some moments a more violent change may be necessary than at others. The problem differs at every period. At some times, a violent revolution may be neither possible nor desirable; at such times, a change which may appear very slight, is the change which the important poet will make. The innovation of Pope, after Dryden, may not seem very great; but it is the mark of the master to be able to make small changes which will be highly significant, as at another time to make radical changes, through which poetry will curve back again to its norm.

There is an early poem, only published in the official biography, which already exhibits Tennyson as a master. According to a note, Tennyson later expressed regret that he had removed the poem from his Juvenilia; it is a fragmentary *Hesperides*, in which only the 'Song of the Three Sisters' is complete. The poem illustrates Tennyson's classical learning and his mastery of metre. The first stanza of 'The Song of the Three Sisters' is as follows:

> The Golden Apple, the Golden Apple, the hallow'd fruit,
> Guard it well, guard it warily,
> Singing airily,
> Standing about the charmèd root.
> Round about all is mute,
> As the snowfield on the mountain peaks,
> As the sandfield at the mountain-foot.
> Crocodiles in briny creeks
> Sleep and stir not; all is mute.
> If ye sing not, if ye make false measure,
> We shall lose eternal pleasure,
> Worth eternal want of rest.
> Laugh not loudly: watch the treasure
> Of the wisdom of the West.
> In a corner wisdom whispers. Five and three
> (Let it not be preach'd abroad) make an awful mystery:
> For the blossom unto threefold music bloweth;
> Evermore it is born anew,
> And the sap to threefold music floweth,
> From the root,
> Drawn in the dark,
> Up to the fruit,
> Creeping under the fragrant bark,
> Liquid gold, honeysweet through and through.
> Keen-eyed Sisters, singing airily,
> Looking warily
> Every way,
> Guard the apple night and day,
> Lest one from the East come and take it away.

A young man who can write like that has not much to learn about metric; and the young man who wrote these lines somewhere between 1828 and 1830 was doing something new. There is something not derived from any of his predecessors. In some of Tennyson's early verse the influence of Keats is visible—in songs and in blank verse; and less successfully, there is the influence of Wordsworth, as in Dora. But in the lines I have just quoted, and in the two Mariana poems, 'The Sea-Fairies', 'The Lotos-Eaters,' 'The Lady of Shalott', and elsewhere, there is something wholly new.

> All day within the dreamy house,
>   The doors upon their hinges creak'd;
>   The blue fly sung in the pane; the mouse
>   Behind the mouldering wainscot shriek'd,
>   Or from the crevice peer'd about.

The blue fly sung in the pane (the line would be ruined if you substituted sang for sung) is enough to tell us that something important has happened.

The reading of long poems is not nowadays much practised: in the age of Tennyson it appears to have been easier. For a good many long poems were not only written but widely circulated; and the level was high: even the second-rate long poems of that time, like The Light of Asia, are better worth reading than most long modern novels. But Tennyson's long poems are not long poems in quite the same sense as those of his contemporaries. They are very different in kind from Sordello or The Ring and the Book, to name the greatest by the greatest of his contemporary poets. Maud and In Memoriam are each a series of poems, given form by the greatest lyrical resourcefulness that a poet has ever shown. The Idylls of the King have merits and defects similar to those of The Princess. An idyll is a 'short poem descriptive of some picturesque scene or incident'; in choosing the name Tennyson perhaps showed an appreciation of his limitations. For his poems are always descriptive, and always picturesque; they are never really narrative. The Idylls of the King are no different in kind from some of his early poems; the Morte d'Arthur is in fact an early poem. The Princess is still an idyll, but an idyll that is too long. Tennyson's versification in this poem is as masterly as elsewhere: it is a poem which we must read, but which we excuse ourselves from reading twice. And it is worth while recognizing the reason why we return again and again, and are always stirred by the lyrics which intersperse it, and which are among the greatest of all poetry of their kind, and yet avoid the poem itself. It is not, as we may think while reading, the outmoded attitude towards the relations of the sexes, the exasperating views on the subjects of matrimony, celibacy, and female education, that make us recoil from The Princess[1] We can swallow the most antipathetic doctrines if we are given an exciting narrative. But for narrative Tennyson had no gift at all. For a static poem, and a moving poem, on the same subject, you have only to compare his 'Ulysses' with the condensed and intensely exciting narrative of that hero in the XXVIth Canto of Dante's Inferno. Dante is telling a story. Tennyson is only stating an elegiac mood. The very greatest poets set before you real men talking, carry you on in real events moving. Tennyson could not tell a story at all. It is not that in The Princess he tries to tell a story and failed: it is rather that an idyll protracted to such length becomes unreadable. So The Princess is a dull poem; one of the poems of which we may say, that they are beautiful but dull.

1. For a revelation of the Victorian mind on these matters, and of opinions to which Tennyson would probably have subscribed, see the Introduction by Sir Edward Strachey, Bt., to his emasculated edition of the Morte D' Arthur of Malory, still current. Sir Edward admired the Idylls of the King.

But in *Maud* and in *In Memoriam*, Tennyson is doing what every conscious artist does, turning his limitations to good purpose. Of the content of *Maud*, I cannot think so highly as does Mr. Humbert Wolfe, in his interesting essay on Tennyson which is largely defence of the supremacy of that poem. For me, *Maud* consists of a few very beautiful lyrics, such as 'O let the solid ground', 'Birds in the high Hall-garden', and 'Go not, happy day', around which the semblance of a dramatic situation has been constructed with the greatest metrical virtuosity. The whole situation is unreal; the ravings of the lover on the edge of insanity sound false, and fail, as do the bellicose bellowings, to make one's flesh creep with sincerity. It would be foolish to suggest that Tennyson ought to have gone through some experience similar to that described: for a poet with dramatic gifts, a situation quite remote from his personal experience may release the strongest emotion. And I do not believe for a moment that Tennyson was a man of mild feelings or weak passions. There is no evidence in his poetry that he knew the experience of violent passion for a woman; but there is plenty of evidence of emotional intensity and violence—but of emotion so deeply suppressed, even from himself, as to tend rather towards the blackest melancholia than towards dramatic action. And it is emotion which, so far as my reading of the poems can discover, attained no ultimate clear purgation. I should reproach Tennyson not for mildness, or tepidity, but rather for lack of serenity.

> Of love that never found his earthly close,
> What sequel?

The fury of *Maud* is shrill rather than deep, though one feels in every passage what exquisite adaptation of metre to the mood Tennyson is attempting to express. I think that the effect of feeble violence, which the poem as a whole produces, is the result of a fundamental error of form. A poet can express his feelings as fully through a dramatic, as through a lyrical form; but *Maud* is neither one thing nor the other: just as *The Princess* is more than an idyll, and less than a narrative. In *Maud*, Tennyson neither identifies himself with the lover, nor identifies the lover with himself: consequently, the real feelings of Tennyson, profound and tumultuous as they are, never arrive at expression.

It is, in my opinion, in *In Memoriam*, that Tennyson finds full expression. Its technical merit alone is enough to ensure its perpetuity. While Tennyson's technical competence is everywhere masterly and satisfying, *In Memoriam* is the most unapproachable of all his poems. Here are one hundred and thirty-two passages, each of several quatrains in the same form, and never monotony or repetition. And the poem has to be comprehended as a whole. We may not memorize a few passages, we cannot find a 'fair sample'; we have to comprehend the whole of a poem which is essentially the length that it is. We may choose to remember:

> Dark house, by which once more I stand
> Here in the long unlovely street,
> Doors, where my heart was used to beat
> So quickly, waiting for a hand,
>
> A hand that can be clasp'd no more—
> Behold me, for I cannot sleep,

And like a guilty thing I creep
At earliest morning to the door.

He is not here; but far away
The noise of life begins again,
And ghastly thro' the drizzling rain
On the bald street breaks the blank day.

This is great poetry, economical of words, a universal emotion in what could only be an English town: and it gives me the shudder that I fail to get from anything in *Maud*. But such a passage, by itself, is not *In Memoriam*: *In Memoriam* is the whole poem. It is unique: it is a long poem made by putting together lyrics, which have only the unity and continuity of a diary, the concentrated diary of a man confessing himself. It is a diary of which we have to read every word.

Apparently Tennyson's contemporaries, once they had accepted *In Memoriam*, regarded it as a message of hope and reassurance to their rather fading Christian faith. It happens now and then that a poet by some strange accident expresses the mood of his generation, at the same time that he is expressing a mood of his own which is quite remote from that of his generation. This is not a question of insincerity: there is an amalgam of yielding and opposition below the level of consciousness. Tennyson himself, on the conscious level of the man who talks to reporters and poses for photographers, to judge from remarks made in conversation and recorded in his son's *Memoir*, consistently asserted a convinced, if somewhat sketchy, Christian belief. And he was a friend of Frederick Denison Maurice—nothing seems odder about that age than the respect which its eminent people felt for each other. Nevertheless, I get a very different impression from *In Memoriam* from that which Tennyson's contemporaries seem to have got. It is of a very much more interesting and tragic Tennyson. His biographers have not failed to remark that he had a good deal of the temperament of the mystic—certainly not at all the mind of the theologian. He was desperately anxious to hold the faith of the believer, without being very clear about what he wanted to believe: he was capable of illumination which he was incapable of understanding. The 'Strong Son of God, immortal Love', with an invocation of whom the poem opens, has only a hazy connection with the Logos, or the Incarnate God. Tennyson is distressed by the idea of a mechanical universe; he is naturally, in lamenting his friend, teased by the hope of immortality and reunion beyond death. Yet the renewal craved for seems at best but a continuance, or a substitute for the joys of friendship upon earth. His desire for immortality never is quite the desire for Eternal Life; his concern is for the loss of man rather than for the gain of God.

shall he,
Man, her last work, who seem'd so fair,
Such splendid purpose in his eyes,
Who roll'd the psalm to wintry skies,
Who built him fanes of fruitless prayer,

Who trusted God was love indeed
And love Creation's final law—
Tho' Nature, red in tooth and claw
With ravine, shriek'd against his creed—

> Who loved, who suffer'd countless ills,
> Who battled for the True, the Just,
> Be blown about the desert dust,
> Or seal'd within the iron hills?

That strange abstraction, 'Nature', becomes a real god or goddess, perhaps more real, at moments, to Tennyson than God ('Are God and Nature then at strife?'). The hope of immortality is confused (typically of the period) with the hope of the gradual and steady improvement of this world. Much has been said of Tennyson's interest in contemporary science, and of the impression of Darwin. *In Memoriam*, in any case, antedates *The Origin of Species* by several years, and the belief in social progress by democracy antedates it by many more; and I suspect that the faith of Tennyson's age in human progress would have been quite as strong even had the discoveries of Darwin been postponed by fifty years. And after all, there is no logical connection: the belief in progress being current already, the discoveries of Darwin were harnessed to it:

> No longer half-akin to brute,
> For all we thought and loved and did,
> And hoped, and suffer'd, is but seed
> Of what in them is flower and fruit;
>
> Whereof the man, that with me trod
> This planet, was a noble type
> Appearing ere the times were ripe,
> That friend of mine who lives in God,
>
> That God, which ever lives and loves,
> One God, one law, one element,
> And one far-off divine event,
> To which the whole creation moves.

These lines show an interesting compromise between the religious attitude and, what is quite a different thing, the belief in human perfectibility; but the contrast was not so apparent to Tennyson's contemporaries. They may have been taken in by it, but I don't think that Tennyson himself was, quite: his feelings were more honest than his mind. There is evidence elsewhere — even in an early poem, 'Locksley Hall', for example — that Tennyson by no means regarded with complacency all the changes that were going on about him in the progress of industrialism and the rise of the mercantile and manufacturing and banking classes; and he may have contemplated the future of England, as his years drew out, with increasing gloom. Temperamentally, he was opposed to the doctrine that he was moved to accept and to praise.[2]

Tennyson's feelings, I have said, were honest; but they were usually a good way below the surface. *In Memoriam* can, I think, justly be called a religious poem, but for another reason than that which made it seem religious to his contemporaries. It is not religious because of the quality of its faith, but because of the quality of its doubt. Its faith is a poor thing, but its doubt is a very intense experience. *In Memoriam* is a poem of despair, but of despair of a religious kind.

---

2. See, in Harold Nicolson's admirable *Tennyson*, pp. 252ff.

And to qualify its despair with the adjective 'religious' is to elevate it above most of its derivatives. For *The City of Dreadful Night*, and the *Shropshire Lad*, and the poems of Thomas Hardy, are small work in comparison with *In Memoriam*: it is greater than they and comprehends them.[3]

In ending we must go back to the beginning and remember that *In Memoriam* would not be a great poem, or Tennyson a great poet, without the technical accomplishment. Tennyson is the great master of metric as well as of melancholia; I do not think any poet in English has ever had a finer ear for vowel sound, as well as a subtler feeling for some moods of anguish:

> Dear as remember'd kisses after death,
> And sweet as those by hopeless fancy feign'd
> On lips that are for others; deep as love,
> Deep as first love, and wild with all regret.

And this technical gift of Tennyson's is no slight thing. Tennyson lived in a time which was already acutely time-conscious: a great many things seemed to be happening, railways were being built, discoveries were being made, the face of the world was changing. That was a time busy in keeping up to date. It had, for the most part, no hold on permanent things, on permanent truths about man and God and life and death. The surface of Tennyson stirred about with his time; and he had nothing to which to hold fast except his unique and unerring feeling for the sounds of words. But in this he had something that no one else had. Tennyson's surface, his technical accomplishment, is intimate with his depths: what we most quickly see about Tennyson is that which moves between the surface and the depths, that which is of slight importance. By looking innocently at the surface we are most likely to come to the depths, to the abyss of sorrow. Tennyson is not only a minor Virgil, he is also with Virgil as Dante saw him, a Virgil among the Shades, the saddest of all English poets, among the Great in Limbo, the most instinctive rebel against the society in which he was the most perfect conformist.

Tennyson seems to have reached the end of his spiritual[4] development with *In Memoriam*; there followed no reconciliation, no resolution.

> And now no sacred staff shall break in blossom,
> No choral salutation lure to light
> A spirit sick with perfume and sweet night,

or rather with twilight, for Tennyson faced neither the darkness nor the light, in his later years. The genius, the technical power, persisted to the end, but the spirit had surrendered. A gloomier end than that of Baudelaire: Tennyson had no *singulier avertissement*. And having turned aside from the journey through the dark night, to become the surface flatterer of his own time, he has been rewarded with the despite of an age that succeeds his own in shallowness.

---

3. There are other kinds of despair. Davidson's great poem, *Thirty Bob a Week*, is not derivative from Tennyson. On the other hand, there are other things derivative from Tennyson besides *Atalanta in Calydon*. Compare the poems of William Morris with *The Voyage of Maeldune*, and *Barrack Room Ballads* with several of Tennyson's later poems.
4. Eliot means the word as intended. But his comment has been misinterpreted to say or imply that Tennyson's intellectual development ceased as well. Especially during the last fifty years or so, reappreciation of *Idylls of the King* and more objective readings of the late poems have made such a position untenable [*Editor*].

ISOBEL ARMSTRONG

The Collapse of Object and Subject: *In Memoriam*[†]

'Lawn Tennyson, gentleman poet'; Tennyson's persistent self-deprecating account of his art as play might be reason enough for endorsing the twice-told joke of Stephen Dedalus and for regarding *In Memoriam* as a delicate, anguished epistemological game. 'And hence, indeed, she sports with words' (XLVIII): 'Or love but play'd with gracious lies': 'A contradiction on the tongue' (CXXV): grief which will 'with symbols play' (LXXXV). His habitual use of the word 'fancy' for imagination, which carries the more restricted, eighteenth-century limitation of meaning and even suggests the idle fancy, a game with poetic artefact, is congruent with the hesitancy which makes him describe the poem as play. But the extraordinarily sophisticated (and daring) version of Catullus, 'O Sorrow, wilt thou live with me?' (LIX), in which sorrow and sexual play are allied— 'I'll have leave at times to play/As with the creature of my love', the understanding of the blind man's minute gesture—'He plays with threads' (LXVI)—as a movement of displaced anxiety, should indicate Tennyson's alertness to the complexities of play. So often in the poem a defensively meticulous technical perfectionism carrying an exposed, openly naked poignancy, continues ingenuously with the cadences of pathos, as if oblivious of the irony and contradictions it is dealing with. The gratuitousness of play grants the poem its freedom to be art, and certainly to be artful: it grants it a freedom to experiment, not to 'close grave doubts' but to liberate possibilities unknown to it except in play. Yet a profounder necessity is at work in the need to play. Play *is* a necessity. The poem has to sport with words in order to enable itself to continue, to bring itself *into* play. The sport is willed to rescue language from collapse by enabling it to continue as a game. 'I do but sing because I *must*.' I *must* implies that song is involuntary and imposed as a duty at one and the same time, willed and unwilled. Involuntary song liberates feeling, '*loosens* from the lip' (XLVIII) the pressure of paralysing emotion. The poem is partly, but only partly, about the psychology of expressive language, about the process of naming a 'something', 'clouds' of 'nameless sorrow' (IV) which can only be named with difficulty. It is a highly studied study of bereavement. 'And with no language but a cry.' Regression to the inarticulate cry is inevitable when words are not adequate to express emotion. There may be no words to use. In that case the continuance of language can perhaps be enabled by a sport which brings it into play, by inventing it as a game.

There is a fundamental anxiety in *In Memoriam* about the dissolution of language altogether. The breakdown of language is collateral with the obliteration of the regulative 'Type' in the external world. 'So careful of the type? But no . . . a dream, / A discord' (LVI). Discord; the consequence of the collapse of relationships is the absence of agreement and correspondence, the absence of syntax. Nature depends merely on the 'dream' of each solipsist subject for its organisation; nature is 'A hollow echo of my own' (III)— a hollow echo of my *own* hollow echoes. 'For words, like Nature, half-reveal

† From Isobel Armstrong, *Language Form in Nineteenth-Century Poetry* (Barnes & Noble Imports). Copyright 1982 by Barnes & Noble. Reprinted by permission of the publisher.

/ And half-conceal the Soul within' (V). The governing analogy between words and Nature is half-concealed in this first poem on language, offered as an aside and interposed almost unnoticed, before the account of the failure of language which occupies it. Half-concealed, perhaps, because nature necessarily breaks down as an analogy. Nature is estranged from language, providing no analogies for it and no connections with it except in so far as it is *like* words, which, the poem shows, are external forms, refusing the vital change of meaning, the soul within, which renews the life of language, because they cannot sustain analogy and relationship. They are 'like Nature', empty of self-renewing life, a discord. If there is a 'soul within' language and Nature it is incompletely realised, half concealed, half revealed. The *world* cannot guarantee the structure of language. Relationships are either arbitrary or break down, and it is the same in the language. The resilience and intelligence of *In Memoriam* lie in its willingness to confront, however reluctantly, the derangement of idealist language with play, to 'frame' words, to invent them, perhaps even, as the secondary possibilities of 'frame' come into play, with some duplicity. The sport with words enables the poem to keep in existence and ultimately to reconstruct both itself and the 'use' of measured language.

The extremity of idealist language in *In Memoriam* is accompanied by a corresponding intensification of artifice. The poem tries to 'fix itself to form' (XXXIII) like the simple faith of the woman in the Lazarus sequence. The fastidious, carefully compacted units of pairing and parallelism, word with word, phrase with phrase, line and line, the 'stepping stones' (I) by which the poems are built up, express the need to make a form in which matching, concord, correspondence, analogy, are possible. The masking circumlocution of poetic diction, artful personification, insist upon the poem as minutely self-conscious verbal artefact, insist that something can be *made*, even if it is the almost unapproachable patina of surface perfection. But the coexistence of an ambiguous syntax with the formal pattern frequently disrupts the poem from within so that the formal organisation of the poem comes to exist independently of its meanings in a self-enclosed separation and autonomy which severs it from the correspondences it tries to make. 'I scarce could brook the strain and stir': the hiatus after his pairing allows the wild conflation of self and world, psychological strain and the stir of the storm in section XV. Because the stanza breaks after 'strain and stir' the condition can belong to the poet as much to the storm. The archaism, 'brook', enables the language not to be sure whether the poet *allows* or suffers upheaval, just as the meticulously parallel verbs are not sure whether they are active or passive, acting or acted upon—cracked, curled, huddled, dashed. 'And but for fancies . . . And but for fear it is not so.' Parallelism veers apart into contradiction. The poet would disintegrate into the storm unless his fancy insisted upon the calm progress of the boat carrying Hallam's body. But because the words 'it is not so' in this deranged syntax relate immediately to the storm the repetition intended to intensify this fancy—'And but for fear'—reads as a fear of calm, and also wills the strain and stir of the storm upon the dead man, forcing him into an identity with it. The poet would disintegrate except (but) for his fear that it is *not* calm, and but for fear that the 'wild unrest' is *not* so, fear that the strain and stir do not belong to the ship. The construction, 'for fear', carries with it the meaning of expectation, even hope. If the ship *were* calm and the dead man not sharing in the storm's and the poet's strain and stir, then

disintegration would follow. The readings of the parallelism are athwart one another, like the movement of the ship placed in strangely obstructive relation to
the sea which carries it, 'Athwart a plane of molten glass'. Either way the poet
and the syntax go mad, making no distinction between self and objects. Undif-
ferentiated, internal unrest and external cloud drag 'a labouring breast', and the
syntax, the cloud, the poet, 'topples' to disintegration with an unclosed phrase
which is not organically part of the sentence—'A looming bastion fringed with
fire'. Poet and storm become inseparable.

> To-night the winds begin to rise
>   And roar from yonder dropping day:
>   The last red leaf is whirl'd away,
> The rooks are blown about the skies;
>
> The forest cracked, the waters curled,
>   The cattle huddled on the lea;
>   And wildly dashed on tower and tree
> The sunbeam strikes along the world:
>
> And but for fancies, which aver
>   That all thy motions gently pass
>   Athwart a plane of molten glass,
> I scarce could brook the strain and stir
>
> That makes the barren branches loud;
>   And but for fear it is not so,
>   The wild unrest that lives in woe
> Would dote and pore on yonder cloud
>
> That rises upward always higher,
>   And onward drags a labouring breast,
>   And topples round the dreary west,
> A looming bastion fringed with fire.
>   (XV)

The derangement of the storm poem ends in dissolution. *In Memoriam* continually threatens itself with termination. 'But that large grief . . . Is given
in outline and *no more*' (V). Language allows grief to be expressed in no
more than an outline, but the poem also categorically discontinues itself. It
can utter grief 'no more'. And it brings itself to a halt. 'I held it truth . . .
That men may rise on stepping-stones / Of their dead selves' (I). Each isolated lyric is a precarious stepping-stone which might not lead to another
when language breaks down.

> Dark house, by which once more I stand
>   Here in the long unlovely street,
>   Doors, where my heart was used to beat
> So quickly, waiting for a hand,
>
> A hand that can be clasp'd no more—
>   Behold me, for I cannot sleep,
>   And like a guilty thing I creep
> At earliest morning to the door.

He is not here; but far away
The noise of life begins again,
And ghastly through the drizzling rain
On the bald street breaks the blank day.
(VII)

'On the bald street breaks the blank day.' Again, the poem can go no further. The day dawns or *fragments*, breaking like something brittle on or against the bald street. The poet, not belonging to the dawn, like the ghost in *Hamlet* (but unlike the ghost, guilty of his exile from life and the day rather than death and the night), fusing the 'blank misgivings' of Wordsworth's 'Immortality Ode' with the blank day, moves about in worlds literally not realised, because the day breaks ambiguously out of, or is only seen *through*, the obstructive drizzle of rain. Breaking day and the hard, resistant street exist in unreactive relation to one another, the light failing to transform the street, the street unresponsive to the day. Bald and blank repel the reciprocity the pairing alliteration attempts to assert. Language fails to establish the correspondence it claims, and offers only a mutual exchange of emptiness. The obstruction of rain, the barrier of the door '*where* my heart was used to beat', by which, and against which, *directly* (with extraordinary physical frankness) the heart-beat knocked to gain entrance, are metaphors of a condition expressed in the organisation of the language of *In Memoriam*. It sets up barriers. Like the self-retarding stanza form, it creates obstructions and blocks against itself. Though the poem longs 'to flood a fresher throat with song' (LXXXIII), and constantly remembers the 'Ode to a Nightingale', it rarely achieves Keats' easeful flow of lyric feeling, because it is halted, and sometimes almost disabled, by an ambiguous syntax which says one thing and its opposite simultaneously, a 'contradiction on the tongue' (CXXV), asserting and negating at one and the same time. Two sentences out of the same words. The double, coalescing Romantic grammar seizes up in contradiction. Parallelism subjects the poem to paralysis. The gaps and transitions which are the life of Romantic language make either voids or barriers. 'O sweet, new year delaying long . . . *Delayest* the sorrow in my blood' (LXXXIII). The delaying spring is accused of the continuance of sorrow and yet at the same time is imperatively asked to delay, to keep sorrow in the blood. The paralysing and the creative energies of grief mutually retard one another.

The poem is most immobilised when it is not sure what form or what language to fix itself to, idealist or non-idealist, mind-moulded or 'matter-moulded' (XCV), actively shaped by the self, passively formed by an external world. It is not even certain whether the distinctions themselves are fixed.

Old Yew, which graspest at the stones
That name the under-lying dead,
Thy fibres net the dreamless head,
Thy roots are wrapt about the bones.

The seasons bring the flower again,
And bring the firstling to the flock;
And in the dust of thee, the clock
Beats out the little lives of men.

O not for thee the glow, the bloom,
   Who changest not in any gale,
   Nor branding summer suns avail
To touch thy thousand years of gloom:

And gazing on thee, sullen tree,
   Sick for thy stubborn hardihood,
   I seem to fail from out my blood
And grow incorporate into thee.

                                       (II)

"And grow incorporate into thee': and grow bodiless, as mind or spirit with the 'dusk' of the yew, or become physically embodied in it. Either way lies the loss of distinction. 'And *in* the *dusk* of thee, the clock/Beats out': external clock, external time, tolls in the shadow of the yew or else, like a heart *in* the dusk of the tree itself, a shadowy, mind-created symbol of unchanging grief, internally registers 'a thousand years of gloom' — darkness and *sadness*. Whether the yew refuses to 'avail' the branding sun of the objective world to touch it, or whether the concrete world itself cannot 'avail' to reach and touch it, are equal and opposite possibilities. The opposites result, not in conflict, but in paralysis.

'To *touch* thy thousand years of gloom'; 'And learns . . . And finds I am not what I see, / And other than the things I *touch*' (XLV). The blocks occur when Tennyson is talking about perception and the relationship between the physical and mental worlds. Consider the connections made between touch and being in sections XLV and XCV: Created out of pronouns, 'I', 'me', the beautifully economical baby poem about the growth of identity uses verbs as stepping-stones to self-consciousness as the baby knows himself as object to himself and discovers the intransigent world of subject and object— 'this is I'.

But as he grows he gathers much,
   And learns the use of 'I' and 'me',
   And finds 'I am not what I see,
And other than the things I touch.'

But as 'he grows he gathers . . . And learns . . . And finds'. 'And learns the use of "I" and "me"': the baby gathers his growing, takes the knowledge of his growing as a fact of awareness, learns by its 'use' and finds what he uses. The emphasis is on an almost tragic imprisonment in the physical self and in the consciousness— 'the frame that *binds* him in' —which is a necessity for the definition of a seperate identity which can relate to the world as other, the not-self, and a necessity for the growth of 'clear memory'. Strictly read, however, the ellipsis of the second parallelism reverses the first and becomes an idealist statement or hypothesis— 'And finds "I am not what I see, / And other than the things I touch"': 'And finds "I am *not* what I see, [And *I* am not] other than the things I touch".' Two possibilities obstruct one another. Isolation, perhaps, grows defined, like an outline, as the self is sealed off from the world, and independent memory evolves. Or perhaps isolation grows defined through an act of mind which includes the other in its definition of self-separation, fusing subject and object in the process of creating relationship. The ambiguous parallelism returns one to the first stanza of the poem. The baby, *pressing* his palm against the breast (pressing himself away from and *into* the breast) has never thought that 'this is I'. This, the pressing palm exerting itself against its first experience of a resistant physical world, the baby's physical entity and consciousness, is 'I' at the first act of awareness and self-consciousness at the breast as the baby comes to understand that it is other to what it feeds upon. On the other hand, the syntax allows that the breast, source of life and literally part of the baby because its milk is taken in by the child, can also be included as 'I': this, the breast, is 'I'. The circle of the breast is outside the suckling child, or baby and breast are included in a circle of interchange and reciprocal being where subject and object are both other to each other and as one.

This, one of the subtlest poems of *In Memoriam*, is perhaps a lyric which finds momentarily a way of transcending the obstructions it creates for itself. But *In Memoriam* is never stable. 'The dead man *touched* me from the past' (XCV): 'I [am not] . . . other than the things I touch' (XLV):

> And strangely on the silence broke
> The silent-speaking words, and strange
> Was love's dumb cry defying change
> To test his worth; and strangely spoke
>
> The faith, the vigour, bold to dwell
> On doubts that drive the coward back,
> And keen through wordy snares to track
> Suggestion to her inmost cell.
>
> So word by word, and line by line,
> The dead man touched me from the past,
> And all at once it seemed at last
> The living soul was flashed on mine . . .
>
> Vague words! but ah, how hard to frame
> In mater-moulded forms of speech,
> Or even for intellect to reach
> Through memory that which I became:

The 'silent-speaking words' which broke on the poet are either the silent words of the dead friend's letter, or words silently reiterated in the poet's consciousness. 'Love's *dumb* cry' cannot be differentiated as belonging to the poet or the writer of the letter, just as 'the faith, the vigour', could belong to each, expressed in written words, or generated in the poet's being. Neither speech, nor even intellect can reach 'Through memory that which I became.' Memory is either creative or passive. The intellect cannot recreate through or by means of memory, but the placing of the words allows a reading, 'that which I became through memory, or the creations of memory'—the 'clear memory' of the baby poem, perhaps, the shaping consciousness itself. Transcendental experience may be given from outside the self or it may be a creation of mind. Experience, and words, may be mind-moulded or they may be matter-*moulded*, formed from the material world. And language may be simply moulded by matter, mere printed marks.

'That which I *became*': 'Thy place is changed; thou *art* the same' (CXXI). The 'double' naming of the Hesper / Phosphor poem simultaneously offers an active and a passive self, a living or a static universe:

> Sad Hesper o'er the buried sun
> And ready, thou, to die with him,

Thou watchest all things ever dim
And dimmer, and a glory done:

The team is loosened from the wain,
The boat is drawn upon the shore;
Thou listenest to the closing door,
And life is darkened in the brain.

Bright Phosphor, fresher for the night,
By thee the world's great work is heard
Beginning, and the wakeful bird;
Behind thee comes the greater light:

The market boat is on the stream,
And voices hail if from the brink;
Thou hear'st the village hammer clink,
And see'st the moving of the team.

Sweet Harper-Phosphor, double name
For what is one, the first, the last,
Thou, like my present and my past,
Thy place is changed; thou art the same.

'Thy place is changed'—by external conditions, fixed and final. Or with the openness of a continuous present, thy place is continually in a state of change. What 'thou art', what being is, is defined simultaneously in two radically opposed ways. Hesper watches over 'a glory done', a glory over or a glory *being made*, a glory ended or self-creating and perhaps even made by the watching Hesper itself. The poem has a double name and double structure, of antithetical, linear beginnings and endings or cyclical renewal. The second and fourth stanzas contrasting cessation and movement, night and day, death and life, are locked in equipoise, miniature pastorals which are virtually inverted images of one another—the team of horses, the boat, the closing door (stanza 2); the boat, the sound of activity, the team. Appropriately, the verbs describing activity and movement are passive in the night pastoral, active in the day pastoral. But paradoxically 'listenest' in the night stanza (like 'watchest' in the first), is a sharper, less involuntary perceptual verb than 'hear'st' and 'see'st in the day stanza. The transforming agent of perception comes into prominence and questions the passivity of experience when it is most subject to necessity. The locked, antithetical opposition is also subverted by the intervening stanza. Phosphor arises 'fresher for the night', fresher for the quietude of night into dawn, and fresher to *encounter* the cyclical renewal of night which follows the 'greater light'. Both structures are subject to necessity—with delicate toughness the cyclical movement of renewal is the renewal of darkness—but one offers a self and a universe capable of transformation while the other does not.

The more fixed to form, the more miniaturist and precise the language of *In Memoriam* seems, the more ambiguous it actually is. The poem discovers the ambiguity of form—solid form, hollow forms, mere form. 'The hills are shadows, and they flow/From form to form' (CXXIII). 'Vague words! but ah, how hard to frame': to frame, to make a solid physical structure like the baby's 'frame' which binds him in, or to invent, to make something new— even with some duplicity. The work of the poem is to overcome the immobility which arises from the discontinuous and uncertain oscillation between an open, reflexive, mind-created world and a binding, subject/object account of experience. It does so by redefining its form. And this redefinition is inextricably bound up with the overcoming of grief, or the acceptance of it, and the liberation of energy. The project the poem discovers is not to recover so much as to construct an idea of death, which is an 'awful *thought*' (XIII)— death to a living man can only be a thought, an act of imagination. This constructing of death can only be done by an act of imagination, defining death against its opposite, life, and creating both anew, redefining 'my present and my past'. Reflexive, idealist language is ultimately the strongest in this project, for all the doubts about it, because it is found to be most capable of keeping words in play and enables the poem to grow. It grows by flowing from form to form, building itself out of itself, contemplating its past, the stepping stones for growth. It arises, above all, out of the collapse of its analogies, out of its dead self, which enables it to find a new account of analogy and metaphor. The struggle of the poem is with discord and concord. The contemplations of analogy finally lead to a redefinition of the idea of form.

Two kinds of poetic form, each a commentary on the other, exist concurrently in the 'fair ship' sequence, often within the same poem. One is linear, narrative, temporal and external, marking the progress of the ship carrying the dead man from Vienna to England. It uses formal, ceremonial 'measured language' of a consciously organised kind more noticeably than any other group in *In Memoriam*. This sequence is the willed, 'sad mechanic exercise' initiated in Section V. The other form is psychological, expressive lyric, non-temporal, marking the vicissitudes of subjective life. Each form criticises the other. Both forms use the barrier of poetic diction as a means almost of neurotic displacement to mask death and the body, the boat, the sea. Conventional, external poetic diction becomes the greatest source of irony, half-revealing and half-concealing the deepest concern of this sequence which is with the collapse of safe and guaranteed order, the dissolving relationship between the internal and external worlds. The kinds of analogy which can be constructed become a crucial preoccupation here. The sequence tries out both the analogy in which objective equivalents for experience are provided by the external world and the analogy in which relationship is constituted by mind. Both fail.

'The Danube to the Severn gave': Section XIX, the last poem in the sequence, is a last attempt to provide a precise and exquisitely fitting image of experience in objective fact which ostensibly matches and illustrates the retarding movement, the ebb and flow of grief which inhibits song. Yet it is a false analogy in spite of the delicate exactitude with which the parallel appears to be made.

> There twice a day the Severn fills;
>   The salt sea-water passes by,
>   And hushes half the babbling Wye,
> And makes a silence in the hills.
>
> The Wye is hushed nor moved along,
>   And hushed my deepest grief of all,
>   When filled with tears that cannot fall,
> I brim with sorrow drowning song.

> The tide flows down, the wave again
> Is vocal in its wooden walls;
> My deeper anguish also falls,
> And I can speak a little then.

Just as the flow of the brimming Wye is blocked at its fullest and highest point by the movement of the Severn, so the poet's grief rises, but is paralysed; his tears cannot fall even through they 'brim' at the brink of falling; he cannot give utterance to grief. 'I brim with sorrow drowning song.' In movement again, the Wye is 'vocal' (the equivalent of Tennyson's song) and 'My deeper anguish also falls, / And I can speak a little then'. The lie of the analogy turns on the word 'falls': tears overflow, if this 'falls' is to become congruent with the earlier 'fall'—'tears that cannot fall'—but the Wye 'falls', not by overflowing, but by falling back to its natural level. The parallels between tears and Wye deviate just when they seem most to match. Again, the poem says two things at once. Poetry can be made possible by the release or overflow of feeling (this is a perfect account of expressive art) or by letting the 'deeper anguish' fall to a lower level of the consciousness (as the Wye falls to its bed), repressing the most powerful emotions and giving voice only to superficial feeling. The Wye is an 'exercise' which fails, and turns into a game with language, a game in which the rules of analogy are subverted so that contradictions emerge. The rigorous serenity of this poem masks the strain.

The antithetical storm and calm poems (XI, XV) try out the possibility of subjective analogy, another kind of consonance, by seeing how far the external world may be a replication of the self, structured by the subject and returning the forms of his consciousness to him as object to himself. Though the poems seem antithetical they are actually complementary. Different emotions, 'calm despair and wild unrest' (XVI), but the same collapse of relationship. The storm poem, I have suggested, discovers the derangement of idealist language. The storm is an objective analogy for psychological upheaval but becomes identified with it. The fusion of the mind of the perceiver is so complete that they become inseparable. When nothing falls outside the self relationship is dissolved, and distinction becomes meaningless. The extremities of incompatible verbs— 'rises' set against 'dropping' in the first stanza, 'looming' set against 'topples' in the last, mark the disappearance of proportion and concord. Everything becomes part of everything else, evrything stands for everything else without distinction in the language of the non-objective world—the poem 'Mingles all without a plan' (XVI).

To mingle. This verb is picked up from the calm lyric by section XVI, which attempts to analyse both it and the storm poem—'Calm and still light on yon great plain / That sweeps . . . To mingle with the bounding main'. Plain and main mingle as rhyme words. The calm poem tries out the possibility of finding the world as an attribute of the self, but whereas the storm poem finds a threatening fusion of subject and object, the calm poem finds only the pathetic fallacy. It cannot evolve the external world from its moods.

> Calm is the morn without a sound,
> Calm as to suit a calmer grief,
> And only through the faded leaf
> The chestnut pattering to the ground:

Calm and deep peace on this high wold,
    And on these dews that drench the furze,
    And all the silvery gossamers
That twinkle into green and gold:

Calm and still light on yon great plain
    That sweeps with all its autumn bowers,
    And crowded farms and lessening towers,
To mingle with the bounding main:

Calm and deep peace in this wide air,
    These leaves that redden to the fall;
    And in my heart, if calm at all,
If any calm, a calm despair:

Calm on the seas, and silver sleep,
    And waves that sway themselves in rest,
    And dead calm in that noble breast
Which heavens but with the heaving deep.

'Calm is the morn . . . Calm and deep peace . . . Calm on the seas':
each stanza repeats 'calm' like the self-mesmerising incantation of a lullaby as
an exercise in self-induced serenity. 'Calm oscillates between being a noun, a
possession of the landscape, and an adjective, a psychological, affective state
which 'mingles', creates an affinity between inner and outer worlds. But the
calm is not penetrative. It is 'on this high wold', 'on yon great plain' or dissipated
'in this wide air'. Finally, calm is refused metaphorical possibilities altogether.
'Dead calm', the customary metaphor for the sea, is transferred to the dead man
and is a literal truth—'And dead calm in that noble breast'. The euphemisms
for death are transferred to the sea—'silver sleep', 'waves that sway themselves
in rest'—ironically pointing the sentimentality of attempts at pyschological
affinity. The dead language of poetic diction opposes the living, suffering 'heart'
of the poet to the 'noble breast' of the dead man which 'heavens' but only with
the mechanical life of the heaving deep. We normally think of the heaving
breast as the sign of expressive feeling and emotion, heaving with sighs, but it
is breathless here, deprived of anything but the inert physical weight of the body
which is a dead form, appropriately describe in a dead form of words—breast.[1]
The psychological adjective, 'deep'—'deep peace'—has been appropriated as a
noun for the sea—'the deep'—space without limit or shape. Calm is death. The
calm lyric is an attempt to impose a psychological reading of the world but
which poignantly recognises its imposture. The activities of the self and world
are neither reciprocal nor fused. The universe, if not dead, continues its activity in dissociation from the poet, the chestnut 'pattering' where the poet discovers a morn 'without a sound', the main 'bounding' in independent life, leaping
in the limitlessness of the present participle, but also the agent of limit and con-
stricting, bounding, the plain. The sea in affinity with calm becomes death,
which resists the understanding of the human imagination. The only fusion of
self and universe occurs in the calm of death. The reiterated 'calm' becomes
not soothing but an obliteration of energy. Repetition is death.

1. This point is made by Alan Sinfield, *The Language of Tennyson's 'In Memoriam'*, Oxford, 1971. I have
learned much from this study.

The haunting possibility that idealist analogy has no content is expressed in the extraordinary analytical lyric (XVI) which follows and is enabled by the calm and storm poems. Sorrow is a 'changeling', inconsistent but, as the double note of 'changeling' suggests, transforming. Then follows the negation of transformation in what is probably the most despairing questioning of the non-objective world in the poem. 'Can sorrow such a changeling be?'

> Or doth she only seem to take
>   The touch of change in calm or storm;
>   But knows no more of transient form
> In her deep self, than some dead lake
>
> That holds the shadow of a lark
>   Hung in the shadow of a heaven?
>   Or has the shock, so harshly given,
> Confused me like the unhappy bark
>
> That strikes by night a craggy shelf,
>   And staggers blindly ere she sink?
>   And stunned me from my power to think
> And all my knowledge of myself;
>
> And made me that delirious man
>   Whose fancy fuses old and new,
>   And flashes into false and true,
> And mingles all without a plan?

The deep self, like some dead lake — deep and dead are changeling words, dead self, deep lake — only seems to register the 'touch' of an external world. But the self or lake create, nothing else, and certainly no other, no object, in place of this illusory relationship. It 'knows' nothing of 'transient form', the living but ephemeral forms of the external world, or 'changeling', internally shaped forms of its own. Not to 'know' is not to know the means of Creating knowledge. The dead lake simply 'holds the shadow of a lark/Hung in the shadow of a heaven'. 'Hold' is a verb almost as important as 'touch' in *In Memoriam*. Here the dead self, the deep lake, fixes its images and keeps them stationary. Hold and hung balance one another, the lark in virtual death, hung. The lark may be a static reflection held in the reflection of sky and clouds, passively received and replicated by the dead consciousness, or worse, as the lyric asserts, it may simply be a *shadow* of the surface held in the larger shadows of sky and clouds which move about it. In this case it is an indistinct, indirect and secondary form which has none of the suggestion of transference implied in the idea of reflection. These shadows are more like the insubstantial internal forms of consciousness in Section IV which cannot be released from the self and given external being — 'Such clouds of nameless trouble cross/All night below the darkened eyes'.

As if to endorse the failure of integration, the final parallelism describing the failure of unintegrated fancy is itself unintegrated. The fancy fuses 'old and new' and 'flashes into false and true'. The metaphor is drawn from gunpowder and chemistry. One disintegrates, the other blends. ('Flashes' is far away from the climactic Section XCV, where the living soul was 'flashed on mine'.) Old and new, false and true, are neither fused as esquivalents nor arranged in meaningful opposition as the arrangement of the pairs would ostensibly insist, line above line, the old falsity, the new truth. The arrangement could equally denote the old truth, the new falsity. It is as unstable as the fancy. The statement about the inconsistency of fancy gives no guarantee even to the stability of the parallel it makes, which falls apart intellectually. What is left is a structure without a content which fall into incoherence, 'without a plan' — without a plan, a projection, a model, a metaphor.

The poems which try out self-reflexive metaphor are the most immediately startling and unsettling in this group. The more formal poems on the ship, suggesting the inexorable progress of a journey, a linear narrative, look conventional. The more formal poems, however, are equally if not more subversive and at the same time paradoxically freer than the purely 'subjective' poems. It is as if the mask of poetic diction grants the poem freedom to 'play' with possibilities which are unreachable by the 'subjective' poems because the formal poems are 'false' as consolation or more outrageous than the 'subjective poems' can ever be. The virtuosity of poetic diction in the Fair Ship series is astonishing. The consolatory, generalised forms of diction 'outlining' grief have a prolific inventiveness and ingenuity which revivifies conventional forms. The inertia of the body and mysteriousness of death for instance, are exquisitely suggested by these circumlocutions — 'a vanished life', 'dark freight' (X), 'mortal ark', 'A weight of nerves without a mind' (XII), 'the burthen' (XIII). But this masking diction is both ingenuous and disingenuous, half-revealing and half-concealing consolation, and a refusal of consolation. Poetic diction asserts the freedom of mind to create its objects with a liberation and equanimity unknown to the expressive, subjective lyric forms. In this diction, Phosphor, the morning star, really can 'glimmer' unimpeded 'through early light' and find its image returned back to itself on 'the dewy decks' (IX) in contrast with the obstructed, unreactive world of the dark house poem. The world can be a reflection of the subject in unperplexed concord. The mind can be released, with an outward projection of the imagination, 'to dart' and 'play' (XII): the fancies 'rise on wing' (XIII) or glance about the object of grief and bring it into being. The mind is liberated to fulfill that longing of the bereaved person, so shocking to the unbereaved, for the physical return of the dead. The single, continuous sentence of section XIV asserts, almost outrageously, that if the dead man got off the ship alive 'I should not feel it to be strange'.

The poetic diction *wishes*, and its artifice conceals its wishes, but outrage, shock, subversiveness, the reversal of conventional expectation, is also the mode of this elaborately euphemistic language. 'More than my brothers are to me': the anti-social statement flagrantly undermining the conventional family priorities, violates the evenness of earlier more conventional parallelisms in Section IX — 'My friend, the brother of my love'. The widower of Section XIII finds in death 'A void where heart on heart reposed': a void in the place of the companion body and heart but, allowably, a void which was always present, unknown to the mourner even when the dead companion was alive. The funeral service and communion are expressed in the more elaborate circumlocutions — 'the ritual of the dead', the kneeling hamlet drains 'The chalice of the grapes of God' (X) — as if to indicate the *obsolete* formalism of a consolatory religious act of burial which merely makes us the 'fools of habit'. Most subversive of all, the syntax of this lyric goes on to tangle, expressing the possibility of suicide simultaneously with the act of religious consolation.

So bring him: we have idle dreams:
This look of quiet flatters thus
Our home-bred fancies: O to us,
The fools of habit, sweeter seems

To rest beneath the clover sod,
That takes the sunshine and the rains,
Or where the kneeling hamlet drains
The chalice of the grapes of God;

Than if with thee the roaring wells
Should gulf him fathom-deep in brine;
And hands so often clasped in mine,
Should toss with tangle and with shells.

For whom, poet or dead man, is it 'sweeter' 'To rest beneath the clover sod'? 'Than if *with thee* the roaring wells/Should gulf him fathom-deep in brine.' The delayed comparative 'than if with thee' strictly refers to the ship carrying the body who is last addressed nearly three stanzas away from this comparative. The delay inextricably tangles and exchanges pronouns, 'with thee', 'him', even 'us' in the search for a relationship less remote and nearer at hand. The pronouns become interchangeably the poet, Hallam. The last line is so severed from its syntactic relationships that is seems to express a preference for remaining dead and unburied. 'Should' becomes an imperative not a subjunctive—'*should* toss with tangle and with shells'. The poet can clasp the hand of the dead again by being dead too, and the syntax tangles to allow him the possibility of doing so.

In *Memoriam* is one of the last great triumphs of idealist language over itself. It both overcomes and founders upon the coalescing, ambiguous forms of Romantic syntax, using these forms to express the problem of articulation and relationship which they engender. It struggles, as earlier nineteenth-century poems do not, with a psychological account of expressive language and the pathetic fallacy which threatens to undermine the firm epistemological base of Romantic poetry. Repeatedly it builds itself out of its collapse by giving full play to the language which threatens its destruction. Classical elegy coexists with psychological, idealist lyric: pastoral landscape with mind-created images. The coexistence of these 'forms' is employed to expose the contradictions inherent in each. *In Memoriam* is a poem about death trying to be a poem about life. It is 'life', not pain, the expected moral truism, which forms the 'firmer mind' (XVIII). On the other hand, 'Doubt and Death' '*let* the fancy fly' (LXXXVI), let the liberated mind free and *allow* or create its freedom, actually bringing it into being. The poem recognises its need for simple longings and consolation while continually investigating and complicating these desires. And so *In Memoriam* can be described as a poem of great intelligence. Its sporting with words, its attempt to set the possibilities of metaphor in play, reveals the problems of the idealist language. It exposes the collapse of relationship inherent in its structure and looks forward beyond the nineteenth century to the problems of language experienced by later poets. It is not surprising that a poem about bereavement, and self without an object, should recognise so acutely the dissolution of idealist language. It is both willing and unwilling to do so, because it is both willing and unwilling to come to terms with death. A world without relationships: to *In Memoriam* to accept idealist language is to accept death.

The nineteenth-century poets I have discussed are in the grip of a series of problems, problems which they were at least partly in possession of, and which extend themselves into the modern period. My intention has been to describe those problems, in which an almost hubristically cognitive account of poetic language slides over into one which is potentially disabling, denying poetry the capacity to create and transform categories virtually in the act of claiming that it does so and suggesting an incipient collapse of relationship. I have proceeded by exploring the connections between epistemology and the structure of poetic language, believing that each implies the other. Questions of epistemology and the structure of poetic language become implicitly elided with or into political and cultural concerns, not because poetic language is forced to reflect some pre-existing ideological pattern in its form, but because it ceaselessly generates complexities and contradictions which, whether directly or by extension and implication, become questions about the word and the world. The configurations of poetic language are thus actively forming and questioning paradigms of relationship and action which are implicitly to do with possibilities and choices, limitations and freedoms, and they play into the extra-linguistic world as much as it plays into them. It must be self-evident that a particular historical period limits the nature and kind of question that can be asked, and that a writer will never be in full possession of his questions or solutions because they themselves are a part of the complex of contradictions he is trying to solve. But it is how these questions are asked in their ceaseless complexity, their mode of existence in poetic discourse through the form and organisation of words, which tells us something about the way in which language and history become part of one another and about the moments at which poetic form and politics intersect. It is a strangely static account of literature (and of ideology) which assumes that a text is caught in a predetermined pattern rather than responding to it and indeed reordering it through the play of language. And if one is prepared to see the language of a text as a play with limit established in and through the ordering of the work itself, one is relieved of the dubious practice of abstracting a fixed set of ideas and procedures from the text and assuming tautologously that they have produced the text.

HERBERT F. TUCKER

Maud and the Doom of Culture[†]

Tennyson was understandably apologetic about The Princess, and even about the faith of In Memoriam he had twinges of bad conscience. Things were dramatically different with Maud. This third panel in the triptych of Tennyson's middle years stayed with him like nothing else he ever wrote, and it invariably stirred his most truculently protective instincts. Tennyson was nettled more by what was harsh in the mixed reviews Maud received than by any of the voluminous criticism his career called forth. Although his

† From Herbert F. Tucker, Tennyson and the Dream of Romanticism (Cambridge, Mass.: Harvard University Press). Copyright 1988 by the President and Fellows of Harvard College. Reprinted by permission of the publisher.

habitual choice of this text for after-dinner recitation may have a compensatory motive, there must have been more than a wish for redress behind the way he flourished *Maud* as a test for all comers. The note of obsession remains audible in the bravura performance of "Come into the garden, Maud" that he chanted into a microphone during his very last years, and no fresh reading of its headlong measures will fail to find it in the written text either. Tennyson had little cause to worry about *Maud's* being, like *In Memoriam*, "too hopeful"—those who disapprove the conclusion, one suspects, are reprehending its grim despair as much as anything else—and he evidently felt that this poem, unlike *The Princess*, was more than "only a medley."[1] Nor did he ever offer much by way of an interpretation. Public recitation, instead, became his defense of poetry; what was required was not to reason why, but to read *Maud* straight through, ideally in polite mixed company.

The poet's insatiable demand for social ratification of this work suggests that he, like the rest of us, found it impossible to endorse *Maud* wholeheartedly. Furthermore, the uniquely social dimension of this text's after-history bears directly on its procedures and themes. For *Maud* is indeed more than a medley: at once love story and social critique, an imperialist tract riddled with anatomies of a sociopathic yet also sociogenic madness, it represents the most complete fusion of private with public codes anywhere in Tennyson. The poem makes the laureate's principal contribution to the Condition of England question, by representing that condition and the condition of its deranged hero as utterly congruent and as reciprocally determined, in a dizzying weave of "cause" with "consequence" (I.x.374) that raises Tennyson's habitual confusion of active and passive moods to a rare analytic instrumentality.[2] *Maud* elaborates a tragically disabling vision of doom, and it remains a radical, perennially disturbing document.

The composition of the poem began, like so much else in the work of Tennyson's maturity, in 1833–34. The stanzaic fragment "Oh! That 'Twere Possible," which found a place eventually in part II of *Maud*, epitomizes the exploratory work of the ten years' silence between 1832 and 1842, with its tension between impulses of inward and outward reference. The opening stanza hearkens back to the English undefiled of "Westron Wind," an anonymous lyric that for centuries has spurred readers to imagine a narrative context for its pure pathos. *Maud* was written in order to provide its lyric germ with such a context, but the original lyric both does and does not lend itself to narrative explanation. While it suggests that the speaker's "true love" (3) is dead to him, the poem leaves unanswered the question of what happened. It interests itself instead in the mood of frustration that an acknowledged impossibility imposes, and its interest for us lies in the scenic juxtapositions whereby Tennyson rendered this mood. For the alternating stanzas of "Oh! That 'Twere Possible" play conventional images of a rural past against something quite new in the canon of English poetry: hypnotically surreal imagery of a desolate urban present. Tennyson

---

1. See James Knowles, "A Personal Reminiscence," *Nineteenth Century* 33 (1893): 182 and Hallam Tennyson, *Alfred Tennyson: A Memoir*, 2 vols. (New York: Macmillan, 1897), II, 70–71.
2. The private side of the monodrama came to Tennyson first, in such lyrics as "Oh! That 'Twere Possible" and "Go Not, Happy Day"; and in the manuscripts it is the elaboration of social detail that gives him the most evident trouble. Issues of causality pertinent to *Maud* are treated, with primary reference to *Idylls of the King*, in James R. Kincaid, *Tennyson's Major Poems: The Comic and Ironic Patterns* (New Haven and London: Yale University Press, 1975), 154; and A. Dwight Culler, *The Poetry of Tennyson* (New Haven and London: Yale University Press, 1977), 239. I cite throughout *The Poems of Tennyson*, ed. Christopher Ricks (London: Longman, 1969).

was aware of the novelty of this imagery, if we may judge from the way he capitalizes on it in Trinity Notebook 21. Already in the first draft the bereaved lover is stealing "Through the hubbub of the market" (42), "Through all that crowd, confused and loud" (45); and decades before his successor J. Alfred Prufrock, he loathes "the squares and streets, / And the faces that one meets" (58–59). These stray early images of the modern city Tennyson systematically expands in the Trinity notebook, inserting new stanzas on "the leagues of lights, / And the roaring of the wheels" (21–22), "the yellow-vapours" (37) and "drifts of lurid smoke / On the misty river-tide" (40–41).[3] These revisions show the poet installing a traditional expression of erotic grief within a markedly modern context, and generalizing that grief into a malaise whose cultural specificity, at the level of imagery, widens its appeal beyond the power of narrative explanation.

Tennyson's only significant publication during the ten years' silence—picked out in 1837 from an array of unpublished manuscripts that few poets can ever have matched—"Oh! That 'Twere Possible" at first seems an odd choice for that honor. But if we reflect that this poem uniquely combines a traditional passion with an unprecedented contemporaneity, we may see it as an unerring choice: a dispatch from the field, a telegraphic progress report on the directions in which Tennyson's explorations of genre were leading him. That progress culminates in *Maud*, and it is fitting that this experimental lyric should have found its home there; for what was a lyric germ in "Oh! That 'Twere Possible" becomes in *Maud* the rampant virus of modern life, "the blighting influence," as the poet later named it, "of a recklessly speculative age."[4] The major analytic innovation of *Maud* is its measured and diffusive contamination, by imagery drawn from economic and political life, of a series of lyrical passions that run the Tennysonian gamut from fury to ecstasy to resignation. We could think of the poet's practice here as a kind of inoculation by the jaundiced eye, if only the poem had the strength, or the naiveté, to imagine a cure. But in this text, where the hero at last donates his body and his intellect in military service to the very interests that have crippled him, the cure *is* the disease. The virulent poem Tennyson wrote has force to resist both the antidote of patriotic sublimation, which his own later glosses would prescribe, and the antibody of liberal and humanitarian criticism, which *Maud* has provoked since the year of its publication.[5]

Before inspecting the text, we might first consider the implications of its genre for the eddying dialectic of its public and private motives. The poem was subtitled *A Monodrama* only in 1875, with a term Tennyson borrowed from reviewers trying to label the *sui generis* production he himself had first issued simply as *Maud*, after toying with a title that despaired of generic classification: *Maud, or the Madness*. The new term appealed to the poet as a match for the

---

3. Chapter 9 of Charles Kingsley's *Alton Locke* (1850) begins with a paragraph suggesting that Kingsley had felt the new effects in Tennyson's experimental lyric: "the roar of wheels, the ceaseless stream of pale, hard faces . . . beneath a lurid, crushing sky of smoke and mist." Two pages later Alton, himself a proletarian poet, devotes a paragraph to praising Tennyson for "the altogether democratic tendency of his poems . . . his handling of the trivial every-day sights and sounds of nature"; here, however, he clearly has the domestic idyllist in mind. See Tennyson's extemporized metaphor of the city, as recorded in FitzGerald's copy of *Poems* (1842): "One Day with A T in St. Paul's — 1842. 'Merely as an enclosed Space in a huge City this is very fine.' And when we got out into the 'central roar' — 'This is the Mind: that, a mood of it'" (135; in Trinity College Library).
4. *Poems*, ed. Ricks, 1039.
5. John Killham, "Tennyson and Victorian Social Values," in *Tennyson*, ed. D. J. Palmer (Athens, Ohio: Ohio University Press, 1973), 172.

generic innovation of his favorite brainchild: "No other poem (a monotone with plenty of change and no weariness) has been made into a drama where successive phases of passion in one person take the place of successive persons."[6] Tennyson's career began with drama in *The Devil and the Lady*, and his sad late attempts to write a stageworthy play let us see in retrospect how important the drama remained to him as a genre affording direct contact with the public. Monodrama offered a version of such contact, as A. Dwight Culler has shown in tracing its descent from the parlor "attitudes" in vogue around the turn of the nineteenth century: intimate performances for select audiences of much the same kind that Emily Tennyson would convene for her husband's reading half a century later.[7]

A failure at drama, Tennyson nonetheless could succeed at monodrama because of just the generic difference his comment on *Maud* emphasizes. In a monodrama he could circumvent his constitutional weakness at imagining other minds and concentrate instead on his forte, the depiction of fixed moods or "phases of passion." Tennyson makes these moods public in two ways. In accordance with the use to which he puts cliché in *The Princess* and *In Memoriam*, he keeps the moods stereotypically standard, as in the Regency "attitude" or the Victorian melodrama. Beyond this, and in sharp contrast to his early mood pieces, Tennyson consistently renders his hero's phases of passion as reactions to stock situations drawn from contemporary life. Thus, while on one hand this monodrama parts company with the social interaction that Tennyson the failed dramatist appears to have craved in vain, on the other hand it repeatedly represents its solitary central consciousness as instinct with a largely unacknowledged social content. The highly individualist generic form of monodrama appears to counteract the poet's unmistakable intention to indict the social consequences of laissez-faire values; yet the form as he deploys it carries his indictment into the very stronghold of individualism, planting conspicuous social codes within the supposed confessional sincerity of the lyrically speaking, lyrically overheard self.[8]

It is never easy to know how much awareness of the social weave of his rhetoric to attribute to Tennyson's hero. The pervasive ambiguity of this issue is one of the features that distinguish the monodrama from the dramatic monologue, where undecidability on this scale would soon burst the generic limits of tolerance. In dramatic monologues we require to know more firmly whether and when speakers know what they are talking about; *Maud* very often leaves this question wide open, so as to open its discourse, and its version of the self, as fully as possible to the influence of the "recklessly speculative age" that not only blights but largely constitutes it. Clearly Tennyson's hero is a rather recklessly speculative type himself when it comes to social analysis, as appears from his version of peace in a "Mammonite" culture (I.i.45) as nothing less than an undeclared civil war of each with all. No class struggle here, because no class consciousness; and therefore no witting solidarity, either, to focus the hero's blurry maledictions. He adopts the pose of a nostalgically anarchic satirist, sharpening on one social object after another the tools of an unsteady Romantic irony that implicates him as well: "Sooner or later I too may passively take

6. Gordon N. Ray, *Tennyson Reads "Maud"* (Vancouver: University of British Columbia, 1968), 43.
7. A. Dwight Culler, "Monodrama and the Dramatic Monologue," *PMLA* 90 (1975): 366–85.
8. Jonas Spatz, "Love and Death in Tennyson's *Maud*," *Texas Studies in Literature and Language* 16 (1974): 506.

the print / Of the golden age—why not? I have neither hope nor trust"
(I.i.29–30). In referring to "the golden age," the hero yokes idealized and mythical with modern and economic associations, in a satirical counterpoint that
chastizes the present with the standard of the past. Within the economic sphere
the hero may also be consciously playing the old and forthright order of "gold"
against the more dubious "printed" currency he will have to "take" as a citizen
in a modern economy. This much is sturdy fulmination of a recognizable sort.
How are we to take it, though, when the scion of a fallen family, manifestly feeling bilked of his inheritance, complains that he has no "trust"? The term implies a relation between his legal and his metaphysical situation, which the plot
insists we entertain later on: if he marries Maud he will be recouping his family's fortune with justice (and with interest). But this same relation, if apparent
to the hero himself, would place his disinterested absorption by the salvific
power of love in a peculiar light indeed.

   We cannot know with any precision, in this entirely representative passage,
how much the hero knows whereof he speaks; and our bafflement arises from
Tennyson's monodramatic rendition of the modern self as lunatic, tidally
swayed by a cycle of passional phases that fall, in turn, under the influence of
the age. When the hero recalls how, upon his father's bankruptcy, "the wind
like a broken worldling wailed, / And the flying gold of the ruined woodlands
drove through the air" (I.i.11–12), we may assume that the economically pathetic fallacy lies within his control. But is a similar assumption justified when
this inhabitant of a world where "only the ledger lives" (35) describes the scene
of his father's suicide as a deranged accountant's entry in the red, where "The
red-ribbed ledges drip with a silent horror of blood" (3)? Jonathan Wordsworth
(1974) and others have noted the sexuality of this primal scene, but the overde-
termination of imagery here and throughout *Maud* seems to call for not just a
Freudian but also a social psychology, an account of manic boom and depres-
sive bust.[9] To take another example, there is bitter wit in the hero's charges that
"a company forges the wine" (36) and that "chalk and alum and plaster are sold
to the poor for bread, / And the spirit of murder works in the very means of life"
(39–40). In conflating the adulteration of subsistence staples with that of the
sacramental elements of eternal life, the hero scores his point with prophetic
keenness. Yet when he turns closer to home and the lyrical sphere of personal
feelings, his language starts veering out of control and into a social orbit: "Maud
with her sweet purse-mouth when my father dangled the grapes" (71). Pursed
lips are sweet, but so are purses, especially in a context that includes the bank-
rupt father. The hero cannot intend such economic associations, yet he cannot
avoid them either—least of all, it seems, in passages that touch on the most private parts of his life.

   Given this pattern of obsessive return, it is no wonder that he has such difficulty imposing upon his inventory of social and personal ills the explanatory
pattern of cause and effect. "Villainy somewhere! whose? One says, we are villains all" (I.i. 17). Like Hamlet, to whom Tennyson liked to compare him, the
hero of *Maud* wants the comfort of clearly assigned virtue and blame. But this
desire is inhibited, first by a Hamlet-like sense of complicity in what he attacks,

   9. Jonathan Wordsworth, "'What Is It, That Has Been Done?': The Central Problem of *Maud*," *Essays in Criticism* 24 (1974): 356–62. See also Roy P. Basler, "Tennyson the Psychologist," *South Atlantic Quar-terly* 43 (1944): 143–59; F. E. L. Priestley, *Language and Structure in Tennyson's Poetry* (London: Deutsch, 1973), 115; Spatz, "Love and Death."

and more generally by a Dickensian vision of universal implication in an un-
beatable system: "We are puppets, Man in his pride, and Beauty fair in her
flower; / Do we move ourselves, or are moved by an unseen hand at a game /
That pushes us off from the board, and others ever succeed?" (I.iv.126–128). If
others ever succeed where we lose, their success is not their doing but that of
the invisible hand; worse yet, those who "succeed" figure not as recipients of
success but merely as later victims in a blind succession. In sum, the galloping
exposition with which *Maud* opens dismantles responsibility and suspends a
baffled passion in its place— thus articulating Tennyson's familiar vision of
doom, but now with a degree of mimetic realism and cultural specificity that is
without parallel in his work.

The hero seeks anesthetic refuge from this condition of passive suffering in
the "passionless peace" of an Epicurean "philosopher's life" (I.iv.150–151). Yet
his philosohy falters when it comes to explaining his alienation in casual terms:
"Do we move ourselves, or are moved?" The explanations the hero produces
contradict each other. At times he seems to himself the victim of his history and
environment,

> Living alone in an empty house,
> Here half-hid in the gleaming wood,
> Where I hear the dead at midday moan,
> And the shrieking rush of the wainscot mouse,
> And my own sad name in corners cried,
> When the shiver of dancing leaves is thrown
> About its echoing chambers wide,
> Till a morbid-hate and horror have grown
> Of a world in which I have hardly mixt.
> (I.vi.257–265)

These circumstances, the hero says, have made him what he is; yet if Tennyson's
Mariana of 1830 were to account for herself in this way, as she could with virtually no change of imagery, we should rightly suspect that the conditioning circumstances were fantastic projections from a self less acted upon than active.
And indeed, when a few sections later a preaching pacifist has come into town,
the hero reverses his behaviorist position and insists on its moral opposite, the
purity of inward discipline:

> This huckster put down war! can he tell
> Whether war be a cause or a consequence?
> Put down the passions that make earth Hell!
> Down with ambition, avarice, pride,
> Jealousy, down! cut off from the mind
> The bitter springs of anger and fear;
> Down too, down at your own fireside,
> With the evil tongue and the evil ear,
> For each is at war with mankind.
> (I.x.373–381)

The chiastic relation between these two passages—private moods arise from circumstances, whereas the public arena evokes an individualistic morality— illustrates the crossing of social upon personal issues that is the poet's larger
theme. Not just the "huckster" but the hero too confuses cause with conse-

quence, in a repeatedly frustrated attempt to grasp, from within, the mono-dramatic dialectic in which he lives and speaks.

The form of monodrama, as a kind of lyrical narration, lends itself particularly well to Tennyson's rendition of the problematic social and individual reciprocity of cause with consequence. Monodrama is a narrative form in which, within the phenomenology of reading, consequences always precede causes. Maud thus situates its hero reactively, his phases of passion having been prompted by some action anterior to the text, usually a social encounter. His speech, which is to say his whole poetic existence, is in this fundamental sense, and with great cumulative force, a product of his social environment. As we read we learn to ask not what he will do next, but what will have happened to him in the interim. Maud thus is a poem not only written backward but inevitably read backward as well, from moment to moment, despite the forward thrust of its plot. This monodramatic retrospection kinks up the chain of cause and effect by compelling us to gather the story by extrapolation from what the hero tells us. Especially given so suspiciously erratic a narrator, this technique emphasizes the arbitrary and inferential nature of the causal linkage involved in understanding any narrative; it lands us, therefore, in uncertainties akin to those that beset the nonplussed hero himself.[1]

It is in representing the pivotal deed, the hero's fatal duel with Maud's brother, that Tennyson exploits the narrative resources of monodrama most brilliantly and makes the question of causality most strikingly problematic:

> "The fault was mine, the fault was mine"—
> Why am I sitting here so stunned and still,
> Plucking the harmless wild-flower on the hill?—
> It is this guilty hand!—
> And there rises ever a passionate cry
> From underneath in the darkening land—
> What is it, that had been done?
>
> (II.i.1–7)

This last question is a version of the one Tennyson's monodrama provokes in its reader throughout, and its passive wording is precisely right. The hero's implication—something uncomprehended has taken its unstoppable course—faithfully reproduces the bewilderment that has suffused his vision since the start. Without dodging responsibility ("It is this guilty hand!"), his narrative of the duel depicts both antagonists as caught up in roles that their high passion assumes by social reflex: roles ordained by "the Christless code" of honor (II.i.26), dated by 1855 but still very much in force, which marshals the vindictive energies of their caste.[2] The doom, and the guilt, that the hero thus shares with his victim are brilliantly presented with the opening line, which is both the most naked admission of responsibility in all of Maud and the most resistant to personal attribution. "The fault was mine"; but the words are whose? They repeat

---

1. See also Priestley, pp. 107–108, and Alan Sinfield, "Tennyson's Imagery," Neophilologus 55 (1976): 476–78. Robert James Mann, the first systematic expositor of Maud, found it necessary to stress this feature of the text: "The object of the poet is evidently not to picture these individuals as they are, but to describe them as they appear to the irritable and morose nature to which they are hostile personalities. . . . It must never be forgotten that it is not the poet, but the chief person of the action, who paints them" (Tennyson's "Maud" Vindicated: An Explanatory Essay [London: Jarrold, 1856], 25–26). Mann was defending his friend against malicious misprision, but he was also pointing to generic features that puzzled readers because they were new.
2. See John R. Reed, Victorian Conventions (Athens, Ohio University Press, 1975), 142–45.

what the brother has said, yet obviously they tell the hero's truth too. However the *beau geste* of Maud's brother was intended, his unimpeachably terminal confession is the noble, Christless code's last cunning article, one that will rivet the hero for life to a fugitive and inexpiable guilt. "'The fault was mine,' he whispered, 'fly!'" (II.i.30). Although winning the duel, the hero has lost by the rules of every code he might stand by: the dictates of human decency, true lover's faith, the biblical commandment—even, now that Maud's brother has upstaged him forever, the standard of honor underlying this most lethal of aristocratic field sports. And yet the hero has played the game: having done wrong, he cannot say where he has *gone* wrong, because he is finally victimized by the confluence of incompatible cultural imperatives.

In a sense this terrible confluence is just bad luck. Luck is the prosaic underside of the doom Tennyson's poetry envisions ("the shocks of Chance," says section XCV of *In Memoriam*, not "Change"); but it is a side he rarely risks exhibiting so nearly as in *Maud*. If the poem escapes the charge of plot contrivance, it does so principally through the very excess of that contrivance. For while from one perspective the monodrama suspends the connection of cause with effect that binds together more traditional narratives (like Tennyson's idylls), from another it furnishes a surplus of explanations. The hero has not one but every reason to quarrel with Maud's brother, to flee the scene of the duel, to take leave of his senses, to enlist at last in the war effort. This causal overload imparts to the poem much of its driven fatalism; to ask motivational questions about any of its main events is to be stormed by a rush of eligible answers—passional, economic, political, clinical—none of them especially convincing, by reason of their very multiplicity and cooperation. It is this interlock of motives, the whole self-reinforcing and self-perpetuating ideological complex, that Tennyson has taken up in *Maud*; and as the poet pursues its strategy across the phases of passion, the poem raises the etiological stakes from happenstance, through the charisma of personal good or bad fortune, toward an inescapable cultural bondage.

The operation of a cultural complex, and not just an Oedipal one, is nowhere stronger or more poignant than where Tennyson's contemporaries would least have expected to find it: in the hero's love affair with Maud. The erotic sphere notoriously served the Victorians as a stay against the allied forces of selfishness and impersonality that a society on the cash nexus had unleashed. The hero of *Maud* certainly regards love in this way, as did his poet when commenting that the hero is "raised to a pure and holy love which elevates his whole nature"; and most criticism has followed suit.[3] Yet when we consider the widespread ideological resistance of Victorian culture to any desecration of its Romantic erotic ideal—a resistance to which Tennyson's comment on "a pure and holy love" shows him also subject— we may surmise that this was the feature of his scandalous poem that aroused the profoundest indignation, as it was also his hardest-won triumph.

The social analysis of love begins where the love story does, as the hero fatally overhears Maud singing by the manorial cedar "an air that is known to me" (I.v.164). In this poem that ends with a decision to enlist, it matters of course that Maud's is "a martial song" (166); but it equally matters that her song is a

3. *Poems*, ed. Ricks, p. 1039.

traditional one, a ballad the hero recognizes at once. Because Maud has not invented the song but found it in the aristocratic past, the hero can deflect his spontaneous devotion from Maud herself onto the nobility that speaks through her: to "adore / Not her, who is neither courtly nor kind, / Not her, not her, but a voice" (187–189).[4] If we compare this passage to Tennyson's lines on the singing bulbul from "Recollections of the Arabian Nights" (1830)—"Not he: but something which possessed / The darkness of the world" (lines 71–72)—we glimpse in little the thoroughness with which in *Maud* the poet has devoted his usual rhetoric of impersonal transcendence to hegemonic conditions of culture. From the beginning the hero loves courtliness, not Maud; and the imagery of stars, flowers, and especially gems in which he consistently represents her, like the singularity of her voice here, points to an imaginative and erotic elitism that is not merely figurative but refers to the constellation of rank and wealth that determines the place of these lovers in the Victorian world.

In view of the events this incident precipitates, it is an awful coincidence for both lovers that he should hear her singing just this song at just this point. And yet, in their time and place, what else should she sing, and how else should he react? This decisive first link in a concatenated plot is already decided before it begins, an entirely natural consequence flowing from who the two principals are, which is to say, from where they are in society and history. A reader who means to condemn the hero in part III for joining troops who "have proved we have hearts in a cause, we are noble still" (III.vi.55) will have to read the judgment backward to this moment of apparently innocuous lyricism, where a song of noble men "in battle array, / Ready in heart" (I.v.169–170), stirs the hero's heart so readily because the codes of nobility are what his heart is ready for.[5] The hero's peroration declares the Crimean War "a cause"; and though his part in it seems less a cause than an irresistible consequence, his declaration rings true. The cause that is "noble still" remains the same cause that has determined the love whose aftermath his soldiering may bring to terminal resolution.

As the love story advances, Maud appears to her lover not a person intrinsically worthy, nor an object of desire, but a sign whose worth arises from the place she holds in a social system. Even physical beauty, the most inalienably personal of possessions, exists in Maud only as it appears to her socially conditioned beholder:

> I kissed her slender hand,
> She took the kiss sedately;
> Maud is not seventeen,
> But she is tall and stately.
> (I.xii.424–427)

Readers have not been kind to this stanza, taking offense at the patronizing decorum of its courtship and its rhyme. But the stiffness of the lovemaking, and of the language that describes it, makes an important point: Maud's beauty *is* her deco-

---

4. Compare I.xvi.549, "Lord of the pulse that is lord of her breast," with an earlier version in Trinity Notebook 36: "Lord of the pulses that move her breast." The more interesting revised line plays down the biological in favor of what Eve Kosofsky Sedgwick calls the hero's "homosocial" desire: to lord it over the lord by obtaining the lady.
5. See A. S. Byatt, "The Lyric Structure of Tennyson's *Maud*," in *The Major Victorian Poets: Reconsiderations*, ed. Isobel Armstrong (London: Routledge and Kegan Paul, 1969), 81; Philip Drew, "Tennyson and the Dramatic Monologue: A Study of *Maud*," in *Tennyson*, ed. D. J. Palmer (Athens, Ohio: Ohio University Press, 1973), 136.

rum, her school-finished poise a cultural accomplishment for which the semi-public "stately" is just *le mot juste*. Here is a young woman bred to receive a courtly kiss as her due; and the hero's patronizing approval of her breeding includes his awareness that, at seventeen or a little older, she will be able to raise him to her estate as a landed paterfamilias. Not her, not her, but a poise, a prize, a place.

The hero's metaphor of choice in describing Maud is the gem or pearl (I.iii.95, v.175, x.352, xviii.640), with its obvious connotations of wealth. More often, though, he describes her metonymically instead, in tropes focused on the associations that make her such a catch.[6] This metonymic displacement, from Maud's proper self to her properties, often leads the hero to dwell on the other men in her life, who are always described in greater detail than Maud herself, for the simple reason that their opinions, doings, and prospects are of greater account. The "dandy-despot" brother (I.vi.231), the "snowy-banded, dilettante, / Delicate-handed priest" (I.viii.310–311), the "padded shape" and "waxen face" of the new suitor he calls "little King Charley snarling" (I.x.358–359, I.xii.441), fix upon the hero's imagination with the fascination of a social taboo; the trappings of their power represent what, for all his philosophy, he cannot help coveting. He finds a warrant for his courtship in a dream memory of "two men," his father and Maud's, plotting their children's future together, their voices spectrally empowered by dream but also by a patriarchal convention that is nowhere and everywhere, "Somewhere, talking of me; / 'Well, if it prove a girl, my boy / Will have plenty: so let it be'" (I.vii.297–300). Even in rare moments of speculation about Maud's mind, the hero assumes that her marriage choice—the one culturally crucial exercise of a Victorian lady's will—must turn on her estimate of a husband's prospective standing in a gentleman's world: "She would not do herself this great wrong, / To take a wanton dissolute boy / For a man and leader of men" (I.x.386–388).

Metonymy is the rhetorical mode of nineteenth-century realism; and since the real, the Tennyson "that which is," (*In Memoriam* XCV) appears in *Maud* as the ideological ordinance of culture, it makes perfect sense that his hero's nervous love should crackle at every synapse with the rhetoric of power. The climactic sections of part I take as their subject the empowerment of love; and it is here, in the realm of erotic fantasy, that Tennyson's experimental interfusion of private with public discourse becomes most acute.

> O beautiful creature, what am I
> That I dare to look her way;
> Think that I may hold dominion sweet,
> Lord of the pulse that is lord of her breast,
> And dream of her beauty with tender dread,
> From the delicate Arab arch of her feet
> To the grace that, bright and light as the crest
> Of a peacock, sits on her shining head,
> And she knows it not: O, if she knew it,
> To know her beauty might half undo it.
> I know it the one bright thing to save
> My yet young life in the wilds of Time.
> (I.xvi.546–557)

---

6. See Pauline Fletcher, "Romantic and Anti-Romantic Gardens in Tennyson and Swinburne," *Studies in Romanticism* 18 (1979): 81–97.

A King Arthur of desire, the hero seeks salvation from "the wilds of Time" in the establishment of just the masculine "dominion" that, in his time, the ideology of gender prescribes. Maud must not "know her beauty," because that is her lover's prerogative. It is he who will *own* it when confessing his love ("For I must tell her"; I.xvi.569), while her part is confined to the giving, keeping, or breaking of "her word" (561–565), yes or no, when man proposes—a version of the passivity, the mere responsiveness to social mandates, from which the hero means to carve himself an escape by asserting the claims of male dominion.

The exotic images the hero imports for Maud's beauty (the "Arab arch," the curiously male peacock's crest) suggest that his fantasies of erotic dominion are imperial fantasies as well. The next section bears this suggestion out very fully indeed. Section xvii, though it has not fared well with critics, seems to me one of Tennyson's tours de force, a chaste imagination of erotic triumph to which images of global hegemony come as if unbidden:

> Go not, happy day,
>   From the shining fields,
> Go not, happy day,
>   Till the maiden yields.
> Rosy is the West,
>   Rosy is the South,
> Roses are her cheeks,
>   And a rose her mouth
> When the happy Yes
>   Falters from her lips,
> Pass and blush the news
>   Over glowing ships;
> Over blowing seas,
>   Over seas at rest,
> Pass the happy news,
>   Blush it through the West;
> Till the red man dance
>   By his red cedar-tree,
> And the red man's babe
>   Leap, beyond the sea.
> Blush from West to East,
>   Blush from East to West,
> Till the West is East,
>   Blush it through the West.
> Rosy is the West,
>   Rosy is the South,
> Roses are her cheeks,
>   And a rose her mouth.

The form and imagery of this poem speak eloquently to the relation between erotic and cultural power, and about both in relation to language. The lines fall into natural quatrain stanzas (as in sections vii and xii), but here the poet has fused his quatrains into a formal continuity that mirrors the seamlessness of a global vision. The most remarkable fusion occurs at the end of the eighth line, which Tennyson consistently left unpunctuated, I think in order to stress a crucial point about the rhetorical power of his hero's metaphor-making in the rose poem tradition.[7] "Rosy," describing the west and south, is either a straight adjective or a buried simile; "Roses are her cheeks" crosses the rhetorical line into metaphor, but metaphor of a weakly conventional sort that suggests rather too many literary girls with roses in their cheeks.[8] The empowered metaphor of this quatrain is the last, "And a rose her mouth"—an image that is wonderfully erotic in itself and that the unusual punctuation shows to be simply irresistible from the vantage of Tennyson's acculturated hero. For Maud's mouth can not only kiss but speak, and thus can bear the news of a surrender whose import is hyperbolically global because the cultural freight behind it is literally global. Love makes the world go round, for Tennyson's hero, as and because the British empire does. That is why the hero breaks through into original metaphor at the point at which eros and culture form one "dominion sweet." Maud's mouth is a rose when it assents to the authority of patriarchal empire, which her faltering blush of submissive pride also confirms, and which the succeeding images of the westering course of commerce ("glowing ships") and of colonial bliss and fecundity ("the red man's babe") expand upon, until a young man's fancy and the first flush of sexual conquest have utterly merged with the Victorian Englishman's proudest boast: that upon his empire—rosy red on any good Victorian map of the world—the sun never sets.

If the shadow of mortality falls across this text, it does so to signal the death of unconditioned subjectivity, the preemption of lyrical by imperial wealth, the cultural doom of romantic—and Romantic—desire. We can catch this fatal shadow best by comparison to Wordsworth's ode on a germane topic, "Intimations of Immortality." In Wordsworth "the Babe leaps up on his Mother's arm" (49) as a culminating figure of communal joy, which the poet joins only after a singular admonition from "a Tree, of many, one" (51) has exiled him to a state of solitary *thought*; from this state, in turn, a visionary memory that sees "the Children sport upon the shore" (166) effects partial restoration, again only "in thought" (171). Precisely the thoughtlessness of *Maud* I.xvii has provoked adverse critical comment; yet it is only its thoughtlessness, its uncritical absorption in a phase of passion, that makes possible its success as an ecstatic lyrical essay in the cultural sublime. The single tree and the leaping babe, which are opposed images for Wordsworth, come back joined in Tennyson's lyric by the rhythm of an imperialist ethnic mythology. With his red babe leaping by his red cedar tree, the red man dances to the rhythm of the white man's burden. Such primitivism locates primal sympathy not in the philosophic mind but in the greater deep of unconscious acculturation, where custom lies upon the self with a weight deep indeed as life.

Insofar as the erotic was the sphere into which Victorian culture most notably domesticated the Romantic ideology of the autonomous self, and insofar as *Maud* deconstructs the self into its cultural constituents, it is appropriately when Tennyson is dwelling on romantic love that he draws most conspicuously on Romantic texts—and draws on them, moreover, as parts of the culture within which he is writing. We have just seen how a revisionist allusion to Wordsworth's ode sharpens the cultural argument of section xvii. Its greater suc-

---

7. In Trinity Notebook 36, fol. 23 there is a period after "mouth" (though none after "yields" four lines above). Evidently the unusual punctuation came to Tennyson late; it occurs in every published edition I have consulted. Compare with Tennyson's lyric Keats's *Hyperion* III.14–22, where a rosy glow passes in the opposite direction, from the rose itself through "the clouds of even and of morn" to culminate in the erotic: "let the maid / Blush keenly, as with some warm kiss surpris'd."
8. See W. David Shaw, *Tennyson's Style* (Ithaca and London: Cornell University Press, 1976), 179.

cessor, section xviii ("I have led her home"), goes beyond allusion, taking Keats's "Ode to a Nightingale" as a central argumentative and imagistic model. The parallels between Tennyson's eight-stanza meditative lyric and Keats's are striking: high Miltonic syntax and purity of diction; the embalmed darkness of a fragrant setting; starlight playing through verdurous glooms; the opposition of human imagination to misery; a flirtation with and then a rejection of mortality; a valedictory bell. Yet all these parallels set off an essential difference, itself different in kind from Tennyson's frequent earlier revisions of this ode. "Ode to a Nightingale" turns on a dialectical relation between imagination and nature, or between the imagining self and its own mortality. But for Tennyson neither term of the Keatsian dialect is simple or stable. He has presented each as subject to mediation by the linguistic structures of consciousness since very early in his career; and when he has alluded to the "Nightingale" ode he has always done so with an eye, or an ear, for some transcendent ground that subtends both the created world and the creative mind that confronts it. In *Maud* this transcendent ground stands revealed, with unique force, as *culture*, in its contemporary Victorian incarnation; and this revelation lets Tennyson rewrite Keats's ode with remarkable fidelity to its images and even to their sequence, but with an altogether original purpose that conduces on occasion to poetic effects more Keatsian than those we find in Keats.

The note of section xviii is acceptance, which if not finally Keats's note is certainly the note Tennyson heard when he read Keats. The hero's blissful calm proceeds from his having found, after hundreds of lines of alienation and nostalgia, "the promised good" (I.xviii.604), a rightful place that justifies the world around him. "I have led her home": whatever has or has not happened this day among the wildflowers by his home, it is now the hero's conviction that Maud's home, within whose grounds he reposes as he speaks, will be his; and that "long-wished-for end" (603) provides the social substrate for the sense of erotic arrival—coming rather than consummation—which the poem also lavishly elaborates: "Maud made my Maud by that long loving kiss" (656). Keats's gifts for recreating the natural world of generation and death, and finding it good, takes in Tennyson's lyric the form of an acceptance of the cultural world. For both poets a full acceptance entails recognition of what is not easily accepted; but where for Keats the obstacles are such natural facts as pain, illness, and death ("Nightingale," 23–30), for Tennyson they inhere in cultural interpretations of nature, "A sad astrology, the boundless plan" that brands "His nothingness into man" (634–638). The hero, who "would die / To save from some slight shame one simple girl" (642–643), seeks an easeful death that is not Keats's blank mortality but an act in a script indited by nineteenth-century chivalry, which he not only would die for but also will kill for soon enough.

The hero's acceptance of love's "madness" and his gallant death wish both illustrate his acquiescence in a cultural role, as the interpolated seventh stanza, based on the seventh stanza of the "Nightingale" ode, makes clear:

Not die; but live of truest breath,
And teach true love to fight with mortal wrongs.
O, why should Love, like men in drinking-songs,
Spice his fair banquet with the dust of death?
Make answer, Maud my bliss,
Maud made my Maud by that long loving kiss,

Life of my life, wilt thou not answer this?
"The dusky strand of Death inwoven here
With dear Love's tie, makes Love himself more dear."
(I.xviii.651–659)

Dying means living the life of a culture hero, which Tennyson risks spoiling his poem by describing in the virtuous bromides of these first two lines. But the stanza executes a handsome recovery in what follows, which complicates its verbal magic with a suggestion that it is the verbal magic of culturally canonical texts that largely inspires the hero's moral reform. "Like men in drinking songs": we would do the "Ode to a Nightingale" no disservice by calling it the finest-toned drinking song in the canon, and the ode receives something like that compliment here from Keats's great port-loving successor. Tennyson finds his way to a meditation on the Keatsian themes of love and death through meditating on the tradition of which the "Nightingale" ode forms a part, and the quoted answer at which the stanza arrives feels like what the Keats of "When I have Fears," "Why Did I laugh?" and "Bright Star" meant but never came out and said.[9]

Just as in its entirety *Maud* treats the Romantic mythology of imaginative immortality as a dusky strand in the fabric of cultural hegemony, so section xviii welcomes the influence of "Ode to a Nightingale" by presenting that influence as part of a cultural tradition. Tennyson at once confirms the ode's Romantic assertion of imaginative priority to natural facts of love and death, and diminishes the saliency of this particular text against the vast tapestry of culture with which it is entangled. This is why the Keatsian tolling bell prompts in Tennyson's hero no anxiety whatsoever: "And hark the clock within, the silver knell / Of twelve sweet hours that past in bridal white, / And died to live, long as my pulses play" (622–664). "No more so all forlorn" (630), he enjoys for the momemt the entire idyllic security of a Victorian man whose love, whose ambition, and whose literary experience all converge in "the promised good," the behavior-reinforcing reward. Finally this satisfaction is intimately and expansively physical; no poem is more sensuous than the "Nightingale" ode, but Tennyson has written one here that is more *corporeal*, in representation of his no longer disaffected hero's blissful merger with the body cultural and politic. Hence the fulfilling bodily imagery that governs the opening and closing stanzas on the "blood" (601), the "heart" (608), and the "pulses" that swell to cosmic dimension: "Beat, happy stars, timing with things below, / Beat with my heart more blest than heart can tell" (679–680).

To be sure, "some dark undercurrent woe" (681) remains to draw the hero back to unsolved problems that the monodramatic narrative holds in store. But when his joy revives in the final love lyric, the hero's body language dances once again to the music of the time, in the appropriately specific form of a Victorian

9. This passage came into existence in one of the most interesting of the Trinity manuscripts. At this point Trinity Notebook 36, fol. 27 moves directly from line 650 to a version of line 660 ("I scarce can think this music but the swell . . . "), which is altered to its final reading on a third try. The curious second version—"What threefold meaning echoes from . . . "—suggests that Tennyson was hearing a reverberant music whose source troubled him. Stanza 7 (which Harvard Notebook 30, fol. 3–4, likewise lack) is first written out on the facing fol. 26v. It is tempting to believe that at this point Tennyson realized his indebtedness to Keats's ode and capitalized upon the debt—"Not die" corresponding to "Thou wast not born for death," and the "drinking-songs" allusion acknowledging, at a higher level, the complexity of the intertextual weave. The writing of stanza 7 then let Tennyson make sense of the "music" that had mystified him before. That music was Keats's enchanted moan: the stanza from the "Nightingale" ode that Tennyson kept uncannily hearing because to that point he had left it out of his brilliant imitation.

polka: "And the soul of the rose went into my blood, / As the music clashed in the hall" (I.xxii.882–883). This pulse resurges most powerfully in the lines that close part I:

> She is coming, my own, my sweet;
> Were it ever so airy a tread,
> My heart would hear her and beat,
> Were it earth in an earthy bed;
> My dust would hear her and beat,
> Had I lain for a century dead;
> Would start and tremble under her feet,
> And blossom in purple and red.
> (I.xxii.916–923)

Well over a century has passed since Tennyson wrote these lines of prophetic rapture, and it is no accident that their reputation has risen and fallen, and now rises again, with readers' sympathy for Victorian tastes. There may be no firmer testimony of Tennyson's intention to explore in *Maud* the pervasiveness of cultural determinants for behavior and feeling than the fact that in this last, climactic expression of love's ecstasy, from the most personally invested of all his major works, this prosodic adept chose to stake so much on the specifically contemporary beat of a popular fad.

From the start of part II, the cultural determinants are dramatically realigned against the hero they have momentarily and capriciously supported at the end of Part I. The ensuing dissonance makes the abandoned hero, "so stunned and still" (II.i.2), begin seeing double. Maud, now irrecoverably lost, becomes a "ghastly Wraith" (II.i.32), a "hard mechanic ghost" (II.ii.82) that the hero explains as "a lying trick of the brain" (II.i.37), or "a juggle born of the brain" (II.ii.90). He is blaming the victim, of course, in the neurophysiological terms of his day.[1] But his ambidexter images of the lie and the juggle point beyond a psychology of self-division to the schism in society that furnishes the germinally twinned imagery of "Oh! That 'Twere Possible." In this long-deferred lyric (now section iv), images of the mutually alien city and country, the "woodland echo" (II.iv.178) and the market "hubbub" (II.iv.208), may meet only in the hero's mind, which is now more plainly than ever a crossroads of contradictory memories and impressions.

The mad scene of section v carries this tendency to its Victorian extreme. Tennyson piqued himself on having drafted the mad scene in twenty minutes, and it is in this most spontaneous poetry that the unreflective mind most forcefully reflects its social victimization. Insanity is a topic, like love, that summons up the deepest privacies, and Tennyson calls upon it in part II in order to practice a sociopathology similar to that whereby he has earlier dissected "the cruel madness of love" (I.iv.156). In describing his passion earlier in the conventional terms of "madness," the hero was surrendering to the beat of culture; so he must do again now in succumbing to madness itself: "And the hoofs of the horses beat, beat, / The hoofs of the horses beat, / Beat in to my scalp and my brain" (II.v.246–248). The rhythms have changed since part I, but it is still the drum of culture that sounds the inevitable tattoo.

---

1. See Ann C. Colley, *Tennyson and Madness* (Athens, Ga.: University of Georgia Press, 1983), 125, 166.

The mad hero's *idée fixe*—that he has died but wants proper burial— affords Tennyson occasions to sustain the urban imagery of the preceding section in a vividly necropolitan mode, and also to venture a reprise of the overt social satire that has been blunted by the coming of love in part I. Churchman, lord, statesman, physician all come under the lash (II.v.266–274), principally for sins of linguistic deviancy. "There is none that does his work, not one" (264); and what fills the space of this unperformed work is language, "chatter," "blabbing," and most significantly "idiot gabble" (257, 274, 279). Etymologically *idiocy* is privacy, and what the hero censures as "idiot gabble" is a cross between autism and bad breeding. The maddening thing about the dead men's chatter, from the hero's standpoint, is its violation of the Victorian decorum that segregates public from private spheres. Tennyson has practiced just this violation since the beginning of *Maud*, as a poetic means of confounding a cardinal Victorian prejudice; but now that the hero shares the poet's secret, it is driving him out of his mind. In its methodical madness section v constitutes the hero's new and crippling consciousness of a breakdown between public and private discourses—a breakdown that unleashes a semiotic bedlam from which he seeks protection. Although he defensively calls the chorus of voices mere "babble" (284), what assails him is rather an excess than a dearth of meaning, an overload of confessional secrets he wants neither to hear nor to have heard by anyone else:

> For I never whispered a private affair
> Within the hearing of cat or mouse,
> No, not to myself in the closet alone,
> But I heard it shouted at once from the top of the house;
> Everything came to be known.
> Who told *him* we were there?
>
> (II.v.285–290)

What is the intolerably open secret from which the hero wants burial? The abortive tryst with Maud to which he suddenly recurs has long since suffered its most devastating exposure; yet it offers a clue, for what was exposed in the exposure of his "private affair" with Maud was the notion of privacy itself. The hero's debacle has exacted his recognition of the inevitably corporate nature of language;[2] and this recognition "Is enough to drive one mad" (II.v.258), into an insanity that is also the poem's most comprehensively public gesture. The subjectively incoherent perspectives of the madman regroup themselves at the level of cultural analysis into an irresistible phalanx that serves Tennyson as the monodramatic equivalent of a tragically fatal objectivity. "Prophet, curse me the blabbing lip, / And curse me the British vermin, the rat" (295–296): simultaneously "prophet" and "vermin"—accuser, criminal, and judge in one breath, as the condensed syntax suggests—the hero can but perpetuate the discourse that entraps him if he is to speak at all.

Placing social invective against the "Wretchedest age, since Time began" (259) in the mouth of a madman serves the poet laureate, of course, as a means of self-defense—a man would have to be crazy to talk about England like that— but it also defends the reader against a too immediate disclosure of a too inti-

---

2. See Samuel E. Schulman, "Mourning and Voice in *Maud*," *Studies in English Literature, 1500–1900* 23 (1983): 645.

mate vision of the pervasive force of culture.[3] The hero requires defense from this vision as well, of course; and since he lacks the dramatic distance available to poet and reader, he pleads insanity. Even this asylum gives no real refuge, however, and he knows it:

> O me, why have they not buried me deep enough?
> Is it kind to have made me a grave so rough,
> Me, that was never a quiet sleeper?
> Maybe still I am but half-dead;
> Then I cannot be wholly dumb;
> I will cry to the steps above my head
> And somebody, surely, some kind heart will come
> To bury me, bury me
> Deeper, ever so little deeper.
>
> (II.v.334–342)

As death represents acculturation in part I, here half-death represents an acculturation tantalizingly unconsummated. The hero "cannot be wholly dumb" until he becomes wholly deaf to the incongruity of the ubiquitous yet personal idiot gabble that circulates around and within him. He cries out for a burial so full, a cultural immersion so total, that he will no longer know that engulfing rite for what it is. More than anything else, the hero wants to lose a mind that he wishes, or suspects, he has never properly possessed. This goal he may achieve only by ceasing to be — or, barring literal suicide, by ceasing to be piercingly aware, as he now is for the only time in the poem, of culture as an otherness that he has internalized, in the tangled nest of public properties that constitutes his private self.

These equivalent modes of oblivion, either of which the hero would prefer to his current torment, come together in the prospect of military self-sacrifice he accepts in part III. Unable to "bury myself in myself" (I.i.75), whether through the cool reason of a philosopher's life or through the irrational escapes of a lunatic's, the hero says at last, "I have felt with my native land, I am alone one with my kind, / I embrace the purpose of God, and the doom assigned" (III.vi.58–59). With the natural images of "my native land" and "my kind," the politicization of any ostensibly natural substrate below culture is complete; and with the invocation of the "purpose of God" and its Tennysonian synonym "the doom assigned," supernatural options for transcending culture are terminally politicized as well. In answer to the pathetic final prayer of part II, the merciful ground of culture has opened to swallow the hero up. He has fallen into the bliss of the state.

Culture never did betray the heart that loved her, not when she is loved as by Tennyson's hero, with "the unselfishness born of a great passion."[4] But great passion is greatly blind, and in awaking to "the better mind" (III. vi.56) the hero has deadened himself to a mass of inconsistencies—something we have watched him do throughout the poem, to be sure, but not yet on this scale or with this urgency of implicit appeal to the reader's conscience. At earlier phases of his passion our hero would have been torn, at some level of awareness, between his claims of sympathy with his "kind" and his zealously bloody inten-

3. See Robert G. Stange, "The Frightened Poets," in *The Victorian City: Images and Realities*, ed. H.J. Dyos and Michael Wolff, II (London and Boston: Routledge and Kegan Paul, 1973), 478; and William B. Thesing, "Tennyson and the City: Historical Tremours and Hysterical Tremblings," *Tennyson Research Bulletin* 3 (1977): 20.
4. *Poems*, ed. Ricks, p. 1039.

tion to go to war; between his dedication to the business interests behind modern warfare and his hatred of the "wrongs and shames" (III.vi.40) of the commercial *Pax Victoriana*. He is not thus torn now; now his cultural entombment
can weather the most Orwellian of contradictions. The abiding horror of part
III arises when the hero's defection into lobotomized jingoism leaves us to take
up the ethical slack, without a clue to imagining a credible alternative course
of events. The hero's unacknowledged contradictions remain, to sear the critical conscience that would free itself of patriotic heroics without falling into step
with some other cultural or countercultural troop.

   "'Maud': I leave before the sad part":[5] Emily Tennyson's discreet exit is understandable but unavailing. We crave excuse from the cultural vision of *Maud*,
but such excuse comes hard once we recognize that its hero has satisfied precisely
this craving, in one fell swoop of moral abdication. We may imagine its poet feeding such a craving, too, in repeatedly indulged yet never quite fulfilling de-
bauches of vicarious abandonment to full acculturation, as he subjected circle
after circle of empire's best and brightest to readings of a poem that held up their
shared eminence to unforgiving scrutiny. "Only once, as it seems to me, (at the
close of 'Maud')," wrote an American culture pilgrim who had undergone the
Tennysonian rite, "has he struck the note of irrepressible emotion, and appeared
to say the thing that must be said at the moment, at any cost."[6] What struck young
Henry James about the close of *Maud* was the reckless extremity of its contemporary commitment: a unique fusion of Tennyson's antinomian, lyrical intensity
with the cultural absorption and finish that always seem so smooth in his idylls
of the hearth or of the king. *Maud* is an achievement of lethal force, one that Tennyson himself seems not to have understood very well and that his career never
repeated. But then he had no cause to repeat this published experiment, because
he was able literally to repeat it in public all the time. The experiment was never
over: *Maud* remained a rhapsode's work-in-progress at each of those command
performances for captive audiences that nobody (Emily Tennyson included)
seems to have rationally willed but that nobody (Alfred Tennyson included)
seems to have been able to escape. Those evenings at Farringford or London or
Aldworth cannot appear more quintessentially Victorian to us than they must
have felt to their participants, who, if they wondered what they were doing there
and minded the poem with even the least attentiveness, must have received some
deeply disquieting answers. Well may the cultural vision of *Maud* sting us still.

CHRISTOPHER RICKS

Idylls of the King, 1859–1885[†]

   In December 1858, Tennyson wrote to his American publisher, 'I wish that
you would disabuse your own minds and those of others, as far as you can, of

5. *Lady Tennyson's Journal*, ed. James O. Hoge (Charlottesville: University Press of Virginia, 1981), 82.
6. Henry James, "Tennyson's Drama," in *Views and Reviews*, ed. LeRoy Phillips (Boston: Bell, 1875), 176.
   See also W. W. Robson, "The Dilemma of Tennyson," rpt. in *Critical Essays on the Poetry of Tennyson*,
   ed. John Killham (New York: Barnes and Noble, 1960), 159–63.
† From Christopher Ricks, *Tennyson*, 2nd ed. (Berkeley: University of California Press). Copyright 1989 by
   the Regents of the University of California and the University of California Press. Reprinted by permission of the publisher.

the fancy that I am about an Epic of King Arthur. I should be crazed to attempt such a thing in the heart of the 19th Century.' Seven months later, Tennyson published *Idylls of the King*.[1] Granted, this was no more than the earliest batch of four ('Enid', 'Vivien', 'Elaine', and 'Guinevere'); they did not constitute an 'Epic', and even the completed enterprise never did—though Tennyson's son was to claim mildly that the *Idylls* achieved 'Epic unity'. Nevertheless, the discrepancy is a revealing one, not because of insincerity but because of vacillation. No other poem of Tennyson's was created with such a central uncertainty as to its shape, style, sequence, and size. Such uncertainty in composition is not in itself any evidence of ultimate uncertainty in achievement. Yet *Idylls of the King* must be judged strikingly uneven, and the indecisions of composition are an index of what went askew.

'Tennyson's Serial Poem', the title which Professor Kathleen Tillotson gave to her detailed study of the *Idylls*, is in danger of overdignifying the compromises and timidities which were engrained in this poetic venture. Tennyson had written his 'Morte d'Arthur' in 1833–4, and had published it in 1842. 'When I was twenty-four I meant to write a whole great poem on it, and began it in the "Morte d'Arthur". I said I should do it in twenty years; but the Reviews stopped me.' More specifically, the *Quarterly Review*, where John Sterling disparaged 'Morte d'Arthur' in September 1842. Tennyson told both his son and William Allingham that by this review 'he was prevented from doing his Arthur Epic'. 'I had it all in my mind, could have done it without any trouble.' He went on, 'But then I thought that a small vessel, built on fine lines, is likely to float further down the stream of Time than a big raft.' A good point (though Tennyson would not have liked us then to apply the term 'a big raft' to the *Idylls*)—but one which already complicates and clouds the initial commitment to 'his Arthur Epic', since the point is an independent act of criticism. A more serious complication is that Tennyson had already manifested a public unease about the epic before Sterling ever reviewed him. For he had framed 'Morte d'Arthur' with one of those poetic wheedlings, those throwings on your mercy, which Leigh Hunt deplored; preceding and succeeding 'Morte d'Arthur' in 1842 was 'The Epic' (which Tennyson wrote probably in 1837–8).

> 'You know,' said Frank, 'he burnt
> His epic, his King Arthur, some twelve books'—
> And then to me demanding why? 'Oh, sir,
> He thought that nothing new was said, or else
> Something so said 'twas nothing—that a truth
> Looks freshest in the fashion of the day . . . .'

'I should be crazed to attempt such a thing in the heart of the 19th Century.' In other words, Sterling's doubts had been explicitly anticipated by Tennyson's own doubts; what distressed him in the review, what made it prevent his going ahead, was not its being a shock but its being a telling corroboration of what he had acutely feared. 'Morte d'Arthur' was plucked from the hearth; though the lines of 'The Epic' had been written and published, the Epic itself had not been written but had been ingeniously burned instead.

In the 1840s, Tennyson 'began to study the epical King Arthur in earnest. . . . But it was not till 1855 that he determined upon the final shape of the

---

1. Tennyson pronounced 'Idyll' with an 'I' as an 'idle'.

poem, and not until 1859 that he published the first instalment, "Enid", "Vivien", "Elaine", "Guinevere".' Even as an instalment, this was far from being in final shape; only the last retained its title, and 'Enid'—with more decisiveness than sensitivity of decision—was to be brusquely divided into two idylls, 'Tthe Marriage of Geraint' and 'Geraint and Enid'.

Hallam Tennyson remarks, 'In spite of the public applause he did not rush headlong into the other *Idylls of the King*, although he had carried a more or less perfected scheme of them in his head over thirty years.' But, as Hallam Tennyson then concedes, there were recalcitrances in the scheme. First, Tennyson said, 'I could scarcely light upon a finer close than that ghostlike passing away of the King'; but this passing away was in 'Guinevere', which therefore had one kind of claim as an ending, and not in 'Morte d'Arthur', which had a conflicting claim. (Moreover, even 'Morte d'Arthur' had originally been thought of as the eleventh, not the twelfth, book.) Second, there was his unease here in 1862: 'I have thought about it for two years and arranged all the intervening Idylls but I dare not set to work for fear of a failure, and time lost.' Third, there was his doubt about whether he would ever be able to undertake the Grail story: 'As to Macaulay's suggestion of the Sangraal I doubt whether such a subject could be handled in these days, without incurring a charge of irreverence. It would be too much like playing with sacred things.' Yet in this same letter Tennyson said that he had once made up—in his head and 'in as good verse as I ever wrote'— a poem on Lancelot's quest of the Grail.

The 'more or less perfected scheme' was fraught with doublings back upon itself. Tennyson's tone in 1868 has something of the haphazard: 'I shall write three or four more of the "Idylls", and link them together as well as I may.' But ten years after the first installment there appeared in 1869 the second: 'The Coming of Arthur', 'The Holy Grail', 'Pelleas and Ettarre', and 'The Passing of Arthur'. This last was 'Morte d'Arthur' now preceded by the last great battle (169 lines) and with a concluding 29 lines. Tennyson in 1862 had resisted the idea of using 'Morte d'Arthur' as the ending, partly because of the passing away in 'Guinevere', and partly because 'the Morte is older in style and suggestive of a less modern social state'. But others denied that there was any incongruity, and in 1869 'The Passing of Arthur' bore a note: 'This last, the earliest written of the Poems, is here connected with the rest in accordance with an early project of the author's.' Readers in 1869 were given too a note on how to order the series.

It seemed—and not only to the unimaginative—that Tennyson was making up an ordering as he went along when in 1871 he published 'The Last Tournament' and in 1872 'Gareth and Lynette'. Whereupon, as Hallam Tennyson says, 'my father thought that he had completed the cycle of the Idylls; but later he felt that some further introduction to "Merlin and Vivien" was necessary, and so wrote "Balin and Balan"'. But even here there was wavering. For one thing, Tennyson said in 1873, 'I must have two more Idylls at the least to make "Vivien" come later into the Poem, as it comes in far too soon as it stands.' A shrewd criticism, since the earliness of 'Merlin and Vivien' has the bad effect of presenting Arthur's court as lamentably corrupted much too early for the moral scheme and for its pathos. Yet, far from adding 'two more Idylls at the least', Tennyson added only 'Balin and Balan'; moreover, he wrote it in 1872–4 and yet did not publish it till 1885, 'whether for the sake of purchasers', suggest Kathleen Tillotson, 'or because he had not decided whether to make it into one or two'. Not that 'Balin or Balan' could have been creatively snipped in two. But the composition and publication of *Idylls of the King,* extending over more than fifty years, are not a record of firm creative decision or of an organic responsiveness.

Large-scale attempts have recently been made to reinstate, or rather, instate *Idylls of the King* as a large-scale achievement. But a reader may find himself concurring with the claims that the *Idylls* are intricately patterned; that they show a subtle and erudite mastery of their sources; that they are a complex allegory and that they anticipate Jungian psychology—without being convinced that they constitute a poetic whole. Was the title *Idylls* defensively modest or truly so? Gladstone saw a discrepancy between the title and the ambitions: 'We are rather disposed to quarrel with the title of Idylls: for no diminutive (εἰδύλλιον) can be adequate to the breath, vigour, and majesty which belongs to the subjects, as well as to the execution, of the volume.' R. H. Hutton similarly deplored the title—and then, as has proved so easy to do, he himself stepped up the claims within the title by giving it, not as *Idylls of the King,* but as *The Idylls of the King:* 'The great poem called, I think with somewhat unfortunate modesty, *The Idylls of the King.* The title misled the public, and the fragmentary mode in which the poem appeared misled it the more.'

The Victorians were not helped by the piecemeal publication to see such unity as the poem may possess. But they were sensitive to the two crucial disappointments which the poem has long elicited, disappointments so fundamental as to vitiate any ambitious advocacy of the *Idylls* which does not incorporate a stylistic advocacy. Elizabeth Barrett Browning wrote to Tennyson's friend Allingham in 1859,

> But the *Idylls.* Am I forced to admit that after the joy of receiving them, other joys fell short, rather?—That the work, as a whole, produced a feeling of disappointment?—It must be admitted, I fear. Perhaps we had been expecting too long—had made too large an idea to fit a reality. Perhaps the breathing, throbbing life around us in this Italy, where a nation is being new-born, may throw King Arthur too far off and flat. But, whatever the cause, the effect was so. The colour, the temperature, the very music, left me cold. Here are exquisite things, but the whole did not affect me as a whole from Tennyson's hands.

Such a criticism cannot be dismissed by an insistence that as yet Mrs Browning had inevitably read only an 'instalment', not the whole. For the defects of the *Idylls* are of a kind that no amount of complex cross-patterning or moral concern can compensate for: they are defects of Tennyson's poetic language. Not only is the style of the *Idylls* extraordinarily uneven in quality, but even at its best the style is too often Tennysonian, mannered and extraneous.

Let me give a list which would indicate where—to one reader at least—the unevenness of achievement is manifest. Of the twelve *Idylls,* three are to me successful both in style and as wholes: 'Merlin and Vivien', 'The Holy Grail', and 'The Passing of Arthur'. Five are a mixture of the successful and the unsuccessful: 'The Coming of Arthur', 'Balin and Balan'. 'Lancelot and Elaine', 'The Last Tournament', and 'Guinevere'. Four are broadly unsuccessful: 'Gareth and Lynette', 'The Marriage of Geraint', 'Geraint and Enid', and 'Pelleas and Ettarre'.

'Here are exquisite things': it is for such things that *Idylls of the King* should last. But the staple of the verse is insensitive and awkward. Such a point is hard to substantiate with a long poem, since denigrators and admirers will merely bandy passages. The claim that such-and-such is representative is especially difficult to get established. Yet some sort of anthology of stylistic demerits is called for, since it is such failure of style which renders vacant or academic or wishful the larger claims made for the *Idylls*.

There is, most surprisingly of all, the failure of Tennyson's ear. Of such a line as 'And thrice the gold for Uther's use thereof', one might say that it should have been spoken not by Arthur but by the battered churl ('Then, sputtering through the hedge of splintered teeth . . . '). Then there are over-insistences, especially in those areas of the poem where Tennyson knew he had failed to create a sense of what the Round Table was in its living vigour:

> And out of bower and casement shyly glanced
> Eyes of *pure* women, *wholesome* stars of love;
> And all about a *healthful* people stept
> As in the presence of a *gracious* king.
> ('Gareth and Lynette')

There is tautology ('young lads'). There is perilous ambiguity:

> To break her will, and make her wed with him:
> And but delays his purport till thou send
> To do the battle with him, thy chief man
> Sir Lancelot whom he trusts to overthrow,
> Then wed, with glory:
> ('Gareth and Lynette')

There is clumsiness: 'A *walk* of roses *ran* from door to door'. There is insensitivity to rhythm and line-ending:

> So Sir Lancelot holp
> To raise the Prince, who rising twice or thrice
> Full sharply smote his knees
> ('Guinevere')

—rising twice or thrice? There is meaning unintended and to be ruled out by the reader's sluggish fellowship, as when we good-naturedly agree to supply the word 'even' for such a line as 'He, reverencing king's blood in a bad man'. There is vacancy of metaphor: nothing will bring 'leavened' into intelligent relationship to 'lay at Arthur's feet' in 'Merlin and Vivien', lines 138–44. There is vacancy of pomp: 'Being mirthful he, but in a stately kind'. There is, most sadly, a rotund insensitivity to those delicate sensualities which Tennyson elsewhere masters: 'An armlet for the roundest arm on earth' is a line which falls like brawn. There is an aimless shattering of the historical past, as in this gratuitous (and syntactically preposterous) introduction of London:

> Now for the central diamond and the last
> And largest, Arthur, holding then his court
> Hard on the river nigh the place which now
> Is this world's hugest, let proclaim a joust
> ('Lancelot and Elaine')

How could Tennyson write such a line as 'Hard on the river nigh the place which now', with its weak overlap of 'hard' and 'nigh', its weak assonance of 'nigh' and 'now', its weak rhythm and its weak line-ending? A full-length cri-tique of the *Idylls*' style would be a dispiriting matter; to me the faults are en-demic, and they imperil the fine things which are often in their vicinity. Two lines after that gaucherie about 'rising twice or thrice', there is a moral vignette which manifests Tennyson's true powers:

> But, ever after, the small violence done
> Rankled in him and ruffled all his heart,
> As the sharp wind that ruffles all day long
> A little bitter pool about a stone
> On the bare coast.
>
>   ('Guinevere')

The central deficiencies of the style are two: that Tennyson has not creatively solved the problem of what the dialogue ought to be in a poem which neces-sarily embodies archaism; and that he has not creatively solved the problem of accommodating his style (what Arnold called his 'curious elaborateness of ex-pression') to the simple exigencies of narrative, the humble essentials which would permit his story to move. Is it possible to be a disinterested admirer of Tennyson and *not* to notice that in the following passage the lines about the hern show genius, while the lines before and after scarcely show talent?

> ' . . .
> And seeing now thy words are fair, methinks
> There rides no knight, not Lancelot, his great self,
> Hath force to quell me.'
>   Nigh upon that hour
> When the lone hern forgets his melancholy,
> Lets down his other leg, and stretching, dreams
> Of goodly supper in the distant pool,
> Then turned the noble damsel smiling at him,
> And told him of a cavern hard at hand
>   ('Gareth and Lynette')

Such unevenness suggests that, though the feeling of manufacture is strong, there are unequal skills in the manufacture. 'Did you ever read such lines?' asked Meredith about 'The Holy Grail': 'The Poet rolls them out like half yards of satin.' But satin is consistently good stuff. 'Why, this stuff is not the Muse, it's Musery.'

The question of archaism was, as Tennyson knew, a crucial one: 'Why take the style of those heroic times? / For nature brings not back the Mastodon' ('The Epic'). But, as the most perceptive Victorians saw, Tennyson did not achieve an imaginative recreation of the past. Matthew Arnold insisted, 'The fault I find with Tennyson in his *Idylls of the King* is that the peculiar charm and aroma of the Middle Age he does not give in them.' Walter Bagehot noticed the wish of the *Idylls* to have it both ways, as in the matter of love at first sight in 'Geraint and Enid': 'It seems hardly fair that a writer should insist on the good side of both species of life; upon being permitted to use the sudden love which arises from not knowing women, and the love-tinged intercourse of thought and fancy which is the result of knowing them, together and at once.' Gerard Manley

Hopkins used the historical tergiversations to launch an attack on the *Idylls* which is probably unanswerable:

> But the want of perfect form in the imagination comes damagingly out when he undertakes longer works of fancy, as his Idylls: they are unreal in motive and incorrect, uncanonical so to say, in detail and keepings. He should have called them *Charades from the Middle Ages* (dedicated by per- mission to H.R.H. etc). The Galahad of one of the later ones is quite a fan- tastic charade-playing trumpery Galahad, merely playing the fool over Christian heroism. Each scene is a triumph of language and of bright pic- turesque, but just like a charade—where real lace and good silks and real jewelry are used, because the actors are private persons and wealthy, but it is acting all the same and not only so but the makeup has less pretence of correct keeping than at Drury Lane.

The moral scheme of the *Idylls*, too, has long been judged vulnerable. There is the sense that both Vivien and Modred are scapegoats more than villains; there is, more crucially, the sense that even Guinevere is too much a scapegoat, in that the doom of the Round Table antedates her adultery. 'First mainly through that sullying of our Queen'—but how mainly is 'mainly'? 'And all through thee!' cries Arthur to Guinevere, with more fire than cogency. Arthur is himself a demon- stration of a root confusion in Tennyson; no critic has ever replied satisfactorily to Swinburne's jibe at 'the Morte d'Albert, or Idylls of the Prince Consort'—or to his fervid and detailed argument that 'Mr Tennyson has lowered the note and deformed the outline of the Arthurian story, by reducing Arthur to the level of a wittol, Guenevere to the level of a woman of intrigue, and Launcelot to the level of a "co-respondent".' Arthur? 'Rather a prig', said Henry James. 'Unfit to be an epic-hero', said Henry Crabb Robinson, 'a *cocu*'. For the undoubted high-mind- edness of the *Idylls* is achieved only by reducing and attenuating the moral con- siderations to the point where they become low-minded. "The sentiments in these poems', said Bagehot, 'are simpler than his sentiments used to be'. You have only to compare Malory, said T.S. Eliot, 'to admire the skill with which Ten- nyson adapted this great British epic material—in Malory's handling hearty, out- spoken and magnificent—to suitable reading for a girls' school: the original ore being so refined that none of the gold is left.' A similar resentment was expressed in 1867 by Carlyle: 'We read, at first, Tennyson's *Idyls*, with profound recogni- tion of the finely elaborated execution, and also of the inward perfection of *va- cancy*, -and, to say truth, with considerable impatience at being treated so very like infants, though the lollipops were so superlative.'

The lollipops are indeed superlative, and the more positive point in insisting on the severe limits of the *Idylls'* success is so that one may sincerely admire the innumerable local felicities which the poem offers. The range of Tennyson's rhythmical mimesis and suggestiveness is extraordinary.

> First as in fear, step after step, she stole
> Down the long tower-stairs, hesitating.
> ('Lancelot and Elaine')

> and Gareth loosed the stone
> From off his neck, then in the mere beside
> Tumbled it; oilily bubbled up the mere.
> ('Gareth and Lynette')

And brought his horse to Lancelot where he lay.
He up the side, sweating with agony, got,
                    ('Lancelot and Elaine')

And I rode on and found a mighty hill,
And on the top, a city walled: the spires
Pricked with incredible pinnacles into heaven.
                    ('The Holy Grail')

Then turned, and so returned, and groaning laid
The naked sword athwart their naked throats,
There left it, and them sleeping; and she lay,
The circlet of the tourney round her brows,
And the sword of the tourney across her throat.
                    ('Pelleas and Ettare')

He spoke: the brawny spearman let his cheek
Bulge with the unswallowed piece, and turning stared;
                    ('Geraint and Enid')

This last, so unexpected an area of virtuosity as to leave Gladstone twice be-
musedly praising its 'good taste', its 'fine taste'.

Throughout the *Idylls* there are those peculiar intangibilities which it might
seem easy to snatch from the air. The spirits of the hills, 'With all their dewy
hair blown back like flame'. Or the shadowy recesses of memory:

He ended: Arthur knew the voice; the face
Wellnigh was helmet-hidden, and the name
Went wandering somewhere darkling in his mind.
                    ('The Last Tournament')

But it is the similes and the descriptions which are the triumphs within the
poem; triumphs which are saddening in that they so seldom relate intimately
to the poem's real concerns, but yet manifesting an eye and ear such as few English poets have possessed. Similes that invoke a complexion 'Wan-sallow as the
plant that feels itself/Root-bitten by white lichen'; or a lake 'Round as the red
eye of an Eagle-owl'; or (especially potent in the *Idylls*) the power and diversity
of the sea. Descriptions that let us glimpse somebody who glimpses 'Dust, and
the points of lances bicker in it'; or 'shattered archway plumed with fern'; or a
spring:

the spring, that down,
From underneath a plume of lady-fern,
Sang, and the sand danced at the bottom of it.
                    ('Balin and Balan')

Best of all, the landscapes which mingle with mood: the journey of Tristam
through the wood in 'The Last Tournament'; the setting of the last battle in
"The Passing of Arthur'; or the dream of Guinevere, which draws (as the *Idylls*
seldom do) upon sources of fearful energy from the earlier Tennyson:

for then she seemed to stand
On some vast plain before a setting sun,
And from the sun there swiftly made at her
A ghastly something, and its shadow flew
Before it, till it touched her, and she turned—

> When lo! her own, that broadening from her feet,
> And blackening, swallowed all the land, and in it
> Far cities burnt, and with a cry she woke.
>   ('Guinevere')

John Ruskin admired the first four *Idylls*, and, yet, 'Nevertheless I am not sure but I feel the art and finish in these poems a little more than I like to feel it.'

>   He looked, and more amazed
> Than if seven men had set upon him, saw
> The maiden standing in the dewy light.
> He had not dreamed she was so beautiful.
> Then came on him a sort of sacred fear
>   ('Lancelot and Elaine')

It is itself beautiful, but is there not something inordinate about its needing to enlist those seven men in order to achieve the sweet directness of 'He had not dreamed she was so beautiful'? And are not the last two lines, for all their legitimate insinuating, something less than the piercing resilience of such a line from *Maud* as 'And dream of her beauty with tender dread'? Yet the *Idylls* have their true poignancies:

> Then, when she heard his horse upon the stones,
> Unclasping flung the casement back, and looked
> Down on his helm, from which her sleeve had gone.
> And Lancelot knew the little clinking sound;
> And she by tact of love was well aware
> That Lancelot knew that she was looking at him.
>   ('Lancelot and Elaine')

The tact, the tenderness, the unmentioned bruises: to me the lines are enduring.

With such gifts devoted to *Idylls of the King*, what went wrong? 'For narrative Tennyson had no gift at all', said T. S. Eliot (who for narrative had no gift at all): 'Tennyson could not tell a story at all.' His best poems show the other side of this; his extraordinary powers over situation and mood, played against a known outcome. But *Idylls of the King* could not be simply idylls; they needed to be narratives, epyllia, as well. Tennyson's awed sense of time lent itself not to narrative, not to charting events and outcomes, but to waiting, to suspense. 'A doom that ever poised itself to fall': this is what tapped Tennyson's deepest fears and imaginings.[2] Which is why the finest lines in the *Idylls* are those which show us Merlin suspended in forethought: while Vivien chattered seductively,

>   he was mute:
> So dark a forethought rolled about his brain,
> As on a dull day in an Ocean cave
> The blind wave feeling round his long sea-hall
> In silence:

Into the cave of the skull, the forethought reaches, its feeling-round beautifully and tentacularly floating through the rhymes and assonances, 'cave' exactly into

---

2. The terrors in 'The Ring' (written 1887) are melodramatic, but one line that rings true evokes this haunting intersection of time and the timeless: 'A noise of falling weights that never fell'. The same poem, in describing the 'creepers crimsoning to the pinnacles', offers the benign version of this paradox: 'As if perpetual sunset lingered there'.

'wave', and then (as the wave begins to separate and dissolve its unity) 'feeling' into 'sea-hall'; fear known in the Cyclopean blindness and the silence; and the delicate creativity of sound in the lines themselves intriguingly played against 'In silence'. After such a sense of Merlin's forethought, what actually happens to him—even though it is a dread that haunted Tennyson, a living death, imprisoned forever, conscious but paralysed, within the hollow oak—cannot but be an anticlimax, a mere incident.

A poem which can include such deep felicities cannot be written off, even though its success must be recognised as sporadic. A critic who is strict with *Idylls of the King* will feel some sympathy with George Eliot, who found that, though she could not capitulate, she needed to recapitulate:

> I had seemed in the unmanageable current of talk to echo a too slight way of speaking about a great poet. I did not mean to say Amen when 'The Idyls of the King' seemed to be judged rather 'de haut en bas'. I only meant that I should value for my own mind 'In Memoriam' as the chief of the larger works, and that while I feel exquisite beauty in passages scattered through the Idyls, I must judge some smaller wholes among the lyrics as the works most decisive of Tennyson's high place among the immortals.

GERTRUDE HIMMELFARB

Household Gods and Goddesses[†]

* * *

If family and home were the repositories of both private and civic virtues, they were also the scene where men and women resided together yet existed in their "separate spheres." Men came home, Froude said, as a refuge from their worldly, workaday lives: "At home, when we come home, we lay aside our mask and drop our tools, and are no longer lawyers, sailors, soldiers, statesmen, clergymen, but only men."[1] Women—at least middle-class women—had no such problem. They did not have to come home; they were at home. And they had no masks to remove, because they were not "lawyers, sailors, soldiers, statesmen, clergymen," but only and always women. That was their entire identity and their sole profession. And the home was their domain, their natural, proper, separate sphere.

To the modern feminist (and to a few Victorian feminists, although they would not have used this language), the identification of women with a separate sphere epitomizes the "patriarchal" ethos that informs Victorian values in general and family values in particular. Whatever the nature of that sphere, however comfortable and congenial it might be for particular women or however exalted as an ideal, it is deemed oppressive and degrading, for it consigns

† From Gertrude Himmelfarb, *The De-Moralization of Society* (New York: Alfred A. Knopf). Copyright 1995 by Gertrude Himmelfarb. Reprinted by permission of the publisher.
1. Froude, *The Nemesis of Faith*, p. 15.

women to a single role and a single place, thus depriving them of the essential human attributes of liberty and equality.

For most Victorians, the idea of a separate domestic sphere for all but the most remarkable women was as natural as the idea of the family itself. And, again for most Victorians (women as well as men), that separate sphere implified the natural inferiority of women and their incapacity for public life. For others, however, including some of the most eminent Victorians, that sphere was seen as separate but equal. And for some it was actually separate and superior. The Reverend Binney, a Congregationalist minister, started by saying that "women are not to be men, in character, ambition, pursuit or achievement"; then went on to explain that "they are to be *more*; they are to be the *makers* of men"; and ended with the startling assertion: "The Mother is the father of the child."[2] To the modern feminist, these distinctions—separate and inferior, separate and equal, separate and superior—are of no account, since any separation is regarded as odious; indeed, the ostensibly equal or superior status is seen as a hypocritical stratagem to ensure the segregation and subordination of women. But to the historian, trying to recover the Victorian ethos as Victorians saw it and experienced it, the nuances of that "separate sphere" are of some moment.

It is difficult to take seriously today such effusions as Coventry Patmore's "The Angel in the House," which catalogues the respective virtues of man and woman, with woman excelling at every point. "She succeeds with cloudless brow" where he agonizingly fails; and "she fails more graciously than he succeeds." She grows lovelier "the more she lives and knows," while he is "never young nor ripe." Her "facile wit" flies straight at the truth, which he "hunts down with pain." "Were she but half of what she is" and "he but twice himself," she is worthier than he; for love is her "special crown," as truth is his, and love is "substance," where truth is "form," and "truth without love were less than nought." In short, her "happy virtues . . . make an Eden in her breast," while his, "disjointed and at strife, . . . do not bring him rest."[3] "The Angel in the House," most critics at the time (and even more today) agreed, was hardly a distinguished poem. But its message cannot be so easily dismissed, for it was enormously popular and reflected sentiments widely held in mid-Victorian England. Patmore, a friend and great admirer of Tennyson, so successfully modeled himself on his mentor that "Coventry Patmore" was thought by some to be a pseudonym of Alfred Tennyson. (It is interesting to note that after Tennyson's death, Patmore recommended a woman poet, Alice Meynell, to succeed him as poet laureate.)

Tennyson himself, as poet laureate, lent his considerable authority to a view of women that was more subtle and complicated than Patmore's, but finally not very different. Several years before "The Angel in the House," Tennyson's "The Princess" appeared. It describes the Princess's passionate desire to found a women's university and the Prince's effort, not to deter her, for he entirely approves of her goal, but to persuade her to be more temperate in pursuing it. A famous passage in the poem has been cited as if it represents Tennyson's own view of the proper roles of men and women.

2. Davidoff and Hall, *Family Fortunes*, p. 116 (quoting from T. Binney, *Address on the Subject of Middle Class Female Education* [1873]).
3. Coventry Patmore, *The Angel in the House* (London, 1885 [1st ed., 1854–63]), pp. 40–42 (canto 5).

Man is the hunter; woman is his game:
The sleek and shining creatures of the chase,
We hunt them for the beauty of their skins;
They love us for it, and we ride them down.
. . . .
Man for the field and woman for the hearth:
Man for the sword and for the needle she:
Man with the head and woman with the heart:
Man to command and woman to obey.[4]

These words, however, are spoken not by the Prince but by his father, a cynical, coarse, and thoroughly unsympathetic figure.

The Prince, on the other hand, the hero of the poem, is so fulsome in his devotion to "the woman's cause" that the poem almost reads like a feminist tract. (Feminists were inspired by it to emulate the Princess and actually establish women's colleges.)

The woman's cause is man's: they rise or sink
Together, dwarf'd or godlike, bond or free:
. . . .
We two will serve them both in aiding her—
Will clear away the parasitic forms
That seem to keep her up but drag her down—
Will leave her space to burgeon out of all
Within her—let her make herself her own
To give or keep, to live and learn and be
All that not harms distinctive womanhood.

Tennyson (like most feminists at the time) did not deny the "distinctive womanhood" of women; he only—a very large only—sought to modify and mitigate it.

For woman is not undevelopt man,
But diverse: could we make her as the man,
Sweet Love were slain: his dearest bond is this,
Not like to like, but like in difference.
Yet in the long years liker must they grow;
The man be more of woman, she of man:
He gain in sweetness and in moral height,
Nor lose the wrestling thews that throw the world;
She mental breadth, nor fail in childward care,
Nor lose the childlike in the larger mind . . .[5]

What is notable about this compendium of virtues is the association of morality with women and intellect with men. For Victorians, who held the moral virtues in the very highest regard, this was tribute indeed. And it was for the sake of these moral virtues—the argument went—to protect women from the tainted atmosphere of man's world that they were placed in their separate sphere.

For Frederic Harrison, the moral superiority of women was a fundamental tenet of the Positivist credo, which assigned women the role of "Moral Provi-

4. Alfred Tennyson, "The Princess," in *The Works of Alfred Lord Tennyson* (London, 1894), pp. 198, 202. John W. Dodds prefaces his quotation of this passage with the comment that Tennyson "gave poetic authority to accepted doctrines." (*The Age of Paradox: A Biography of England, 1841–1851* [London, 1953], p. 70.)
5. Tennyson, p. 214.

dence" and located them at the very highest rung of the hierarchy. In his enthusiasm, he also credited them with being the "intellectual" genius of man's life, which gave women a place in the next rung of the hierarchy as well, that of "Intellectual Providence." Yet these considerable powers were to be exercised within the home, for only there could the "womanliness of woman" be ensured.

> Our true ideal of the emancipation of Woman is to enlarge in all things the spiritual, moral, affective influence of Woman; to withdraw her more and more from the exhaustion, the contamination, the vulgarity of mill-work and professional work; to make her more and more the free, cherished mistress of the home, more and more the intellectual, moral, and spiritual genius of man's life.[6]

It was from a very different philosophical perspective that John Ruskin came to much the same position. In lectures delivered in 1865 and reprinted that year in his most popular book, *Sesame and Lilies*, Ruskin introduced the much quoted metaphors for men and women: the "Kings' Treasuries" and the "Queens' Gardens." Unlike Harrison's "Moral Providence," which was deemed superior to the "Intellectual Providence," Ruskin's metaphors suggest that the Queens' "Gardens" were of lesser importance than the Kings' "Treasuries" — an adornment, not a place of power. And unlike Tennyson, who saw the sexes as converging at least to some extent ("liker must they grow"), Ruskin had a more rigidly separatist view of their respective spheres: "Each has what the other has not; each completes the other, and is completed by the other: they are in nothing alike, and the happiness and perfection of both depends on each asking and receiving from the other what the other only can give."[7]

Like Tennyson and Harrison, Ruskin was a great advocate of women's education, insisting that a woman should study every subject a man did (with the exception of theology, which was too "dangerous" for the female sensibility). But she should study them all in a different fashion and for a different purpose — not frivolously or shallowly, but differently.

> All such knowledge should be given her as may enable her to understand, and even to aid, the work of men: and yet it should be given, not as knowledge, — not as if it were, or could be, for her an object to know; but only to feel, and to judge. It is of no moment, as a matter of pride or perfectness in herself, whether she knows many languages or one; but is of the utmost, that she should be able to show kindness to a stranger, and to understand the sweetness of a stranger's tongue.[8]

And so with all other subjects: science should be studied not to master a particular discipline but to be trained in "habits of accurate thought" and to understand the "loveliness of natural laws"; or history, not to know the dates of events or names of celebrated persons but to "apprehend, with her fine instincts, the pathetic circumstances and dramatic relations, which the historian too often only eclipses by his reasoning."[9]

---

6. Frederick Harrison, *Realities and Ideals: Social, Political, Literary and Artistic* (New York, 1970), pp. 103–4, 77. (Although the volume was first published in 1908, the essays had been written over a period of forty years.)
7. Ruskin, *Sesame and Lilies*, pp. 58–59.
8. Ibid., p. 62.
9. Ibid., p. 63.

In the light of Ruskin's personal life—not only his much publicized impotency but also his mode of life and career—it is ironic to read his description of the "manly nature": "the doer, the creator, the discoverer, the defender"; "active, progressive, defensive"; displaying an "energy for adventure, for war, and for conquest." The woman's power, by contrast, is "for rule, not for battle"; her intellect "not for invention or creation but for sweet ordering, arrangement, and decision"; she "enters no contest, but infallibly adjudges the crown of contest,"[1] It is to guard her from the perils that beset man in the "open world," as well as to give him a haven from that world, that woman is confined to the home. "This is the true nature of home—it is the place of Peace; the shelter, not only from all injury, but from all terror, doubt, and division."[2] (This too is ironic, for Ruskin's own home was anything but tranquil. Indeed, the whole of this essay is almost a reverse image of this own life.)

The superiority of women, Ruskin said, was attested by all great literature. Shakespeare, for example, "has no heroes . . . only heroines"; in every play the catastrophe is caused by "the folly or fault of a man," whereas redemption comes from "the wisdom and virtue of a woman"; his women are "infallibly faithful and wise counsellors,—incorruptibly just and pure examples—strong always to sanctify, even when they cannot save"; there is only one "weak woman" (Ophelia) and three "wicked women" (Lady Macbeth, Regan, and Goneril), the latter being "frighful exceptions to the ordinary laws of life."[3]

The view of woman as an exalted, almost divine being was so prevalent among Victorian writers that it acquired a name: "woman-worship." If Chesterton is right in saying that the Victorians worshipped "the hearth without the altar," one might also say that a good many of them professed to worship a Goddess rather than a God. The religious metaphor is apt, for it echoes a theme heard over and over again: in Patmore's eulogy of the "Angel" in the house; or Tennyson's description of the Prince's mother "dipt in Angel instincts . . . interpreter between the Gods and men"; or Charles Kingsley's portrayal of woman as "the natural and therefore divine guide, purifier, inspirer of the man";[4] or Beatrice Webb's reflections on "the holiness of motherhood."[5]

1. Ibid., p. 59. As late as 1889, two eminent scientists, Patrick Geddes and J. Arthur Thomson, in *The Evolution of Sex*, described the differences between the sexes: the man "katabolic"—active, energetic, variable; the woman "anabolic"—passive, sluggish, stable. These differences were said to be innate and immutable. "What was decided among the prehistoric Protozoa cannot be annulled by Act of Parliament." Quoted by David Rubinstein, *Before the Suffragettes: Women's Emancipation in the 1890s* (New York, 1986), p. 4.
2. Ruskin, *Sesame and Lilies*, p. 59.
3. Ibid., pp. 50–53.
4. Charles Kingsley, *Letters and Memories* (New York, 1973 [1st ed., 1877]), II, 330. I am indebted to Walter E. Houghton, *The Victorian Frame of Mind, 1830–1870* (New Haven, 1957), for suggesting this and several other sources. This book is an invaluable compilation of quotations and, more important, bibliographical references.
5. *The Diary of Beatrice Webb*, ed. Norman and Jeanne MacKenzie (Cambridge, Mass., 1983), II, 52 (July 25, 1894). Beatrice Webb's identification of "womanhood" with motherhood is most interesting, because it comes from one of the most driven intellectuals of her time (to say nothing of her sex), who was not herself, to her great regret, a mother. Before her marriage, Webb had suggested that the only way women could show their power was for "women with strong natures to remain celibate, so that the special force of womanhood—motherly feeling—may be forced into public work." After her marriage she was dubious about how many women could fulfill themselves in that fashion. The highest mission of a woman, she then said, was to fulfill the "genius of motherhood." A woman should be encouraged to cultivate her mind, for without that she would be capable only of "the animal office of bearing children, not of rearing them." But no woman should be encouraged to forgo motherhood in favor of a purely intellectual life (as she herself had done, she explained, because of her late marriage and too many years of a "purely brainworking and sexless life), because that would be to deny her very nature. In any case, no woman, however well trained, would ever attain that "fullness of intellectual life which distinguishes the really able man." [The quotes are from] Beatrice Webb, *My Apprenticeship* (Penguin ed., London, 1971 [1st ed., 1926]), p. 223;

It was against these woman-worshippers—"philogynists," he called them— that T. H. Huxley protested. In seeking to refute the antiquated views of the misogynists, he said, they became equally fanatical in insisting that woman was "the higher type of humanity"; that her intellect was "the clearer and the quicker, if not the stronger," than the male's and her moral sense "the purer and nobler"; and that man should "abdicate his usurped sovereignty over Nature in favour of the female line." One need not make such excessive claims, Huxley argued, in order to advocate the same education for girls as for boys. One need only believe that girls and boys had the same "senses, perceptions, feelings, reasoning powers, emotions," and that intellectually the average girl differed less from the average boy than one boy from another. For himself, neither philogynist nor misogynist, Huxley preferred to believe "that the ideal of womanhood lies neither in the fair saint nor in the fair sinner; that the female type of character is neither better nor worse than the male, but only weaker; that women are meant neither to be men's guides nor their playthings, but their comrades, their fellows, and their equals, so far as Nature puts no bar to that equality."[6]

Most Victorians were neither "woman-worshippers" nor egalitarians. Many, if not most, took the separate-spheres idea to mean that women were inferior to men morally as well as intellectually—not angels in the house but servants in the house, not divine beings placed on a pedestal but lowly creatures capable of little more than menial tasks in the kitchen and dutiful submission in bed. This is the stereotype of the Victorian family, and there is a good deal of truth in it.[7]

But there was also a powerful countercurrent of thought that belied that view. This countercurrent played into the hands of the Victorian feminists, if only to break up the stereotype and make room for other ideas of the proper relations of men and women. The separate spheres were never as separate in practice as in theory; in reality there were intermediate areas, a "social borderland," where they overlapped. But even in theory the separation was less firm, less inviolable, than some would have liked. However committed the woman-worshippers were to the notion that women could exercise their special and superior virtues only in the home, they unwittingly subverted their cause, for they opened the door to the claim that women so elevated could not and should not be confined to so restricted a sphere, that the angel in the house would not so easily be corrupted if she ventured outside the house, and that she might even have a duty to bestow upon all of society those gifts which were now the exclusive privilege of her family.

If men and women were presumed to have distinctive attributes and virtues, it might be supposed that they were governed by different standards of behavior—a double standard, as the conventional view has it. Here too there is some truth, but only a partial truth, for if it describes a not uncommon practice, it does not at all describe

---

Diary, I, 214 (August 29, 1887); [and] *Diary*, II, 52 (July 25, 1894). Some years later, she seemed more reconciled to her motherless state, saying that "on the whole" she did not regret the decision not to have children. But this was expressed with great diffidence and reservations (ibid., p. 193 [Jan 1, 1901]).

6. T. H. Huxley, "Emancipation—Black and White" (1865), in *The Essence of T. H. Huxley*, ed. Cyril Bibby (New York, 1967), pp. 194–96.

7. Virginia Woolf described the angel in the house as an "intensely sympathetic," "immensely charming," "utterly unselfish" woman, who "sacrificed herself daily." "If there was chicken, she took the leg; if there was a draught she sat in it." She was also totally "pure," so pure as not to have a mind of her own. "Had I not killed her, she would have killed me," Woolf said. "Killing the Angel in the House was part of the occupation of a woman writer." Virginia Woolf, "Professions for Women," in *Collected Essays* (New York, 1967), II, 285–86.

the principle to which most people subscribed. That principle, the ideal of moral conduct, found its most dramatic expression in Tennyson's *Idylls of the King*. This long poem, one of Tennyson's most admired and popular works, is a paean to chastity (in the familiar sense not of celibacy but of fidelity and modesty)—for men as much as women. It is curious to find that single standard ascribed not to the court of Queen Victoria, where it would have seemed perfectly natural, but to the court of King Arthur. One might have thought that the virtues associated with the king would be the traditionally masculine ones of the battlefield: heroism, courage, spirit, audacity, virility. The virtues celebrated in the *Idylls*, however, are those more often identified with women and domesticity: love, sweetness, gentleness, faithfulness, chastity. Yet it is the knights, not the ladies of the court, who are enjoined to cultivate these virtues, for these are "all that makes a man."

> To lead sweet lives in purest chastity,
> To love one maiden only, cleave to her,
> And worship her by years of noble deeds,
> Until they won her; for indeed I knew
> Of no more subtle master under heaven
> Than is the maiden passion for a maid,
> Not only to keep down the base in man,
> But teach high thought, and amiable words,
> And courtliness, and the desire of fame
> And love of truth, all that makes a man.[8]

The violation of this sexual code by Sir Lancelot and Queen Guinevere signals the fall from grace, the dissolution of the knightly ideal and of Camelot itself. Another knight, Sir Tristram, is emboldened to make a virtue out of their vice; what the lovers have done out of passion and weakness, he does arrogantly and willfully, thereby creating a new moral code, a code of immorality, so to speak. The knightly ideal of "high thought, and amiable words" is perverted into a coarse braggadocio and a gross libertinism. Tristram threatens to set up a rival court in the north, boasting that it will be full of knights who are adulterers and women who are whores. In the last tournament, the king—the "woman-worshipper," as he is mockingly called, who "fain had clipt free manhood from the world,"—is mortally wounded, and Camelot is doomed. "The old order changeth, yielding place to new"[9]—a new order, it is implied, that has abandoned the old virtues and verities.

Tennyson's was not the only account of the Arthurian story. William Morris's "The Defence of Guenevere" was just that—a defence of illicit love. (The sequel, however, "King Arthur's Tomb," has Guenevere painfully aware of having sinned against Arthur and against society.) But it was Tennyson's tale that became the authorized Victorian version. And it was Arthur whom Gladstone extolled as "a selfless man and stainless gentleman, . . . the great pillar of the moral order."[1]

One may question Tennyson's reliability as a witness to the manners and morals of his time, after all, a poet, an incorrigibly romantic one, and Poet Laureate to boot. But one may be more trusting of foreigners who had no *parti pris* and who testified to the same ethos. Ralph Waldo Emerson visited England a few years

8. Tennyson, "Idylls of the King," in *Works*, p. 463.
9. Ibid., pp. 451, 473.
1. Mark Girouard, *The Return to Camelot: Chivalry and the English Gentleman* (New Haven, 1981), p. 184.

before Victoria came to the throne, and again a decade into her reign. In *English Traits*, published in 1856, he reflected on the Englishman's passion for family and home: "Domesticity is the taproot which enables the English to branch wide and high. The motive and end of their trade and empire is to guard the independence and privacy of their homes." That passion, Emerson speculated, may have been produced by the vagaries of the climate, which keep the English indoors, but for whatever reason, the Englishman "dearly loves his house." He loves its furnishings, heirlooms, silver—and its inhabitants, tied together by some "invisible ligature." He especially loves the women of the house, who "inspire and refine" him. "Nothing can be more delicate without being fantastical, nothing more firm and based in nature and sentiment, than the courtship and mutual carriage of the sexes." William Cobbett, Emerson recalled, attributed the huge popularity of the then prime minister, Spencer Perceval, to the fact that he went to church every Sunday, "with a large quarto gilt prayer-book under one arm, his wife hanging on the other, and followed by a long brood of children."[2]

Hippolyte Taine, visiting England some years later, was no less impressed by the domesticity and sexual propriety of the English. In France too, he assured his readers, adultery was relatively rare, but it was not treated as solemnly as in England, where marriage was regarded with such profound respect that even in private conversation among men, adultery was regarded as a crime. He had been told that he could frequent every known salon in England over a period of many months without hearing of any case of adultery. Reminded of the French novels and comic papers where adultery was a subject of levity, he went through the bound volumes of *Punch* and found not a single cartoon on infidelity; instead they were full of scenes of conjugal bliss.[3]

Taine was especially, and agreeably, surprised by the fidelity of women. To account for that curious fact, he contrasted the lives of middle-class English women with those of their French counterparts. Having enjoyed more freedom as children, English women were used to exercising self-control; brought up in the company of young men, they were less given to illusions and romantic dreams; being better educated, they thought for themselves and were sensible; living in the country for a good part of the year, they were removed from temptation; having many children and a large staff to supervise, they were fully occupied; reading the same books as men, engaged in philanthropic work, traveling, physically active, they had little time or energy for "unwholesome ideas." (Taine might have added, as did other observers, that arranged marriages were rare in England, so that couples were united by sentiment and love as well as practical considerations.)

* * *

2. Ralph Waldo Emerson, *English Traits* (Boston, 1858 [1st ed., 1856]), pp. 112–13. The idea that the climate was responsible for the Englishman's love of home was common at the time. Samuel Smiles gave the same explanation: "It is said that comfort is the household god in England—that the English worship comfort. Perhaps this comes from the raw and changeable weather, which drives people within-doors." (*Life and Labor, or Characteristics of Men of Industry, Culture and Genius* [New York, 1888], p. 376.)
3. Hippolyte Taine, *Notes on England*, trans. Edward Hyams (London, 1957), pp. 79–80, 197–98. Every now and then one finds a surprising lapse of reverence, even on the part of the most proper Victorian. Samuel Smiles quoted Coleridge (who was echoing Montaigne): "The most happy marriage I can imagine or picture to myself would be the union of a deaf man to a blind woman"—to which Smiles added: "It would probably have been well if Coleridge's wife had been deaf as well as blind," an illusion to his incessant monologues. Smiles's lists of unmarried geniuses, in philosophy, science, art, poetry, history, and politics, may also have given his readers pause. Smiles, *Life and Labor*, pp. 373–377.

[The works of] other historians and contemporary memoirs [allow us to] appreciate the gratifications, as well as the hardships, of working-class lives.[4] It was not only middle-class moralists like Samuel Smiles who assured hardworking mothers that the home was "the most influential school of civilization" and that "one good mother" was "worth a hundred schoolmasters."[5] Working-class memoirs are full tributes to the mother: "My mother, a model housewife, kept everything tidy, and did her best to protect me"—to protect him, that is, from becoming a "rough" and thereby losing all claim to respectability and the opportunity for a decent life for himself and his children.[6] Another laborer apologized for his poor hand and spelling:

> My mother was a big strong Woman, and not cast down with a little thing, but strugled through with a family of seven Sons and tow daughters, with a man that did not seem to take very little interest in home Matters, We were all under controle of the Mother who held a Masterly hand.[7]

It is also now possible to put to rest some of the stereotypes that have distorted our view of the Victorian working classes. Their family values—most notably, the idea of the separate spheres—may not be ours, but neither were they as oppressively patriarchal as they have been made out to be. Nor was working-class life the unrelieved, joyless toil one might think it. Family life was much enhanced by the general rise in the standard of living and social conditions in the course of the century; the five-and-a-half-day workweek that became the norm in mid-Victorian times ("*la semaine anglaise*," as it was enviously known on the Continent), the August bank holiday officially instituted in 1871, the paid summer holidays common by the end of the century, cheap excursion rates on trains, Cook's bus tours (to the Great Exhibition of 1851, for example, when Londoners were pleasantly surprised by the good behavior of the "trippers"). All of these had the effect, if not the intention, of enhancing a family-centered culture. So did such other amenities, common in the latter part of the century, as family allotments for gardening, private privies for working-class houses, a parlor reserved for solemn family occasions, or a piano (to be found in many working-class homes, even in the country, by the end of the century).

Victorian poets and preachers surely overromanticized the family, but they did not overemphasize it. "Family values" were indeed at the heart of Victorian culture and society.

4. See, for example, Childs, *Labour's Apprentices*; Meacham, *A Life Apart*; John Burnett, ed., *Annals of Labour: Autobiographies of British Working-Class People, 1820–1920* (Bloomington, Ind., 1974); Perkin, *Women and Marriage* and *Victorian Women*. Robert Roberts, *The Classic Slum: Salford Life in the First Quarter of the Century* (Manchester, 1971), and Paul Thompson, *The Edwardians: The Remaking of British Society* (Bloomington, Ind., 1975), deal with the Edwardian period primarily but have implications for the late-Victorian period as well.
5. Quoted by F. M. L. Thompson, *The Rise of Respectable Society: A Social History of Victorian Britain* (Cambridge, Mass., 1988), p. 151.
6. Brian Harrison, *Peaceable Kingdom: Stability and Change in Modern Britain* (Oxford, 1982), p. 172.
7. *Annals of Labour*, p. 290.

R. W. HILL JR.

A Familiar Lesson from the Victorians[†]

The mortal moan begot of sentience
— HARDY

An infant crying in the night;
An infant crying for the light
And with no language but a cry.
— TENNYSON

I

The Darwinian hypothesis—that man and ape were biologically descended from some common ancestor—was a hard pill for the Victorians to swallow. Well before *The Origin of Species* appeared, however, they had already become highly sensitized to any association between animal and human behavior, particularly of a sexual nature. In Dr. Thomas Bowdler's *The Family Shakespeare* (1818) Iago's "an old black ram is tupping your white ewe" or they're "making the beast with two backs" was not proper parlor parlance, most assuredly not with ladies and children present. But what has seemed to us of this century to be dismissable as excessive prudery was not that at all. However much their language and manners may seem to deserve the adjective *prudish*, underneath lay a deep dread that animalistic license in human conduct would or could become fatal to the species, beginning with the dissolution of the family. Especially within the last decade or so, studies in sociobiology, which argue that there is a biological basis for social behavior, along with the new science of evolutionary psychology, have given scientific credibility to the Victorians' worst nightmares and premonitions. Whatever else one may think of the Victorians "they did their human best," as Richard Altick presciently stated, "in their various ways and according to their various lights, to bequeath us a stabler, happier world."[1] Can the same be said of our intentions and achievements in this century? To answer that question negatively in evolutionary terms has implications we must heed now.

First, though, I should say that I am not unaware of current or past indictments of attempting just what I shall attempt here. In *Academic Questions*, a professor of philosophy reported:

> The pathology of English departments over the past quarter century is quite mysterious. Many of their denizens give every sign of having lost interest in literature (making one wonder why they got degrees in it) and eager to grasp the discarded, often disdained crumbs of philosophy, politics, psychology, cardboard history, developmental economics, and such popularizations of science as they might comprehend. It's a dreary business.[2]

Tennyson once responded to a hostile, ad hominem attack on his poem *Maud*—"Adulterer I may be, fornicator I may be, murderer I may be, suicide,

† First published in this Norton Critical Edition.
1. Richard D. Altick, *Victorian People and Ideas* (New York, 1973), p. 309.
2. Barry R. Gross, Review in *Academic Questions*, 8, no. 3 (summer 1995), p. 93.

I am not yet."[3] To the above, I respond: pathologies I admit to; denizen of an English department I surely am (though the word rather suggests an animal trapped in a rat hole); lost interest in literature, absolutely not. But I know, or think I know, exactly where that professor is coming from; and furthermore I quite agree with his generalization.

What set me to this task is a single sentence from Robert Wright's *The Moral Animal* (1994), a book on the new science of evolutionary psychology: "Some of the conservative norms that prevailed in Victorian England reflect, if obliquely, a surer grasp of human nature than has prevailed in the social sciences for most of this century." Wright goes on to assert that "the resurgent moral conservatism of the past decade, especially in the realm of sex, rests on an implicit rediscovery of truths about human nature that have long been denied."[4] In other words, those of the so-called sexual revolution, generally accepted as roughly spanning the twenty-five years form 1960 to 1985, are revealed to have known far less about human sexuality and its consequences than did the Victorians a hundred years earlier, centered as they were on family solidarity. It's a phenomenon that puts an ironic spin on Santayana's famous saw: "those who cannot remember the past are condemned to repeat it": those who were most certain the past had it wrong have ended up themselves being wrong or, if you will, twice wrong.

Last, by way of introductory comment, I should refamiliarize us all with the major tenet of the Darwinian hypothesis. Natural Selection is, of course, the engine that drives the entire theory—the evolutionary process by which individuals in any species develop characteristics enabling them to become better adapted to their specific environment. Through the struggle for existence, or in Spencer's phrase, "survival of the fittest" (which Darwin himself preferred), those less able to adapt are killed, eaten, or simply die out, for only a relatively small number survive. Conversely, in Darwin's words, "Natural Selection can act only through and for the good of each being."[5] For example, the weasel that changes its coat to white in winter has a higher survival potential than does the weasel that remains brown. Sexual selection, again in Darwin's words, is "the struggle between the individuals of one sex, generally the males, for the possession of the other sex. The result is not death to the unsuccessful competitor, but few or no offspring,"[6] i.e., what we know as genetic death. Darwin had, of course, no knowledge of genetics and was wrong in believing acquired traits could be inherited, promoted as "pangenesis," but that ignorance of fact in no way compromised the theory itself—that "variations, however slight and from whatever cause,"[7] will be inherited by the offspring, with large future consequences for enhancing their survival.

II

"Mawnkey!" "Mawnkey!" "Mawnkey!" The undergraduates are literally hanging from the rafters. More than seven hundred students, among other in-

3. Charles Tennyson, *Alfred Tennyson* (New York, 1949), p. 286.
4. Robert Wright, *The Moral Animal* (New York, 1994), p. 13.
5. Charles Darwin, *The Origin of Species* (1859; New York, 1958), p. 91. Thomas Huxley always worried over "the unfortunate ambiguity of the phrase 'survival of the fittest.' 'Fittest' has a connotation of 'best'; and about 'best' there hangs a moral flavor" (see *Evolution and Ethics*). First published as "Ethics and Evolution" (1893).
6. *Ibid.*, p. 94.
7. *Ibid.*, p. 74.

vited public, are chanting in unison "Mawnkey!" "Mawnkey!" "Mawnkey!" Scheduled at a smaller room, the event has been moved to a large library-lectural hall, Oxford, end of June 1860. Two other speakers have been shouted down and a most unfortunate don has risen to offer a mathematical proof in defense of Darwin's *Origin* published in the previous year. He's at the blackboard with his pointer saying of his diagram, "Let this point A be man, and let that point B be the mawnkey."[8] And that was as far as *he* got. "Mawnkey!" "Mawnkey!" "Mawnkey!" Bishop Wilberforce, eminent Victorian, is the one they are waiting for, the great man himself, who will presumably demolish the Darwinian hypothesis speaking extemporaneously on a book he has not read. But no matter, all the power and authority of the Church of England are invested in his person at this moment.

We're twenty-three years into Victoria's reign and a scant two years away from Coventry Patmore's publication of the first parts of *The Angel in the House*, which proves to become an immensely popular poem celebrating mother as a Madonna figure. Tennyson, thirteen years earlier, had helped to do his part as a founder of the Madonna complex, when he had his hero in *The Princess* reminisce on his mother saying of her: "No Angel, but a dearer being, all dipt / In Angel instincts, breathing Paradise."[9] Five years later in 1865 with his essay "Lilies of Queen's Garden," John Ruskin would weigh in on the subject with what arguably qualifies as being the last word on the matter. Mother, Angel in the House, Madonna, in her moral presence not only did no wrong, "she must—as far as one can use such terms of a human creature—be incapable of error."[1] Facile and ill-informed though he was (not unlike an ex-university president who recently dismissed Robert Wright as a "down-scale hedgehog"),[2] the bishop was no mean orator. He certainly well knew the values the Victorians placed on motherhood, and he thought he knew his audience. Nearing his conclusion, he appealed unctuously to the assembly at large "asking whether woman, as well as man, was supposed to be derived from a beast?" Now, for one man to, say, call another a son-of-a-bitch, or some like allusion to a beast, depends for its insult value on how literally the statement is meant to be taken— and is taken. The forum, of course, also matters a great deal, whether public or private, and whether uttered by friend or foe, and in what tone. The insult most depends, however, on what and how one thinks of *mother*. A universal gasp, one imagines, filled the place. Well pleased with himself and intent on demolishing as well the next speaker, his primary antagonist, Thomas Henry Huxley, he put the infamous question turning directly at him: "Was it through your grandfather or your grandmother that you claim descent from a monkey?" Instantaneously, the whole purpose of the debate—that Darwin's theory was a contradiction of God's word—became all but irrelevant. As in the Scopes Trial, aka the "monkey trial" as dubbed by H.L. Mencken precisely sixty-five years later, it was Wilberforce versus Huxley, as it would be William Jennings Bryan

8. Gertrude Himmelfarb, *Darwin and the Darwinian Revolution* (New York, 1968), p. 290. Here and in what immediately follows, I am obviously indebted to this seminal work.

9. Tennyson, *The Princess* VII, lines 301–02. Since easily located, citations from Tennyson are identified by poem and line numbers.

1. John Ruskin, *Sesame and Lilies* (New York, 1888), p. 103.

2. Dennis O'Brien, "Outfoxing the Hedgehogs," *Commonweal*, June 2, 1995, p. 26. Hardly lending credence to expertise, the article has *The Origin of Species* published in 1858 and is five years off on J. S. Mill's publication of *Utilitarianism* as well (1863 not 1858). "Down-scale hedgehogs are convinced that the meaning of the whole is in the fundamental parts." Darwin would be pleased to have himself thus specified.

versus Clarence Darrow, ideologue versus intellect, ignorance and prejudice against knowledge and reason. Huxley whispers to his neighbor: "The Lord hath delivered him into mine hands."

After a reasoned and carefully crafted argument, patiently explaining that Darwinian theory as properly understood claimed only that man and ape shared a common ancestor thousands of generations ago, and without deigning to look at his adversary, Huxley delivered the coup de grace:

> I asserted—and I repeat—that a man has no reason to be ashamed of having an ape for his grandfather. If there were an ancestor whom I should feel shame in recalling, it would rather be a *man*, a man of restless and versatile intellect, who, not content with an equivocal success in his own sphere of activity, plunges into scientific questions with which he had no real acquaintance, only to obscure them by aimless rhetoric, and distract the attention of his hearers from the real point at issue by eloquent digressions and skilled appeals to religious prejudice.[3]

Bishops are not accustomed to such treatment; the place went berserk. "One lady fainted and had to be carried out."[4] From Wilberforce himself, the rest was silence. Accurately assessed by one evaluator, "Huxley had committed forensic murder."[5]

The roar that lies on the other side of that moment of silence is, however, still too much with us late and soon. One day, years later, Huxley was seen by Carlyle, that ever cantankerous, old transcendentalist; and Huxley crossed the street to speak to him. "You're Huxley, aren't you? the man that says we are all descended from monkeys."[6] And with that, the dour Scot, who, during his literary career had figuratively been riding up hills perpendicular or shooting Niagara, shuffled on his lonely way to dusty death. William, Darwin's eldest son, wrote a letter to his father in which he reports Thomas Carlyle had said to him: "*The Origin of Species* is nothing to me."[7] It may have been nothing to Carlyle (a most dubious assertion) but for much of the world the concept of "natural selection" became and is, arguably, the single most profound, far-reaching idea in humankind's recorded history. But if that opening salvo between Huxley and Wilberforce would become another shot heard round the world, its reverberations are still very much with us:

> Those who for ideological, political, economic, or other such reasons interfere with the delicate but highly generative process of transforming individual ideas into widely useful scientific truths may well end up having neither one nor the other.[8]

3. Himmelfarb, *Darwin*, p. 291. In private, numerous anecdotes exist, one of the best being Alexander Dumas (*père*) responding to a snide remark on his heritage: "My father was a mulatto, my grandmother was a Negress, and my great grandparents were monkeys. My pedigree begins where yours ends."
4. *Ibid.*
5. William Irvine, *Apes, Angels and Victorians* (Cleveland, 1968), p. 13.
6. *Ibid.*, p. 243.
7. *Ibid.*, p. 217.
8. Gerald Holton, "'Jumpers,' 'Splitters,' and Scientific Progress," *Academic Questions*, 8, no 2 (spring 1995), p. 19. "In point of fact, even though Wilberforce has long since been reckoned as hunted to extinction after his famous gaffe, he remained an Anglican hero whose wounds of battle with infidel science helped elect him Bishop of Winchester as well as Oxford, although his opposition to the theology of *Essays and Reviews*, expressed in his own severe review that same year (1860) probably helped even more. His name appeared frequently in the Anglican hymnals and prayer books for more than a century, before the most recent round of modernization. The goat of one camp seems to have been the peacock of another" (contributed by Donald Lawler).

It sounds a bit like Huxley, does it not? The writer is Gerald Holton, Mallinckrodt Professor of Physics at Harvard, spring 1995.

To question what this extended anecdote has to do with evolutionary psychology, biological determinism, and the moral animal is to be forgiven even should one suspect that there is less here than meets the eye. These associations are, however, best eased into, for I shan't so easily get out of them. Edward R. Murrow once said: "The obscure we see eventually; the completely apparent takes longer." Huxley, upon completion of his third reading of the book Wilberforce never read, remarked (specifically of natural selection), "How extremely stupid not to have thought of that."[9] Alfred Russell Wallace, of course, had; and he and Hooker were the first clearly deserving recipients of the Darwin Medal. Huxley, the third recipient, protesting in the last year of his life that, as no longer a practicing scientist he was unworthy, was perhaps the most deserving of all, before or since. Call it synchronicity, Huxley's final essay, Evolution and Ethics (1894) — The Moral Animal (1994) — anticipates by a lot what the term sociobiology encompasses as presently understood. As has been tersely stated: "Darwin caused history and Huxley made it."[1] But if "Carlyle couldn't swallow the monkeys,"[2] neither have a number of others been able to. Consider the following as representative of what I shall derisively call our age of enlightenment (1960–85):

> This monkey mythology of Darwin is the cause of permissiveness, promiscuity, pills, prophylactics, perversions, pregnancies, abortions, porno-therapy, pollution, poisoning, and proliferation of crimes of all types.

Thus spoke Georgia Judge Braswell Deen as reported in Time magazine, March 16, 1981. With whatever irregular success they may have sought to prevail, sane voices were also present, such as George Gaylord Simpson's in The Biological Nature of Man (1966):

> The point I want to make now is that all attempts to answer that question [what is man?] before 1859 are worthless and that we will be better off if we ignore them completely.[3]

Or, as put more recently and citing Simpson, "There is such a thing as being just plain wrong, and that is what, before 1859, all answers to [such] questions were."[4] To argue otherwise is equivalent to quarreling with the statement that "today the theory of evolution is about as much open to doubt as the theory that the earth goes round the sun."[5]

Huxley, "Darwin's Bulldog," had done his best to correct the obviously still lasting and certainly the Victorians' major misreading of Darwin — that man was directly descended from the ape, a monkey in a gown, preferably an academic one. Tennyson was hardly alone when, nine years before The Origin appeared, he asserted an essentially fundamentalist belief:

> Let him, the wiser man who springs
> Hereafter, up from childhood shape

---

9. Wright, Moral Animal, p. 23.
1. Irvine, Apes, Angels and Victorians, p. 8.
2. Ibid., p. 217.
3. Richard Dawkins, The Selfish Gene (Oxford, 1989), p. 1.
4. Ibid., p. 267.
5. Ibid., p. 1. [In 1992 the papacy officially recanted its injunction against Galileo Galilei (1564–1642).]

His actions like the greater ape,
But I was *born* to other things.[6]

It was between 1875 and 1878 that the poet italicized the word *born*, the only underlining in the entire poem. Darwin had published his *Descent of Man* in 1871; and since then, Tennyson, more enlightened and well read in science than many of his contemporaries, had accepted, however grudgingly, the biological hypothesis of natural selection and the transmutation of species. It seems likely that it was that very acceptance which prompted the italics. Mankind may have evolved physically from the lower species, but at some point God had entered in and invested human beings with souls, that which distinguishes our conduct from the amorality of the other beasts that take their "license in the field of time"[7] unfettered by a moral sense. "No evolutionist," Tennyson once said to Tyndall, "is able to explain the mind of Man or how any physiological change of tissue can produce conscious thought."[8] To Darwin's horror, no less a scientist than Wallace himself, co-inventor of the theory of evolution, agreed with Tennyson. Natural selection, Wallace wrote, could account for the development of all other organisms but cannot have created the human brain, an event that called for divine intervention. Darwin wrote Wallace: "I hope you have not murdered too completely your own and my child."[9] That single sentence goes a long way toward accounting for why so-called neo-Darwinism, sociobiology, and evolutionary psychology are now comprehensive, if not synonymous terms. In other words, biological evolution cannot be dissociated from the evolution of the human brain and human behavior. That, though perhaps obvious, is the most loaded statement in this essay.

Man is an animal. How and why did he become a self-conscious animal? What conceivable evolutionary purpose does self-awareness or self-reflection serve? Natural selection, we must remember, is utterly futureblind. Are self-consciousness and a sense of ethics somehow complementary? Could we have one without the other? In the struggle for existence of what possible value are altruism, compassion, a notion of mercy or justice? Is there a gene or combination of genes for such traits? If so, how could they possibly have emerged where survival belongs to the fittest? In *The Hour of Our Delight: Cosmic Evolution, Order and Complexity* (1991), Hubert Reeves urgently pleads that in a secular world "sooner or later [people] must find what can only be called a moral reason for their lives." He places in our context what the Victorians most feared:

> Mankind is the accidental product of a series of incoherent processes. Total selfishness is the one rational behavior if human existence has no meaning. Looking out for number one is the only thing that counts. People and other objects are meant to be used or consumed. . . . What should be the basis for ethical behavior?[1]

6. Alfred Tennyson, *In Memoriam* 120. [Unless clear from the text, hereafter cited as *IM*.]
7. *IM* 27.
8. Hallam Tennyson, *Alfred Lord Tennyson: A Memoir by His Son* (London, 1897), I, 323. [Hereafter cited as *Memoir*.]
9. Adrian Desmond and James Moore, *Darwin* (New York, 1994), p. 569. Also see pp. 522 and 538 for the Darwin-Wallace split. Also cited by Stephen Jay Gould, *An Urchin in the Storm* (New York, 1987), p. 121.
1. Herbert Reeves, *The Hour of Our Delight: Cosmic Evolution, Order and Complexity* (New York, 1991), pp. 180–81.

That is a difficult question to answer, but "to take our license in the field of time" is to deny that there is an answer, a basis for ethical conduct, that there is any purpose in self-consciousness. Hardy's last novel, *Jude the Obscure* (1894–95), being written all but contemporaneously with Huxley's *Evolution and Ethics*, throws the problem at us relentlessly. From the outset, he introduces young Jude: "He was the sort of man who was born to ache a good deal before the fall of the curtain upon his unnecessary life should signify that all was well with him again." Throughout, to the closing death scene wrapped in the Book of Job, the novelist staggers us with the costs of self-consciousness. "'Let the day perish wherein I was born, and the night in which it was said, There is a man child conceived'"—the *only* event in our own life over which we have had no control.

We often hear precisely Tennyson's and Wallace's point about consciousness echoed today, here from the physicist Brian Pippard, once Cavendish Professor of Physics at Cambridge: "What is surely impossible is that a theoretical physicist, given unlimited computing power, should deduce from the laws of physics that a certain complex structure is aware of its own existence."[2] Biologists, I have learned, have a similar problem with the laws of probability; sociobiologists have even bigger problems. The chance that a DNA molecule, the building block for life, could come into existence spontaneously has been graphically dramatized as equivalent to a pile of junk self-organizing itself into a functioning Boeing 747. It has been seriously proposed, and not by kooks either, that earth was seeded with living organisms from outer space, our 3.5 to 4 billion years of life-sustaining history simply not being enough time for DNA to have evolved. Thomas Hardy was probably the first poet who seriously toyed with the idea: "I thought a germ of consciousness / Escaped on an aërolite / Ions ago / From some far globe."[3] The difficulty here is that you need a second- or third-generation sun to assemble the elements necessary for life out of the supernova of first-generation stars. Fascinating as that topic is, I must shortcut it by saying simply that the probable 15 billion years of the universe's existence does limit the time available, however immense. Life exists, and very probably it takes just about 15 billion years for any self-aware species to evolve, here or wherever else in the universe. Tennyson's assertion was correct and still is; biological evolutionists can't explain how conscious thought developed, but they are closing in fast perhaps on being able to do so. *The New York Times* (May 10, 1998) reports that we may know the complete human genome by 2001, four years ahead of schedule. And, though I may not, many will live to see the day when the origin of life, DNA, and self-awareness are fully accounted for and explainable to a seventh grader, who easily comprehends the earth's circuit of the sun.

Those last couple of sentences should begin to identify where I stand. However encumbered by ignorance in hard science, and especially, as Henry Adams acknowledged of himself in *The Education*, by "the fatal handicap of ignorance in mathematics";[4] however dim the lights and tangled the circumstances; however painful and costly to what I would *like* to believe—I confess to being a reductionist, inescapably a believer in determinism as driven by natural selection and, of necessity, an atheist. In the analogy thread-

2. Steven Weinberg, *Dreams of a Final Theory* (New York, 1992), p. 44.
3. Thomas Hardy, "The Aërolite."
4. Henry Adams, *The Education of Henry Adams* (New York, 1931), p. 449.

ing *In Memoriam*, aren't we all infants crying in the night, crying for the light with no language but a cry, calling for our parents? The parents can't come because they are not there. Steven Weinberg has said in his fine book *Dreams of a Final Theory* (1992):

> The reductionist world view is chilling and impersonal. It has to be accepted as it is, not because we like it, but because that is the way the world works.[5]

The universe or Nature has no prior or conscious design for itself and there is no God — no father figure in the sky or anywhere else. The question that haunts Tennyson's great elegy for Hallam, "Are God and Nature then at strife?"[6] is irrelevant, on both counts. Of course, "we long for a parent to care for us, to forgive us our errors, to save us from childish mistakes. But knowledge is preferable to ignorance. Better by far to embrace the hard truth than a reassuring fable."[7] No poet has put our acceptance of that hard truth more poignantly than Wallace Stevens:

> To see the gods dispelled in mid-air and dissolve like clouds is one of the great human experiences. It is not as if they had gone over the horizon to disappear for a time. It is simply that they came to nothing. It was their annihilation, not ours, and yet it left us feeling dispossessed and alone in solitude, like children without parents, in a home that seemed deserted, in which the amical rooms and halls had taken on a look of hardness and emptiness.[8]

As anyone familiar with Tennyson knows, he was no stranger to the position that Weinberg presses on us again in the sentence: "All our experience throughout the history of science has tended toward a chilling impersonality in the laws of nature." He locates the key moment in the demystification of the heavens as being "Newton's observation that the same law of gravitation governs the motion of the moon around the earth and a falling body on the surface of the earth."[9] (Perhaps less noticed is that this may also roughly mark another key moment — how we habitually use language in conscious contradiction of reality. Not many of us looking with awe and wonder at the western sky, exclaim, "Hey! what a beautiful earth turn *that* was tonight.") The stars, the voice of Sorrow whispers in *In Memoriam*, blindly run; and, had Tennyson known about it, the theory of quantum mechanics would have only verified randomness, the alarm over which brought him to "the night of fear." "Nature red in tooth and claw," Nature that brings of a hundred seeds but one to bear, the Nature that speaks in *In Memoriam* of the human species and had seemed so careful of the type, asserts: "A thousand types are gone; / I care for nothing, all shall go."[1] So, what, then, is so special about the human race? What's special, only to us, of course, is the evolution of consciousness. Richard Dawkins in *The Selfish Gene* puts the issue well:

5. Weinberg, *Dreams*, p. 53.
6. *IM* 55.
7. Carl Sagan, *Pale Blue Dot* (New York, 1994), p. 57.
8. Wallace Stevens, *Opus Posthumous* (New York, 1982), pp. 206–07.
9. Weinberg, *Dreams*, p. 245.
1. *IM* 56.

The evolution of the capacity to simulate seems to have culminated in subjective consciousness. Why this should have happened is, to me, the most profound mystery facing modern biology.[2]

Thomas Hardy thought it no mystery, just an excessively cruel accident of fate, a point of view that does not leave much playing room.

Of Tennyson, A. C. Bradley observed long ago:

> We live, and civilized man must continue to live, in an age of science. But with the exception of Shelley, Tennyson is the only one of our great poets whose attitude towards the sciences of Nature was what a modern poet's ought to be . . . the only one to whose habitual way of seeing, imagining, or thinking, it makes any real difference that Laplace, or for that matter, Corpernicus, ever lived.[3]

A contemporary of Tennyson's, Thomas Huxley again—and from whom it was high praise indeed—named the poet the only nonscientist of the century who really comprehended the magnitude of the issues; and he strongly praised *In Memoriam* for its "insight into the scientific method."[4] Today we are similarly impressed by how remarkably close Tennyson can be to a Weinberg's or Dawkins's articulations, the former's most quoted occurring in his book *The First Three Minutes:* "The more the universe seems comprehensible, the more it also seems pointless."[5] How extraordinarily Tennysonian! In March 1833, when he and Hallam were looking through microscopes at "moth's wings, gnat's heads, and all the lions and tigers which lie perdus in a drop of spring water," Tennyson said, 'Strange that these wonders should draw some men to God and repel others. No more reason in one than in the other.'"[6] Repelled he most certainly was. "If we look at Nature alone, full of perfection and imperfection, she tells us that God is disease, murder and rapine."[7] Weinberg, looking at birds, reflects:

> Although I understand pretty well how brightly colored feathers evolved out of a competition for mates, it is almost irresistible to imagine that all this beauty was somehow laid on for our benefit. But the God of birds and trees would have to be also the God of birth defects and cancer.[8]

How accurately Tennyson reflects in language and tone the concerns of so many scientists today who are sensitized to the human dimensions of their work. W. H. Auden's vacuous remark that "Tennyson had perhaps the finest ear of all English poets; he was also undoubtedly the stupidest,"[9] seems in this context to be undoubtedly the stupidest comment one poet has ever made about another.

---

2. Dawkins, *Selfish Gene*, p. 59.
3. A. C. Bradley, *A Miscellany* (London, 1931), pp. 30–31.
4. *Memoir* II, 143.
5. Steven Weinberg, *The First Three Minutes* (New York, 1993), p. 154. Long before, Thomas Hardy had come to a similar conclusion, in a letter, saying: "What we gain by science is, after all, sadness. . . . The more we know of the laws and nature of the Universe, the more ghastly a business one perceives it all to be." John I. M. Stewart, *Thomas Hardy: A Critical Biography* (Norfolk, UK, 1971), p. 35.
6. *Memoir* I, 102.
7. *Memoir* I, 314.
8. Weinberg, *Dreams*, p. 250.
9. W. H. Auden, ed., *A Selection from the Poems of Alfred Tennyson* (New York, 1944), p. x.

III

As I move further into my central thesis concerning human behavior and sociobiology, I want to take another glance at *In Memoriam*. Tennyson, speaking for, and to the whole human race, urges:

> Move upward, working out the beast,
> And let the ape and tiger die.[1]

He put the matter figuratively; Dawkins, Reeves, and Wright do so literally. Unless the human race somehow contrives to create a moral social order that suppresses the reptilian genes still active in the limbic brain, the aggressiveness that once served us so well in the struggle for survival, we as a species are in for deep trouble. As Carl Sagan recently warned, that is "if we continue to accumulate only power and not wisdom." Sagan is as clear as one can get: "It is only a matter of natural selection. If we become even slightly more violent, shortsighted, ignorant, and selfish than we are now, almost certainly we will have no future."[2] The phrase "only a matter of natural selection" places him, too, squarely among the reductionists. Clams, fleas, and cockroaches have been around unaltered for hundreds of millions of years. The average lifetime for any species is about a million years, as many as eight million for mammalian species. We are approximately halfway through our allotted span and we're the only species so far to be conscious of that fact. Sagan speculates, "Maybe civilizations arise all the time, but wipe themselves out as soon as they are able."[3] Among theoretical physicists, Stephen Hawking has put straight to us the issue with deadly seriousness: "Unless we can use our intelligence to control our aggressions, there is not much chance for the human race."[4]

To round the figure off, for over fifty years Tennyson asked himself and us what Hawking would mean by "unless." Unless we control our aggression. "So many a million of ages have gone to the making of man: / He now is first, but is he the last? is he not too base?"[5] ponders the speaker of *Maud*. What if the dead were indeed aware of our innermost feelings and desires: "Is there no baseness we would hide? / No inner vileness that we dread?"[6] When Tennyson uses the word *base* in this context, he invariably, if obliquely, is referring to the sexual impulse. The act of procreation, making the beast with two backs, indelibly identifies us with animals and irrevocably locates us within the natural world. The bestial impulse must be regulated somehow to preserve our species as *Homo sapiens* in a Malthusian world of population explosions. To move upward, to tame "the wild beast within," would also involve the creation of a "moral reason" for our existence. Monogamy (though not unknown, rare in the rest of the mammalian kingdom) must be our sexual practice if there is to be, indeed, a chance for the long-term continuation of our species.

The assertion that the Victorians had a surer grasp of human nature than has prevailed throughout most of this century is particularly apt if we focus on the quarter century from 1960 to 1985. So I will now record without comment three of Tennyson's more purple passages on the subjects, which are assuredly among

---

1. *IM* 18.
2. Sagan, *Pale Blue Dot*, p. 397.
3. Sagan, *Pale Blue Dot*, p. 397.
4. Stephen Hawking, *Black Holes and Baby Universes* (New York, 1993), p. 137.
5. *Maud*, I, IV, lines 136–37.
6. *IM* 51. (See the notes to this section, p. 235.)

those having been the most derided during the past hundred years. Just how abundantly they reflect the Victorian temper, specifically the moral values associated with monogamy—one husband, one wife, forever—will be obvious. The more one may be provoked to smile or even to ridicule, the better; for I shall later examine them with selected commentary on current theories about evolutionary psychology and the science of biological determinism.

Here, then, are the three passages, the first, ironically enough, published in 1859. I know, the poet asserts,

> Of no more subtle master under heaven
> Than is the maiden passion for a maid,
> Not only to keep down the base in man,
> But teach high thoughts, and amiable words
> And courtliness, and the desire of fame,
> And love of truth, and all that makes a man.[7]

Some twenty-six years later, then long since poet laureate and commanding the largest audience that had ever existed for a living poet, he celebrates

> Love for the maiden, crown'd with marriage
>   no regrets for aught that has been,
> Household happiness, gracious children, debtless
>   competence, golden mean.[8]

Third, here's a passage on adultery, to my knowledge the single most scoffed at and maligned poetry in all of Tennyson's works:

> I hold that man the worst of public foes
> Who either for his own or children's sake,
> To save his blood from scandal, lets the wife
> Whom he knows false abide and rule the home.[9]

Now, briefly, I'll offer a few comments on matters informing current scientific inquiry into evolutionary psychology and then move back to these passages with specific commentary on each.

IV

First, what we can't really comprehend but must be aware of is geological time. Dawkins in *The Selfish Gene* makes the unarguable point. "Genes," he observes, "are denizens of geological time: Genes are forever . . . a DNA molecule could theoretically live on in the form of *copies* of itself for a hundred million years."[1] In the physical sense they *are* our immortality. Our bodies, purely in their reproductive capacities, are merely mortal coils temporarily to house those genes—maybe twenty-five years for a female, perhaps fifty or so for a male—then back to be "cast as rubbish to the void,"[2] to cite Tennyson. Here is one way to try to visualize human time versus geological time: since life began on this planet, human history, as we know it, is equivalent to stretching our arm and with a nail file taking a single swipe across the index finger.[3] Biological de-

---

7. *Idylls of the King*, "Guinevere," lines 475–80.
8. *Vastness*, lines 23–24.
9. *Idylls of the King*, "Guinevere," lines 509–12.
1. Dawkins, *Selfish Gene*, p. 35.
2. IM 54.
3. Peter Coveney and Roger Highfield, *The Arrow of Time* (New York, 1990), p. 250.

terminism does its work in a time frame that is all but unimaginable. Tennyson tried his best, as no poet before him had attempted: "There where the long street roars hath been / The stillness of the central sea."[4] Only Tennyson, well read in Lyell's *The Principles of Geology* (1830–33), could imagistically conceive of wind and water "sowing the dust of continents to be."[5]

Second, about evolutionary psychology I must stress that we're talking about genes in geological time—the preservation of a copied gene in the human animal, or through the human animal, to be precise. "*Most* men are probably better off in a monogamous system and *most* women worse off."[6] These are Wright's words; here is his model, which he defends as scientifically, analytically valid, however, as he admits, crude and offensive:

> Suppose 2,000 people live in a monogamous society and each woman is engaged to marry the man who shares her ranking. She'd like to marry a higher-ranking man, but they're all taken by competitors who outrank her. The men too would like to marry up, but for the same reasons can't. Now, before any of these engaged couples get married, let's legalize polygyny and magically banish its stigma. And let's suppose that at least one woman who is mildly more desirable than average—a quite attractive but not overly bright woman with a ranking of, say 400—dumps her fiancé (male # 400, a shoe salesman) and agrees to become the second wife of a successful lawyer (male # 40.) This isn't wildly implausible—forsaking a family income of around $40,000 a year, some of which she would have to earn herself by working part-time at a Pizza Hut, for maybe $100,000 a year and no job requirement (not to mention the fact the male # 40 is a better dancer than male # 400).
>
> Even this first trickle of polygynous upward mobility makes most women better off and most men worse off. All 600 women who ranked below the deserter move up one notch to fill the vacuum; they still get a husband all to themselves, and a better husband at that. Meanwhile 599 men wind up with a wife slightly inferior to their former fiancées—and one man now gets no wife at all.[7]

That last man is a most dangerous animal. Genetically speaking, what's in the self-interest for a female is to link up with the alpha male; what's in the self-interest for a male is to get his genes into as many different women as possible. In sociobiological terms, neither self-interest is best for the survival of the species; a compromise is necessary. As Shaw put it almost a century ago in a wittier and, for the times, probably even more offensive comment:

> Polygamy [he means more precisely polygyny], when tried under modern democratic conditions, as by the Mormons, is wrecked by the revolt of the mass of inferior men who are condemned to celibacy by it; for the maternal instinct leads a woman to prefer a tenth share in a first rate man to the exclusive possession of a third rate one. Polyandry has not been tried under these conditions.[8]

For "maternal instinct" read today the unconscious motivation of the woman to do what is most favorable for the continuation of her own genes. Polyandry (or

4. *IM* 123.
5. *IM* 36.
6. Wright, *Moral Animal*, p. 96.
7. *Ibid.*, p. 97.
8. George Bernard Shaw, *Man and Superman* (New York, 1963), III, p. 734.

females with more than one husband) has been tried in a few cultures—is indeed highly favorable for women—but just won't do for civilization at large because it is so highly unfavorable to males. The point I most want to focus on is from Dawkins again: "One of the surprising consequences of the modern version of Darwinian theory is that apparently trivial tiny influences on survival probability can have a major impact on evolution. This is because of the enormous time available for such influences to make themselves felt."[9]

V

Now consider again the first passage from Tennyson. I know

> Of no more subtle master under heaven
> Than is the maiden passion for a maid,
> Not only to keep down the base in man,
> But teach high thought, and amiable words
> And courtliness, and the desire of fame,
> And love of truth, and all that makes a man.

These lines may require, I think, one gloss—the second line, "the maiden passion for a maid." Maiden passion presumes male virginity as well, a Victorian ideal indeed, often unrealized, but not as often as one cynically might think. "There may have been [however] a bit of wisdom in the Victorian disapproval of premarital sex,"[1] Wright deliberately understates. Consequences of pregnancy for females are immense; for the male, spending, say, fifteen minutes failing to impregnate a female is of no evolutionary consequence whatsoever—no different from idling away fifteen minutes admiring the sunset. Of course, if he was too enraptured he may have gotten pounced on by a leopard—in either activity.

A highly consequential gender distinction exists here. Pretending that one does not is simply willful denial. As is well known in evolutionary terms, it is very costly genetically for a woman to have intercourse with a man she does not want. A couple of minutes with a calculator can be revealing; and, recall, tiny influences have huge evolutionary impacts. A man gets a woman pregnant and, following his genetic predisposition, trots off in search of another female. She didn't check him out on the male parental investment scale (MPI), which, as we shall see, is a most important quality. The woman brings her fetus to term—fifteen minutes is to nine months and her investment is 26,000 to 1 for the male. Somehow, against the odds and without her mate she manages to get her offspring to child-bearing age: her investment is 551,500 to 1. A tiny matter, fifteen minutes, has cost her about half her life.

Look at this from another angle. "In one experiment, three fourths of the men approached by an unknown woman on a college campus agreed to have sex with her, whereas none of the women approached by an unknown man were willing."[2] She's not thinking "should I or shouldn't I"; the choice has already been made for her, psychology driven by natural selection. The distinction gets subtler when men and women were asked about the minimal level of intelligence they would accept in a person they were dating. The average response for both male and female was average intelligence. When it came down to whom

9. Dawkins, Selfish Gene, p. 4.
1. Wright, Moral Animal, p. 123.
2. Ibid., p. 43.

they would sleep with, the women responded, "Markedly *above* average." The men said, "Oh, in that case, markedly *below* average."[3]

It would not be a happy consequence were the future of our species left exclusively to male choices. In a questionnaire at a college, "I would be happy to have sexual relations with someone I didn't like if he or she had a great body," only 4 percent of women said yes versus 54 percent for men. The gist here is that women *are* the choosers, whether consciously or not. "She can refuse to copulate. She is in demand, in a seller's market. That is because she brings the dowry of a large, nutritious egg. Once she has copulated, she has played her ace."[4] What she is searching for is a mate who will stay around, which significantly increases the survival probabilities of her offspring.

In proper Victorian fashion, Tennyson's maid is expected to be coy: "Feminine coyness is in fact very common among animals."[5] She's in a position to drive a hard bargain; and, what's more, the male respects her for it. Before committing themselves to a marriage, men are highly suspicious of loose women for a very good reason: her sexual behavior after marriage is of the utmost importance to him. "Can anyone find a single culture in which women with unrestrained sexual appetites *aren't* viewed as more aberrant than comparably libidinous men?"[6] For the male, look to her closely if you have eyes to see, for if she has deceived others, she may thee. Even at this relatively late evolutionary date, such decisions and behavior are driven at an unconscious level. A woman doesn't size up a man and think of him as a worthy contributor to the genetics of her offspring. "All the thinking has been done—unconsciously, metaphorically—by natural selection."[7] But she is the chooser—that's the important point, whether she knows it or not, as so comically dramatized in Shaw's *Man and Superman*.

One other matter in this passage—this, too, a major one—the maid keeps down the base in man. What a quaint, neatly formulaic Victorian notion until . . . listen once more to Wright: "Male violence can be dampened by circumstance. And one circumstance is a mate. An unmarried man between 24 and 35 years of age is about three times as likely to murder another male as is a married man the same age."[8] And we can't say of that, what a splendidly antiquated notion, how Tennysonian! In *The De-Moralization of Society* (1995) Gertrude Himmelfarb has observed the sixfold rise in illegitimacy in only three decades (in both Britain and the United States).[9] This fact neatly parallels the fivefold increase in violent crime since 1960. No sane person would call these figures "apparently trivial." "The increase in wantonly violent behavior is, without a doubt, one of the most disturbing phenomena of the past few decades."[1] To call that remark from Reeves an understatement is, believe it or not, possible. It is important, therefore, to take a closer look at some of Himmelfarb's statistics to suggest why, as well as to promote contrasts with Victorian England.

Almost precisely as bracketed by Victoria's reign from 1837 to 1901, out-of-wedlock births decreased from a mere 6 to 4 percent. Crime, indictable of-

---

3. *Ibid.*, p. 64.
4. Dawkins, *Selfish Gene*, p. 149. Without contraceptive devices, "4 percent" would change to zero.
5. *Ibid.*
6. Wright, *Moral Animal*, p. 45.
7. *Ibid.* p. 37.
8. Wright, *Moral Animal*, p. 100.
9. Gertrude Himmelfarb, *The De-Moralization of Society* (New York, 1995), p. 223. See the "Epilogue" for what follows as I won't note each page source.
1. Reeves, *Hour of Our Delight*, p. 180.

fenses, decreased from about five hundred per one hundred thousand to less than three hundred. The point here is that already low figures by our standards were becoming even lower. Now, when we look back at our last three and a half decades, the graph becomes appalling. From 1961 to the present, out-of-wed-lock births have gone from a flat 5 percent or so to more than 30 percent. Crime (that's all indictable offenses, including violent ones) has gone up to an in-credible ten thousand per one hundred thousand. (The figures are similar for this country.) By the year 2000 there are projected to be more people in prisons in the United States than there are undergraduates in all of our colleges and universities. Among so-called developed cultures, the *New York Times* (May 30, 1995) gives statistics on global family decay, the divorce rate in the United States peaking at just above 60 percent in 1980. There were, as well, half a mil-lion unmarried couples in 1970—three million in 1990, less than ideal condi-tions for the children's prospects. But back to divorce: Gladstone opposed the Divorce Act of 1857, saying "it would lead to the degradation of women"; or, as an Irish woman put it a century later, "a woman voting for divorce is like a turkey voting for Christmas." However much supported by modern feminists, "divorce is often a raw deal for women."[2] No-fault divorce in this country during the last two or three decades has, especially if one projects it in Darwinian terms, been an unqualified disaster for women and children, with horrendous implications for the well-being of the species. In Wright's view, we have created, de facto, a polygonous society, but of a kind unfavorable to women, i.e., serial monogamy, which is the "worst of all worlds."

Our prisons are gorged with dangerous males. No one can predict with any accuracy just what the Darwinian consequences of this state of affairs will be, yet it would be simply stupid to believe that the evolutionary effects will be other than profoundly and broadly negative. Natural selection, I repeat, is future-blind, but are we blind as well? It may be an intelligence from elsewhere pe-rusing these graphs who will ponder the question: Didn't they *see* it coming? *It* being the extinction of *Homo sapiens*—rather an ironic piece of nomenclature. If Carl Sagan *is* right, that civilizations may wipe themselves out as soon as they are able, paradoxically as a result of overpopulation, we certainly have already accumulated some rather convincing evidence for a strong start to that end.

"Hail wedded love," intones Milton, introducing us to Adam and Eve in paradise. So, if not quite in such epic proportions, back to Tennyson's sec-ond passage:

> Love for the maiden, crown'd with marriage,
>   no regrets for aught that has been,
> Household happiness, gracious children, debtless
>   competence, golden mean.

Here I first want to do just a little bit of probing—where is perhaps obvious—into the line "no regrets for aught that has been." In Victorian times, the Angel in the House is the wife; what also pertains in modern terminology is the Madonna-whore complex. Yes, the double-standard is very much in evidence. The husband may have fooled around in his bachelorhood, but those days are past, or so he would most ardently assert. Of the marital state, Dawkins notes: "If there are loose females in the population, prepared to welcome males who

2. Wright, *Moral Animal*, p. 134.

have deserted their wives, then it would pay a male to desert his wife, no matter how much he has already invested in her children."[3] The Victorian married
male may yet again fool around, but on grounds very different from those we
play on today. He may now and again have a prostitute at Picadilly Circus (or,
if he can afford it, a mistress), but never, never (or hardly ever) will he desert his
wife and children. The Victorian placed the highest priority on male faithfulness or MPI—one reason divorce rates were all but negligible in the nineteenth
century, even after the Divorce Act. "Hypocrisy," we say, "pure Victorian
hypocrisy." The male is free to take his license in the fields of lust. Double-standard. True. But if we stop with that, we are simply wrong—or perhaps one
wishes to make the claim that hypocrisy no longer exists.

Fundamentally, what Tennyson's lines are addressing is respect— the Victorian husband's respect for his wife as a person and as mother of his children.
Whatever his lapses of the flesh, his respect for the person of his wife was spiritually etched in granite—permanent, unequivocal, the female's greatest single
asset in a male. Wright makes the point: "If by *respect* you mean what the Victorians meant when they urged respect for women—not treating them as objects of sexual conquest—the respect has probably dropped since 1970 (and it
certainly has since 1960)."[4] True enough, the Victorians believed there were innate differences between men and women, but the last thought a Victorian
male ever had was of his wife as a sexual object for conquest:

> One long-standard and utterly non-Darwinian doctrine of psychology—
> that there are no important innate mental differences between men and
> women on courtship and sex— seems to have caused a fair amount of suf-
> fering over the past few decades. And it depended on the lowest imagin-
> able "standards of evidence"—no real evidence whatsoever, not to
> mention the blatant and arrogant disregard of folk wisdom in every culture
> on the planet.[5]

Who would want to launch an attack on Victorian morality from a culture, particularly in America, which has so blatantly failed to support stability and economic viability in family life?

Last, but certainly not least, again Tennyson's passage on adultery:

> I hold that man the worst of public foes
> Who either for his own or children's sake
> To save blood from scandal, lets the wife
> Whom he knows false abide and rule the house.

Throughout most of this century, the Victorians' obsession with female adultery has seemed as senseless as it was preposterous. In Victorian England, Himmelfarb reminds us, "marriage was regarded with such profound respect that
even in private conversation among men, adultery was regarded as a crime."[6]
Tennyson spends some forty years on and off writing his *Idylls of the King* as a
sort of parable of how a single act of adultery between Lancelot and Queen
Guinevere could bring down an entire society and, by allusion, the British Empire at its height. We laughed, derided, felt immensely superior and far more
knowledgeable. And we were completely wrong, just about as wrong as one can

3. Dawkins, *Selfish Gene*, p. 150.
4. Wright, *Moral Animal*, p. 135.
5. *Ibid.*, p. 150.
6. Himmelfarb, *De-Moralization*, p. 77.

possibly get. Here are the plain facts; the major four in outline are (1) a wife's promiscuity is directly proportional to the male's incertitude over whether the baby she is carrying is carrying his genes; (2) all women know what all men can't—that whoever the father, her offspring carries her genes; (3) the high genetic costs cuckoldry bring the male are, in Darwinian terms, tremendous, for raising children not his own terminates him genetically; (4) a seemingly tiny event in human time can have huge consequences for the long-term evolution of the species.

A male's investment in children not his own is, then, in current lingo, a zero-sum game. It is finally, obviously, in the male interest to favor and insist on monogamy. Wright argues that feminists (and here I would insert the term *gender feminists* as used by Christina Hoff Sommers) "will not be convinced that polygyny liberates down-trodden women." Furthermore, feminists, "who actively resist special moral consideration (by men for women) as patronizing, which it sometimes is, and certainly was in Victorian England,"[7] ignorantly cooperate in destroying what is genetically in women's best interest, or MPI. We once looked back at Victorian times with, at best, veiled tolerance and at worst contempt. A century later we are taking a hard, second look. Just how will the children of the future age look back on our contributions during the last three decades with our millions of fatherless households? "The fatherless family of the United States in the twentieth century is a social invention of the most daring and untested design. It represents a radical departure from virtually all of human history and experience." [8] Should we flunk the test, it could well be the last one we shall ever have to take.

VI

Athough it would be an exaggeration to claim that Tennyson was a sociobiologist a century before the word became currency, nevertheless he was asking many of the most important questions in circulation today. Are "we poor orphans of nothing—alone on that lonely shore— / Born of the brainless Nature who knew not what she bore? . . . Come from the brute, poor souls—no souls—and to die with the brute"? Will "the homeless planet at length . . . be wheel'd thro' the silence of space, / Motherless evermore of an ever vanishing race"?[9] Be reminded that in the British system a billion is a million million when he asks, "As this poor earth's pale history runs,— / What is it all but a trouble of ants in the gleam of a million million suns."[1] Until the 1920s our galaxy was thought to be the entire universe, four hundred billion stars, and Tennyson's notion of that vastness was not far off. "What is it all, if we all of us end but in being our own corpse-coffins at last? / Swallow'd in Vastness, lost in Silence, Drown'd in the deeps of a meaningless past?"[2] "Chaos, Cosmos! Cosmos, Chaos! who can tell how all will end? . . . but dream not that the hour will last."[3] The past has determined the present just as surely as the present shall determine the future, through natural selection; and so we'd better pay heed to the here and now. Although "my body come from Brutes," must not the Soul

7. Wright, *Moral Animal,* p. 136.
8. David Blankenhorn, *Fatherless America* (New York, 1995), p. 49.
9. *"Despair,"* lines 33–36 and 83–84.
1. "Vastness," lines 3–4.
2. *Ibid.,* lines 33–34.
3. "Locksley Hall Sixty Years After," lines 103–06.

"hold the scepter . . . and rule the province of the brute?"[4] From the 1830s the question had haunted him with increasing persistence as he himself neared his own end. When, he asks, "shall we lay / The ghost of the Brute that is walking and haunting us yet, and be free . . . what will our children be / The man of a hundred thousand, a million summers away?"[5] And yet again, "Where is one that, born of woman, altogether can escape / From the lower world within him, moods of tiger, or of ape?"[6] Will the "fiery clash of meteorites" or "the rush of Suns, and roll of systems" extinguish "my tiny spark of being?"[7]—and the entire human species along with it?

Indeed, behind all these questions, which I have rather jammed together from a number of the late poems, lies Tennyson's craving for some manifest cosmic purpose. But he became increasingly persuaded that we must discover for ourselves a worthy goal for the future. After all, "every single, tiny, blindly taken step either happens to make sense in immediate terms of genetic self-interest or it doesn't. And if it doesn't, you won't be reading about it a million years later."[8] What control of the future can human beings bring to such processes? Tennyson came more and more to acknowledge during the last years of his life that "the one, far-off, divine event / To which the whole creation moves"[9] was not going to be realized without human intervention. Edward O. Wilson has proposed in his key thesis a "largely unknown evolutionary process we have called gene-culture coevolution: it is a complicated, fascinating interaction in which culture is generated and shaped by biological imperatives while biological traits are simultaneously altered by genetic evolution in response to cultural innovation."[1] Tennyson would have had less trouble with that complex theory than some apparently have today, for he would have properly focused on our duty to provide cultural innovaton, for our own and the future's sake. We are, after all, the only species so far capable of even knowing that there is a future. That's the easy part. Are we wise enough, at least to try to ensure that we have one? Tennyson certainly had his doubts. I certainly have mine. Yet most assuredly "to scoff at [the Victorians] is to overestimate our own moral advancement."[2] I am, however, most emphatically not proposing a return to the whole system of Victorian ethics. But I am urging the pressing necessity of re-examining our own under the pressure of objective comparison. Futhermore, I subscribe to Weinberg's position, as would Tennyson: "The effort to understand the universe is one of the very few things that lifts human life a little above the level of farce, and gives it some of the grace of tragedy."[3]

In our century, Bertrand Russell, face to face with the immutable Second Law of Thermodynamics, put the challenge to us as unflinchingly as possible—

4. "By an Evolutionist," lines 13–16.
5. "The Dawn," lines 23–25.
6. "The Making of Man," lines 1–2.
7. "God and the Universe," lines 1–3.
8. Wright, Moral Animal, p. 56.
9. IM, conclusion.
1. Cited in Gould, Urchin, p. 107. For the most up-to-date outline version of the theory, see Edward O. Wilson, Consilience: The Unity of Knowlege (New York, 1998), p. 127:
     Culture is created by the communal mind, and each mind in turn is the product of the genetically structured human brain. Genes and culture are therefore inseverably linked. But the linkage is flexible, to a degree still mostly unmeasured. The linkage is also tortuous: Genes prescribe epigenetic rules, which are neural pathways and regularities in the cognitive development by which the individual mind assembles itself. The mind grows from birth to death by absorbing parts of the existing culture available to it, with selection guided through epigenetic rules inherited by the individual brain [emphasis in the original].
2. Wright, Moral Animal, p. 25.
3. Weinberg, First Three Minutes, p. 154.

short of despair. From the passages we have just seen, do we not hear Tennyson's voice echoing behind every phrase of Russell's?

> That Man is the product of causes which had no prevision of the end they were achieving; that his origin, his growth, his hopes and fears, his loves and his beliefs, are but the outcome of accidental collocations of atoms; that no fire, no heroism, no intensity of thought and feeling, can preserve an individual life beyond the grave; that all the labours of the ages, all the devotion, all the inspiration, all the noonday brightness of human genius, are destined to extinction in the vast death of the solar system, and that the whole temple of Man's achievement must inevitably be buried beneath the debris of a universe in ruins—all these things, if not quite beyond dispute, are yet so nearly certain, that no philosophy which rejects them can hope to stand. Only within the scaffolding of these truths, only on the firm foundation of unyielding despair, can the soul's habitation henceforth be safely built.[4]

Every time I read these words, two passages particularly, from *In Memoriam*, are instantly present in my mind's ear, as indeed, for ought I know, they may have been in Russell's as he penned them. Shall

> Man, her last work, who seem'd so fair,
>   Such splendid purpose in his eyes,
>   Who roll'd the psalm to wintry skies,
> Who built him fanes of fruitless prayer,
>
> Who trusted God was love indeed
>   And love Creation's final law—
>   Tho' Nature, red in tooth and claw
> With ravine, shriek'd against his creed—
>
> Who loved, who suffer'd countless ills,
>   Who battled for the True, the Just,
>   Be blown about the desert dust,
> Or seal'd within the iron hills?[5]

The second, a mere five and a half lines, projects with unnerving accuracy the destruction of our planet as decribed by astrophysicists today envisioning the earth's someday inevitable collision with a ten-kilometer-wide comet or asteroid:

> . . . the sustaining crags:
> The spires of ice are toppled down,
>
> And molten up, and roar in flood;
>   The fortress crashes from on high,
>   The brute earth lightens to the sky,
> And the great Eeon sinks in blood.[6]

Tennyson probably got his imagery from the Book of Revelation, but the scientist Paul Davies didn't:

> Directly above ground zero, the sky splits open. A thousand cubic miles of air are blasted aside. A finger of searing flame wider than a city arcs ground-

---

4. See Heinz R. Pagels, *Perfect Symmetry* (New York, 1985), p. 363.
5. *IM* 56.
6. *IM* 126.

ward and fifteen seconds later lances the earth. The planet shudders with the force of ten thousand earthquakes. A shock wave of displaced air sweeps over the surface of the globe, flattening all structures, pulverizing everything in its path. The flat terrain around the impact site rises in a ring of liquid mountains several miles high, exposing the bowels of the Earth in a crater a hundred miles across. The wall of molten rock ripples outward, tossing the landscape about like a blanket flicked in slow motion.[7]

In *The Last Three Minutes* (1994), Davies's version is of a predictable event perhaps every hundred million years, like the one that wiped out the dinosaurs and an estimated 50 percent of the rest of earth's species some sixty-five million years ago, leaving some sort of shrew-like creature for us to evolve from. One wonders what Bishop Wilberforce could have made out of that? Unlike a Russell or Tennyson, some find it pointless, or even silly, to contemplate such matters or worry about them. I don't. It's part of our *"education to reality,"* as Freud would say: "As for the great necessities of Fate, against which there is no help, they will learn to endure them with resignation" for "men cannot remain children for ever"[8]—we, poor orphans of nothing.

In Freud's figurative sense, are we children capable of growing up? One has one's doubts. In 1954, Carl Sagan noted that 75 percent of people polled said that the sun was not alive. In 1989, spanning our age of enlightenment, 70 percent thought the sun *was* alive. In 1954, 90 percent denied that automobile tires can "feel anything." In 1989, 27 percent thought tires had feelings.[9] Should the study of evolution in our public schools allow equal time for the promotion of creationism? President Reagan thought so. Should human sociobiology be dissociated from evolutionary biology as applied to animals? "The prevailing view in the social sciences in the seventies was essentially that there is no biologically based human nature, that human behavior is almost entirely sociocultural in origin,"[1] writes Wilson today; and I suspect he may be overly optimistic in his belief that that day has passed. As recently as 1987, Stephen Jay Gould in *An Urchin in the Storm* supported that very position against Wilson's thesis in *Sociobiology, the New Synthesis,* and he is still doing so as I write. It is, to say the least, discouraging that an evolutionist of Gould's stature is still arguing against the synthesis of biological evolution with the evolution of human nature, that sociobiology works only for animals and not human creatures. That part of the Victorians' dilemma is still around and gives one pause for deepest thought. To deny, as many do, that "inequality of endowments, including intelligence is a reality" and "trying to pretend that inequality does not really exist has led to disaster."[2] But if you wish to believe that automobile tires have feelings, by all means be free to go ahead and think so.

VII

In sum, I would simply point out that, just as the Victorians had all but insurmountable difficulties with the notion that man (his brain included) was but a species of animal descended like the apes from a common ancestor, so do we

---

7. Paul Davies, *The Last Three Minutes* (New York, 1994), p. 1.
8. See Sigmund Freud, *The Future of an Illusion,* trans. James Strachey (New York, 1989), p. 63.
9. Sagan, *Pale Blue Dot,* p. 32.
1. Edward O. Wilson, "Science and Ideology," *Academic Questions,* 8, no. 3 (summer 1995), p. 76.
2. Charles Murray and Richard Herrnstein, *The Bell Curve* (New York, 1994), p. 551.

today continue to resist the theory that sociobiology predominately determines
human behavior. Current studies of long-separated identical twins showing the
undeniable, predominant effects of genetic coding would seem, by all logic, to
put the issue beyond dispute. But "again and again, when genetic research turns
toward human nature, and away from simple biology, politics swamps the discussion, and often sinks the research efforts."[3] Yet the achievement of the Victorians can, I think, be clearly stated. If man is but an animal, it is imperative
to put into place a moral code, a system of ethics, as Huxley so persuasively argued in Evolution and Ethics, that would distinguish us and our conduct from
animals, bestial behavior, and natural law. Tennyson was unique, Francis Golffing said presciently in 1966, "envisioning a social order which would embrace
all mankind, and which would be based on a rational technology and a thoroughly humanized science." He added, "That may sound like a rather dreary
program for a poet to tackle,"[4] but it stands as part, a major part, of the Victorians' effort to bequeath us a stabler and happier world. We, to the contrary, in
our obdurate denial of genetic distinction among us and innate behavioral differences between the sexes have bequeathed to our next generations a social
wasteland, which is just now being recognized as the horror it truly is, as an evolutionary nightmare.

"It is manifest that, during the time men live without a common power to
keep them in awe, they are in that condition which is called war; and such a
war as is of every man against every man . . . where every man is enemy to
every man . . . consequent to the time wherein men live without other security,"[5] Do those words of Hobbes's in 1651 not apply to inner-city existence
today, equivalent to a presocial world ruled by teenage street gangs? The Victorians sought for and provided security; the literal father was at home; the
"common power" was their code of ethics, and it was indeed awe inspiring. Current scholarship on the Victorians has increasingly come round to defining the
center for that code: "Tennyson stresses the unit of the family, sees it as a microcosm of the nation and the universe, and is willing to wait, seeing hope in
the future."[6] Are we not, perhaps, simply rediscovering the obvious?

For the first time in three and a half billion years mankind has the wherewithal directly to influence, if not significantly to alter, the otherwise future-
blind, biologically determined course of evolution. A short while ago the comet
Swift-Tuttle was projected to hit this planet on August 21, 2126. Recalculations
suggest there will be apparently a two-week miss. The chance that a baby born
today will die along with the entire human species may be one in two thousand.
A Shoemaker-Levy–type comet could, coming from nowhere, easily strike earth
and not Jupiter. Would you climb aboard an airplane with those odds? Are we,
as a species, so unimaginative and dumb, so profoundly prejudiced by our own
ideologies and myths that we are incapable of responding to less precisely cata-
strophic and specifically spectacular evidence of our sure extinction? Yes, the
obscure we see eventually; the completely apparent does indeed take longer.

3. Lawrence Wright, "Double Mystery," The New Yorker (Aug. 7, 1995), p. 49. Also see Robert M. May's review of Wilson's newest book, Consilience: The Unity of Knowledge (New York, 1998) in Scientific American (June 1998). Here we are properly reminded that after the publication of Sociobiology: The New
   Synthesis, reviewers and letters in the mid-1970s compared "Wilson's idea with those of the Nazis."
4. Francis Golffing, "Tennyson's Last Phase: The Poet as Seer," The Southern Review II (1966), pp. 264–85.
5. Thomas Hobbes, Leviathan (New York, 1958), pp. 106–07.
6. Michael Timko, Carlyle and Tennyson (Iowa, 1988), p. 67. And see, of course, the concluding sentences
   of Himmelfarb's article on p. 675.

Tennyson: A Chronology

1809   Born August 6 at Somersby, Lincolnshire. His father, the Reverend George Clayton Tennyson, had been disinherited in favor of a younger brother, Charles, who later changed his last name to d'Eyncourt.

1816   Studied at Louth Grammar School, where his older brothers Frederick (b. 1807) and Charles (b. 1808) had enrolled.

1820   Leaves school to be privately educated at home by his father, whose alcoholism and deep moods of despondency took a toll on the child.

1823–24   Writes "Translation from Claudian's 'Proserpine'" and *The Devil and the Lady*, a play largely an imitation of Elizabethan dramatists, especially Beaumont and Fletcher.

1827   Published *Poems by Two Brothers* in April, containing contributions by his brother Charles and a few by his brother Frederick. Enters Trinity College Cambridge in November.

1828   Arthur Henry Hallam (b. 1811) enters Trinity College in October.

1829   Tennyson wins the Chancellor's Medal in June with the prize poem *Timbuctoo*. Elected to the Apostles, the undergraduate literary-political debating society. Hallam meets Tennyson's younger sister Emily, whether in December or April of the following year is debated.

1830   *Poems, Chiefly Lyrical* is published in June. Travels to the Pyrenees with Hallam, July through September.

1831   Tennyson's father dies in March; Tennyson leaves Cambridge without his degree. Hallam's essay on Tennyson is published in August.

1832   John Wilson's ("Christopher North") hostile but tempered review of *Poems* (1830) appears in *Blackwood's Magazine* (May). Tennyson travels to Rhine country with Hallam in July. In the autumn, Hallam's engagement to Emily is reluctantly recognized by his parents. Publishes *Poems* (dated 1833) in December.

1833   Croker's savage review of *Poems* appears in April's *Quarterly Review*. Hallam dies suddenly from cerebral hemorrhage while in Vienna with his father, September 15.

1834   Infatuation with Rosa Baring.

1835   Tennyson's older brother Charles inherits an estate and changes his name to Turner.

1836   Charles Tennyson Turner marries Louisa Sellwood in May; Tennyson falls in love with Louisa's sister Emily, met in 1830.

1837   The Tennyson family moves from Somersby to High Beech, Epping; his engagement to Emily recognized by both families.

1840   Breaks off engagement, in part at least out of financial concerns.

1841   Invests about £3,000 in a mechanized wood-carving venture, which goes under in 1843, substantially losing his whole fortune. In today's currency, *very* roughly about $250,000.

1842   *Poems* in two volumes published in May: the first included reworked selections from the 1830 and 1832 volumes with a few written ca. 1833–34; the second volume contained all new pieces.

1845   In September, granted a Civil List Pension of £200 per year, first proposed by Carlyle, but secured by Hallam's father.

1847   *The Princess* published in December.

1849   In letters renews relationship with Emily Sellwood.

1850   *In Memoriam* published anonymously in May. Marries Emily in June. Appointed poet laureate in November. Wordsworth had died in April; Samuel Rogers, eighty-seven, refused the offer on grounds of his age and infirmities. Elizabeth Browning and Leigh Hunt had also been contenders. Tennyson had the backing of the Prince Consort.

1851   During July and into October with his wife visits Italy, to help recover from loss of a still-born baby boy.

1852   Hallam Tennyson born in August.

1853   Moves to "Farringford" on the Isle of Wight. He purchases the house three years later.

1854   Lionel Tennyson born in March.

1855   *Maud* published.

1859   Publishes first four *Idylls of the King* in July. Darwin's *Origin of Species* published.

1862   New edition of *Idylls of the King* dedicated to the memory of Prince Albert (d. December 1861).

1864   *Enoch Arden* published in August; its huge success earns him the title "Poet of the People."

1865   Tennyson's mother dies in February.

1868   Begins construction of his second country home, "Aldworth," in Haslemere, named after the town where his wife's ancestors had lived.

1869   *The Holy Grail and Other Poems* (dated 1870) published in December.

1872   Assembles *Idylls of the King* with new epilogue: "To the Queen."

1875   Begins career as a playwright, publishing *Queen Mary*. Much of these later years were taken up with dramas, some successfully produced, some not. A listing of their publications and productions can easily be had elsewhere. The thinness following should not be construed to be idleness.

1879   Charles Tennyson Turner dies in April.

1883   Accepts offer of a barony, having refused offers of a baronetcy in 1865, 1874, and 1880.

1886   Death of Lionel from "jungle fever" on board ship returning from India in April.

1888   Life-threatening illness. According to his doctors, as near death as a man could get.

1890   With Edison's initiative, records some of his poems on wax discs in May. Miraculously, they survived after being stored next to a heat register.

1892   Dies at Aldworth on October 6.

Selected Bibliography

(The distinction between biography and biographical criticism can often be an arbitrary one; so for biography see also works listed under "Critical Studies.")

• indicates works included or excerpted in this Norton Critical Edition.

Editions

The Complete Poetical Words of Tennyson. Ed. W. J. Rolfe. Boston: Houghton-Mifflin, 1898.
The Works of Tennyson. Ed. Hallam Tennyson. 9 vols. London: Macmillan, 1908 (The Eversley Edition).
The Poems of Tennyson. Ed. Christopher Ricks. 3 vols. Berkeley: University of California Press, 1987.
Poems by Two Brothers. Ed. Hallam Tennyson. London: Macmillan, 1893.
The Devil and the Lady and Unpublished Early Poems. Ed. Charles Tennyson. Blomington: Indiana University Press, 1964.
A Variorum Edition of Tennyson's "Idylls of the King." Ed. John Pfordresher. New York: Columbia University Press, 1973.
Tennyson: In Memoriam. Ed. Susan Shatto and Marion Shaw. Oxford, UK: Clarendon Press, 1982.
Tennyson's Maud. Ed. Susan Shatto. Norman: University of Oklahoma Press, 1986.

Biography

Buckley, Jerome H. *Tennyson: The Growth of a Poet.* Cambridge, Mass.: Harvard University Press, 1960.
Levi, Peter. *Tennyson.* New York: Scribner's, 1993.
Martin, Robert Bernard. *Tennyson: The Unquiet Heart.* New York: Oxford University Press, 1980.
Richardson, Joanna. *The Pre-Eminent Victorian.* London: J. Cape, 1962.
• Ricks, Christopher. *Tennyson.* Berkeley: University of California Press, 1989.
Tennyson, Sir Charles. *Alfred Tennyson.* New York: Macmillan, 1949.
Tennyson, Hallam. *Alfred Lord Tennyson: A Memoir.* 2 vols. New York: Macmillan, 1897.
Turner, Paul. *Tennyson.* London: Routledge, 1976.

Letters

The Letters of Alfred, Lord Tennyson, vol. 1, *1821–1850.* Ed. Cecil Y. Lang and Edgar F. Shannon. Cambridge, Mass.: Harvard University Press, 1981.
The Letters of Alfred, Lord Tennyson, vol. 2, *1851–1870,* and vol. 3, *1871–1892.* Ed. Cecil Y. Lang and Edgar F. Shannon. Oxford, UK: Clarendon Press, 1987, 1990.
The Letters of Arthur Henry Hallam. Ed. Jack Kolb. Columbus: Ohio State University Press, 1981.

Critical Studies: Books, Periodicals, and Chapters in Books

Adams, James Eli. "Harlots and Base Interpreters: Scandal and Slander in *Idylls of the King.*" *Victorian Poetry* 30, no. 3–4 (1992), 421–40.
• Armstrong, Isobel. "The Collapse of Object and Subject: *In Memoriam.*" *Language as Living Form in Nineteenth-Century Poetry.* New York: Barnes & Noble/Harvester-Wheatsheaf, 1982.
——. *Victorian Poetry: Poetry, Poetics and Politics.* London: Routledge, 1993.
Bush, Douglas. *Mythology and the Romantic Tradition in English Literature.* Cambridge, Mass.: Harvard University Press, 1937.
Carr, J. Arthur. "Tennyson as a Modern Poet." *University of Toronto Quarterly* 19 (1949), 361–82.
Christ, Carol T. *The Finer Optic: The Aesthetic of Particularity in Victorian Poetry.* New Haven, Conn.: Yale University Press, 1975.
Culler, A. Dwight. *The Poetry of Tennyson.* New Haven, Conn.: Yale University Press, 1977.
Dean, D. R. *Tennyson and Geology.* Lincoln, Nebr.: Tennyson Society, Tennyson Research Centre, 1985.
• Eliot, T. S. "*In Memoriam.*" *Selected Essays.* London: Faber & Faber Ltd. (1932), 286–95.
Engleberg, Edward. "The Beast Image in Tennyson's *Idylls of the King.*" *ELH* 22 (1955), 287–92.
Golffing, Francis. "Tennyson's Last Phase: The Poet as Seer." *The Southern Review* 2 (1966), 264–85.
Gray, J. M. *Thro' the Vision of the Night: A Study of the Source, Evolution and Structure in Tennyson's "Idylls of the King."* Edinburgh, Scotland: For the Edinburgh University Press, 1980.
Himmelfarb, Gertrude. *Darwin and the Darwinian Revolution.* New York: Norton, 1959 (I. R. Dee, 1996).

• ———. *The De-Moralization of Society*. New York: Knopf, 1995.

Hughes, Linda K. *The Many-faced Glass: Tennyson's Dramatic Monologues*. Athens: Ohio University Press, 1988.

Kennedy, Edward Arthur. *King Arthur: A Casebook*. New York: Garland, 1996.

Kiernan, Victor. "Tennyson, King Arthur and Imperialism." *Culture, Ideology and Politics*. Ed. Raphael Samuel and Gareth Stedman Jones. London: Routledge, 1982.

Killham, John. *Tennyson and "The Princess": Reflections of an Age*. London: University of London, Althone Press, 1958.

Lang, Cecil Y. *Tennyson's Arthurian Psycho-drama*. Lincoln, Nebr.: Tennyson Society, Tennyson Research Centre, 1983.

Langbaum, Robert. *The Poetry of Experience*. New York: Norton, 1957.

Nunakawa, Jeff. "*In Memoriam* and the Extinction of the Homosexual." *ELH* 58, no. 2 (1991), 427–38.

Paden, W. D. *Tennyson in Egypt: A Study of the Imagery in His Earlier Work*. Lawrence: University of Kansas Press, 1942.

Peterson, Linda H. "Sappho and the Making of Tennysonian Lyric." *ELH* 61, no. 1 (1994), 121–37.

Priestley, F. E. L. "Tennyson's *Idylls*." *University of Toronto Quarterly* 19 (1949), 35–49.

Rader, Ralph Wilson. *Tennyson's "Maud": The Biographical Genesis*. Berkeley: University of California Press, 1963.

Roppen, George. "The Crowning Race." *Evolution and Poetic Belief: A Study in Some Victorian and Modern Writers*. No. 5 in *Norwegian Studies in English*. Oslo: Universitetsforlaget, 1965, 83–112.

• Sedgwick, Eve Kosofsky. "Tennyson's *Princess*: One Bride for Seven Brothers." *Between Men: English Literature and the Male Homosocial Desire*. New York: Columbia University Press, 1985.

Shannon, Edgar Finley, ed. *Tennyson and the Reviewers*. Cambridge, Mass.: Harvard University Press, 1952.

Shaw, Marion. "Tennyson's Dark Continent." *Victorian Poetry* 32, no. 2 (1994), 157–169.

Shires, Linda M. "*Maud*, Masculinity and Poetic Identity." *A Quarterly for Literature and the Arts* 29, no. 3 (1987), 269–90.

Stevenson, Lionel. *Darwin among the Poets*. Chicago: University of Chicago Press, 1932.

———. "The Pertinacious Victorian Poets." *University of Toronto Quarterly* 21 (1952), 232–45.

Tennyson, Charles. *Six Tennyson Essays*. London: Casell, 1954.

Timko, Michael. *Carlyle and Tennyson*. Iowa City: University of Iowa Press, 1988.

• Tucker, Herbert F. *Tennyson and the Dream of Romanticism*. Cambridge, Mass.: Harvard University Press, 1988.

———. "Columbus in Chains: Tennyson and the Conquests of Monologue." *Harvard Library Bulletin* 4, no. 4 (1993), 43–64.

———, ed. *Critical Essays on Alfred Lord Tennyson*. New York: Macmillan, 1993.

Turner, Paul. "Tennyson." *English Literature: 1832–1890, Excluding the Novel*. Oxford, UK: Clarendon Press, 1989, pp. 18–38.

Wickens, G. G. "The Two Sides of Early Victorian Science and the Unity of *The Princess*." *Victorian Studies* 23 (1980), 369–88.

Index of Poems
and First Lines